Praise for Jonathan Maberry and His Acclaimed Pine Deep Novels

"I first met Jonathan when he was a teenager, and I predicted great things then. And look, he has achieved great things. Jonathan Maberry is a writer whose works will be read for many, many years to come."
—Ray Bradbury

"Maberry has the unique gift of spinning great stories in any genre he chooses. His Pine Deep vampire novels are unique and masterful."
—Richard Matheson

GHOST ROAD BLUES
Winner of the Stoker Award for Best First Novel

"Jonathan Maberry rushes headlong toward the front of the pack, proving that he has the chops to craft stories at once intimate, epic, real, and horrific."
—Bentley Little

"Reminiscent of Stephen King . . . Maberry supplies plenty of chills in this atmospheric novel. . . . This is horror on a grand scale."
—*Publishers Weekly*

"Every so often, you discover an author whose writing is so lyrical that it transcends mere storytelling. Jonathan Maberry is just such an author."
—Tess Gerritsen, *New York Times* bestselling author of *The Mephisto Club*

"It is hard to believe this is Jonathan Maberry's debut novel because his writing is of such a high caliber and his story line is comparable to that of a master writer of horror. Great action scenes, a growing sense of foreboding, and fine characterizations make this a one-sitting reading experience."
—*Midwest Book Review*

"Jonathan Maberry writes in the grand poetic horror tradition of Poe and Robert McCammon. His novel is not just a frightening tale but one in which the reader can truly identify with both the characters. The language and descriptions are vivid, threatening, and beautiful. Maberry belongs with the big names including King and Koontz."
—**Stuart Kaminsky**

"A chilling tale about the staying power of evil. As lyrical, melodic, and dark as the music that provides the imaginary soundtrack. Maberry breathes new life into modern horror fiction."
—**Scott Nicholson**

"Maberry knows that true horror lies in the dark, hidden places in the human heart, and to take this journey with him is genuinely chilling."
—**T. J. MacGregor**

"If I were asked to select only one new voice in horror fiction to read today, it would be Jonathan Maberry. *Ghost Road Blues* jumps so easily out of his blend of words, images, and characters that you hardly realize you're reading a novel rather than watching a movie."
—**Katherine Ramsland**

"*Ghost Road Blues* is a hell of a book—complex, sprawling, and spooky . . . with strong characters and a setting that's pure Americana Halloween hell. A satisfying chunk of creepy, visceral horror storytelling—I'd recommend this to anyone who loves the works of Stephen King."
—Jemiah Jefferson

"Reading Maberry is like listening to the blues in a graveyard at the stroke of midnight—the dead surround you, your pounding heart keeps steady rhythm with the dark, melodic prose, and the scares just keep coming. You find yourself wondering if it's the wind howling through the cold, foreboding landscape of gray slate tombstones or whether it's Howlin' Wolf's scratchy voice singing 'Evil.' "
—Fred Wiehe

"Get ready to be totally hooked, because it's all here: incredible atmosphere, characters you truly care about, and a level of pure suspense that gets higher with every page. Jonathan Maberry is writing as well as anyone in the business right now, and I'll be counting the days until his next book."
—Steve Hamilton

"Maberry's *Ghost Road Blues* leads with a hard left hook and never lets up, full of good, strong writing and complex characters who step right off the page and into readers' heads. It's a lyrical, frightening, and often astonishing read. Although Pine Deep is not a place you'd like to call home, you'll feel as if you've been there before. A wonderful novel from a fresh new voice in the genre."
—Nate Kenyon

"Maberry weaves words of mesmeric power. Gruesome, scary, and bloody good fun."
—Simon Clark

"A wild mélange of soulful blues music and gut-wrenching horror! Through vivid characters and clever descriptions, Jonathan Maberry carefully crafts a very special town that any horror fan would love to live in—that is, until it starts to get ugly . . . *really* ugly. He brings terror to life in a uniquely contemporary way. I'll be so excited to read the second book in his trilogy!"
—Brinke Stevens

"*Ghost Road Blues* is epic horror that puts you in mind of *The Stand, It, Boys' Life,* and *They Thirst,* but beats its own scary path. Nicely tied to the blues and the dark magic of Halloween, it is the first of an impressive new trilogy by Jonathan Maberry, whose vivid prose hits the right rhythms and whose creeping horrors will feed your nightmares until the next installment—and maybe forever. High-octane storytelling meant for chilly, full-moon nights."
—W. D. Gagliani

"Prepare to be scared. Maberry frightens, amuses, and makes you think, often on the same page. The horror is pervasive, but so is a deeply entrenched sense of fun. Move over, Stephen King."
—J. A. Konrath

"Jonathan Maberry writes with the assured hand of a veteran wordsmith. His voice is a confident one, his stories possessed of the kind of rhythmic, lyrical quality one might find in the work of Cady, Conrad, or even Faulkner. And yet such comparisons, though hard to avoid when sitting around Maberry's campfire and hearing his voice, are not entirely fair, for there is a uniqueness here that is exciting to behold. Jonathan Maberry is reaping a crop all his own, and I for one eagerly await the fruit of future harvests."
—Kealan Patrick Burke

"Maberry writes a vivid, fast-paced prose, creating characters and events that are memorable and often frightening. If you like your fiction compelling and deliciously dark, this is an author you should get to know."
—Bruce Boston

"*Ghost Road Blues* begins with more horror than one can imagine and ends savagely beautiful, intricately and deftly written. Don't start this book unless you can finish it!"
—Jack Fisher

"Like Stephen King in *'Salem's Lot*, Jonathan Maberry creates a small town where the everyday flesh-and-blood brutality of the citizens seems to call forth a deeper, more supernatural evil . . . The cliffhanger ending will make you impatient for the next installment of this trilogy!"
—E. F. Watkins

"Terrifying. Maberry gets deep into the heads of his troubled characters—and ours. The small-town horror feels like it's right next door."
—Jim Fusilli

"Stunning, powerful . . . a complex, heart-pounding read. It deserves the Stoker for Best First Novel."
—Kim Paffenroth

"As a horror fan, I loved *Ghost Road Blues* with its great storytelling and memorable cast of characters. As a music fan, I loved Maberry's references to classic blues and rock recordings. There may very well have been hellhounds on Robert Johnson's trail."
—Andrew Burns

"Riveting, bristling with scares, rich with atmosphere . . . brings to mind early Stephen King. Highly recommended!"
—Jay Bonansinga

"Without a doubt this prolific author is the next Stephen King. Maberry deserves more then a Bram Stoker Award for this; he deserves Bram Stoker to rise from his grave and shake his hand."
—Chad Wendell

"A must for anyone who enjoys a literary roller-coaster ride with a deliciously grotesque streak."
—Litara Angeli, *Dark Realms* magazine

DEAD MAN'S SONG

"Maberry takes us on another chilling roller-coaster ride through the cursed town of Pine Deep. You might want to keep the night-light on for this one. Really."
—Laura Schrock

"A fabulously written novel that grips you from its first line to its last. Jonathan Maberry's writing runs from dark and beautiful to sharp and thought-provoking, and his books should be on everyone's must-read list."
—Yvonne Navarro

BAD MOON RISING

"One of the best supernatural thrillers of recent years."
—John Connolly

OTHER BOOKS BY JONATHAN MABERRY

PINE DEEP NOVELS

Ghost Road Blues
Dead Man's Song

JOE LEDGER NOVELS

Patient Zero
Dragon Factory
King of Plagues
Assassin's Code
Extinction Machine
Code Zero

ROT & RUIN NOVELS

Rot & Ruin
Dust & Decay
Flesh & Bone
Fire & Ash
Bits & Pieces

DEAD OF NIGHT NOVELS

Dead of Night
Fall of Night

The Nightsiders: The Orphan Army
The Wolfman

BAD MOON RISING

A Pine Deep Novel

JONATHAN MABERRY

KENSINGTON BOOKS
www.kensingtonbooks.com

KENSINGTON BOOKS are published by

Kensington Publishing Corp.
119 West 40th Street
New York, NY 10018

All Kensington titles, imprints, and distributed lines are available at special quantity discounts for bulk purchases for sales promotions, premiums, fund-raising, educational, or institutional use.

Special book excerpts or customized printings can also be created to fit specific needs. For details, write or phone the office of the Kensington sales manager: Kensington Publishing Corp., 119 West 40th Street, New York, NY 10018, attn: Sales Department; phone 1-800-221-2647.

ISBN-13: 978-1-4967-0541-9
ISBN-10: 1-4967-0541-6

First Pinnacle Mass Market Printing: May 2008
First Trade Paperback Printing: January 2017

10 9 8 7 6 5 4 3 2

Printed in the United States of America

First Electronic Edition: January 2017

ISBN-13: 978-1-4967-0544-0
ISBN-10: 1-4967-0544-0

To Alvy & Kittie West

Bad Moon Rising: An Introduction

BY JONATHAN MABERRY

I'm a little weird.

Let's be up front about that; let's put it on the table. You don't write the kinds of things I write without there being some questionable wiring behind the baseboards and maybe an infestation of *desmodus rotundus* in the ol' belfry. Anyone who visits my office can tell that right off. Among the curios on my bookshelves they'd find the skull of a housecat, a megalodon tooth, a collection of fighting knives, tiny robots, a rubber brain, a blood-spattered plastic hand, action figures of Dana Scully and Fox Mulder, a statue of Wolverine as a zombie, a stuffed Cthulhu in a Hawaiian shirt and straw hat, a copy of the shooting script for *Night of the Living Dead* signed by George Romero and John Russo, a bobble-head statue of Edgar Allan Poe, a statue of Godzilla (Japanese version, not the revisionist U.S. critter), several gargoyles, several statues of the Hindu god Ganesha (I'm not Hindu, but he's the patron god of writers), two steampunk pistols, a Beanie Babies bat, brass knuckles, a TARDIS coin bank, a statue of Anubis, several antique Halloween figures, action figures of both the Lon Chaney, Jr., and Benicio del Toro versions of the Wolf Man, voodoo dolls, a replica of the planet Mars on a glass pedestal, several Day of the Dead musicians, a Navajo storyteller figure, a hand-carved Malaysian bat, a mask from Mardi Gras, a roll of crime-scene tape, fifteen different kinds of rocks and crystals, a trophy from my induction into the

Martial Arts Hall of Fame, a wind-up Dalek, a magic 8-Ball I have been known to consult on serious business issues, a miniature Tom Servo from *Mystery Science Theater 3000,* a jack-o'-lantern squeeze ball, a perfect replica of a human skull, and several glow-in-the-dark zombies. Oh, yeah, and there's a whole bunch of multicolored tentacles that sprout from the top of my penholder, which also contains a replica of Dumbledore's wand, a tiny and very sharp samurai sword, and a throwing knife that I use as a letter opener.

I spend my days writing about zombies, vampires, ghosts, werewolves, demons, weird science, corrupt politics, the end of the world, mass murder, possession, revenge, and alien invasion. Most of my friends are in some aspect of the same business, ranging from writers of horror, thrillers, mysteries and suspense to the comic book crowd to movie and TV people.

So, sure. Weird.

Which brings us to *Bad Moon Rising*, the third and final book of the Pine Deep Trilogy. It's the follow-up to *Ghost Road Blues* and *Dead Man's Song.* It was also the third novel I ever wrote. I started writing it in 2006, the same year that my first novel—and the first in the trilogy—debuted. I started writing it, in fact, before I had any idea how that first book would do. I wrote it while waiting to make my first footprint in the fiction world. This was before *Ghost Road Blues* hit the stores, long before it was nominated for the Bram Stoker Award, and a full year before it won that award.

A lot's changed in the ten years since I began writing *Bad Moon Rising.* The world's gotten stranger and more dangerous. My circle of friends has expanded to include many of the writers whose books I read before I'd made my first fiction sale. Politics have crossed the line into some kind of scary sitcom. My son has gone from high school to college graduate to world traveler to businessman. My wife and I have relocated from one end of the country to the other. Friends have died. Other friends have brought new life into the world. I've gotten grayer.

And I've gotten a little weirder each year. Which is fun.

When I finished *Bad Moon Rising* I thought, *Okay, that's done, that's out of my system. I've told that story and it's time to say good-bye to Crow, Val, Iron Mike Sweeney, the Bone Man, and the rest of the residents of that unfortunate little town.*

But . . . the thing is, the town is every bit as weird as I am. It won't let me leave. I keep driving to the edge of town, and then I have to turn around or stop to change a tire, or I remember something I forgot. A town like Pine Deep is weird by nature. It cannot be normal, which means that even after three thick novels, there are stories left to tell. Some of them have since been told as short stories. These tales range from prequels set in the years before, when Crow, Val and Terry were kids ("Property Condemned"), and some take place years after the events of the book you're holding ("The Trouble"). Some tell stories totally unrelated to the story of Ubel Griswold, and some tell of how that monster and the darkness he conjured polluted the lives of others in the town.

The town wants me to keep telling its story. It has weirdness to share. Right now I'm working on a script for a possible TV pilot set in Pine Deep. It's partly an adaptation of these books, and it's partly new stuff. New strangeness.

Pine Deep, though, is not entirely a fictional town. Nope. It's based on a very real place—well, two places. The model for the town is New Hope, Pennsylvania, which is north of Philadelphia, right on the Delaware River, across from Lambertville, New Jersey. When I was a teenager in high school—and we're talking the mid 1970s here—my friends and I would drive out to New Hope with illicit bottles of beer and wine, and we'd go deep into the endless cornfields to drink, make out, and try to scare each other with ghost stories. The town of New Hope was famous for ghost stories. It was once named the "most haunted town in America," and it has an incredible variety of ghost stories associated with it, some of them going all the way back to the Lenape Indians and the European settlers who came and crowded them out.

The other place that helped form the substance of Pine Deep was Upper Black Eddy, a few miles farther north along Route 32. There used to be an amazing haunted hayride there. I took bunches of my friends there, and we all laughed and screamed and had hellacious fun.

But times have changed. The New Hope of the twenty-first century has far fewer farms. The cornfields and pumpkin patches have dwindled and been replaced by the infill of suburban sprawl. The ghosts have been ignored and have become hushed. Mostly hushed, that is. Ask some of the old-timers there and they'll tell you that some things never quite go away.

As for the haunted hayride . . . it's gone. Closed and shuttered, and the land sold to developers. The haunted attractions have all been dismantled and packed away, taking their thrills and chills with them. It's become less weird. So sad. What a loss.

So when I sat down to write *Bad Moon Rising* and its predecessors, I conjured the spirit of those towns and, in doing so, have let the darkness out of its cage. I've let that whole region be as weird as it could be, and thereby accomplished two things. First, I've had wicked fun, because it's always fun to be weird. Second, I've surprised myself. Even though I had meticulously plotted the three books of the Pine Deep Trilogy all the way to the end, the story and its characters pulled away at times, going places I didn't expect, doing things I was shocked to observe even as I typed.

Fiction does that when you allow it to become alive as it's being written. Kind of weird, kind of cool.

And since the town of the story is based in many ways on real places, I decided to extend that conceit to smudge the line between fictional characters and real people. The celebrities who visit Pine Deep for the Halloween Festival are all real people. And, yes, they know that I wrote them into the story. They were all willing participants, so we all had a little fun. In the story you'll meet James Gunn, who—at the time I wrote this—was best known as the screenwriter for Zack Snyder's remake of *Dawn of the Dead* and writer-director of the alien-zombie horror comedy *Slither*, which starred very young actors Nathan Fillion (*Firefly*, *Castle*), Elizabeth Banks (*The Hunger Games*, *Pitch Perfect*), Jenna Fischer (*The Office*), and Michael Rooker (*The Walking Dead*, *Henry: Portrait of a Serial Killer*). Jim Gunn went on to write and direct the *Guardians of the Galaxy* movies. You'll meet Tom Savini, the make-up effects master who scared the crap out of the whole world with his work on *Dawn of the Dead, Creepshow, Day of the Dead*, and a zillion others; legendary drive-in movie critic Joe Bob Briggs; screenwriter Stephen Susco (*The Grudge, Grudge 2*); actor-screenwriter-director Jim O'Rear (*The Vampire Wars, Don't Look in the Basement 2*); actor Ken Foree (Peter from George Romero's original *Dawn of the Dead*); and scream queens Debbie Rochon (*Tromeo and Juliet, Playmate of the Apes*) and Brinke Stevens (*The Slumber Party Massacre, Slave Girls from Beyond Infinity*). All of them were good sports and allowed me to bring them to Pine Deep just in time for very, very bad things to happen.

Which is another way of saying that my friends are weird, too.

And *you're* holding the book, reading this intro . . . Good chance you read the first two. Very good chance you're a little weird, too.

That makes me happy. We've all come a long, long way together. And I'm just about finished writing my twenty-seventh novel. By the time you read this, I will have written at least two more, possibly three. In the ten years since *Ghost Road Blues* debuted, I wrote five nonfiction books and fifteen graphic novels, and published nearly a hundred short stories and novellas. Many of those stories have been gathered into a dozen print and/or audio collections. I've edited a dozen anthologies ranging from dark fantasy (*Out of Tune*) to media tie-in (*The X-Files*). I have seven novels sold and waiting to be written. I have movie and TV options in place for some of them. I even have my own board game out based on books and comics I've written—*V-Wars: A Game of Blood and Betrayal*. My whole life has gotten very, very weird.

In all the right ways.

And what's most fun is that you've come along for the ride. So, c'mon, let's turn on our flashlights and go prowling the back roads by the light of the harvest moon. Who knows what we'll find?

Let's go be weird together.

March 31, 2016

AUTHOR'S NOTE (2008)

Welcome to Pine Deep!

Bad Moon Rising is my third novel about the pleasant little town of Pine Deep, Pennsylvania, where a lot of *un*-pleasant things seem to happen. It can be read as a stand-alone novel or as part of the complete Pine Deep Trilogy. If you want to take the whole ride, start with *Ghost Road Blues* (which, I'm delighted to say, won the Bram Stoker Award for Best First Novel of 2006 and was also nominated for Novel of the Year, though it was edged out by Stephen King).

That book tells the story of Karl Ruger, a psychotic killer who wrecks his car in Pine Deep while on the run from both the mob and the law. In truth Ruger is drawn to Pine Deep by an even worse killer, Ubel Griswold, one who cut a bloody swath through the town thirty years ago and whose body is buried deep below the swampy mud of Dark Hollow. In Pine Deep, however, the dead don't always rest easy and Griswold's particular brand of evil is vast, powerful and ancient.

Griswold was brought down by an itinerant farmworker and sometime blues singer named Oren Morse, or as the kids called him, the Bone Man. The Bone Man recognized Griswold for the monster that he was and risked his life to stop the killer's reign of evil; but although he killed Griswold the Bone Man was framed for the murders and beaten to death by the town fathers. He, too, rested uneasy in his grave and when Griswold's power began to reassert itself the Bone Man returned as a ghost to try and stop him. The real problem there was that Griswold understands how to be a supernatural being and the Bone Man, sadly, does not. Alone, unseen, nearly powerless, the Bone Man has been trying to communicate with the living and help them in their fight against Griswold's growing power.

Ghost Road Blues is also the story of a handful of people in the town whose lives were touched by the slaughter thirty years ago and are tainted again by more recent events. Malcolm Crow's brother was one of Griswold's early victims and Crow himself was very nearly killed (saved by a timely appearance by the Bone Man), and he alone understands that something dreadful and unnatural is still at work in his town. His fiancée, Val Guthrie, lost an uncle to Griswold years ago and more recently saw her father gunned down by Ruger.

Dr. Saul Weinstock, the chief medical examiner and Crow's friend, has begun to suspect that something is seriously wrong in Pine Deep and has begun to compile evidence that points to an impossible and horrifying explanation.

Terry Wolfe, Crow's oldest friend and the mayor of Pine Deep, lost a sister to Griswold and received terrible wounds himself. Now, as Griswold's power reawakens, Terry feels his mind begin to fracture: is he going insane or is there some supernatural taint in his blood that is transforming him, night after night, into a monster?

And Mike Sweeney, a fourteen-year-old newsboy, has been caught up in the events as Griswold's power grows. He is the victim of appalling ongoing physical abuse by his stepfather, Vic Wingate. Vic, unknown to everyone except Ruger, is the slave and right hand of Griswold; and it is Vic who has labored for thirty years to set in motions the events that will launch Griswold's Red Wave: an attack on the town, and on humanity itself. But Mike is a much more complex person than anyone knows: he has a twisted bloodline that ties him to both the forces of good and evil, and as he struggles to survive the abuse and punishment he begins to undergo a transformation into something *else*.

Karl Ruger repeatedly attacks Val Guthrie and Crow, and each time—even though he is defeated—he seems stronger. Way too strong, as if death no longer has a hold over him. Even after Crow guns him down for the second time he lies in his morgue drawer, quietly waiting for Griswold to call him forth. Ruger's companion, the normally mousy Boyd, has also been transformed by Griswold's power, though, unlike Ruger, Boyd no longer possesses any traces of humanity. He becomes a shambling and murderous hulk.

In the second book, *Dead Man's Song*, as Dr. Weinstock continues his investigation Crow decides to confront his demons by laying the entire story out to news reporter Willard Fowler Newton. He tells Newton about the massacre thirty years ago and then takes him on an adventure: a trip down into Dark Hollow, where Griswold's abandoned house waits among the shadows. The two men are foiled in their attempts to penetrate the house and are ultimately driven off by a bristling wave of cockroaches—tens of thousands of them. They flee Dark Hollow in terrified defeat.

Throughout the entire Pine Deep story there is another tale, that of Tow-Truck Eddie, a brute of a man who believes that the voice in his head is that of God ordering him to track down the Antichrist. God tells him that Mike Sweeney is the Beast and Eddie tries over and over again to murder the boy. The voice he hears, though, is that of Ubel Griswold. Only the ghostly Bone Man—and Mike's own developing powers—save the boy from slaughter.

Meanwhile death has come again to Val's family. Her brother is savagely attacked by the now-monstrous Boyd, and after a bloody battle in which Val's friends and family are torn apart, Val manages to kill the monster. It's a very near thing.

The second book ends with the battle at Guthrie Farm.

Bad Moon Rising is the tale of the Red Wave and how ordinary people try and take a stand against an impossibly powerful and very dark enemy. Crow, Val, Mike, Dr. Weinstock, Newton and a handful of others are pitted against a true army of darkness. On Halloween night a very bad moon indeed will rise over Pine Deep.

There's another note at the end of this book, so I'll see you on the other side.

—JM

From *The Black Marsh Sentinel,* **September 28**

AMERICA'S HAUNTED HOLIDAYLAND

By Willard Fowler Newton

For most small towns a reputation for being haunted would turn away tourists and vacationers. But for Pine Deep, Pennsylvania, tucked into the wooded hills of Bucks County, the haunts are what draw the tourists by the tens of thousands. Several years ago Newsweek Magazine published a list of the "Most Haunted Towns in America," and Pine Deep landed solidly in the top spot. More hauntings and weird happenings per capita than any other town in America, and that includes Salem, Massachusetts.

Since Colonial times Pine Deep has been the scene of strange happenings—murders, disappearances, odd behavior, and poltergeists. The town celebrates this reputation with a variety of spooky events designed to send chills up the spines of even the heartiest trick-or-treater. Pine Deep Authentic Candy Corn is the number-one treat for the little monsters that come around on Halloween; and pumpkin muffins and cakes are made locally and served on tables from Allentown to Philadelphia.

The Pine Deep Haunted Hayride, owned by town mayor Terry Wolfe, is the largest and most elaborate attraction of its kind in the country; and the accompanying Haunted House of Horrors has won the award for the Best Haunted House four years running from Attraction Industry magazine. All during October the Dead-End Drive-In features classic horror films from dusk till dawn, and the movie theaters in town and on the campus of Pinelands College hold continuous monster movie marathons.

The centerpiece of Pine Deep's creepy celebrations is the Halloween Festival, which kicks off on Mischief Night and rolls on until dawn on November 1. This is a huge event that brings in many thousands of tourists and includes a parade, magic shows, dramatic re-enactments of classic moments from horror film, and much more. Topping the bill this year will be appearances by a number of celebrities from the world of horror entertainment, including special makeup effects master Tom Savini (who created the effects for most of the zombie films by *Night of the Living Dead* director George A. Romero); Ken Foree (star of the original *Dawn of the Dead*), James Gunn (screenwriter for the remake of *Dawn of the Dead*), Stephen Susco (screenwriter of the *Grudge* films), film critic Joe Bob Briggs, Hollywood stuntman and haunted-attraction consultant Jim O'Rear, and a pair of femme fatale scream queens, Brinke Stevens and Debbie Rochon.

Malcolm Crow, owner of the Crow's Nest Craft Shop—which sells everything from Halloween costumes to scary novels to DVDs of classic horror films, is the man responsible for much of Pine Deep's ghoulish fun. "Mayor Wolfe's an old friend of mine," he told reporters during a press conference for the Festival, "and he knows I have way too much interest in these spooky kinds of things. So . . . he hired me to amp up the shocks and frights at the Hayride and I've been helping to bring in the coolest horror industry celebrities so that this year's Festival will be the best ever."

It promises to be a terrifyingly good time for all!

For more information visit the Festival's website at www.ghostroadblues.com/pine_deep_ halloween.

BUCKS COUNTY MANHUNT
FOR COP KILLER

PHILADELPHIA—Three men are being sought by police following a deadly shoot-out in Philadelphia that left several people dead, including one officer. Names of the victims are being withheld pending notification of next of kin.

Details are still sketchy, but sources close to the commissioner's office say that a drug buy between members of the Menditto crime family of South Philadelphia and a posse of Jamaicans from West Philly ended in a gun battle that left at least eleven dead. An as yet unnamed Philadelphia undercover narcotics officer was caught in the crossfire and was pronounced dead on arrival at Episcopal Hospital.

Witnesses say that three men were observed fleeing the scene, and at least one of them appeared to be badly injured.

From *The Black Marsh Sentinel,* September 30

MURDER IN PINE DEEP
By *Willard Fowler Newton*

Tragedy struck Pine Deep, Pennsylvania, last night as three armed gunmen, fleeing from a shoot-out with police in Philadelphia, brought violence and bloodshed to this sleepy rural town. The suspects have been tentatively identified as Karl Andermann Ruger, Kenneth Boyd, and Anthony Macchio—all reputed to be members of the Menditto crime family of South Philly.

Police sources say that the gunmen eluded police roadblocks but were forced to stop in Pine Deep when their car broke down. Macchio's mutilated body was found by the wrecked car. It is *speculated* that Karl Ruger, the leader of the crew, killed Macchio after a dispute over the split of money and drugs. A few torn bags of cocaine and bundles of bloodstained money were discovered at the scene.

From here the story took a bizarre and tragic turn as Ruger broke into the farmhouse of Henry Guthrie, one of Pine Deep's most prominent and important farmers. Ruger took the whole Guthrie family hostage, including Guthrie, 65; daughter Val, 41; son Mark, 38; and daughter-in-law Connie, 37. After brutalizing the captives for several hours, Ruger took Guthrie and Val out into the cornfields on the pretense that he needed their help with Boyd, whom Ruger claimed had broken his leg in a rabbit hole. When they reached the spot where Boyd was supposed to be resting, the other gunman was gone, along with all of the money and cocaine.

Ruger flew into a rage. Guthrie, fearing for his family, tried to lure Ruger into a chase through the cornfields while Val headed back to the farmhouse to free her brother and sister-in-law. However Ruger coldly gunned down Henry Guthrie, leaving him to die in the rainstorm that assaulted the town that night.

"It's a great tragedy," said Mayor Terry Wolfe, a close family friend. "Henry Guthrie was the finest man I've ever known."

Ruger got to the farmhouse first and after savagely beating Mark Guthrie, he attempted to sexually assault Connie. Val was able to interrupt the attack and draw Ruger outside, but was unable to elude the killer, who caught her in the yard and attempted to strangle her.

Luckily for her and the others in the town, Val Guthrie's fiancé, Malcolm Crow, owner of a local craft shop and a former Pine Deep police officer, arrived in the very nick of time. Crow and Ruger fought in the rain and though details of the encounter are sketchy, it seems clear that Crow was able to overcome the killer. Police arrived shortly thereafter and in the confusion Ruger managed to pull a gun. During a brief gun battle Officer Rhoda Thomas was shot twice in the chest and shoulder and is listed in stable condition. Crow was grazed by two bullets and was hospitalized from wounds received in the fight. Val, Mark, and Connie Guthrie were also admitted for treatment.

Though Crow and officer Jerry Head, a Philadelphia officer in Pine Deep to participate in the manhunt, both claim to have shot Karl Ruger, the killer escaped.

"We'll get him," insists Pine Deep Sheriff Gus Bernhardt. "We have Detectives Frank Ferro and Vince LaMastra from Philadelphia working with us and we've put together a big task force to hunt these men down."

From *The Black Marsh Sentinel,* October 1

SHOOT-OUT AT PINELANDS HOSPITAL
By Willard Fowler Newton

Late last night Karl Ruger, the gunman sought by police for several murders including those of Philadelphia police officer Michael Johnston and beloved local farmer Henry Guthrie, made a second attempt on the lives of Val Guthrie and Malcolm Crow. According to a statement by Sheriff Gus Bernhardt, "Karl Ruger broke into Pinelands Hospital late last night. He attacked the maintenance supervisor and disabled the hospital's main and emergency generators. While the lights were out he proceeded to the hospital room of Malcolm Crow and assaulted him and his fiancée, Valerie Guthrie. Ruger also seriously injured Norris Shanks, a Pine Deep volunteer police officer. During the struggle Crow and Ms. Guthrie managed to secure Officer Shanks' standard sidearm and backup pistol, with which they fatally wounded Ruger."

Sheriff declined to provide further comments but promised a more detailed formal statement after Crow and Guthrie were treated for wounds received in the fight and were able to give complete depositions.

CAPE MAY KILLER IN PINE DEEP!

By Willard Fowler Newton

The Karl Ruger murder case took a far more bizarre and chilling turn when this reporter discovered that the man responsible for the murder of Henry Guthrie has been positively identified as the mass murderer known widely as the Cape May Killer.

The Cape May Killer has been wanted by police and the FBI for the murders of eighteen senior citizens who were visiting the Cape May Lighthouse last year. Two of the victims, Maria and Vincent Menditto, were the grandparents of Philadelphia mob boss Little Nicky Menditto. FBI sources have speculated that the murders had been part of the turf war that rocked Philadelphia for three years following the death of the former don. One unnamed source in Philadelphia's Major Crimes Unit speculates that the murders were an attempt to discourage Little Nicky from pursuing his goal of running the crime families of Philly, but that the extreme nature of the murders had an opposite effect, making Little Nicky more determined and causing the other crime lords to step up in support of him, as a way of turning the focus of blame away from themselves. Until now no suspect had ever been named.

This reporter has heard from a number of reliable sources within the investigation, however, that Karl Ruger was the leading—if not indeed the only—suspect in the case and that a warrant for his arrest was being sought when Ruger got wind of the suspicion and fled, more from the wrath of Little Nicky than from the police. It is now believed that Ruger orchestrated the drug buy between his crew and the Jamaican posses, then deliberately provoked a gun battle so that he could get away with both the drugs and the money.

Considering the extreme danger this madman posed to the citizens of Pine Deep, Black Marsh, and Crestville, it seems odd and perhaps criminal that the mayor and police chose not to inform the public. *The Black Marsh Sentinel* is calling for an immediate investigation into the mishandling of this case.

From *The Black Marsh Sentinel*, October 1

TWO OFFICERS SLAIN AT GUTHRIE FARM
By Willard Fowler Newton

Early this morning two police officers were brutally murdered at the Guthrie Farm, the scene of another murder just days ago. The officers have been identified as James Castle of Crestville Police Department—on loan to Pine Deep during the Karl Ruger manhunt—and Nelson Cowan of Pine Deep. The degree of savagery inflicted upon the officers was described by one witness as "beyond brutal."

Sources close to the investigation indicate that Kenneth Boyd, a confederate of Karl Ruger, is being sought as the lead suspect in the murders, though this degree of brutality does not seem to fit the picture of Boyd given to the press during earlier statements by Detective Sergeant Frank Ferro of Philadelphia PD, who described him as "a relatively minor figure" in the Menditto crime family who was probably accompanying Ruger under duress. According to Ferro's partner, Detective Vince LaMastra, "Boyd's what we call a 'travel agent.' He arranges to get other criminals out of the country. He's a small fish. It's Ruger we really want."

Now, with Ruger dead, that assessment seems strangely premature.

In a statement to the press, Mayor Terry Wolfe said, "Kenneth Boyd is now being sought as the primary suspect in the murders of Officers Cowan and Castle. Police departments in Pennsylvania, New Jersey, and New York are working together to spread a net so finely meshed that I can guarantee you Boyd will not slip through."

From *The Black Marsh Sentinel,* October 14

MORE TRAGEDY AT GUTHRIE FARM
By Willard Fowler Newton

Once more death and horror struck Pine Deep, and once more blood was spilled on the Guthrie Farm. Two weeks ago Henry Guthrie, 65, the patriarch of the Guthrie clan and the owner of the region's largest corn farm, was brutally murdered by Karl Ruger, who was later revealed to be the infamous Cape May Killer. Two days later two police officers, James Castle of Crestville Police Department and Nelson Cowan of Pine Deep, were killed and mutilated by Kenneth Boyd, a known compatriot of Ruger. But last evening Boyd returned to Pine Deep and once more attacked the Guthrie family.

Boyd murdered Mark Guthrie, 38 and attempted to murder his sister, Val, 41, and Mark's wife, Connie, 37. During the ensuing struggle three farm employees, José Ramos, 25, Tyrone Gibbs, 23, and Diego Santiago, 52, rushed in to try and overcome Boyd. However things went badly wrong. Boyd killed Gibbs and critically wounded Ramos and Connie Guthrie. Santiago received a head wound and is listed in stable condition. Hospital sources indicate that Ramos received severe spinal trauma and is feared to be paralyzed. Connie Guthrie received extensive throat wounds and is on life support.

In an ironic twist of events, Val Guthrie, who was also injured during the attack, was able to bring down the killer using the handgun once owned by her father.

From *The Black Marsh Sentinel,* October 14

PINE DEEP MAYOR
IN CRITICAL CONDITION
FOLLOWING SUICIDE ATTEMPT

By Willard Fowler Newton

Pine Deep, Pennsylvania, does not seem to be able to get a breather from the ongoing violence that has rocked the town since the end of September. In the latest chapter of this ongoing tragedy the town's beloved and respected mayor, Terry Wolfe, attempted to take his own life last night by throwing himself out his second-floor window onto concrete flagstones.

Sources say that Wolfe has been under tremendous pressure since the beginning of this season's crop blight that has brought many of the town's farms to the brink of financial ruin. "The poor man's been a wreck," said Deputy Mayor Harry LeBeau. "First the blight and then the attacks on the Guthries. He's always been very close with them, ever since he and Val were an item back in school."

Sarah Wolfe, the wife of the mayor and a career politician herself, made only a brief statement: "Terry has been working night and day to try and save Pine Deep from economic ruin. This town means everything to him and I ask that everyone in town joins me in praying for my husband."

Sheriff Gus Bernhardt released a brief statement: "Mayor Wolfe is in critical condition and is in surgery at this time. The nature and cause of his injuries are under investigation. It has been a very tragic night for the people of Pine Deep."

PROLOGUE

Diggin' in the graveyard—finding all
them secrets out
I'm digging in the graveyard—I'll be finding all
your secrets out

—Oren Morse, "Midnight Graveyard Blues"

This is a cruel cruel cruel world
You have to live in each and every day
You can't hardly trust your next-door neighbor
Or they just might steal your life away

—Eddy "The Chief" Clearwater, "Messed Up World"

The Bone Man was as thin as a whisper; he was a scarecrow from a blighted field. He stood on the edge of the hospital roof, toes jutting out over the gutter, his trousers fluttering against the stick slimness of his legs. His coat flaps snapped vigorously but silently around his emaciated hips. The only sound the wind made as it whipped by him and through him was a faint plaintive whine as it caressed the silvery strings of the guitar slung behind his back.

Far below, the parking lot faded back from the glow of the emergency room doors, spreading out in a big half-circle that had been cut acres-deep into the surrounding sea of pines. Even this late there were dozens of cars down there, dusted with moonlight but asleep. All around the town there was a ring of black clouds that were invisible against the night, but above the Bone Man the stars flickered and glimmered by the thousand.

For three hours he had sat cross-legged on the roof, playing his songs, humming and sometimes singing, coaxing the sad blues out of the ghost of an old guitar that Charley Patton had once used to play "Mississippi Boweavil Blues" at a church picnic in Bentonia, Mississippi. Another time the Bone Man's father, old Virgil Morse, had used that guitar to play backup on a couple of Sun Records sides by Mose Vinson. The guitar had history. It had life, even though it was no more real than he was. A ghost of a guitar in a dead man's hands, playing music almost no one could hear.

He'd sat there and played and listened to the whispers and cries and moans from inside the hospital, hearing the beep of the machine that breathed for Connie Guthrie. Hearing the sewing-circle whisper of needles and thread as the doctors stitched Terry Wolfe's skin, and the faint grinding sound as they set his bones. He heard the whimper of hopelessness from the throat of José Ramos as the doctors stood by his bed and explained to his mother that his back was broken, and then the scream as the enormity of that pronouncement drove a knife into his mother's heart. He heard the dreadful terror as Dr. Saul Weinstock murmured, "Dear God," over and over again as he knelt alone in the bathroom of his office, hands on either side of the toilet bowl, his face streaked with tears and his lips wet with vomit.

He heard all of these things while he played, and then he heard the hospital slowly fall quiet as drugs or shock or alcohol took each of them into their private pits of darkness. That's when the Bone Man had stopped playing and rose to stand on the edge of the roof, staring across blacktop and car hoods and trees at the moon.

It was an ugly quarter moon, stained yellow-red like bruised flesh, and its sickle tip seemed to slash at the treetops. The sky above the trees was thick with agitated night birds that flapped and cawed, hectoring him like Romans at the circus.

(2)

"Where are you now?"

Jim Polk cupped his hand around his cell and pitched his voice to a whisper. "At the hospital, like you said. Back loading dock."

"Anyone see you?"

"Jesus, Vic, you think I'm that stupid?"

Vic Wingate's voice tightened a notch. "Did anyone *see* you?"

"No, okay? No one saw me."

"You're sure?"

Polk almost mouthed off again, but caught himself. A half beat later he said, "I'm sure."

"Then open the door. We're here."

The hallway was still dark and empty. He'd already disabled the alarms and the video cameras, permanently this time per Vic's instructions. He pocketed his cell and fished for his keys, his fingers shaking badly. His nerves were shot and getting worse every time Vic asked him to do something like this. There was no letup, always some other shit to do, always something that was tightening the noose around his neck. The McDonald's fish in his stomach felt like it was congealing.

He turned the key, but before Polk could push it open the door was whipped out of his hand and Karl Ruger shouldered his way in, pausing just enough to give Polk a slow, hungry up and down. He smiled a wide, white smile that showed two rows of jagged teeth that were wet with spit. The greasy slush in Polk's belly gave another sickening lurch. Vic was bad enough, but looking into Ruger's eyes was like looking into a dark well that was drilled all the way down to Hell. He fell back a step, stammering something useless, and twitched an arm nervously toward the morgue door halfway down the hall.

Ruger's mouth twitched. "Yeah," he whispered, "I know the way."

Polk flattened back against the wall, not wanting to even let Ruger's shadow touch him. Two other men came in—beefy college kids in Pinelands Scarecrows sweatshirts—their faces as white as Ruger's, their mouths filled with long white teeth. Vic was the last to enter and he pulled the door shut behind him and stood next to Polk, watching the three of them pad noiselessly down the hall.

"Yo!" Vic called softly and the college kids turned. "Quick and dirty. Mess the place up, paint some goofy frat-boy shit on the wall, break some stuff, and then haul Boyd's sorry ass out of here." He looked at his watch. "Five minutes and we're gone."

The college kids grinned at him for a moment and then pulled open the morgue door and vanished inside. Ruger lingered in the doorway.

Vic said to him, "They can handle it, Sport. You don't need to bother."

Even from that distance Polk could see Ruger's thin smile, and he felt Vic stiffen next to him. *Jesus Christ,* Polk thought, *Vic's afraid of him, too.*

"Mark Guthrie's in there." Ruger's tongue flicked out and lapped spit off his lips. "I want to pay my respects."

With a dry little laugh Ruger turned and went into the morgue.

Polk looked at Vic, who took a cigarette from his shirt pocket and slowly screwed it into his mouth, his eyes narrowed and thoughtful. Absently Vic began patting his pockets for a match and Polk pulled his own lighter and clicked it. Vic cut him a quick look, then gave a short nod and bent to the light, dragging in a deep chestful of smoke.

"Vic . . . ?"

Vic said nothing. Polk licked his lips. "Vic . . . is this all going to work out? I mean . . . is this all going to be okay for us?"

Vic Wingate exhaled as he turned to Polk, and in the darkness of the hallway his eyes were just as black and bottomless as Ruger's. "Couple hours ago I'd have told you we were screwed. Royally screwed." He plucked a fleck of tobacco from his tongue-tip and flicked it away. "But a lot's happened since then." He took another drag.

"Does that mean we're okay now? Does that mean we're safe?"

A lot of thoughts seemed to flit back and forth behind the black glass of Vic's eyes. "Depends on what you mean," he said with a smile, and then he headed down the hallway toward the morgue.

PART I
America's Haunted Holidayland

October 14 to October 16

*Hope is the worst of evils, for it prolongs the
torment of man.*

—Friedrich Nietzsche

*Walking that Ghost Road is like walkin' down to Hell
Walking the Ghost Road—it's taking me
down to Hell.
I'm walking it once, won't walk it no more
Tonight I'm walking down to Hell . . .*

—Oren Morse, "Ghost Road to Hell"

Chapter 1

Malcolm Crow wanted to kill someone. He wanted to take a gun, a knife, his *hands* . . . and murder someone. He wanted it to hurt, and he wanted it to last. He wanted to run up and down the hospital hallways and find someone who needed killing, some black-hearted bastard whose death would mark the line between the way things were and the way they used to be. Or *should* be.

Waiting was excruciating. It had been hours since he'd ridden with his fiancée Val in the ambulance to Pinelands Hospital and then watched the ER team take her away. He'd tried to bully his way in so that he could be with her while they checked to see how badly she'd been hurt—Val and the tiny baby just starting to grow inside of her. *Their* baby. Crow had tried to stay by her side, but the doctors had been insistent, telling him that he needed to leave, needed to let them work. Yeah, well . . . what he really wanted was a villain he could find and hurt. He needed to have a big summer blockbuster ending to this madness, with explosions, CGI effects, a big body count, and the sun shining on the good guys as the bad guys lay scattered around them. Defeated, once and for all. That's what he needed, and he needed it bad.

A snowball had a better chance of making it through August in Hell.

The voice in his head was giving him a badass sneer and telling him he'd come too late to this dogfight. It was all over and if the good guys won, it had nothing to do with him. Not in this latest round. He stood looking at his reflection in the darkened window, seeing a small man, barely five-seven, slim, with a scuffle of black hair. He knew he was tougher than he looked, but toughness hadn't been enough to get him to Val's side in time to help her. To his eyes he just looked as weak as he felt.

Karl Ruger was already dead—okay, to be fair Crow had killed him two weeks ago, right in this very hospital, but that was yesterday's news. Kenneth Boyd was dead, too, but Crow had no hand in that, though he wished he could fly counterclockwise around the world like Superman and roll time back to last night so he could change the way things happened. It would have been so much better if he had been the one to face Boyd down there at the Guthrie farm. Him . . . rather than Val.

It was crazy. Ruger was supposed to be the stone killer, not Boyd—his crooked but relatively harmless chum. But after Ruger died Boyd suddenly steps up and takes a shot at being Sick Psycho of the Year by killing two local cops at Val's farm, breaking into the hospital to steal Ruger's corpse from the morgue—and Crow didn't even want to *think* about what that was all about—and then, to really seal the deal, the rat-bastard tried to kill everyone at Val's farm. It had been a true bloodbath.

Val's brother, Mark, was the first victim. He'd stormed off after a spat with his wife, Connie, and had apparently been sulking in the barn where he'd run into Boyd. For no sane reason that Crow could imagine, Boyd murdered him. Tore his throat out with his teeth. Drank his blood. Actually drank his blood. Every time Crow thought about that a sick shiver rippled through him and gooseflesh pebbled every inch of his skin. He got up from his chair and stared out the window at the featureless black of the middle of the night.

Val was taking Connie out for a cool-down stroll when Boyd attacked them. Connie—poor Connie, who was never much cut out for the real world and had very nearly been raped by Ruger—was overwhelmed by Boyd. He bit her, too. Not immediately fatal, but bad enough. From what little Crow had been able to find out from harassed nurses, Connie's throat was a ruin and she was fighting for every breath, every heartbeat. No one seemed hopeful about her chances.

Three of Val's farm hands—big, tough sons of bitches—had come pelting up and tackled Boyd. They should have been able to stomp the living shit out of him, and that should have been the end of it; but two seconds later Tyrone Gibbs was dead, José was down with a broken neck—alive but paralyzed for life—and the foreman, Diego, was knocked senseless.

That left only Val.

Crow closed his eyes hard, trying to squeeze the image out of his head, but it worked on his mind like rat's teeth. Boyd tried to kill her, and the thought of her facing down the murdering monster was too much to bear. Rage kept spiking up and Crow was sure his blood pressure could blow half-inch bolts out of plate steel. Thank God Val had been carrying her father's old .45 Colt Commander ever since Ruger invaded the farm at the end of September. It was too heavy a gun for a woman, even a tall, strong farm woman like Val, but heavy or not she must have been pumping adrenaline by the quart. She held her ground and used that heavy pistol to blow the living hell out of Boyd.

The thing was—more gooseflesh rippled along Crow's arms—Boyd didn't go down like he should have. That .45 should have punched him down and dead on the first shot. *Maybe* the second, if Boyd was totally whacked out . . . but Val shot him over and over again until finally a shot to the head snapped off his switch.

While they were waiting for the ambulance last night, Val told him, "That's when I knew."

"Knew what, baby?"

"That he wasn't human. That he was . . . dead."

Crow understood. Who better to understand such things? The dread of just that sort of stuff had been haunting him since he was a kid, and it was almost funny because in Pine Deep it was *okay* to believe in ghosts. Hauntings brought in the tourists. Problem was, Boyd was no ghost—he'd killed Mark for his blood. He tore grown men apart. He'd taken bullet after bullet and kept coming. Boyd was something else entirely.

Crow knew that, of anyone in town, he was the only one

who was predisposed to accept that kind of thing as possible . . . even likely. During the Massacre when he and Val were kids, he alone had seen the face of the killer and had understood that the terrible menace in Pine Deep was not just a serial killer. Crow had looked into the face of local farmer Ubel Griswold and had seen that face begin to change from human . . . to wolf. Only the sudden arrival of Oren Morse, the guy all the kids called the Bone Man, had saved Crow. Griswold hadn't completely transformed and, before he could complete the murder, the scuffle with the Bone Man had roused all the neighbors. Griswold had vanished into the darkness; no one else had seen what he was.

The truth was that no one else even suspected Griswold of the crimes. The man had immigrated to the States from Germany and had purchased a large tract of land in the borough's most remote spot—way down past Dark Hollow. There he'd set up a cattle farm and stayed to himself, paying his taxes and maintaining only a few friends. But Griswold never sold any of the cattle he raised. Crow suspected that Griswold used them to satisfy his peculiar *hungers*; that he hunted them the way a wolf would, and that those killings kept his appetites in check. It was only after a season of blight and disease had wiped out all of the town's livestock, Griswold's included, that bloodlust forced Griswold to hunt beyond his own lands. Still no one suspected because Griswold was sly and careful.

It was only chance that the migrant worker and blues singer Oren Morse discovered Griswold's true nature. Morse was hunting the killer that night years ago and had arrived in the nick of time to save Crow's life; but no one was ready to believe the word of a homeless day laborer—especially a black one in mid-1970s rural Pennsylvania. Not that Crow was believed, either; he told his father about Griswold and was rewarded by a savage beating. The elder Crow was one of a select group of young men who were completely devoted to Griswold. The beating left the young Crow too afraid to tell the truth; and shortly after that Oren Morse tracked Griswold down and killed him, or so Crow believed. Crow's father and a handful of other men—Vic Wingate, Jim Polk, Gus Bernhardt, and a few others—captured

Morse, beat him to death, and hung him on a scarecrow post out in the corn. From that point on everyone believed that Morse had been the killer all along. The truth had never come out.

The town recovered from the disaster and changed, transforming from a blue-collar hick town into an upscale arts community. The Bone Man became an urban legend, the local bogeyman who was blamed for all of the killings of that Dark Harvest Autumn of 1976. The name of Ubel Griswold was forgotten.

Just yesterday, while death was stalking Val and her family, Crow had gone down into Dark Hollow, the remotest spot in the whole borough, dragging Newton along with him—the two of them on a stupid quest to somehow try and prove Crow's tale of thirty years ago. Down in the Hollow they'd found Griswold's house, but they hadn't found a werewolf or even a man. Maybe they'd found a ghost, even Crow wasn't sure, but when they tried to enter the house they were driven back. First by the porch roof that collapsed and nearly crushed them—strange timing for a roof that had been sagging for three decades—and then from the rubble a swarm of bristling black roaches attacked them. Hundreds of thousands of them. Crow and the reporter had dropped everything and run. Heroics be damned. It was only the presence of patchy sunlight that had given them a chance to escape. The insects would not cross from shadow into light, and so Crow and Newton ran back through the woods and climbed the hill.

Now, looking back on it with vision filtered through his rage, Crow realized that everything that had happened down in the Hollow must have been some kind of delaying tactic, keeping Crow out of play so that Val and her family would be vulnerable. It had worked, too. Crow got there way too late.

So, it galled Crow that Val had been forced to do it alone, just as it galled him that he wasn't the one to swoop down like Captain Avenger and save the day. Val had done that. Pregnant, injured, grief-torn Val. Not him, not Crow. Her.

"You are a stupid day-late and a dollar-short chauvinist jackass," he told himself. He burned to be able to step back one day and change this. Save Mark and Connie and the others if he could; but as guilty as it made him feel, those concerns were secondary to wanting to take that experience away from Val. It was beside the point, there were no villains left to kill. All the bad guys were dead. The show was over. All that was left for him to do was wait while the doctors and nurses did what they did; wait until Val was brought up here to her room . . . and even then it wouldn't be Captain Avenger she'd need. Val would be grieving, and he would need to be her rock.

Behind him, Newton, the dumpy little reporter, stirred in his sleep and shifted to a less uncomfortable position in the comfortless guest chair of what would be Val's room when they finally brought her up from the ER.

Crow looked at the clock. Three-thirty in the morning. What was taking the doctors so long? Was it a "no news is good news" deal? From his own memories of hospitals he didn't think so. Val had been hit in the head by Ruger—first a pistol-whipping, then a punch that cracked her eye socket; then Boyd had hit her even harder. There was a danger, Crow knew, of her losing the sight in that eye.

Would she lose the baby, too? The thought sent buckets of ice water sloshing down through Crow's bowels.

There was a discreet tap on the door and Crow leapt up, hope flaring in his chest that it was Val being brought in, but as soon as he saw the look on the face of the young doctor in the hall his heart crashed.

"Mr. Crow . . . ?"

"What's wrong? Is it Val? How is she, is something wrong?" He took a fistful of the doctor's scrub shirt.

"Mr. Crow, please," the doctor said, lightly touching his wrist. "This isn't about Ms. Guthrie. She's still in the ER, and the last I heard is that her condition is listed as stable."

"Thank God—"

"Dr. Weinstock told me to tell you about the other Ms. Guthrie . . . Mrs. Connie Guthrie. He said you're more or less family? Next of kin?"

"Close enough. I'm engaged to Val. Connie's her sister-in-law."

The doctor looked sad. "Mr. Crow . . . I'm sorry to tell you this, but Mrs. Guthrie passed away."

"What?" He couldn't process what the doctor just told him.

"Her wounds were too severe, there was extensive damage to her airway and . . ." He faltered and shook his head. "We did everything we could. I'm so sorry." He left very quietly.

Crow had no memory of walking into the bathroom, but he suddenly found himself sitting on the floor between the toilet and the sink, dizzy and sick. He clamped his hands together, laced his fingers tightly over his knuckles, and bent his head, mumbling prayers to a God he'd long since come to doubt, or at best mistrust. He wanted to pray, tried to put it in words, but there had been too many bad nights and too many broken years since he last believed, and he found that he'd lost the knack of it. So all he did was squeeze his eyes shut and say the only words that he could muster, making the only argument that made any sense to him.

"Take me if you want," he pleaded, "but not Val. Not her, too. Not our baby. Do whatever you want to me, but save my family." When he added, "Please!" it sounded like the word had been pulled out of his mouth with pliers.

(2)

Jim Polk was in charge of the police detail at the hospital. He was Sheriff Gus Bernhardt's right-hand man, the department's only sergeant, and getting what he wanted was easy. Gus was an idiot and even Gus knew it, just as Gus knew that if it wasn't for Polk's efficiency, energy, and attention to detail the whole department would be a total wreck. So, what Polk wanted, Polk got.

Even Brad Maynard, head of hospital security, deferred to Polk, especially in light of the hospital's appalling track record lately. First Ruger had broken into the hospital and disabled both main and backup generators so he could try and kill Crow and Val; then the very next day Boyd broke in and stole Ruger's body from the morgue. It was an open secret that Maynard was going to have to face the hospital's board and no one was putting hot money on his chances for keeping his job.

All of this was Polk's doing. Ordered by Vic, of course, but planned and executed by Polk. *I should just request a revolving door for the morgue,* he thought as he poured ten sugar packets into the cup of cafeteria coffee he'd sent one of the hospital guards to fetch for him.

It was coming on 4:00 A.M. when his cell phone vibrated in his pocket. Polk didn't even have to look at it to know who it was. He jerked his chin for the hospital guard to come over. "Duke, I'm gonna go catch a smoke. You stay here. Remember—no one talks to Val Guthrie unless I personally say it's okay. No exceptions."

"What about Crow?"

Polk gave him a Clint Eastwood squint. The one Clint uses when he's trying to figure out how to explain to some total idiot the difference between shit and Shinola. Vic had given him that same look too damn many times. "Just do what you're told, okay?"

Polk turned on his heel the way he'd seen Clint, and Vic, do and strolled out of the ER and into the fire tower. He jogged up a flight and then down a flight to make sure no one else was around and then pulled out his cell and hit speed-dial. Vic answered on the first ring. "What the hell took you so long?"

"I was with people."

"Gimme a status report on Mayor Wolfe. He going to make it?"

The town's mayor, Terry Wolfe, had attempted suicide by hurling himself out of his second-floor window. The drop was not far enough to kill him, but almost.

"He's a mess. Forty broken bones, couple of 'em compound. Shattered skull. Brain's probably chopped liver. He's in a coma right now. Guess we're going to need a new mayor."

"So he's definitely out of the picture for the moment."

"What about Val Guthrie? What shape did Boyd leave her in?"

"Might go blind in one eye. They just ran a bunch of tests, but right now they got an OB-GYN in with her. Turns out she's pregnant and they're checking to see if she's going to lose the baby."

Vic grunted. "Bun in the oven, huh? Let me think on that some, maybe it's something we can use. Call me if you need anything else."

"Sure, but what—?"

Vic hung up on him.

(3)

Feeling wretched about Connie and desperately alone, Crow headed down to the ER in hopes of getting a glimpse of Val or Weinstock, but instead he ran into Sarah Wolfe, the mayor's wife, who sat alone on a hard plastic hallway chair, looking small and lost, her lap scattered with crumpled tissues.

"Hey, sweetie . . . how are you? Or is that the dumbest question ever asked?" He screwed on a genial smile and it fit so badly that it hurt his cheeks. She opened her mouth to say something, but her first word turned into a sob and her face crumpled. Crow bent to her, drew her into his arms, guided her around a corner and into an empty triage room.

"Have they told you how he is yet?" he asked when her sobs slowed.

"I talked to Saul just a few minutes ago. He's been running in and out of surgeries. He said that Terry's lucky to be alive. Lucky"—Sarah gave a wretched nod—"that's a funny word to use."

"Yeah. Really cheers you up, doesn't it?" He shook his head. "Sarah, honey . . . what set Terry off? I talked to him the day before and sure he was stressed, but he didn't seem this far gone. What triggered it?"

Terry's nightmares and paranoia had gotten much worse over the last few weeks, and lately he'd been claiming that he saw his dead sister Mandy everywhere he went. "He finally confessed to me that Mandy was trying to convince him to commit suicide. I know it sounds ridiculous," Sarah said, forcing a ghastly smile, "but I believe he really *saw* Mandy. He believed she was actually there. He would turn to face her, to look at a spot in the room as if she was standing right there. You'll think I'm crazy, too, but I swear there were times I could feel her myself. Nuts, huh?"

Crow made a noncommittal sound and tried not to let the horror show on his face.

"There was one moment, Crow, where I swear to God I thought Terry was going to attack me. He started stalking me across the bedroom floor. It was so . . . weird; it was like he stopped being Terry and became some kind of, oh—I don't know—some kind of animal. He moved like an animal, you know? He told me about the conversation you two had about his dreams, where you said that he was probably dreaming of becoming an animal—a wolf—because of our last name. I mean, let's face it, you've been calling him 'Wolfman' since you two were little kids. So . . . maybe that's what happened. Maybe his psychosis, his damage, whatever it is . . . maybe it just took that path. Maybe for a few minutes up there in our room he thought he was a wolf. Or something like that. Is this making any sense? Am I just rambling?"

"Sarah, honey, I think it's those pills he's been popping," Crow lied. "When this is all sorted out I think we're going to find that he was probably taking too much of the wrong prescription and it just threw him out of whack. That . . . plus everything that's been happening in town, the blight, the whole Ruger thing. Terry holds this town together."

"Maybe," she said doubtfully, "but that still doesn't explain what started him down that road. He's only been on meds for the last four or five months. The dreams started almost a year ago."

"I know . . . but we're going to have to let the docs figure that out. Right now we have to just focus our minds on the thought that he's going to pull through, that he'll be okay."

"God . . . do you think so? I mean . . . really?"

"Sure," he said, pushing the lie in her path. "Everything's going to be fine. Terry will pull through and he'll be kicking my ass on the back nine by spring. Val, too. We're all going to be fine. It's all over now . . . from here on, everything gets better."

(4)

Tow-Truck Eddie knelt there in a pool of his own blood, his naked torso streaked with sweat, his face burned dark with red rage, his hands pressed together in prayer. His knuckles were raw hamburger, chopped and lacerated, with flaps of skin hanging open. Blood ran in slow lines down his forearms and dripped from his abraded elbows.

Around him his living room demonstrated his fury. The couch was overturned, its wooden bones shattered, each pillow bitten open and ripped apart. One metal foot of the heavy recliner was buried inches deep into the drywall by the dining room door, still canted at the awkward angle into which it had settled after Eddie picked it up and hurled it half the length of the room. The coffee table was a mass of mahogany splinters scattered in a fan pattern around the shaft of the floor lamp Eddie had used to smash it.

"I'm sorry!" he said, and it was maybe the hundredth time he'd said it. It was all he had said since he'd come home late last night ashamed, furious, and defeated.

Hours earlier he'd had to call his boss, Shanahan, to tell him that he had driven the company's best wrecker off the road into a ditch near Shandy's Curve out on Route A-32.

Shanahan was furious. "Are you friggin' kidding me here, Eddie?"

"No sir," Eddie whispered back, his shame so huge that it was like a pounding surf smashing down on him.

There was a long pause on the line. "You hurt?" Shanahan asked, his concern grudging.

"Nothing to worry about." In fact his knee was badly bruised, the muscles in his neck were sore, and he had a slowly pounding headache that suggested whiplash. But he would never say it, couldn't bear to hear sympathy. The undertone of disapproval and disappointment was bad enough. "I need another truck to pull me out."

"How bad's the wrecker?"

"Not too bad. I'll fix what I can and you can dock the rest out of my pay."

"I'm insured. But—damn it, Eddie, how'd the hell you put the thing into a ditch?" Before Eddie could invent an excuse, Shanahan said, "Give me half an hour and I'll come fetch you."

Eddie sat on the side of the ditch waiting, murderous with humiliation as Shanahan pulled the wrecker out. But that was not the real source of Eddie's shame—it was the sure knowledge that he had betrayed the trust his Father had shown him. For weeks now Eddie had been hearing the voice of God whispering to him in his head, telling him wonderful things, revealing to him that Eddie was the Messiah come again and, even more wonderfully, that Eddie was the Sword of God! It confirmed what Eddie had always suspected, but hearing the Voice of God speaking to him . . . to *him* . . . was beyond glorious.

God told him that the New Age was coming, that a New Covenant was about to be made between mankind and the Divine All, but that the Beast—the Antichrist in human disguise—had manifested on Earth to try and thwart God's holy plan. Eddie's mission had been to seek out this monster and strike him down to the furtherance of His glory. But the mission was far more difficult than Eddie had thought because the Beast wore a costume of flesh and bone that looked like a boy, and he rode around town on an ordinary bicycle. Such a clever disguise, but Tow-Truck Eddie had ultimately seen through it and had hunted the roads for him for two weeks. Last night he had received a whisper from God Himself, telling him to wait for the Beast out there on the road. He'd known the time, the place, the *moment*. It should all have gone smoothly; but nothing had gone right and Eddie, through his mortal weakness, had let the Beast defeat him with ridiculous ease, tricking him into that ditch.

Since then Eddie had begged, wept, and cried aloud to his Father, trying to explain, to seek forgiveness of his great sin . . . but God's voice had been silent since the accident. Not one word, not even a reproof. Nothing. Just an aching silence so profound that Eddie could feel his heart break bit by bit. All through the long, long night he had alternately prayed and pleaded, and then as dawn broke over his house and the interior shadows shifted from black to a muddy gray, Eddie's heartache and shame had boiled up from his gut to his brain and he had gone berserk, screaming, raging up and down the stairs, smashing everything that would break, punching holes through plaster, crushing, all the time crying out to his Father for some answer.

When the volcano of fury burned down, the hours of sleeplessness, the aches in his body, and the weight of his grief collapsed him down to his knees amid the debris. He had nothing left, he *was* nothing. Tears streaked his face, drool hung from his rubbery lips. In his ears he could hear the pounding of his heart—it sounded like someone hitting a bass drum with a fist wrapped in gauze.

"I'm sorry," he blubbered, hanging his head. "I'm so sorry."

The Bone Man lingered in the shadows of the destroyed living room. He'd enjoyed Eddie's frustrated rage. Such a damn shame it stopped short of the big man just plain killing himself. He pretended to sigh.

"That's one round to us," he said, though his voice was as soundless as he was invisible.

Even so, Tow-Truck Eddie's head jerked up as if he had heard those words. The Bone Man froze, afraid to even move as Eddie looked around in confusion, pawing tears from his eyes, brow knitted. It was a long minute before Eddie's scowl faltered and his eyes lost their hawklike intensity. He bent again to his prayers and his pleas, and the Bone Man backed carefully out through the wall.

(5)

Crow slipped away when Sarah's sister Rose arrived from Brooklyn. He drifted to the nurse's station and begged for information, but instead of a doctor Jim Polk came smirking out of the ER.

Polk said, "You're going to have to stop harassing the nurses, pal."

Startled, Crow said, "What the hell are you talking about? Val's my—"

"Val's a material witness in a murder case. Once the doctors are done with her we have to take her statement. Until we do no one gets to see her."

Polk wasn't a big man, but he was taller and heavier than Crow, and he wore a hyena smile as he spoke, slowly chewing a wad of pink gum. His teeth were wet and his eyes looked piggish. Crow wanted to stuff him into a laundry chute.

"Look, Jim," he began, trying to be reasonable, "it's not like I don't know the drill here. How about a little professional courtesy?"

"You're not a cop anymore."

"Actually, I think I am. Terry swore me back onto the department during the Ruger manhunt. He never swore me out again, so technically—"

Polk took a half step closer and lowered his voice. "Terry Wolfe is a hophead schizo who didn't have enough brains to even commit suicide. Who the hell cares what he did or didn't do?"

Polk's words stunned Crow. "Hey, Jim, let's dial it down here."

Polk tapped Crow's chest with a stiffened index finger. "Dial your own shit down, Crow. You're not a cop in this town, and your butt-buddy Terry Wolfe isn't around to hold your hand. Right now all you are is a pain in the ass and a potential nuisance to a police investigation. You got no rights and you got no say. Are we clear on that?" With every other word he jabbed Crow in the chest.

With each tap more of the shock drained out of Crow as cold fury took its place. He looked down at the finger pressing against his chest and then slowly raised his eyes to meet Polk's. For a few seconds he said nothing, just letting the hardness of his stare work on Polk, and Crow could see the tough-guy façade lose some of its fastenings. Very softly he said, "Jim . . . I don't know what bug crawled up your ass, but I'm going to tell you only once to move that finger before I break it off. Maybe you opened a box of Cracker Jacks and the toy surprise was a new set of balls, but believe me when I tell you that today is not the best day to get in my face."

Polk gave him a hard-ass sneer, but he lowered his hand. "Get your ass out of here, Crow. When we want you, we'll call 1-800-dial-a-drunk." With that he turned away and reached to push open the ER door.

"That's it?" Crow said, laughing before he could catch himself. "That's really the best exit line you can think of? Dial-a-drunk? That wasn't even funny when I *was* a drunk, you dumb-ass hick, and now it's just . . . lame."

Polk almost turned around; it was there in his mind and he even had a hitch in his step, but they both knew he wouldn't. Instead he pushed angrily through the swinging doors and let them flap shut behind him.

Crow went and peered through the crack between the doors, but all he could see was another cop's back. *Shit.*

Totally perplexed by what had just happened—and feeling anger burn on his cheeks and ears—Crow turned away and trudged back to Val's room, grinding his teeth all the while. Newton was still asleep in the chair, and Crow crossed to the empty bed and sat down, feeling weak and defeated.

Chapter 2

Vic Wingate pulled his midnight-blue pickup into the slot behind his house and killed the lights. The sun was setting brush fires on the horizon, but the back alley was still shrouded in bruise-colored shadows. He lit a cigarette from the dashboard lighter and looked up and down the street. Nothing moved; even the pear trees in his neighbor's backyard seemed frozen in time.

"It's clear," he said, but Ruger was already getting out of the car like he didn't give a shit.

Inside, Ruger sank down into Vic's Barcalounger with a volume of Eastern European folklore. Vic went to the wet bar at the foot of the stairs and poured himself a C&C and ginger ale without ice. He took a small sip, rinsing it around to clear out the acid taste in his mouth, swallowed, and then took a larger gulp. When he lowered the glass he saw that Ruger was not reading but was instead staring up at the ceiling. It was only then that Vic could hear the muffled footsteps above, followed by the bang of a pan on the stove. Lois, up early.

"Smells good," Ruger said in his whispery voice.

"You can smell her cooking all the way down here?"

"No," Ruger said, his eyes dreamy and unfocused, "I can smell her." He closed his eyes; one corner of his mouth hooked up in a smile as thin and curled as a dentist's hook. "Full-blooded bitch."

"Hey, Sport," Vic snapped, "that's my wife you're talking about."

Ruger waited maybe five whole seconds before he opened his eyes. All color in the irises had melted into a featureless black. It was like looking into the eyes of a shark. His smile never wavered and he said nothing; all he did was lower his head and pick up his book.

Vic stared at him for a while, then cut a sharp look at the ceiling, angry at Lois for no reason. He slammed back the rest of his drink and built another, searching in the shadows of his mind for that little thread of contact, that indefinable conduit that would link him to the Man. It was getting harder and harder to touch the Man, which made no damn sense since with things moving like this it should be getting easier. The Man was feeding every day now, taking the discharge of pain and terror from each kill that Ruger and his goon squad made. Every day he got stronger, so it should be easy for Vic to reach him. Behind him he heard the soft rustle as Ruger turned a page.

He paused, the mouth of the whiskey bottle hovering over the rim of his glass, the liquid sloshing softly as he gave Ruger a long, calculating appraisal. He didn't like the thoughts that were forming in his brain.

"Son of a bitch," he breathed.

Ruger said, "You say something?"

Vic set the bottle down very carefully, screwed the cap back on, and turned with his drink, forcing his hands to hold the glass steady, forcing his mouth to smile a smile that was just as thin, just as icy as Ruger's.

"No, Sport, I didn't say a goddamn thing."

They looked at each other, two sharks smiling across the sea of eddying shadows, seeing each other with perfect clarity.

After a moment Vic said, "At some point you and I might have to sit down and have a heart-to-heart talk about some shit, you dig? But right now we both have bigger fish to fry."

Ruger kept giving him *the look* for another couple of seconds, then his eyes seemed to lose some of their heat. "Okay."

"The Red Wave launches in two weeks. We're nowhere near ready."

"We're not behind schedule, far as I know."

"Yeah? Last night we should have cut down the opposition and increased troop strength. Tell me how you figure we're on schedule?"

Ruger didn't comment.

"Not one damn thing went as planned. We didn't kill Val Guthrie, the Man didn't kill Crow . . . which is probably a good thing since that pussy Terry Wolfe tried to kill himself."

"Maybe the Man knew Wolfe was going to take the plunge and laid off of Crow," Ruger offered. "After all, we got to have one of them alive until the big day."

"Maybe, but I smell a nigger in the woodpile. I think something went *wrong* down in the Hollow."

Ruger said nothing.

"And since I don't hear Lois up there wailing and gnashing her teeth I can pretty much guess Tow-Truck Eddie didn't kill Mike. Bottom line, we drew a complete blank last night. Maybe even a setback."

"You waste too much time on that kid, Vic ol' buddy. Instead of trying to get that moron Eddie to kill your asshole stepson, why not just do it yourself?"

"I told you already . . . I can't. He has to die by a clean hand. That's why the Man wants Eddie to do it."

"Eddie's clean? How the hell do you figure that? He works for the Man just like we do."

Vic shook his head. "No, he don't. Eddie thinks he's hearing the voice of God in his head. Eddie's this whole-milk-drinking, on-his-knees praying, Bible-thumping child of Jesus, so the Man's been riffing off that, twisting his faith even more while at the same time making him think he's the avenging son of Heaven or some shit."

That nudged an appreciative chuckle out of Ruger. "Sweet."

"Point is, if one of us—especially one of your bunch—kills Mike, then what he is, his *essence* will be released to the whole town. Once that happens every stick, stone, and blade of grass will be like a holy weapon. It will be like everything was radioactive—none of you could even walk here, and the Man wouldn't be able to *rise*."

"That's what being a *dhampyr* means?"

There was a flicker of hesitation before Vic answered, "It's part of what it means. It's in the folklore, in the traditions. I don't want to get it into right now, either . . . that's not part of your end of things except that you just make sure your crowd doesn't put the chomp on him. We clear on that?" Vic pursed his lips for a moment. "If Eddie can't get the job done by, say, next week, then I'll just take a baseball bat to the kid's knees just so he's not in the game during the Wave. Been wanting to do that for some time. Kid's a serious disappointment."

"Maybe he has too much of his father in him."

"Watch your mouth—"

"Not *him*, dumbass, I meant the—whaddya call it?—the biological father. Maybe he picked up the pussy goody-two-shoes gene or something."

"Yeah," Vic conceded grudgingly. "Maybe. Genetics and the supernatural make a weird cocktail. You can sure as hell bet no one's ever studied it, so all of us, even the Man, are making some of this shit up as we go. Sometimes you never know how things'll turn out."

"In a pinch you could always handcuff the little punk to the radiator come Halloween morning. Let him just sit the whole thing out. Ever thought of something as simple as that, Einstein?"

"Of course I have." Vic felt his face flush because it was so simple a solution that he'd overthought the situation. So, apparently, had the Man. "We're getting off the point here. About the only thing we managed to get right yesterday was stealing Boyd's body . . . though we'd both better hope that our little bit of stage dressing is going to do the trick."

"We gotta consider spin control here. Crow and that faggot reporter saw too much down in the Hollow. We have to keep him quiet. Maybe take the Guthrie bitch and hold her hostage to force him to keep his mouth shut, or threaten her and the baby she's carrying."

"Be a tricky play, Sport. Do it too soon it would mean having to hold her for two weeks. You got to remember that Crow was a cop and he's still cop-connected. There's ten thousand ways that could go south on us. On the other hand, if we wait too long he'll probably be poking his nose where it don't belong."

"That Guthrie bitch probably knows what Boyd is . . . or *was*, I mean."

"Yeah, damn it." Vic sipped his drink. "We have to slow down any attempts they make to investigate things. I have the Man's house rigged, but that's only if they get there closer to the Wave. Until then we have to make things look ordinary so nothing screws up the tourist flow."

"If we have to we can move the nest out of there. Or we can tweak the scene, make it look like Boyd was using it as a hideout. That'll sell if Polk can handle playing an actual cop."

"Polk'll do whatever he's told, but there's another potential player in all this and he's someone people will listen to—that Jew doctor . . . Weinstock."

"What about him? We stole Boyd's body . . . he don't have jack shit."

"Don't you ever watch *CSI* or any of them shows?"

"No, jackass, I actually have a life."

"Not anymore," Vic said and there was a long moment when the two of them stared hard at each other, then Ruger's lip twitched and they both burst out laughing. Ruger beat the arm of his chair as he howled and Vic had to set down his drink to keep from spilling it down his shirtfront.

"Okay, okay, that's one for you, you son of a bitch," Ruger said as the laughter died down. "Get to where you were going, though. How's the doctor going to be a problem?"

"Forensic evidence. He autopsied those two cops Boyd killed. Castle and Cowan. He's got to have lab reports and shit. And Polk told us they had morgue video of Boyd stealing your body . . . what if there's tape of Cowan and Castle getting up to go out for a stroll?"

"Balls. Even so, we certainly can't kill him right now. There's no one to pin it on and it'd draw the wrong kind of attention."

Vic nodded. "Plus, he's a good friend of Crow and Guthrie. It'd be way too high profile, too many of the wrong connections, and it would just strengthen anything Crow had to say."

Ruger's mouth gave an ugly tremble. "I could turn him."

Vic considered, but then shook his head. "Too chancy. We run the risk of him going brain dead."

"Yeah . . . which is something I don't quite get. About one in five of the people I turn wakes up with 'No Sale' written on his eyeballs. Like Boyd, only worse in a lot of cases. It's a pain in the ass, and it's dangerous to the plan. They don't like following orders, even if they *understand* the orders, which I friggin' doubt. When they're not milling around groaning like extras from *Night of the Living Dead*, they're trying to break out to go hunt. I had to put a few of them down 'cause they were just too unruly. You're the expert . . . what's with that shit?"

"Hell if I know. Some vampires are like that. Not everyone wakes up smart and charming. Look at you, for instance."

Ruger shot him the finger. He said, "Are you sure they're actual vampires? They're more like zombies."

"Supposed to be vamps, according to the Man. Just different. Just like some of you guys have retractable fangs and some don't. Some of you guys have these oversized chompers that look like walrus teeth, and some don't and can pass for Joe Normal. Lots of different species. Maybe it has something to do with ethnic background, who knows? The only ones that are a real problem are those Dead Heads like Boyd. At first I thought he was a fluke but, you're right, it seems to be a pattern, and that could hurt us if it gets out of hand." He shook his head. "So, I guess, we can't risk having it happen to the Jew. Not yet."

"Well, then the answer's pretty obvious—we have to find out if he has any forensic stuff, find out where he keeps it, and then get rid of it. Simple as that. Steal his files, fry his hard drive. Your boy Polk's supposed to be a computer geek, right? He could find out what the doc has stored. Delete it or some shit."

Vic looked thoughtful as he sipped his whiskey. "That's not bad. Another job for Jimmy-boy. And in the meantime I have to make a decision about Cowan and Castle. Much as we need soldiers we don't need liabilities."

"Let me handle that end of things. Those guys belong to me."

"You mean they belong to the Man," Vic said, a warning edge in his voice.

Ruger smiled. "That's what I meant."

(2)

Crow heard someone call his name and looked up from the hallway water fountain to see Saul Weinstock coming out of the elevator, his clothes sweat-stained and soiled and his face as gray as five-day-old steak. Crow stepped forward, offering his hand, but Weinstock clamped a hand around his bicep, spun him, and dragged him back down the hall to Val's room. "We have to talk . . . right now."

Once they were inside Crow pulled his arm free. "I've been trying to get to you all night. How's Val?"

"She's fine, she's fine . . . look, there's something else I have to—"

Crow put his palm flat on Weinstock's chest and gave him the smallest of pushes—not hard, but hard enough. "Saul . . . tell me about Val. Now."

Weinstock blinked in confusion for a moment, then his face cleared. "Right, sorry, man . . . you can't imagine the kind of night I've had. Can I at least give you the short version?"

"Shortish, but tell me something before the big vein in my head pops."

"All right, all right . . . Val has a fracture of the medial wall of the orbit and a mild concussion. We did a CT scan and there's no evidence of a subdural hematoma and though there is some damage to the maxillary sinus there's been no blowout injury—which is a fairly common result of the kind of injury she sustained." He looked at his watch. "I have a neurologist coming in at nine this morning to do a more complete workup. Val's probably going to have headaches for a while, some loss of balance, double vision, maybe some short-term memory loss. We've been worried about retinal detachment, but it's looking better, though we're still waiting on that report from Dr. Barrett. I told them to page me the second he's done with her, and they'll be bringing her up here. Should be pretty soon. If the retina's good, then there may not even be any vision loss. Considering the trauma she's had, she's got luck on her side."

"Luck's relative," Crow said. "You told Sarah that Terry was lucky."

Weinstock looked pained. "Yeah, well, around here any time a doctor gets to give news that's not worst-case scenario 'luck' is a good word to use. Believe me, we don't get to use it enough. But I hear what you're saying, what with Mark and Connie and all."

Crow gripped Weinstock's sleeve. "What about the baby? I've been terrified to even ask. She didn't . . . lose it?"

Weinstock brightened. "No, thank God. For a slender woman Val has the constitution of a bison. We ran every test in the book and even made up a few new ones, and as far as our OB resident is concerned everything is looking good. Even so, Gail Somerfield will be here later this morning and there's no better OB-GYN in the state. I love Val, and I'll be damned if after all that's happened I will let anything happen to her or her baby." He paused and gave Crow a warm smile. "Your baby."

Crow closed his eyes and a great dark wave of tension seemed to roll out of him.

"So, yes—lucky in that regard," Weinstock said, "but there's still everything that went on at the farm last night. You'll have to really be there for her, buddy. More than ever, what with Mark and Connie and all . . ."

"I know. About Connie . . . did she suffer much?"

"I doubt she was even aware of anything from the time she was attacked."

"God. I just can't believe this. It's like Ruger and Boyd had some kind of vendetta going. Why them, though?"

Weinstock shook his head. "Who the hell knows what goes on in minds like that?"

"Is there anything new on Terry?"

"Not much. They moved him out of surgery and into ICU but—"

"Are you talking about Mayor Wolfe?" a voice asked.

Weinstock stopped and wheeled around to where Newton was struggling to sit up in the chair by the window. The little reporter blinked like a turtle and fisted sleep out of his eyes.

"You!" Weinstock said, pointing a finger at him. "Whoever you are, get out."

"Whoa," Crow said, stepping between them. "Ease up, Saul—Newton's a reporter. You know him, the guy that broke the Ruger story."

Weinstock inhaled through his nose. "In that case get the *hell* out. And I mean now."

"Hold on, Newt's with me," Crow said, waving Newton back to his seat.

Weinstock's face was alight with anger. "Crow . . . there are some things I want to tell you that I'm sure you're not going to want him to hear. Trust me on this."

"Don't be too sure. A lot of stuff happened yesterday and Newt was with me. You can speak openly."

"No way . . . not in front of a reporter."

"Saul, I don't think there's anything you can tell me that he won't be ready to hear."

"No." This time it was Newton who said it.

Crow and Weinstock both looked at him. "Hey, Newt, you can't bail out on me now."

"Crow . . . honestly, I don't know how much more of this I can take. I haven't even gotten my head wrapped around what we saw yesterday. I need to stop thinking about this. It's all too . . ." He stopped and just stood there, small and defeated, hands jammed defensively into his pockets.

Weinstock arched an eyebrow at Crow, who sighed. "S'okay, dude. I guess I didn't give you a lot of time to prepare for this, and what we went through yesterday . . . well, I'm just glad I had a friend with me."

Newton looked at him in surprise, his eyes searching Crow's

face for the lie, but not finding it. "Thanks," he mumbled, his eyes wet.

"Why don't you go home, get some sleep, and meet me back here later today? Try to put this stuff out of your mind for a while."

Newton smiled at the absurdity of the concept. "What do you think the chances are that I'll ever be able to do that?" He sketched a wave, picked up his soiled jacket, and shambled out of the room.

"Poor bastard," Crow said. "He's a pretty good guy, Saul. A little fussy at first, but he kind of stepped up. It's just that yesterday was . . . well, when I tell you the whole thing you'll understand."

Crow sat down on the edge of the bed and Weinstock dragged the chair over. For a full minute neither said a word, their eyes meeting for a second at a time and falling away. Crow leaned on his forearms and stared at the floor between his hiking boots; Weinstock leaned back and studied the blankness of the speckled acoustic ceiling tiles.

After a while Crow took a breath. "You want to start?"

Weinstock barked an ugly little laugh. "Not really."

"Me neither."

The tide of silence washed back and forth between them for a while before Weinstock finally said, "The problem is, now that I'm right up to it I don't know *how* to start."

"There's that." Crow chewed his lip for a second. "On the other hand, brother, do you have the same feeling I have that we both want to say the same thing but are just too damn scared about how we'll each react?"

Weinstock stopped looking at the ceiling. "No, but that sounds encouraging."

"There's a word that's in my head here, Saul, and I wonder if you're thinking about the same word."

There was another long time of silence, but this time they kept eye contact. Finally, Weinstock licked his lips and, very softly, said, "Does your word start with a *v*?"

"I'm sorry as hell to say it does."

Weinstock closed his eyes. "Oh . . . shit."

Chapter 3

In his dreams he was Iron Mike Sweeney, the Enemy of Evil. In his dreams he was tall and powerful, his hand was strong and sure, his courage a constant. In his dreams Mike rode through the burning town on a cut-down Harley, a Japanese *katana* slung across his back, matching pistols strapped to his hips, the fire of purpose burning in his eyes. In those dreams he sought out the killers and the predators, the monsters and the madmen, the dragons and the demons—and he slew them all.

That's what happened in Mike Sweeney's dreams.

Last night he stopped having those dreams, and never in this life would he have them again. The interior world of fantasy and heroics, of drama and excitement was gone, completely burned out of him by a process of change that had begun the night Karl Ruger came to town. For a while his dream life had intensified as new dreams had snuck into his mind, dreams in which he was chased down by a madman in a monstrous gleaming wrecker—chased and then run down, ground to red pulp beneath its wheels—or dreams in which he walked through Pine Deep as it burned, as everyone he knew and loved died around him.

The heroic dreams were gone. The dream of the wrecker was gone, too.

Only the dream of the burning town remained.

All through the night, as blood was spilled on the Guthrie farm, and as the doctors labored to save the lives of people Mike

knew and didn't know, Mike phased in and out of a dissociative
fugue state. Memories flashed before his dreaming mind that his
waking mind would not remember. Well, not for a while anyway. Halloween was coming, and that would change everything
for Mike, as it would for the rest of Pine Deep. The part of him
that was emerging, the chrysalis forming in the shadows of his
deepest mind—that part of him knew everything—but it was
still unable to communicate with Mike's conscious mind. Unable, and unready.

Mike slept through that night of pain and death and most of
who he was burned off, fading like morning fog will as the sun
rises. The part that was left, the memories and personality that
was truly Mike Sweeney had become thinner, just a veneer over
the face of the *dhampyr* who fought to emerge. Yet both boy and
dhampyr shared the dreams, the former unaware of the presence
of the other, and the latter indifferent, but both caught up in the
remaining dream as it played out over and over again as the night
ground to its end.

When Mike woke only one image remained in his conscious
mind, and it lingered there, enigmatic yet strangely calming. In it
Mike stood in a clearing by a ramshackle old farmhouse that
was overgrown with sickly vines and fecund moss. Behind the
farmhouse was the wall of the forest, but in front of it was a big
field that had gone wild with neglect. Mike stood in the clearing, just a few feet from the house, and he heard a sound that
made him turn and look up to see a sight that took his breath
away. Overhead, from horizon to horizon, filling the sky like
blackened embers from a fire, were crows. Tens of thousands of
them, perhaps hundreds of thousands. Featureless and dark, flapping silently in the still air, and Mike turned to watch them as
the carrion birds flew from west to east, heading toward the forest, which was burning out of control. The last image Mike had
before he woke was the silhouettes of the swarm of night birds
painted against the swollen face of a gigantic harvest moon.

"This is what Hell looks like," Mike heard himself say. "The
Red Wave is coming . . . and the black wind follows."

(2)

After he left the hospital Willard Fowler Newton did not drive home. He walked the six blocks to where his car was parked outside of Crow's store, fished in his pocket for the keys, unlocked it, climbed in, pulled the door shut, and locked it. The interior of the Civic smelled of stale air, old coffee, dried autumn leaves, and sweat. He didn't roll down the windows, didn't start the engine.

For twenty minutes he just sat there, his keys lying on the passenger seat, the engine off and cold. At this time of day Corn Hill was empty except for an occasional car rolling past as someone went off to start an early day at work, or drifted home after the graveyard shift. There was no foot traffic, no one to take notice of him, no one to see a man sitting alone in his car in the early morning of October 14. No one to observe a young man sitting with his face buried in bruised and filthy hands, his shoulders hunched and trembling as he wept.

(3)

"You're up early, Mikey."

Mike Sweeney stood in the shadows of the doorway, silhouetted by the light filling the hallway from the foyer window. Lois Wingate turned from the stove and looked at her son. "You want some breakfast? I'm making pancakes."

"Not hungry," he said and walked slowly over to the fridge, opened it, and fished around for the orange juice.

"You look tired, Mikey. Your eyes are so bloodshot."

He swirled the orange juice around in its carton, then opened it and drank at least a pint, wiped his mouth, and tossed the empty carton into the trash. "I'm going out. I have to work at the store today."

"It's only seven o'clock."

He headed back toward the hallway. "I'll ride my bike for a bit."

"Mike," Lois said, reaching out a hand to touch his shoulder as he passed. He stopped but didn't turn toward her. She smelled of last night's gin and Vic's cigarettes, and the pancakes smelled burnt. "Mike, are you okay?"

Mike looked at her and their eyes met. His mom looked into his eyes—dark blue eyes flecked with red with thin gold rings around the irises. She blinked at him in surprise and took a small involuntary step backward, her own eyes widening, her mouth sagging open.

"Michael . . . ?"

There were no bruises on Mike's face, no sign of the savage beatings he'd received from Vic over the last couple of weeks. His skin was pale and unmarked except by his splash of freckles, his mouth thin and sad. Every line and curve of his face was the same as it should have been—though the absence of bruises was strange—but all Lois could see were those eyes. The blue of them looked like they'd been spattered with tiny droplets of blood; the gold rings gave them a totally alien cast.

Mike bent forward and kissed her forehead; she tried to pull back, but he held her close. "I love you, Mom," he whispered, then he turned and hurried down the hall, opened the door, and went out into the bright morning.

His mother stood there, hand to her open mouth, totally oblivious to the burning pancakes. Nor did she see the cellar door open just the tiniest crack and other eyes watching her. These eyes were a much darker red and they burned with a hungry light.

(4)

Newton grabbed a wad of Starbucks napkins out of the glove compartment, dried his eyes, and then angrily scrubbed away all traces of the tears on his cheeks. He cursed continually under his breath, a steady stream of the foulest words that bubbled onto his tongue; then he wadded up the napkins and threw them against the windshield as his muttering suddenly spiked into a single shriek: "NO!"

He punched the dashboard and then pounded his fists on his

thighs until the pain shot through his muscles all the way to his bones. "No, goddamn it!"

Newton reached out, gave the ignition a violent turn, and the car coughed itself awake; he slammed it into Drive and pulled away from the curb. He didn't head home, but instead did a screeching U-turn in the middle of the street, ignoring the bleat of horns, and when he stamped down on the gas the Civic lurched forward in the direction of his office. He needed a good computer and a better Internet connection than the dial-up he had at home. He needed to get some answers, and he needed them now.

He ran two red lights and a stop sign as he barreled out of town, down A-32, past the dirt road that led down to Dark Hollow—which sent a chill through him despite his anger—past the Guthrie farm, all the way to the Black Marsh Bridge. In his pocket, forgotten in the midst of everything else, the old coin he'd found on the slopes of the Dark Hollow pitch jingled among the newer change. It was a weatherworn dime someone had once drilled a hole through so a Louisiana aunt could put a string through it and tie it around the ankle of her nephew from Mississippi. A charm against evil that Oren Morse had worn until the day he died. A charm that he'd lost just minutes before the town fathers of Pine Deep had beaten him to death.

With all the residual hot-blood flush in his thighs from where he'd pounded out his rage, Newton did not feel the dime flare to mild heat as he drove. Later on he would remember that dime, and a toss of that coin would decide the life or death of a lot of people in Pine Deep. Including Newton.

(5)

"What the hell are you doing up there?"

Vic's voice caught him unaware and Ruger stiffened, but he composed his face into a bland smile before he turned and looked down the stairs to where Vic stood on the basement floor, fists on hips, glowering.

"I smelled cooking," Ruger said as he slowly descended the steps, making it a slow roll, making it look casual, like Vic's hard look was nothing.

Vic looked at him and then up at the near side of the cellar door. "Cooking, my ass. You're still sniffing after Lois."

Ruger said nothing as he brushed by him, making sure to use one hard shoulder to clip Vic on the pass-by. Ruger knew he was a lot stronger than Vic and he wanted to leave a bruise. Like the Indians used to do in the books he used to read. Counting coup.

"I'm talking to you, asshole," Vic snarled. The bump had knocked him off balance but he recovered cat-quick and gave Ruger a hard one-handed shove that knocked the cold-skinned man into the corner of the workbench. Ruger rebounded from the desk and spun so fast that he appeared to melt into shadows; one moment he was by the desk, the next he was beside Vic with one icy hand clamped around the man's throat.

"You don't lay hands on me, motherfucker . . . not ever. I'll tear your heart out and wipe my ass with it."

There was a small metallic click and then Ruger felt a touch even colder than his own as the barrel of a pistol pressed upward beneath his chin. "You really want to dance, Sport?" Vic said; his voice was a choked whisper, but the hand holding the gun barrel was rock solid.

Ruger's eyes had gone totally dark again and they burned into Vic as the moment stretched itself thin around them. Vic could feel Ruger's hunger, his power, prowling around in his mind, could feel the shadowy charisma of that stare as if it were a physical thing, but he kept his gun hand steady. Upstairs Lois put a pan in the sink and started the water, each sound clear and distinct. Both men involuntarily shifted their eyes upward, held their gazes there for a moment, and then awareness kicked in and they noticed each other's look. Their eyes met and lowered together.

"Take your hand off me, Sport, or I'll paint the ceiling with what's left of your brains."

For a microsecond Ruger's hand tightened, but then he abruptly let go. "Like you even care about that bitch."

Vic almost reached his free hand up to massage his throat, but restrained it—that would look weak—but he couldn't control the involuntary swallow. His throat hurt like hell. He jabbed Ruger hard with the pistol barrel. "I don't give a leaping shit about Lois . . . but she's my property, Sport. *Mine.*"

Ruger said nothing, but he sneered and slapped the pistol barrel away—which Vic allowed—and turned away to hide a hungry little smile.

(6)

Crow watched as Weinstock got up and walked into the bathroom to splash cold water on his face. He reappeared in a minute, dabbing at his eyes with wads of paper towels, leaned his shoulder against the door frame, and threw a quick look at the door to make sure it was firmly closed.

"I can't believe we are having this conversation," he said. "I can't believe I'm having a conversation with the word 'vampire' in it."

"Welcome to my world."

"It's my world, too, damn it. I've been living this nightmare for weeks now, ever since I did the autopsies on Jimmy Castle and Nels Cowan."

"Not that I want to play who's the bigger dog, Saul, but I sure as hell got you beat there because mine starts back in 1976, during the Black Harvest."

Weinstock winced. "Oh man . . . don't even try to tell me that the Massacre is tied into all this. I don't want to hear that. I don't want to *know* that." He came over and sank down in the chair. "Okay, okay . . . tell me everything."

So Crow told him. He started with Ubel Griswold moving into the town, talked about the 1976 blight that destroyed the town's crops and killed most of the livestock—including all of Griswold's cattle—and how the Massacre began shortly afterward.

"What are you saying? That Griswold was a vampire, too?"

"No . . . I don't think that was it." Crow licked his lips. "I think Griswold was a werewolf."

Weinstock sat back and studied him. "Okay. Right. Fine. A werewolf. Peachy. Our conversation now includes vampires *and* werewolves. Why don't we throw in ghosts and the Jersey Devil, too, then I can go and blow my brains out and no one will blame me."

"You want to hear this or not?"

Weinstock sighed. "Not really," he said, but he made a twirling motion with his index finger to indicate that Crow should continue.

"For whatever reason Griswold moved here, if we at least for the sake of argument accept that he was a . . . werewolf . . ." Even Crow had a hard time saying the word. It felt clunky in his mouth and its edges caught in his throat. "Then he must have come here to lay low. Raising and killing the cattle kept him off the radar until the blight killed the cattle and all of the other local livestock. When the urge to hunt came on him where else did he have to turn but people? Even then he tried to keep it on the QT by preying on tramps and hobos, but I think the lust for human blood got the better of him and he just started hunting anyone he could find. Val's uncle was killed, my brother Billy. Terry's little sister, Mandy . . . and remember, Griswold almost killed Terry, too. He was in a coma for weeks."

"God . . ."

"I would have been killed, too, 'cause he came after me, but Oren Morse—the guy we used to call the Bone Man—he saved my life. Griswold hadn't completely transformed yet and the Bone Man was able to stop him. He tried to tell people about it, but nobody listened to him. Far as the rednecks in the town were concerned—my own father among them—Morse was just a black draft-dodging tramp. This was thirty years ago, Saul, and no one paid any attention. When I told my father he kicked the shit out of me. You got to remember, he was one of those young jackasses who hung out at Griswold's all the time. Griswold was their hero."

"I seem to remember not shedding a tear when your dad died, hope that doesn't offend."

"Nah, Dad was a complete tool. Point is, he either didn't believe me or didn't want to believe me, and he put such a fear of God into me that I didn't tell anyone else about it."

"What about Morse? Wasn't he supposed to be tight with Val's dad? Did he talk to Henry about this?"

"Probably, but Henry and I never talked about it, and Morse was murdered not long after."

Weinstock chewed his lip. "How sure are you that Griswold was a werewolf? I mean, serial killers are well known for following the moon, for cannibalizing their victims, yada yada . . . it's a known pathology."

"I saw his face, Saul. I'm not talking about a man's . . . I saw his face as it was changing."

"Crap . . . I was afraid you'd say something like that." Weinstock got up and walked over to the window and stared out into the new morning, which was bright and clear, with puffy clouds coasting across the vast blue. Without turning he said, "Even if you saw what you say you saw and all your guesswork is right . . . what does that have to do with what's been happening in town?" He turned around and sat on the edge of the air conditioner. "It doesn't fit with the stuff I've been seeing—not at all. Not even with the killings at the Guthrie farm. None of this says 'werewolf' to me, even if I was ready to believe in that sort of thing. Full moon was last Friday . . . the two cops were killed on the first. We're not following the lunar cycle."

"I know, but like I said, I don't think we're dealing with a werewolf right now. From what I've been able to put together, we seem to be in vampire territory."

"Did that statement sound as stupid to you as it did to me?"

"Probably," Crow admitted. "There's more. When Ruger attacked Val and me here in the hospital that night he said something before he died. Something Val didn't hear, but I did, and it's been like a needle stuck in my brain ever since." Crow closed his eyes for a second, took a breath, and then looked hard at Weinstock as he spoke, "He said, 'Ubel Griswold sends his regards.'"

"Ruger said that? He actually said Griswold's name?"

"Uh-huh, and when we were fighting . . . he was way too strong. I mean stronger than anyone I've ever met, and I've been in the martial arts since I was a kid. I know what muscle strong is like, and I know what wiry strong is like, and this was something completely different. Off the scale . . . strong in a way nothing rational can describe."

"Man, I think we left rational behind by a couple of miles."

"No joke. Ruger's eyes were weird, too. They seemed to change color while we were fighting. Don't laugh, but I swear they turned yellow and then red."

"I'm not laughing," Weinstock said. "I may never laugh again. Ever."

Crow told Weinstock about how he met Newton, and about the long interview he'd given him. He told him how they had cooked up a plan to scale down the pitch at Dark Hollow and head through the woods to try and find Griswold's house. He spoke about the strangeness of the swampy area around Dark Hollow, and how they had been forced to cut their way through foul-smelling vines and sticker bushes before they found the house. "I really wanted to find an old, abandoned pile of sticks, but that's not what we found. The place was in good shape, like it had been maintained. All the doors and windows were covered up with plywood that was still green, and the front and back doors were chained shut with the locks on the *inside* of the house. Only someone inside could lock or unlock those chains."

"Oh my God . . ."

"Then, while we were on the porch examining those locks, the whole porch roof just suddenly collapses down." He snapped his fingers. "Just like that. Damn near killed us. Don't you think that's a little strange?"

"A 'little strange'?" Weinstock echoed hoarsely. His color was horrible.

"Well, buckle up 'cause it gets stranger." Crow told him about the swarm of roaches that attacked them. "Now here's the last part of it. When I was standing there on the porch, before the roof fell and the roaches attacked us, I thought I heard a voice in my head. Very faint, but definitely there—and before you start making jokes about me hearing voices, here's what it said, '*She is going to die and there is nothing you can do to save her.*'"

Weinstock stared at him in horror. "This was last night? You had that in your head while—"

"While Val was walking into the trap with Boyd. I was being teased with it, as if he knew I'd never get back to Val's farm in time to save her from Boyd."

"'He'? Are you saying that this was Griswold's voice?"

"I don't know. I mean . . . I think the bastard's dead. Thirty years dead, probably buried by the Bone Man in an unmarked grave, and there haven't been any attacks around that you could point to as being like Griswold's."

"Unless he isn't dead and maybe moved away for a while," Weinstock ventured. "He could have moved over to Jersey or up to the Poconos, started another farm, kept himself in check all these years, and maybe now he's come back."

"I thought about that, and it's certainly a possibility—but I *feel* like he's dead, that he's been dead since 1976. Just a gut thing, but it's what I believe."

"So whose voice was it?"

Crow shook his head. "That's just it. I suppose it might have been Boyd doing a kind of vampire mind-fuck on me, but my gut still tells me it was Griswold."

"Which makes sense only if, somehow, Griswold is still here. As . . . what, though? A ghost? Are we finally adding them to the mix?"

"Hell if I know. I guess that very last part of it, at least from my end, is the whole Boyd thing. I saw his body, and apart from all the rounds Val pumped into him he had a whole bunch of other bullet wounds. Nine, to be exact, and all of them pretty well healed over. Remember, Jimmy Castle emptied his gun into him, hit him every damn time."

"Jeez . . . don't tell me that. I haven't even had a chance to view the body yet."

"Now," Crow said, "now let's hear your side of this."

Weinstock gave him a long, flat stare. "You won't like it."

Crow made a rude noise. "I knew that before we started talking. But I have to know."

Weinstock told him everything. Crow didn't like it.

Chapter 4

The silence between Vic and Ruger was thick as mud. Vic went back to his workbench and tried to concentrate on how many sticks of dynamite it would take to bring down the cellular phone relay tower. When he was done with that he had to go out and meet a candy maker he knew who was doing some work for him. Treats for Halloween night. There was a ton of other stuff needing attention, and Vic was feeling the pressure.

Ruger was in the recliner reading a battered old copy of Emily Gerard's *The Land Beyond the Forest*. Someone had made extensive handwritten notes in the margin of every page.

Into the stony silence, Ruger murmured, "I'm getting hungry."

Vic's right finger paused over the Enter key on his calculator; his left hand twitched in the direction of the pistol lying on the table. "It's still light out," he said, not turning.

Ruger was quiet for a while, then very softly—so softly Vic barely heard him even though he was straining to hear any sounds coming from that end of the cellar—the killer whispered, "Hungry."

The word haunted the air in that dark cellar.

(2)

Weinstock rubbed his tired eyes. "How much of this does Val know?"

"She knows the backstory, the Massacre and that stuff. She

knows my theories. I didn't have time to tell her what happened down in the Hollow yesterday. Not after what she went through herself, still she has to know there's something strange is happening. You know Val—she's not stupid or given to hysterics. She knows what she saw last night when Boyd came after her. She kept shooting him and Boyd kept wading through the shots."

"Not all of them, apparently."

"No," Crow agreed, "and let's thank God for that. Apparently the one thing they can't shake off is half a clip in the skull."

"Important to remember," Weinstock said, almost to himself. "Did either of you mention the . . . um . . . 'V-word'?"

"No, but before the ambulance guys took her she told me that she knew that Boyd was dead. She knew it when he was still on his feet and coming after her. Maybe she hasn't put the name to it yet, but she knows." He stared at the closed door as if he could already see Val. "I'm not sure if that's going to make it easier or harder."

"Seems to me that it should make it easier."

Crow looked at Weinstock, and there was raw pain in his eyes. "Saul, Boyd didn't just kill Mark . . . he *bit* him. Connie, too."

Crow saw the meaning of that register on Weinstock's face. *"Holy God."*

"I think we have to tell her everything. She's lost her entire family to this. She has a bigger stake in it than anyone. We have to be straight with her."

At that moment there was a tap on the door and a nurse popped her head in. "Doctor? We'd like to bring Ms. Guthrie in, is that okay?"

Both men leapt to their feet as two orderlies wheeled Val in on a gurney. Her right eye and most of her head was turbaned in thick bandages, and most of the exposed flesh of her cheek, nose, and chin were puffy with dark red bruises. She was dressed in a white ER gown patterned with tiny cornflowers. She saw Crow and her eye widened, but before she could even say his name he'd pushed past the nurse and bent over her.

"Val!" Crow cried, shouldering past the orderlies. He bent to

her, murmuring her name over and over again, kissing her forehead, her cheek, her lips. "Oh, baby! How are you?"

Val kissed him back, tears spilling from her eye. In a shattered
voice she said, "Mark!" and then her voice disintegrated into
sobs as he held her.

After a minute or so Weinstock gently pulled Crow away, and
Val was transferred to the bed, hooked up to a fresh saline drip,
and plugged into monitors. Weinstock shooed everyone but
Crow out of the room. Polk appeared in the doorway, glaring at
Crow.

"Hey, I thought I told you that you weren't supposed to talk
to my witness?"

Crow wheeled on him and was just about to tear into him when
Weinstock stepped between them. "What's the problem, Jim?"

Polk's eyes narrowed on the doctor. "The problem, *sir*, is that
I specifically told Crow that Valerie Guthrie was a witness and
that no one was supposed to talk to her until—"

"Oh for God's sake," Weinstock snarled and pushed Polk out
into the hall and pulled the door shut. "Not even you can be
that thick, Jim. Or am I wrong about that? Are you that much of
a blockhead?" Before Polk could answer, Weinstock plowed
ahead. "Miss Guthrie is my patient and she is the victim of a
crime. Crow is a deputy, last I heard, and until Sheriff Bernhardt
himself revokes that designation, then I'll continue to regard
him as such. In the meantime, this is my goddamn hospital. If I
hear one more word out of you I swear I'll have security escort
you off the premises and I will file formal chares of trespassing,
harassment, and anything else I can get my good friend Judge
Shermer to agree to. And I'll be talking to Gus about this. Now
get the hell out of my face before I ask Crow to bounce you off
the walls just to make us all feel better."

Polk was livid and his balled fists trembled at his sides. Crow
shifted position to be within reach of Polk, hoping to God that
the cop would take a swing. Bouncing him off the walls really
would make him feel better.

"Crow . . . ?" It was Val's voice, faint through the closed door,
but still an arrow in Crow's heart.

Polk pointed a finger at Crow. "This isn't over," he said with a hiss.

"Yes it is," Weinstock said, beating Crow to it. "It had better be or I promise you, Jim, that you will regret it. Don't push me on this."

Polk made a rude noise and turned away. He stalked down the hall under a cloud. The other two cops exchanged looks with each other and then looked at Weinstock.

"Do either of you have a problem with Crow being here?"

"No sir," said the oldest of the two, "we surely don't."

Weinstock touched Crow on the arm. "I'll leave you two alone. Don't tax her, buddy, okay?" With a parting glare at the cops, the doctor stalked off. Both cops gave Crow a palms-out "no problem" gesture as Crow opened the door and went inside.

Crow sat on the edge of the bed and for a long time he and Val, finally alone, just clung together as she wept for her brother and Connie. Crow wept with her—even for Mark, whom he barely liked? Maybe. In part, certainly. Mark was an officious ass at times, but he had been a good guy at heart, and he'd suffered the same loss that Val had when Henry had been murdered; now he was dead, too. And Connie was a total innocent; life never gave her a chance. Crow ached for them both, and for the whole town.

It was half an hour later, after tears and more tears, after soft words and silent times, that he finally worked up the nerve to bring up the events of last night. When he saw the aching, weary grief in her eye he almost didn't. He looked down at Val, touched the stain of tears on her cheek, and absently licked the tears from his finger.

"Val . . . honey . . . we need to talk about some stuff. I need to tell you some things, but first I need you tell me what happened last night. Are you up to this?"

In the space of a heartbeat the look in Val's eye changed from wretched pain to an almost reptilian coldness. "It's long past time that we talked about this. All night I've been thinking

about this, Crow, needing to talk to you. God knows I had nothing else to do while they fussed around me. I'm pregnant, so
they couldn't give me sedatives. They wouldn't let me see you,
and that jackass Polk kept trying to ask me questions, so I just
tuned him out and thought about what I saw." Her grip was
tightened like a vise on his wrist. "I wanted it to be straight in
my head. I wanted to try and make some kind of sense out of
what happened, put it together in my mind, try to be cold and
clinical about it. I had time to think it through." She took a
breath and studied him. "You know I don't believe most of that
supernatural crap—zombies and hobgoblins and all. You're into
it, but you know that I never . . . I mean, I don't—"

"It doesn't matter, baby. I don't believe most of it myself. A lot
of this is just for fun. Spooky movies and Halloween dollars in
America's Haunted Holidayland."

"Maybe . . . but what if it's true?" She gave his arm a final
squeeze and then let go, giving his wrist a defiant push as she
did so. "What if a lot of it is true?"

There was such coldness in Val's voice that it made Crow
flinch.

"The papers always joke about Pine Deep being the most
haunted town in America. It's on all of our tourist pamphlets.
We *bank* on it. So, you tell me . . . what if it's true? What if we
really are the *most* haunted town? There's no other explanation
for what we both saw here in the hospital two weeks ago, and
what I saw last night. And no one is going to tell me I imagined
it. Not unless they want their asses kicked, 'cause I'm not going
to take any of that crap from *anyone*. I know what I saw. I know
what happened."

"I saw some things, too, baby," he said, and told her about
what happened down in Dark Hollow. As Val listened her face
went paler, but the hunting hawk glare in her eye intensified.

"God," she said. "So, we're now looking at something that
started when we were kids. You always believed it, and now I do,
too. I'd say I'm sorry for doubting you, but I don't think that
really matters now, does it?"

"No, baby, it sure as hell doesn't."

"So where does it leave us? Vampires . . . and whatever the hell it was down in the Hollow. Would you call it a ghost? Griswold's ghost?"

"I think so," Crow said tentatively.

"I'm fighting so hard right now to stay solid, to not break apart, and I have to keep this as logical as possible because if I take one little step off the intellectual facts-and-figures plane I'm going to totally lose it."

"Hey . . . Val . . . it's okay. It's over now, no one expects you to be a rock all the time."

"No, it's not okay, damn it! I can't break down. Not until I know where this is all going, not until I understand what really happened to Mark and Connie and what it might mean. I have to hold it together."

But those last words punched a hole in the dam and the pent-up tons of grief finally smashed through. From one second to the next Val's face went from stern control to shattered grief and the tears burst from her and the sobs tore her from the inside out. She cried out her brother's name and clawed Crow to her in her need to be sheltered, weeping brokenly against his chest as he held her.

Chapter 5

Mike Sweeney biked down to the Crow's Nest and used his key to let himself in. The store wasn't scheduled to open until nine-thirty, but he had nowhere else to go. He was only half aware of the process of locking up his bike, opening the shop, counting the money in the till, restocking the shelves, and sweeping the floor. On some level he was aware that he was doing these things, but it was more process than deliberate action, and even though he'd only worked at the shop for two weeks he did everything right, made no errors, felt no hesitation. Autopilot with just the occasional glance from the person behind the wheel.

Then Mike went into the small employees-only bathroom to get the dustpan and peripherally caught sight of himself in the mirror. What he saw jolted him out of the unconscious rhythm and he froze for a discordant moment because the face there in the glass was not his own.

It was . . . and then again it wasn't. Déjà vu flared and he knew that he had seen this other face, this other *version* of his own face somewhere else. Recently. He straightened slowly, afraid to move too fast in case it somehow changed what he was seeing in the mirror. Carefully, like he was trying not to spook a skittish deer, he moved toward the mirror and looked at the face, watched as it moved with him, normal in the seamless way it mimicked his every movement but totally unnatural in what it showed. The face that looked back at him was older, with a stronger jaw and skin that was gaunt and stretched over a sharply etched brow and cheekbones. The lips of this stranger's mouth were thin and hard as if he was fighting a grimace of pain, and the upper lip was cut by a thick white scar. The eyes were the most compelling, though. They were blue, flecked with blood-colored drops of red and totally ringed with gold. Strange eyes. Alien. If there was anything human about those eyes, Mike Sweeney could not find it. There was no way Mike could have known it, but those were the eyes his mother had seen that morning in the kitchen. Mike hadn't looked at his own reflection that morning in the bathroom; he'd just stumbled in, washed his mouth with Scope, and used the toilet. Had he looked then he would have seen the same eyes that stared out of the mirror at him now.

Hard eyes, cold, without remorse, without pity. Without hope.

"Dead eyes," he murmured, and the sound of his own voice was equally unfamiliar. It had grown deeper, sadder, more harsh. There was a cynical sneer in the sound of it.

The face in the mirror stared at him, hard as fists, cold as night.

Mike blinked to clear his eyes—and that fast the spell was broken. In the microsecond of the blink the face was there—and then it was gone. He blinked again, but all he saw was his own face. Fourteen going on never grow up. That's how he thought of himself, and that's what he now saw. Just his own face. Tired and pale, splashed with freckles, smoother bones in brow and cheeks, hair more garishly red, chin still childlike, lips unscarred. He leaned closer, letting the light above the mirror fall on his face. He searched the mirror for any trace of what he had seen, and all he saw—and that only for a moment—was the alien color of his eyes. Fiery gold rings around blue ice, flecked with blood. He blinked again . . . and his eyes were ordinary blue. No trace of fire or blood—merely a cold and hopeless blue.

He stood there, peering at himself for several minutes, then he closed his eyes and stared at the darkness behind his lids for a slow count of thirty. When he opened his eyes, they were still ordinary eyes.

Mike straightened, turned, picked up the dustpan, and walked out of the bathroom. By the time he'd swept the floor the whole incident was gone from his conscious mind. Secretly and quietly shoved down by some unknown hand into a darker and less accessible place inside. He did not even remember that he couldn't remember. He finished his chores by eight-thirty, picked a magazine off the rack, and sat down on the stool behind the counter to wait for the day to start.

At nine o'clock precisely, the bell above the door tinkled and Mike looked up from the latest copy of *Cemetery Dance* to see a police officer enter the shop. He was a big, brawny, blond-haired cop with a very neatly pressed uniform, highly polished leather gun belt, and gleaming chrome cuffs that jingled as he walked. The blacking on his shoes looked like polished coal, but despite his fastidious clothing he walked with a noticeable limp and both of his hands were lightly bandaged.

Mike's heart froze in his chest.

It was Tow-Truck Eddie.

(2)

Newton sat at his desk with his main computer on in front of him and his laptop open to his left. He had several Google search pages open on each and a half dozen Word documents. His fourth cup of coffee was cooling to tepid sludge as his fingers blurred over the keys, typing in search arguments, scrolling through the lists of web pages, cutting and pasting information and URLs. He'd been at this for hours now, ever since driving back from the hospital. No shower, no change of clothes, no food except for the cups of coffee that had long since turned his stomach to acid.

Willard Fowler Newton was furious. He was hurt and scared, too, but mostly he was absolutely livid. Twenty-four hours ago he was just another third-string reporter in a fifth-rate town like Black Marsh. A day ago he was, he knew, a geek. Nerdy and kind of annoying—insights often provided for him by people he met, even strangers. He was content to be a geek. He could *do* geek without effort.

Now he was caught up in something that involved vampires. Actual *vampires*.

That's what made Fowler so furious. Vampires should not be in any part of the world in which he lived. Vampires were TV and movies. Buffy and Blade and Barnabas-fricking-Collins. Vampires were Halloween costumes and Count Chocula. Vampires were fiction. At worst they were supposed to be myths and legends. Vampires weren't real. Vampires and geeks do not belong in the same reality, of that he was quite certain.

In vampire stories there were only two kinds of characters— victims and heroes. Newton knew that there was nothing remotely heroic in his nature, but he sure as hell did not want to be a victim.

Waking up and discovering that the world now included vampires and werewolves—*let's not forget werewolves*—was too much to ask. Not just one . . . but two monsters . . . the big two. The classics. Right here in River City. Shit.

Crow was the hero, Newton knew. He'd already shown that by facing Ruger twice. Val was a hero, too. She'd fought Ruger herself, and she'd killed Boyd. At best, Newton knew, he was the squatty sidekick who would probably not make it to the final reel. Like George from *Seinfeld*, with a stake and hammer. Yeah, there were good odds on *that* game.

But what could he do? Running was an option, and he gave that a lot of thought. No one would blame him; no one ever blames the geek for being a coward. After all . . . we were talking supernatural monsters here. He didn't have a black belt like Crow or a will of iron and a big-ass pistol like Val. All he had was . . . what?

That was the thought process that took him from sitting in his car after leaving the hospital—crying like a baby and praying to a God he hadn't said "boo!" to since his bar mitzvah—to where he was right now. Parked at his computer, working the Net, working sources. Finding stuff out. It's what a geek would do.

He kept at it for hours, researching everything he could find, punishing the keys with stabbing finger hits. He searched on vampires and werewolves, and at first the enormity of the available information nearly stopped him in his tracks. When he typed "Vampire" into Google the search told him there were 54,200,000 hits.

"Holy shit!" he breathed, then tried adding an "s" to make it "Vampires." That dropped the number of websites down to 18 million. "Werewolf" 11,400,000 hits. He chewed a plastic pen cap for a few moments, then he tried it as "vampire folklore" which eliminated most of the film and fiction references and that dropped it down to 773,000 sites. On a whim he refined it even more by adding the word "university," hoping to score experts. That dropped it down even further to 276,000 sites, and from there Newton plowed through it, looking for thesis papers, studies, published works, and for names that popped up over and over again. Ohe was J. N. Corbiel, an assistant professor of folklore at the University of Pennsylvania.

Newton recognized that name and pulled open his file drawer for the folder of notes he'd made when researching material following his interview with Crow. He riffled the pages until he found one whose contents jarred him. One he'd read but put out of his mind at the time—could that just be a day or two ago? The printout was a historical account of a man named Peeter Stubbe, known in folklore as the Werewolf of Bedburg, a mass murderer executed in 1589 following the most famous werewolf trial in history. Under brutal torture Stubbe confessed to having been a sorcerer and lycanthrope who had practiced black magic since boyhood and who transformed regularly into a savage wolf for the purpose of hunting humans for sport and food. The article also gave the many aliases Stubbe used over the years: Peter Stubb, Peter Stumpf, Abel Greenwyck, Abel Griswald . . . and *Ubel Griswold.*

His skin crawled.

There was a URL on the printout and he typed it in, bring-

ing up a page with a lot of history about that and similar werewolf trials, most of which had been conducted by the Inquisition. Dr. Corbiel had a typically dry and detailed academic style,
but the case details were nonetheless bloody and sensational.

Newton sat back in his chair and considered this, tapping his
lower teeth with the cap of his pen. U of P was in Philly, maybe
fifty, sixty miles from where he sat. Maybe he could meet with
this Professor Corbiel, pick his brain. Pretend to be doing a story
on the folklore behind the pop culture, something like that. Or
maybe writing a pop-culture book.

He looked for an e-mail address and found it on the staff di-
rectory, and clicked on it to load an e-mail screen. Jcorbiel
@sas.upenn.edu.

"Dear Professor Corbiel," he began.

(3)

Before Weinstock even had the door closed, Val said, "Crow
told me everything."

"Okay," he said carefully, glancing at Crow.

Crow nodded. "She knows what we know."

"That was fast, don't you think? Val needs rest and—"

"Listen to me, the both of you," Val interrupted. "I know I'm
hurt, I know I'm pregnant, and I know that Mark and Connie's
deaths haven't really hit me yet, not like they will . . . but if either of you starts walking softly around me, or hides stuff from
me because you don't want to upset me or some such crap, I'll
skin you both alive. You know I'm not joking here. My family is
dead and I need to understand why . . . and how."

She looked at each of them in turn.

Crow took the lead. "Believe me, sweetie, this isn't a matter of
the manly men not wanting to upset the womenfolk. The real
problem, at least for me, is that I don't know *how* to talk about
this."

Weinstock nodded agreement.

Val nodded. "Then that's a problem we're going to have to

solve right now, boys. Are we talking past or present tense?" When they looked perplexed, she added, "Did Boyd's death end it, or does . . . what happened last night . . . indicate that this is *still* happening?"

"We've been chewing on that all morning," Weinstock said.

"The way I see it," Crow said, "this part of it—the, um, *vampire*, part of it—started with Ruger and Boyd coming to town."

"You know that or are you guessing?" Weinstock asked.

"Guessing, but before they got here we didn't have vampires."

"Oh?" Val said. "And how do you know that?"

"I . . . well . . ."

Weinstock jumped in on Val's side. "We can't make assumptions here. Are you suggesting that Ruger and Boyd were vampires already?"

"No," Crow said. "At least Ruger wasn't."

"He wasn't," Val agreed. "Not when he was at our house, not that first night. I think I would have known . . . and he probably wouldn't have bothered with a gun."

Crow nodded. "Absolutely. When he and I fought outside your house he was human enough, but when he showed up at the hospital it was like fighting a whole other person."

"So what happened during those two days?" Weinstock pursed his lips. "I mean . . . I've seen enough Dracula films to know how vampires are made, but doesn't it take three or four days?"

Crow shook his head. "I doubt we can trust what's in the movies. I mean . . . this is real, and when it comes to vampires being real, what do we actually know? What *are* vampires, after all? I've read a lot of books . . . nonfiction stuff, folklore, and there are all sorts of vampires out there, all the way back through history. Hundreds of different kinds in different cultures. The whole idea of a vampire being some guy in a tuxedo and an opera cloak is for the movies. Even in the novel *Dracula*, the vampire was different than they showed in the films. I don't even think they staked him in the book. It's been a while since I read it, but I seem to remember that Dracula was stabbed or something."

"That doesn't fit with what's been happening here," Val said. "I shot Boyd over and over again, and he lived through it, if 'lived' is the right word. It was only after I shot him in the head that he went down and stayed down."

"That's more like those zombies in those Living Dead films," Weinstock offered.

"They were undead ghouls, not zombies," Crow corrected.

Weinstock shot him a look. "Really? Nitpicking? Now?"

Val interrupted, "Are we sure Boyd's actually dead?"

"Baby," Crow said with a smile, "you blew most of his head off."

Her eye was icy and she spaced each word out. "Are. We. Sure. Boyd's. Actually. Dead?"

Crow and Weinstock looked at each other. The doctor cleared his throat. "I guess we could go and check?"

"Yeah," Val said coldly. "Maybe you ought to."

Neither of the men made a move to get up.

"What about Mark?" Val asked and her voice cracked on his name. They looked at her. "If Boyd is what we think he is—or was—then what about Mark? And Connie, too, for that matter."

"Oh shit," Weinstock said. Crow just closed his eyes and sighed.

"Crow . . . Saul . . . listen to me," Val said, her tone cool but reasonable, "I know you're both as freaked out about this as I am. It's unreal . . . surreal—but my family was murdered last night by a monster. An actual monster." She took a breath. "If there is even the slightest chance that my brother is somehow infected . . ." The word hung in the air like a bright flare and no one could bear to look at it. "If there is even the slightest chance that he and Connie could become like Boyd . . . then I want to know about it, and I want to know right now."

Crow struggled to his feet and looked down at her. He was filthy and exhausted, his eyes were glassy with fear and shock, and his face was the color of old milk. He licked his lips. "Okay," he said. "Okay . . . I think we'd better go check. Saul?"

The doctor nodded tiredly and stood, but suddenly swayed and sat down hard again on the bed. The jolt made Val hiss with pain. Weinstock grabbed the metal rail of the bed to steady himself, too frightened to be ashamed. Tears broke from his eyes and rolled down his cheeks and when he raised his hands to touch the wetness his fingers quivered with palsy.

"God . . ." he breathed and his voice broke into a sob. "I don't know if I can do this . . ."

Crow stood by wretchedly and watched, but Val reached up with one hand and touched Weinstock's chest, her palm flat. The doctor looked down at her slender tan hand, his lips trembling into a small smile at the tenderness of the gesture. "Val . . . I—"

Then Val's hand closed into a fist around a knotted wad of his lab coat and with a grunt she jerked him down to her level so that his face was inches from hers. Aghast, Crow saw her mouth twist into a harsh mask. Her voice was a whisper filled with razor wire. "Don't you fucking *dare*! My brother is *dead*! My *sister-in-law* is dead! Friends of mine are dead. Don't you dare wig out on me now, you son of a bitch."

Weinstock stared at her in total shocked horror. That one blue eye seemed to radiate heat and he was burned by it. His own eyes bugged and his mouth hung open in a soundless O.

"Now you get your ass down to the morgue and you do whatever you have to do to make sure that bastard Boyd is dead . . . and you see to my brother, or so help me God, Saul, I'll—"

"Val . . ." Crow said it softly, but it was enough. Val cut a hard look at him, and then her glare softened, just a bit. She pulled Weinstock two inches closer.

"Please," she said, and this time it was a whisper of urgent need. "Please."

Weinstock could feel his face change in that moment. Shock drained away and the buttery lines of his chin and mouth firmed up; shame and anger warred in his chest. Val pulled him one last inch closer, then leaned her head up and kissed his cheek. Weinstock closed his eyes for one long moment then nodded. "Yes," he said, and kissed her; then he straightened and went into the bathroom to throw water on his face. When he was done, he stood in the doorway, patting his face dry with a wad of paper towels. "Crow . . . I'll wait for you in the hall." He shambled out.

When the door closed, Val looked at Crow and even managed a small smile. "See what you got yourself into when you proposed to me?"

He sucked his teeth. "Yep. It's all clear to me now—you're a complete psychopath. I'm on the first bus outta here." He grinned. "Crazy or not, I really do love you, Valerie Guthrie."

"You'd better," Val said and somewhere behind the stern lines of her face there was a tremble, a flutter in her voice that he could only just hear. "I don't have anyone else left."

Crow kissed her and went out to where Weinstock stood, hands deep in his lab-coat pockets, giving the hallway the thousand-yard stare. Without another word the two of them headed down to the morgue.

(4)

Polk's voice was a shrill whisper. "You want me to do *what*?"

"You heard me. Search his office, his files, and his computer. Whatever he has that relates to what's going on has to be completely destroyed. You hearing me? Everything."

"I'll get caught, Vic. There's no way I can break into his office without someone noticing. He's here all day and at night. Someone'd see the lights through his window."

He heard Vic sigh and there was a pause as if Vic was slowly working through a slow ten-count. "Jim," Vic said tiredly, "believe it or not I actually get tired of having to threaten you every time I want something done, so, let's just take it as read that you're going to do this because you don't want to face the consequences of really, truly pissing me off."

Polk sat down on the third step and rubbed his face with one hand. "Yeah," he said tiredly, "okay. Only . . . I really don't know how much more of this stuff I can take, Vic. My nerves are shot. My hands are shaking all the time, I got diarrhea now everyday, my gut feels like it's full of broken glass."

"Tell you what, you hold the phone while I go open me up a fresh can of I-don't-give-a-shit."

"Thanks, Vic . . . you're a real pal."

Vic was laughing when he hung up. Polk stared at the mottled gray-white of the concrete of the stairwell landing, conscious of the weight of his sidearm in its holster, heavy with promise.

Chapter 6

Mike stood frozen to the spot as Tow-Truck Eddie entered the shop. A panicky voice screamed in his head, *Run . . . run . . . RUN!* but his legs were concrete, his body stunned into an immobile mass.

He'd only seen Eddie up close twice before and that memory didn't match this one at all. The first was maybe two years ago when his mom had made Mike drop off a lunch for Vic. Eddie had seemed big enough, but he'd worn a gentle smile and had given Mike an amiable wink. The second time was a couple of weeks ago, as they passed one another in the lobby of the hospital after Crow had been shot. He'd almost seemed ordinary then. Now the man seemed ten feet tall and five feet wide. Eddie's police uniform was well tailored but it did nothing to hide the weightlifter's chest and arms. He had huge sloping shoulders that tapered right up to his head, making it look like he had no neck at all. And though he had to be in his early fifties he showed no signs of age except for some crow's-feet at the corners of his piercing blue eyes. An Arnold Schwarzenegger cop, Mike thought, a Pine Deep Terminator. The name OSWALD was engraved in white on a black plastic name tag pinned to his chest, and Mike realized that he had never known the man's last name before.

Eddie Oswald closed the door slowly, his gaze intent on Mike, and then walked slowly across the floor of the shop, big hands swinging easily, almost no expression on his face except for tiny bits of muscle at his jaw that bunched and flexed.

For just a second, though, something odd happened and Mike was aware of it on a detached, almost remote level. The air between Officer Oswald and himself seemed to shimmer as if heat vapor were rising from the floor. It gave the big man a distorted appearance, like a mirage of some giant seen across desert sands.

Mike knew he couldn't run. The big man could catch him easily before he could fish out the key and duck through into Crow's apartment. Mike wondered if the cop recognized him. Maybe out there on the road the big man hadn't had a good look at him, so he played on that and turned on a bright, helpful smile that was so fake it made his cheeks hurt. "Uh . . . can I help you, Officer?"

The cop stood there, frowning now as he looked at Mike, all of his force and swagger diminishing second by second. He peered at Mike, eyes narrowed to slits, but there was no recognition on his face. When he spoke, though, his voice carried a different and far more accusatory weight.

"You work here, boy?" Tow-Truck Eddie's voice was as raw as scraped knuckles.

"Yes, sir," Mike whispered through a dry throat. "Is there anything I can do for you . . . Officer? Um . . . d'you want me to get the owner?" Crow hadn't come in yet, but Mike hoped the promise of it might protect him from whatever this madman had planned.

"No," said the cop quietly. "No, don't bother him. I want to ask you a couple of questions." He leaned on the word *you.*

"Me?" asked Mike, and his adolescent voice broke from tenor to soprano on that one word. "Me? Uh . . . About what?"

The cop removed a notebook from his pocket and consulted it. Mike watched him, and he had the strangest impression that the cop wasn't really reading notes on the book, but was just staring at it. The officer's lips moved slightly, not as if reading aloud with the words, but as if speaking to himself. Finally, the big man raised his eyes and stared long and hard at Mike. "There have been some reports of kids harassing drivers on A-32, play-ing chicken with cars and trucks out on the highway. Would you know anything about that?"

"Kids playing chicken? No."

"You're sure?"

"Yeah. I don't know anything about anything like that."

The cop stared hard in his direction, but kept squinting as if he was having a hard time focusing on him. "Do you have a bi-cycle, son?"

"Sure." The word came out before he could stop it.

"Do you ever ride it on Route A-32?"

Mike hesitated, trying to make it look like he was consider-ing it. "No sir."

The cop took a ballpoint pen from his pocket and made a note in his book. Or pretended to. "Are you telling me that you never ride your bicycle on Route A-32 at night?"

Mike hedged. "Not . . . really."

"What does 'not really' mean? Do you or don't you?"

"I guess I do sometimes, like during the summer, but not re-cently."

The cop made another note, and Mike saw him peek upward as he pretended to write, as if hoping to catch a clearer look. For a moment the cop tilted his head as if listening, wincing as he did so, and again confusion clouded his face. "Now tell me, son, have you ever seen other kids riding their bicycles there at night?"

Mike hesitated. "I guess."

"What was that, son?"

"Yes, sir." Mike avoided direct eye contact. "Sometimes I see other kids, sure."

"Have you ever seen any kids playing chicken with cars or trucks on Route A-32 at night?"

"No . . . no, nothing like that."

"Never?"

"No."

The cop winced again. "Would you mind turning down the music so we can talk?

Mike just looked at him. He hadn't turned on the Halloween CDs yet; the store was quiet. "Music?" he asked.

The cop blinked as if surprised either of them had said anything about music. He looked at his notepad for a moment and then shook his head like a dog being harassed by flies. "Look at me, son," said the cop quietly, and Mike reluctantly raised his eyes. The shimmer in the air between them seemed to intensify.

Could he see it? Mike wondered. He tensed, his legs trembling with the urge to run.

The cop looked at him with blue eyes that were as hard as fists. "Tell me this, son, have *you* ever played chicken with a car?"

"No."

". . . or truck . . ."

"No, never!"

". . . or any vehicle of any kind on Route A-32 at night?"

"I swear, Officer, I never did. Nothing like that."

The cop looked skeptical, and he inflicted silence on Mike for several long seconds. "You know, son, one of these punk kids actually caused an accident on the road the other night."

"Um . . . really? What happened?" Mike couldn't believe he was asking that question.

The cop put a finger in his ear and jiggled it around like a swimmer trying to get rid of water. He realized he was doing it, cleared his throat, and consulted his notebook. "Some kid . . . some evil, nasty little son of a bitch of a kid . . . was playing chicken with a truck on the road."

"A truck?"

"Yes," said the cop gravely. "A tow truck."

Mike mouthed the phrase "tow truck," but didn't put any sound to it.

"A brand-new tow truck. Very large and very expensive."

"What happened?" There it was again, his fool mouth asking questions while the rest of him wanted to run and hide.

"Well, son, the tow truck was just driving along, the driver minding his own business, when this punk kid dodges right out in front of him. Dodges right out so unexpectedly that the driver had to swerve to keep from running him over. And do you know what happened then?" When Mike shook his head, Oswald continued. "Since the driver had to swerve so violently to keep from hurting the kid, he lost control of his tow truck and went off the road and into a ditch. The driver was pretty badly banged up. The tow truck itself sustained several thousand dollars' worth of damage. Now, isn't that terrible?"

"I . . . I guess."

The cop bent suddenly forward, his eyes blazing. "You *guess*?"

Mike recoiled, but the cop came so close that he could smell the man's breath. It was awful, like spoiled meat.

"You guess?" the cop snarled again. "Well, let me tell you something, you young piece of shit, that man could have been killed. Killed! Do you understand that? Do you think it's just all right for punk bastards to try and kill honest citizens?"

"No! No, sir . . . of course not."

"Oh, good, then you're a good, upstanding citizen, aren't you?" the cop said, suddenly smiling, straightening, and once more consulting his notebook. He absently pawed at his ear. "It's too loud," he muttered to himself, then looked at Mike again, his smile brightening. "Do you go to church?"

The question came out of complete left field, and Mike just stared at him. *He's out of his freaking mind,* he thought, but on the heels of that came the certain knowledge that the cop didn't recognize him. It made no real sense, but there it was.

"I guess . . ." He caught himself. "Sure," he lied. "Every Sunday."

Tow-Truck Eddie reached out with one of his bandaged hands and tousled Mike's hair. "You're a good boy, I can tell that. If you did know something about that incident, you would tell me, wouldn't you?" The transition to Officer Friendly was just as scary as the seething vehemence had been a moment before. Dumbfounded, Mike just nodded. "I'm sorry, son, I didn't catch that." Just the slightest edge there.

"Yes . . . yes, sir, if I knew something about it, I'd tell you."

"Good boy." The cop stood there and for a few seconds, consulting whatever notes he had written in his notebook and staring at the top sheet unblinkingly. He turned without comment and walked to the door, but as his big hand was touching the handle he paused and looked back at Mike. "You're . . . not him," he asked. His voice was infused with sadness, perhaps loss. "Are you?"

Mike's throat was as hot and dry as Hell's back door. "No," he said. "No . . . I'm not him."

"Okay then," he said, paused, and then added, "God bless you."

"Um," Mike said. "You . . . too?"

The cop flashed him a tired grin, and then he was gone.

Mike sagged back away from the counter, took two wobbly steps, and sat down hard on the floor, numb even to the shock of the impact. Bees and termites seemed to be crawling around the inside of his stomach and there were fireworks exploding in his eyes.

"God!" he gasped, and then tumbled over onto his hands and knees and vomited into a small plastic trash can. His guts clenched and spasmed and his whole body bucked with the effort as the fireworks turned to blooming black flowers and his blood roared in his ears. When his stomach was empty he crawled under the counter, curled into a ball with arms wrapped around his bowed head, and began shivering uncontrollably.

The convulsions didn't start for at least another ten minutes.

In the middle of the store, halfway between the counter and the front door, the air shimmered again and again, and if Mike had been in any condition to pay attention he might have caught just the faintest ghostly echo of the fading notes of a wailing blues riff and an even fainter sound of bitter laughter.

The shimmer wafted like heat vapor toward the door and in the harsh intensity of the morning sunlight it melted away into nothingness.

(2)

A long time ago, back when Vic had started schooling him on his role in the Red Wave, Polk had managed to steal a set of passkeys for the hospital, copy them, and return the originals before anyone noticed they were gone. There was no part of the hospital, not even the private offices of the senior staff, that he couldn't enter. When he saw Saul Weinstock and Crow enter the elevator, he took that moment to use his master key and slip into Weinstock's office, slipped on a pair of latex gloves, and in three quick minutes made a fast and thorough search of desk, cabinets, and files. Whatever else he might be, Polk was efficient.

In the bottom left drawer of the doctor's desk he found an accordion folder marked *Ruger et al.* that was crammed with notes, lab reports on Cowan and Castle, photos, and medical records. It was exactly what Vic had told him to find. There were computer disks and several security camera digital tapes in there as well. The whole shebang.

"Sweet," he said, but the second he said it the word turned sour on his tongue and doubt took a giant step into his heart. This was the stuff Vic had told him—*ordered* him—to get and destroy. On the other hand there was no way to make this stuff vanish without making things worse. No way in the world. If he took it, then somehow the shit was going to land on him. Polk knew that as sure as he knew dogs didn't fart gold coins. It wouldn't be Vic's ass on the line . . . it would be his.

He chewed his lip, glancing from folder to desk clock to closed door and back to folder, but he knew the decision had already been made. Maybe even before he broke in here. The bottom line, as he saw it, was that Vic wasn't paying him enough to take a fall for this. Taking one for the team was not part of Polk's game plan, no way José. Plus, doubt had been growing in him like a brushfire, fueled by the fact that Vic never quite detailed what Polk's role would be once the Red Wave had swept through Pine Deep. Too often when he probed Vic on that subject, the coldhearted bastard just gave him a crocodile smile and a wink, saying some shit like, "We always take care of our friends, Jimmy Boy."

"You know what, Vic?" he murmured, "You can kiss my ass." He put the folder back as neatly as he'd found it, closed and locked the desk. Maybe it was good enough to know where it was in case *he* needed the leverage. He slipped out of the office, stripped off the gloves, and shoved them into a pocket, then ducked into the fire stairs.

Two flights down he stopped, checked the stairs, and punched Vic's number on speed dial. "Vic? It's me," Polk whispered.

"Yeah? And?"

"Nothing. I checked Weinstock's office from top to bottom. No files, no evidence. Nothing."

There was a pause and Polk felt little jabs of stress pain under his heart.

"Okay," Vic said. "You're sure? You checked everywhere?"

"Maybe it's at his house. Or . . . um, in a safety deposit box. Maybe he gave it to someone. Maybe he gave it to Crow."

Another pause. "Shit," Vic said at last, "that sounds about right. Damn it."

"What do you want me to do?" He took a risk, guessing what Vic would say. "You want me to creep his place?"

"No. Not at the moment. Just go back to watching the hospital and I'll get back to you."

Vic hung up and Polk sagged against the wall. His armpits were soaked and he felt sick to his stomach. With Vic it was never easy to tell whether he believed something or not. Not until Vic brought it up face-to-face. Polk fumbled a bottle of aspirin out of his pocket and dry-swallowed three of them before pulling the door open.

(3)

"That's funny," Weinstock said as he reached for the doorknob, "this should be locked."

The door was open just a crack, showing a vertical line of shadows inside the morgue. Crow saw it and immediately pushed Weinstock's hand away. "No! Don't."

"You don't think—"

"I don't like this one bit, Saul. So let's just back away," Crow said softly as he pulled his friend away from the door. Together they moved to the far side of the hallway and Crow looked up and down the corridor, seeing things he hadn't seen when they'd first come off the elevator. The concrete was scuffed with dirt and mud that had been tracked in from the access door to the outside. There was a beer can on the ground and a couple of cigarette butts. He squatted down to examine them. No, not cigarette butts—they were the roach ends of a couple of joints. "What the hell?" He glanced at the door as he straightened. "Saul, call security. Get some guards down here."

Weinstock gave a curt nod and hurried back up the corridor to where a white plastic phone was inset into the cinderblock wall. He lifted the handset and punched in a three-digit code.

"Security," a crisp female voice answered. "Molly Sims."

"Molly, this is Dr. Weinstock. I'm outside the morgue. It looks like there's been a break-in."

"Another one?" Her voice rose three octaves.

"Get somebody down here right now!" He slammed down the phone and crept back to join Crow, who was peering at the mud. Mixed in with ordinary dirt there was a darker, more viscous substance that was a dark red fading to chocolate brown.

"I think some of this is blood," Crow said softly. "Christ, are we looking at just another break-in, or is did something break *out*?"

Weinstock paled. "I really wish you wouldn't say things like that." He shifted to try and peer through the narrow crack, but the room beyond was completely dark. "You thinking Boyd?"

"Yeah," Crow said. *Or Mark*, he thought, but didn't say it. "Wait here." He hurried back to the elevator end of the hall to where a heavy fire ax was mounted on clips behind a glass door. He smashed the glass and took the ax.

Weinstock nodded approval. "Should do the trick if anything comes out of there, but I sure hope you're not thinking of going in."

Crow smiled faintly. "Dude, in the movies the hero always walks into some dark place all alone, and you *know* something fangy and hairy is going to jump out. Doesn't work for me— I'm not a total idiot and I'm comfortably chickenshit, so I'll wait for the cavalry to arrive. This," he hefted the ax again, "is to make me feel better while we wait."

They waited. Every other second one of them would shoot a look over at the elevator, waiting for the little white light above the door to go *bing!* Long seconds passed.

"Your security team kinda blows with the whole rapid-response thing."

Weinstock was scowling at the elevator. "Ever since we got down here my balls have been slowly climbing up into my pelvis. If my nuts make it all the way to my chest cavity by the time those guards get here, heads will roll." He nodded at the ax. "And I don't mean layoffs."

The elevator pinged and the doors slid open as five people burst out into the hall—three hospital security officers and two cops. Polk was one of the cops. Everyone had their guns drawn and they raced down the hall, pistol barrels pointed up to the ceiling, eyes shifting back and forth, moving just like each of them had seen real cops do on TV.

"We're saved," Crow said dryly.

Weinstock sighed. "Whoopee."

Though Crow didn't like Polk, he had to admire the smooth efficiency with which the officer led his men into the room, where they fanned out and covered every corner. It was very workmanlike.

"Clear!" Polk called. As he holstered his pistol he gestured for Weinstock and Crow to come in. "Nobody's home, but it looks like there was one hell of a party."

The place had been trashed. Tables overturned, glass shattered, closets torn off the walls, and contents dumped. The walls were covered with crude graffiti—naked women with huge breasts, men with gigantic penises, and slogans like "Pine Deep Scarecrows Rule!" and "Blow Me!" On the floor someone had used a pint of whole blood to create splash art, and there were footprints patterned all the way through it.

"That explains the blood in the hallway," Weinstock said, but he sounded more hopeful than certain. Crow merely grunted.

"I'll call for a crime scene team down here," Polk said and went out into the hall.

Crow and Weinstock barely registered the comment. They were both staring at the rows of stainless-steel doors behind which bodies were stored on sliding metal trays. All the doors stood open. Mark Guthrie lay on one of them; Connie was two drawers down. Tyrone Gibbs was in the one at the far end, and an old lady who had died of a coronary was in the drawer next to him.

"Saul . . . tell me, please, that Boyd's body was stored somewhere else."

Weinstock scrambled around, kicking through the debris until he found a clipboard. He riffled through the pages and then just stood there, his face going dead.

Crow closed his eyes. "Oh . . . shit."

Boyd's body was gone.

Chapter 7

He drifted through the forest on silent feet while above and around him the air was filled with the scream of crows. The ragged black birds carted and wheeled above the Bone Man's head, sometimes landing in rows along the arthritic arms of trees, sometimes gathering in gossiping clusters on the ground. Several hundred more of the night birds lined a twisted path, standing like diners at a buffet to peck at the rotting remains of ten thousand squashed roaches—the debris from the hysterical flight of Crow and Newton the day before.

The Bone Man smiled at the birds. He liked them, they were his friends in this. His eyes, sometimes, his ears. Why these ragged carrion birds could see him when no one else could was something even he didn't know. Maybe they were doomed, too. Henry Guthrie had seen him that night because Henry was knocking on Heaven's door, but then a lot of people had seen him that first night. Henry's little girl, Val. Li'l Miss Bosslady he used to call her. She'd seen him out there in the corn when Ruger was hunting for her. The boy, the *dhampyr*, had seen him on the road that night, but that was when the Bone Man was being a fool and using up the little power he'd brought from the grave, being stupid and wasteful, trying to be symbolic when straightforward would have worked better—showing himself as a white stag instead of just speaking to the kid. The Bone Man shook his head as he walked, torn by the opportunities missed.

Well it's not like you gave me a goddamn handbook on this shit! he yelled at God.

He kept walking, heading deeper into the forest, thinking about the other times the boy saw him. He was sure the kid had seen him over and over again, but it was during those weird fugues that were changing Mike from what he was to what he was going to be and who the hell knows what the kid was aware of during those moments? The Bone Man guessed, but he didn't know. Anymore than Griswold knew—or so he hoped.

And on that topic, he shouted in his soundless voice, *where the hell are you—you cowardly piece of shit?*

Griswold—his personality, his *presence,* whatever the hell you call it . . . the Bone Man hadn't sensed him since late last night. Not since Val Guthrie had shot the living hell out of that son of a bitch Boyd. Griswold—*the "Man" my ass,* the Bone Man thought— had gotten his mouth slapped with that one, sure enough. He may have taken down Mark Guthrie, who was always a weak sister, but not Val.

The Bone Man was grinning about that when he reached the edge of the swamp. He stopped there and the crows flocked around him, settling in the trees, fluttering their oily wings, clicking their beaks in expectation. Despite the chill of mid-October, the swamp was always warm and wet. Flies as big as bees flew low and heavy across the rippled surface, sometimes getting caught in the pop of a bubble of sulfur or methane. There were snakes in the brown grass and worms as thick a child's finger wriggling in the tangles of rotting vegetation that choked the edges of the slough. Even to a dead man the place was unnatural and vile, and the Bone Man winced at the stink of it.

He moved slowly to the edge of the mire and looked at it. Thirty years ago he and Griswold had fought here. Right here, down deep in the shadows of Dark Hollow, while beyond the mountains the moon was clawing its way into the sky. The Bone Man had gone hunting for the man, knowing—if no one else in town did—that Griswold was the murdering bastard behind the killings that had torn the heart out of Pine Deep. The Bone

Man had stabbed him with the broken neck of his guitar and then dragged his body into that mud and pushed it down with a stick until Ubel Griswold had vanished forever beneath the sludge. After thirty years in that kind of muck there would be nothing left but some fragments of bones. The mud of that swamp was filled with worms and every other kind of thing that eats. Griswold was worm food long ago.

So where was he now? Why was there no *sense* of him around?

The Bone Man stood there, smiling darkly down at the swamp. "Maybe you're off sulking, you cowardly piece of shit," he shouted. The birds squawked their support like Baptists in a revival tent. "Val Guthrie handed your boy Boyd his ass. How d'you like that? You wanted her dead—something new for your collection. You already got Billy and you got Mandy. You probably got Terry Wolfe, 'cause he's sinking low and maybe that's where you are . . . down in the dark waiting for Terry to let go and stop fighting so you can take him. You tried to get Val and you tried to get Crow, but you ain't got *shit!*" The Bone Man tried to summon up moisture so he could spit on the swampy grave, but there was just dust in his throat. He'd have loved to piss on the mud, but he couldn't do that, either. He could laugh, though, and there was no bluesman who ever lived who didn't know how to laugh at the craziness of life.

Now he was laughing at the foolishness of the dead.

"We quite a pair, ain't we, *Mr. Man?* A ghost who don't know how to be a ghost, and a bloodsucker with no teeth who can't bite what he wants to bite. Must really piss you off. After being the cock of the walk all them years ago it must really bite your ass to be just a shadow in the back of sick minds like Wingate and Ruger's." He chuckled. "And they're a half-step shy of being too stupid to wipe they own asses . . . couldn't even kill Val Guthrie. Hell, much as it pains me to say it . . . you, at least, were dangerous. Now you got no teeth, no claws, and no dick, and you gotta watch these clowns try and do your screwin' for you. That just makes me laugh!"

The Bone Man was bent over laughing, slapping his knees, shaking with it as if he really had a body, his eyes shut and his head shaking back and forth as he howled. The birds in the trees cackled with him.

Far beneath the surface of the swamp, lost in an infinity of verminous earth and polluted rainwater, Ubel Griswold listened to the sound of the Bone Man's mocking laughter. His rage was terrible.

Chapter 8

Eddie Oswald sat in the front seat of his patrol car and stared numbly through the windshield, listening to the absolute silence in his head. His bandaged hands lay like broken birds in his lap, his lower lip drooped slack and rubbery. The windows were rolled up, the radio turned off, the engine silent. He'd sat like that for twenty minutes.

When he first left the Crow's Nest he was confused. He had been so sure that Mike Sweeney worked there at the store. Positive. Days ago God Himself had told him where he would find the child. What could be more certain? Yet every time he drove by the store all he saw through the window was Crow, and sometimes another boy, but the face was never clear. There was always something blocking his view. Sunlight, a smear on the glass, shadows. So, today, with the deafening silence of his Father's disdain hammering at the inside of his head, Eddie had gone straight into the store, had confronted the boy, ready to do what was necessary, ready to complete his Holy Mission. The Sword of God had been drawn, ready to cut down the Beast.

Then something had happened. The lighting in the store must have been bad, or maybe it was that annoying wailing music that made it so hard to concentrate, but try as he might Eddie never seemed to be able to get a clear look at the kid. Even when he saw him somewhat better there was a veil of doubt. This couldn't have been the Beast; this could not have been the false suit of skin the Beast had used into order to work his evil magic here in Pine Deep. This child, this boy in the store . . . there was no reek of evil about him; there was no crackle of demonic energy that Eddie believed must be present in the Beast. He'd felt it, even at a distance, out there on A-32 last night. The dark energies had burned his fingertips as he reached for the boy there on the road; it was like an ozone stink in the air as he chased him in his truck and on foot.

Not today, though. This boy—*why couldn't he see the kid's face?*—was just an ordinary child. He said he went to church. He was a good kid. Eddie sensed that, as surely as he sensed the evil power of the Beast last night on the road.

He needed clarity. He needed his Father's voice speaking to him from within the infinite universe of his mind. He needed direction.

Eddie sat in his car as the minutes ticked past, and gradually his mind shut down, like someone clicking off lights by flicking one switch after another, dropping more and more of his awareness into soft, untroubled, uncomplicated shadows.

It was then, as an armada of clouds sailed across the sky and blotted out the sun, that something happened. It was then that his Father . . . *spoke.*

It was not in language. It was a single, guttural, howling scream of absolute rage that shrieked into his mind like the explosion of a thousand tons of TNT. Instant, immediate, impossibly loud— a hoarse cry of such unimaginable fury that every muscle in Eddie's body locked into a spasm of agonized awareness. His sinews contracted, muscle fibers clenched, his nerve endings seemed to ignite with the sheer intensity of it as Eddie convulsed in pain so intense, so white-hot that it was even beyond his body's ability to scream it out. Blood sprayed from his nose and ears and he vomited black ichor, bile, and blood all over the inside of his car.

His Father's rage struck him down with all the wrath of a furious and disappointed God. Eddie's eyes glazed over and he toppled sideways into blackness.

(2)

Ruger had gotten up to take another book down from Vic's shelf when his body suddenly snapped straight as if he were coming to attention. His arms and legs twitched and jerked like a million volts of electricity were being channeled through him. A terrible scream ripped loose from his throat—dry and searing and then wet as blood spewed out of him. Tears of blood sprang into his eyes and rolled down over his cheeks, his eardrums nearly burst, his head felt like it was being smashed by an iron mallet. He could not speak, could not move, could do nothing in that moment but scream as pain beyond anything he had ever endured, beyond anything he had ever imagined, burned through every cell. He was not even aware that fifteen feet away Vic Wingate had collapsed onto the floor, howling with his own agony. The air was stained with foulness as Vic's bladder and sphincter let loose; the fecund stink mixed with the sheared-copper smell of blood to create a perfume of shame.

For a handful of seconds the world was defined by pain.

Then it was gone. Not gradual, not ebbing like a tide or subsiding like the pain of a smashed finger. It was there, and then it was not there.

Ruger took one staggering step and then like a marionette with severed strings he crashed to the floor, bleeding and dazed. His head struck the edge of the armchair as he fell and his cheekbone cracked audibly; his body collapsed into a boneless heap mere yards from the stinking, wretched mess that was Vic Wingate.

They lay in a world where time had no meaning, no sense or order. It did not matter that one was alive and one was undead—they shared that moment like two birds shot with the same gun, and though they could not know it, all across the square miles of Pine Deep, in shadowy barns and locked cellars, in shallow graves and shuttered attics, in the trunks of cars and in empty corn silos, the legions of Ubel Griswold were all sharing the same experience. Every one of them, from the living to the blood drinkers to the mindless flesh eaters, they all writhed in the aftershock of the moment. As that moment passed and sense crept into blasted minds, even the smallest intelligence among them was aware of the meaning of that eloquent message. This was payment for the mistakes of last night. No further mistakes would be permitted.

The Man was *pissed*.

Chapter 9

Five customers came into the Crow's Nest in the two hours Mike lay under the counter. Three of them peered around, saw that no one was there, and left. The fourth—his friend Brandon from school—called Crow's name, got no reply, and left. The fifth was a kid from Mike's homeroom who wanted to buy some comic books. After spending ten minutes in the store, browsing through Daredevil and Thor books while surreptitiously checking for staff or security cameras, he tucked thirty dollars' worth of Marvel comics under his sweatshirt and sauntered out as if he owned the world. On the way out, just for the hell of it, he flipped over the sign on the door so that it now read CLOSED.

The store settled into silence. Mike was not crying anymore. The convulsions had put an end to that. He wasn't twitching anymore, either. He lay there, cold and still, eyes open and dry from not blinking. His chest barely moved, his breathing very shallow and slow, his pulse slower.

When the change started, it happened very slowly, with no great hurry. It started with a hitch in his chest as he took a single sharp, deep breath, like a dead person who was suddenly reacting to the defibrillator paddles. His body didn't arch or jump, just that single gasp, after which his breath became deeper, more regular. Then nothing for five minutes.

The next thing that happened was a blink. His dry lids scraped over the arid surface of his eyes once, then again. The second time was easier; there was more moisture. Then a third, a fourth as the eyes moistened. There was no sign of focus, no hint of intelligence or awareness. The blink, like the breath, was a process kicking in, a link in the organic chain of system reboots.

It was just over two hours from the time that Tow-Truck Eddie had walked out that Mike Sweeney came back. One moment his eyes were open and empty and the next, bridged by another blink, Mike was there behind those blue windows. Like water filling a submerged cup, life flooded instantly in and filled his body.

As he gradually became aware of his body, Mike began the process of thinking. He thought about who he was, and that took a while before he remembered. He thought about why his body hurt, and he came up blank on that one—but he was aware that he didn't know, which was a step toward full consciousness. He thought about where he was, and very slowly he went from small picture—he was on a floor under the counter—to a more moderate view—he was in someplace that was not his home— to a larger view—he was in Crow's store.

Crow. The name of the store came to him more quickly than the identity of its owner, though as he lay there, becoming increasingly more aware of something sticky on his face and throat, of the way his clothing was uncomfortably twisted, of the cramps in muscles, the face of Malcolm Crow gradually formed in his mind.

"Crow . . ." Mike said, his voice just a whisper. Saying the name fleshed out Crow's complete personality in his mind, and that tumbled the last pieces into place. He was in Crow's store, it was daytime. Crow wasn't here . . . no one was here.

Why was he here?

Mike took a steadying breath and then slowly, carefully, he unclenched the knotted fist that was his curled body. Pain seemed to be a humming presence within it, constantly throbbing. He was on his side and he rolled over onto his elbows and knees. Beneath him the floor seemed to buckle and ripple in a nauseating way, but as consciousness blossomed he grew to understand that this was just the effects of—

Of what? He didn't know, wasn't sure he wanted to know.

From his knees he straightened his torso so that he could look over the edge of the counter. The store was empty; the outside light looked like late morning. There was traffic outside, people and cars. Mike leaned his hands on the counter to steady himself, and the touch of the solid wood and Formica had a nicely steadying effect on the whole room and an equally calming effect on his stomach. Solid reality. It felt good enough to risk standing up and he gave that a shot, using both hands to pull himself up, first to one foot and then to both. The room, agreeably, did not start dancing around again.

There was a horrible taste in his mouth and he looked around for something to drink. He saw the trash can, saw that he'd thrown up in it.

"Swell," he said and carefully walked over to the small bathroom. As before, the face in the mirror was one he didn't recognize, but this time it was not an hallucination of his own, older face; now it was just his normal face but his skin was greenish and there was puke dried on his chin, throat, and upper shirtfront. "Swell," he said again, and reached for the tap.

When he had cleaned himself up, he felt better, stronger. He emptied the trash can and washed it, then mopped the floor behind the counter, which was stained with vomit and sweat. He removed all traces of what had happened, embarrassed by it without understanding what had happened or if there was any shame he should feel. Probably not, but guilt was a reflex for him.

It was nearly an hour before he realized that the sign on the door was hung the wrong way. A lucky break, he thought as he went over to flip it to OPEN.

Still no sign of Crow. He thought about calling him, but something inside told him not to. Not now, not yet.

He got a bottle of Yoo-hoo from Crow's apartment fridge, pulled the stool to the end of the counter, picked up the copy of *Cemetery Dance* that he had started reading. The entire encounter with Tow-Truck Eddie was buried down deep, buried along with a lot of other things that were stored in the shadows in the back of his brain. Stored out of sight, but not gone.

(2)

Crow sat in the plastic visitor's chair, sloshing around the cold dregs of hospital coffee in a cardboard cup and watching the sky outside thicken from gray to purple as another storm front pushed in from the west. Val was finally asleep, her face turned away from him so that all he could see was the lumpy mountain of bandages that covered the right half of her head. Her hands twitched as she slept. *Bad dreams*, he thought, knowing that right now there were no other kinds of dreams she could be having.

Boyd's body was missing. Exhausted as she was, the news had nearly broken her. She dissolved into frustrated, horrified tears and went on and on until Crow began to fear that she was having a breakdown. How much could one person take, after all? There was nothing the nurses could do; she was pregnant, so sedatives were out of the question, and there's only so much emotional mileage you can get from a cup of chamomile tea. So, Crow had held her while the storms of fear and hurt raged in her heart, and it was close to three o'clock before pain and exhaustion dragged her down into a rough and troubled sleep. He doubted she would find much restoration there, and he hated the thought of what shapes lumbered through her nightmares.

Just after five there was a soft tap on the door and Crow got up quietly and padded over, opening the door softly to see Sarah Wolfe standing there. She looked as smashed down and weary as Val. She started to say something, but he put a finger to his lips as he stepped out into the hall and closed the door behind him.

"Sarah . . . how's Terry?"

She offered him a brave smile. "The same. Stable, if that really means anything."

"You know Val and I are praying for the big guy."

A quick nod, then, "Crow, I need to speak to you about something and I don't want you to hate me for it."

"Wow, that's a hell of an opening."

"It's about the Halloween Festival." When he looked blank, she said, "The party, the movie marathons, the whole—"

"Sarah, sweetie . . . don't get me wrong but . . . who the hell *cares* anymore?"

"Terry wanted you to run things if he couldn't. He's been telling me that over and over again these last few weeks as he's gotten . . . well, sicker."

Crow just looked at her. "Sarah, do you know what's been happening lately? Mark and Connie are dead."

"I know, and I heard that some creeps from the college broke in and stole the body of that horrible man—"

"Sarah . . . with all that's happened to Val and her family I couldn't give a rat's ass about Halloween right now."

She took his hand and held it in both of hers. "Crow, this is hard for me to ask because I know how stupid and trivial it sounds, but please hear me out. Okay? You know how bad this crop blight is for the farmers in town. They're on the verge of losing everything—their farms, their homes. Terry loaned out some money to those that were hardest hit. He's mortgaged our house, his businesses, and even the Hayride up to the hilt. And there have been a lot of deals made between the farmers and the businesses in town, a lot of loans swapped back and forth, and what the banks couldn't guarantee, Terry did."

"Christ, Sarah . . . why the hell did he do that?"

"Because he loves this town, Crow. He loves it so much that he feels responsible for it, that if he lets it fail, then it'll be a personal failure. I think that's why he's been seeing his sister. You know he nearly died trying to save Mandy when they were attacked. I think on some damaged level Terry is trying to save her all over again by trying so hard to save the town."

"Maybe," Crow said cautiously. He had other thoughts on Terry and Mandy.

"If the Halloween Festival fails, then Terry won't be able to make good on the loans. He'll be ruined, and it will destroy the economy of Pine Deep. Completely. A few people will survive, but the town as we know it will become a wasteland of foreclosures and bankruptcies." Her eyes were bloodshot and when she had reapplied her lipstick she'd done a shaky job of it. "Crow, we need that Festival to happen. This isn't just a money thing, and it's not just about Terry's—and my—financial future. This is really about the survival of Pine Deep."

"I get that, Sarah, I really do . . . but what the hell can I do? No way I'm going to leave Val here and go off to play spooks and specters with the tourists."

She shook her head. "Terry has plenty of staff to run the day-to-day operations, but you were the one who set up most of the events, you've been the liaison for all of the celebrities, you're the one who has the contacts and knows how every part of this festival runs. If I had another month I might be able to train a couple of people to handle this, but we don't. Halloween is two weeks away."

"I get it, I get it . . . but—"

"If you're going to be here at the hospital, then I can have Terry's laptop and files brought here. You could send some e-mails, make some phone calls . . . basically keep things on track. The Festival this year promises to be the biggest ever, which means that money is going to pour into Pine Deep. If we can just keep everything running smoothly, then we can accomplish what Terry staked everything he has to achieve." Her eyes searched his face, and she still held his right hand.

Crow gently disentangled his hand and walked a couple of paces away, shaking his head and rubbing the back of his neck. "Jeez, Sarah . . . I don't know. So much of this depends on what's happening here in town. We're going to be arranging funerals and all."

She managed a weak smile. "Well, I did start this off by asking you not to hate me." She came over and gave him a hug. "Just think about it, okay? I'm going to have Terry's computer and files brought in anyway . . . just in case."

He grinned, too. "But no pressure."

"Oh, heavens no. Pressure? Here in bucolic Pine Deep, where the nights are quiet and sleepy and nothing ever happens and everyone's just happy as clams."

"Yep, that's us, that's Pine Deep." He sighed. "Whoever coined that phrase 'America's Haunted Holidayland' should be stood against a wall and shot."

She patted him on the cheek. "That was you, sweetie. Ten years ago when you were interviewed by Don Polec for *Action News*."

"Yeah, well," he said, remembering, "it sounded good at the time."

"And now?"

"Now it just sounds too much like truth in advertising." Down the hall he saw Saul Weinstock and Gus Bernhardt coming out of the elevator. "Okay, Sarah, let me think about it, and when Val wakes up, I'll run it by her. No promises, though, so if you have another backup plan you should start looking into it."

"There's no other—" she started to say, then stopped, nodded, and said thanks.

Crow watched her head down the hall, saw Weinstock give her a reassuring smile, and then she was gone. Crow saw that the smile lingered on Weinstock's face and that made a frown form on his own.

"Hey, Crow!" Weinstock said as they came to stop in front of him.

"Any word on—" Crow began, but Gus cut him off.

"No," Weinstock said, "Gus thinks that it really was those jackasses from the college."

"Little Halloween is bigger than Mischief Night around here," Gus observed. The Pine Deep police chief was a big, sloppy fat man with a perpetually sweaty face and boiled-red complexion. "This whole morgue break-in is turning out to be a Little Halloween stunt. We were dealing with crap like this all night. Trash can fires, webcams hidden in the girl's bathroom at the dorms, the doors to the school bus arc-welded shut."

"But, Boyd . . ." Crow began.

"We'll find him eventually." Gus shook his head. "These college jocks love their friggin' jokes."

"Glad they think it's funny. Personally I'd like to kick their asses. Better yet, wait until Val's on her feet and then lock them in a room with her. That'd teach them."

"Speaking of which," Gus said awkwardly, "tell her that I'm, you know, sorry for her loss and all. Mark was pretty okay. Connie, too."

"Sure, Gus, I'll tell her. Your guys learn anything more from the crime scene? Like . . . how they got in?"

"Yeah, well we're working on that. Got a few things locked down, though, like the security camera. Someone poured a cup of coffee into the switching box that runs all the cameras on the basement level. That doesn't require any kind of special access except getting into the electrical room, and since Ruger broke in a couple of weeks ago and shut all the power down, that door's been left open more often than not because of all the work they're doing to reinforce the locks and frame."

Crow smiled. "Let me get this straight . . . while working on improving security to a sensitive area of the hospital physical plant they left the door open . . . for convenience?"

Weinstock's face went red. "Yes," he said slowly, "and when I say heads will roll, I mean actual heads will be on the floor."

"Christ on a stick." Crow shook his head.

"The hospital morgue is still a crime scene," Gus said. "I posted a guard, and the doc here has authorized installation of a new video security system. There's a guy coming up from Lower Makefield to install it today."

"Screw the budget committee," Weinstock growled. "I'm tired of this place being a laughingstock."

"A little late for that. Well, see you guys. I'll keep you posted." Gus gave them a cheery wave and headed off.

"Jackass," Weinstock muttered under his breath. He and Crow headed down the hall to the solarium and bought Cokes from the machine. The room was empty, and Weinstock closed the door.

"Before you even ask," he began, "I examined Mark and Connie as completely as I could—ostensibly to check for damage as a result of the prank—and as far as I can tell they're actually dead."

Crow looked skeptical. "You're telling me you know how to check to see if someone's a vampire?"

Weinstock sipped his soda. "Not as such, no. It's just that they are both in phases of the rigor process consistent with normal corpses who've been dead as long as each of them has been."

"Which tells us what?"

"Hell if I know. It might surprise you to know that they don't cover vampirism in medical school, not even in Pine Deep. But . . . I thought you're the expert, you're Mr. Halloween. You tell me how I'm supposed to tell."

"I've been thinking about that all night, but the folklore and the fiction just contradict each other. I don't know what to believe."

"Give me something I can try, damn it."

"Well . . . vampires aren't supposed to have reflections, so we could try a mirror."

"Good . . . that's easy enough."

"After that, most of the rest of the stuff are things we can try if we're face-to-face with one. I mean, crosses, garlic, holy water . . . that sort of stuff."

That didn't sit well with Weinstock. "If it gets to the point where we are actually face-to-face with a vampire who is awake and smiling all toothy at us, I think I might want something a little more substantial than a piece of garlic. And, news flash, Einstein, I'm Jewish. We're notoriously short on crosses and holy water."

"There's that." Crow thought about it. "There's always, um, the whole 'stake' thing."

"I was waiting for you to get to that, and I would love to hear how you're going to explain to Val that you want to drive a stake through her dead brother's heart."

"She knows what's going on."

"Go on, tell her you want to stake Mark. I'll watch."

"Isn't there something you can do during the autopsies to kind of ensure that they're dead?"

"Considering the fact that I autopsied both Cowan and Castle and determined with all medical certainty that they were dead, and then caught them on morgue video walking around, I'd say no."

"Val's going to want to cremate him anyway. Connie, too, since Val was her only family. Maybe we should just convince her to expedite that process. She might go for that a lot more than . . . other methods." Crow rubbed his eyes. "Or is any of this necessary?"

"Meaning?"

"Like I said earlier . . . is this over? Did the problem start with Ruger and Boyd? If so, now that they're dead is the situation over?"

"Maybe they started it, I don't know. With Cowan and Castle we know that there were at least two more of them. That's why I'm so concerned about Mark . . . he was killed by Boyd, who also killed those two cops."

"Yeah, on that subject—Cowan and Castle were buried. Have you checked their graves?"

"Have I dug them up? No. Have I checked to see if their graves look like someone crawled out . . . then, yes, actually," Weinstock said, surprising him. "Every morning I check Castle's grave in Crestville, every afternoon I swing by Rosewood Memorial here in town to look at Cowan's. The graves look undisturbed, but we're talking recent burials—bare earth, nothing growing there yet—so they could have been dug up and re-buried, and as long as the job was done neatly, then who would know?"

"Damn."

"Which means that we're going to have to check."

"Check how? Dig them up?"

Weinstock gave him a silent, steady look.

"Oh, crap," Crow said.

Chapter 10

Weinstock went to do some paperwork and Crow spent some time with Val, who was awake again. They talked about Sarah's request and then Val drifted off again, so Crow went back to the solarium to make some calls. His first was to his store and Mike answered on the fourth ring, "Crow's Nest. We have everything you need for a happy Halloween."

"You sound chipper, young Jedi."

"Crow? Hey! Your friend Dave Kramer just stopped in to get some stuff for the Hayride and he told me what happened last night! I can't believe it. How's Val?"

"She'll be okay." Crow gave Mike an abbreviated version of what had happened, sparing him the more lurid details and all of the backstory. Mike kept telling him how sorry he was and to give his best to Val.

"I'll tell her, kiddo . . . but listen, there's no way I'm coming in today, and probably not tomorrow, either. You good there? I know it's a lot to ask . . ."

There was a brief pause before Mike answered. "Sure, Crow . . . I got the routine down now. I can handle things."

"Terrific. You know I'll take care of you come payday."

"Man . . . don't even go there. I'm having fun here."

"So, you're telling me retail sales is your heart's desire?"

"Duh, no . . . it's just that I like doing this. I like being here. I feel . . . I don't know . . . *safe* here." Mike immediately added, "I know that sounds stupid and all—"

"No, it doesn't, kiddo." The moment turned awkward and to cover it Crow said, "Take some cash from the drawer and have food delivered. Whatever you want. There's a whole bunch of menus in the third file drawer. You need a break, just lock the place up."

"I got it. Thanks, Crow. Look, there's a couple customers coming in. I gotta go." Mike hung up.

Crow frowned at the phone for a moment, then saw Sarah Wolfe coming toward him. "How's Val?"

"Sleeping."

"Sounds like what we should all be doing. I'm heading home now to see the kids, get showered, and find some fresh clothes. I feel like I've been wearing these for a month."

"I should probably do the same," he agreed. "I must stink like a skunk."

"A little bit worse than a skunk," she said, trying for a joke. The effort was an encouraging sign and he gave her a smile. Sarah touched his arm. "Have you given any thought to what I asked you?"

"Yeah. About running the Festival? Sure. I talked it over with Val, and she thinks I should do it, but I still don't know if it's a good idea, Sarah. With all that's happening, I'm not so sure bringing in more tourists is a good thing."

"We *have* to, or the town will—"

"I know, I know." He felt frustrated and hamstrung by having his fears on one hand and the realities of the town's needs on the other. Sarah stood there, looking into his eyes, her need as strident as if she were shouting it. He sighed. "Oh, hell, sure. Why not?"

Sarah gave him a short, fierce hug. "Thank you, Crow . . . I know it doesn't feel like it matters, not with Val and Mark and all. With what's happening with Terry I feel the same way. But it's what the town needs. It'll help all of our friends. You're doing the right thing."

So why does it feel like I just made the worst mistake of my life? he asked himself, but to her he just smiled and nodded.

Sarah gave him another quick peck on the cheek and left. He got up and bought a Yoo-hoo from the machine, shook it, cracked it open, and drank half of it down as he sank back onto the couch, punching in another number on his phone.

"Hey, Newt? It's me."

"Crow . . . what's . . . um, happening? Is there anything new?" The reporter sounded wary, and Crow couldn't blame him.

"What condition are you in?"

"I'm a train wreck. What the hell do you think?"

"Well, maybe this will help." He brought Newton up to speed on everything, emphasizing their belief that the whole thing was pretty much over except for Boyd's missing body.

"Doesn't feel over," Newton said.

"That's 'cause we stepped in it in the last inning."

"Still doesn't feel over."

Crow said, "Whether it is or isn't, we need to know more than we do right now. I hate like hell fumbling around in the dark. Which brings me to my next question. Are you in any condition to help me out with what's going on?"

"If that means tramping around through graveyards with a Gladstone bag filled with stakes and holy water, then . . . no, I'm not. On the other hand, if you want me to help with research and that sort of thing, then I'm way ahead of you. Since I left the hospital I've been doing nothing but surfing the Net and sending e-mails. I've tracked down about twenty people, just in this end of the country, who are considered top experts on . . . *these* subjects."

"Anything we can use?"

"The one person who seems to be the absolute golden boy of this particular kind of folklore is a guy from U of P, Professor Jonathan Corbiel. Do you remember me telling you yesterday about a website I was at that mentioned you-know-who down in Dark Hollow?"

"Sure. Something about a werewolf trial a couple hundred years ago."

"We agreed it was either an ancestor of our boy, or he took the name symbolically. In any case, Corbiel is a real expert on that case. The Peeter Stubbe case." He spelled the name. "The more of the case I read the stranger it gets. I've forwarded a lot of it to your Yahoo account."

"Can we talk to this Corbiel guy?"

"I already sent him an e-mail. Carefully worded. I'm pretending that I'm writing a pop-culture book on the haunted history of Pine Deep and want a folklore expert I can footnote. Haven't heard back yet, but maybe we can get him to meet us for dinner somewhere." He paused. "Somewhere that's not Pine Deep."

"Works for me," Crow said, "but before you go, there's more stuff happening around here." He told him about the morgue and the missing bodies.

Newton's voice was a whisper. "Are you sure that Boyd didn't just get up and walk off?"

"I'm pretty sure."

"Pretty sure?" Newton said. "Oh, man . . ."

He hung up.

Crow made a few more calls, then walked back to Val's room. She was only dozing and woke as soon as he entered. She turned toward him and offered him a tight smile.

"Get any sleep?" he asked, parking a haunch on the side of the bed.

"In and out."

"I'm heading home for a bit. I got to get cleaned up, but I'll be back here in an hour or two. Will you be okay?"

"I'll be fine. Just . . . be careful," she said, glancing at the window. "It's dark out."

"I will. Be back soon." He kissed her, and left.

He met Weinstock by the elevator; he was heading home, too. Crow told him about his call to Newton.

"That sounds promising," Weinstock said.

"It may be past time for getting proactive, but it's better to be safe than sorry."

"No kidding." The elevator was nearly to the bottom floor when Weinstock opened his coat and turned his hip so Crow could see the handle of a big pistol snugged into a belt clip. Crow cocked an eyebrow, then the elevator chimed and Weinstock dropped the coat flap.

As they crossed the nearly empty lobby, Crow asked, "You any good with it?"

"I fired a couple of rounds off when I bought it."

"Swell." They exited the lobby and stepped out into the parking lot. There were still dozens of cars parked in neat rows, their colors muted by the darkness except where sodium vapor lamps spilled down swatches of light.

"But I have a little edge, just in case." Saul said, leaning close. "I had some silver bullets made. No, don't give me that look—I know silver is for werewolves, but I figure I've got both bases covered. No matter what jumps out at me I'll park one of these hollowpoints in his brainpan. Werewolf, vampire—I'm pretty sure that's going to settle his hash."

Crow smiled." 'Settle his hash'? And you say I watch too much TV?" He tilted his head and cocked an eye at Weinstock. "I can't say much for your choice of handgun, though."

"Why not? It's a damn .44!"

"It's a Ruger Blackhawk. A *Ruger*, Saul, really?"

"Jeez . . . I didn't even think . . ."

A voice said, "You fellows okay there?"

They turned to the first row of cars to see a pair of local cops leaning against the side of a parked ambulance. Shirley O'Keefe and Dave Golub. Good kids, new to Pine Deep PD. The pair of them stood just outside the spill of light from the entrance. Golub, a big man, had his arms folded and his hat pulled low. O'Keefe wore no hat but her face was shadowed by her frizzy mane of red hair. The stark lighting made both of them look dark-eyed and pale.

"Hey Dave," Crow said with a smile, "Shirley."

Shirley said nothing, but she gave Crow a slow nod. She wore a quirky little knowing smile that seemed out of place on her freckled face. It made her look impish rater than elfin.

"How's Val?" Golub asked.

"Well as can be expected."

"Shame about Mark and his wife, though," Golub said.

"Dave," Weinstock asked, "any news on finding Boyd's body yet?"

"No . . . but I'm sure it'll turn up."

"Ask Gus to call me first thing if it does."

Golub gave him a smile and a nod. "Will do, Doc."

(2)

Vic was out for hours, sprawled in a tangle of arms and legs, reeking of shit, a pool of brown urine going cold and stale under him. His nose and ears were no longer bleeding, but the dried blood caked his nostrils and streaked the side of his face. Every once in a while one of his fingers would twitch. That it was his trigger finger was not coincidental and spoke of the dreams that burned in his mind as he slept off the effects of Griswold's rage.

Ruger was only out for a few minutes. He was wired differently now, his nerves and synapses firing on different fuel. When he came awake it was like the flick of a switch, with full awareness returning in a crystalline rush of clarity. He knew who he was, where he was, and why he had been smashed flat. He felt the pain was his due, and he wore the invisible stripes of the Man's lash humbly, honored to be noticed enough even to have been struck down.

Ruger was on his back when he became aware and he lay there for a moment drinking in the room. He smelled Vic and that made him smile. He was allowed to smile at the pain of others, even at Vic's pain. The house above was almost silent, but he could hear the clink of ice in a glass and smell the faint juniper tang of Lois's gin. Even through the smell of Vic's shit and piss, he could smell that, just as he could smell the woman who sat alone, drinking the day away. He put those thoughts away for later.

Ruger sat up, crossing his legs and folding them under him so that sitting moved into kneeling. He placed his palms on the floor and closed his dark eyes as he bowed his head to the cool concrete. In the posture of the supplicant he had never been in life, Karl Ruger bowed before the raw, boundless power that was the Man.

"Forgive," he begged in a whisper.

He remained in that posture for hours. All the while the only thing that burned as intensely within him as his need for forgiveness was his aching, burning desire to feed. Night had fallen heavily over Pine Deep. Ruger could *feel* it, a silky wet darkness that was alive with predator and prey. His body was on fire to run into the shadows, to melt with them, seeking the human heat in the dark cold of October, but he would not move, would not even budge. Even when he heard Vic get up, cursing and groggy, weeping with pain and humiliation as he staggered to the cellar steps and climbed unsteadily up to get cleaned up— even then Ruger remained bowed in supplication as the nothingness screamed in his head.

Then, like the faintest breath of a cool breeze on scorched skin it came. Not a word, not even a whisper, nothing articulate or shaped. Just the softest, sweetest, most subtle of touches, mind to mind. Kind to kind. After the lash, a caress of forgiveness. And of consent.

Ruger's fetid blood screamed for black joy.

Chapter 11

Weinstock dropped Crow off outside his store and headed home, anxious to be out of the night and behind his own locked doors. Crow watched him go, and in the time it took Weinstock to drive two blocks and make a left the enormity of everything that had happened in the last day and a half suddenly caught up and hit him like a freight train. He staggered backward and leaned against a parking meter as a wave of nausea swirled sickeningly around his head. Gagging, he twisted around to throw up into the gutter but could only manage dry heaves. The corners of his eyes tingled as if little spiders were crawling on his cheekbones and he had to grip the meter to keep from falling into the street.

Three shoppers gave him disgusted looks as they passed, and Crow distinctly heard the word "drunk" from one of them. It made him furious, but that only intensified the nausea. He held on to the meter for dear life.

Mike looked up as the bell above the door jangled and he saw Crow come in looking dirty and defeated.

"Crow!" He hurried over, and actually had to support Crow across the floor to the tall chair behind the counter. "What's wrong?"

Crow sat on the chair, arms on thighs, head low, breathing like he'd just finished a marathon. "Sorry, kiddo," he gasped when he could manage it. "Feeling a little out of it. No sleep, no food, bad hospital coffee."

"Stay here," Mike ordered, then went over and locked the front door, came back, and helped Crow into the adjoining apartment and down onto the couch. Crow's three cats, Pinetop, Muddy Whiskers, and Koko, rushed over but then slowed to a stop when they smelled Crow's clothes. One by one they sniffed, turned up their noses, and stalked off. Crow, steadier now that he was sitting down, looked at them and then at Mike. "When you stink so bad you offend animals that lick their balls for fun and sniff each other's asses, then you really are in sorry shape."

"Well," Mike said, "fair's fair. You smell pretty bad."

"Thanks, kid, I knew you'd have my back." Crow picked up the CD remote and aimed it at the big Nakamichi Home Audio system. He had five disks in the trays, a mix of classic rock and blues. Leadbelly started it off by singing "Bourgeois Blues," and the disks that followed went from The Ides of March's "Vehicle" to Pink Floyd's "Wish You Were Here" to Albert King's "Born under a Bad Sign," all of it wrapped up by Big Bill Broonzy singing about "Trouble in Mind." It was the music he'd listened to before setting out to Dark Hollow with Newton, and he almost turned it off, but didn't. The music wasn't any kind of threat. The music was a safe place and even the first few notes of Leadbelly's rough voice were immensely soothing.

Mike brought him a bottle of Gatorade and a PowerBar. "Here, these might help until I can get some food delivered."

"Thanks, Mike." He looked at the bottle. "My favorite flavor. Green."

Mike sat on the arm of the guest chair. "Do you want to talk about, um, anything? I mean, I heard some stuff on the news, and a lot of customers came in asking about you, and you told me some stuff, but—"

"Can it wait until I have a shower?"

"Sure," Mike said. "You don't . . . uh . . . need help in the bathroom or anything, do you?"

"No, and let us both give thanks for that."

"Amen," Mike said, and went back into the store.

(2)

Vic finished his shower and dressed in fresh clothes, going slowly through the steps of washing, drying, and dressing. His body hurt as if he'd been stomped by ten skinheads wearing Doc Martens. When he pissed his urine stream was tinted red, and when he brushed his teeth he spit as much blood as toothpaste into the sink. He blew his nose carefully to clear away the clots of blood, and used a rag and then Q-tips to clean his ears. His old clothes—stained with shit, piss, and blood—he dumped in a black plastic trash bag he got from the hall closet. He wouldn't even bother making Lois clean them up. He'd just throw them the hell out. Shoes, too. He wanted to traces, no reminders. Never, not once in his whole life, not since he'd first met Ubel Griswold in 1970, had Vic been punished. The memory of it—what he could remember after the blackout—was so humiliating, so traumatic that all he felt inside was a vast empty sadness.

He finished buttoning his shirt and then sat down on the edge of the bed, putting his face in his hands, feeling lower than he ever had.

"What do I have to do to make it up to you?" he whispered. "You tell me, Boss, and I'll tear down Heaven for you. I'll burn this whole town to ashes. Anything. You just tell me what I have to do to make it right."

The voice—that sweet, dark voice—was there in an instant. The presence of it after so much terrible silence was almost as jarring as that scream of rage had been and Vic toppled forward onto hands and knees, then collapsed onto his forearms so that his brow was pressed into the carpet.

"Tell me!" he begged.

With a whisper as soft as bat wings on an autumn night, Ubel Griswold named the price for redemption. It hit Vic hard—harder than he thought it would. Nevertheless he closed his eyes and kissed the floor. He would do anything—even that—for his god.

(3)

Ruger touched the handle, feeling the roiling darkness beyond the door. Vic be damned, he was going out to hunt. To kill and to recruit; to build the armies of the Red Wave. He turned the knob, forcing it against the tumblers that twisted and screamed beneath his hand. Metal pinged and snapped and the door sagged open in defeat.

With a snarl of delight he pushed the door open and vanished into the night.

(4)

Terry Wolfe's face was bruised meat, his body debris. He was ruined, smashed, nearly gone. The vitals on the machines sagged, and the brain activity was just above the level where families begin to discuss pulling the plug.

Yet there are some levels of the brain, some chambers of the sleep center that have thicker doors, stouter walls, fewer entries. The deepest dreams live there, playing out in shadowed corridors and in cellars where no light has ever shone. There are cobwebs and spiders down there; there are blind rats in those catacombs, and colorless things that wriggle in the relentless dark. No machine can record those dreams, no meter will ping or beep when something scampers through those places.

When the doctors and nurses came into his room to look at the patterns on his charts their faces fell into sadness, their eyes showed the defeat each of them felt. Everyone loved Terry, everyone respected him. He *was* Pine Deep, but it was pretty clear that Terry Wolfe had left them, had caught the night train out of town, and now all they could do—the sum effect of their years of training, their collective experience, the weight of their science—was to watch and wait for him to die. Because Terry had left.

Yet, he hadn't. Nor had the beast.

Over and over again, through lightless passageways and darkened dungeon rooms, into one blind alley after another, in the doorless maze of his own inner oubliette, Terry Wolfe ran screaming and the beast, always hungry, followed after.

Chapter 12

Weinstock glanced at Crow and then turned a hard look on the caretaker. "There's some risk of contagion here. Please, stand back."

"Contagion?" the man said, eyes flaring wide as he did indeed step back. "From what? I thought this fella was murdered."

Weinstock's eyes were hard as flint, but even so they had a shifty flicker to them. Crow wore Wayfarers against the glare of the Sunday morning sun and he kept his face blank. Weinstock wore a heavy topcoat; Crow was in a bomber jacket and jeans. He held the clipboard with the exhumation papers on them, signed by Weinstock himself right over the signature of Nels Cowan's wife. Her hand had trembled when she'd signed it and it made her handwriting look like that of a five-year-old. There were two small circles on the page where her tears had fallen and puckered the paper.

Weinstock licked his lips. "Not all of the blood work on Officer Cowan was completed at the time of interment. Our tests detected traces of a highly dangerous virus."

"Virus?" The caretaker's name was Holliston and his seamed face was a study in skepticism. He rested his shoulder against the bucket of the front-end loader and folded his arms. "Nels Cowan didn't die of no virus, he was killed by that Boyd fellow."

"I didn't say he did, Mr. Holliston," Weinstock said frostily. "I said traces of a virus were detected in his blood. Tests have suggested that the alleged killer may have been infected, and that during the struggle he was wounded. There may have been an inadvertent exchange of blood during the struggle. It is vitally important to establish if this is the case. Among other things, I am the liaison between the town of Pine Deep and the local office of the CDC."

"What's that?"

"The Centers for Disease Control. So, it's important that I conduct this test under the proper conditions." He pulled a surgical mask out of his bag and slipped it on, and then began squirming his hands into latex gloves. Holliston yielded and walked a few dozen yards away.

Crow waited until Holliston was far enough away and then said, "We are so going to go to jail for this shit."

"Joanie Cowan signed the paper and I'm the county coroner. It's all more or less legal."

"More or less is not a comfortable phrase."

"It's what we have."

"Any of that CDC stuff on the level?"

Weinstock shrugged. "More or less."

"Swell."

They looked around. For a Sunday morning the cemetery was remarkably empty; church probably hadn't let out yet.

"You ready?" Weinstock asked, and Crow slipped his hand inside his jacket and pulled his Beretta nine half out of the shoulder rig. "If there's anything in that coffin except a dead guy I'm going to empty this thing in it."

"Just don't shoot me."

"Don't get in the line of fire."

"Fair enough."

On the drive home from the hospital they'd cooked up the plan, going on the basis that if something was still happening in Pine Deep they needed to know sooner rather than later, so by the next morning they were ready. Weinstock printed out the exhumation papers and cooked up the infection story—he'd deal with chain of evidence later—and then called Joanie Cowan at seven-thirty on that Sunday morning, waking her out of a deep sleep in order to break her heart all over again. Overwhelmed by

Weinstock's medical double-talk, she had disintegrated into tears and signed the papers, and the two of them slunk away like thieves.

"This is so wrong," Crow said as they approached the coffin, which sat on the bucket of a big front-end loader. He brushed away clods of cold dirt and started twisting the wingnuts that held the lid on. His hands shook so bad his fingers slipped on the cold metal.

Weinstock stopped him and handed him a mask. "He's been dead for two weeks . . . this is going to be bad. You don't want to breathe it. Remember . . . smell is particulate."

"Oh man. I really could have gotten through the day without knowing that."

"Welcome to the field of medicine."

"This isn't medicine, brother," Crow said, adjusting the rubber band that secured the mask. "This is black magic."

They worked together to make a fast job of it. Even without opening the lid it smelled bad. Like rotting meat and raw sewage poured over molasses. Crow gagged.

Weinstock glanced around. The caretaker was ten rows down busy with the task of cutting the turf to dig a fresh grave. The doctor looked across the casket to Crow. "You ready?"

"Not really. You?"

Weinstock tried to laugh and bungled it.

Crow said, "We're burning daylight, Saul. Let's do this or go home."

"Shit." Weinstock steeled himself and gripped one corner of the lid as Crow told hold of the other. "God help us if we're wrong about this."

But Crow shook his head. "God help us if we're right."

The lid resisted for a moment, but then it yielded to their combined strength and opened; they pulled it up and daylight splashed down on the silk-lined interior.

They stood there looking into the coffin for over a minute, saying nothing, lost in their own thoughts, each of their faces set into heavy frowns.

"Well," Crow said. "Now we know."

"Yeah," Weinstock said hoarsely.

"What does it mean?"

The doctor shook his head. "As God is my witness, Crow, I honestly don't know."

Nels Cowan had been buried in his Pine Deep police uniform. His hands, bloated with decomposition, lay folded on his stomach with the brim of his uniform hat set between the thick, white fingers. The flesh of Cowan's face was purplish, distended with gas.

"There's no chance this is not him" Crow ventured.

"It's him." Even so he took a sample of skin tissue just in case they needed a DNA match.

Crow lowered the lid.

"So—what's happening, Doc?" called the caretaker. He was wiping his hands with a rag as he strolled across the graves toward them. "Did he have something catching?"

Weinstock began tightening the wingnuts. "Apparently not," he said.

"Well, hell," Holliston said with a grin. "Guess we can all be happy about that. With all that's happening 'round here we don't need no new troubles, now do we?"

Weinstock wore a poker face as he tightened one nut and started on the next. "No, we don't," he said.

Across from him, Crow worked in silence.

When they were back in Weinstock's car they sat for a while, sipping Starbucks coffee and staring out at the morning. The trees seemed unusually thick with crows and the birds sent up a continuous cackle. John Lee Hooker was singing "Boogie Chillen"—from the only blues CD Weinstock owned, a gift from Crow that only came out of the glove box when Crow was riding shotgun.

"I don't know how to think about this, Crow. I mean . . . I know what I saw on those morgue tapes. I know I saw Castle and Cowan walking around after they were dead. I'm not hallucinating."

"I believe you, Saul. You showed me the tapes. I know what you saw."

"But that was definitely Cowan in that coffin, and he is in a state of decomposition consistent with having been dead for a couple of weeks."

"Which means that he's dead."

"So what did I see on those tapes?"

"I don't know . . . I believe you, of course, but I don't know what it means. Maybe Ruger or Boyd tried to convert them into vampires and it worked for a while but somehow, and for some reason, they died again. Died for real."

"Maybe. We don't know enough about this stuff to understand if that's even possible."

"I know one thing, though," Crow said and he pulled his sunglasses out of his shirt pocket and put them on.

"What's that?"

"Before I move one inch toward believing that this whole thing is over I want to see Jimmy Castle's body."

Weinstock started the car. "Me, too, and I want to get that done while we still have daylight. I'm not going anywhere near his body at night."

(2)

Mike worked at the store all day Sunday, gradually phasing in and out of lucidity. There was a steady stream of customers and Mike was able to wear a smiling face, answer their questions, fill their orders, and ring up their sales; but below the surface his mind was blank more than it was filled by thought. He knew it, too, but on some other level. It was like standing on a balcony and looking down on his life, and the feeling totally creeped him out.

"I'm really going crazy," he said to the cash register at one point.

The customer he was ringing up—Brandon Strauss, a kid from Mike's own class—said, "Mike . . . hello? Earth calling Mike."

Mike blinked at Brandon. "Huh?" He realized that instead of

bagging the Robert Jordan novel his friend had bought he was trying to stuff it into the drawer of the cash register.

"You bent the cover, man," Brandon said.

"Um . . . sorry."

"I'll get another off the rack." Brandon swapped the battered copy for a new one and peered at Mike while he finished ringing it up and bagging it. He held it out and Brandon plucked it from his fingers as if afraid Mike would mangle this one, too.

"Sorry," Mike said.

Brandon paused, his scowl softening. "You okay, Mike? You sick or something?"

Mike pasted on a smile. "Sorry, I just started a new allergy medicine. Makes me kinda goofy for a bit."

"You're always goofy," Brandon said, but he smiled back and shot Mike with his finger. "See you in school. Ms. Rainer's subbing for Donaldson again. Woo-hoo!" Natalie Rainer was the favorite substitute teacher for all the boys in the county. She looked like Kate Beckinsale and always wore tight clothes. It didn't matter that she taught math, no one's favorite subject; she could have taught advanced calculus and not one of their friends would have missed her class.

Mike promised he'd be there and smiled as Brandon left. As soon as the door jingled shut, Mike leaned back against the wall and closed his eyes. It was getting harder and harder to stay focused, to stay present.

"I really am going crazy," he said aloud, and this time there was no one to comment on it, or to refute it.

(3)

"Father! Why have you forsaken me?"

The silent emptiness in Tow-Truck Eddie's heart was enormous, vast. Tears streamed down his face as he drove down A-32 in his police cruiser. Yesterday he had gone into Crow's store to confront—he thought—the Beast, but instead all he saw was a boy. Just an ordinary boy. Not the Beast, not evil incarnate, not the Antichrist. It didn't make sense to him.

"I am still your Sword, Father. I am still the avenging lamb!" He cried out these words, but they lacked conviction, even to his own ears. "Please, Father, show me the way."

The boy in the store—Eddie had not even been able to see him very clearly. The light must have been bad, or something. How different from the Beast: Eddie had always been able to see the Beast with total, holy clarity. When hunting for him on the road, or searching for him in the town, Eddie had never faltered in the purity or certainty of his sacred purpose. His Father had told him that this boy, the child in the store, was the Beast, but when Eddie looked at him he could not see the evil there.

Doubt was a thorn in his brain, a spike in his heart.

(4)

Weinstock got the call while he and Crow were heading back to the hospital. He listened for a minute, said, "Thanks, we'll be right there!" and hung up.

"They found Boyd's body. Turn around, it's down by the Black Marsh Bridge."

"Damn," Crow said and spun the wheel.

(5)

She stood in the shadows near the foot of Terry's bed for days. No one saw her. No one noticed her, even though her little dress was torn and her face and throat were streaked with blood. They walked right by her, and sometimes they walked right through her. When that happened, whoever did it—nurse, orderly, visitor, or doctor—would give a small involuntary shiver as if they had just caught an icy breath of wind on the vulnerable back of their neck. The feeling would be gone in less than a heartbeat and they would forget about it because there was nothing, and no one, in the room to take note of.

Since they had brought Terry in here in the evening of October thirteenth and hooked him up to all of the machines, Mandy

Wolfe had been there, keeping her silent vigil. Sometimes she wept, and then the tears would flow and mingle with the blood, diluting it, turning it pink on her cheeks. Most of the time she just stood and watched her brother, aching with guilt and grief. Now that he had tried to do what she wanted, now that he had thrown himself out of his window but failed to kill himself, Mandy didn't know what to do next. No one else could see her, no one else could hear her.

The fear that reared up in her was immense.

"Terry," she said in a voice quieter than the soft rustle of dried leaves on the autumn trees outside his window. "Terry . . . I'm so sorry."

Terry could not hear her. No one could. Except *him*. And as Mandy wept for her failure, Ubel Griswold listened, and laughed.

(6)

With the Sunday tourist traffic it was twenty minutes down to the Black Marsh Bridge and they could see the knot of police and crime scene vehicles as they crested one of the last hill. "Looks like a party," Crow said.

Tow-Truck Eddie Oswald was directing traffic, his uniform uncharacteristically rumpled and his face haggard. Eddie was usually neat as a pin. Once he recognized them, he waved them through and told them where to park. As they got out they could see Chief Gus Bernhardt standing at the crest of the embankment that led down to the river and beyond him the near leg of the old iron Black Marsh Bridge. Smoke curled sluggishly up between Gus and the bridge. Crow shot a look at Weinstock, who shrugged, and they crunched over gravel to the grassy hill to join Gus, who was in animated conversation with a couple of firefighters.

"Hey, fellas," Gus said as Crow and Weinstock joined him. "I hope you brought some weenies for roasting." His pink face was alight with pleasure as he turned and swept an arm down the hill like an emcee introducing a headline act. "Voilà!"

"Holy jumping frog shit," Crow said.

Gus clamped Crow on the shoulder. "I think we can pretty much close the file on Kenneth Boyd."

At the base of the bridge support, tied to the concrete block that anchored the big steel leg, a body stood wreathed in wisps of smoke, the arms and legs twisted into dry sticks, the skin black and papery, the head nothing more than a leering skull covered in hot ash. A crudely lettered and soot-stained sign had been affixed to the support by bungee cords. It read: DON'T FUCK WITH PINE DEEP!

Weinstock whistled softly between his teeth. "Ho-lee shit."

Gus beamed. "I guess the local boys got sick and tired of that Philly piece of shit kicking up dust out here. Pine Deep," he said with pride that threatened to pop the buttons on his straining shirtfront, "you can hurt us, but you can't beat us."

"Oh, for Christ's sake," Crow muttered and pushed past him. Weinstock shot the chief a look as he followed.

"What?" Gus asked, totally perplexed.

"You sure that's Boyd?" Crow asked.

"I sure as hell hope so," Gus said.

A state police criminalist, Judy Sanchez, was working the scene and turned when she sensed Weinstock and Crow approaching. She knew Weinstock from when Boyd had broken into the morgue to steal Ruger's body; she knew Crow from AA, though they just acknowledged each other with a slight nod.

"What can you tell me?" Weinstock asked, nodding at the corpse. "Any ID?"

She gave a short laugh. "Beyond the fact that he's probably male and probably human, no. Those college boys torched him good."

"They want to know if that's Boyd down there," Gus said, still having a blast with this.

"You figure college kids for it, Judy?" Crow said.

"Looks like it. We got joints, beer cans, lots of sneaker prints. Little Halloween doesn't let go around here very fast, does it?"

Little Halloween was Pine Deep's unique holiday, celebrated only when Friday the 13th occurred in October; it was like

Mischief Night on steroids. Each one was legendary, and when it showed up the kids at the college went out of their way to outdo the pranks of previous classes. The current tally included three bonfires—two of them built around cars belonging to hated teachers—a game of nude touch football between a sorority and a frat that was likely going to end in expulsions and, very probably, a lawsuit; a rock concert played so loud that fish in the Floyd Pond died; a spate of bricks thrown through store windows; a school bus being completely disassembled, with all of the parts placed neatly on the high school soccer field; the vandalizing of the Pinelands Hospital Morgue; and the subsequent burning—in fact rather than effigy—of Kenneth Boyd.

"It's a fun-loving town," Crow said sourly.

"Pine Deep," Weinstock said sotto voce, "a great place to visit. Bring the whole family."

They stood there looking at the corpse, thankful that the breeze carried the cooked-meat stink out toward the river. Sanchez said, "So . . . yeah, it's probably Boyd. Even with all the charring you can tell that the head has received several gunshot wounds." She looked at Crow. "Your fiancée's doing well, I hear."

"Yep."

"Tough chick."

"She is that," Crow agreed.

Weinstock blew his nose noisily, "We're going to need dental records or DNA on it." He cut a look at Crow, but Crow was wearing his best poker face.

Back in the car they drove in silence for several miles before Weinstock said, "So, are we buying that this is a fraternity stunt?"

"I don't know. Does it seem like something a vampire would do?"

Weinstock looked at him. "Not really. Somehow I don't equate the living dead with juvenile prankishness. Even cruel-hearted and extreme juvenile prankishness."

"In the movies, do vampires come back from the dead if they've been incinerated?"

"Not usually. Fire's always one of those fallback plans. Like beheading."

"So, Boyd's toast in real point of fact."

Crow grinned. "I guess."

He took a tin of Altoids out of his pocket and put three of them in his mouth, then offered the tin to Crow, who shook it off. Crow put a Leonard Cohen CD into the player and they listened to that while the cornfields—lush or blighted—whisked by on either side.

They were back at the hospital by sunset and the two of them sat in chairs on either side of Val's bed. A night's sleep had transformed her from an emotional wreck back into a semblance of her stolid self, and her strength helped steady Crow and Weinstock.

They told her everything and then watched her process it. Val had a tough, analytical brain and Crow knew that engaging her in a complex problem was one of the best ways to keep her from getting too far into grief for Mark and Connie. There would be plenty of time for that later.

Val said, "Let's go over it. Every bit of it, step by step."

They did, and each of them played devil's advocate for any thought, observation, or experience the others brought up. They picked it apart, dissecting it, chewed the bones of it as the sun burned itself to a cinder and left the sky a charred black. Dinner came and went, friends stopped by to visit or deliver flowers and fruit baskets. The phone kept ringing—friends, relatives, the press. Val and Crow both turned the ringers off on their cells. Every time a nurse left or guests made their farewells, the three of them went right back into it, picking up where they left off.

Night painted the window black and the three of them eventually ran out of things to say. Val probed the bandages around her eye as she thought it through. "The question we keep asking is . . . is this thing over?"

Weinstock looked at Crow, who shrugged.

"Boyd and Ruger are dead, Castle and Nels Cowan are dead and buried. Mark is not . . . one of *them*. You're sure of that?"

"As sure as I can be. And though my gut tells me that this is all over, I think that we should keep Mark and Connie here in, um . . . storage . . . until we find some way of medically determining if they are infected or not."Val shot him a hard look, but Weinstock held up his hand. "Let me finish. I can stall Gus on this—he's stupid enough to buy any dumb excuse I make up. Maybe I'll tell him that there was a chance that Boyd was carrying a disease and I need to do more tests to make sure that it's nothing that will affect the town."

"That's ridiculous,"Val said. "Nobody'd believe that."

"Gus?"Weinstock said, arching his eyebrows.

"Okay, okay," she conceded.

"In the meantime," Crow said, "I think we should make sure the bodies are secure. Locks on their freezer doors and maybe restraints of some kind. Newton's working on the research. We should know in a few days . . . a couple weeks tops."

Val closed her eye for a moment, took a breath, then nodded. "Okay. That makes sense."

Crow patted her thigh. "I think whatever this madness was, we kind of came at it from an angle, and by the time we knew what it was, it was over. There's nothing that indicates that this went further than Boyd. As far as the morgue break-in . . . if college kids did this as a Little Halloween stunt or some macho Pine Deep rah-rah bullshit, then we're done. Fat Lady's finished her aria and gone home and we can all take a nice deep breath and try to forget this all ever happened."

"That'd be nice,"Val said. "On the other hand, if it wasn't frat boys, then we have to consider that burning the body is the one way to destroy any trace of physical evidence that Boyd was anything more than a psychotic killer."

"There's that,"Weinstock agreed.

"Problem is . . . we might not ever know the truth."

"Uh-huh."

"So what do we do?" she asked.

"I don't know,Val. I mean . . . I still have the videotapes and lab reports, but now I have nothing to back them up, and I don't know how much mileage I can get out of that stuff. Even if I could make a case for each individual bit of evidence being faulty, or tainted. I'm not willing to risk my whole career on it at the moment, not if there's a chance this thing is actually over."

Crow nodded and glanced at Val. "So what do you think we should do?"

Val didn't answer right away, but her eye was flinty. "I guess," she said at last, "what I'm going to do is hope for the best."

"Okay."

"And from now on, and maybe for the rest of my life . . . I'm going to keep all my guns loaded."

Weinstock and Crow looked at her.

"This is still Pine Deep, boys," she said. "Far as I'm concerned, it'll never be over. Crow, I think you should see what you can do to beef up security for the Festival, and as often as we can we should brainstorm with Newton. Even if this is over we should all learn everything we can about vampires. From now on we need to be prepared. If—and I only say if because I hope like hell it *is* over—if we run into another one of these bloodsucking bastards again, then I want the story to have a happier ending. I'm tired of being in the dark, and I'm tired of being blindsided." When they said nothing to that, she added, "I'm going to have a baby. I want that baby born into a safer world."

Weinstock smiled at her. "I hear garlic's good for your health."

Crow gave him half a smile. "I heard that, too."

After a moment Val managed a smile. "Then I guess I'd better learn to cook Italian."

INTERLUDE

The first thing Paul Ruffin did after he threw his suitcase on the motel bed was call the pizza joint the manager had suggested, then he switched on the big screen, popped the top on a Coors, and scooched over to the center of the big bed. His sigh was enormous. After eight hours on the road nothing felt as good as a cold beer, a hot pizza, and nothing in particular to do. Tomorrow he would be busy with his camera, taking photos of the Haunted Hayride and all the spook-film celebrities for a major horror magazine. He was doing a whole spread on scream queen Brinke Stevens, and he was psyched. She'd factored in his fantasies for a lot of years.

The place had cable, so he surfed for a while, amazed as always at how many stations seemed to broadcast either reruns or mind-numbing shit that no one could possibly want to watch. He cruised along the airwaves, then slammed on the brakes as he discovered that yet another service provided by the Pinelands Motel was Showtime. On the screen Carmen Electra was running slow motion down a beach. It was quite something to see, though it had to be at least ten years old—not that it mattered even a teensy bit. He smiled as he sipped his beer. Now there was something he would like to have taken pictures of—her breasts were something out of science fiction.

Balancing his beer can on his stomach, he lay back and watched the image change from Carmen Electra and her breasts running on the beach to Carmen Electra and her breasts taking a bath. As

Ruffin saw it, she took one hell of a bath. Just as Carmen Electra and her breasts began playing billiards, someone knocked on the door. Ruffin muted the TV, set down the beer, and fished for his wallet as he opened the door. "Come on in. What are the damages?" He looked up from his wallet and his smile bled away.

The person standing just inside the doorway was not dressed in a pizza delivery uniform of any kind, and he held no steaming cardboard box. He was a tall, pale man with black hair that dipped down in a widow's peak and a face like a stage magician's. Paul Ruffin looked confused by what he saw, and the confusion tumbled quickly into unease and then fear. The person standing in the door was smiling. It was the wrong kind of smile for a relaxing kick-back kind of evening.

"Welcome to Pine Deep," whispered Ruger as he pushed his way into the room.

On the TV Carmen Electra and her breasts were riding a horse, smiling at the camera without a trace of concern, even when the bright splash of arterial blood stitched red splatters all across her nipples.

PART II
Born Under a Bad Sign

I don't mind them graveyards, and it ain't 'cause
I'm no kind of brave;
Said I don't mind no graveyard, but I ain't no man
that is brave.
'Cause the ghosts of the past, they are harder to face than any-
thing comes from a grave.

—A. L. Sirois and Kindred Spirit, "Ghost Road Blues"

You ain't hearing nothing, don't mean
nothing's going down,
You ain't hearing nothing, don't mean
nothing's going down
You ain't hearing nothing . . . don't mean the
Devil done left town.

—Oren Morse, "Silent Night Blues"

Chapter 13

Very early Tuesday morning Crow was seated in Val's guest chair sorting through e-mails on Terry's laptop, putting out fires for the Festival. Val was reading estate papers her lawyer had brought by, when there was a quick knock on her door and then a very tall woman breezed in. The woman was in her mid-sixties, with a straight back, a long face set with intelligent gray eyes, and lots of wavy red hair caught up in a sloppy bun. Her hair was threaded with silver, but her face and energy were youthful. She wore a lab coat with a nameplate that read: G. SOMERFIELD, MD—CHIEF OF OBSTETRIC MEDICINE.

"Hello, cupcake!" she said brightly, plucking Val's chart from the foot of her bed.

"I think she means you," Weinstock said, touching Val's shoulder.

"Well, Saul, I certainly don't refer to you as cupcake," Somerfield murmured as she scanned the chart. "Not to your face anyway." She peered over her granny glasses at Crow. "Let me guess . . . you're the father?"

"Malcolm Crow," he said, reaching over the laptop to offer his hand. Somerfield gave him a firm shake with a hand that was bigger than his.

"Gail Somerfield. Call me Gail."

"So?" Val asked, and the decisive edge that had been in her voice just moments before had softened. She looked scared and Crow took her hand and kissed it.

"Well, if I was our esteemed chief of medicine here"—and

she shot Weinstock a look—"I'd lead off with one of his famous 'I've got good news and bad news' openers, but since I'm not an overpaid bureaucrat who only *thinks* he's a doctor . . ."

"She really loves and respects me," Weinstock said. "Ask anyone."

"Ask someone whose paycheck you don't sign. Hush now, women are talking." She leaned a hip against the bottom of the bed frame, laid the chart against her chest, and folded her arms over that. "The bottom line is this, Val . . . your baby is fine."

Val closed her eye and let out a breath that had been cooking in her lungs since Somerfield walked in; Crow bent over and hugged her and whispered, "Thank God!" in her ear. Weinstock grinned at Somerfield, who gave him a quick wink.

"At some point," Somerfield said, "I'll bore you with all of the technical details of the tests we've run and the results we've gotten, but in my judgment the recent trauma you've suffered has not adversely affected the developing fetus. You're a strong woman, Val. Many women would not have come through this as well as you have, especially in light of the other issues. Of course I have to caution you to take it easy for the next few weeks. You have sustained other injuries and your body is dealing with those. You're not going to have much of a reserve of strength for a while. You need lots of rest and lots of TLC."

"She'll get both," Crow promised.

"See to it, or you'll answer to me, little fellow." Ignoring Crow's crestfallen expression, she added, "I would advise you, however, that you do whatever you can do to avoid physical or emotional stress as much as possible. And, yes, I do know what's going on and you certainly have my deepest sympathies, but at the risk of sounding harsh, your concerns are now with the living, with new life. By all means do what you have to do for your brother and sister-in-law, but then you need to focus only on getting healthy, staying healthy, and allowing your baby to develop with no further trauma. I can't stress enough how important this is." She paused. "Saul tells me that you and Mr. Crow here are recently engaged?"

"Just two weeks ago."

"Then make that part of your focus. Baby, marriage, health, home. All the stuff you see in *Ladies' Home Journal.*"

"I will," Val said, but Crow thought he heard doubt in her voice.

Taking a risk, Crow said, "Doc . . . were you being serious earlier about the good news bad news thing? If so . . . what's the bad news?"

In perfect deadpan, Somerfield said, "You're short . . . your kid might be a runt as well. A sad truth, but there it is."

"Ouch," Crow winced.

Val burst out laughing.

Somerfield gave Val a quick hug, winked at Crow, and smiled at Weinstock as she left.

When the door closed, Weinstock beamed at Val. "Did I tell you she was the best?"

"I love her," Val said.

"Everyone does," Weinstock agreed. "She's top of the line, too. She's from Long Island originally, but did a long stint overseas with Doctors Without Borders and then came here to teach. She's everything the rest of us quacks aspire to."

Val wasn't listening. "My baby is okay," she said softly, laying her palms flat on her stomach. "That's one thing those bastards didn't take from me. Thank God."

Crow kissed her on the forehead.

A few minutes later he said, " 'Little fellow'? I'm almost five-eight, damn it."

Val and Weinstock cracked up.

"It's not that funny," Crow protested, but he might as well have been talking to himself.

Chapter 14

Val was scheduled for more tests, so Crow headed out to run some errands. It was only four, but the day seemed in a hurry to end early. It depressed Crow. For about the zillionth day in a row it was mostly overcast and as the lights of Pine Deep came on they seemed distant and weak. The air was thick with humidity even though a frost was predicted; the wind felt raw and mean. Crow jammed his hands down into the pockets of his bomber jacket and hunched his shoulders to protect his ears as he walked to his car. Even the sounds of the tourist cars on Corn Hill and Main Street were muted, distorted as if more distant than they were. The tread of his sneakers made strange sucking sounds on the damp asphalt.

He unlocked his car, slid behind the wheel, and pulled the door shut, happy to be inside the familiar shell. Here were smells he knew—old vinyl, oil, the stale aroma of the pine tree deodorizer. Not pleasant smells, but familiar ones. He keyed the engine and as the car warmed up he pulled his cell phone out and punched in a number.

"Yo," said a voice after the third ring.

"BK? It's Crow."

"Hey hey, man. I've been seeing you all over the news. What the hell's happening out there in the sticks?" BK was Bentley Kingsman, an old martial arts buddy of Crow's. They had trained briefly under the same instructor back in the mid-1980s, and had crossed paths so often at tournaments that they'd become friends. Not that they'd ever faced each other on the mat—BK at six-four and built like a phone booth was roughly twice Crow's size—but students of theirs had traded some kicks over the years. BK worked as a cooler, or head bouncer, at one of Philadelphia's most popular strip bars.

"Yeah, things have been pretty crazy out here." He gave BK the necessarily edited version of all that had happened.

"Damn, brother . . . that's some rough shit. Give Val my best."

"Will do. Look, BK, the reason I'm calling is that I've been asked to oversee our big Halloween Festival. You know the one."

"Sure, the Hayride and all. It's been in the papers, too."

"Well, with everything that's happened I've gotten a bit spooked, so I want to beef up security for Halloween, just to make sure everything's cool."

"Spooked . . . or you know something's up?"

"Just spooked, but I could use some muscle for Mischief Night and Halloween. I've got twelve different venues to cover—the Hayride, three different movie marathons, a bunch of celebrity appearances, a parade, and a blues concert. Any chance you could help me out?"

"Volunteer or pay gig?"

"Definitely a pay gig, so I need top of the line."

"I know some guys. Depends on what you need."

Crow outlined his needs.

BK whistled. "That's a lot of feet on the ground. I can probably get Jim Winterbottom and some of his JKD guys; maybe Rick Robinson—he has that big jujutsu school over in White Marsh. Dave Pantano and some of his Kenpo boys. Maybe a few off-duty cops, too, if you don't mind paying them under the table. I assume you're looking for guys who can keep it cool, right?"

"I want you there, too."

"Jeez . . . Halloween's a big night at the club."

Crow said nothing, letting BK think about it.

"Yeah, okay, I'll get someone to cover for me. I'll be there, and I'll bring Billy, too." Billy Christmas was BK's best friend, a fellow bouncer who looked like a male model but fought like a junkyard dog. They made a colorful team.

"Thanks, BK . . . I owe you one."

"Hey, as long as the check clears you don't owe me shit, brother."

They sorted out a few details and then Crow hung up, feeling much more relieved. BK would put together a tight team for him, he knew that, and knowing it made the problem seem a lot less vast. He fished in the glove box and came out with Eddy "The Chief" Clearwater's *Reservation Blues* and slid it into the player, and as the first cut "Winds of Change" began with its moody guitars and brooding horns, Crow put the car in gear and headed out of town.

He didn't head home though, at least not yet. Instead he took the side road that led out of town and as soon as he cleared the jam of tourist cars he found himself out on the highway, rolling along the undulating black ribbon of A-32 out into the farmlands. A few fields were still thick with tall corn, the last of the season; but most had either been harvested down to brown stubble or razed and plowed under to try and halt the advance of the blight. Only a few of the roadside farm stands were open, the ones that could afford to import goods for resale. A few stayed open with their own products, but they were rare; among them, Guthrie Farm-goods, staffed by family members of farms that had been badly hit. More of Henry's goodwill.

Crow brooded on that as he drove. Henry and Terry, the town's two most successful men and the ones with the biggest hearts. One dead, the other dying as the Black Harvest ground along.

He passed Tow-Truck Eddie in his wrecker and tooted his horn, but Eddie either didn't see him or didn't recognize him and the big machine thundered past, heading toward town. Crow also passed Vic Wingate's midnight-blue pickup truck. Behind the glare of the headlights he could see two shadowy silhouettes in the cab, but he couldn't see their faces. Vic and some other asshole who apparently possessed the ability to tolerate Vic's company. Crow didn't toot or wave, but just drove on.

When he came to Val's farm he saw that the police guard was no longer stationed at the entrance. No one and nothing left to protect. Crow's mood soured even more as he made the left and crunched slowly up the gravel drive to the house. He switched off the lights and engine and sat there in the silence, watching the house. There were a few lights on, some cops probably not bothering to switch them off as they left. Those yellow rectangles of light usually looked so homey, but now they felt so remote, empty of all of their promise of warmth and acceptance. The whole house seemed drained, like a battery that's almost run down—not quite dead—but with only enough energy to be frustrating, or a cheat.

He got out and walked to the back of his car, opened the trunk, took his Beretta out of a plastic tackle box, shrugged out of his jacket, slipped on the shoulder rig, hung the Beretta in the clamshell holster, and pulled the jacket back on. He didn't ask himself why, with all the players off the board, he felt the need to wear the pistol; part of him didn't want to delve that deeply. Not at the moment.

He crossed the driveway, then slowed to a stop as something far to his left caught his eye. Crow peered into the gloom, seeing what he first thought—bizarrely—were tendrils, like the waving arms of an octopus or squid, but then he grunted as he realized that he was seeing the torn ends of crime scene tape fluttering in the wind down by the barn. In the distance the tape seemed to move in eerie slow motion.

"Jeez," he muttered and headed to the house, climbed the wide wooden steps where thirty years ago he and Boppin' Bill, Val, Terry, and Mandy would all sit clustered around the Bone Man, listening to the blues, learning about life far beyond Pine Deep.

The front door was locked, but Crow had his own key and let himself in. There was no sound except the ticking of the big grandfather clock at the foot of the stairs and the muffled scrunch of his sneakers as he moved into the living room. He stopped, looking to his right, through the dining room and into the kitchen—Connie's domain, where she'd happily cooked a thousand meals for the family with all of the charm of a TV house-wife, maybe that redhead from *Desperate Housewives*. Everything always had to be perfect. Though nothing would be anymore.

To his left was the big office Henry had used to run the farm and his other holdings, and next to that Mark's slightly smaller office. The doors to both stood ajar, left open by some cop, the lights on, the occupants never to return.

Crow headed upstairs, stepping lightly, keeping his back to the wall and his eyes cutting back and forth through the gloom of the second floor. At the end of the hallway was the master bedroom where Henry and Bess had slept for forty-six years of marriage. Bess had gone first two years ago, taken by cancer, and who would have thought cancer would be the kinder, gentler way out? Henry had gone down with Ruger's bullet in his back and had died alone out in the rain.

Crow turned. At the other end of the hall was Mark and Connie's bedroom.

Shaking his head Crow climbed the stairs to the big bedroom on the third floor where Val had lived her whole life; Crow knew that her old stuffed toys and dolls were all carefully packed away in one of the closets. He sat on the edge of the bed, running his palm over the comforter and finding precious little comfort. And yet this was the bed where he and Val had made love so many times, where they had almost certainly conceived their child.

"Val," he whispered, and her name seemed to chase the shadows back like a talisman held in the face of some ancient evil. "Val."

Crow sat for a long time, soaking up the energy of the room—the only vital energy left in the whole house. Up here he couldn't hear the ticking of the clock, but there was the soft rustle of the damp October wind through the trees and the skit-ter of dry leaves on the shingled roof. He sighed heavily and got up, packed a big suitcase of clothes, toiletries, and makeup for Val, and went downstairs. No way was he going to bring Val back here when she was released from the hospital; he'd convince her to stay with him. Maybe even try to get her to consider sell-ing the farm. There was nothing left there but ghosts anyway.

He turned off most of the lights and locked the door behind him and left that house of the dead.

(2)

In his dreams Terry Wolfe ran and ran and ran, and the beast ran after. Always following, never tiring, always getting closer. Hour by hour, minute by minute, the beast closed the distance between them as Terry ran through the lightless corridors of the oubliette. There was an infinity of hallways and passages, but no matter which one he chose his running feet—slapping bare on the clammy stone floor—would circle him back to the central chamber and there, bathed in the only light that shone in that forgotten place, his body lay on its hospital bed, surrounded by useless and incomprehensible machines. Each time he staggered out of a side tunnel and skidded to a terrified halt in front of his bed, in front of his own naked and battered body, he would pause just for a second—he couldn't risk longer than that because the beast was always just around the last bend—and he could see that his body was dying.

And that it was changing.

As the life ebbed out of him, as the life force that made him who he was drained away, the meat and muscle and bone of that physical form in the bed changed. The nails were darker, thicker, longer. Just in the last few minutes his jaw had changed, elongated, stretching to allow more teeth. His forehead had become lumpy, thrusting out a heavy brow while the skull flattened above it, sloping back. There was more hair on the face, thicker hair on the chest and arms. Beneath the lids his eyes twitched and flicked.

"That's not me!" Terry yelled as he turned and fled away down another hallway.

The echo that chased him repeated only the last word: "Me! Me! Me!"

Behind him, just past the pursuing wave of echoes, the beast growled in red fury.

(3)

Mike came to the hospital to see Val, but her room was empty and Crow was nowhere to be found. A nurse told him that Val was expected back in twenty minutes or so and asked if he'd like to wait. He told her he'd be back and just wandered the halls for a while. It was visiting hours, so none of the nurses or doctors gave him so much as a glance, even when he went downstairs into the ICU wing, which smelled of disinfectant, sickness, and fear. Mike didn't like the smell, or the way it made him feel, and he almost turned around, but something kept him moving down the hall, as if an invisible hand pushed him gently from behind.

There were twenty-four small bedroom units, each with a big glass window to allow for maximum visibility. Mike drifted along slowly, peering through the glass into each room. Most of the units were empty, a few had old people in them, most of whom already looked dead; one had a young Hispanic man who was bound up in a complicated series of harnesses. Mike wondered if that was José Ramos, the guy who worked for Val. The one who'd gotten his neck snapped by Boyd. The thought tumbled around in Mike's brain for a bit, stirring up different emotions. At first he felt a wave of fear—Mike could imagine almost any kind of pain, having felt so much of it himself—then the fear congealed into sadness, and he crept away, hoping that Vic never went so far overboard that he broke his neck. To be helpless like that, just trapped in a dead body, totally vulnerable, unable to even lift a hand to block the slaps or punches, or to halt the other even more terrible things that Vic could do—that would be the worst thing. He didn't want to look at that thought and moved quickly away from that room as if distance could keep him from the dreadful images that rose up in his mind.

The next unit was ICU #322 and the patient there was also heavily bandaged and had his limbs in casts supported by straps. Mike slowed to a stop, not sure why, and stared through the open doorway at the man. The air around him seemed to shimmer, but Mike's whole concentration was focused on that patient.

He blinked his eyes once, twice, and suddenly he realized that he wasn't in the doorway anymore. He had walked inside all the way to the foot of the bed without any conscious awareness of the action of the passage of time. Those seconds were just *gone.*

The patient's head was heavily bandaged and the visible face was just bruised meat, the skin painted black and purple, the lips puffed, the swollen eyes closed. There was no trace of dreaming movement behind those lids. Despite the beeping of the machines Mike had to watch the man's chest for a full minute to convince himself this person was even alive. Only his face, his throat, and his fingers were visible. The arm nearest him was raised, the white cast bent at the elbow, slings supporting it off the bed so that the fingers of that hand were inches from Mike's face. Big fingers; a big man. Mike stared in fascination at the hand. The nails were neatly manicured, the fingers showing no calluses or scars; on the back of the hand there were curls of red hair. For no good reason he could think of, Mike raised his own hand and held it near to the man's, comparing the hairs, which were a little darker than his own. The width of the palm, the shape of the knuckles, the proportionate length of the fingers, though, were very similar to his own. Mike had never known his father, Big John Sweeney, but he always imagined that he and his dad would look alike, and this man's hand looked like it could be his own in twenty or thirty years. Big and strong, despite the injuries. The red hair gone darker with age.

FUGUE.

The face that had looked at him from the bathroom mirror in Crow's store was an older version of himself, with a stronger jaw and gaunt skin stretched over sharply etched brow and cheekbones. Thin, hard lips in an unsmiling mouth. Dark red-brown hair. Strange eyes. Alien.

Mike almost reached out and touched this man's eyelids to raise them, feeling a strange compulsion to see what color those eyes were. Would they be blue shot with red and ringed with fiery gold? Mike was afraid they would be.

He did not know that he was going to touch this man's hand, would never have deliberately done so, but it was as if some unseen hand just nudged his forward. Without warning his fingers reached out and curled around the pinky and ring finger of the comatose man.

FUGUE.

Mike Sweeney, for all intents and purposes, evaporated into mist at the point of contact. The room in which he stood, the house around the room, the world around the hospital just melted into a featureless blur, faded to darkness, and then winked out.

FUGUE.

He was not Mike Sweeney anymore. He was . . . nothing. A shell casing where inside something that was not Mike Sweeney shifted and groaned. Time was meaningless. If there was air he did not breathe it, or could not feel himself inhale or exhale. If there was light, then either he was blind or could not process the concept of vision. He remained still, just a husk.

He heard another squelching sound and turned quickly, freezing at once into shocked immobility as a huge white stag paced around him in a wide, slow circle. It was snow white, with just a scattering of brick-red flecks on its haunches and eyes that burned with orange fire. The rack was huge, glistening with moisture from the damp air. It moved slowly, looking at him with calm intensity. Mike knew that animal, had seen it once before, that night on the road when it had stood between him and the section of cornfield where a car had gone off the road and plowed itself deep into the field. Mike had wanted to check it out, to see if anyone had been hurt, but this deer—an albino stag—had come out of the night and had stood between him and the wreck, barring his way. With all that had happened later that night, and all that had happened since, Mike had barely remembered the animal until now, and yet here it was.

But where was here?

Mike turned his head and saw that he stood on a gravel driveway leading up to the battered hulk of an abandoned house. Above the house the sky was bruise-blue fading to blackness in the distance. Lightning burned continuously around him, charging the air with ozone, but there was no thunder—just the constant strobe-flicker of lightning above and beyond the house. It was a house he knew, though when he had seen it the shutters had been freshly painted and secure, not hanging from rusted hinges; the windows had been whole, not yawning like jagged mouths, dusty gray on the outside of the each broken pane and ink black inside the maw. On this house the shingles had been shed like scabs from old wounds, and the door hung twisted, sagging down to a porch whose boards had all buckled and warped.

Aware that the stag was watching him, Mike turned away from the house, feeling and hating the deadness of the place. He looked down a wet farm road to where a barn had stood, but it was just a charred frame from which the last few tendrils of smoke curled without enthusiasm. Beside and beyond the burned-out barn were cornfields whose leaves were potholed by insects and whose corn hung fat and pendulous, swollen with disease and rippling with maggots. Strangely, the air around him suddenly felt calmer and he thought he heard the blend of musical notes as some unseen hand fanned down over the strings of a guitar. It came from behind him, where the stag had stood, and Mike turned quickly back, and his mouth opened in a soundless "O." The stag was gone, antlers, dark spots, footprints, and all.

"You the one," said a voice that seemed to come from the middle of the air. It was deep, soft, flavored with a Southern accent. "You the one we all got to pay close mind to now, you know that?"

Mike didn't know where his mouth was or how to make thought into sound. He tried to move but felt himself frozen in place.

"Go ahead, son . . . you can speak." The voice now came from behind him. He heard the sound of fingers lightly strumming guitar strings and the sound was so soothing, so . . . *safe*.

Just like that, Mike could. Cool air rushed into his mouth and down into his lungs. "What's going on?" he blurted.

"You dreaming, young son. You lost in the dreamworld, just like me."

Mike braced himself to fight the immobility, but when he tried to turn it was easy; all restrictions were gone. He turned to see a black man in a dirty suit sitting on the top step of a flight of wooden stairs that led to the big wooden porch of the old farmhouse. The man's skin was dark but ashy-gray and his hair was styled in an old-fashioned Afro, nappy with dirt and rainwater. The man smiled at him, and though his face was kindly his eyes were unblinking and covered with a thin film of dust.

"What the hell's going on?" Mike demanded, angry and confused. "Who are you?"

The man picked out a couple of notes with his long fingers; on the forefinger of his left hand was a glass slide made from the neck of a whiskey bottle, and he drew this down the neck of the guitar to turn the notes into a wail.

"Who are you?" Mike asked again, his tone wavering between demand and plea.

"I ain't hardly nobody no more, but you can call me Mr. Morse."

"I don't understand this. I don't understand what's going on. How'd I get here? I was at the hospital . . . at least I think I was . . ."

"You was . . . and you still is. This ain't real, Mike, this is all a dream." Mr. Morse smiled at him. He had a nice smile, but he looked very sad and tired. "You know what a shaman is, boy?"

"Sure. It's like an Indian medicine man or something."

"Or something, yeah. Well, a shaman would call what we got here a vision, and you're on a vision quest."

"I don't know what that means."

"Yeah, you do, but you don't know you do. Y'see, Mike, you been having visions for a good long time now." He played a few notes, the break of an old Ida Cox tune. "You call 'em dreams, but they are bona fide visions."

"How . . . ?"

"You been dreaming about this town just burning itself up, burning down to the ground."

"How do you know that?"

"I know," said Mr. Morse. "And you been having dreams of *him*."

"Who?"

"You know who. You may not know his name, but his blood screams in your veins, boy. His breath burns in your throat." The man stopped playing and leaned forward. "Look here, boy, you got to listen to me real good, because a whole lotta folks are sitting right there on the edge of that knife blade. You go the wrong way, you make the wrong choice . . . or worse yet, you don't do nothing, and they all gonna die."

"No," Mike insisted, shaking his head.

"We don't have to like something to make it so. Believe me, I know. Hell, yes, old Oren Morse he knows."

"I don't want to be responsible for people dying. I don't want that. That's not fair."

Mr. Morse sighed and gave a sorry shake of his head. "Fair got nothing to do with this. This is Heaven and Hell. This is the bad times come to Pine Deep and everybody here got to play their part."

"I don't want to."

"Well," Mr. Morse said, leaning back and picking out some more notes, "that's your choice. Everybody got a choice, even them bad ones—even they got a choice. It's what we do with our choices that makes us or breaks us. The whole world is spinning right now on the choice you got to make."

"I don't *want* to."

"Well that's as may be. But your father is about to do some bad shit here in town, and Crow and Val, strong as they is, ain't enough to stop him. Not alone. Not without you. I can't see everything that's gonna happen—an' maybe that's a good thing an' maybe it's not—but I know this, Mike Sweeney—if you don't make your choice, if you don't take your stand, then the Red Wave is going to wash over this town. It'll start here . . . it'll start in Dark Hollow, and it'll start at the hospital, right there in that bed with your daddy in it, and it'll start right on Corn Hill. The Red Wave will start here and there all over this town, all at once, and it'll gain momentum and force and it'll get so strong the boundaries of water won't stop it, and it'll wash out across this whole country."

"My dad's dead. My dad is John Sweeney and he—"

"Boy, it breaks my heart to break your heart, but Big John, good man as he was, he wasn't never your daddy. Big John didn't know it, but another mule been kicking in his stall."

"Stop saying that! You're a liar!"

Mr. Morse set down his guitar and stood up. He towered over Mike, covering him with his shadow, and his eyes were fierce. He placed his hands on Mike's shoulders and when Mike tried to turn away Mr. Morse held him fast. His gaze was as hot as a blowtorch. "Now you listen to me good, Mike, you listen like a man, not like a boy. You listen like what you hear and what you do about what you hear *matters*. Don't turn away from me, son, and don't you dare call me a liar. You don't know who I am, boy, but I *died* for this goddamn town. I died for it and my memory's been spit on for thirty years. You think a man can rest quiet in his grave when every time his name is spoke there's a lie and a curse put to it?"

Mike stared at him, shocked to silence, confused, his mind reeling. Mr. Morse's hands were like hot irons on his shoulders.

Mr. Morse never blinked. Not once, and his dusty eyes were filled with a weird light. "Boy, I want you to listen to me for your own soul's sake, even though what I'm going to tell you might take away what little love for this world you got left. I know that pain, boy, and I lost my own love and most of my hope, but by God I'm standing right here. I made my choice, and I'll take my stand, come Heaven or Hell. Now . . . you going to listen?"

Mike didn't want to. He wanted to block his ears, he wanted to hit this man, to push him away, to turn and run. He didn't want to hear anything this man had to say. Rage mingled with terror in his chest and it felt like his heart would burst. When he opened his mouth he wanted to scream at the man, to tell him to go away, to leave him be.

What he said was, "Okay." Just that.

That agreement unmasked a terrible sadness in Mr. Morse's face, and for a moment he lowered his head, murmuring, "I'm sorry, boy. Believe me when I tell you that I mean you no harm."

"Okay," Mike said again.

Mr. Morse told him everything. Mike listened, and he listened, and he listened, and then he screamed. Sometimes the truth doesn't set you free.

Chapter 15

"The eye is not permanently damaged," said Weinstock, distilling for Crow and Val the information he'd gotten from the tests and the specialists. Neither Crow nor Val said anything, their faces not yet showing relief. "The orbit is cracked even worse now that it was before, but that'll heal. So, even though we have to be very, very careful it's better news than we hoped."

"But . . . ?" Val asked. "Drop the other shoe."

"No, that's it. You must have been moving when Boyd hit you, so you actually didn't get as serious an injury as you might have, especially considering the preexisting damage. If you hadn't already had an injury there, this might have been moderately minor. Of course, you have to add shock, general stress, overall trauma . . . and the emotional component." He cleared his throat. "Seeing Mark and all."

Val touched the bandage over her eye, her expression pensive.

"Damn," Crow said with a release of tension that seemed to deflate his whole body. He leaned over and kissed Val on the forehead.

"Thanks, Saul," Val said. "When can I get out of here?"

Weinstock shrugged. "No reason we can't cut you loose first thing tomorrow morning." He held up a finger. "Providing you take it easy, and I mean really easy." He reached over and jabbed Crow in the chest. "And that means no hanky-panky for a few days, too."

"We'll behave ourselves," Val assured him.

★   ★   ★

After Weinstock left Val leaned back and blew a huge lungful of air up at the ceiling. Crow crawled onto the bed and she turned to him.

"Soon as we blow this joint I want you to stay at my place," Crow said. He didn't mention her house or her farm—the enormity of it was always right there with them.

Val just nodded. "I think that's best."

There was a tentative knock on the door and they turned to see Newton peering in. "Is this a bad time?"

"For once," Val said, "it's not. Come in, have a seat."

Newton was an awkward man at the best of times and in situations like this was nearly spastic. He perched on the edge of a guest chair with all the skittishness of a high school kid waiting for his prom date.

Crow handed him a juice carton. "You find out anything useful on the Net?"

"Quite a lot, actually, though at this point it might just serve as backstory since you all seem to think this is all over and done with." He pulled a thick file of computer printouts out of his briefcase. "Aside from the ton of stuff I downloaded about . . ." He looked around and then used his two hooked index fingers to simulate fangs and gave Crow a big stage wink as if the pantomime wasn't enough. "I also e-mailed Dr. Corbiel at U of P. Turns out it isn't Jonathan Corbiel, it's *Jonatha.* No 'n,' a woman. Like the singer Jonatha Brooke."

"Okay."

"We talked on the phone for a couple of hours, and I told her I was doing a book on the haunted history of Pine Deep, yada yada, and asked her if she would be willing to come up here and sit down with us."

"Really?" Val asked. "What'd she say?"

"She said she'd love to, though she said she can't get away until the twenty-ninth because she's giving midterms. I know it's a long time to wait, but in the meantime we can still tap her for info via phone and e-mail."

"Okay, fair enough. Where are we meeting her?"

"She didn't really want to drive all the way here, so I compromised and told her we'd meet her halfway. I set it up for the Red Lion Diner in Warrington."

"Okay, perfect."

(2)

The nurses came back, this time to change Val's IV and fuss over her and even though there was nothing they were doing that was actually too private or official enough to warrant kicking Crow out he still somehow found himself in the hallway on the other side of a closed door. Newton gave Crow a CD with his research notes and headed home to get some rest. Crow was slouching down to the solarium to buy a Yoo-hoo when he spotted Mike Sweeney coming out of the ICU wing.

"Hey," Crow said, "you get lost or something?"

The kid stopped walking and peered at Crow with eyes that seemed at once shocked and dreamy—the pupils were pinpoints, his eyes wide. Crow waved a hand in front of Mike's eyes, expecting the kid to snap out of his reverie with a sheepish grin. Crow had seen him woolgathering a number of times before, but it took Mike at least thirty seconds to come back to planet Earth. Crow could see the process happen. The boy's eyes went from blank to confused to shifty and Mike's rubbery lips congealed into two tight lines.

"Crow?" Mike said in a voice that was unusually hoarse, the way someone sounds after they've been yelling.

"Yo, kiddo . . . what planet were you orbiting?"

"What?"

"You okay? You look like you're out of it."

"Do I?" Mike rubbed his eyes and then looked at his fingers as if expecting to see something on them. What? Grit? Tears?

"Mike," Crow said slowly, touching the kid on the shoulder. "Are you okay?" He eyed the kid, looking for fresh bruises. Maybe he'd had a run-in with Vic.

"I'm good," he said. "Just having kind of a weird day."

"Bad weird or just weird weird?"

"Pine Deep weird," Mike said, and when Crow continued to stare at him, he added, "Soon as I'm old enough, man, I am so out of this frigging town."

Crow snorted. "Soon as you're old enough, kiddo, I'll drive you."

(3)

Mike left the hospital, unchained his bike, and fled onto the back streets of Pine Deep, whisking down the crooked lanes and shadowed alleys, aware of the tourist crowds thinning as he raced toward the farmlands and the forest. He made the last turn, cutting a sharp left off Alvy Lane onto West Road and headed south, leaving the last of the houses behind and rolling through a countryside that was open and vulnerable.

Though it was mid-October it was a November-colored day. There was green, but it huddled low against the ground as thinning islands of grass in a swelling sea of brown dirt. The treetops had been blown to crooked gray sticks by the constant topwind, and invisible snakes of current leapt off the fields and snapped at him, trying to push his bike over. He kept pedaling, his eyes locked on the center of the road thirty feet ahead, his head fixed forward, and only his peripheral vision took slices of the vista to either side and fed it into that nameless place in his mind that hung suspended between the conscious and subconscious.

He had nowhere to be. Crow said that the store would be closed for the rest of the day while he got Val settled in, and Mike didn't have to be home for hours. He was free, the time was his, but he still felt like an escaped prisoner trying to outrun . . .

Outrun what?

He had snapped out of the fugue in Terry Wolfe's room over an hour ago, and much of what he had seen—

Seen
Dreamed
Imagined

—was still with him. Mike did not know how to think about what had happened there in that room; there in his head. Mr. Morse was as real to him as someone he'd actually met. He could smell the earthy stink of dirt on the man's clothes, could smell his sweat. In his head the crystal purity of Morse's silvery guitar notes played over and over again with such precise clarity that Mike was sure that if he had a guitar of his own he could pick out the opening of that song.

Cold wet air abraded his cheeks, making them burn both cold and hot. Despite the chill there was a trickle of warm sweat wriggling down his spine and gathering between his buttocks as his legs pumped and pumped.

What Mr. Morse had said was impossible. More than impossible. Terry Wolfe was the mayor of Pine Deep. He was Crow's friend.

John Sweeney was Mike's father. He knew that; everyone knew that. Big John Sweeney, who was a stand-up guy. Every time Mike ran into one of his dad's old buddies, that's what they said. Big John was a stand-up guy. You knew where you were with him. When the moment broke and you needed someone at your back, Big John was always there. One of the good guys.

Boy, it breaks my heart to break your heart, but Big John, good man as he was, he wasn't never your daddy.

Those words put iron in Mike's legs and stoked the fires that made his feet blur as he pumped up and down on the pedals.

The second after the fugue had snapped Mike realized he had been holding two fingers of Terry Wolfe's hand, and had snatched his own hand away like he'd been holding a hot coal. For five whole minutes he just stood there, staring at the bruised face of the battered mayor, searching for any hint of truth in what Mr. Morse had told him.

Big John didn't know it but another mule been kicking in his stall.

Mr. Morse didn't have to translate what that meant, and Mike didn't have to ask if Morse meant that Vic had been fooling around with Mike's mom. It wasn't Vic. It was never Vic.

Mike had turned and lurched into the bathroom in Terry's room and spent at least as many minutes staring into the mirror.

The curly red hair. Terry's was red-brown. Mike's would be. In time. The same blue eyes. The same cheekbones and jaw. Mike's was softer, younger, but it would change.

There was a little of Mike's mom in his features, just enough so that Mike did not look like a clone of Terry Wolfe—and it was thirty years since Terry had been a boy—but there was too much of Terry's face in his own. Way too much.

Big John wasn't never your daddy.

That might have been okay. If it was just a case of Terry Wolfe being his real father, it might have been okay. As Mike rode on past the fields of dying grass he knew that it might have been okay. Awkward, sure. A little weird, definitely . . . but in the end it would have been okay. A Hallmark moment come next Christmas, maybe.

Mike's life had never been filled with many Hallmark moments and this wasn't going to start a new tradition. This wasn't an After School Special, either. This was late-night scary-movie double-feature stuff. It was damn near *Star Wars,* and as he rode Mike thought about that, trying to find a splinter of fun in it; but it was like looking at the welling blood from a skinned knee and trying to glean from it the fun of bright colors.

Morse had gone on to say, *Boy, I want you to listen to me for your own soul's sake, even though what I'm going to tell you might take away some of the little love for this world you got.*

Yeah, Mike thought, *you got that shit right.* A car came out of a side road and instead of braking Mike poured on more speed and shot across the mouth of the road inches ahead of the bumper, the horn shrieking at him as the driver stamped down on the brakes.

There was precious little in the world Mike loved. His mom, maybe, but in light of the things Mr. Morse had told him that was even more confused and polluted than ever. Mom belonged to Vic, and Vic belonged to . . .

Believe me when I tell you that I mean you no harm. Morse had said that, and Mike believed him—then and now—but it didn't change a thing. Big John Sweeney was no longer his father. At most he was a guy who was around for a bit when Mike was born, and died before Mike had ever gotten a chance to form a clear image of him. Anything Mike had ever believed about how Big John's strength and dignity, his honor and good nature had all been passed down to Mike, filtered perhaps through Mom's gin-soaked genes, was all for shit. *Big John wasn't never your daddy.*

Terry Wolfe was. And at the same time, he wasn't.

Mike raced on, trying to outrun the insanity of it all, the sheer unscalable impossibility of it all, but it chased him down the road, running like a hellhound, never tiring, as focused on Mike as he was on the road ahead, as dauntless as truths often are.

Terry Wolfe? Sure, he was Mike's father, but only in the strictest sense of empty biology. Mike was a realist, he could accept—however much it hurt—that Terry Wolfe had slept with his mother. In the scheme of things, so what? Shit happens, and it happened a long time ago. So, that was just the first incision. The really deep cut, the one that had marked him, the one that hurt in so many ways that Mike did not know how to react, did not know how to feel the pain of it, was knowing that Terry Wolfe was not his *only* father.

Yeah, that was a total bitch.

The afternoon sky above him was darkening as the high winds pulled sheets of gray clouds over the mountains toward the town.

What was the word Mr. Morse had used to describe Terry? A *vessel.* Another person—Mike's *other* father—had come sneaking in like a mist through Terry's pores, sinking deep into the flesh, and as Terry sank into drunken stupor, this other presence just simply took over. Like stealing a car. Going for a joyride. With Mike's mom.

The thought alone was so disgusting Mike would have skidded his bike to a stop and thrown up his guts by the side of the road, but his stomach was as empty as his hope, and he rode on.

Terry Wolfe was his biological father. Okay, done deal. Someone else was his—spiritual father? *Spiritual? Was that the way to look at it?* It felt completely wrong because Mike knew that it was completely correct. Mike could have accepted being Terry

Wolfe's son. There was no shame in being the son of a guy like that, not even a bastard son.

His real father, the father of Mike's own *soul*, well, that was another thing. That was a thing that sat in the center of his own soul and screamed in a voice of pure darkness and pure rage. His mom had a saying she used—the apple doesn't fall too far from the tree.

The tears ran down his burning cheeks, snot ran from both nostrils, and in his ears all he heard was a steady roar of white noise like a blank TV station with the volume turned all the way up. Blood vessels burst in his eyes, painting the landscape ahead of him in a hundred shades of red as blackness crept in around the edges. In his chest his heart was beating 160 beats a minute. 170. 180.

He raced on, feeling his throat closing, feeling the air fighting its way into his lungs and scorching its way back out. Blood mingled with the snot as it seeped out of his nose and a single bloody teardrop broke from his left eye and collided with the regular tears, staining them and his face an angry pink.

The father of his soul.

Mr. Morse had shown him who that was . . . and *what* it was.

So Mike raced on and on into the murky landscape fleeing the thing he carried with him, trying to outrace the poisonous contamination of his own soul.

(4)

The Bone Man felt the darkness rising from the ground like cemetery mist. He stood in the middle of A-32 and watched the sun fail and he fancied that he could hear the night cry out in triumph. No, not triumph . . . more like a challenge. A hunting call.

Above and around him the night birds took to the sky, startled into flight, terrified of the thickening shadows. The Bone Man turned as a whole flock of them rose and headed away from Dark Hollow in a mass as thick as locusts. Only one bird stayed with him, landing on the top rail of a wooden farm fence.

He looked down the road and saw Mike Sweeney riding as if hellhounds were biting at the tires of his bike.

"I tried to tell him." The bird cocked its head at him and regarded him with one obsidian eye. "I tried to warn him, to make him understand . . ."

The bird shivered its wings and cawed once, high and shrill. "Instead," the Bone Man said, "I think I might have gone and killed that boy."

The crow looked at him, his eye penetrating, accusing.

"It's going to be bad," asked the Bone Man. "Ain't it?" The bird just turned away and watched the boy. "Yeah," the Bone Man said, answering his own question, "it's going to be bad."

(5)

Mike was barely even aware of the road as he shot along it like a suicide bullet. His heart was a screaming red explosion in his chest and he could taste blood in his mouth. Air tasted like acid in his mouth and throat. When he hit the broken tree branch lying in the middle of the road and his bike left the ground he closed his eyes, feeling the lift as he began to fly, hoping he was going to die. Maybe he would never feel the impact, maybe he would. It didn't much matter as long as at the end of that moment there would be nothing.

Time vanished around him. He had no sense of movement, no sense of the ground either falling away or rising to meet him. With his eyes closed and the wind now a soft stroke on his cheek, everything was peaceful.

Then he hit the tree from which the branch had fallen.

Chapter 16

"Where the hell are we?" Josh was looking for roadside signs. His wife Deb was hunched forward using her cell phone's meager display light to try and read a map. The dome light of their car hadn't worked in four years. "I think we're near some town called Black Marsh."

"Never heard of it. We just passed a sign for a bridge," he said, looking in the rearview, though behind them everything was black.

"Good, take that. We'll cross back into Pennsylvania and go through . . . um, looks like something called Pine Deep."

"Yeah, that's that dumb tourist place that's been on the news. All that Halloween crap." Josh was getting cranky. The two of them had driven from Erie for a wedding in Ocean City, New Jersey, and had gotten directions off the Internet. So far those directions had failed them three times, and for the last hour they had been Brailling their way through back roads in New Jersey. The little finger of the gas gauge was pointing accusingly at E, needling Josh for not filling up when he had the chance

"They ought to have a gas station or two. Being, you know, a tourist place and all."

Josh said nothing.

"If not . . . we have Triple-A."

Josh hadn't renewed the AAA membership and didn't want to have to tell her, so he just concentrated on the road. Their car, a battered Jeep Cherokee that had seen better decades, rolled onto the heavy timbers of the bridge and rattled across the Delaware River into the borough of Pine Deep. In the darkness of the cab, both Deb and Josh Meyers shivered. Neither noticed the other do so. It was an instinctive reaction, a trembling as if in the face of a chill wind, but their windows were rolled up and though set on low the Jeep's heater was on.

They drove on, climbing up to the tops of the long hills and then dropping down the other sides, plunging into darkness, chasing the spill of the Jeep's headlights. At the top of a particularly steep hill, just as the Jeep pitched toward the drop, Deb said, "Look, there's a cop car."

"Finally!"

They descended the hill toward a police cruiser parked on the shoulder, the light bar lit but not flashing—the way a lot of small-town cops did when writing reports or just making their presence known. As the Jeep coasted toward the cruiser, they could see the officer in silhouette, bent down over something, apparently writing on a pad. Josh tooted the horn, a single short beep, as he slowed to a stop. The cop didn't look up.

"Gimme the map," Josh said, "and wait here. I'll see what he says." He jerked open the door, stepped out into the cold air, hunched in to the wind and jog-walked over to the cruiser. "Hello? Uh . . . excuse me? Officer?"

The cop still sat with his head bent over a writing tablet. From the angle at which he sat, and with the masking presence of the man's uniform hat, Josh could not see the cop's features.

"Officer . . . ?"

There was no movement, and Josh began to wonder if the cop was sound asleep. Tentatively he reached out and tapped the closed window. Nothing.

He tried again, and again called, "Officer? I need to get some directions."

The officer's head moved slightly. Josh rapped on the glass again. Like most people he was afraid of cops, not because he had done anything at all illegal, but just because he was Joe Public and cops were cops. His action, just simply wanting to know directions to a gas station, was deferential, even apologetic. Even the way he tapped on the glass implied apology for disturbing the officer.

"Please, can you tell me where I can find a gas station?"

The cop's head came up, but he was facing away from Josh, appearing to stare out the window into darkness. The officer slowly held up a hand, one finger extended in a mild command for Josh to wait. The officer set down his notebook and, though still looking in the other direction, jerked the door handle open.

Josh stepped back from the door and watched the cop get out. He was frowning. The cop was getting out of the car in a very strange fashion. He would not turn his face toward Josh, so in a way he actually bent forward and backed out of the car. His motions were jerky, peculiar, as if he was unused to moving his own body. As his head cleared the door frame, the hat caught on the edge and was swept from his head as he straightened. The hat fluttered into the car and the cop made no move to retrieve it. The officer's hair was tangled and unkempt, and there appeared to be something dark and moist clotted into the tangle at the back of his head. The red and blue dome lights made nonsense of colors, but Josh had the thought that it could be blood glistening on the back of the cop's head.

Josh's frown deepened, and he was caught between the sudden rush of ordinary concern and a fearful uncertainty that rooted him to the spot. Then it came to him. The cop must have been in some kind of accident. Maybe he banged his head and that's why he was so unresponsive and groggy. Josh could see no damage to the car, but maybe the whole other side of the car was punched in.

"Officer . . . are you all right?"

The cop lost balance for a moment and had to reach out and grab the door frame to keep from falling. Josh automatically reached out with both hands to support him, catching him by the elbow and under the armpit.

"Jesus! You're hurt. What happened?"

The cop steadied himself, and even lifted one hand to wave Josh back.

"Officer? Hey . . . you okay?"

"I'll . . ." the cop began. His voice was thick and distorted. "I'll . . . be . . ."

"Are you hurt?"

"I'll . . . be . . . fine. Just . . . give me a moment." He barely whispered the words.

Josh looked over his shoulder to where Deb was peering at him through the windshield. She made a questioning gesture and he shrugged, shaking his head.

"Um," Josh said uncertainly, "look . . . if you're hurt maybe I can help." He bent close, saw something dark and glistening on the cop's face. "Jeez, you're bleeding!"

Josh put his hand on the officer's shoulder and gently pulled, trying to turn the man, wanting to see how badly the officer was injured. His first-aid knowledge was on a purely "get a Band-Aid" or "put ice on it" level. But what if this guy had a concussion? What if he was really hurt? The patrol car didn't look damaged, but maybe he hit something, a deer perhaps, and then cracked his head on the steering wheel. It seemed like the only likely answer. Josh didn't know if he would be able to work a police microphone to ask for help. He pulled on the cop's shoulder, and then hesitated. The officer was trembling, his big body shaking spasmodically. Was he . . . crying?

Jesus, he thought, *the poor guy*.

He pulled on the shoulder as gently as he could, but still firmly enough to turn the cop. The man resisted with surprising strength. "Let me help," Josh said softly. "C'mon, let me see . . ."

"You . . . want to see?" the officer said, and Josh felt a chill race up and down his spine. As the cop had spoken, it had become clear he wasn't crying at all.

He was laughing.

Josh's hand faltered and he opened his mouth to say something; he was confused, trying to understand. The cop turned then. Not with Josh's assistance, but with his own effort. It was fast—so fast that all Josh saw was a blur of gray cotton, a brief glint of headlights on a gold wristwatch, the hot red flash of a high school ring, and then Josh felt the officer's white hand clamp around his throat. The pressure was instant and enormous, and Josh felt himself rising to his toes, then beyond all sanity he felt the ground dropping away under his shoes. Even as it was happening the part of his mind that required logic was saying, *That can't be right.* His feet kicked in empty space, and yet the cop still held him, still maintained that crushing grip on his throat. Josh tried to scream. The glare from the Jeep's driving lights splashed against the cop's face, showing his features at last and with stark clarity illuminating horror.

The officer's eyes were a furious red set in dark pits of bruised flesh. His mouth was a gaping, laughing impossibility of wicked white teeth. His throat was a ragged ruin caked with blood.

Darkness swarmed around Josh; his senses became confused. He thought he saw two more figures rush out of the darkness beneath the trees that lined the side of the road. His mind was closing down and all that he could be sure of was a vagueness of white faces and empty eyes, and beneath the roaring in his ears he thought he heard a desperate, hungry moaning. These shapes did not come to rescue him, nor did they come to hurt him— they moved away from the police cruiser, toward the Jeep. Dimly, distantly he heard Deb yelling his name, and then she began screaming in long inarticulate wails. She jammed her hands against the horn and the blare rose like a banshee.

Josh tried to call her name, tried to reach for her, but he could feel his own strength fading away. He saw the figures tear open the car doors, saw the shapes come at Deb from both sides. They grabbed her arms and for a moment Josh's darkening brain thought that the attackers were playing a kids' game. Tug-of-war. And then Deb's scream rose to a supersonic shriek as the monsters tore her apart. Her blood splashed against the inside of the windshield and painted it an opaque red-black. Deb's screams gurgled to a wet nothing and all Josh could hear was a sound like lions tearing apart a zebra with their teeth.

The hand holding him gave a tighter squeeze and Josh saw, with fading vision and awareness, the name tag on the cop's uniform: D. McVey. It meant nothing to him except that it was the last thing he ever saw before the pain in his throat blossomed into a dripping darkness tinged with scarlet.

(2)

Vic's cell phone rang and he picked it up from where it lay on a table, saw that the screen display said POLK, and flipped it open. "Yeah?"

"Back door."

Without comment Vic flipped the phone shut and went to open the door, pausing only long enough to peer through the spy hole to confirm that it was Polk, and that he was alone.

"Hope this ain't a social call, Jimmy."

Licking his lips nervously, Polk held up a finger and then retreated to his parked car, which was angled in toward the garage door, and removed a large cardboard box from the trunk. Vic noted that Polk had used enough common sense to remove the bulb from the trunk light, and decided that was worth some brownie points. Polk handed the box to Vic and in a hushed voice said, "Detonators, rolls of fuse wire, and some timers. Everything you asked for, plus I got a couple extra of each."

Nodding in appreciation, Vic turned and set the box inside the door. He did not invite Polk in. Turning back, he said, "And the dynamite?"

"I'll have it next week, but I don't want to bring it here. I can meet you somewhere out of town, if that's okay."

"Yeah, that's good. Keep your cell handy and once you get it, give me a call. I'll tell you where and when to meet."

"Okay."

Polk's face was shining with sweat despite the chill, and he kept licking his lips in a way that reminded Vic of a nervous Chihuahua. If he'd had a dog biscuit he would have bet he could have made Polk sit up and beg.

"Kenny said he needed seventy-five percent up front before he turns over the stuff, though, and the rest on delivery."

"Fair enough," Vic said. "Wait here." He left Polk standing outside in the cold darkness while he went back into his den and to a wall safe that was behind a framed photo of Heinrich Himmler, punched in a code, and when the door popped open he took out several stacks of bills that had been bundled into

five-thousand–dollar bricks and secured with green rubber bands.
He counted out two hundred thousand and dumped the bills into
a zippered vinyl bag that read STRIKE IT BIG AT PINELANDS LANES.
As an afterthought he took more bricks of bundled twenties and
carried them and the bag back outside. Handing off the bag, he
said, "This is for your cousin Kenny. And this," he added, holding out the ten grand, "is for you."

Polk looked at it narrowly as if he expected some kind of
nasty trick. "Why?"

"Because you're doing your job, Jimmy-my-boy. Unless you
don't want it?" Vic pretended to pull it back, but Polk snatched
at it, catching one bundle of five thousand and causing the other
to fall. He bent down and picked it up off the ground from in
front of Vic's feet and as he rose he unzipped his jacket and
stuffed the money inside.

"Now, what do you say?" Vic asked mildly.

"Um . . . thanks, Vic."

"Good dog," Vic said, and turned and went back inside.

(3)

Ruger absently wiped his mouth with the back of his hand,
caught sight of the bright-red smear, and licked it off, savoring
the taste. Blood was so much sweeter when it was still fresh, before the cells thickened and died. After that the taste was drab,
like sucking on wet cardboard. He'd known that even before the
change, and now he felt like a connoisseur.

On the ground, the young woman moaned, struggling to turn
over, fighting to find a thread of breath amid the smashed debris
of her throat. Red bubbles formed on her lips and popped, staining her face with tiny misty droplets. She lifted a fluttering hand
to her throat, touching with featherlight fingers the irregular
line of blood-drenched skin that should have been smooth.
Blood seeped in sluggish pulses; her life pushed out of her with
each fading beat of her heart.

Ruger squatted down and looked at her. The fluttering hand

entertained him; it reminded him of a hummingbird, and he smiled. He reached out and scooped another fingerful of blood from her throat, licking it the way a kid would lick a finger's worth of cookie batter.

"Please . . ." the woman whispered and just managing that single word cost her breath she didn't have left to spend. Ruger smiled and brushed a strand of hair out of her eyes. She had pretty eyes—honey brown with gold flecks. Even now, even after all that he'd done to her, her eyes still held a glimmer of in-nocent hope, as if he could take it all back, make it all better again. "Please," she said again and even tried to give him a trem-bling, hopeful smile.

Karl Ruger looked into those brown eyes and gave her a smile of his own, warm, encouraging, and he could see her spirit rise toward it, her hope blossoming as he pressed his fingers to her throat, closing the wound.

"H . . . help me . . ." she whispered in what was left of her voice.

He bent close so that his lips were inches from hers. His black eyes filled her vision. "Fuck you, bitch," he murmured, and then curled his fingers and tore her throat apart.

The last of her spilled out with her blood.

Ruger bent closer still and licked up that last pulse of blood. That final moment of life was as precious as the first beat of an infant's heart, and it was his to own forever.

He rose, deeply satisfied, powerfully aroused.

Around him there was still some movement, though all of the desperate scrambling was done. A final scream tore through the night but it was cut off and ended with a gurgle, overlapped by someone's laughter. Six cars were parked in the clearing at Pas-sion Pit on Dark Hollow Road, each tucked under sheltering trees; one old 1980s-style custom van was side-on to Ruger, the driver's door open and a man's body, naked from the waist down, lay with head and shoulders hanging limp, arms wide, the backs of the hands touching the ground. The air was heavy with the coppery scent of blood, and Ruger felt intoxicated. Everywhere he looked there was young flesh, much of it bared to the inspection of the moonlight, white skin and red blood and wide, empty eyes. Ruger was hard as a rock.

The young woman and her date had provided some genuine entertainment. The man was stretched across the hood of the Lexus. His fly was open and his limp penis poked like a thick white grub through the folds of his trousers. The dead woman's blouse was unbuttoned, her white bra pushed up; she wore no panties. Ruger had watched from the shadows as the young couple fumbled in the little shell of the car. It was a real kick to watch the man cajole her into going down on him, sometimes pleading, sometimes browbeating her. It jazzed Ruger to hear the man's almost feminine shriek as he had come in her mouth, his hands clamped down on the back of her head, ignoring her struggles and gagging coughs. It had been obvious to Ruger that it was the young woman's first foray into oral sex, and she hadn't been all that fond of the experience. Ruger had known women who had been spoiled for it forever because some tough guy had held her head down with strong fingers, all the time promising he wouldn't come in her mouth. Hell, Ruger had done it himself enough times, loving the struggle, loving the fact that the blow job he was getting would be the last one the woman would probably ever willingly give. It made such events rare and special for him, especially the knowledge that he could actually reach into a woman's mind and leave his own mark, a scar that could never be erased. That was a rush better than the resulting orgasm.

The young woman—teenager actually—he'd watched had been going through that process, and while it was fun to watch, it wasn't Ruger himself who was leaving the mark but some pimple-faced young jock who was only getting some because he had his daddy's fancy car. Ruger couldn't just sit by forever and let the bozo have all the fun. So, just as the jock came, Ruger rose up beside the car and yanked the door open and the jock fell halfway out. Ruger caught him by the hair and jerked him the rest of the way out of the car, handing him back to the hungry ones behind him. The twins and the Carby kids. They didn't go for the kill right away—they beat the living shit out of him first. Just for fun.

This was not the first hunt for the Carbys, Jilly and Tyler, whose farm had been overrun by Ruger's first recruits two weeks ago, or for the twins Demian and Adrian, who had been turned a few days later. Each of them had been involved in group hunts and solo kills, but there was always something new to learn from Ruger. Everyone worshipped Ruger. He was like a rock star to them. The actual Cape May Killer and Ubel Griswold's cold left hand.

The Carbys had brought along their cousin, Chad, whom they had turned last night, and they wanted him to learn the art of the kill from a kickass bloodletter like Ruger. Over the last few nights Ruger had let all the kids make kills, but more than that he'd let them kick the shit out of the victims. Even the twins, who were just grade-school kids, had been fully blooded on Ruger's field trips. Now it was Chad's turn, and Ruger had made him watch as twelve of the youngest members of the Red Wave swept through the Passion Pit, kicking ass, taking lives. Having a grand fucking time of it.

Now all the sweating, huffing, moaning young lovers were dead. Ruger snapped his long, thin fingers, the sound firecracker sharp in the cold air. A dozen faces, pale as the watching moon, turned toward him, expectant and silent.

"Clean it up," he told them. "No traces."

They looked disappointed. One of them, one of the newer ones, spoke up. "Why? We can wake them up, get them to clean up their own shit. Why do we have to do it?"

Ruger turned toward Chad and fixed him with the full impact of his stare. "Because I said so, Chad," he said, inflecting the boy's name with contempt, smiling like a crocodile, his top row of teeth like a serrated knife.

Chad Carby shrank visibly, but still he held his ground. Some of the others smirked at the speaker's discomfiture, but Ruger kind of admired the kid's spunk. It was even okay, in the scheme of things, because this was the way it worked. The alpha teaching the pups how the pack works.

Ruger turned in a slow circle, making brief but scintillating eye contact with each of them. Like a good general he knew how to rally as well as how to chastise, and he laid a cold hand on Chad's shoulder. "Just be patient, kiddo," he said with his icy whisper. "A good soldier knows when to go quiet and dark and when to burn the trees. Until Halloween, it's all about keeping it on the down-low. You with me, pardner?"

"I . . . guess so," Chad said, his eyes shifting toward Ruger's and then falling away.

Ruger pretended to find a drop of blood at the corner of his mouth, dabbed it off, and licked it with a darting tongue. "Tell you boys what we can do," he said. "Once we clean this shit up . . . why don't you wake up the girls first?" He gave Chad a wicked wink, making sure the others saw it, too.

They all laughed, low and mean and hungry.

"Halloween's coming soon, kids," he said, and then nodded to Chad. "You know what Halloween is, don't you?"

Chad Carby lifted his eyes to meet Ruger's. "You told us it would be trick or treat."

Ruger chuckled softly. "Lots of tricks," he murmured, "and lots of treats." He gave Chad another quick wink. "Now let's clean this shit up and have some fun."

(4)

Vic's cell rang again and this time the display said GOLUB. He set down the timing switch he'd been tinkering with and flipped it open.

"This had better be important."

"Vic? Look, we had a bit of problem out here. Karl had me swing by to check on Dixie McVey. He was doing some car stops near the Black Marsh Bridge. Dix had some of the Dead Heads with him and he faked out a couple of tourists. Young couple from Erie, no local ties, at least as far as I can tell."

"I don't give a shit. Get to a point or get off the line."

"Dix did okay—he took out the guy and we've already recruited him—but the Dead Heads jumped the schedule and hit the woman."

"Meaning?"

"Well, they went all George Romero on her."

Vic sighed. He hated the fact that every jackass in this god-damned town loved to throw pop-culture references around as if it made them cool. Even recruits like Golub. Vic would love to just push the plunger and nuke the whole frigging lot of them. Fanboy assholes. "What did they do?" he asked, though he thought he already knew.

"Well . . . they kind of *ate* her."

"Shit."

"There's not enough left to recruit. Tore her arms off, tore her . . ."

"All right, all right. Son of a bitch." He rubbed his eyes. "Put McVey on."

There was a rustle and then McVey spoke. "Hey, boss, sorry for the screwup." Unlike Golub, who could pass, McVey was a different species of vampire and his teeth had already grown so huge that his voice was muffled by trying to talk around them. Worse than Ruger.

"Where are those assholes now?"

"Dave and I quieted them down, got them sitting in the woods just off the road. We had to cuff them together around a tree."

"How bad's the mess?"

"Bad enough, but Dave and I both brought cleanup stuff in our car, like you told us to."

"I don't like hearing that you let this get out of hand." Silence on the other end of the phone. "You understand me?"

"Sure," McVey said, his voice thick. "But . . . those Dead Heads are pretty hard to handle. Won't listen, and sometimes they just go off, y'know? They don't even drink, not the right way—all they want to do is eat. I'm not even sure they can think, let alone take orders—"

"You think you just called 1-800-IGiveAShit? Just clean it up and make damn sure you don't put a foot wrong again. I don't want to have to tell you a second time."

"Yes, sir," McVey said. The "sir" was a suck-up gambit, but Vic liked it.

"One more thing. Get some body bags and pop a cap in two useless meatheads. Headshots only, and use sound-suppressors. Then bury 'em somewhere quiet. Spread the word about it, too. You step outside of the Plan, you die. Even Dead Heads should be able to process that." He hung up.

"Shit!" he growled and very nearly hurled his cell phone against the wall.

Chapter 17

Val was discharged the next morning and Crow took her home. His home, not hers.

The nurses wheeled her to the front door and she rode in a brooding silence, the cane lying across her thighs, her face stony and set. Crow walked beside her, holding one hand, and as the automatic doors opened before them he jerked them all to a halt. The parking lot was packed with reporters who surged forward to stick microphones in Val's face as cameramen jostled each other for the best shot. Crow was only marginally relieved to see that Newton was not among them. There were cops there, too, but none of them were engaged in any visible crowd control. Scanning the crowd, Crow saw Polk leaning against a patrol car, legs crossed at the ankles, arms folded across his chest, a shit-eating grin on his face. When Crow shot him a look of pure loathing, Polk responded by giving him a nasty wink.

Prick, Crow thought, and filed that away for future consideration.

As the questions thundered around them, overlapping into a rumbling blur of meaningless words, Crow turned and bent to Val and whispered, "Don't say anything. Let's just push through."

The glasses hid her eyes but there was as much hurt in the set of her jaw as there was offense and anger. Crow helped her out of the wheelchair and put one strong arm around her and used the other to push his way through the crowd. Both of them staring stolidly ahead, they headed toward Crow's car, Missy. Every reporter tried to be the one to break Val's silence, and over and over again one would shout a provocative question like, "How do you feel about your brother being killed?" or "Are you devastated now that you've lost your whole family?" All designed to gouge a comment out of her, but she bit down on her rage and clutched Crow's supporting arm like a vise and they eventually got to Crow's car. Even then, even when they were inside and buckled up, with the car in gear and rolling slowly, the reporters knocked on the glass, even tried the door handles, shouting as loud as they could to be heard and to get through to her. Most people crack; most people get mad and shout, or dissolve into tears, all of which makes for great vidcaps; but Val was Val—she wore her grief like armor and carried her rage like a shield, and she endured it.

More than a dozen film crews followed her out of the parking lot, the news teams scrambling like fighter pilots during an air raid, screeching into turns and pursuing them as Polk and his cronies just watched. Crow didn't try to lose them, didn't race down the streets. That would be theater, too, and he didn't want to give them anything. Beside him Val was a statue, looking neither left nor right, just staring out of the window as the blocks rolled past and the circus followed.

When he pulled up to the Crow's Nest, the news crews double-parked and hustled out to make another run at a sound bite. Again Crow had to shove past them, and again neither he nor Val said a word or even made eye contact with them. They wrestled their way to the front door of the store; Crow unlocked it and ushered Val inside. When some reporters tried to barge in with them, Crow closed the door on them. Slowly, but with force, pushing them back inch by reluctant inch, then turning the locks. Without a pause he and Val went straight through the store, past the counter, through the rear door that opened into Crow's apartment. He closed and locked that, too.

"The phone," she said. They were the first words she'd spoken since the hospital. Crow went over to the phone and switched the ringer off. He drew the blinds on the back windows, made sure the back door was locked, and when he turned around Val was gone. He went quickly into the bedroom and found her sitting on the edge of the bed.

It was only then that she started to cry, and she cried for a long time.

(2)

"Where are you, Sport?"

Ruger took a cold cigarette from between even colder lips. "I'm at Carby's place."

"Okay. Might as well stay there today," Vic said. "It's almost dawn. You don't want to get caught by daylight."

"Nope," Ruger said. Vic knew that sunlight was not fatal to Ruger as it was to some species of vampires; all it did was hurt him. But Ruger was still supposed to be dead and his face had been on every newspaper, magazine, and Internet news feed for weeks now. Staying in the shadows meant staying off the radar. "I'll keep out of sight, don't worry."

"You know about that cluster-fuck out on A-32?"

"Yeah. Friggin' Dead Heads."

"We can't have more of that, Sport. Not now. You could do us both a favor and lock all those assholes up until the Wave."

"I'll see to it," Ruger said, his voice a whisper.

"Make sure you do. Right now I gotta get going. Mike didn't come home last night and I need to look into it. If we're lucky, Tow-Truck Eddie got him."

"You think so?"

"I should be so lucky . . . but something sure as hell happened and I need to know what. I'll be in touch."

Ruger flipped his phone shut and tapped it thoughtfully against his chin for a moment, still smiling. Dawn was coming, but it was still dark, so he settled into the shadows to wait. The song "Time Is on My Side" occurred to him and he killed some time letting it play in his head. Corny, sure, but fun corny—and this was going to be fun. His smile never faded as the minutes of night dropped like cigarette ash on the ground around him.

At five-twenty in the morning the door across from him opened and Vic stepped out, dressed in a jeans and a big Eagles Windbreaker. Ruger didn't move, confident of the shadows around him. He watched Vic lock his back door, check the street, then climb into his pickup and drive up the alley. Vic's eyes were human eyes—weak and stupid. Ruger kept smiling as Vic's careful stare rolled right over him without a flicker.

The truck passed within a few yards of where Ruger stood, arms folded, leaning on one shoulder deep in the mouth of a neighbor's side yard. Ruger grinned as the pickup turned the corner.

"Asshole," he whispered in a voice like a dead Clint Eastwood, and crossed the street. He had no key, but the lock was nothing to him. He put a palm flat on the wood next to the door handle and gave a single short shove. Wood splintered and the dead bolt worked like a lever to tear the entire strike plate out of the frame.

"Oops," he said, grinning like a kid. He pushed the door shut behind him and tilted a chair under the handle to keep it shut. *Have to keep up appearances.*

The cellar was dark and silent, but Ruger could hear sounds in the house. He knew that if Vic was up and out, then Lois had to be up. Vic didn't cook his own breakfast or make his own coffee. He stood at the foot of the stairs and listened to the scuff of her feet on the kitchen floor. Bare feet, no slippers. He liked that. There was a clank of a pan—Ruger caught the whiff of eggs—and then the clink of a bottle. Definitely a gin bottle; he could smell the sharp juniper aroma as she poured. Lois was starting early today.

"Goodie," he said. And it was. Drunk would work.

He climbed the stairs. It was high time he showed Vic who really was the big dog. More to the point, it was time he showed that sneering prick who was really the Man's favored son. The door to the kitchen was also locked and it mattered just as little. Ruger wrapped his long white fingers around the doorknob and with no effort at all pulled the whole lock set right through the hole, splintering the wood and snapping wood screws with gunshot sounds. Beyond the door Lois Wingate screamed in shock.

As he pushed through into the kitchen Ruger's smile grew into a hungry grin. He liked the sound of that scream, his mouth watering with the knowledge that it would be the first of many.

(3)

They slept through the night, but as dawn approached Val woke up. She lay for a long time staring upward into the empty shadows above Crow's bed, feeling the weight and solidity of his arm and aware that his need to protect her meant so little in the scheme of things. To her heart, sure, it was wonderful, but to her mind—a machine grinding on its own gears—nothing was strong enough to protect her. Not against her own thoughts. There was nothing that Crow could do—nothing anyone could do—to protect her from the truth of her loss. The town was polluted; there was blight on almost all the crops. Except hers, but the Guthrie farm had suffered its share of pestilence. At that moment, if she could have accomplished it she would have razed all of the crops and every building including her own house to the ground and sown the ground with salt. Not for fear of the crop diseases, but in fear of that other plague. The plague that had made Boyd what he was, which was perhaps the same plague that had drawn Boyd and Ruger to Pine Deep in the first place.

Mark's body was in the morgue. Cold and empty, without Mark's soul in it. Just flesh, she told herself. Not Mark at all . . . just an empty shell . . . and yet Mark had been killed by Boyd. And Boyd was a vampire. It didn't matter that Weinstock checked on him three times a day; it didn't matter that neither Mark or Connie showed any signs of being anything more than corpses. In a movie she'd seen once a vampire had said something about outliving his enemies by simply going to sleep for a century and then rising after they were dust. What if that sort of thing was possible? What if Mark, cold and dead as he appeared, was only waiting for some dark call to awaken him?

It was a stupid thought, she knew. Stupid, and fanciful, and utterly terrible. Val lay there and stared out through the lightless window into the blank blackness of the night and thought lots of such thoughts.

(4)

Mike knew that everything was broken, but he didn't care. He didn't know how to care anymore. The impact with the tree had smashed almost every thought out of his mind, and filtered what little remained into a single piece of understanding. "I'm dying," he said in a wet voice.

He coughed and felt blood splash out of his mouth onto his chin. There was pain. Of course there was pain, but it was a remote island way off on the horizon of his perception. It had been there for hours, ever since he'd crashed, and it had done all the harm to him that it could. Now it was just *there*. He didn't care about that, either.

"I'm dying," he said again, smiling. It was the safest he'd felt in years.

Time, as meaningless as the rest of it, had long ago ceased to move . . . and yet the sky had changed. Mike couldn't move his head and had been staring at the featureless black above him forever. Maybe he slept at times, maybe he just stared, but now the sky was less pervasively black, now there was just the faintest hint of color. A brick-red tinge dabbed here and there on the underside of the clouds.

The wind stirred, pushing some leaves around. One leaf blew against his cheek and stuck to the blood, quivering as if struggling to escape. Mike turned his eyes to look at it, saw its jagged brown edges vibrating, and it took him a few seconds to realize that he could see the color. He tried to lift one hand, wanting to see if there was enough light to see his fingers and was surprised when his hand moved. When he had tried to move his hand before it had not so much as trembled; there hadn't been a single flicker of sensation from anything below his shoulders. That had changed now, but Mike still didn't care. He was too busy trying to die.

There was the rustle of more leaves off to his left, not in the path of the wind, and Mike turned his eyes that way—and his whole head turned, too. His neck was no longer locked into immobility. Over there, just beyond where his bike lay, there was a man.

Mike looked at him, trying to pick out details in the gloom, but the light was still bad. At first Mike thought he was looking at a scarecrow, because the man was dressed in filthy rags whose tatters flapped in the breeze, but there was no post, no fence to support a scarecrow. And then the man took a step toward him. Such a strange step, and even in his semidaze Mike thought it was odd. A stiff and staggering step, more like the Tin Man from Oz than the Scarecrow. That thought flitted through his mind and Mike almost smiled at the absurdity of it. Another step, managed with equal awkwardness, as if the man's knees were inflexible or unused to walking.

The dawn was filling in the world with colors, defining shapes, painting the day, and as he lay there Mike could see more of the man. He frowned. The stranger was truly a raggedy man, his clothes nothing but mismatched castoffs. A soiled pair of patched work pants, two different shoes—a sneaker and a woman's low-heeled pump—a checked shirt that was torn in a dozen places. Heavy cotton work gloves. And some kind of mask, but it was still too dark to make out what it was. It was dark and shiny and the material it was made from rippled in the wind.

Daylight swelled by another degree and though the cloud cover kept any rays from touching the man, the quality of light increased but still the mask made no sense to Mike. There were no holes for eyes. It was just a swirling complexity of wrinkles that writhed and twisted with the steady breeze. The man took another jerky step forward. Mike had no urge, no desire to ask for help. The dying don't need help to die, and if this guy wanted to be a witness, then that was on him. Mike felt removed from thoughts of help and safety, even of right and wrong.

He just wanted to die and he didn't care if anyone—especially a raggedy man—stood by and watched. Another step and now the man was no more than twenty feet away. Two more steps, another, another. Ten feet now and the rosy glow of the dawn washed him in crimson from his shoes to his face.

To his . . . face? Suddenly terror struck Mike like a fist over the heart. In a single moment all of his detachment fractured and fell away. His whole body convulsed, arching belly-up to the sky like a heart attack patient getting the paddles. Every wound, every splintered bone, every inch of torn flesh, every nerve ending screamed in desperate, howling agony and terror. The shriek burst from his throat in a spray of bloodstained spit. If someone had sprayed him with gasoline and tossed a match on him the pain could not have been more comprehensive or intense. His scream went on and on and on. Hordes of crows exploded from the trees and raced in panic across the sky above him, sweeping in vast circles above the field. The sparse green grass that patched the dirt around him withered into sickly yellow twists and curled in on themselves to die. In the soil beneath him the sleepy October worms swelled and burst as if boiled.

The scream ended. Mike sagged to the ground, limp and exhausted. His eyes—more red than blue now—cast wildly about to find the Raggedy Man.

He was there. Right there, right next to him, looming over, looking down. Mike could see that face, that mask—which was not a mask at all, not some wrinkled dark cloth rippling in the breeze. It was his face that rippled, that . . . *writhed*. There were no eyeholes because there were no eyes—not human eyes; no mouth either—not a human mouth. What there was, what composed the man's entire face, was a black, roiling, chitinous swarm of bristling insects. Roaches and beetles. Slugs, maggots, centipedes. Flies and termites. In the gaps between his gloves and his sleeves the exposed arm was the same—every foul creature of the shadows wriggling together to form a wrist. Between shoes and cuffs, the same. Wasps and earwigs, lice and locusts.

"No!" After the scream Mike's voice was a frayed whisper. Overhead the crows circled and circled in terrible silence.

The Raggedy Man raised his left hand as if to reach for Mike. It was not a threatening movement, but everything about it was dark with *wrongness*. Mike screamed again, weakly this time, a croak in a torn throat. "Help me!"

Instantly the sky around him was filled with whispery noise as the flocks of circling crows hurtled down toward him. The leading rank of night birds struck with such force that several of the birds died, their necks snapped on impact, but the sheer mass of them surged forward . . . not at Mike, but at the Raggedy Man. The birds slammed into him and drove him backward, the beaks of the birds slashing and stabbing at the old clothes, their cries tearing the air. The Raggedy Man staggered and for just a moment he seemed to catch his footing, to hold his ground, but the night birds hit him in wave after implacable wave, and then the Raggedy Man *exploded,* losing whatever power it had to retain the man shape, and the hundreds of thousands of insects that made up its hand, its arm, its shoulder, burst apart into their separate selves and showered Mike, landing on his chest, his face, crawling on him, crawling into his nose and mouth and . . .

FUGUE.

Mike's mind burned out like a cinder.

Above him the clouds overhead paled from rose red to gray as the dawn took hold on the day. The crows swarmed over Mike, beaks darting here and there, snatching at the bugs, tearing through carapace and shell in a savage frenzy of killing and eating. They fed and fed and fed. As the sun rose it bored a single hole through the clouds and punched a hard beam of cold yellow light down onto the field. Then another, and another until the morning sky stretched into a blue forever that was clean and hard.

Soon a stillness settled over the place where Mike lay, silent and unmoving. Sunlight sparkled on the dewy tips of the dying grass and turned the morning mist to a ghostly blue-white opacity. The light gleamed on the blue tubing of the bicycle lying by the side of the road. It caressed the freckled cheek of the boy who lay sprawled among the dry autumn leaves. And it glittered on the edges of the broken shells and cracked antennae of ten thousand insects whose corpses lay scattered across fifty yards in all directions from where the boy lay. In the center of this slaughter, the ground around the boy was completely empty except for the tatters of some old torn clothing as all the birds flew away into the trees.

All but one, a single crow that stood on the boy's sternum.

Everything was as still as death. There was not the slightest tremble under the bird's feet. The crow tilted its head, angling one black-within-black eye to stare at the boy's slack face. The smell of blood was everywhere. The music rode the breeze, a little stronger now, the blues melody plaintive. The mist retreated all the way to the road.

The boy took a breath, and the crow cawed quietly.

A full minute passed. The boy took another breath. Then another. The crow hopped down from his chest and walked away, angling to keep an eye on the boy.

FUGUE.

From a blackened cinder Mike's mind coalesced into living awareness once again.

Minutes floated past on the breeze and gradually sense returned to him along with awareness of his body. He no longer felt helpless and wrecked. It took a while and it took a hell of a lot of effort, but Mike gradually sat up. He shook his head like a drunk, lips slack and rubbery, nose running, eyes going in and out of focus as he stared at the withered grass between his knees. Awareness came back with slow reluctance. His body hurt in a dozen places, his head worst of all. Mike probed his scalp, found lumps. He explored his mouth with his tongue and tasted old blood, but found no cuts. Memory was sluggish and it hurt to try and pull it out of the junk closet of his mind. He looked around, saw that he was in a field, saw his bike lying nearby. He vaguely remembered racing down the road, remembered hitting something in the dark and then falling. But after that . . . nothing.

He had no idea what time it was. It looked like morning, but that was ridiculous. His last clear memory was biking toward the hospital to visit Val, but . . . had he gotten there? Mike wasn't sure. Everything was weird, and his head felt like it had been ransacked, all the drawers pulled out and dumped, everything just thrown onto the floor.

He plucked at his shirt, saw that it was crusted with dried blood, but he couldn't find any cuts on his body. Some bruises, sure, but not even a scrape on his arms or legs or body. Could that much blood have come from a nosebleed? He doubted it, but when he touched his nose it felt eggshell fragile and sore. Some blood caked around the nostrils, though not as much as he expected to find. More blood on his chin and throat. He flexed his hands, pressed his fingers against bones and ribs. There was pain just about everywhere, but nothing seemed broken. Except maybe his head, because that pounded like a psychopath doing a drum solo.

Mike climbed carefully to his feet, swaying a bit, watching the field tilt and whirl like a carnival ride; but after a moment it slowed, steadied, stopped. There was a rustle behind him and he turned to see a crow standing in the grass a dozen feet away. Without knowing why Mike smiled at it. The crow cawed softly. Mike thought he heard music on the breeze, but ignored it. He always heard music. He figured it was just part of being crazy.

On unsteady feet, Mike trudged over to his bike, picked it up, spun the wheels to make sure they were true, and walked it back to the road. He stood there for a moment, looking up and down A-32. There were no cars this early and in the dips and hollows of the road there was the faintness of a dwindling fog. He swung one leg over, wincing with the effort, then turned and looked back to the field. He felt—on some level *knew*—that he should be more worried about all this than he was, but he couldn't make himself care about it. His head hurt too much. The strangeness of it all made it hard to think.

"Vic will kill me," he said, and the crow cawed again.

Vic's house rules didn't allow him to be late, let alone out all night, but that wasn't something he could control. It would mean a beating, but that was okay. He'd had plenty of beatings; he could handle another. He pushed off and began his slow, creaking way back to town. With each mile it became less and less important to try and remember what happened.

(5)

The Bone Man sat on the wooden rail of the farm fence and watched Mike ride by. He wasn't sure if the boy was able to see him now. The boy probably could, the Bone Man considered, because from what little he knew of ghosts from his days down in the superstitious South the dying were supposed to be able to see the dead. Death was a window, his aunt had told him. He was pretty sure Val Guthrie had seen him that night in the rain, but not since; maybe she'd had one foot on the ghost road and then stepped off. He knew for certain Henry Guthrie had as he lay dying in the rain.

The kid looked bad as he biked by. Sick and thin, bloody and gaunt. He looked mostly dead now, but he never even turned his head toward the Bone Man, so the point was moot.

The last crow came over and perched on the rail next to him, and the Bone Man stared into its black eye for a long time. "I wish you could talk, little brother," the Bone Man said. "I'll bet you know a lot more about this than I do."

The bird opened its mouth and gave a nearly silent caw, almost of agreement.

"Least now I can know whose side you're on." He smiled. "It ain't no good to be alone all the time."

The bird rustled its wings. They both turned to look down the road.

The Bone Man knew full well that Griswold had not sent the Raggedy Man to hurt Mike—that would have been suicidal—but he wasn't sure why it was sent at all. Maybe some kind of test, an attempt to gauge how strong Mike was. Well, he mused, I wonder what he'll make of what just happened. "Bet you didn't expect that to happen, did you?" he asked the wind, hoping Griswold could hear him. Now Griswold really had something to think about.

So, he realized, did the Bone Man himself, because what he just saw didn't fit into anything he knew about what a *dhampyr* was or could do. Maybe *dhampyr* wasn't even the right word to use anymore. Maybe there just wasn't a word to describe what Mike Sweeney was becoming.

That thought sat uneasily on him as he watched the figure vanish into the distance. A *dhampyr* was something he understood, and a *dhampyr* had hope built into it, but if Mike was becoming something *else*, then maybe the last little of bit of hope Pine Deep had was going to leak down the drain. Maybe there was nothing standing between the Red Wave and Pine Deep. Beside him the bird cawed again; the Bone Man looked at him and frowned. Or . . . maybe there was.

Chapter 18

Mike got home at nine-thirty and he pedaled around back to see if Vic's truck was there. It wasn't, but he did not know if that was good news or bad. He chained his bike to the side-yard fence and went inside. The house was quiet and still. It had an empty quality. He went into the kitchen, took the orange juice out and drank half of it from the carton, put it back. As he turned to go he heard a sound. He stopped, looking at the door to the basement. Mike had never been down there; it was Vic's domain and more than once Vic had promised the world's worst beating if Mike so much as thought about going down there. Mike never thought about it. Pissing off Vic was not a hobby.

But there was that sound. Like a muffled grunt. Not of pain or effort. Just a human sound, like someone might make walking into a chair. A kind of oomph. Then nothing.

He moved closer to the door and listened. Vic's truck wasn't out back, and he was sure Vic was not home. Vic never lent his truck to anyone, either. Mike pressed an ear to the wood and as he did so the door shifted. He stepped back like he'd been burned and looked at it. The door was closed, but it wasn't locked and now that he was paying attention to it he could see that the lock was broken. There were splinters of wood sticking out—small ones, but telltale. More splinters littered the floor. The door was closed, but there was no lock to hold it firm, so it had swung out on its hinges maybe a half inch, and Mike's leaning against it had made it thump back against the frame.

Mike quickly backed away, not liking this at all. Either this was some new trick Vic was playing, a trap to make him break the house rule about going downstairs, or else someone had busted that door. Mom? Would she have done that? *Could* she have done it? Even had she been sober Mike doubted it, and Mom was never sober. Besides, she'd told him yesterday that she would be in Doylestown all day today, something about a craft show that started early.

Then what was left? A burglar?

He almost smiled at the thought. Here in Pine Deep, after all that had happened, a simple breaking and entering seemed comical. The smile almost took root on his face, but didn't. This was Pine Deep, after all, and nothing was ever that simple. Certainly not something like this.

A tingling sensation began behind his eyes. It was like the feeling he had when one of his headaches was coming on and a hairy ball of sick dread began forming in his throat.

No, this was bad. Whatever it was, whatever it would turn out to be, this was bad.

Without making a sound Mike backed away, backed out of the kitchen. When he was in the hallway he spun and sprinted for the stairs, taking them two at a time. He raced to his room, yanked open a drawer, and pulled out clean underwear, a sweat-shirt, jeans, and socks and stuffed them into a nylon gym bag. He opened his window and dropped the bag down into the side yard, closed the window quietly, and then went into the bathroom. He stuffed a deodorant stick into one pocket and his toothbrush and toothpaste into another. Then he crept back down the stairs, all the time listening for sounds from the basement.

For an agonizing moment he wondered if maybe that was his mom down there, that maybe she hadn't gone to Doylestown. That maybe whoever this was down there had come in before she left and . . .

No. His instincts—perhaps his fears—said no to that. Mike was pretty good about reading the energy at his own house. He knew when Vic was home, knew when his mother was home. Always. None of what he sensed at home felt like Mom's energy. Everything just felt . . . *wrong*.

Mike opened the front door very quietly, slipped outside, and then raced to grab his gym bag and his bike. He'd stop on the way to school and pull on his sweatshirt to hide the blood, then clean up in the boy's bathroom. If anyone asked, he would say he fell off his bike on the way to school and had a bloody nose. He'd change, drift into homeroom, and pretend this had never happened. Let Vic sort it out. That sounded good, sounded like a plan, even though he knew it was all total bullshit. He raced away into the morning.

(2)

Ruger heard the kid moving around upstairs. He could smell blood on the kid's clothes and it made him smile. Lois heard him, too. When Mike was upstairs, while Ruger was paused in an attitude of listening, face turned toward the ceiling, Lois had tried to make her move.

She drove her elbow back and into his stomach as hard as she could, slamming it into him with a terrible and desperate fury, and lunged forward, trying to break free of his arms, kicking away from the lounge chair. She was fast, she was vicious, and she wanted to hurt him as much as she wanted to try and warn Mike. She almost made it, but Ruger was much, much faster, and the blow had only surprised him. It hadn't hurt him at all. As she lunged forward he snaked out a hand and caught her by the wrist, locking his icy white fingers so hard that she was snapped back and spun around and came crashing back down on top of him. Air whooshed out of her as she collapsed down, and before she could scream Ruger clamped a hand over her mouth, bending forward fast and close.

"Make a single sound, you silly bitch, and I'll kill your boy." His voice was a reptilian whisper that froze her heart. His mouth was smiling, but his eyes told her the truth of his threat. Black eyes with no whites, no color other than red shadows. "I'll use him worse than I used you, sweetheart, and I'll make you watch."

Lois felt the world tightening around her like a noose. "No . . ." she whispered. Just a faintness of a sound. "God, no."

Ruger pulled her closer and ran his cold tongue up her throat and over her chin. There was blood on her face and he licked it off. "Smart move, sweet piece."

Lois closed her eyes. They were naked, entwined in an ugly way on the lounger. She had blood on her face and throat and breasts. Blood streaked her thighs and buttocks. Her pale skin was splotched with the livid outlines of his open hand. Her nipples were torn and there were bite marks on her hips and stomach. Ruger had not taken much, just a taste here and there, drawing it out, making it last, loving the terror he tasted on her skin and the disgust he saw in her eyes.

The rape was bad enough, but Lois lived with Vic and he had never wanted anything she gave willingly. He had always taken it, enjoying the fight, the win. Hard and vicious use had become her life, and mostly the gin could blunt it. But Ruger was not Vic. By contrast Vic was almost kind. He was cruel and brutal, but he was a man.

What Ruger did . . . what he forced her to do . . . was beyond anything Vic *could* do to her. The thought of Ruger turning those appetites on Mike was too horrible to even think about, and Lois's soul collapsed in on itself. "No," she kept saying, over and over again, a mantra against Ruger's hungers. She lay still and they listened to Mike's footsteps upstairs and then heard the front door. Above them the house settled into empty stillness.

Ruger pushed Lois off him and she landed hard on palms and knees as he rose to stand over her. His skin was so white it was almost translucent and he stood above her, naked, indomitable, relentless.

"Hey," he said, "want to learn a new game?" But since she didn't answer he showed her anyway. Now that the house was empty it didn't matter that she screamed. And screamed.

(3)

Vic stood in the doorway to the cellar and watched Ruger stand up and, without cleaning any of the blood from his skin, begin slowly pulling on his clothes. All the while Ruger smiled. Ruger picked up Lois's robe and tossed it over her, the bulk of it covering her face and chest, leaving the rest of her exposed to Vic's stare.

The gun in Vic's hand hung there, a dead and forgotten weight at the end of his arm, barrel pointing at the floor. Vic could have killed Ruger right then, shot him point-blank. The special loads in that gun would have snuffed Ruger out like a candle, yet the gun just hung there as Ruger tucked his penis into his pants and zipped up the fly. He took his time about it, too, staring at Vic, smiling with bloody lips.

It wasn't Ruger's smile that hurt Vic so deeply. It wasn't even that Ruger had broken his house rules, had taken what belonged to him. Had taken his *wife*. It wasn't that as much as it was the steady, slow, very soft laughter that echoed in his brain. *His* laughter. Not Ruger's. *His*.

"Penance is a bitch," Ruger said as he buttoned his shirt. He started to turn away and then paused, looking down at Lois. Then, glancing up at Vic as he did so Ruger sucked up a mouthful of bloody phlegm and spit on Lois.

And still Vic did not, could not, lift that gun.

"It's a new world, pal," Ruger whispered with his graveyard voice, "and it must be a real kick in the nuts—especially after all these years and all you've done—to realize that you're on the wrong end of the food chain." Ruger tucked in his shirttails, then licked his fingers and used them to smooth back the hair from his widow's peak.

"Griswold is my god," he said, and turned away.

Chapter 19

Mike got to school early and managed to slip into the bathroom and clean himself up without being noticed. He drifted through the rest of the day in a kind of haze and at lunch sat with his friend Brandon and talked about comics. Mike could do that on autopilot. When Brandon shifted onto last night's episode of *Heroes*, Mike just listened and nodded whenever he thought he should. He hadn't seen the show last night and could not for the life of him remember what he had done. He knew that not knowing should bother him more than it did, but somehow he could not work up the energy to care.

One thing he did care about, one thing that wasn't blunted by the apathetic glaze that seemed to be coated over everything in his mind, was his mom. He hadn't liked the sound he heard in the cellar. He hadn't liked that one bit, and even though he knew that she was supposed to be out—and that she never went down into Vic's cellar willingly—that knowledge did little to ease that gnawing doubt.

"I gotta make a call," he said abruptly, standing. Brandon, caught in midsentence, just stared at him. "I'll be right back."

Mike turned and headed to the far side of the cafeteria where the pay phones were. No one much used them—everyone but Mike had a cell phone. He fitted some quarters into the slot and punched his home number. The phone rang six times and went straight to the answering machine. Mike slapped the receiver down, fed in more quarters, and dialed again. Maybe she just hadn't gotten to the phone in time.

"C'mon, Mom," he breathed, "pick up. . . ."

Again the machine picked up. He hung up and leaned against the wall, staring across the cafeteria into nothingness.

After school he sped home on his bike, but as he was rounding the corner on his street he saw Vic walk through the side yard and into the front of the house. He was carrying a toolbox in one hand and under his other arm he had folded shutters. Mike slowed to a stop behind a parked SUV and watched.

Vic had a ladder against the front of the house and Mike saw that he'd already installed heavy slatted shutters on the porch windows and one of the upstairs master bedroom windows. He set the toolbox down and fished in it for a hammer, then climbed the ladder one-handed, the shutters still under his arm.

Vic was a very thorough craftsman. Mike knew that much about him, and he never did anything around the house that was slipshod. When he installed shelves for his DVD collection— mostly World War II movies and westerns—everything was precisely measured, perfectly cut, and as straight as an arrow. When something broke down, like the time the lawn mower crapped out, Vic worked on it with meticulous care and ever since the machine had never so much as sputtered.

What Mike was seeing now, however, was a completely different Vic Wingate. Standing on the ladder Vic pounded nails with sloppy force, brutalizing the wood around the nailheads. Mike looked at each shutter and not one of them hung completely straight. Mike could have done better himself and he barely knew which end of a hammer to hold. Vic's love of tools had engendered in Mike a dislike of them.

He stood there, watching in perplexed concern, as Vic clumsied the shutters up and battered them into place. He had no idea what to make of it.

When Vic finished, he just pulled the ladder down and let it fall onto the front lawn. Snatching up his toolbox, he stomped up the steps and jerked open the front door. "There! You happy now, you stupid bitch?"

Those words rolled all the way down the street to where Mike hid. When Vic slammed the door the echo ricocheted off every house front on the block.

Mike picked his bike up and turned it around and headed back toward Corn Hill and the Crow's Nest. As he rode away Vic's vicious words pounded in his head. Vic always called his mom horrible names, but there was something worse about this. It felt worse somehow; it felt *meaner*, if that was even possible for Vic. As he pedaled away he could feel a sinking dread for his mother's safety forming in the pit of his stomach; but at the same time he felt a white-hot scalding rage building in his hands and behind his eyes.

If he, or anyone else, had seen his eyes at that moment they would have been terribly afraid. All of the blue was gone, as was most of the white. What was left was a mingled cloud of black, like a storm cloud, veined with bloody flashes of red.

(2)

"How are his vitals?" Weinstock asked as he entered Terry's room.

"Same," said the nurse. "No change since this morning." She recited the numbers. Nothing encouraging, but nothing discouraging. A gloomy status quo.

Weinstock went through a cursory examination, but there was nothing new to see, nothing to learn. Nothing to tell Sarah that would bring her out of the funk she'd been sliding into.

He made a note on Terry's chart. "Keep me posted."

He and the nurse left and Terry's room settled back into stillness.

Except for the tiny figure who stepped out of the shadows in the corner and walked up to the side of Terry's bed. Mandy's eyes were wet and her torn throat trembled with silent sobs.

She rose onto her toes and stretched to kiss Terry on the cheek.

There was a strangled little sound in her brother's throat and he turned his head slowly from side to side—less a negating motion than one of an animal struggling to pull free from a leash. Mandy stepped back, looking scared.

"Fight it, Terry!" she said, but her voice was silent and Terry was deep, deep down in the dark of his mind where all he could hear was the roar of the beast. Mandy put her tiny bloodstained hands to her mouth and stood there, watching moment by moment as Terry lost his fight.

(3)

Midmorning Sarah Wolfe came by to pick up Val. They wanted some time with each other and they both had a lot of things to handle in the aftermath of Little Halloween. Since Mark and Connie were not going to be buried right away, Val had to arrange a memorial service. Mark was well liked in the community and had been an influential businessman. There would be a lot of people who would want to pay their respects. Setting that up was going to take a lot of detail work, but Crow knew that detail work kept Val steady, so he kissed her good-bye, hugged Sarah, walked them to Sarah's big Humvee Alpha, and watched as they headed into the stream of traffic.

The Crow's Nest was slow that morning, which was good because Crow had a million things to do to stay on top of the Festival preparations. He called all of the hotels to make sure that the arrangements for the visiting celebrities were in place; then called half a dozen airports to check on bookings. He spent some time on the phone with BK, working through the details for the security measures he wanted to have in place for Halloween. BK had managed to round up a solid crew of bouncers, off-duty cops, and martial arts guys to work the gig and the ticket was going to cost the township—and the Wolfe family—a bundle. Crow didn't sweat that . . . any additional disasters would cost everyone more.

He used Terry's laptop to log into his friend's e-mail and spent two hours sorting through the mass that had piled up. There were so many people needing to be reassured that things would go well even with Terry in the hospital, and Crow gave what assurances he could, and he lied a little here and there.

He called John West, an amusement park consultant and general fix-it man, and asked him to spend the next few days going over every inch of the Hayride and the Haunted House. West, who used to oversee the Cyclone roller coaster up in Coney Island and who now ran a general consulting firm in Lahaska, was pleased to take the job. They'd worked together a number of times at the Hayride and where Crow was able to conceptualize the spooky stuff, West was able to make it work.

"We can't afford so much as a tourist getting a splinter this season, John," Crow said.

"Okay, buddy, I hear you. Leave it to me." And Crow was content to do just that.

By the time Crow finished with all of the Festival matters, it was midafternoon and he was waiting on Mike. Before things went to hell on Little Halloween, Crow had been teaching Mike some jujutsu. Not the deeper secrets or the more esoteric aspects of the art—just the hard-core take-no-prisoners hand-to-hand stuff. Mike had been reluctant to study, largely because it made him confront, however obliquely, the fact that Vic was abusing him. Crow knew about it, but Mike would not be drawn into an open discussion on the subject. He did, however, start training, and Crow was impressed with his progress. The kid had a real talent for it, and he picked up the moves extremely quickly, something Crow attributed to genuine motivation. He looked at the wall clock. Mike was supposed to come in early today so they could pick up where they left off, but the kid was more than fifteen minutes late.

A knot of middle-school kids came in to buy Halloween costumes and by the time Crow had helped them make their judicious selections Mike was there. He wandered into the store as silent as a ghost, looking pale and worn.

"You okay, young Jedi?" Crow asked as the kids left.

Mike shrugged. "Sorry I'm late."

When Mike was like this Crow knew that something bad had happened at home. There were no visible bruises on Mike's face, though, and he didn't wince as he walked over and dumped his backpack behind the counter. Crow looked at the clock. "You up for a little backyard Fight Club?" he asked, expecting Mike to say no.

But Mike surprised him. Straightening from behind the counter, Mike gave him a long, steely look. "Yeah," he said. "Yeah, I could really use that."

Crow closed the shop for an hour and they went out through his apartment into the yard. Crow took him through some warm-ups and stretches, and Mike followed along, silent and intense. He did his bends and reaches, his twists and reps, matching Crow and keeping up without effort.

Either I'm getting old or he's getting better, Crow thought as they did side-by-side push-ups. The boy's body went up and down, straight as a board, with no more than a small grunt of effort with each push away from the ground.

"Let's start with some evasions," Crow said as they got to their feet. "I'll throw some punches and kicks and you just evade them. Block only if you can't slip the shot, okay?"

Mike nodded and settled into the defensive crouch Crow had shown him: weight on the balls of the feet and evenly distributed, knees slightly bent, the whole body springy, hands raised but loose. Crow began prowling a slow circle around him, watching as the boy turned to keep his body angled away to protect belly, throat, and groin. Crow faked a punch and Mike twitched his head back—but it wasn't the frightened-rabbit flinch Mike typically did when he was surprised; this was a classic boxing slip. That was a good sign.

He threw a looping right at about half speed and Mike just

stepped back away from it as if he'd seen it coming yesterday. *Okay, fair enough*, Crow thought and dialed it up a bit. He added more speed to his punches and kept the arcs and lines of each blow shorter, still deliberately leading with his shoulder to give Mike a chance, but doing that less and less as Mike slipped and bobbed away or under each hit. Crow faked a jab-overhand right combination and then pivoted to throw a roundhouse kick that missed Mike's hip by an inch as the boy spun away. Without putting his leg down Crow shuffled sideways on one foot and fired three more roundkicks, chasing Mike across the yard. Only the last one tagged him, and even then Mike blocked most of it with his elbow.

Crow grinned at Mike and gave him a thumbs-up for that, but Mike's face was a mask. There was sweat on his face and in the glare of the late afternoon sunlight the kid's eyes looked funny. Almost red.

They moved like that for five more minutes and then Crow stepped back, palms up and out. Out of nearly a hundred attempted kicks and punches he tapped Mike only eight times. Even though Crow was not going at full speed or power it was exceptional, and Crow said so.

Mike just made a face and shook his head. "That means you hit me eight times. It's not the ones you evade, it's the ones you don't that matter."

"What jackass told you that?"

"You did, the first day we worked out."

"You shouldn't listen to strangers, Mike." That got a tiny flicker of an artificial smile. "Okay," Crow said, turning to get some padded mitts from his equipment bag. "Let's see how you like hitting back." He fitted on two gloves that had thick flat foam pads covered in black leather. "I'll move around, changing the position and angle of the targets. You hit and kick them as many times as you can. Don't worry about power—concentrate on speed—and don't let up, even if I back off. When you're winning a fight you press the attack until your opponent is down. Fighters who get a good one in and then step back like good sports to give their opponents a chance to collect himself deserve to lose the fight."

"No mercy," Mike said under his breath.

"Well . . . I'm not sure I'd go as far as that. Let's just call it the will to win."

"Whatever." Mike raised his hands and began moving forward before Crow even had his pads up.

"Whenever you're—"

Mike's fists slammed into the pads before he could finish, and even through the thick pad Crow could feel the brutal power of the blows. Hard. Much too hard for the weight and muscle Mike carried. As they moved Crow watched the boy's hips and legs and feet, and he saw that on each punch he was shifting his weight and torquing his hips to put body weight behind each blow, and the speed gave each shot more foot-pounds of impact. It was right, it was perfect; and Crow was not really sure he had ever shown Mike how to do that.

Mike hit without a sound except for his fists and palms and elbows slamming into the targets. His face was bright with exertion and sweat, and all the while his upper lip was curled back away from his teeth in a feral snarl of hate.

Jesus Christ, Crow thought, *this kid is in hell.*

(4)

It became a busy night in the store and Crow never found a good moment to talk to Mike, and as the evening wore on the boy seemed more and more like his old affable and comfortably geeky self. Crow let it go.

At closing, Crow and Mike parted with a few jokes and with that it felt easier, more like normal. Mike rode his bike away through the tourist traffic as Crow locked up and shut off the lights. Val tapped on the door just as Crow was heading back to his apartment and he let her in. They kissed in the doorway and then walked hand in hand back to the apartment.

"How was your day?

"We have the memorial all set for Friday night. The Rotary wanted to host it, so we'll be using their hall, and the college asked if they could cater it."

"Nice of them."

"Mark had a lot of friends," Val said. "Everyone wants to make a gesture."

"How are you with all of this?"

Val shrugged. "Better than I thought I'd be. I stuffed my purse with tissues thinking it was going to be that kind of a day, but I didn't use a single one. Now, Sarah, on the other hand . . . she pretty much cleaned me out."

"Yeah, she looked pretty rocky."

Val sank down on the couch. "She's keeping it together, but only just. No change at all with Terry."

"I know, I spoke to Saul a couple of times today."

They sat with those thoughts for a while. Val broke the silence by saying, "Twelve days."

He looked at her. "What?"

"Newton's folklorist friend will be here on the twenty-ninth. Then we can find out what we have to do to put Mark to rest. The thought of him just lying there in that drawer . . ." She shivered.

"I know, but we'll have to be pretty careful with how we ask her. Just 'cause she's a folklore professor doesn't mean she believes any of this."

Val nodded. "We'll be careful, but I intend to find out one way or another."

"I'll look through my books again tonight when Newt gets here. Maybe there's something I missed."

"You looked, honey. Newton looked. I looked, too. It's not there. Your stuff, good as it is, is mostly the pop-culture version of folklore. We need to go a lot deeper than that."

The doorbell rang. "That's him."

Crow let Newton in. The little reporter, looking seedier and more haggard than ever, slumped down into a chair and set a bag down between his sneakered feet. The contents of the bag clinked. Crow knew that sound and came to point like a bird-dog.

Val beat him to the punch. "Newt . . . you do know Crow doesn't drink."

Newton gave her a bleary stare that for once was neither deferential nor accommodating. "I do," he said, and reached down into the bag and brought out a longneck bottle of Hop Devil, twisted off the cap, and drank about half of it down. "And don't bother getting mad at me . . . I didn't bring it to share." True to his word, he did not offer one to her.

Val opened her mouth to say something, but Crow touched her arm and shook his head.

"We were just talking about Dr. Corbiel," Crow said. "And Mark."

The bottle paused halfway to Newton's mouth, hovered there for a moment, and then he took another long swig. "I talked with her about that today. No—don't look at me like that, I'm not hideously stupid. I told her I was researching a chapter for my book and wanted to know about how vam . . . how these things happen. I told her about what I knew from movies and stuff and she pretty much dismissed all of it."

"What did she say?" asked Val.

Newton looked over the mouth of his bottle at her for a long moment. "She said that there were a lot of ways, but that if I wanted a definitive answer I'd have to know what kind of . . . *thing* . . . did the attack."

"Oh, Christ, Newton say the frigging word," Crow snapped. The smell of the beer was making his stomach churn and his mouth water.

Newton gave him an evil look. "Okay, she said we'd have to know what kind of vampire bit him." The room went quiet. Newton took another pull. "Jonatha said that in folklore different vampires have different methods of predation and different methods of, um . . . recruitment." He finished the first beer and took a second from the bag. "The thing in the movies where a vampire drinks someone's blood and then makes them drink theirs—that's a distortion. She said that most transformations don't even require a sharing of blood. Others require that the victim be willing to drink the vampire's blood. In a lot of them a person can be transformed by a bite, but even if they revive as a vampire they aren't evil unless they drink human blood, willingly or not. Apparently there are blood rituals to force a reanimated person to become a vampire. But in some cases there's no bite at all."

"What do you mean?" Val asked.

"In some cultures a person isn't turned into a vampire by other vampires. It's based on a bunch of other stuff. Dying unrepentant is a big one, dying by violence is another. Being born on certain days of the year. Holy days, I think, but she was going pretty fast and I missed some stuff. It's a wonder we're not assdeep in vampires."

"Yes," Val said, her eyes thoughtful.

"So, bottom line is that we don't know which kind of vampire Boyd was. If we did, then the folklore from that country would tell us what we need to know."

"I don't think it's that simple," Crow said. "From what I read . . . and I'm admitting I'm no scholar here, but the problem is more complex than that because we don't know how many of the folkloric vampires were even real. All we know about is Ruger and Boyd, Cowan and Castle, and even there we don't know that much."

Val got up and crossed to where Newton sat in the overstuffed chair. "Beer," she said and held out her hand. He obeyed without a hesitation and even twisted off the cap for her.

"Whoa!" Crow said. He patted his stomach. "I think the phrase is 'eating for two,' not 'drinking for two.'"

Val shot him a thoroughly vile look and thrust the beer back into Newton's hand. "You shouldn't have brought that," she snapped.

Newton shrugged. "I shouldn't have moved to Black Marsh and shouldn't have met you two. Life's funny sometimes." He set one bottle down on the side table and sipped from the other.

Standing, arms folded under her breasts, face set, Val said, "If we don't know what kind of vampire Boyd was . . . and if we can't ever know because he was burned so badly, then we have to find some way of testing Connie and Mark."

"Jesus Christ," Crow said, and Newton blanched.

(5)

Mike was careful putting the key in the front door lock, was careful opening the door, was careful stepping into the hall. He didn't want to make any sound, didn't want to do any of the thousand things that could set Vic off. The hall was all in somber brown tones, barely lit by the baseboard night-light near the coatrack. Ahead of him the stairs drifted up into shadows; to his right a doorway opened to the hall to the kitchen and, closer, into the big living room. Both rooms were dark. No TV sounds, no radio. The framed photos on the wall—people from his mom's family that Mike had never met—brooded behind their glass windows.

He moved toward the stairs, had a foot raised to step, but something made him stop. He listened to the house, then turned toward the doorway to the darkened living room. *Was that a sound?*

"Mom . . . ?"

Something moved in the shadows, shifting on the couch. He took a step toward the doorway, and peered through the gloom. He squeezed his eyes shut for a second to try and kick in his night vision and it worked enough so that he could now see that the living room shadows ranged from medium black by the windows to a softer golden brown by the doorway. As his eyes became accustomed to the darkness Mike could now see his mother's figure sitting on the end of the couch, shoulders hunched forward, head bent low.

"Mom, are you okay?"

Mike took a step into the living room, but jerked to a stop. The air in there was so thick it was as if the shadows were made of some viscous matter that choked and pushed against him. His muscles twitched as if they had a will of their own and wanted to flee, but Mike forced himself to stay there, kept his eyes locked on the silhouetted form of his mother. What the hell had happened here? What had Vic done to her?

"Mom . . . what's going on?"

Her head turn slightly. "M . . . Mike?"

"Yeah, Mom. Are you all right? Are you sick?" He stood behind the couch, not ten feet from her, still too conditioned to go any further into the room. Another of Vic's rules.

"Mike?"

"Why are you sitting here in the dark, Mom?" He took a determined step forward through the resistant gloom. "Look, let me turn on the light . . ."

"NO!" she shrieked as she recoiled from him. "Just leave me be."

"Come on, Mom, what's going on?"

She huddled into herself, turning away from him so that he couldn't even see the silhouette of her face. "You shouldn't be in here, Mike, you know Vic doesn't like you to be in the living room."

"Mom, if you're sick or . . . hurt . . . then we need to get some help—"

She made a sound and it took Mike a moment to realize that she had laughed. A short, bitter bark of a laugh. "I think we can all agree it's a little late for that," she said in a faux light tone that was ghastly to hear.

"Mom?"

"I'm okay. Just leave me alone, Mike. Just go to your room. Do your homework."

Mike stood there, uncertain. "Well . . . can I fix you something? Are you hungry?"

She turned farther away from him. He thought he heard her say "Yes," but he just as easily could have imagined it.

"How about some tea? You want me to make you a cup of tea?"

"I think I heard her say go to your room," Vic said from behind him.

Mike cried out and jumped as he turned. Vic stood there in the kitchen hallway, arms folded, leaning one shoulder against the wall. He was wearing a tank top and jeans and his arms and chest were cut with wiry muscle.

The moment hung in space and Mike waited for the first blow.

"Now," Vic said. His voice never rose above a conversational tone.

Mike half turned. "Mom . . . ?"

"Do as you're told, Mike," she said. "Everything's fine."

Mike turned back to Vic, who was not looking at him; instead Vic was staring into the living room at the figure hunched over in the dark.

"Go on," Vic said and still there was no heat, no edge to his voice.

Defeated by confusion, Mike nodded and backed away, then turned and ran up the stairs. In his room he crouched by his bedroom door, listening through a crack for any sound of yelling, of hitting, of a fight resumed. But everything downstairs was silent.

After twenty minutes Mike closed his door.

Chapter 20

Two days before Halloween

Newton sat for over an hour on the hard bench at the Warminster train station, chewing butter-rum Life Savers and drumming his fingers. A paperback book on vampire folklore was open on his lap, but he was too jittery to read. Commuters looked at him with his rumpled outdoor clothes and his razor-stubbled face and assumed he was homeless and gave him a wide berth. Newton was aware of their stares, but didn't care. In the three weeks since Little Halloween and the trip down into Dark Hollow he hadn't slept more than three hours at a stretch. Insomnia kept him up, too much coffee jangled his nerves, and when he did drift off the dreams kicked in. It was better to be sort of awake and wasted than to be asleep and at the mercy of his overactive imagination.

For the hundredth time he looked up at the wall clock above the ticket booth. Just shy of three o'clock. Jonatha Corbiel was nearly half an hour late. As each northbound train pulled into the station he stood up and searched the faces of the debarking passengers. Jonatha had given him only a vague and sketchy idea of what she looked like. "I'm tall, dark, and top-heavy." Amused and intrigued by her description, he conjured images of a leggy beauty with a deep-water tan and a grad-student's wire-framed glasses. Something like a brainy Jennifer Tilly or a scholarly Jennifer Connelly with olive skin. Maybe someone with the delicacy of a Maggie Gyllenhaal but with lots of wild curling black hair, dressed in the jeans, flannel lumberjack shirt, and Dr. Martens that comprised the dress code of the understipened Ph.D. candidate.

Thus self-conditioned, he was totally unprepared for the woman who suddenly loomed over him like a skyscraper. He had seen her get off the train, but had not even thought that she might be Jonatha despite the fact that she did, indeed, fit the description of tall, dark, and top-heavy. She smiled down at him and in a thick Louisiana accent said, "Let me guess. Willard Fowler Newton, or what's left of him?"

He stared up at her. "Uh . . . Jonatha . . . ?" he stammered, rising.

"In the flesh."

He goggled. Jonatha Corbiel was certainly tall, and at six-one she towered over Newton's five-seven. She was certainly dark: her skin was an exquisite and flawless blue-black, as richly dark as that of her Ashanti ancestors. And she was certainly top-heavy, with large breasts straining at the fabric of her faded gray U of P sweatshirt, distorting both letters. Standing at his full height his eyes came to just above her chest and try as he might, he could not help but stare.

"Might as well get it over with," Jonatha said with tolerant amusement.

"Er . . . what?"

"I have really big boobs. Take a good look and get it out of your system."

His eyes leapt immediately away from her chest and up to meet hers, which were filled with humor. He felt his skin ignite to a fiery red.

"Sorry," he mumbled. "You must hate that."

"I've been used to it since I was fourteen." She looked around. "Where are your friends?"

"We're meeting them at the diner. Couple blocks from here. My car's over there . . ." He gestured vaguely in the direction of the parking lot and reached for the small suitcase that stood next to her. She let him carry it, but opted to hold on to her laptop case, which she wore slung over one shoulder.

"Let's go, then." Her tone was on the affable side of matter of fact, and he turned and led the way to the lot, trying not to cut looks at her as they walked. Jonatha Corbiel was a knockout and

Newton had no experience at all around women of that level of beauty. None at all. In the thirty yards between the bench and his car he managed to bang his knee into the *Intelligencer* news box and trip down two of the three steps from the platform. When they were in the car, Newton drove slowly and badly and tried not to study her face in the rearview mirror. She wore seven earrings in her right ear and four in her left and silver rings flashed on each of her long fingers; she wore no makeup, and he thought she was the most beautiful woman he'd ever seen.

"I . . . really want to thank you for coming up here. I know it's a lot to ask."

She shrugged. "I've had it on my list to visit Pine Deep at some point." She smiled and held her hands out like she was reading a movie marquee. "Pine Deep, Pennsylvania: The Most Haunted Town in America. To a folklorist that's like the mothership calling me home."

"The charm wears off once you live here for a while."

"Maybe," she said. "I'm interested in this book you're writing on vampire and werewolf legends in Pennsylvania. I don't think anyone's ever done a folklore book as specific as that for this area."

"Seems to be a theme with us," Newton said dryly.

"In the last ten years I've done over fifty field investigations of reported vampirism in eleven states, and fourteen of were-wolfism. You'd be amazed how often these things are reported. All of them were duds, dead ends. It always turns out that the witnesses were untrustworthy, or the evidence faked or simply misidentified."

Instead of replying to that, he said, "We're here." He pulled into the lot of the Red Lion, a Greek diner on the corner of County Line Road and Route 611, and parked next to Val's two-year-old Dodge Viper. Inside, Gus, the owner, gave him a friendly grin.

"You looking for Val and Crow? They're in the back." He picked up two menus and ushered them into a nearly empty dining room. Newton made introductions and everyone shook hands.

"Thanks for agreeing to come up here," Val said after they'd ordered coffees.

"Well, Mr. Newton piqued my interest with his book. A mass-market trade paperback deal is something we academics only dream of, so being extensively quoted and footnoted in one is actually a good career move."

Newton's cover story was only partly a lie because Newton did plan to write a book, leveraging his celebrity as the reporter who broke the Karl Ruger/Cape May Killer story. Even his editor, Dick Hangood—who was not Newton's biggest fan— thought a book deal would be a no-brainer, but no actual deal yet existed.

Crow sipped his coffee. "Newt's been tapping me for info since he started on the project. Up till now I've been the local spook expert."

"I know," Jonatha said. "I Googled you and saw how many times you've been quoted."

"Then you'll know that most of it has been related to hauntings and such," he said, nodding.

"You've been quoted a few times in articles about werewolf legends, but just in passing. Do you have a folklore background?"

"Not really. I've read a lot of books and when you live in Pine Deep you tend to pick up on things."

Newton watched Jonatha as she studied Crow. She had shrewd eyes and didn't blink until after Crow finished talking. Newton recognized that as an interviewer's trick. She was looking for a "tell." If you blink you can miss small changes in the other person's expression, pupilary dilation, nostril flaring, thinning of the lips, angle of gaze—all of which could reveal a lot more about the subject than words or tone of voice. Newton had seen cops use the same tricks. So far Crow seemed to be doing pretty good.

Newton said, "I've been collecting some oral stories—things that have not yet been recorded and some weird things have come up that are outside of my own experience."

"Outside mine, too," Crow said.

The waitress came and they ordered. Cheese omelets for Crow

and Jonatha, a stack of French toast for Newton, and a bagel with whitefish for Val. Everyone had second coffees.

"If you don't mind me asking, Ms. Guthrie," Jonatha said, "what's your involvement in this?"

"Val, please, and I'm an interested observer."

"Crow and Val are engaged," Newton explained.

Jonatha stirred Splenda into her coffee. Her eyes lingered on Val's. "I read the last few week's worth of papers. Please accept my condolences."

"Thanks."

"I read that the mayor of the town is in a coma."

Val paused. "Yes."

"Unrelated events?"

"Yes."

"But on the same day as the attacks on your brother and his wife."

Val said nothing.

"Which is the same day you shot and killed that criminal, I believe?"

"Are you going somewhere with this, Dr. Corbiel?"

"Jonatha. No, I'm just trying to put the pieces together. You've all been through a terrible series of events. It's pretty amazing that you can find the peace of mind to work together on a pop-culture book."

The food arrived, which gave Newton, Crow, and Val time to share some brief eye contact. All of them were hustling to reevaluate Jonatha Corbiel. When the waitress left, Crow said, "Distraction is useful under stress, don't you think?"

"Distraction? That's a funny word to put on the pursuit of a book on vampires. I would have thought you'd have had enough of monsters by now. Human monsters, I mean, which I think we can all agree are much worse than anything we find in film, fiction, or folklore."

Val tore off a piece of bagel and put it in her mouth as she leaned back in her chair and assessed Jonatha. "Is this going to be a problem? Would you rather not help us out with this?"

Jonatha gave them all a big smile that was pure charm and

about a molecule deep. "Not at all. I'm rather interested to hear what you have to say."

They all digested that as they ate, but it was Jonatha who again broke the silence. "So . . . who wants to start?"

"Why don't I give it a shot?" Crow said.

She waggled a corner of toast. "Fire away."

"Okay, if you've been reading about Pine Deep, then you've read about the Massacre of 1976."

"The Black Harvest and the Reaper murders, yes."

"Um . . . right. Well, since the seventies there have been a lot of urban myths built up around what happened. Have you heard of the Bone Man?"

"Sure. That's the nickname given to Oren Morse, the migrant worker who was falsely accused of the crimes."

That threw Crow. "Falsely . . . ?"

"I have copies of the news stories, Crow," she said. "When Newton told me that the records from the Pine Deep newspapers had been destroyed in a fire I just probed a little deeper. Crimes of that kind are widely reported, and I have photocopies of the stories as reported by the Doylestown *Intelligencer* and the *Philadelphia Inquirer*. Some *Daily News* and *Bulletin* articles as well. Prior to his own murder, Morse was quoted in an *Intelligencer* article. It was just after your brother was murdered."

If she had tossed a hand grenade onto the table she could not have hit Crow harder.

"What?" Val and Newton both exclaimed.

"Your father was also quoted in four separate articles, Val," Jonatha said, "beginning with the murder of your uncle."

The three of them sat in stunned silence, gawking at her.

Jonatha finished her toast and cut a piece of omelet. "Mmm, good food here," she said as she chewed. The silence persisted and finally Jonatha put down her fork. "You didn't know your father was in the papers, did you?"

"No," Val said. Her face had gone pale.

Jonatha folded her hands in her lap and looked at them in turn. Some of her smile had faded. "Okay, let's cut the bullshit, shall we? Val, you and Crow lost family to the Reaper. According to the news stories you were friends with Morse, who worked for some time for your father. Your town's mayor, Terry Wolfe, lost a sister to the killer and was himself hospitalized. All through this there was a terrible blight . . . the Black Harvest in question. Now, thirty years later we have another blight, another series of brutal murders, and violence again hitting the same three families. Even some of the dimmer news affiliates have remarked on the coincidence, but they left it as coincidence." She pursed her lips. "I don't much believe in coincidence."

Crow opened his mouth to say something, but Jonatha held up a hand. "Let me finish. After Newton contacted me about this . . . about his *book*, I started reading up. I read everything I could find, including everything about Ruger and Boyd. That makes for some interesting reading." Her dark eyes glittered. "The news stories say that Crow and a Philly cop named Jerry Head both shot Ruger—and this is after Crow kicked the stuffing out of him—but the guy not only manages to flee the scene and elude a concentrated manhunt but then shows up a couple of days later and attacks again. Stronger than ever. How many bullets did it take to bring him down the second time?"

Instead of answering, Val just said, "Go on."

"Then Boyd attacks and kills two police officers on your farm. The news report—Mr. Newton's own news report—states that one of the officers emptied his gun, apparently during the struggle. All those shots without hitting the suspect? A week or so later he attacks your brother and sister-in-law, kills one of your employees, and almost kills you and you have to empty an entire clip into him to bring him down."

None of them said a word.

"Then Newton here contacts me for backstory on the folklore of vampires and werewolves, wanting specifically to know how to identify a vampire *after* it has been killed." She drained her coffee cup and set it down on the saucer. "Folks . . . how stupid do you really think I am?"

After almost half a minute of silence, Val said, "Well, well."

To which Crow added, "Holy shit."

"Okay," Val said softly, "then what do *you* think is going on?"

Jonatha shrugged. "It seems pretty clear to me that you all think you have, or possibly *had*, a vampire here in Pine Deep." She arched her eyebrows. "Am I right, Val? Crow?" They said nothing. "And very probably a werewolf, too."

Crow opened his mouth to reply, but Val touched his arm. Her eyes bored into Jonatha's. "What if we were to agree? What would you do if we said that we thought that we were dealing with something supernatural here in Pine Deep?"

"Then," Jonatha said, "I'd say that you'd better tell me absolutely everything. Everything that's happened, everything you suspect."

"And if we do?"

"First," she said, "I'd have to believe you. Meaning I'd have to believe that you are telling me all of it and telling me what you believe."

"Okay," Newton said.

"Then I'll tell you if I think this is over or not."

"From the way you're talking," Crow said, "it almost sounds like you believe in this stuff."

Jonatha didn't answer. She cut another piece of omelet, speared a piece of grilled potato, dipped it in ketchup, and ate it while staring him right in the eye.

"Tell me first," she said.

(2)

"Well . . . that's kind of weird."

Nurse Emma Childs looked up from the chart on which she had been recording the doctor's notes. Pen poised above the paper she said, "Excuse me, doctor?"

The young resident, Dr. Pankrit, was bending over Terry Wolfe, gently moving aside bandages in order to examine the man's lacerations and surgical wounds. "Look at this. I've never seen a surgical scar heal that fast."

Childs leaned past Pankrit's shoulder. "Wow. I changed that dressing yesterday. This is wonderful!"

Pankrit turned and gave her an enigmatic stare for a moment, then bent lower to peer at the sides of Terry's face. "I . . . guess." He sounded dubious. "It's just so fast . . . and look, see that? That was a deep incision and the scar should be livid. This scar looks like it's six months old. That's just . . . weird." He put the bandages back in place. "Let's run this by Dr. Weinstock. He said he wanted to be notified of any changes to the mayor's condition."

"Well, surely if the mayor is healing fast it must be a good sign. His system must be getting stronger."

Pankrit gave her another of those odd looks. "Let's run it by Dr. Weinstock."

(3)

Bentley Kingsman, known to everyone as BK, walked the whole route of the Haunted Hayride, pausing every once in a while to make notes on a map of the attraction he carried on a clipboard. He and his friend, Billy Christmas, had driven into town the previous night, stayed at the Harvestman Inn on the town's dime, and were out at the Hayride by seven in the morning. Crow had met them, introduced them to Coop and a few of the management staff, then left for another meeting.

BK was set to handle security for Mischief Night and Halloween at the Hayride, the Dead-End Drive-In, the College Campus, the movie theater in town, and the main Festival that covered three full blocks in the center of town. BK had a lot of muscle coming in that afternoon and by then he wanted to view every site himself and make decisions on who should go where.

They stopped at a slope that led down to a man-made swamp in which the silvery disk of a spaceship appeared to rise from the muddy water. BK read from the clipboard. "Alien Attack. Five staff as aliens, two as victims, plus mannequins as deceased victims."

"Cute," Billy said, sipping from a Venti Starbucks triple espresso. "What happens here?"

"The flatbed stops up there on the road and a lightshow kicks in. Blue and white lights plus a strobe over behind the saucer. The aliens chase the two actors up the slope and shoot them down with ray guns right about where we're standing, then they start coming after the kids on the flatbed. The driver guns the engine and the flatbed slips away just in the nick of time."

Billy grunted. "Kids buy that shit?"

"By the busload, apparently. Crow said this is the biggest one of these in the country. Place makes a ton of cash."

"We're in the wrong business, Kemo Sabe." Billy was tall and wiry, with lean hips and long ropey arms. He looked more like a dancer than a bouncer, and two nights a week he did climb onto the stage for ladies' night male stripper revues. He was tanned and handsome, with white-blond hair, cat-green eyes, and a smile that BK had seem him use to melt just about any woman who crossed his path.

BK was taller, broader, heavier, and darker. Brown hair and eyes, a short beard, and forty more pounds than he would have liked to carry. He was built on a huge frame, though, and carried the extra weight lightly. He did look like a bouncer.

The two of them worked at Strip-Search, the biggest of Philly's go-go bars. BK was the cooler and Billy was his main backup. Like Crow they were old hands in the Middle Atlantic States martial arts scene. BK studied the same art as Crow, traditional Japanese jujutsu; Billy had years invested in a number of systems, including Muay Thai kickboxing and Wing Chun kung-fu.

"How many guys you figure for this spot?" Billy asked.

"This is the most remote spot, but I think we can get away with three guys for this scene and the next two. One here, one a quarter mile along the path, and one walking the line between the two."

"That'll work."

There was a lot of activity around the saucer. Attractions consultant John West and his team were involved in a thorough wiring safety check, so BK didn't bother them. He and Billy moved on, strolling past the Graveyard of the Ghouls, through the Corn Maze, and into the final trap, the Grotto of the Living Dead. "This is where one of the kids gets pulled out of the flatbed. He pretends to be a tourist and an actress plays his girlfriend. Some zombies sneak up and drag him off into the bushes and tear him up. The girl screams her lungs out and the zombies attack the flatbed, almost catching it as the tractor pulls away. Then it swings around the big bend in the road and back to the starting point where they offload the kids."

BK consulted the clipboard. "I figure it'll take fifteen guys to secure this entire attraction."

Billy whistled. "I hope somebody around here's got some deep-ass pockets."

"From what Crow says, they do."

"It'd piss me off if the check bounces."

"Amen, brother."

(4)

They took turns telling her the story. Crow started and told her everything about the Massacre, everything about Griswold and the Bone Man. Val picked it up with what happened at her farm, first when Ruger invaded her house and took her family hostage—and mercilessly gunned down her father—to Boyd's murderous attack. Newton filled in the backstory of the Cape May Killer, the police handling of the case, and what he had found out through Internet searches. It took well over an hour and they were so wired from caffeine that they'd switched to decaf. The owner, Gus, came by several times to see if they needed anything, but the seriousness of their faces and the fact that they immediately stopped talking as soon as he came into the back room finally convinced him that they were involved in something private and important. He stopped seating customers in that part of the diner.

Throughout the discourse Jonatha said very little except to clarify a point, a name, or a date. She made no notes, offered no opinions. When Newton finished his part of it, she leaned her elbows on the table and steepled her long fingers. "Wow," she said. "And the only other person who knows about this is this Dr. Weinstock?"

"Yes," Val said, "and we'd like to keep it that way."

"Have you seen Dr. Weinstock's evidence? The tapes, the lab reports?"

Crow nodded. "He said that each single element could probably be disproved, or at least discredited if someone wanted to work hard enough at it, but taken en masse it's pretty damned compelling."

To Val, Jonatha said, "So, as far I can tell, you three brought me here because of what happened to your brother and his wife, is that correct?"

"Not entirely," Val said. "Mark is the most important reason to me, of course. I need to know that he's going to be at rest. That he isn't infected . . . but we also need to know if the town itself is safe. We *think* this is over, but how can we ever tell? I don't want to have to live in fear every day and night for the rest of my life. Crow and I are expecting a baby . . . we need to know that this town is going to be a safe place for our baby to grow up." Crow reached over and gave her hand a squeeze.

"Wow," Jonatha said again.

"We've been pretty candid with you, Jonatha," Val said. "Now it's your turn. You seem remarkably calm after hearing the story we've just told. Frankly, I expected you to laugh in our faces and storm out. But here you are."

"Here I am."

"So what does that mean?" Crow asked.

"It means, Crow," Jonatha said, "that it's a good thing Newton here didn't contact my thesis advisor first. Or the department chair."

"Why's that?" Newton asked.

"Because neither of those gentlemen believes in vampires."

"And you do?"

Jonatha paused. "Yes," she said. "I do." She shook her head. "Before you ask, though . . . no, it doesn't mean that I've ever met a vampire. I'm not Van Helsing's illegitimate daughter. I have never in my life encountered the supernatural. Not once."

"So . . . why?"

She shrugged. "Not everyone gets into folklore because of an academic drive. Some of us—quite a lot of us, actually—pursue folklore because we do believe in some kind of *larger* world. I'm from Louisiana . . . from the real backwoods Louisiana. Before starting college I had a Cajun accent so thick you couldn't cut it with a knife, but thanks to some undergraduate theater classes I learned to get rid of that. Where I grew up everyone believes in something, even those who swear up and down that they don't. My grandmother and mother were as much vodoun as Catholic. In Louisiana we have plenty of legends of the loup-garou. I believed those stories as a kid, and still believe some of them."

"Some?"

"Sure, most of these stories are fake, or tall tales whose origins got lost over time and drifted into pop culture and folklore."

Val said, "What's a loup-garou?"

"It's French for werewolf," Crow explained.

"Right," Jonatha agreed, "and it's because of that part of your story that I'm here. You see, after Newton here contacted me and I started reading up on Pine Deep's history, I saw the name of the last known victim of the Massacre. Or, at least the person most of your town believes was the last victim." She paused. "Ubel Griswold is why I'm here."

Crow winced at the name.

"I'm not following this," Newton admitted.

"Ubel Griswold is a fake name. It's one of several false identities used by the most famous werewolf in European history."

"Peeter Stubbe," Crow and Newton both said together.

"Bonus points to you for knowing that. Most of the pop-culture books on werewolves mention Peeter Stubbe, though often the accounts are missing many details that can, however, be found in the scholarly literature, among which is Stubbe's probable birthplace."

"I thought he was German," Crow said.

She shook her head. "No, and that's part of the problem. He started using the name Peeter Stubbe when he moved to Germany, but he had already committed a series of murders in several countries before that. The earliest accounts of Stubbe's crimes date back to the fourteenth century, and that and other historical details suggest that Serbia, or possibly what is now know as Belarus, is where he was born."

"I'm sorry," Val said, "but isn't this all rather beside the point?"

"Oh, no, Val . . . it's not. It's the reason I believe so much of your story."

"Then you'll have to explain, because I haven't read many of these books."

"Okay, the short version is that there are hundreds of different werewolf and vampire legends. They occur in every country, and except in the case of folklore following population migrations, these creatures are all different. The Japanese vampire and the Chilean vampire bear almost no similarities. You with me? Well, the werewolf legends of Belarus and Serbia are different from those of Germany, and if Stubbe was born in one of those countries, and if he *was* actually a werewolf, then he would have very likely possessed the qualities of the *Vlkodlak* of Serbia or the *Mjertovjec* of Belarus. Those are the dominant species of werewolflike creature from those nations. Now, the thing is that even though most of the qualities of those two monsters are different, they share one really dreadful thing in common."

"And what is that?" Val asked. Tension etched lines in her face.

"In both countries, when either a *Vlkodlak* or a *Mjertovjec* werewolf dies and is not properly buried, it comes back to life . . . as a vampire."

Val's face lost all color and she gripped Crow's hand with desperate force.

"Holy mother of God," Crow whispered.

"That," Jonatha said, "is why I believe you."

Chapter 21

Crow said nothing as he drove. He just put a Solomon Burke disk in and headed north. The sunny morning had given way to a thin cloud cover that was starting to thicken as they drove. Val used her cell to fill Weinstock in on what they'd learned.

"She said that the psychic vampire is the root of the word *nosferatu*. It's funny, after all those Dracula movies I thought that *nosferatu* meant 'undead.' I guess we can't trust any of what's in fiction."

"So what does it mean?" Weinstock asked.

"Jonatha said that at least a third of the world's folkloric vampires were bodiless and invisible spirits who spread disease. The Romanian word *nosferatu* actually translates as 'plague carrier,' which she thinks might explain our blight."

"Swell."

"The main thing is, if Griswold was one of the werewolf species from Belarus or Serbia, and if he was killed, as Crow suspects, by the Bone Man somewhere in Dark Hollow, then it's likely he's the one who somehow turned Boyd and the others into vampires."

She told him the rest of it and then made arrangements to meet later on. For the next ten minutes of the drive north, Val stared out at the cars passing in the other direction, her fingers tracing the outline of the small silver cross she wore around her neck. Crow knew that she must be in hell. If Griswold's spirit was lingering in town, then Mark and Connie might also be caught in the polluted etheric tidewaters of Pine Deep.

"Whatever it takes," he said, giving her thigh a reassuring squeeze, "we'll take care of Mark—"

"I want to go back to the farm," Val interrupted. "Now. On the way back to town."

Crow nodded. "Okay. Any particular reason?"

"Dad's guns."

He studied her face for a moment and then looked at the dark clouds building in the direction they were headed. "Works for me," he said.

(2)

Newton used his credit card to pay for Jonatha's room at the Harvestman Inn and trailed behind her as she opened her door and went in. Like all of the rooms at Pine Deep's premier hotel, it was spacious, accented in autumn colors, and very expensive. The numbers on the bill caused Newton real pain.

"I'll be back to pick you up at six," he said, fidgeting in the doorway.

Jonatha turned around and sat down on the edge of the big queen bed that dominated the room. They had barely spoken a word since she dropped her bomb at the restaurant, and now she sat there and chewed her lip, giving him a long and thoughtful look.

"Tell me something, Newton."

"Call me Newt. Everyone does."

"Okay. Tell me . . . what are you and the others going to do now? With everything that's happening, I mean?"

"I don't know. I think Crow will want to go down to Dark Hollow again, to Griswold's house."

"Why? If he's a ghost, or some kind of psychic vampire spirit, then what do you think you'll be able to accomplish? You can't shoot him and you can't dig him up and run him out of town on a rail."

"I don't know what we can do. Spray garlic over his house, or set it on fire."

"Was he buried there? At the house, I mean?"

"I don't know. Does it matter?"

"Sure. What good would burning his house down do for us if he's buried on the other side of town?"

Newton frowned. "Well . . . we told you what happened to us. The bugs and all. Something's there. Crow saw that the doors were all locked from the inside. He figures Boyd was using it as a hideout. Maybe Griswold's buried in the cellar or bricked up in a wall or something."

"That would be very convenient, and if this was an Edgar Allan Poe story I'd even say likely . . . but something tells me it's not going to be that easy."

He gave her a tired smile. "This is Pine Deep . . . nothing here is ever easy."

(3)

He wanted to do one thousand cuts and then go back inside and work the store, but he lost count somewhere in the three hundreds and that was forty minutes ago. The sword handle was starting to slip in his sweaty palms and Mike's shoulders ached as he raised the wooden blade over his head and brought it down, over and over again. He strived for the rhythm that Crow always had when he used the *bokken*, the hardwood training sword, but knew that his blows were clumsier, rougher, driven more by rage than art. Each time the dull edge whacked the leather wrapping of the striking post the shock through his wrists and up his arms; the ache that had started early on had blossomed into burning bands of pain that tore across his chest with each blow. Lactic acid coursed through him; his blood was a hellish cocktail of adrenaline, endorphins, and pure hate.

His eyes had long ago turned from blue to red and black flowers seemed to bloom in his vision as he hit and hit and hit.

One blow was for Vic.

The next was for his *father*.

The next for Vic; the one after that for his father. Over and over again, as the minutes shattered into fragments under the blows, Mike's face twitched and snarled as he struck. A hundred blows back his nose had started to bleed, and although Mike was aware of that on some level, he just didn't give a shit. The rage felt good. The violence—however much a sham—felt good.

The burn in his muscles felt good. Felt great. Hate felt *wonderful*.

The sword rose and then slammed down, first on the right side of the post, then up and down on the left side. The leather was beaten black and then pale and finally it split. Threads of it jumped into the air with each blow.

His cuts had started sloppy, had been a child's attempt to do a man's cut. That was two or three thousand cuts ago. Now the sword rose and struck, rose, changed angle and struck; the wood was a blur, the rhythm far better than Mike thought it was. The timing and angle and efficiency of each cut was better than it should have been.

Far, far better.

If Crow had been there, if he could have seen the unrelenting frenzy of Mike's attack on the forging post. If he had seen the demonic fury in Mike's eyes and the sneering brutality on his face, he would have done anything he could to stop him. He would have seen the *dhampyr* crouching inside the boy, and the nameless *other* crouching inside the *dhampyr*. Had Crow seen that he would have been more than just terrified for Mike . . . he would have been terrified *of* him.

(4)

It wasn't until they pulled into the parking lot of the hospital that Val broke the long silence that had endured while they'd gone to her house to get the weapons and ammunition that once belonged to Henry Guthrie. She rubbed her palms over her face, careful of her battered eye socket, then looked at her hands for a moment as if she expected to see something there.

"Where the hell are we?" she asked as Crow turned off the

engine. "I mean . . . I don't know about you but I'm ready to go on a bear hunt here, but how do you hunt a ghost?"

"Damn if I know, baby. This is new territory for me. I went down to Griswold's place and got run off by cockroaches. That's as much as I know about what he is and what he can do."

"As frightening as that must have been, Griswold doesn't seem to have had that much actual power. He dropped the porch and sent the bugs, but you and Newton escaped."

"Seemed like a pretty big deal at the time. But I see your point. If he was all that strong, wouldn't he have just snuffed me out like that?" He snapped his fingers. "The whole bug thing didn't really do me that much harm. Mind you, I'll have a case of the butt-rattling shivers forever, but it's not like I lost a leg or anything."

"When this is all over I'll buy you some shares in Raid."

"I'm a Black Flag man myself, ma'am."

She gave him a spoonful of a smile, which was a larger portion than he'd seen since Mark's death. "My point is, honey," she said, "that I don't know how much of a real threat Griswold is."

"He made Boyd and Ruger into vampires. Jonatha said that psychic vampires can make ordinary humans into vampires."

"True, but she didn't know *how* that was done," she said. "Maybe it involves actually *going* to that house or those woods. Maybe when Ruger was on the run after the fight at the farm he somehow found—or was drawn to—that place. Jonatha said that all it takes is for a person to die evil and unrepentant. Well if you wounded Ruger badly enough and he died there, then maybe that's how it happened. If so . . . it's the first time in what, thirty years?"

"But then Ruger probably bit Boyd and Boyd bit Cowan and Castle. It just takes one Typhoid Mary to start a plague."

"Okay, so where are you going with this? Do we put up signs saying No Trespassing—Danger of Vampire Infection—all over the Hollow?"

She shot him a look. "No, I'm saying that maybe what needs to happen is that we find some way to sterilize that place. Some kind of ritual, or something. Maybe find a way to bring a couple of pieces of heavy equipment and tear that house down, maybe a backhoe to dig up the swamp. Till the soil and plant garlic everywhere. Something like that."

"I love you, Valerie Guthrie. I love your strength and I love your practical mind. Those are great ideas."

"Great ideas, but not practical," she said. "Getting the equipment down there will take some doing . . . but before we go in and bust everything up I think someone needs to go back to Griswold's house and search it from top to bottom. If he's buried there, then we can bury him with the rituals Jonatha talked about. If he's not, maybe there's something else of use. Evidence, books, I don't know what, but we should find out."

"Roaches?"

She waved a hand. "Insects can be dealt with, that's not the main problem, Crow. Man power is. Literally *man* power. I can't do it right now—between my head and the baby I wouldn't be any use. Newt's . . . well, he's Newt, and I don't think he should go down there again. I doubt Jonatha would go, and Weinstock's not the backwoods type."

"Who's that leave other than me?"

Val shrugged. "I think it's time we called the cops."

(5)

The trees grew close and blocked the sunlight, keeping the Hollow in shadows. Not that it mattered. Only a few of them were vulnerable to sunlight, and any one of those would have gladly, gleefully ignited himself if *he* asked it of them.

All through the morning and into the afternoon they came to him. Creeping through the forest, picking their way through sticker bush and vines, hurrying to be in his presence. They clustered around the swamp in a loose circle, each one dropping to his or her knees as they came close, their eyes fluttering closed with ecstasy as he called them and whispered to them. There was a long, continuous moan as the faithful flocked to their master, and in ranks they swayed back and forth like cornstalks in the wind.

There were hundreds of them now.

Hundreds.

Ruger walked among them, his face protected from the direct sunlight by a broad-brimmed hat, his long white fingers snugged into leather gloves. The sun caused him pain but no damage. He was smiling as he walked the inner circle of the first ring of worshippers. He could feel their passion, could taste their bloody intensity on the air, and his own heart lifted in glory.

A murmur of delight suddenly went up and Ruger turned to see the surface of the swamp bulge upward, methane bubbles bursting, steam rising from the muck as the Man moved. Ruger was well pleased. He had worked hard for this, had made sure everything was done just right.

With every kill the Man's army got stronger, but more than that—far, far more than that—with every kill the Man *himself* got stronger. The release of energy from fear and despair and the horror of death—all of that was channeled along unseen energy lines to this Hollow. As each of the faithful killed and fed on blood or flesh, the Man fed on the psychic energy, growing stronger minute by minute, forming, taking shape.

Becoming.

Ruger turned and surveyed the masses. "The Red Wave!" he yelled, and they screamed it back to him.

"The Red Wave!" Louder, his voice shaking the withered leaves on the trees.

They chorused it back to him, their voices shivering the bark from the trees.

He went on yelling it and they kept replying in the litany of the damned. Each time those words pummeled the clearing the great, shifting mass that was Ubel Griswold trembled with red joy.

It was near sunset on October 29. In two days the Red Wave would wash the town of Pine Deep in blood. In two days Ubel Griswold would rise. Pine Deep would die. The world would scream.

Chapter 22

He picked up the phone on the second ring. "Ferro."

"Frank? It's . . . Saul."

Ferro murmured distractedly. "Saul . . . who?" He held the phone in left hand and with his right he was ticking off items on an elaborate expense account that was due in an hour.

"Saul Weinstock."

"Mm-hmm," Ferro said absently, underlining an item he thought might be disallowed.

"From Pine Deep," said the voice on the phone.

Ferro paused, smiling as he recognized the voice. "Hey! Saul, how are you?"

Instead of answering, Weinstock said, "Look, is there any way we can get together to talk?"

"About what?"

"About what's happening in Pine Deep. About the thing with Boyd and Ruger."

"Saul, that case is pretty much closed, at least as far as my involvement in it. Our homicide guys are working with the FBI on it. My partner Vince and I were only dragged into it by circumstance, following the drug angle out of Philly, so with Ruger and Boyd both dead . . . well, our involvement dried up—"

"It's not over!" Weinstock barked. "It's still happening."

Ferro set down his pen. "What's that supposed to mean?"

"You thought everything was over when Boyd died, huh?

Well, let me tell you, Frank, that was just the start of it. Things have been happening here in town you should know about."

"Like what?"

"Like . . . well, I really don't want to go into this over the phone."

Oh brother, Ferro thought. "Why not? Are you afraid someone might be monitoring your call?"

"No, it isn't that."

"What, then?"

"What I have to say involves a lot of very detailed material. Forensic evidence. X-rays, test results, stuff you should come and take a look at."

"It's not my case anymore. The FBI is in charge now."

"Oh, please . . . those two jokers who were here during the manhunt? Neither of them could find his butt with both hands and a map. *You* ran that investigation."

"I helped to coordinate it, but—"

"You ran it. Look, Frank, I'm really not in the mood to mince words. I'm under one hell of a lot of pressure right now, and to tell you the truth, I'm pretty scared."

"Scared?" Ferro echoed, half-smiling. He leaned back in his chair and put his crossed ankles up on his desk. "Scared of what?"

Again that long silence. "Of what I found out during my autopsies . . . and what I've discovered since then."

"Have you discussed this with Sheriff Bernhardt?"

"Oh, of course not. He's hopeless, and you know it. The mayor's still in a coma, so there's no one here to talk to except Malcolm Crow and Val Guthrie and both of them are sitting here in my office right now. We all want to talk with you."

"They're both there?"

"Yes," Weinstock. "Look, I know it's a lot to ask, but if you could just meet us, let us share our concerns with you."

Ferro sighed and rubbed his eyes. "Saul . . . I just can't see how I can manage that."

"What if I told you I found some of the missing cocaine?"

"Say that again?"

"Would you be interested if I found some of the cocaine that Ruger misplaced somewhere here in Pine Deep?"

"Are you saying you have found some?"

"Would it make a difference if I have? Would it get you to come back to Pine Deep? Would *you* be reassigned to the case?"

"I could request it," Ferro said cautiously. "If, and I say *if*, you actually had located some of the missing coke. I want to be really clear on that."

There was some low conversation at the other end and then a new voice spoke. "Frank? Crow here. You're on speakerphone. Look, I don't want to try and bullshit you with some fairy tale about finding the coke. We didn't find any, but we did find some other stuff and we need to talk to you. I know about the whole jurisdictional thing, but trust me when I tell you that this is important. Vitally important."

"Crow . . ."

"People are dying here, Frank."

"You have a police force."

"No," said a third voice—Val's. "No, Detective Ferro I don't think we do. I think we're all alone here and we need your help."

Ferro said nothing.

"Detective Ferro . . . Frank," Val said, "you told me that at my father's funeral that if there was ever anything you could do. I know people say that because they don't know what else to say, but I'm going to take you at your word. I'm going to make you live up to your word. You said you'd help if I needed it, and I need it. What's your word worth?"

"That's pretty damned—"

"Answer the question," she snapped. "What is your word worth? I've lost my father, my brother, and my sister-in-law, and one of my best friends is in a coma. Doesn't that give me enough of a right to ask for help?"

Ferro felt heat bloom in his cheeks. "That's a low blow, Ms. Guthrie."

"I don't care. At this point I'd do anything to get you to come out here. Believe me when I say that."

"Okay," he said. "I do believe you."

"Will you come?"

He sighed in disgust. "Oh, all right, I'll come out. But you get to play this card once and that's it."

"Thank you, Frank," she said.

Crow said, "Can we do this tomorrow morning? Meet for lunch?"

"Why?"

"Because we may not have a lot of time with this. Look, Warrington's about halfway . . . why don't you meet us at Graeme Pizza? You know where that is?"

"Across from the movie theater? On County Line Road, just off 611?"

"Yeah. Noon okay?"

"Not really," Ferro said, "but we'll be there."

He slammed down the phone.

"Shit!

(2)

"Is this all of it?" Vic said, pulling open the panel truck's back door. It was filled with cartons floor to ceiling.

"Everything you asked for," said the driver. He was a weasel-faced man name Trent who owned a minority share in a candy company in Crestville. The truck was backed into an empty bay at Shanahan's garage. Trent looked around, but there was no one else in sight.

Vic pulled one box down and tore it open. Inside were forty one-pound bags of Pine Deep Authentic Candy Corn. He took the clipboard from Trent's hand and scanned down the list. Fifteen boxes of candy corn; forty boxes of marshmallow Peeps— ten each of bats, pumpkins, ghosts, and black cats; twenty boxes of Gummi worms; and the rest were cartons of rolled sugar dots in Halloween colors.

"Looks good." He handed the clipboard back. "Okay, leave the truck here and I'll have some of my boys offload this shit. I'll drive you to the Black Marsh train station. You packed?"

Trent gave a nervous bob. "By the time anyone starts tripping on these goodies I'll be in Rio."

"Sounds fun. Don't send me a postcard."

"No way, José. Now . . . just to put me at ease . . . you're going to take care of everything, right? You won't leave anything that'll tie me to this?"

"Yeah, I'll handle everything." Vic fished a cigarillo from his shirt pocket. "Got a light?"

"Sorry, don't smoke."

"No problem," Vic said, and kicked him in the groin. Trent's eyes goggled with surprise and sudden agony; he made a strangled squeak and dropped to his knees. Vic kicked him in the face and then stood over him and stomped him nearly to death. He smiled all the time.

A figure stepped out from the far side of the truck. The embroidered patch on his shirt said *Shanahan*. "Jeez, Vic . . . he screw you over or something?"

Vic turned. He was breathing heavy. "Nah . . . just working out some frustrations." He nodded at what was left of Trent. "You hungry?"

Shanahan smiled a toothy smile. "Sure," he said, "I could eat."

"Help yourself. I got to head home."

(3)

Mike stopped home between school and his shift at the Crow's Nest to get a sweater. The afternoon had gone suddenly cold and his light Windbreaker was nowhere near warm enough. He leaned his bike against the steps, climbed onto the porch, and had just turned the handle when he heard Vic yelling. Mike froze in an attitude of listening, head cocked to one side.

"You're such a pain in the ass, Lois, I swear to God! All you do anymore is bitch about how hungry you are, but you won't frigging eat anything we bring you."

We? Mike thought.

He heard his mother reply, but her words were too faint to make out.

"Well, I don't care . . . and I'm not going to go get you something from Trinian's. You think I'm the goddamn maid?"

Trinian's was the butcher shop in town. Mike thought it was weird that mom was asking Vic to go shopping. Vic never did anything like that. He didn't even buy his own beer. Besides . . . Mike had been rooting in the fridge earlier and there was plenty of food, including pork chops and ground turkey. Why was she making a fuss about something from Trinian's?

"Well, you can starve for all I care." There was a crashing sound and Mike had the feeling Vic had hurled something against the wall. He was a big one for throwing shit. "I'll be downstairs. You know what you need to do, you silly bitch. When you come to your senses and want to feed, then send me a frigging postcard . . . otherwise you can kiss my white ass."

There was the sound of fast, stomping footsteps and then the distinctive heavy slam of the cellar door. Mike gave it a few seconds and then pushed the door open and stepped quietly into the foyer.

Going into the living room was a major sin against Vic's house rules, but this was driving him nuts. Every night all his mom did was sit in the living room. No lights, no TV. She seldom answered when he called to her, and sometimes she said nothing at all. It was weird and it scared Mike.

He lingered uncertainly in the doorway.

"Mom? Are you all right? Are you sick?"

No answer. He took a deep breath as he stepped into the living room, standing behind the couch, not ten feet from her. The fear of Vic's wrath was a stink in the air. "How come you always sit in the dark like this?" When she didn't answer he said, "Look, let me turn on the light . . ."

He heard her gasp. "No, Mike . . . please don't . . ."

"Come on, Mom, you're freaking me out here."

She turned away from him just like she did the other day, clearly not wanting him to see her face, and Mike wondered just how badly had Vic beaten her that she hid her face for over a week?

"Mom . . . listen to me . . . if you're sick or hurt we need to get you to a doctor."

"Mike, if you love me, then please just leave me alone. Go to your room, go to Crow's store . . . just leave me alone."

Mike stood there, uncertain. "I heard you tell Vic that you were hungry. You should eat something."

He saw her body cave over as if his words had hit her like a punch in the stomach.

"Why don't I go get some Chinese? I'll get the lemon chicken you like . . ."

"Go away!" she said, and this time there was an edge to her voice and and it scared Mike to hear it. It hardly sounded like her at all.

A month ago he would have turned and fled from the sound of that voice, but he wasn't the same boy he had been a month ago. He wasn't even the same boy he had been that morning. Now he took a half step forward, beginning the motion of raising his hand to touch her, to reassure her, to comfort her with his presence.

"Why, you disrespectful little shit!"

The voice slashed through the shadows and Mike turned to see Vic's bulk filling the doorway behind him. He hadn't heard Vic come upstairs, hadn't heard the cellar door open, but there he was, all puffed up with righteous rage, standing wide-legged, fists on hips like a poster of Superman.

"Mom's sick," Mike said hastily.

"Sicker than you think, shithead. Get the hell out of there."

But Mike held his ground. "What's that supposed to mean?"

"It means that she's a sloppy drunk and a lousy lay, and if she'd just take her medicine like she's been told she wouldn't be mooning around the house like she was at death's door." Vic chuckled and repeated, "Like she was at death's door. Ha!"

Mike didn't understand what was funny about that, and didn't care. He stood his ground. "If she's sick, then she ought to go to the doctor."

Vic laughed again. "Well, I think it's a little too late for the doctor, kiddo. Isn't it, Lois honey? Too late for the ol' doctor? Still, she knows where the medicine is, and she knows how to get it, but she won't, 'cause she's a stupid, stubborn old cow."

"Don't talk like that about my mother," Mike warned.

Vic looked at Mike for a second, then burst out laughing. "I'll say whatever I damn well want in my own house, and you, my little piece of shit, are just going to have to listen and like it."

"I'm telling you—"

"No, shithead, I'm telling you! Since when did you grow a pair of balls? What, you think you're standing up for your mother's honor? That's a frigging joke! I was screwing her long before your father rolled his car off Shandy's Curve. I was sticking it to her day and night while your dumbass father was out working his balls off. Christ, what a shithead he was!"

"You're a liar!" Mike felt his hands balling up into fists.

"Hell I am," Vic snapped back. He was smiling, enjoying this. "And I'm here to tell you, boy, ol' Lois there used to be a sweet piece, no matter what hole you'd take her from. And head? Damn, she could suck a golf ball through a twenty-foot garden hose. Jeeez-us! Man, those were some good times. Your dad'd call home to say he was working overtime and Lois here'd call me up not ten seconds later, talking all sweet about how she wants my cock in her and she can't get enough of it and how she's all wet and wants me over there. Back then, kid, I'd be over here in a hot minute. You'd be sucking your thumb upstairs and your mom'd be sucking my root down here."

"Shut your lying mouth!"

"Hell, boy, I was taking her up the ass when the chief's office called to say that John Sweeney was Spam in a can off Shandy's Curve. You know what? We finished screwing before we went out to the accident. How's that for good old Mom?"

Mike took a definite step toward Vic, who didn't budge.

Behind him, Mike could hear his mother quietly weeping.

Mike looked over his shoulder at her huddled form. He tried to muster anger at her, tried to conjure hate, but he couldn't. Maybe there would be a time for that, but right now all he felt for her was sadness. Still, as he turned back to face Vic, a searing white-hot hatred sprang up in his heart, charring his soul.

"Yeah," Vic said in an offhand way, "Lois'd ball anything with a dick back then." Vic leaned forward and gave Mike a secretive leer. "How do you know John Sweeney was even your dad?"

"He *was* my father, asshole!" Mike snapped, though he knew it was a lie.

"John Sweeney was a useless piece of shit who did the whole world a favor by rolling his car down the hill. Kid, if I was you I'd be embarrassed to tell anyone that I was even related to that loser, let alone scream that he's your father." He gave Mike a knowing sneer. "You couldn't begin to understand who your father is. Or what he is! You should be ashamed of yourself, you little faggot, for being such a weak, miserable piece of crap, when your father is—"

He never finished his sentence because against all logic and expectation Mike Sweeney hit him so fast and hard that Vic never saw it coming. It caught Vic in the mouth and ground his inner lips against the teeth of his laughing mouth and knocked him back three steps so that he slammed against the living room doorway. Vic touched his mouth and looked at the hot blood on his fingertips.

For a moment he stood there and stared through shocked eyes at Mike. The boy's chest heaved, hands clenching and unclenching, and there was a look of mingled fury and surprise in his eyes.

"Oh, God, Mike . . . no!" his mother cried from the shadows.

Slowly Vic's eyes rose from his bloodstained fingers to stare at Mike, and Mike swore he could see a crimson veil of fury fall over his stepfather's gaze.

"You just killed yourself, you stupid shit," he said and hurled himself off the wall, looping a hard right hook that broke a big white bell in Mike's head and sent him crashing into an over-stuffed chair. Mike slid to his knees as blood ran into his left eye.

"Fucking hit *me*?" Vic said, still overwhelmed by it. He moved toward Mike, bringing his hands up into a boxer's guard.

Mike scrambled to his feet and backed away as he brought his own hands up the way Crow had taught him, remembering the advice he'd learned: "The best block is to not be there."

Vic started throwing jabs and short hooks, uppercuts and backhands, tagging Mike in the biceps and shoulders, trying to beat down his guard. Mike blocked and parried as best he could, but his head was ringing so badly that he couldn't think. Vic's hands were pistons, driving Mike back into the living room, into shadows, toward the edge of the couch.

Mike felt the back of the couch against his thighs as he was battered backward. He almost overbalanced and fell over, but Vic darted out a hand and caught his shirt, holding him upright as he delivered a short hook to the ribs that knocked all the air out of the room. Mike's head swirled with pain and disorientation. This had been a mistake. Stupid, and probably fatal. *Well*, he thought as the beating continued, *at least I hit him, at least I made him bleed.*

Vic cuffed him again in the head, but this new blow had a weird effect. Instead of worsening the disorientation it seemed to hit some kind of internal circuit breaker and suddenly all of his interior lights came back on, all at once. Crow's voice seemed to whisper in his ear: "Never hold someone with one hand and hit him with the other. It limits you. The hand that's holding on can't hit and the punching one can't block. Use both hands because otherwise it leaves half of your body wide open." How Mike was able to remember that at such a time was beyond understanding, but suddenly that germ of information was there. He had looked at what Vic was doing and somehow managed to analyze it for a flaw—and found that flaw. From his perspective, despite the constant blows, Mike could see what Crow was trying to tell him. He could see how vulnerable that whole side of Vic's body was.

FUGUE.

Before he even knew he was going to do it, both of his hands moved at once. With his left he blocked the incoming high hook, meeting it at the source and jamming the swing of Vic's shoulders so that the punch never generated any power; and at the same instant Mike's right hand lashed out, palm foremost, and caught Vic on the side of the head, just at the curve of the eye socket where eyebrow meets temple. This time the blow was delivered the right way, and Mike even used one foot to push himself away from the couch and turn into the blow as he delivered it. This combination of movement was unexpected and immensely powerful; it spun Vic halfway around so that he had to let go of Mike and flail his arms to keep from falling as he took three staggering sideways steps.

Mike stepped in and kicked Vic in the back of the knee with the edge of his foot, jolting the knee into such an extreme bend that Vic's legs buckled, and as he went down Mike hit him with two overhand rights, one after the other, that smashed Vic's nose and nearly tore his ear from his head.

Vic crashed down onto hands and knees, shaking his head, trying to fight through explosions of light and shadows to understand what had just happened. Blood poured down his face and neck and splattered on the floor. Mike surged forward and landed a football placekick that caught Vic in the floating ribs, half-lifting him off the ground. Vic flipped over onto his back, wrapped his arms protectively over the point of impact, and struck the floor with a crash that knocked decorative plates off the shelves in the living room.

Vic was vulnerable and Mike stepped forward to kick him again, had actually raised his foot to do it . . .

. . . and hesitated.

Vic was bleeding, dazed, down.

Don't stop! Don't stop now! His own voice screamed in his head, but he didn't listen. Instead he turned, searching the shadows for his mother, wanting to grab her, pull her out of here, run while Vic was dazed. He saw her; she was on her feet now, a dark shape against the greater darkness of the room.

"What have you done?" she demanded in a voice filled with dread.

"Mom . . . I had to . . ."

She didn't move. "Oh, Mike," she said softly, but her words were strangely muffled.

A metallic clicking sound saved Mike's life. Vic had pulled out his clasp knife and with a flick of his wrist he snapped the four-inch blade into place. The gleaming metal seemed to fill the whole room. Mike saw his death on that gleaming blade as it slashed at him. He ran backward out of the way, but he was in the middle of the living room now and Vic was between him and the front door.

"Oh boy . . ." Vic crooned softly, "Oh boy. Here it comes, now. Here it comes. Oh boy. Here it comes." Vic held the knife, guarded by his other hand, the way an expert would hold it. Mike had seen Crow hold a knife just that way. Crow probably knew how to take a knife from someone. Mike did not. Their lessons hadn't gotten that far. He wished he had a sword, even the blunt-edged *bokken*.

He was going to die. After all that he had survived, he was going to die.

"Here it comes, now. Here it comes." Vic's eyes were insane. Blood dripped from his mouth and torn ear, it streaked his grinning teeth. "Oh boy. Here it comes, now."

Vic advanced on Mike, the knife slicing at the air between them as if he was cutting a path toward Mike's heart. Mike knew in that instant, without any reason for knowing it, that Vic had killed people, and he wondered how many people had seen Vic smile just that way before they died.

Mike didn't know what to do or where to go. There was no other exit from the living room but the doorway, and Vic's crouched body blocked it entirely.

"Here it comes, now. Here we go."

Mike didn't want to cry. He didn't want to just give up and collapse and be killed with no way left to fight. He wanted to fight, even if it meant going down fighting, but he didn't know how. Not against a knife, not against this.

Suddenly something smashed him out of the way even as Vic lunged in to bury the knife in his throat. As he fell, Mike saw something dark blur past him and crash into Vic, driving him backward, crashing him out into the hallway, propelling him down onto the bottom steps of the staircase.

He stared, dazed with unbelief, *"Mom?"*

She had leapt over the sofa and slammed Vic down, taking his knife wrist in one of her slim hands. Mike watched in horror, waiting for the moment in which Vic would tear his wrist free and slash her to death, but try as he might Vic couldn't get free. With his other hand, though, he hit her, shoved her . . . but all to no effect.

"Mom?"

She shouted at him. "Run!"

"But, Mom!"

"Run, for God's sake!"

It was impossible that she had held him even this long—Vic was twice her size, many times her strength—yet somehow, impossibly, she kept him pinned there with his knife arm hard against the floor.

"Run!" she screamed.

"Mom!" He took a step toward her, desperate to help.

Lois Wingate whipped her head around toward him, and for the first time in days he saw her face. Her skin was as white as new milk; her eyes were as red as fresh blood. Her mouth was a snarling mask of curled lips and bared teeth.

Mike felt every molecule in his body turn to ice. He wanted to scream, couldn't remember how to do it.

In a voice that shook the walls of the house, a voice that was a bellow of sheer force and volume that it literally staggered him back a pace, his mother screamed, "RUN!"

He ran. Of course he ran.

He screamed as he backed away and then turned and ran out of the house. He was still screaming when he grabbed his bike and jumped on it and tore away into the night. He did not remember doing that, he did not remember the nightmare ride down the street past neighbors who stood on their porches and stared at him, or stared at Vic's place. No one called the cops. No one on that block dared.

Mike tore down the street. His mind was black with shock except for the clear and vivid memory of his mother's face.

Her white, white face.

Her eyes, her skin. Her teeth.

Oh, God, he thought as he fled into the darkness, *her teeth.*

Chapter 23

They all met for coffee in Weinstock's office. Val, Crow, Jonatha, and Newton were seated on a ring of chairs pulled around Weinstock's desk, which was covered with the evidence he had collected. Weinstock had gone over it step by step for Jonatha's benefit. The morgue videos had rattled her, and she accepted the doctor's offer of a stiff knock of Scotch in her coffee.

After she'd downed half of it, she said, "I've been on the Net all afternoon, and I've made a number of calls to friends and colleagues who are deeper into the vampire folklore than I am. I told them the story that I was doing deep background work for a book, and now they all want to be footnoted. I made a lot of promises here, so our boy Newton here had better write that book."

"Did you find out anything new we need to know?" Val asked.

"Nothing you'll like."

"No offense, Jonatha," said Crow, "but we haven't liked anything you've told us so far."

"Okay, I know we're all pressed for time here," she began—and Crow noted that she used "we." He cocked an eye at Val, who had registered it, too, and she gave him a tiny nod.

"First, Professor Allenby at Rutgers, who's written the definitive book on Peeter Stubbe, said that the likelihood that Stubbe was born in Serbia is near to one hundred percent, not in Bedburg as most books claim. There are records in Serbia of the

Stubbe family—under a variety of name variations—dating back as early as the 1420s. He wasn't known in Bedburg until around 1589. That means that he was at least one hundred and fifty years old when he was put on trial for werewolfism."

Weinstock whistled.

"That would mean that he is likely to be a *Vlkodlak*, the dominant werewolf species of that part of Eastern Europe, and one widely believed—in folklore before now—to come back to life as a vampire."

"I'm confused about something," Val said. "I was looking through some of Crow's books and they seemed to indicate that Stubbe, or Stumpp as they called him, was brutally executed. Why didn't he come back as a vampire then?"

"Allenby's theory is that like many of the more powerful vampires, some werewolves were known to have human familiars and confidants. It's entirely likely that Stubbe, who was known for being extremely charismatic, suborned some local yokel and— since Stubbe was not truly a native of Bedburg—used that other person as a kind of stand-in or body double. Maybe he appealed to their religious mania—kind of like Manson or Jim Jones. In such cases the person under the charismatic control is more than willing to die for their master, even to the point of undergoing torture. Like a martyr. Even in ordinary psychology there are plenty of cases of it. Add to that some degree of supernatural persuasion and, well, there you go."

"That fits with what we know of Griswold," Crow said. "He had a whole crew of local guys who pretty much worshipped the ground he walked on. My own father was one of them. When Oren Morse killed Griswold, it's a pretty good bet that these followers were the ones who murdered Morse."

"Reasonable," Jonatha said. "Scary as hell, but reasonable. How many of them are still around?"

"Except for my father? All of them."

"Then we are going to have to work them into the equation . . . take a good hard look at them."

Val said, "Did you find out anything more concrete about the process of becoming a vampire?"

"Well, the consensus from among my colleagues is that, folklorically speaking, a psychic vampire like Griswold would be able to create other vampires at will. As I mentioned before, all he needs to do is impose his will on anyone who has recently died through violence."

"You mean anyone bitten by a vampire?"

"No . . . not exactly. There are as many ways to become a vampire as there are vampire species, but I think we can distil that down to the three most common methods," Jonatha said. "The first is also the oldest. A person has to die with a corrupt heart and unrepentant. That creates a kind of schism between them and the next world—call it Heaven or whatever. An evil person who dies, typically by violence, and who does not repent of their sins is likely to come back as a vampire of one kind or another. We see this in the folklore of dozens of nations."

"That could explain Ruger easily enough," Crow said.

"And probably does."

"But Boyd was corrupt rather than evil," Weinstock said, "at least according to what the cops told us."

"Which brings us to the second most common cause of vampirism worldwide—death by violence. Any death, any kind of violence. There isn't a lot of commentary on why this is, but generally I take it as a feeling of unresolved anger at having died and the need for some kind of revenge for having been killed. In Boyd's case it appears that somebody killed him. Maybe even Ruger, who knows? When he rose from death he was a vampire, but for some reason we don't know his anger was not directed at Ruger but at humans."

"Griswold?" Val ventured.

"Could be," Jonatha agreed. "If he is the directing force behind this, then his will would be strong enough to turn Boyd's anger and aim it like a gun."

"At my family."

"You told me your dad was no friend of Griswold's, and he was a friend of Oren Morse. Griswold also killed your uncle. Maybe there are other reasons he doesn't like your family, but clearly he wants you all dead."

Val said nothing but the muscles at the sides of her jaws flexed and bunched.

Crow said, "What's the third method?"

"That one is closer to the traditional view," Jonatha said. "In the more modern stories, meaning those from parts of Europe beginning in the early eighteenth century, we see a pattern of vampire stories being built around a bite and an exchange of blood. Not the willing and bizarrely sensual exchange you see in movies where Dracula bites some chick and then she drinks his blood—that's a Hollywood distortion. No, once a person has been killed by a vampire, then any human blood will reactivate them, so to speak. Not animal blood . . . it has to be human, according to the stories. Even a few drops will do it."

"Otherwise they stay dead?" Val asked. She took Crow's hand and held it.

"Well, that's a bit cloudy. In about half of the stories the vampire's victim is caught between Earth and Heaven in a kind of purgatory. Some even rise as ghosts, but they have little or no power."

"God . . ." Val said, touching her cross.

"In the other stories the victim is just plain dead unless human blood is poured into their mouth. At that point a demonic spirit enters into them and reanimates their flesh. They have all of the memories and personality of the person they were before they died, but that's all a trick. What's inside is pure demon, or ghost, depending on who you talk to."

"Damn," Crow said. "So we don't know what state Mark's in."

"No, we don't," Jonatha said, "and bear in mind, we don't know how much of the vampire legend is even true. We're really fishing in the dark here and for every bit of reliable folklore—if we can call it that—there's a hundred times as much nonsense, bullshit, and storytelling embellishment. We could be wrong about all of this."

"Swell."

"Now, there's one more thing. In a few of the older stories, if a person is brought to the point of death but not killed outright they can simply transition into a vampiric state without going through the process of actual death. You follow me? In those cases the person retains their soul and true personality only as long as they drink animal blood, but should they take so much as a taste of human blood their human soul is pushed out and the demonic spirit takes over forever." She paused. "I know this doesn't apply to your brother or sister-in-law, Val . . . but in going over everything with Newt I can see that we don't actually have proof positive that Ruger or Boyd actually died prior to becoming vampires. They could have transitioned."

"So what?" Crow asked. "Does any of that matter?"

"Well, the vulnerabilities are different. A vampire who has transitioned instead of dying is usually stronger. Much stronger . . . and the more they feed the stronger they'll become. So if Ruger transitioned, then he could be even stronger now than he was when you last encountered him."

Crow sighed and bent forward so he could bang his forehead on the desk a couple of times.

Newton said. "What do you want us to do now? You want us to go with you to meet the cops?"

Crow looked at Val, who shook her head. "No," he said. "Why don't you find out everything you can about how to stop these bastards? I mean, can we rely on any of the usual stuff? Crosses, holy water . . . ?"

"No, that's all Bram Stoker stuff. Fiction."

"What I figured."

"Garlic is good, though. It's deadly poison to vampires. It weakens them and if it gets into their bloodstream it might be fatal. I'll ask some of my guys about it."

"Good, we'll offer them garlic bread next time we see one."

"I'm sorry, Crow . . . Val . . . I thought I'd be able to find something comforting . . ."

"Actually," Val said, her voice tight, "you've at least told me what I need to know for now. Keep researching this, Jonatha. Right now you're the most important person in the world to us."

Jonatha looked at her, head tilted to one side. "But . . . no pressure, right?"

Val actually smiled. "No, of course not. Another sunny day here in Pine Deep, America's Haunted Holidayland."

"I should have stayed in Louisiana. All we have there are killer hurricanes."

Crow and Val turned to Weinstock, who had been silent throughout, his face buried in his hands. "Saul?" Crow asked.

Weinstock raised his head and gave them the bleakest stare they'd ever seen. "I need to get Rachel and the kids out of this godforsaken place."

Val nodded.

"Can we stop the Festival somehow?" Newton asked.

"No," Crow said. "Sarah Wolfe won't even discuss the matter. All she says is that the town lives or dies on this Halloween."

"Christ," said Newton, "she's not joking there."

(2)

Mike fled into the night as if all the demons of Hell were in close pursuit. His life seemed to be nothing but horror and flight from it. No matter how far he went, no matter what direction he took, it always seemed to circle back around to another, far worse horror.

And now this, the worst of all.

Legs pumped the pedals, hands clutched the ribbed rubber grips, lungs heaved, and pulse hammered furiously. His shirt snapped and fluttered as he rode, and though he was unaware of the chill of the air against his bare forearms, his heart was heavy with black ice.

With each hill he climbed, his legs ached more and more.

He could not think. Could not bear to think.

All he could do was fly. From horror toward nowhere, through the shadows that opened wide to receive him.

The Bone Man stood in the road and watched the boy fly, feeling the eerie déjà vu that was actually memory. He had stood here before, had watched the boy flee before. It had ended badly that time.

It would be worse this time. Halloween was in two days. There was no turning back for anyone now.

(3)

When the manhunt for Ruger and Boyd was at full burn, all of the town's former and inactive police officers had been called back to duty, but just as the threat diminished the Halloween season kicked into full gear and most of the officers remained on the job. Tow-Truck Eddie Oswald liked working as a part-time cop, partly because he loved his town—despite its tradition of celebrating the pagan holiday—and he hated the wretched excesses of the un-Christian tourists who had to be kept from running amok. The other reason he liked the job was that it gave him yet another reason to be prowling the streets and roads of the borough in his hunt for the Beast. He needed to complete that task to both honor and appease his Father, whose wrath had turned to a cold and disappointed silence in Eddie's head.

He drove the main drag now, alone in his cruiser, neat and tidy in his crisp uniform, his sidearm a comforting weight at his hip. His mind, however, was an untidy mess—a ransacked room where hope and trust in his own judgment had been thrown to the floor. Doubt seemed painted inside his brain like some vandal's graffiti. For a while he thought he'd known the direction of his purpose; for a while he thought he'd known exactly who the Beast was and in which body he was hiding. Now the only thing of which he was certain was that he was now completely *un*certain . . . and uncertainty in his holy purpose filled him with shame.

"Base to four." The sudden squawk of the radio made Eddie twitch and he snatched the handset up.

"Four," he said, "what's up, Ginny?"

"Got a job for you, Eddie. Domestic disturbance."

Great, just what I need. Eddie sighed. "Give me the rundown."

"It was just called in a few minutes ago. FedEx guy heard a fight, someone screaming, and then saw this kid go running out of the house, face all bloody."

So what? "Give me the address."

"Oh, no, you don't have to go there. Polk's already there. He called in and told me to tell you to go looking for the kid. Jimmy said you're the only one free, so you catch this one. Lucky you, huh?"

"Yes, lucky me. Okay, Ginny, do you have anything on the kid? Name, description . . ."

"Name is Sweeney. Michael Sweeney. Age fourteen, red and blue, five-six, slim build. Probably on a bicycle."

Eddie jerked upright. "Repeat that name, please?"

"That was Michael Sweeney. Last seen wearing a short-sleeved T-shirt with some band label, FedEx guy thinks it might have been The Killers. The neighbor said the kid had a bloody nose and there was blood on his hands and the front of his shirt. He was reported to have left the scene on a black mountain bike."

"Michael Sweeney," Eddie said, tasting each honey-sweet syllable.

"Last seen heading south toward A-32. Probably making for a friend's house."

"Out into farm country," Eddie murmured. "How long since he fled the scene?"

"Say ten minutes. If he's heading out to one of the farms you should have no problem finding him."

"I'm on it," he said and hung up.

Michael Sweeney. Covered in blood. The image was so delicious that tears filled his eyes.

In his mind it was as if a series of relays clicked into place and a current of pure cognitive energy flowed uninterrupted for the first time in weeks. Of course it was Michael Sweeney. Vic Wingate's stepson. Eddie had even *seen* the boy at the garage once or twice. So why had it been so hard to identify him at

Crow's shop? A devil's mind trick, that had to be. The Beast was, after all, the Father of Lies . . . it wasn't so hard to assume those lies could have been more subtle than words. Hadn't the air shimmered like heat vapors from hell? That was all part of a glamour put on him by the Beast. He hadn't seen it then, hadn't grasped it fully, but now everything made sense. Now everything was crystal clear.

Michael Sweeney was the Beast and he was out there now, soaked in blood, probably laughing as he fled into the farmlands. The soulless bastard!

No wonder God had sickened of him and turned His back. How could He not when His son was so weak that the Beast could thwart him with such a simple conjuring trick.

"Forgive me, Father, for I am most heartily sorry for my sins." He recited a dozen different prayers of humility and confession, then threw his car into gear and headed out of town.

(4)

Vic Wingate chain-lit his eighth cigarette and between puffs probed experimentally at his nose and ear. A plastic bag of ice cubes lay on the floor by his feet. He saw Polk's stare. "What?" he snarled.

They were alone in the living room. Lois was upstairs, and the neighbors had been shooed unceremoniously back to their houses. Polk had taken the call alone, making very sure that no other deputies set foot in Wingate's house. That would lead to all sorts of complications. He perched on the edge of Vic's overstuffed wing chair and jiggled his uniform cap in his hands.

Polk cleared his throat. "How bad is this going to be for us?"

Bitterly, Vic said, "Dumb bitch helped him get away. She showed herself to him."

Polk's eyes went wide. "She . . . showed her . . . ? I don't get it, if she's one of *them* why'd she help him?"

"She ain't gone over to *Him*, yet. Bitch has been living on neighborhood dogs and beef blood from the butcher's. Still got her frigging *soul*, as if that matters to her. Shit, she never used it before."

Polk swallowed the rock in his throat.

The door banged open and Polk leapt to his feet as Ruger walked in from the kitchen carrying the limp body of a teenage girl in his arms. The sight of him made Polk's balls climb up into his body.

"Hey hey, welcome to the funhouse, Polkie."

Polk couldn't answer. He was staring at what Ruger held in his arms—a teenage girl, head lolling, eyes closed, her face and throat smeared with bright blood.

"Oh, Jesus," Polk whispered and almost—*almost*—crossed himself.

Ruger ignored Polk and glanced up the stairs. "She still acting out?"

Vic took a drag, eyes narrow and hard, said nothing. Smoke leaked out of his nostrils. Ruger snorted. The girl he carried could not have been more than thirteen. Her T-shirt was torn, exposing one cup of a functional white bra. Her blond hair hung over Ruger's arm and nearly to the floor. He hefted her like she weighed nothing. "Well, maybe we can whet her appetite." He put one foot on the bottom step and glanced back at Vic. "Your face looks like shit."

"Blow me."

"Maybe the kid's turning into something like his old man after all."

Vic picked a fleck of dried blood from his nostril and wiped it on the arm of his chair. "Yeah," he said, "maybe. Maybe that's the only way a pussy like him'd ever get a sly one in on me."

"Good thing you didn't cut him," Ruger said, nodding to the knife on the coffee table. "If Lois hadn't stepped in . . ."

"I wasn't going to kill him, asshole . . . I was just going to carve my initials on his balls. Maybe take an ear off, or a finger. I wasn't going to kill the little shit."

"The Man's going to really be pissed." He gave Vic a wink

and carried the girl upstairs. Vic and Polk stared at the ceiling for a long time. They could hear Ruger's muffled voice and Lois's scream, high and shrill. Polk cut his eyes toward Vic and saw an expression he didn't expect to see: hurt. When Vic caught him watching he put on a poker-face scowl.

"We have to find the kid," Vic said, "before Halloween."

"I put Tow-Truck Eddie on it. He'll catch him."

Upstairs Lois gave another long scream, and this time it rose like a banshee wail, filled with such horror that Polk lowered his head and pressed his palms to his ears until it stopped. The scream rose and rose and then suddenly cut off. For a long while there was no sound at all except the vague creaking of the timbers and the twilight wind outside whispering through the slits in the shutters.

Polk rubbed his eyes. "This is getting to be too much," he said. "I don't know how much more I can take."

Taking a long drag, Vic squinted at him through the blue smoke that filled the living room. "Yeah, well . . . it'll all be over soon," he said.

Those words tightened around Polk's heart like a vise.

(5)

Iron Mike Sweeney was the Enemy of Evil.

At least, that was how he had once thought of himself, back when his inner fantasy life was a safe and exciting escape hatch from the real world. That was before, when evil was an abstract concept from comic books and TV and movies—granted, a concept enhanced by the hard hands of his stepfather, but still abstract. That was before evil had become an actual thing, a presence, a force, a reality that chased him through the gloom of the cold October afternoon and the darkness of his cold, shrieking thoughts.

Now evil was a thing that drew a knife and came at him with burning eyes and a whispering voice. Now evil was a thing that roared at him with his mother's mouth and a monster's voice. Now evil was more than just real, it was unreal. Titanic, overwhelming, impossible—and he fled before it.

He tore along the roads, not aiming for any particular place. Just away. Away from town. Away from Vic. Away from *home* and from what that word no longer meant, and what it now meant.

The farthest away he had ever been by himself was the dark stretch of A-32, and so he went that way. Not because he chose to, but because the path was programmed into him and his mind was a small cringing thing that hid from conscious thought. Inside him the chrysalis writhed. Cracks appeared in the cocoon that was wrapped around his transforming soul.

Behind him, Mike felt the vastness of nowhere to go; back there was everything he had ever known and nowhere that he wanted to be. A sudden realization blindsided him with the force of a runaway train and he skidded and slewed his bike to a stop on the verge, kicking up gravel and a plume of dust.

He could never go home again.

Never.

Not just because of Vic, but because of Mom. Tears fell like hot rain and he bent forward over the pain, buried his face in his arms as he hunched down over the handlebars. His lips tried to speak, but they were twisted with weeping, streaked with phlegm. He managed only one word, but he said it over and over again, trying to rediscover its lost meaning.

"Mom!"

The gathering twilight painted him and the surrounding fields in shades of bloody red. He was still crying, oblivious to the rest of the world, when the police cruiser crested the hill behind him.

Chapter 24

He still had his face buried in his arms, so Mike did not even know he was in mortal danger until the cruiser leapt over the crest of the hill and hurtled at him.

Then he heard it: a fierce and immediate bellow as the police car's heavy engine revved to a screeching pitch. Mike jerked his head up and twisted around to see the white dragon's eyes of the headlights not twenty yards away; the lights flared to high-beam brightness, piercing him like lasers.

"No," Mike breathed. "Not now."

The cruiser came barreling at him, and even though it was not the monstrous wrecker, Mike knew full well who it was. He instantly leapt off his bike and jumped down into the drainage gully, dragging the bike with him as the cruiser struck the empty air where he'd been—with such force that the vacuum sucked Mike off balance. He was showered with gravel and dirt as he fell into a heap at the bottom of the ditch.

Eddie slammed on the brakes, but it took fifty yards for the car to fishtail to a stop. He threw it into reverse, accelerated back to where the boy was scrambling up onto the field side of the ditch, skidded to a stop, slammed it into park, and was out of the car in an instant. He raced around the car and leapt the ditch. The boy was out of the ditch and running hard for the cornfield beyond. Eddie considered drawing his sidearm, but didn't. Though the road was empty now, tourist cars would certainly be coming.

Besides, it would be more holy to do this by hand. With the voice of God shouting in his head with every step, he ran after the boy.

Deep inside the cornfield Mike slowed from a run to a walk and then stopped, keeping his labored breathing as quiet as possible while he listened to the sounds. He could hear Tow-Truck Eddie crashing through the stalks about forty yards from him, going in the wrong direction. Despite everything Mike grinned. "Asshole."

He crept back the way he came, shortening the route to try and find the path to the road. Halfway there he saw something up ahead that made him smile even more. There was a rusted red wheelbarrow standing in a lane between the rows. Inside was a spool of chicken wire, a pair of wire cutters, and four three-foot lengths of pine used for supporting damaged cornstalks.

Mike stuffed the cutters into his back pocket and hefted one of the staves. Not as long or as strong as the *bokken*, but better than nothing. He started to turn away when something—some instinct—made him turn back and take the spool of wire. It was the size of a big apple and fit into his jacket pocket.

Feeling marginally more confident, he started once more toward the road, trying not to do a comparison between his makeshift arsenal and the weapons the big man would have. Gun, nightstick, maybe a Taser. And about a hundred and fifty pounds of muscle and mass more than he had. Holding the stick like a sword, he crept back toward the road.

Eddie slowed to a stop and listened, straining his senses forward through the field to try and locate the Beast, but there was nothing, no sound.

The voice of God in his head hissed in inarticulate rage and Eddie could almost feel himself being spun around by invisible hands. *Back!* The single word was shouted in his head. The voice of God, so long absent, now roared at him, warning him of another mistake. Tow-Truck Eddie realized that he had been underestimating the Beast.

"The Father of Lies," he murmured, and he ran back toward the road.

Mike was nearly to the edge of the field when he jolted to a stop, realizing with horror that he could no longer hear the distant thrashing of Tow-Truck Eddie deeper in the field.

Where was he? He turned in a slow circle, peering between the tightly planted rows of corn, but with the light breeze the stalks were constantly moving, the sun was just about to set, and the whole field was dissolving from red-gold sunset to the featureless purple of twilight.

Mike felt a hand close around his shoulder—he let out a shriek and spun around, swinging wildly with the stick—but there was no one there.

A shiver of dread passed through him. Mike could still feel the residual imprint of those fingers—icy and strong.

Then Tow-Truck Eddie stepped out of the corn, grinning.

"What's wrong with you?" Mike screamed. "Why are you doing this?"

Eddie's smile brightened into one of terrible joy. "Into my hands is delivered the Beast!" Mike had no idea what that meant and he tightened his grip on the stick, ready to fight.

"Leave me alone. I didn't do anything!"

Eddie craned his head forward. "You *exist*! You are an abomination in the eyes of God."

There was such a crushing weight of certainty in the cop's voice that Mike took a single stunned step backward. It was everything he had ever feared, every doubt that had ever burned the inside of his mind put into words. The ugly secrets that Mr. Morse had told him flooded back into his consciousness and the weight of them almost buckled his knees.

"No . . ." he said, but his protest sounded weak and empty even to his own ears; the big man, hearing that single word, raised his hands to heaven.

"And through the lies of the Beast shall we know his face and know the truth! Praise God."

"It's not my fault," Mike protested, tears gathering in the corners of his eyes. "I didn't mean to—"

Then a voice, as disembodied as the unseen hand, whispered a single word in his ear: "*Run!*"

It was as good as a slap in the face. Without understanding what ghostly hand had made him turn or who had spoken to him, Mike nonetheless spun and raced for the road.

Howling with glory, Tow-Truck Eddie ran after him.

(2)

The Bone Man stood in the cornfield and watched Tow-Truck Eddie, that monster of a man, one of the men who had beaten him to death all those years ago, chase down Mike Sweeney. Time was running out for them all, the Bone Man knew, just as he knew that this day was going to end badly.

(3)

Mike thought he was going to make it, that he was yards ahead, but just as he started to leap for the ditch Eddie's hand closed around his jacket hem and jerked him violently backward. He hit the big man's chest and it was like smashing into brick. Eddie spun him around and backhanded him to the ground. It wasn't a hard blow—Mike was already moving away from it— but it brought him to his knees.

Mike didn't wait for a harder blow. He rammed the stick backward into Eddie's gut and was rewarded by a deep grunt of pain. Mike spun fast and brought the end of the stick around in a hard, tight arc like a soldier would do with the stock of his rifle and he caught Eddie under the chin. Blood sprayed from Eddie's chin as he reeled back and went down hard on his rump.

Run! Again the voice screamed in Mike's ear, but Mike didn't run. Instead he stepped forward, and taking the stick in a two-handed grip, he swung it like a baseball bat, aiming for Eddie's temple. All the fear from his fight with Vic, all the terrible awareness of what his mother had become, all of his own confusion and sense of abandonment by the whole world went into that swing and it was a killing blow.

But Eddie was just too damn quick. Despite the stars in his eyes, he brought up his hands and caught the stick in two callused palms. The abrupt stop to the swing sent shock waves up Mike's arms and his hands spasmed open. Mike staggered sideways and went down to one knee.

With blood dripping freely onto his uniform shirt, Eddie got to his feet and loomed over Mike, hands clenching and re-clenching, rehearsing the murder he ached to perform.

"I am the Sword of God," he said in a voice that was eerily calm. He took the stick and broke it over his knee and tossed the jagged ends behind him.

He started to close in for the necessary kill when he saw something that jerked him to a stop as surely as his grab had stopped the boy a few seconds before. The boy was staring at him and as Eddie watched the child's eyes *changed*. The pure and innocent blue darkened as red specks appeared and then instantly blossomed so that within the space of a few heartbeats those eyes were completely red. As red as hellfire and Satan himself glared out at Eddie through veils of blood.

Eddie gasped and any last shreds of doubt that had clung like cobwebs in his mind were blown clear. "You are the Beast of the Apocalypse!"

"Whatever," Mike said and with one smooth movement he pulled the wire spool from his pocket and hurled it right at Eddie's face; it struck square in the middle of his forehead and Eddie dropped like a felled oak.

Mike didn't wait to see how badly the big son of a bitch was hurt; he just turned and ran.

(4)

Newton took Jonatha out to dinner, leaving the others behind in Weinstock's office. For a while Weinstock himself went out, wanting to go down to the ICU to check on Terry. When he came back he was frowning deeply.

"I'm not sure if we should be happy about this or sad," he said, "but the residents in ICU are all but throwing a party because of how well Terry's doing. He's still in a coma, but his bones are setting and his surgical scars are healing—all at remarkable rates."

"Isn't that a good thing?" Crow asked. "I mean . . . isn't that some kind of sign that the bad times are passing."

Val turned and stared at him. "Sometimes you're even too much of a romantic fool for me, honeybunch."

"What?"

"She's right," Weinstock agreed sourly. "Believe me when I say this, Crow, nobody heals that fast. Nobody. I ordered a full set of X-rays this morning and they show that his bones are nearly knitted. The femur, which was a compound fracture, looks like the tail-end of a healed hairline fracture. Two of the doctors are so pumped by this that they want to do a paper on it. They think this is an episode of *House*, but let me tell you, anyone who heals that fast is not doing so in a way covered by known science. End of story."

Val touched her cross and closed her eyes.

After a moment, Crow said, "Sarah told you that she thought Terry was going to attack her. Then he throws himself out the window. Okay, benefit of the doubt, maybe Terry realized what was happening to him and tried to kill himself to save Sarah."

"I can believe that," Val said. "Terry loves her very much. Her and the kids."

"Point is, Val, we have a victim of a you-know-what who has been having dreams of becoming a you-know-what who is now healing at an *unnatural* rate."

"Then what do we do, Saul?" Val asked.

"I . . ." he hesitated. "Actually, I don't know. He's still in a coma, so we can't mess with him too much or we could kill him. Comas are tricky."

Crow looked past Saul at the door as if he could see all the way to the ICU. "What about when he wakes up?"

Weinstock shook his head. "As for that . . . I'm no longer sure that's what I'm hoping for."

(5)

Later Crow tried several times to get Mike on the phone. He called the store and got his own answering machine, then called a friend who had a shop near his, but was told that the Crow's Nest had been closed all day. Strange. Finally Crow called Mike's house, hoping to get the boy or, at worst, his mom, but Vic Wingate answered.

"Yeah."

"Vic?"

"Yeah, who's this?"

"It's Crow. I'm looking for Mike. Just wanted to see if he was coming in to work tonight."

"How the hell should I know?" Vic said, and hung up.

"Prick," Crow mumbled. His next call was to BK to check on the security for the Festival.

"Everything's fine, Crow," BK assured him. "Stop acting like my Aunt Tessie. We got the whole thing under control."

"Good . . . but listen to me for a minute here, okay? There's a very, very remote chance that there might be some trouble this weekend. Not sure what, exactly, but tell your boys to stay on their toes. No one goofs off, no one slacks. Eyes open and combat ready."

"Jeez, Crow, you getting twitchy in your old age or have you heard something?"

"Just a heads-up from local law enforcement," Crow lied. "Been some sketchy characters in the area. You know how it is when there's tourists."

"Yep, it always draws the goon squad, too. Okay, chief, we're on it. I got enough tough guys out there to kick any ass that needs kicking."

"What I want to hear. Look, man, there's one more thing. Big favor. I was supposed to host a dinner for the celebs, but with Val and all. . . . Can you and Billy cover for me?"

"Let me think . . . you got two gorgeous scream queens, movie stars, free food, and an open bar. Yeah, brother, I think things'll go just fine. I'll play host to them, but Billy's gonna want a table all to himself with that Brinke Stevens and the other babe. He's been talking about it all day."

"Well, good luck to him. Just because they lose their clothes in the movies doesn't mean they're easy targets."

"Have you *met* Billy? He could charm the britches off the Queen of England."

"And on that truly, truly appalling thought, I'll say good-bye."

(6)

Mike Sweeney stood up from the weeds and scanned the road. No cars.

As soon as he'd fled from where he left Tow-Truck Eddie, he took a risk and went off the road on the far side, just over the hill; it was lined with gravel and he would leave no tracks. There was a big Halloween display made from hay bales and a pair of scarecrows—male and female—holding a sign for the Haunted Hayride. Mike dragged his bike behind the bales and then flattened down to wait.

The cruiser came past slowly a few minutes later but didn't even pause. Mike wasn't fooled, though; he waited ten minutes and during that time the cruiser came past twice more. Finally it vanished over the hill and was gone, heading farther along A-32 toward the Black Marsh Bridge.

Mike was cold and scared, and his heart was a black ball of pain in his chest.

He looked up and down the road, weighing his options. There was no way he could risk going back to town, not even to try and find Crow. He wished he owned a cell phone. Tow-Truck Eddie knew where he worked and Mike didn't think he'd be so lucky again if the maniac cornered him at the Crow's Nest. Home was impossible. He knew he could never go there again. *Mom.*

The thought of her was a knife in his gut. What had happened to her? There were words for what he had seen—after all Mike Sweeney lived in Pine Deep—but he could not bear to put those labels on his mother. Not now . . . not ever.

Mike wrenched his mind away from those thoughts as he turned and looked the other way. Black Marsh was just a couple of miles, but how could he reach the bridge without using A-32? Tow-Truck Eddie owned that road. Plus he was a cop. He could call for backup, make up some kind of story for the other cops. No, that way was closed to him, too. So, what did that leave?

He closed his eyes to try and orient himself, drawing a map in his mind. The Kroger farm was over the hill, and beyond that, on the left side of the road was the Guthrie place. On the same side as Kroger's was the Carby place and the back roads that would take him to the fringes of the college campus.

"Mom," he said aloud, without realizing the word was there.

He wrapped his arms around his chest and shivered, surprised at the loud sound his chattering teeth made. He didn't even know he was that cold. His shirt was soaked with sweat and he zipped up his jacket and pulled the hood up, cinching it tight under his chin with the drawstring. He did not know enough about physiology to recognize the warning signs of shock, and simply cursed the cold air. Overhead, there was the long, drawn-out call of a nightbird.

"I'm gonna freeze," he told himself. He bent to pick up his bike, and paused, cocking an ear to listen. "Oh, shit!" he said.

The breeze carried the distant drone of a car, still far away, coming closer.

Was it him?

He crouched down again and waited, but it was a tourist car. Another behind that, and another. Evening had fallen now and the tourists would be pouring in for the parties.

Still crouching, Mike turned and surveyed the field behind

him, which was a pumpkin patch that lapped up against the wall of the state forest. The black bumps of the pumpkins stretched away into infinite night, blending with the darkness of trees and hills and the lofty sky. The sky was marginally paler, washed to gray by the moon which, though not yet over the hill, still infected the whole of the sky with its own sickly pallor. It was too dark to ride fast without wrecking his bike, so Mike started walking slowly, heading into the field, aiming for the line of trees.

The road behind him was becoming a steady line of headlights and taillights with no way to identify one car from another. One of them was surely going to be the police car.

The exercise of walking warmed him marginally and he quickened his pace.

The cruiser came back and prowled the road again, but by the time Eddie's searchlight washed across the Haunted Hayride sign Mike was more than a mile away, lost in darkness and distance, heading away from the road.

With every step the boy drew closer to Dark Hollow.

Chapter 25

Mischief Night—October 30

"They're here," Val said, and Crow looked up from the menu as two tall men were ushered into the dining room by Erin, the wife of the restaurant's owner. She brought them to the table, gave the detectives menus, and took orders for coffee—decaf for Ferro, espresso for his partner, Vince LaMastra.

Ferro looked like a younger, less good-humored Morgan Freeman and had an undertaker's dour face and the hard shark's eyes of a longtime cop. LaMastra looked every bit the ex–college football player he was, with broad shoulders, blond hair that was cut high and tight, and an out-of-season tan. Crow remembered LaMastra as a jokester, always smiling, but right now he looked as serious as his partner.

"Are we eating and talking, or just talking?" Ferro asked.

"I'm hungry," said LaMastra. "What's good here?"

"Everything," Crow said, "but I can really recommend the pizza. Best anywhere."

"That works," Ferro said and they ordered two pies, one with the works, one plain, both well done. The dining room was large, with grapevines painted on the walls and a widescreen plasma TV showing Portuguese soccer. Danny, the owner, came by to shake hands with Crow and his friends, flashing everyone a brilliant smile, and left them with a big bowl of steaming baked garlic knots. Crow had ordered them with double garlic.

"Long drive up here," Ferro said when they were alone. "Lots of traffic."

Val leaned her forearms on the table and said, "Then let's cut right to it."

"Works for me," LaMastra agreed, tearing into the garlic knots.

Ferro said, "Where's Dr. Weinstock?"

"He had some personal business," Crow said. "We'll see him later."

"Well . . . that remains to be seen."

Val took a folder out of an old leather briefcase that sat on an empty chair, flipped it open, and handed Ferro the top pages. "This is the report from the State Police crime scene investigator who participated in the cleanup after Boyd killed my brother."

Ferro hesitated a moment before taking it. "How did you get this?"

"From Saul."

"You're not allowed to have this, you know."

"You can arrest me later. Read it, Frank."

Ferro gave her a narrow stare before putting on a pair of reading glasses. "Why am I looking at this?"

"Just read it."

He did, with LaMastra leaning sideways to read past his shoulders. Ferro started frowning first, but LaMastra caught up. "This is questionable reportage," Ferro said.

"Yeah," agreed LaMastra. "Says here that Boyd had a large number of healed-over injuries consistent with bullet wounds." He looked up. " 'A large number'?"

"Interesting," Val said, "isn't it?"

Crow reached out and tapped a paragraph. "It also says that from initial inspection it looked like Boyd had a partially healed broken leg."

The pizzas arrived and Crow served slices. Nobody spoke until the waitress was well out of earshot.

Ferro sprinkled hot peppers on his pizza. "Okay . . . so are you reporting a case of improper crime scene assessment? That's a state matter."

Val's pizza sat untouched on her plate. "That's just it, Frank. The crime scene assessment was one hundred percent accurate."

Both detectives paused in the midst of chewing.

"What?" LaMastra said around a mouthful of pizza.

(2)

Vic banged on the door and waited until the padlocks inside were keyed and the chains pulled through; then he opened the door and went in, a toolbox in each hand. The white-faced figures moved back away from him as he entered, knowing not to speak unless spoken to. One of Vic's house rules, especially in *this* house.

Griswold's house was gloomy and dark, but over the years Vic's night vision had improved, and besides no one knew this house better than he did. Long before Griswold had awakened from his long sleep, long before the Red Wave had even been conceived, he'd walked here.

He set the toolboxes down and looked around, feeling the energy of the place. It was here where Vic went after he'd orchestrated the murder of Oren Morse. That had been such a terrible, terrible night. As soon as Vic saw Morse he knew that Griswold had to be dead, that the nigger had killed him. Even now, thirty years later that thought filled him with crimson rage. Once that black bastard had paid for that murder and been nailed to the scarecrow post, Vic had come down here to the house in the Hollow, had opened this very door, and then gone inside. All that night he had lain curled in a fetal ball of pain at the foot of Griswold's bed, weeping and lost, torn to pieces by Griswold's death.

None of the other men had come with him. Not even Polk or Jimmy Crow. Like the apostles after the arrest of Christ they'd lost faith and fled, and only Vic had come to his master's house. Alone there in the wretched darkness of that first night he had prayed for hours—not to God, because that would be an insult to the Man—but to darker, less defined powers. Had Vic known at the time where Morse had buried Griswold's body he would have dug him up, washed and dressed him in the old Reichsleader uniform—his favorite, Griswold told him many times, of all the many uniforms he'd worn over the years. Then he would have buried him properly, with the correct rites read over him so that his return would have been assured, and so it would have been much faster. By the time he learned where Griswold was actually buried it was both too late and no longer the right thing to do. Funny how that worked out.

As it was, years passed before the Man awoke, and that sweet night seventeen years ago when that glorious voice first spoke in his head was Vic's most precious memory. The very first word the Man spoke after those years of nothingness was "Vic."

Calling him, calling the one who always loved him, who always believed in him.

So much had happened since then. Vic moved through the living room, ignoring the pale-faced figures that moved aside to let him pass. Avoiding certain spots—tripwires and hidden floor triggers that he'd installed himself—Vic went into the kitchen, opened the fridge, and took out a beer. There was no electricity in the house, but blocks of ice kept his beer cold. He twisted off the top and dropped it into a trash can. Vic never littered, especially here.

He fired up a small Coleman lantern and turned it up to medium and set it on the table. Drinking his beer, Vic looked around at the walls, the paintings of Hitler and other great thinkers of the twentieth century. Vic felt a stirring in his heart and in his loins. He'd have to make sure those paintings were removed, sent to one of his storage units.

He sensed someone behind him and turned. Dave Golub was there, a big moonfaced hulk of a kid who had always been something of a clumsy goof, but Vic hadn't heard him approach. They were all like that. Ghost-footed. Vic just gave him an uptick of his chin.

"Karl said you wanted a count." He handed over a sheet of paper that showed the location of every nest in town. Beside each location there was a number, and a tally at the bottom of the page.

"That's everyone?"

"Yes, sir. Less about ten of the Dead Heads that Karl wanted put down. Ones who wouldn't listen."

Vic frowned. "Still a lot of mouths to feed."

Golub stared at him for a moment, perplexed, then when he realized that Vic had made a joke he laughed. It was a bad fake of a laugh, but it showed respect and Vic appreciated the gesture.

"You and McVey all set to handle the candy?"

"Sure. We have about eight guys with us. None of the ones with too much teeth. Guys like me and Shanahan who can blend in."

"No Dead Heads either."

"Oh, no sir. The ones who are still left are locked up."

"Any word on Mike?"

"No. I had everyone out looking last night, and those guys who can take sunlight are still out there. Nobody's seen him." Golub paused. "Is that going to be okay for us? If we don't find him, I mean?"

Vic sucked on the mouth of the beer bottle. "Let's just say it'd be better for all of us if we found him."

He dismissed Golub with a curt nod and sipped his beer. His face still hurt from Mike's lucky punches. Little bastard. God, how he wished he could just do what he wanted to do to that kid and have done with it. Two or three hours and some power tools would be a nice way to punch his ticket. Make him pay for the hurt and the humiliation. Yeah, that would be sweet. That'd take the sting out.

He sat down at the kitchen table and took out his notebook. Tomorrow was Halloween. Even though he'd worked so hard for all these years to bring the Plan to this point, it was hard to believe that it was all ready to launch. Tonight he'd set the dynamite and wire the radio detonators. The boxes of candy would be distributed all throughout the town, and a few in the neighboring towns of Crestville and Black Marsh. Spreading joy, Vic thought.

The candy was not precisely part of the Plan, but Vic had put it into play as a backup. The Plan was complicated and something could go wrong. If the Plan failed, or if any part of it misfired and the authorities came in before the Man rose, then the candy would be part of a cover story. And even if the Plan worked according to the Man's vision and intention, it would be useful to muddy the waters for a while, at least until the Red Wave took hold and started sweeping toward both coasts. Ultra-high doses of hallucinogens were in the candy, more would be dumped into the town's water supply, and at least a quarter of all the bottled water that would be sold to tourists was spiked with LSD or haloperidol.

Vic also had caches of white supremacist flyers hidden where the authorities could find them once an investigation started. An excellent cover story. Not towel-head terrorists but homegrown stuff. Very plausible, and Vic didn't feel so much as a twinge of sympathy for his buddies in the white leagues who would take the hit for all this. Once the Man rose there would be a whole New Order and old loyalties wouldn't mean a thing. All human connections would be broken forever.

Without warning an image of Lois popped into his head. It happened so suddenly that it jolted Vic, even though it was the fifth or sixth time it had happened today. Lois. For sixteen years she'd been his whore and his punch, and never once had he ever given a single moment's serious consideration to the possibility that there were any genuine feelings for her anywhere in his heart. A month ago Vic would have laughed at the thought. Now she belonged to Ruger and suddenly there were conflicted feelings in Vic that he would have liked to reach in and tear out by the roots.

He didn't want to feel a goddamn thing for her, or for anyone except the Man, yet there it was. The Man must have known all along, or must have gotten wind of it the way he does, because when Little Halloween went all to hell and Griswold vented his rage at Vic, Ruger, and all the others, there had been a special twist of the blade for Vic. To appease the Man, to earn back his favor, Vic had been asked for a sacrifice. The Man wanted him to give up Lois. Not just give her up—he wanted Vic to let Ruger have her.

That shouldn't have hurt. Sure, maybe it should have stung

his pride a bit, like the alpha dog having to yield up a favorite toy to a new puppy in the house, but it should not have hurt him deep inside.

He swallowed more beer and stared at his list without really reading the entries. It did hurt, though. It actually hurt.

(3)

Ferro said, "What's this bullshit all about?"

Val leaned back in her chair and gave him a long, calculating look. "Frank, I want you and Vince to come with us to the hospital. Saul Weinstock has all of the forensics and video information and he's willing to show you everything."

"Why should we go anywhere with you?"

"Because now that you've read that report you have to know the rest."

"No, we don't," said LaMastra, "it's not our case anymore. What part of that can't you people process?"

Ferro met Val's stare and after a minute he said, "Be quiet, Vince."

LaMastra pivoted in his seat and stared at him. "What?"

"She's right," Ferro said. "There's something very wrong here and we have to know what's going on."

Crow exhaled a long breath, but Val didn't look convinced. "Are you saying that you understand what's going on . . . that you understand what those reports indicate?"

"No," Ferro snapped. "I'm saying that someone has either screwed up a crucial phase of the investigation, or else these folks are pulling some kind of shit. In either case I want to know what's going on." He looked hard at Val. "And if there's something hinky with this don't think my sympathies for your losses are going to cut you any slack."

"All we want you to do is look at the evidence," she said.

"Okay. We'll go that far, but as of now I'm putting you all on notice. This is police business and you are a bunch of local yokels who are not cops." He stared hard at Crow. "And I don't give a rat's ass if you used to wear a badge, Mr. Crow. That was then, this is now."

"Frank," said Val, her blue eyes dark and unblinking, "if, after seeing what Dr. Weinstock has, you want to arrest us, then so be it. If we can't convince you with what we have to show, then jail is going to be the safest place for all of us to be."

"What's that supposed to mean?" Ferro demanded.

Val just gave him an enigmatic smile and called for the check.

(4)

Sergeant Jim Polk finished his coffee and stepped out into the sunlight of October 30. Though the forecast called for a storm later, the sky of early afternoon was a cold blue dome dotted with crows circling high above. The sunlight was warm on his face and Polk indulged himself by standing there, face tilted upward, eyes closed, enjoying the warmth.

"Trying to get a tan, Jim?"

Polk opened his eye to see Gus Bernhardt's florid, sweating face beaming at him from the passenger window of Unit C1, the command vehicle of the town's small fleet of cruisers. Gus was chewing a mouthful of gum so big he looked like a cow with a cud and Polk resisted the urge to spit on him. Instead he pasted on a genial smile.

"Afternoon, Chief," he said. "Nice day for it, huh?"

"Sunshine brings in the tourists," Gus said, as if that's what Polk meant; and at least that much was true because the town around them had swollen to bursting with tourists. Thousands upon thousands of them—overnighters and day-trippers, kids and adults, families and school groups. They were everywhere, going in and out of the stores like lines of worker ants. Laughing, all of them. Everyone seemed to be having tremendous fun.

Polk hated them all. He hated the smiles on their faces, he hated the hands that lovers held, he hated the grins on the faces of the kids as they showed each other the costumes they'd bought for tomorrow night. Speakers on the lampposts played music, and

Polk swore to himself that if he heard one more goddamn rendition of "Monster Mash" he was going to take his hunting rifle and climb to the top of the Methodist Church and just plain open up.

"You drink your lunch today, Jim?"

Polk blinked and refocused on Gus. "What?"

"I been talking to you for a whole minute and you're just staring shit-faced at the crowd. What's with you today?"

"Late night," Polk said. "Burning the midnight oil."

"Midnight oil, huh? Well, I hope she had big tits," Gus laughed at his own joke and signaled his driver to go. Polk stepped into the street and watched the cruiser head south.

South was a good direction, he mused. Maybe he should head south, too. Maybe *before* tomorrow night. Once this party got started Pine Deep was going to be a really bad place to be found loitering. Polk knew that he was a fool, but he wasn't fool enough to really believe that his neck would be safe once Ruger and those *others* started their shenanigans. What was the phrase he heard on TV so often? "Ethnic cleansing?" Tomorrow night was going to be all about *them*, and Polk didn't belong to that club and sure as hell didn't want to. Not that he felt any kinship with the throngs of bleating sheep that flocked all around him.

Yeah, getting out of Dodge was a great idea, and south was as good a direction as any. Somewhere nice and hot, where there was a lot of sunshine. He had plenty of cash now. He could go now, not even bother to pack. Just get in the car and drive.

He snorted, mocking the thought even as he had it. Sure, it was a nice idea, except if Vic caught up to him. Or Ruger.

He thought about the evidence in Saul Weinstock's office—the evidence he told Vic wasn't there. He wondered if he should tell Vic now. Make up a story, say he went back and checked and found it. Would Vic reward him for that? Maybe, maybe not. Vic was hard to predict; he never jumped the way you'd expect.

Or should he go drop a dime to someone? Maybe that Philly cop, Ferro. Drive down to Doylestown or Newtown and use a pay phone. Put a rag over the mouthpiece and leave an anonymous tip. God, it would nice to screw things up for Vic. Might even work, he thought. Probably *would* work. Polk looked around. It would save a lot of people, too. People like him. *Ethnic cleansing.* Them against us.

Polk thought long and hard about making that call. Fifty cents in a pay phone and the Red Wave might come crashing down before it got rolling. Tell Ferro about the evidence and a whole lot more besides. Name names, give locations. Polk knew enough to bring it all down.

He looked at his watch. Nearly two in the afternoon. He smiled as he looked at the people around him, trying to feel what they felt, trying to see the day through their eyes. He should make that call.

"Vic would kill me," he said aloud. A passerby flicked him a glance, but as Polk was in uniform the tourist said nothing. Polk turned and watched him go. "Vic would kill me."

The speakers began playing "Monster Mash."

Or worse than kill me, he thought, and that was really the decider. Polk knew too much, and it included way too much about Ruger and his kind. There were fates worse than death, Polk knew, and that was no joke.

He jingled the coins in his pockets, feeling with the pad of his thumb the faces of a couple of quarters mingled in with the pennies, nickels, and dimes. His car was parked across the street. Tank was almost full; the gym bag with the cash was hidden in the wheel well. Hours and hours until sunset.

"God help me," he said softly, and he turned and walked up the street, away from his car, back toward the station.

(5)

"Thank God!" Weinstock said and gave Ferro's proffered hand a vigorous shake. Then he seized LaMastra's and wrung that. "Come in, come in. I can't tell you how glad I am to see you fellows. Thanks so much for coming."

Ferro gave him a stern glare. "To be honest, Dr. Weinstock,

we're not happy to be here and the clock is ticking on my patience."

"Understandable, understandable, sure. Well, you guys should sit down and get comfortable. There's a lot to go over."

The two detectives sat; the doctor went around behind the desk and perched on the edge like a frightened pigeon ready to take flight. He looked like hell, with dark smudges under his eyes, three visible cuts from a botched job of shaving, and a case of the shakes that made LaMastra glad that Weinstock wasn't about to operate on him.

"Before we get started, I want both of you to swear to me that everything I tell you, everything we discuss here today is going to stay between us."

Ferro pursed his lips and drummed his fingers on the desk top before saying, "I'm not sure we can make that promise."

"You got that right," LaMastra agreed. "Doc, let's do it this way—you shoot straight with us and we give you our word that we will play fair with you. We can't promise anything more than that."

After a long moment, Weinstock nodded. "Okay, okay . . . whatever. I just need to get this out. Frank . . . Vince . . . please, you have to help us save our town!"

Chapter 26

After fleeing the highway the night before, Mike slept in a barn on the Sackmore farm, a spread that been one of the hardest hit by the blight and had sold out in early August, their place now deserted. Mike tried the house, but it was too cold and drafty—just hardwood floors and no heat. The barn, at least, had old hay and he burrowed into it; it kept enough heat in his skin to keep him alive.

Twice in the night pale-faced figures crept past the barn, not hunting him, but hunting nonetheless. If they smelled the blood in his veins it did not lure them inside. The second one lingered longest, listening to the strange melody that rode the night wind and seemed to come from nowhere. But it wasn't just the ghostly blues that drove him off. When he was within a dozen yards of the barn he heard a sound and looked up to see that the entire sloping roof of the vast old barn was black with the close-packed bodies of thousands of crows. The trees all around rustled and hissed with them as their wings brushed against each other.

The white-faced night hunters fled, first one and then the other, disliking the music and the sea of bottomless black eyes that watched from every tree branch and roof shingle.

Inside, Mike slept on through the night and into the late morning, unknowing, and drifting from haunted dreams of his mother into deeper levels of coma in which the chrysalis inside him struggled toward birth.

(2)

Vic Wingate got home late from his morning round of errands and found the mess that Ruger and Lois had left for him. Just the blood spatters downstairs were bad enough and he went into the kitchen and drank two beers for brunch before going upstairs to see how bad it was. The bloodstains began about halfway up the stairs. There were long artistic smears, flecks and splotches, dots arranged in arterial spray patterns, and here and there were handprints. One of the prints was Ruger's, Vic knew, but the others were smaller. Lois's.

Lois and Ruger were gone, but they'd left him a real mess to clean up. Vic smoked a cigarette while leaning against the bedroom door staring at the bed.

He changed into soiled work clothes from the hamper, wrapped plastic bags around his shoes, and fetched a yellow rubber rain slicker from the hall closet. He lined the hamper with a double layer of plastic trash bags and took it with him.

The first of the body parts was at the top of the stairs. Well, not so much a part, just a lump, really. It didn't look like anything Vic recognized.

Vic bent down and picked up the meat and tossed it into the hamper. As he worked, he thought about Ruger, remembering the things Ruger'd said.

It's a new world, pal, and it must be a real kick in the nuts—especially after all these years and all you've done—to realize that you're on the wrong end of the food chain.

Ruger wouldn't have been so bold, made such a statement, if he hadn't gotten at least a provisional nod from the Man. That troubled Vic so much he wanted to cry. Not just the implied betrayal of the Man, or—if betrayal wasn't the right word, then what was? Disfavor?

Vic moved down the hall, collecting pieces that he figured would eventually add up to two teenage girls. He'd seen a lot of carnage, had created a good deal of it himself, but this was over the top. What the hell had happened to Lois since the change? She hadn't just come awake like the others. She was more like

Ruger. Powerful . . . way past what the other vampires were like. Crazier, too, and ten times more savage.

Not for the first time he wondered if the Man had made a mistake in bringing Ruger on board as his general. As his *left* hand. Vic felt sure right from the beginning that it had been a bad move. He looked at the crimson junk in the hamper and fought the urge to shiver.

The Red Wave, he thought . . . and hoped that it wasn't he who had made a mistake.

(3)

"This doesn't make a lot of sense," LaMastra said as he shuffled through the papers Weinstock kept handing them. "I see bloodwork, reports on saliva samples, forensic dentistry reports on bite marks . . . but so what? I mean, we already know that Boyd attacked those two officers. We know he bit them, et cetera, et cetera . . . so why the hoopla?"

"It'll make sense," Val assured him.

"It had better make sense soon," Ferro said, slapping down one stack of papers and snatching the next set out of Weinstock's hands. "My patience is wearing pretty damn thin."

"Bear with me," Weinstock said. His voice was steadier than it had been, but his eyes were jumpy and looked feverish. He picked up another folder. "I have here the autopsy report on both men. Full workup. In it I recorded the exact cause of death for both men."

"Saul," said Ferro, "if you remember, we saw the bodies. We know the cause of death."

"Do you? Okay, then what was it?"

LaMastra said, "They were attacked by person or persons unknown—though Boyd seems to be the only possible suspect—and aside from other physical trauma, they had their throats ripped out. I guess they just died from blood loss."

"Blood loss," murmured Weinstock. "Yes, that about covers it. But what would you say if I told you that the majority of the damage done to the throat, the tearing of the flesh and tendons and such, were done postmortem."

Ferro shrugged. "It's not unusual for a killer to perpetrate additional damage to a victim. Many sociopathic killers even dismember their victims."

"I know. Still, the damage to the throats of both victims was not done just to satisfy some kind of maniacal frenzy."

"How do you know?"

"Because I know *why* it was done."

"Okay. Why?"

"To hide the puncture wounds on the throat."

"Puncture wounds? You mean stab wounds?"

Weinstock gave them a twisted smile and flipped open the folder, turning it around so they could both see the glossy black-and-white photo. It was a very clear shot, a close-up on the throat of Nels Cowan, identified by a note paper-clipped to the edge. The detectives bent forward and stared. "I had to press the flesh back together, fitting the pieces carefully to reconstruct the throat. As you can see there are two ragged punctures just over the left carotid artery."

"Jesus . . ." said LaMastra. "What the hell did he use? Looks like one of those two-pronged forks you roast hot dogs with."

Ferro looked hard at Weinstock. "And this was the cause of death? These . . . uh, stab wounds?"

"No. The actual cause of death of both men was a nearly total exsanguination. They were both completely drained of blood."

"When you say 'completely'. . . ?" Ferro arched an eyebrow.

"During the autopsy, I was able to recover a total of forty-eight cc's of blood. That would fill a large syringe, gentlemen, and that is all I recovered in total from both bodies. In essence, the bodies were sucked dry."

Ferro began shaking his head, and LaMastra burst out laughing. "Oh, come on, Doc! What are you selling here, that they guys were offed by a *vampire*?"

Weinstock did not laugh, didn't even smile. He leaned back in his chair and folded his arms over his chest, and just looked at them.

Ferro rolled his eyes. "I think we're done here."

Val got to her feet to block him from standing. "Frank, please just hear him out."

"I don't want to hear any more of this nonsense—"

"I can prove this," Weinstock said.

LaMastra was still grinning. "You're going to prove to us that there are vampires in Pine Deep?"

Dr. Weinstock returned the smile, but his was cold and humorless. "Yes."

Ferro folded his arms and tilted his head to one side, giving him a challenging, mocking look. Weinstock reached for another folder, but Crow interrupted him. "Saul, just show them the fricking tape."

"What tape?" LaMastra wanted to know.

Weinstock opened his top desk drawer and removed a Sony digital cassette still in its cardboard jacket. "Surveillance camera tape from the security camera at the morgue."

"Of what? The autopsy?" Ferro asked.

"Not exactly." Weinstock handed the tape to Crow, who put it in the machine. "This was recorded automatically by the morgue cameras the night after Boyd stole Ruger's body," explained Weinstock. On the screen, the time display read 8:00 P.M. "The security guard patrolling the hospital changes all of the tapes every day and each tape records just twenty-four hours of footage. Unlike the tapes from the hall camera, the morgue tapes are never actually viewed unless there is an autopsy in progress or some reason to believe an event has occurred, such as when we discovered Ruger's body missing from the morgue. This tape would never have been looked at except for the fact that I noticed some irregularities the next day when I was doing routine work in the morgue."

"What kind of irregularities?" asked Ferro.

"When Boyd broke in to steal Ruger's body he messed with the corpses of Cowan and Castle. I wanted to do a detailed examination of each man so we'd have a detailed record of any additional postmortem mutilation. Mind you, at this point even I didn't believe what the evidence was trying to tell me. I was putting together a puzzle without knowing the picture. When I got in that morning the morgue doors were locked and at first everything looked kosher. It wasn't until I wheeled Castle out of his cold storage and brought him into the autopsy room that I saw the changes."

"Changes?"

"Physical changes. At first I thought it was just the lighting, but even with changing the angle of the lights, there were definite physical changes."

"Such as?"

"Skin color, for one. Instead of the waxy, blue-white skin typical of a postautopsied corpse, I was looking at what appeared to be normal skin tone."

"Normal for a dead man, you mean?"

"No, normal for a living person. There were no signs of pallor, the skin was pink as if flushed with blood. Even the lips seemed red and swollen. Because of the apparent lividity I decided to check for trace amounts of blood in the skin."

"I thought you said the corpses had been totally drained of blood."

"They had," Weinstock said. "They had. But when I cut into Jimmy Castle's skin that morning, real blood welled out of the wound."

Ferro frowned. "Welled out, you say?"

"Yes. Not drained out. It welled out of the surface of the skin."

"But . . . how can that be? If the heart has stopped pumping . . ."

"Right, there's not going to be any blood in the surface of the skin, especially on elevated sections of the body, no hydrostatic pressure in the veins. The place I made my incision was just below the navel, just off center of the big Y-incision I made during the previous night's autopsy."

"And blood came out."

"A lot of it."

"That isn't possible," Ferro said, shaking his head.

"No," said Weinstock, "it isn't. Nor is the fact that when I cut through the sutures holding my autopsy incision together the wound itself had nearly sealed itself shut. It was sealed enough to become watertight, so to speak. I reopened the incision, and saw something else that defied all logic or explanation."

"Oh, I can't wait to hear this," murmured LaMastra.

"In an autopsy we cut away a section of the rib cage and then remove each of the internal organs, weigh them, do some tests on them to determine the presence of toxins, trauma, that sort of thing. After we're finished, we pack them in a plastic bag and more or less just cram them back into the body cavity, lay the cut-away sections of rib on top of them, and just sew the whole mess together so that the body is as intact as it needs to be when it's sent to the mortuary for funeral preparation. There's no reason to arrange the internal organs in any kind of order, especially since they'd each been severed from the connective tissue that had held them in place. When I'd done my autopsy on Jimmy Castle, I'd done just that. I'd been pretty thorough about it since I was on the hunt for the blood that I never found. So his internal organs should have been a jumble of dead tissue inside the body cavity."

LaMastra was looking green; Ferro unwrapped a stick of gum and chewed it slowly, the muscles in the corners of his jaw flexing.

"That morning, when I reopened Castle's body, the internal organs—each and every goddamned one of them—was in the right place."

Ferro's face was a stone. LaMastra looked like he'd just taken a mouthful of sour milk.

"It was as if I'd never performed that autopsy. Only the presence of the Y-incision showed that I had even opened the body. Plus, the body—every vein, every artery, every organ—was gorged with blood. Not just filled, but filled nearly to bursting."

LaMastra was slowly shaking his head. He really did not want to hear this.

"I assume," said Ferro dryly, "that you did some kind of examination on the blood? Typed it, that sort of thing?"

"Of course. I had to try and determine what had happened. I

mean, here was a corpse I know damn well was dead. A corpse I had autopsied in the presence of a registered nurse, and now it was as fresh as if it had died just that moment."

"It was actually dead, I trust?"

"I checked all the vitals again and again. Castle was dead, no doubt about it. His BP was zero, which doesn't explain how the blood remained in the veins or had the pressure to bleed out." Strain was making Weinstock's voice hoarse. "Castle was your basic O-positive type, but the blood in his veins was a soup. Mostly O-positive, but a bunch of other types mixed in."

"I don't want to know this," LaMastra said to the ceiling.

Ferro glanced at Val and Crow, who sat on the doctor's couch, holding hands, saying nothing. To Weinstock he said, "Is that what's on the tape? Your examination of the body?"

"No."

"Then why are we watching a video of an empty morgue? How is this going to corroborate what you're trying to tell us?"

"Frank, Vince, try to put yourselves in my shoes for a minute. Imagine how I felt during all this. I was shocked and scared and I didn't know where to turn. I had to sit down and think about it for a while. While I was trying to work it out, I just happened to catch sight of the security camera and suddenly I realized that whatever had happened to the two bodies must have occurred the previous night, after Barney and I had left. Understand, I was still at this point trying to convince myself that somehow someone had come in and tampered somehow with the bodies, filling the bodies with a mixture of blood for some reason, maybe a prank, maybe some kind of weird fraternity stunt. I don't know what I believed at the time, but I knew that the event had to have been recorded on the cameras. So I called security and got the tape."

"How do we know this is the legitimate tape?" asked LaMastra.

"The ID number is hologram-stamped into the case, the case itself is sealed with a tamperproof label that changes color if the seals are broken, and the time signature on the tape itself cannot in any way be altered."

Ferro said, "We can check on that."

"By all means check. Double-check. But for right now, just watch the tape." Weinstock raised the remote and pointed its electric eye at the VCR. "Nothing happens for the first forty minutes, so I'll have to fast-forward. It'll take some time, so bear with me."

"Why not stop it and fast-forward?" asked LaMastra irritably. "It's faster that way."

"No," said Ferro, "I see what he's doing. Fast-forwarding visually will show us the continuity, will show that there are no breaks where other footage could have been spliced in."

"Plus, you can see the timer in the corner. It's progressing normally, and you can see that even when I fast-forward."

The video image of the empty morgue rolled on, minutes transformed into seconds, with the shadows remaining constant except for the distortion caused by the enhanced speed. Except for the constant unreeling of the chronometer, the image might have been a still photograph. Then, abruptly, the image changed.

Ferro and LaMastra watched the video image with faces that had become white, not just from the reflection of the black-and-white video image, but from shock and a growing, gnawing horror.

Chapter 27

The image on Weinstock's TV showed an unreal world of flat grays and whites and blacks. The stainless steel gleamed without twinkling; the shadows were precise and unchanging geometric shapes; the dim security lights were surrounded by frozen clouds of light. Only the inexorable count of the digital clock at the lower right-hand corner of the screen argued the reality of the passage of time. The stillness of the scene was ordinary at first, just a reflection of an event as detached from the present as something recorded on a cave wall twenty-five thousand years ago.

Dr. Weinstock raised one hand, finger extended, and pointed. His whole arm trembled. In a whisper he said, "There."

The detectives looked at him briefly and then back at the video image and saw nothing. At first. Then there was a brief moment of vibration; then a muffled thud from somewhere off-screen, then a long silence broken by a second thump.

Nothing happened for nearly a full minute. Then there was another movement. It began as a tremble, a hesitant shift of the left-hand door that led from the autopsy suite to the adjoining cold room. The door shifted as if pressed, but it did not open, as if the pushing hand were uncertain, or confused. It began to open, dropped closed, began again to open. Closed again. Then abruptly it banged open hard and fast, reeling away from a powerful blow. The swinging door flew to the end of its closer, jolted to a halt, and then began to fall back toward the frame, but now something was blocking the way, and the closing door bounced off the hard shoulder of something that moved in a slow and plodding way.

LaMastra gasped out loud, leaning sharply forward.

"Oh my . . . God!" breathed Ferro.

In the doorway, blocking the close of the door, stood a man. He was naked and tall. Fair hair stuck out in all directions, tacky with fluids. He stood there, swaying slightly, staring with eyes that seemed to be dazed from sleep. His skin was milk white, turned to a luminescent blue by the videotape. The door hid half of his body, but the center of his torso was clearly visible, and both detectives could see the long lines of lightly stitched incisions. One stretched from shoulder to shoulder all the way across the chest in a lazy line that sagged toward the middle of the breastbone, where it met the longer cut that dropped all the way down past chest and stomach to the groin. The horrible Y-shaped ventral incision was held together only with temporary stitches, and in the gaps dark and unsavory shapes of organs and muscles bunched and shifted in their plastic bag with each step. The throat was the worst thing, though. The flesh there was a mass of torn strips of skin, ripped and shredded, held in place only by thin lengths of surgical tape.

With slow and uncertain steps, the figure moved into the autopsy suite, staggering a bit as it walked, as if uncertain how to use its legs. The milk-white hands twitched as if stung by live electrical wires, and the figure's mouth hung open, lips slack and rubbery. The eyes stared as if newly awakened, a bulging fixity of focus, but as the figure moved closer to the camera, those eyes seemed almost artificial, like the glass eyes of a stuffed deer.

"Dear sweet God," murmured Ferro. "That . . . that's Jimmy Castle!"

Someone made a gagging sound, and Weinstock looked over at LaMastra, who had his hands clamped to his mouth. Crow rose and handed him a plastic trash can. LaMastra took it without comment and wrapped both arms around it, holding his head over it, eyes fixed with manic concentration on the TV. He did not throw up, though he gagged again and again.

Castle stumbled, tripping over his own feet, and pitched forward almost out of shot, falling hard but making no attempt to stop his fall or protect himself. There was a horrible meaty thud as Castle's cheekbone struck the unyielding corner of the nearest surgical table. He toppled off and vanished out of frame.

"No . . ." said Ferro, his dark brown skin sickened to a toxic gray.

There was more movement. Not from the figure that had fallen, but from the doorway, where a second figure was slowly pushing through the door. It, too, was naked, but was darker, heavier, taller, with coarse black hair that matted its milky skin like an animal's pelt. This second figure had the same long and terrible Y-shaped ventral incision and the same mass of torn skin on its throat held in place by adhesive strips. Ferro and LaMastra watched in stunned horror as Nels Cowan shambled into the room. Cowan stared blindly at the security camera for a while, not with any deliberate focus, but because his face was in line with the lens. Cowan's face was horrible. The features were slack as if the muscle and flesh just hung from the skull with no internal anchor, a mask draped loosely over a set of empty bones. There was a long incision across the top of the scalp from ear to ear, stitched now to stay in place. Ferro knew, even if LaMastra was spared the knowledge, that during an autopsy the whole front section of the scalp was peeled forward to expose the skull, then the front of the skull itself sawn off to allow the pathologist access for removing the brain. The long line of sutures showed where Weinstock had reattached the lower part of the scalp and all of the forehead flesh. LaMastra's stomach writhed with icy worms and sour sickness.

Cowan's face filled the screen and for a while did nothing but stand there, but that was horrifying enough. That face, empty of life but filled with an impossible animation, dominated the whole of Weinstock's office from where it looked out of the TV screen.

Behind Cowan, blurry now that the auto-focus had shifted to Cowan, something moved. Ferro leaned forward to see, and watched in horror as Jimmy Castle slowly got to his feet. It was an effort of incredible clumsiness, as if the muscles and bones and tendons of Castle's body had no single point of direction, no memory of how to work in concert. It was a parody of human movement that nonetheless possessed no scrap of comedy. Castle flailed and thrashed, flopping three or four times back onto the floor, each time with a hard-bone crack but no grunt of pain or gasp of effort. There was no humanity to the action, just an effort of a construct to master the mechanics of standing, but even seeing it in such an antiseptic way did not keep the grotesque horror of it from making Ferro's mind reel and LaMastra's stomach churn.

Both detectives were sweating badly. Weinstock opened his desk drawer and took out a full bottle of Glenlivet and three paper cups. As he unscrewed the top his eyes were locked on the screen, seeing the images he had watched over and over again, seeing them new again through the eyes of the cops.

Jimmy Castle managed to get to its feet, and somehow in its last efforts there had been some kind of a change, some improvement in the link between body and directing force, as if the flesh had remembered the way in which it was supposed to work. Muscles bunched under the pale, pale skin, and the figure rose slowly from an awkward crouch, straightening inch by inch to stand on firm footing. The body swayed but did not fall.

In the foreground, the face of Nels Cowan had taken on a different cast. Where moments before the eyes had been as lifeless and empty as marbles, now there was something . . . a faintness of life, a subtle flickering of energy, and as they all watched those eyes seemed to come to a slow and very gradual focus, actually seeing the camera instead of just pointing in the that direction. There was no specific recognition of what the camera was, it was more that the camera was simply the very first thing those eyes noticed. Cowan's eyes were black windows that looked into a vast, dark space, but now something in that darkness moved. Those eyes stared and stared, and then, slowly, they shifted as if Cowan had discovered that there were muscles that could make the eyes move. He looked right and left, up and down, just experimenting with the mechanics, then found a new and specific focus as Cowan raised his hands to eye level. He looked down at the hands, as white as candle wax and wasted from the massive loss of blood and other body fluids.

For just a moment, it seemed to Ferro and LaMastra that expression flickered through those eyes, something like awareness, or shock, or fear; but if those emotions were there they lingered only briefly and then flitted away as Cowan turned his hands over and peered at them closely. He closed his hands into fists and there was a dry cracking sound as the unlubricated tendons creaked and popped. Opening the fingers, Cowan stared at his palms, and that left the backs of the hands clearly visible to the camera's unwinking eye.

LaMastra gasped. "Frank, look at his nails!"

Ferro nodded mutely, too stunned to speak. Each of Nels Cowan's fingernails had changed, had become thicker, darker, almost black, the new growth of nail splitting the flesh of each finger, curling out like talons. Not as long as an animal's nails, or even as long as many women wore them, but too long for the hands of a man who had been a working cop, and the thickness and sharpness of them was alien and awful.

Cowan opened and closed his hands several times, turning them to stare at them with a kind of animalistic wonder. His face showed the very first flicker of emotion as he considered his taloned hands. There was just the barest hint of a smile on his blue-white lips, just enough to show the even edges of his white teeth. Even, except for the incisors.

"No," said LaMastra firmly. "Fucking no!"

The incisors were long. Far longer than they should have been, far longer than they had any right to be. Too long. Impossibly, insanely long for a human mouth.

"Goddamn it—*NO!*" yelled LaMastra. He slammed the trash can down on the floor and wheeled on Weinstock. "This is bullshit, man. This is some kind of stupid Halloween bullshit!"

Weinstock didn't answer. What could he say? He threw an imploring look at Val and Crow, but she was looking down at the lacings of her shoes and Crow was giving the TV a thousand-yard stare.

Ferro reached a hand out to touch LaMastra on the shoulder, but the younger man just shook it off.

On the TV screen, Cowan had turned away and was lumbering toward Castle. They stood there, regarding each other. Cowan was still smiling, but Castle's face looked almost sad. It didn't last, though, as Cowan and he scrutinized each other, the look of sad dismay on Jimmy Castle's face crumbled and fell away and soon he, too, was smiling. That smile was wrong in every possible way.

Suddenly both men—if men they were—stopped and froze with their heads cocked to listen. They stood like that for a very long time, though the microphone of the security camera picked up no trace at all of anything they might have heard. Their smiles widened, became the leering, grinning mouths of animals, losing any last resemblance to humanity. Then, as if responding to a call, both of them turned and walked toward the door. Walked now, not lumbering like machines. They moved with something approaching grace. It was still not a manlike way of walking, but instead it possessed the smooth stalking fluidity of predatory hunters. They crept to the door, listened, opened it, and vanished into the hall.

Once again the autopsy room was frozen into the silence and immobility of a still photograph except for the constantly changing clock. After a while, Weinstock raised the remote and pressed Stop, reducing the image to static and softly hissing white noise.

He looked at the two detectives, feeling sorry for them, feeling helpless as if showing them this was some kind of betrayal of trust.

Ferro sat with his face in his hands, shaking his head slowly; beside him LaMastra was beating one bunched fist forcefully against his thigh. Weinstock knew that the blows had to hurt. Perhaps LaMastra needed the pain to keep from flying apart. That was something he could well understand.

Without asking he poured them each a measure of Scotch, then walked around the desk to hand one to each, saying, "Here."

LaMastra took the Scotch and sipped at it, winced, and took another sip, letting the alcohol burn play surrogate for the pounding fist.

Ferro looked into the cup and said, "I don't drink Scotch." Then he drank it down in two gulps, hissing at the fumes. He held the cup out for a refill, which Weinstock provided.

"There's more of it," Weinstock said softly.

"The hell there is!" growled LaMastra. "The bloody hell there is!"

"It shows them coming back. It's on the next tape. It shows them coming back." He wiped his mouth with a shaky hand. "It shows them all . . . bloated. Shows them going back into the cold room."

"Go fuck yourself!" snarled LaMastra jabbing a finger at Weinstock.

"I'm sorry," said Weinstock.

LaMastra looked up at him, then he wheeled on Crow and Val and they saw tears in the young man's eyes. "Why'd you have to do this?" he demanded with as much desperation as ferocity.

There was nothing to say to that, so Weinstock gestured with the bottle. Both detectives held out their cups for more. Weinstock filled the cups and set the bottle down on the edge of the desk. He slumped down on the edge of the desk next to the bottle, arms folded protectively across his chest, ankles crossed, head slumped forward. "I'm sorry."

"What you showed us . . ." began Ferro, stopped, tried again. "This is just . . ."

"I know."

"This can't be what it is," said Ferro, then corrected himself. "What it looks like. That can't be. It can't."

"I know."

LaMastra wiped angrily at his eyes. "There is just no way I just saw that. You just get that out of your head, Doc."

Weinstock nodded.

"It's absurd," said Ferro, trying for a trace of his air of cool command. "What we saw was some kind of prank. Highly convincing, sure, but not real. No way, not possible."

"Okay," said Val softly.

"Just a lot of bullshit!" agreed LaMastra.

"Someone's idea of a sick joke," concluded Ferro.

"Sure," said Crow.

Ferro looked at Weinstock, whose face was weary beyond words, and grave; he looked at LaMastra, who was flushed and fighting to keep tears out of his eyes. He looked at Val, who nodded silently.

"Oh, God . . ." he said at length.

Chapter 28

The bottle of Scotch was half empty. Ferro got up and walked over to the couch and stared hard at Crow.

"Why?" he asked.

"Why what, Frank?"

Ferro's hand snaked out and took a fistful of Crow's shirt and pulled him roughly to his feet. He was six inches taller than Crow and his face was filled with fury. "Why did you bring us into this . . . this . . . ?"

Crow began to say something but Val stood and put her hand on Ferro's wrist. "No, Frank," she said. His eyes snapped toward her and they seemed to generate heat. Val raised her other hand and put her palm on his cheek. "No."

Ferro's eyes went moist. He let go of Crow and stepped back.

Val said, "We brought you in because we're scared and we're desperate and we didn't know where else to turn. You and Vince are outsiders, which means we can trust you. We can't say as much for the police here. Gus is a fool and Polk . . . well, there's a possibility that Polk is involved."

"It was wrong of you to call us," Ferro insisted, but his voice lacked conviction.

"I won't apologize, Frank," Val said. "I've lost too many of the people I love to want to play it coy. I'll do anything I have to do in order to stop this. Anything."

Ferro tried to hold her gaze, tried to win the contest, but

there was just no way. His eyes dropped and he turned away, swatting at the air as if he could put the whole thing behind him.

Crow cleared his throat. "We have other help on this." He told them about Jonatha Corbiel and filled them in on all of the information she'd dug up. "She's doing the deep research for us, her and that reporter, Newton. Maybe she'll come up with something."

"Frank . . . Vince," Val said, "sit down. We have to tell you all of it now. From the very beginning."

Their faces registered the horror that each of them felt at the thought that there was more, but Val was implacable. She waited them out and they did sit down. Then she and Crow told them about Griswold and what they believed he was; about the Bone Man; about everything they knew and believed. Weinstock brewed a pot of coffee and everyone had a cup. When they were about three-quarters through the story Newton and Jonatha joined them, crowding the office. The detectives' greeting was less than cordial.

"This is like a plague," Crow said. "And the plague started with a single vampire. The main vampire."

"In folklore the paradigm is known as the 'vampire overlord,'" Jonatha said.

"This is getting out of hand," growled LaMastra. Anger was replacing shock by slow degrees. "Vampires, werewolves, *and* ghosts?"

Ferro held up a hand. "There's something wrong with your theory about this, Crow. All the stories about werewolves I ever heard of say that whoever gets bitten by one becomes one. So why didn't the mayor ever turn into a werewolf after all this time?"

Jonatha fielded that one. "There is very little in the folklore that suggests that the bloodline of a werewolf follows through victims of their bite. That's a fictional device. Like vampires, werewolfism is something that manifests based on a person's nature. An evil, twisted person can become a werewolf. Unlike a vampire, though, this can happen while the person is still alive."

"So, Mayor Wolfe—and excuse me if I don't think that his

name is just too goddamn bizarre—is *not* in danger of becoming a werewolf?"

"I didn't say that. Actually, we don't know. From what Crow and Val said, he was going through a terrible psychological breakdown, including intense dreams about *becoming* a monster."

"Shit," Crow said.

"So if he does carry the curse—or infection, to use Val's word—then his own good nature has probably been at war with the werewolf nature all these years."

"That's why he tried to kill himself," Val said, her eyes going wide. "My God . . . he thought he was losing the struggle. He tried to kill himself to save Sarah."

Weinstock covered his mouth with his hands. "Dear God."

"On the other hand," Jonatha said, "there is evidence in the folklore to support the theory that a werewolf is not inherently evil. Take the case of the *Benendanti* of Italy. They are ancient families who claimed that they became werewolves at night and descended into Hell to fight vampires and other monsters. Some were put on trial by the Inquisition, and there's at least one case where a *Benendanti* was acquitted because the inquisitors could not prove—either through evidence or coercion—that the werewolf was not a servant of God."

"I read about them in a couple of books," Crow said. "The name means . . ."

" 'Good walker,' " Jonatha said. "Though their nicknames are 'The Hounds of God.' "

"You think that's what Terry was?" Val asked.

"Oh, I have no idea," Jonatha admitted. "I'm shooting in the dark here, trying to make what's happening fit somewhere into what's in the folklore."

"Christ," said Crow, "I don't think Terry tried to kill himself just to protect Sarah . . . maybe he was afraid of the beast getting out and starting a new series of murders, like the Massacre. I think he did it to protect the town!"

"I feel sick," LaMastra said looking into the bottom of his empty coffee cup.

Val said, "So what we're dealing with is both the werewolf's bloodline in Terry and with the fact that after thirty years, the monster that killed my uncle and Crow's brother and all those other people has come back as a vampire. Only now he's stronger. He's making more like himself. And it's pretty clear that he's doing a lot of this on the QT."

"How do you figure that?" Ferro asked.

"Look at it. It's been going on for a while and we're only just putting it together now, and we wouldn't even be this far if it hadn't been for the lucky accident of the morgue's video cameras."

" 'Lucky accident,' he says," complained LaMastra.

"It makes me wonder how much else is going on that we don't know about," Crow concluded.

"Well, we know some of it," said Newton. He shot a look at Crow, who nodded and gave Newton a wan smile of encouragement. "We know he's organized, and we know he has help. Probably human help."

Ferro shot him a glance. "Human help? How do you figure that?"

Quickly Newton related the trip down to Griswold's house and all that happened there. After the horrified reactions had calmed down, he said, "Crow pointed out that the lumber was fresh, and so was that chain. Can you see a vampire going to a lumberyard and a hardware store?"

Ferro shook his head.

Crow said, "Then we should assume the presence of human help. I mean, in the books and movies about vampires, doesn't he always have someone who looks after things during the day? A Renfield sort of character. So, either we have a human handyman, or we have a vampire that likes to use tools."

"That can give us a starting place, can't it?" asked LaMastra, but Val shook her head.

"In farming country nearly everyone knows some basic carpentry. No, the point is that the helper is probably someone local."

Ferro scanned the faces of the others. "So . . . does anyone have a useful suggestion for what we should do now? We have to be careful about how we release this information. You have a full town here, and we could be wrong . . . I mean, sure there may be vampires, God help us, but Ruger could actually be dead and rotting out in some shallow grave and this whole thing could be over."

"That'd be nice," Newton said. "Crow and the Doc dug up those two cops and they seem to be pretty well dead. So, maybe this is all after the fact."

"Regardless," Ferro said, "I don't think it's wise to tell anyone about this just yet."

"What are you talking about?" LaMastra said, goggling. "I intend to tell every frigging person in the tristate area. This is not the time to play it close to our vest."

"It could cause a panic. We can't risk that."

"Well fine then, Frank. Let's *have* a panic. Let's do 'er up pretty, too. Let's have everyone in this end of the country running around with crosses and stakes. Hey, I'm all for the whole villagers with torches thing here."

"If we have a panic," Ferro said patiently, "it will be impossible to control the situation."

"Control it? Christ, Frank, we are not in control of it now. Like, I'm all for calling the National Guard and maybe even the Vatican. Let's have a Vampire Slaying party. Invite your friends. Control it? Jesus, you're right out of the movies."

"No, Vince," said Val quietly, "Frank's right. If people start panicking, then how are we going to try and organize our attack?"

"Our attack on *whom*?"

"Why . . . on the vampires," Val said so softly that it chilled everyone in the room. After a moment Crow, Weinstock, and Newton all nodded.

LaMastra folded his arms and sat back in his chair. There was an enigmatic smile on his lips. "Have you guys been smoking crack? You just told us that Griswold dropped a porch on you and then called up a couple billion friggin' roaches to run you off. You never even got inside. Who knows what would have happened if you had and Boyd or Ruger had been there. You'd both probably still be there with beer taps in your necks."

"Yeah," Newton snorted, "we were so damn lucky."

Jonatha nodded gravely. "Luckier than you think. We don't know what these things can really do. In folklore there are all sorts of powers associated with vampires, and if only a tenth of it is true then we're in real trouble." Everyone turned to look at her, each face registering a different degree of distress. She plunged ahead. "Here's what we already know—from what Crow, Val, and Dr. Weinstock have observed. Vampires are stronger than us, though if we're dealing with more than one species the level of strength may vary. Some of them are smarter than humans, too, though the literature suggests that the intelligence increases because of longevity. Immortals, for lack of a better word, have more time to learn."

"Ruger was crafty," Crow said, "but nothing he did suggests he was Einstein with fangs."

"Boyd was more like a zombie," Val said. "A killing machine, which sounds corny, but believe me there was nothing corny about him."

Jonatha nodded, continued. "Some vampires can call on storms and affect the weather."

Val looked at Crow, her eyebrows arched. "That might fit. We've had a lot of storms this past month, and more cloudy days than sunny."

"Right," Crow agreed, "and that started the night before Ruger and Boyd came to town." He looked inquiringly at Jonatha. "Griswold?"

"If he's a true psychic vampire, then, yes, that would fit."

"How bad can these storms get?" Val asked.

"I don't know. The stories are often exaggerated. I mean, some vampires are supposed to be able to cause eclipses, which is of course impossible."

"Even for something . . . supernatural?" LaMastra asked.

Jonatha smiled. "Bringing corpses back to life is one thing, causing storms is another . . . but moving the sun and the planets seems a bit much even for a vampire."

"Well, thank God for small favors," Ferro muttered.

"In the movies," Crow said, "Dracula can command rats and bugs. Considering the whole army of roaches thing I think we can assume Griswold has that ability, too."

"What about shape-shifting?" Newton asked. "Dracula turns into a bat and a wolf . . ."

"Oddly, in folklore vampires never turn into either bats or wolves. Those vampires that are theriomorphic are—"

"That are what?" Ferro asked.

"Sorry. Shape-shifters. Theriomorphs are what we call creatures that are able to change their shape, or at least their appearance. I don't know if our vampires can do that, though since Griswold was once a werewolf we can't rule it out."

Ferro reached for the coffeepot. "This conversation has become surreal."

LaMastra held out his cup. "Hit me."

"What else?" Weinstock asked as he poured.

"Please"—Jonatha said, holding up a slim hand—"please remember that this is all speculation."

"Yes, we get that. Go on."

Jonatha folded her arms. "Hmm. I don't suppose anyone has mapped the ley lines of this town, have they?"

"What the hell are ley lines?" demanded LaMastra.

"It's a belief held by some that there is a kind of energy grid covering the world, somewhat like the imaginary lines of latitude and longitude, but acting more like the lines of energy in the human body they call meridians. In healing arts like acupuncture and acupressure the belief is that energy flows through the body along invisible pathways and disease comes from blockages in the normal flow and health is restored by removing those blocks. Ley lines are similar in that spiritual earth energy flows along them. Now, there have been folkloric studies of ley lines and in places where the normal flow is somehow blocked there have been all sorts of phenomena like hauntings, plagues, and blights."

"Hmm," Crow said.

"You and Newt said that you felt a very negative energy in Dark Hollow, right? Well, I wouldn't be at all surprised to find that the natural flow of earth energy probably warps around that spot."

"How does this New Age crap help us?" LaMastra said.

"It might not," Jonatha admitted, "except to help understand the scope of this thing. Do you have a map of the town, Doctor?"

"Sure." Weinstock took a book from a shelf, a big glossy history of the town. He rifled the pages then stopped at a two-page aerial photo.

As Jonatha bent over it, Crow tapped a few spots. "Okay, here's Dark Hollow, and there's Griswold's farm."

"What's here?" Jonatha asked tracing a line in a semicircle that skirted the Hollow.

"Well, the center section here is Val's place. Then there's some sections of the campus, some forest, and a few farms." He named the farms.

Jonatha looked at Val. "Your farm wasn't affected by the blight, was it?"

"No."

"What about these others?"

As Val looked at the map deep frown lines formed between her brows. "God . . . !"

"What?" Newton asked.

"Holy crap," Crow said. "Those are the only farms unaffected by the blight." There was a stunned silence.

Jonatha nodded. "I'd bet my tenure that the natural ley line warps around the Hollow and crosses each of those farms, and because those farms—and only those—would in essence be pinched between the next natural ley line and the warped one, they sit in a zone of higher natural energy. That intensified energy kept them safe from the blight."

LaMastra looked from the map to Ferro. "You buying any of this bullshit?"

"Actually," Ferro said softly, "I'm starting to." He sat back in his chair and swirled the coffee around in his cup. "However, as fascinating as the backstory is, Dr. Corbiel, I think we need to determine two things right now. No, make that three things. First, we need to know how to kill these bastards."

"I'll drink to that," said LaMastra, and did.

"Then we need to know where they are," Ferro continued. "And finally, we need to know how they're created. If that's a process we can identify, then maybe we can cut it off. Like when you're getting rid of termites in a house . . . if you can kill off one breeding cycle you kill the infestation."

"Well," Jonatha said, "as far as where they are . . . I think Dark Hollow has to be the hub. Griswold's almost certainly buried somewhere down there."

Ferro looked at his watch. "There's not enough daylight to go out there today, but I think we should plan on going there tomorrow."

"I take it you're signing on," Crow asked.

Ferro gave him a withering look. "Yes, and when this is over I hope to Christ that I never see any of you again."

"Amen," agreed LaMastra. "When this is over I'm moving to Florida."

"Why Florida?" Newton asked.

"Why not?"

"The second point is killing them," Jonatha said, "and that might be some good news. The folklore has a lot to say about that."

"What, we need to get a bunch of hammers and stakes?" LaMastra asked.

"No," Weinstock interjected. "Val's pretty much shown us that severe brain trauma will do the job. Though it's possible that spinal damage might be a factor. At least one of Val's shots severed Boyd's upper spine and also broke his neck. All of those are possible or even probable methods of killing them. When in doubt, aim for the brain stem."

"Beheading should work, too," Jonatha said, "and we can probably count on fire."

"Burn baby burn," LaMastra said under his breath. Crow reached over and offered a high-five, which LaMastra, to his surprise, returned.

"And don't forget garlic, that's very important. In every culture where there are vampires, garlic is used both to ward them off and to kill them. I'm not sure how we'd introduce it into their bodies, though."

"Garlic oil," Weinstock said, looking at Ferro. "Could we use that somehow? Some kind of weapon?"

"Doable," said the detective thoughtfully. "Definitely doable."

"What about the last point," Val asked quietly. "That matters most to me because of Mark. Can we do a test to determine if Mark is infected?"

Jonatha looked at her for a long time before she answered. "Yes," she said slowly. "There is a way . . . but it's dangerous."

"So what else is new?" asked Newton sourly.

(2)

After Jonatha outlined her plan, Val said she needed some time. Crow walked her down to the hospital's chapel, but at the door she stopped him with a gentle hand on his chest. "Honey, I need a few minutes to myself. I have to think this through . . . and maybe talk to Daddy about it."

He nodded. "You don't have to be there when we do this. Saul and I can do it. We have the two cops . . ."

"No."

"You're pregnant, Val . . . Crow Junior doesn't need his mom to—"

"I said no, Crow." She put a finger to his lips, then kissed him, sweetly and long. "Give me fifteen minutes, okay?"

Crow sighed, nodded, hating it.

Back in Weinstock's office, he saw that Newton and Jonatha were gone—out to get sandwiches for everyone—and the others were watching TV coverage of the Halloween parties that were in full swing in town.

"There's a lot of people in town," Ferro said dubiously. "I don't like it."

"Tomorrow it will be even crazier," Weinstock said.

"That's just peachy." LaMastra rubbed his eyes. "No way to keep control of this."

Ferro said, "We've established that the Halloween stuff is going to happen. What precautions have you taken?"

Crow told them about the security team he'd brought into town. Ferro was familiar with BK and Billy Christmas. "They did security a couple of times for some big-ticket election events in Philly. BK's a levelheaded guy."

To Ferro, Weinstock said, "Are you concerned that something is going to happen during the holiday activities?"

Ferro pursed his lips, then shook his head. "I doubt it. With all the media coverage . . . it'd be too high profile. But with all that's going on, we'll have no way of seeing what is going on behind the scenes. There'll be no way to keep track of who goes missing, which means we have to take a closer look at those statistics you've been keeping over the last month, Saul. You've logged an increase in mortality rates, and although each of them individually appears to be normal—house fires, car accidents, heart attacks, and such, in light of what we now know we have to ask ourselves whether any of these could have been attacks by Ruger or Boyd. And, if so, are any of these people also likely to be infected?"

"There's also tourists. How would we know if any of them went missing?" LaMastra asked.

Crow looked at Weinstock. "Saul, how many people do you actually think may have been attacked?"

Weinstock licked his lips with a nervous tongue. "There's no way to know for sure. I didn't examine everyone. And I couldn't arrange for all of them to be exhumed."

"That's not good," LaMastra said. "If there are even one or two more of these things out there . . ."

Crow nodded. "I know."

"Hey," LaMastra asked, snapping his fingers, "what about holy water and crosses?"

"Jonatha said that wouldn't work. At best it would depend on the faith of the vampire—not, as is sometimes mentioned in fiction, on the faith of the person holding the cross. At worst they won't work at all. Besides, even if the vampire is religious, it's a crucifix, not a cross."

"Not if the vampire is a Protestant," Ferro offered. "They don't use the crucifix, they go for the empty cross, symbolic of the resurrection, not the whole death-for-sins thing."

"Sure," said LaMastra. "Plus, the vampire could be Amish or a Mormon, or even a Jehovah's Witness."

"Or Muslim or Buddhist or Hindu," Crow said.

"Or Jewish," Weinstock offered hopefully.

"Great," snapped LaMastra. "Go wave a Star of David at Ruger." Weinstock shook his head. "Actually a mezuzah would be better. It's symbolic of the torah and the laws of Moses. Far more religiously significant than the Star."

"Oh."

"But even so," Weinstock continued thoughtfully, "would that protect men against a vampire who didn't believe in Judaism?"

Crow said, "My, my, here we are discussing the actual power of God." He smiled and shook his head. "I mean, think about it. We are discussing which symbols of God will stop vampires. That's quite a topic. And doesn't it suggest that God is actually real? That He has power that can actually affect things in our world?"

"Well no shit," said LaMastra. "What's your problem? Don't you believe in God?"

"Not much, no."

Ferro asked, "What were you before you lost your faith?"

Crow's eyes were like flint. "A child," he said. "I had it beaten out of me at an early age."

"I'll stick with fire," Weinstock said. "Fire purifies, as the saying goes."

"It would be interesting," said Ferro, "to see how we could

burn them without burning down your whole town and all the surrounding forestland."

They sat and thought about that for a while. Crow said, "Okay, this is farm country. Getting plenty of garlic is not a problem. We ought to be able to rustle up a hundred tons of it if we have to."

"I'm toying with the idea of bathing in it," said LaMastra.

To Crow, Ferro said, "Is your fiancée going to be okay with this? With what we have to do to her brother?"

"It was her idea in the first place."

"She's a pretty tough lady."

"You have no idea, Frank."

Ferro nodded. "You agree we have to do this, right?"

"Yeah, damn it."

"Mark is my brother," Val said from the doorway. They could all see that she'd been crying, but her mouth was a hard line. "He's . . . dead, and that's something I'll have to live with, but I can't go on without knowing if he . . . if he . . ." Even she could not say it. No one blamed her. "But we have a responsibility to this town. If Mark and Connie are infected we have to know. I have to know. I owe it to the town, and to my baby."

"I'm sorry," Ferro said softly.

She nodded, accepting it. "It's getting dark. If we have to do this, let's do it now." She paused and stifled a sob.

"Val," said Ferro, "you should probably stay here while we—"

"No!" she snapped. "Listen to me, Frank. All of you listen. Mark is *my* brother. I love him. Do you think I'll let him be alone through this?" Her voice was as harsh as a slap across Ferro's face, and he winced. "Jonatha said that in order to test him we have to make him taste blood, that we have to put it in his mouth. Well, here's what we're going to do. Crow, you and Vince are going to hustle your asses out to the closest farm stand and buy all the garlic they have. As soon as you get back we're going to go right down to the morgue, and you men are going to hold him down, and I am going to cut open my thumb and spill my blood, my family's blood, into my brother's mouth. That is what's going to happen. Don't you dare try to tell me it's not."

The men stared at her in amazement, each one of them trying to measure their personal courage to see if it came close to matching hers. At that moment, there was not a man in that room who wouldn't have died for her.

"And if my brother is one of them, if he's become a . . . a . . ."

"Val," Crow whispered, touching her.

She looked down at his hand then into his eyes. "If Mark is a vampire," she said in a deadly whisper, "then we will do what needs to be done!" She paused for a moment. "And may God have mercy on us all."

Chapter 29

By the time Crow and LaMastra got back from the farm goods stand, the others had things ready to go. Val was on the far side of the morgue, standing by one of the room's two large stainless-steel surgical tables, arms folded under her breasts, head bowed, staring down at a body completely covered by a clean white sheet.

Ferro said, "What did you get?"

"Cloves and a couple of big jars of garlic oil in gelcaps. I had a brainstorm while I was out."

"Hit me."

"If we took a syringe and drew the oil out of the gelcaps and then injected them into shotgun shells, then maybe used a lighter to seal the punctures . . ."

"That might just be brilliant," Ferro said.

"It'll gum up the guns," LaMasta said, "but who cares?"

Jonatha joined them and took one of the sacks of garlic bulbs LaMasta carried. "I'll get to work." She and Newton used a mortar and pestle to smash the bulbs into a lumpy paste and then smeared the door frame.

Weinstock fished in the other sack for a big bulb and began peeling off the papery skin. "We should all eat a couple of cloves," he said, handing them out.

"I hate garlic," Newton said, "it makes me sick."

"Consider your alternatives." Weinstock held out the clove,

and Newton took it. Nobody liked the taste, but they all had seconds and thirds.

Ferro and LaMastra went to work on the shotgun shells and Crow went over to Val. He touched her face. She didn't react, and he realized that tenderness was probably the last thing she needed right now, so he cleared his throat and withdrew his hand. "We'll be ready soon," he said.

Weinstock joined them, "Val, I don't like the idea of you cutting yourself and dripping blood all over, so I'm going to use a syringe and draw off a few cc's. I think it'll be safer that way. No telling what kind of infection we might be dealing with here."

"Okay," Val said. She held out her arm and Weinstock wrapped a rubber tourniquet around it, swabbed her with alcohol, slapped her inner arm to get a vein, and drew off a full syringe. He put a Band-Aid over the puncture and gave her some cloves to chew.

Val lifted the bottom corner of the sheet to show Crow what they'd done. Mark's ankles were tied to the table with several turns of thick surgical gauze. "Wrists, too," she said. Though her eyes were dry there was a strange deadness to her voice that scared Crow.

"We're just about ready," Ferro called.

Val touched Crow's arm. "Give me just another minute with him, honey, okay?"

"Sure, baby, whatever you need." He kissed her cheek and led Weinstock over to where the cops were working. As the detectives finished doctoring the shells Crow loaded them into the shotgun.

Very quietly LaMastra said, "Tell you one thing, Crow, and don't take no offense."

"Yeah?"

"Your lady has more balls than any of us."

Crow grinned.

"Seriously," LaMastra said, "you're a lucky guy."

Crow glanced over to where Val stood looking down at her dead brother. "Yes I am," Crow said. He slid the last shell in and handed the weapon to Ferro.

Ferro took a deep breath and let it out slowly, then jacked a round into the chamber. Val looked up at the sound. "Ready," he said.

Everyone came and stood in a loose circle around the table. LaMastra crossed himself, drew his Sig Sauer 9mm, and racked the slide.

Val looked at Newton, who held two handfuls of the pulped garlic. Mush dripped from between his fingers. He nodded, genuinely unable to speak for the dry stricture of his throat.

"Saul?" she asked.

He raised the syringe. "Ready as I can be."

Crow took a position by Val's side. "I'm here, babe." In his left hand he had one of the knobby uncrushed garlic bulbs, and in the other his Beretta 92F. "Let's go," he said, "let's get it done."

Faced with the moment of truth, even Val's nerve wavered, but slightly. She reached out to touch the sheet that had been folded up to cover Mark's chest and face. She paused, closed her eyes, and murmured something, perhaps a brief prayer, perhaps only her brother's name, then she took the edge of the sheet between her strong fingers, made a white-knuckled fist, and pulled back the cloth.

If she expected to see a monster, she was wrong. Mark looked dead, and that was frightening enough, but nothing about him was actually fearsome. His familiar features were distorted to a waxy whiteness and a gauntness that was the result of a total loss of blood. He seemed much older, more like her father than ever, and shrunken. Weinstock had wrapped some gauze around his throat to hide the savage wounds, but Val could see the lumpy roughness along the left side just below the chin.

"Oh, Mark," she whispered brokenly and bent forward to kiss his forehead.

Weinstock suddenly reached for her. "Val . . . don't!"

She stopped, looked at Weinstock for a moment, then nodded and straightened. "Right," she said. "You're right." She sniffed and angrily brushed away a tear.

Crow wanted to take her in his arms, hold her, tell her that it was going to be all right and be able to mean it. Instead he ground his teeth as a wave of bilious hatred for Ubel Griswold boiled up from deep inside. No hell would be deep enough or hot enough to punish his black, murderous soul.

"Okay, Saul," Val said, "give me the needle."

"I'd rather do it myself . . ."

"Saul. This is mine to do."

Weinstock reluctantly handed over the syringe. Val held it up, looking at the dark red blood that filled its barrel, then turned the tip of the needle downward.

"Okay, troops," warned Crow, "stay sharp."

Val touched Mark's face with the fingertips of her other hand. She stroked his cheek lightly, placed her fingers on his lips, and parted them gently, then she carefully inserted the needle between the dry teeth. LaMastra, Ferro, and Crow each slipped their fingers into the trigger guards of their weapons. Everyone was sweating heavily. Val's breath was rasping as if she had been running for miles under a hot sun. There was a bright feverish quality to her face as she took one last steadying breath and depressed the plunger. Her own salty, clean, innocent blood sprayed into the open mouth of her dead brother.

Crow leaned forward, pointing his pistol at Mark's temple. Ferro stood at the foot of the table, aiming the shotgun at the ceiling because Val and Crow were in the line of fire. Sweat dripped into his eyes. On the wall the, each tick of the clock was as sharp as the snap of dry twigs.

Mark did not move. Nothing flinched, nothing changed. As Val removed the needle from between his teeth a single drop fell onto his lower lip. It glistened in the fluorescent light.

"Step back," Ferro said, and Val and Crow shifted out of the line of fire; Ferro brought the shotgun down and aimed it at Mark's head. The barrel shook visibly as tension vibrated in every cell of Ferro's body. The lines beside his mouth were taut as fiddle strings. Beside him, LaMastra held his pistol in a two-hand shooter's grip and whispered, "Hail Mary, Mother of grace . . ."

Newton stood apart, his eyes filling with tears of fear and tension.

A full minute passed.

Nothing happened. Another minute. Two. Three.

"It's not happening," whispered LaMastra. "Goddamn. God-damn."

Another minute passed. The room remained still, the dead stayed dead.

Val Guthrie exhaled a lungful of air that had been burning in her chest. She sagged forward, laying her hands on Mark's chest as she closed her eyes in exhausted relief. "Thank God!" she said, and meant it. "It's over." She burst into tears.

That seemed to break the spell. They all breathed out huge lungfuls of air, their bodies slumping, guns lowering, faces breaking into triumphant smiles. They grinned and slapped each other on the back as if they had just won a great victory.

LaMastra prodded Mark with his pistol, but the only movement he saw was the movement he caused. Smiling, he reholstered his gun and dragged his forearm across his face. Newton abruptly laughed out loud, and though such a thing was horribly inappropriate, Weinstock and LaMastra found themselves laughing, too. Their laughter and Val's tears meant the same, felt the same, and cost as much. Ferro slumped back against a worktable and lowered his gun. He looked fifteen years older and he struggled to unwrap a stick of gum with badly shaking hands.

Val huddled over Mark, laying the side of her face on his chest, and wept brokenly.

Only Crow stood completely apart from it all. He felt the same tension, but didn't share the release. He slowly slid his pistol into the holster, placed a hand on Val's back, and failed to think of one single useful thing to say.

Val leaned over to kiss Mark's forehead, daring it now that she knew it was safe. Distantly she knew that the true impact of his death would hit her now; now the true storms of grief would come slashing. Her lips lightly brushed the cold flesh of his brow. "Go to sleep, baby brother," she murmured in a small voice that came close to breaking Crow's heart.

And then Mark Guthrie's eyes snapped open.

With a snarl of inhuman rage and hunger he reared up, snapping the gauze bindings as if they were crepe paper, and lunged off the table at Val.

Val screamed in total horror and recoiled, but Mark's hands caught her elbow and the shoulder of her shirt. His grip was as hard as iron and as cold as arctic ice.

"Watch!" Ferro yelled and swung the shotgun around, trying to find a line of sight to get a clear shot, but Val was in the way.

Crow ripped his gun out of its holster and launched himself at Mark, pistol-whipping him across the face, opening a deep three-inch gash on Mark's cheek that did not bleed. Mark let go of Val's elbow and backhanded Crow with a blow so hard and fast that it lifted him and sent him crashing into Newton. They both went down in a painful tangle of limbs. Newton's head hit the hard floor with a meaty crunch.

Growling, Mark pulled Val to him, grabbing her short black hair and yanking her head back to expose her throat. His teeth snapped at her, but she jammed her hands against his chest and fought the pull, screaming all the while. Ferro still could not get his shot and tried shifting around, bellowing at Val to move out of the way even though it was impossible. Yanking out his gun, LaMastra snapped off a shot, but Weinstock knocked his arm upward and the shot went high and wide, shattering the clock.

"You'll hit Val!" Weinstock yelled, and together he and a furious LaMastra leapt across the table at Mark. The doctor grabbed Mark's arms and tried to wrench his grip away from the struggling Val; LaMastra caught Mark around the head in a powerful judo choke that would have rendered any strong man helpless in seconds by cutting off all blood to the brain. Unfortunately there was no flow of blood anywhere in Mark's body and the choke, despite all of LaMastra's considerable strength, was useless. Spitting with fury, Mark released Val with one hand and reached over his shoulder to take hold of LaMastra's shirt collar. Mark whipped his arm forward and LaMastra felt himself flying through the air, propelled with incredible force. He crashed into the medicine chest with an explosion of jagged glass splinters and twisted metal, but in his flight his big right shoe caught Ferro perfectly on the point of the jaw and spun him around and his finger jerked the trigger of the shotgun, sending garlic-soaked pellets into the concrete ceiling. Ferro slumped against the counter and began to sag down to his knees, the room swimming around him. He landed next to LaMastra, who was dazed and bleeding from glass cuts on his face.

Weinstock had thrown his body directly between Mark and Val, literally lying on the one arm that still held Val. He punched at Mark with both fists, even as Val sought to tear at the waxy hand that held her like a vise. Since he could no longer get to Val, Mark darted his head forward, fast as a snake, and sank his teeth right through the white lab coat and into the meat of Saul Weinstock's shoulder.

The doctor screamed at the searing agony as blood exploded from his arm, drenching his sleeve and spraying Mark's face with a fine crimson mist. The smell and taste of blood drove Mark into an absolute frenzy.

"GET HIM OFF ME!" shrieked Weinstock, beating at Mark's face with his fists, smashing cartilage and tearing flesh, but accomplishing nothing.

Jonatha stepped up behind him and swung a fire extinguisher at Mark's back. The blow bounced off him, but the force was enough to make him release his hold on Weinstock. Still screaming, Weinstock dropped to the floor and scuttled away from him. Released from Mark's grip, Val overbalanced and fell the other way, landing painfully on elbow and spine.

Jonatha raised the red fire extinguisher again but as she swung it, Mark swatted it out of the air so hard that the tank flew ten feet across the room and buried itself in the wall. The force of Mark's blow spun Jonatha around and she pirouetted right into the near wall, struck her forehead, and sagged to the floor, out cold.

By now Ferro and Crow had both struggled to their feet and rushed in to attack. Ferro grabbed his shotgun and slammed Mark with the stock, a blow that would have killed an ordinary man, and even though the blow shattered Mark's jaw and partially tore away his right ear, it did not stop him. The force of the blow spun Ferro, and he slipped on Weinstock's blood and almost fell. Crow, more agile, scooped up a garlic bulb as he ran and threw it without breaking stride as deftly as any third baseman plucking a line drive and throwing to first to pick off the runner. The garlic struck Mark in the eye, and it was the first thing that had gotten any response. Mark staggered back, clapping both hands to his eye.

"SHOOT HIM!" screamed Val, struggling to sit up despite the searing pain in her spine; but Ferro was already bringing up the gun. It took only a second to snap it up to his shoulder and aim it, but in that second Mark slapped it out of Ferro's hand with a savage blow, then Mark grabbed Ferro's throat with both hands and began to to pull him toward his broken, gaping mouth.

Crow leapt at Mark, jumping into the air for a powerful kick that packed all of Crow's weight and speed into it. The kick caught Mark on the side of the chest and knocked him back several feet, but he kept his hold on Ferro. Crow landed, spun, and kicked Mark in the knee, trying to cripple his leg, hoping for damage to do what mere pain could not. Mark's leg twisted, but did not collapse despite the audible crunch of bone and cartilage. Before Crow could attack the same leg again, Mark snapped out with one hand and caught Crow by the shirtfront and slammed Ferro and Crow together once, twice, and then swept his hands apart, hurling them into opposite walls. Both men fell bonelessly to the floor.

Mark threw back his head and howled like a triumphant wolf, the sound of it making the whole room tremble, but the howl ended in a low, mean laugh. He took a menacing step forward toward Val, hands clutching the air between them with unholy need.

Val rose from behind the autopsy table and in her hands she held Ferro's shotgun.

"God forgive me," she whispered as she raised it to her shoulder and fired.

From four feet away the hard lead pellets and viscous garlic oil took the vampire full in the face and blew him back to Hell.

INTERLUDE

Final Fugue

Mike Sweeney squirmed out from beneath the hay and sat blank-eyed for an hour before he realized who he was and where he was. He zipped his jacket up to his chin and crept out of the barn into the frigid afternoon. Beyond the fields was the dark green wall of the state forest, so Mike went that way, heading in a wandering zigzag course through the woods until he stumbled to a stop at a drop-off that fell away into utter blackness. Going back was out of the question, going left would take him through a dozen farms and then back to town. If he went right he was pretty sure he could make it to Val Guthrie's farm before full dark.

But he lingered for a while at the drop-off, staring down into the lightless void of Dark Hollow. He wondered what would happen if he just . . . stepped off? How far would he fall? Would it be a long enough drop so that the fall would kill him? That would be nice. A long drop down into nothingness and to become nothing at the end of it all.

"Mom . . . ," he said, and just saying it made the lure of the darkness all the stronger.

The air in front of him shimmered and Mike felt as if invisible hands were pushing on him. Not pushing him toward the long dark, but away from it.

A thought came into his head, and it was a strange one because it didn't feel like one of his own thoughts, but there it was. The thought was *if you take that step he'll win.*

He? Mike didn't know if his inner voice meant Vic or Tow-Truck Eddie. Or did it mean his *father?*

Mike stood at the edge of the abyss and listened for more from that inner voice, but there was only silence inside. Every tree around him was filled with crows; they were invisible in the shadows, but Mike could hear the soft rustle of their wings.

If you take that step he'll win.

The voice again, and now he realized that it was a voice, not a thought. It was the same voice that had warned him to run earlier. It was the voice of the man from his waking dream. Mr. Morse.

The crows cawed as if in chorus to that warning.

"You're not real," Mike said, addressing the voice in his head.

No. Not anymore.

"Why is this happening to me?" Mike pleaded. "Why me?"

Why not?

"That's a stupid answer."

It is what it is.

"I don't want to be who I am," Mike said.

Who do you think you are?

"I . . . I'm a monster. Isn't that what Tow-Truck Eddie called me? The Beast?"

Damn, son, you can't listen to what that fool says. His mind is on fire.

"So's mine!" Mike pawed a tear out of his eye. "I don't want to do this. I don't want to be who I am. I don't want that man to be my father." A sob broke from his chest. "I want my mom!"

He fell to his knees but the edge of the drop-off crumbled under him, the soil washed out of the roots by all the recent rain. Mike cried out and spread his arms to catch the tangled weeds at the edge of death and the moment froze. Even the crows in the trees held their breath as natural erosion nearly did what Tow-Truck Eddie and Vic and all of Griswold's armies could not do. Mike fought for balance and nearly—so nearly—fell.

But he didn't fall. He heaved himself backward onto the grass and fell flat on his back, staring up through the spiderweb tracery of the barren trees at the stars above.

It's not your fault who your parents are, said Mr. Morse.

"It's not fair."

No, it ain't.

"I don't want to be like him. I can't be like my father."

Then don't *be.*

Mike sat up slowly. "What?"

Don't be like him. Don't be like Vic. Don't be like your mamma, either.

Mike said nothing, listening.

None of them know who you really are, Mike. They want you to be like them, but they're afraid that you won't be. You hear me, boy? They are afraid that you won't be like them.

"Afraid? That's stupid. Who would be afraid of me? I'm no one."

In his mind Mr. Morse laughed, all the crows sent up a cackle. *Who do you want to be?*

"I . . . ," Mike's voice failed. He had no idea how to answer that question. Instead he lay back and asked, "Why are they afraid of me?"

You know.

"No, I don't."

Yes, you do. Look inside, Mike. It's gonna hurt—but they already done hurt you worse than anything else could do. You want to know why they're afraid, just open up and look deep inside.

"I don't know how."

I can help you, if you let me. You got to trust me.

"I'm scared."

So am I, son. So are we all.

Mike lay for a while and watched heaven spin on its axis. The birds rustled and whispered to one another; Mr. Morse held his tongue.

"Okay," Mike said at last, and it took nearly everything he had to say that one word.

A sound rippled through the trees above him as if each of the thousand crows uttered a long sigh. Then, as the stars glittered and the crows held their breath, Mr. Morse—the Bone Man—

fulfilled his mission on Earth and told Mike everything that he knew. He didn't know all of it—there were such huge gaps in his own knowledge—but what he knew for sure hit the boy like a shotgun blast.

At first Mike listened in silent horror, and then he wept, and finally he screamed.

Down below, far down in the shadows of the Hollow, the swamp shuddered as things twitched in fury and fear beneath the mud.

When the telling was done, Mike Sweeney did not speak. He could not. He lay there with his eyes open, his lips parted in a soundless *O* of terrible surprise. His body was sprawled in a rough cruciform, arms out to either side, heels dangling over the edge of forever. His chest barely lifted with each breath, and deep inside his heart struggled for each next beat until, as the moon drifted behind a veil of clouds, his broken heart just did not take the next beat, and his lungs did not struggle to fill.

And Mike Sweeney, the Enemy of Evil, died.

PART III
The Red Wave

October 30 (Mischief Night) to
October 31 (Halloween)

And we all know death someday comes
Life was never all that certain . . .

—Harry Manx, "Weary When You Run"

With every weary step, you one step closer to the grave;
With every single step, on every broken-hearted day
you one step closer to the grave.
Lay down and die and let the worms have their way.

—Oren Morse, "Cemetery Blues"

Chapter 30

For twenty-four hours now Tow-Truck Eddie had been cruising the roads around Pine Deep. When his shift was over he swapped the cruiser for his wrecker and went back out on the road, but there was no sign at all of the Beast. As each moment passed he felt the twin fists of tension and despair beat at him.

He was failing in his Holy Mission. The Beast had actually been in his grasp and he'd lost him. Blood boiled in his veins, and he gripped the steering wheel of the wrecker with such force that the knobbed wheel was slowly being twisted out of shape. Hulking in the cab of the wrecker, he drove through the noisy crowds, praying for guidance, begging for the chance to let his work begin.

(2)

The official version that Ferro concocted was that a pair of criminals in ski masks broke into the morgue, ostensibly to steal medical supplies, and Val and Crow happened to be there discussing the release of her brother's body with Dr. Weinstock. Ferro and LaMastra had come back up from Philly to interview Ms. Guthrie and officially close the Ruger/Boyd case. The morgue video cameras were still out of commission and the criminals turned off the lights and in the ensuing confusion shots were fired but luckily the only person struck was the already dead Mark

Guthrie. However, in the darkness everyone was generally knocked about, and Dr. Weinstock was bitten by one of the assailants. The attackers fled and their identities were still unknown.

It was a load of horseshit, but they only had to sell it to Gus Bernhardt and he would buy swamp real estate from a guy in a shiny suit. Weinstock, injured as he was, was lucid enough to browbeat the hospital staff, and no one questioned Weinstock on anything anyway. Jonatha and Newton were too difficult to fit into the scenario, so they left before Weinstock called it in.

LaMastra was surprised that everyone seemed to buy the story, but Crow pointed out, "Dude, after everything that's happened since Ruger came to town, this shit actually sounds reasonable."

Weinstock was admitted into his own hospital. His shoulder needed twenty-two stitches, and he was scheduled for an MRI to see what kind of damage was done to the tendons. Even as he was being wheeled into the ER he was diagnosing himself, bullying the residents and nurses, and generally making a pain in the ass of himself.

One of the residents put five stitches in the glass cut on LaMastra's jaw, and nurses handed out ice packs to Crow and Ferro. Val was hurt, too, but not in a way that required treatment. She sat in Crow's ER unit and just stared into the middle distance, and Crow could guess what she was seeing. When the ER docs were done with him, Crow dragged a chair over and sat down next to Val, pulling her close, whispering soothing words to her over and over again.

"I'm so sorry, baby . . . but you did what you had to do."

It was maybe the fiftieth time he had said that during the four hours they were in the ER, and Val finally pushed herself back and Crow could see the fierce hurt in her eyes. Pitching her voice low, she said, "I know that, damn it!"

Crow's next words died on his tongue.

"I know what I did was right. God, Crow . . . do you think I'm sitting here torn up with self-loathing for what happened? I thought you knew me by now."

She turned her angry face away and stared at the wall for a while.

Crow almost said, "I'm sorry," but didn't. He was learning.

After a while she turned back. Her eyes were as cold as any Crow had ever seen.

"Honey . . . listen to me. Do you understand what I'm feeling? Can you guess what's tearing me up inside?"

He took a moment with that, then said, "Yeah, I think I can." He licked his lips. "You want to find Ruger, don't you?"

"Yes," she said in an almost inhuman whisper, filled with urgency. "If he's still alive, if he's one of *them*, then yes, I want to find him."

"And Griswold?"

"Yes!" she hissed, and took his hands in hers, squeezing them with painful force. "Dear God in Heaven, but I want to find them and I want to make them *pay*!"

Crow nodded slowly and bent and kissed her hands.

"Then that's what we're going to do."

(3)

Newton and Jonatha left the hospital and headed back to her hotel room. During the short drive neither said a word, and they remained silent until she had closed and locked her door. She engaged both locks and then stepped aside as Newton dragged over one of the room's two overstuffed chairs and wedged its back under the doorknob. When he gave it a shake and saw how steady it was, she nodded. Then they checked the window. It was a big picture window and was not designed to be opened. The glass was thick and heavy; there was no balcony, so no need for a sliding door. There were no other windows or doors in the room.

Jonatha went around and turned on all the lights. They turned on the television and sat there, she on the edge of her bed, Newton on the other chair. Newton channel surfed. They watched *Everybody Hates Chris* and even though the studio audience was howling, neither of them cracked so much as a smile. They watched some of *Deal or No Deal*. They watched ten minutes of a Patriots-Vikings game on ESPN though neither of them knew a thing about football. They watched *The Dog Whisperer*. They took none of it in. They didn't speak at all.

At around ten-thirty Jonatha got up and went into the bathroom. She closed the door and was in there for a long time. Newton could hear the shower running and it made him look at his own hands and clothes. He was filthy. He reeked of garlic and stank of sweat and dried blood. His head hurt terribly where he had struck the floor. He hurt all over. Inside and out.

They had seen a vampire. An actual *vampire*. Not a hypothetical one, but right there in the flesh. It had *touched* him. Newton felt unbearably unclean.

In his mind it wasn't Val's brother—Newton had only ever seen him a few times around town and didn't know him—but even if he had he was sure that what he had seen tonight was not Mark Guthrie. This had been a monster.

He shivered once, then again, and the second time it was a whole frigid body ripple that popped gooseflesh along his skin, stood his hair up on end, and made him feel desperately cold to the core of his being. "Oh God . . . ," he moaned, but his teeth were chattering so bad they sounded like knuckles knocking on glass.

Newton didn't hear the bathroom door open. "Newt . . . ?"

He turned at the sound of her voice; Jonatha stood there in a blue terrycloth robe that was pulled close at the throat and cinched tight around her waist. She came and knelt next to him. "What's wrong?"

He opened his mouth, tried to tell her that he was cold, tried to tell her that she looked beautiful, tried to tell her that it was all over, tried to tell her that he was sorry. A dozen thoughts collided in his head and none of them made it to his lips. His teeth were chattering so bad he couldn't talk.

Jonatha grabbed the comforter off the bed and wrapped it around Newton even as she pulled him down out of the chair and onto the floor, pulled him close, wrapped him up in a co-

coon of the blanket and her own radiant heat. He did not embrace her, or cling to her; but he let himself be gathered in, shivering and shaking as the waves of shock crashed over him. She
kept pulling him close and kept shimmying away from the chair
until they were both tucked into the corner formed by the big
wooden breakfront that served as TV stand and bureau and the
wall. Jonatha pulled the blanket tighter and tighter around them
and then pulled it over their heads just as the shivers started to
hit her, too.

(4)

Ten-thirty on Mischief Night, and the town was lost in a sea
of sound and movement. Beyond the parking lot and the iron
fences the town was in full revel as Mischief Night burned its
way toward midnight. Music blared from the streetlight-hung
speakers. Traffic was stopped on Corn Hill to allow a continuous
rolling block party. It was Mischief Madness & Mayhem, Pine
Deep's legendary night before Halloween blast, modeled after
Mardi Gras and powered by the lingering real-world adrenaline
rush of the post–Ruger and Boyd massacre. Instead of driving
tourists away, now that the killings were over, the town attracted
three times the usual number of merrymakers; everyone wanted
to suck in a chestful of real danger, real mystery, real frights—so
long as they didn't actually get hurt and there was beer.

The entire starting lineup of the Pine Deep Scarecrows,
wearing only their football helmets, streaked down ten blocks of
Corn Hill and then scattered into the crowds, which opened to
receive them. Everyone loved it.

BK and Billy Christmas held court at the banquet hall at
Harvestman Inn. BK was at the head table, flanked by two
screenwriters—Stephen Susco and James Gunn. The three of
them were shouting over the noise to discuss the Quentin
Tarantino flick *Grindhouse*. Across from him, Billy was in his
glory, with Brinke Stevens on his left and Debbie Rochon on
his right. He looked like a kid on Christmas morning. Brinke

was a petite brunette with big dark eyes and a wicked smile; Debbie was bustier and had an infectious laugh. Both of them had a stack of racy studio 8x10s in front of them and there were lines of eager fans stretching all the way down the hall and out into the street. Next to Debbie sat John Bloom, who, as faux redneck Joe Bob Briggs, wrote reviews of classic drive-in movies that were legendary. He kept telling jokes in his lazy Texas drawl that had the other three laughing so hard they looked like they were going to stroke out.

Jim O'Rear, a stuntman and fight choreographer who also freelanced as a haunted attraction consultant, was talking movie fight scenes with Sam and Mischa, two of the kids who played monsters at the Hayride. The two adjoining tables were packed with members of the Horror Writers Association and a delegation from the Garden State Horror Writers, all of whom were firing horror trivia at each other faster than automatic gunfire. Whoever lost had to do a shot of tequila. Nobody minded losing.

The other corner of the room had a small stage where Mem Shannon and the Membership were whipping out down-and-dirty blues that had over two hundred people dancing and sweating.

On all four walls there were huge rear-projection screens on which horror films played. Susco's *The Grudge* 2 on one screen; Gunn's *Slither* on another; the original *Dawn of the Dead* played out over the table where its star, Ken Foree, sat in sober conversation with two theater grad students from the college; and opposite that Brinke Stevens was losing her clothes in the legendary B-film *Sorority Babes in the Slimeball Bowl-O-Rama*, an event that sent up a howl from the audience loud enough to rattle the windows.

Outside the Inn, the party rolled back and forth, up and down every side street and out into the countryside. There were continuous horror movie marathons at the Dead End Drive-In and on the grounds of the Hayride, and the campus football field was one big blues-rock slam party as Al Sirois and Kindred Spirit set fire to the night.

The members of BK's team who didn't draw the long straws that allowed them to come to the gala at the Harvestman Inn were patrolling in pairs on the campus and at the Hayride. A few of them, despite all warnings and threats from BK, were drunk, and the rest were feeling lighthearted and loose. There were a few trouble spots—a pickpocket working the crowds at the concert, a few shoving matches between irritable drunks, some pranks that got out of hand—but nothing the team couldn't handle. Everything got handled.

Every time BK used his cell phone to call one of his team the only response he ever got was "It's all good."

Karl Ruger made damn sure that was all that got onto the radar. Wearing a Count Dracula rubber mask and costume, he wandered through the revelers. His own point men—Golub, Carby, McVey, and a few others—were positioned in key spots around town. Even Polk walked the streets, wriggling through the crowds, keeping an eye out, reporting in as ordered. Lois Wingate, dressed as Buffy the Vampire Slayer, walked arm in arm with Ruger. They made a charming couple.

The Dead Heads were all locked up safe and sound. The vampires who couldn't pass for human were in the nests. Ruger's orders for the evening were simple: "Nobody hunts, nobody dies."

Not tonight; not on Mischief Night.

Tomorrow was Halloween and that was when the killing would begin again. *Yeah*, Ruger thought as he walked hand in hand with Lois, *that's when the real party starts.*

Chapter 31

Midnight

Crow and Val sat on opposite sides of Weinstock's bed. They were dressed in clean hospital scrubs—a loan from one of the many doctors they'd gotten to know during their recent stays. Their own soiled clothes were in a plastic bag.

"They say you're going to be fine," Crow said. "They don't think the rotator cuff's torn."

Weinstock looked at him for a moment and then turned away. "What does it matter?"

Crow frowned. "What's that supposed to mean?"

"I was bitten!" he said in a tortured voice.

"Saul . . ."

Weinstock turned sharply, eyes flaring. "Don't you understand? I was bitten by a vampire!"

"He just bit you, Saul," said Val. "He didn't kill you."

"I'm going to die! I'm going to come back as . . . as . . ."

"No you're not!" she snapped.

"I'm damned! Don't you get it? I'm going to die and then I'm going to come back as a freaking vampire and—"

Val bent forward and stared at Weinstock until he stopped talking. She bent and kissed him on the tip of the nose. "You are not damned, you dope! Jonatha told us that you have to die by a vampire's bite and then either be forced to drink blood or drink it when you revive. Neither of those things happened. This is just a wound. Right now you're hurt and you're scared. We're all scared." Her smiling mouth started to tremble. "Mark only bit you. He didn't drain your blood, he didn't kill you, and he didn't make you drink his blood. You're not going to turn into what he was."

Weinstock stared at her for a long moment, then he wrapped his uninjured arm around her and pulled her close. After a moment she sat back on the bed and fished for a tissue in her pocket, didn't find one; Crow held one out without comment. He handed a second one to Weinstock.

The TV was on and they all pretended to watch ABC's coverage of the town's Mischief Night festivities. After a minute Weinstock said, "I need to call Rachel. I need to get her and the kids out of town."

"It's the middle of the night, Saul . . ." Val began, but let it go. She understood, and she sat with him while he made the call, listening as Saul concocted a complete piece of nonsense about an outbreak of avian flu that was just discovered. Saul pleaded, he cajoled, he even yelled, but in the end he convinced her. When he hung up he looked ten years older, but greatly relieved.

Later, Crow said, "We have to decide what to do about Connie."

Without looking at him, Val replied, "I want her cremated. I'll call the Murphy Brothers tomorrow; they can come for her and take care of it. Mark, too. Jonatha says fire will work, so let's end it with that."

There was a light knock on the door and Ferro came in with a cardboard carrier heavy with Starbucks cups. He looked like five miles of bad road, and Crow told him as much. Ferro's attempt at a smile was ghastly.

"You okay?" he asked Val, offering her a cup.

She waggled her hand back and forth. "Where's Vince?" she asked, taking the coffee.

"Throwing up," Ferro said. "Again. He said he might go to the hospital chapel for a while."

Val nodded.

Ferro cleared his throat. "Look, Crow, Val . . . as soon as Vince is fit to travel we're heading back to Philly. No, no, don't look at me like that—we're not jumping ship. We talked it over and the bottom line is that we all got hurt in there because we were under-prepared. No way am I letting that happen again, so we're heading back to the city to get some more reliable armament. Kevlar vests, ammunition, the works. I figure we tweak Crow's shotgun-shell idea and put a drop of garlic oil in the tips of hollow-point rounds and seal them somehow."

"I have plenty of sealing wax at my store," Crow said

"Outstanding." He sipped his coffee, winced, and set the cup down. "While we're gone, maybe you can pick up some garlic oil, and anything else you can think of. I'm sure Saul can arrange for us to use one of the rooms here as a staging area."

"Anything you need," Weinstock agreed.

Ferro looked at his watch. "Should take us about six hours. We should try to get some sleep . . . but I don't know how that's going to happen. We'll pick up No-Doz or something on the way." He leaned back in his chair and looked at Val. "In the morgue . . . that was, well . . . that was bad. We were there to protect you and we let you down. That won't happen again, I give you my word."

Val nodded but said nothing.

"I'm sorry for what you had to go through and what you had to do. You're an incredible woman, Val, and I'm proud to know you."

"Thank you, Frank."

To Crow he said, "I hope you'll be ready when we get back because I want to saddle up, get down to Dark Hollow, and see if we can finish this."

"Frank . . . we don't know if Ruger's even down there, or if he's even alive. We don't know if we'll find anything down there."

Ferro stared at him for a long moment. "He's out there. I know it. You know it."

Crow just looked at him.

"If he's not down at Griswold's house, if he's not in Dark Hollow, then we have to hunt him down and kill him no matter where he is, no matter where he's hiding. We *have* to. The alternative is just too . . ."

He stopped, shook his head, and and left.

(2)

They gave Weinstock a sedative, which he grumbled about taking, and he drifted off. Crow looked at his watch. "I'd better get moving, baby. If I'm going to be ready when they get back I've got to get a bunch of things done."

"I wish I was going with you today," Val said as Crow fished his car keys out of the plastic bag that held his clothes. "Oh, don't look at me like that. I know I'm pregnant, I know I'm too delicate." She hooked quotation marks around that last word and her tone was mocking.

"Honey," Crow said, straightening, "believe me when I tell you that if you weren't pregnant with Crow Junior I'd want you riding shotgun . . . and I mean that exactly."

"Why do you always think our baby is going to be a boy?"

"Because you're going to want another guy you can boss around."

She stuck out her tongue. "You will pay for that remark."

"Vince, Frank, and I can handle this part of it. By the way, I called Newt, but Jonatha answered his cell. She said he was asleep."

Val arched an eyebrow. "Asleep? With her?"

"I didn't ask for details. I told her the plan and she said that she and Newt would try and meet us back here before first light to help us get ready. She sounded pretty rocky. Not everyone's as tough as you, baby," Crow said. "Look . . . I'd better go."

"God," she said, "this is never going to be over. I can feel it."

"No! We're going to end it today." He kissed her, long and sweetly, and then knelt and kissed her stomach. Rising, he hitched up as confident a smile as he could manage. "Trust me, Val. We're going to win."

"I trust you," she said softly.

He kissed her again and left.

(3)

Crow drove out to Val's farm, pulled up to the big toolshed near the barn, trained the high beams on the door, and got out of his car holding Ferro's shotgun. It still held four shells doctored with garlic, and he approached the shed cautiously until he was sure it was safe. He unlocked the shed and removed four yellow 4.6-gallon backpack-style sprayer tanks that were used for liquid fertilizer; they were exactly where Val said he'd find them. He poured out their contents and wiped each one down.

He filled them at the farm gas pump and tested the sprayers; each one worked fine.

"Hope the gas doesn't melt these puppies," he murmured as he stowed them in his car.

Next he drove to the Haunted Hayride grounds. It was past two o'clock and everything was shut down, but Crow let himself in and drove to the barn where a dozen ATVs stood in a row. The ones Crow wanted were in the back, three nearly new bright yellow Renegade 800s. Four-wheelers with 800cc, four-stroke v-twins. Less than six hundred pounds each and as tough as Bradley Fighting Vehicles.

"Sweet."

It took him an hour to load three of them onto a flatbed, drive out to the Passion Pit, offload everything, and drive back to get his car. He left a note for Coop, the Hayride's manager, and then headed up the road to Millie's Farm Stand. Crow had called before midnight and told Millie that he wanted every drop of garlic oil she had plus six big sacks of garlic bulbs. When she asked why, he told her it was for the Halloween Festival.

Millie was waiting up for him, bleary-eyed but amused. Everything was in boxes and Crow crammed them into his car and tied the sacks of bulbs to his roof.

"For the Festival, you say?" she asked as Crow wrote out a hefty check.

Crow kept his face bland as he tore off the check. "Life's always a little different in Pine Deep."

"Mm-hmm," Millie agreed, her face equally bland. "Always is."

As his car was rolling over the gravel and onto the blacktop, Oscar ambled over and stood by his wife. Unlike Millie, Oscar was not a native of Pine Deep, having been raised on lobster boats off the Maine coast, and despite his forty years in Pennsylvania, he still maintained his laconic New England drawl.

"Was that Crow driving off just now?"

"Mm-hmm," she said. "He bought ten gallons of extract and three hundred pounds of bulbs."

"Ayuh?" he murmured.

"Awful lot of garlic."

"Ayuh."

"I mean, for someone who owns a craft store."

"Ayuh."

"And he was here with a policeman last night to buy some, too. I told you about how he was in a terrible hurry. Worked up into such a state."

Oscar nodded and wrapped his arm around her shoulder as they watched Crow's car dwindle to a dot and vanish around a curve.

"Still seems to be in a hurry," she observed.

"Ayuh."

"So, why do you think he needs all that garlic?"

Oscar squinted up into the moonlit sky for a moment and then back at the road. "Probably something to do with the damn vampires, if y'ask me."

"You think so?"

"Ayuh."

(4)

Crow got home well before dawn, parked outside of his shop, and hurried inside, door key in one hand, pistol in the other. Once inside he locked up again and went straight through the store into his apartment, locking that door behind him, too. His three cats crowded around him, scolding him for being away so long. Their cat box needed changing, their water bowl was dry, and they were hungry.

As he took care of their needs he wondered for the thousandth time where Mike was. "C'mon, kiddo . . . be okay," he murmured, but he had nowhere to go with his concerns, and no time to spend on them. He showered—first hot and then very cold—and dressed for a hard day in heavy-duty cargo pants with lots of pockets, North Face hiking shoes, thermal undershirt, his shoulder holster, and a Temple Owls hoody that zippered up the front and was baggy enough to hide his shoulder rig. Appraising himself in the mirror he thought he looked like a street kid getting ready to rob a liquor store.

He stuffed his pockets with a lighter, Swiss Army knife, gum, two PowerBars, a small first-aid kit, and extra magazines for the Beretta, and clipped on a Buck 888 Combat Knife in a black Cordura sheath. It was a real killer, with a 4¾-inch blade, but it weighed only eleven ounces. Crow was as much an artist with a knife as he was with his sword. He took the sword, too, a Paul Chen *katana*, one of the Orchid series, that had cost well over a thousand dollars and with which Crow had practiced tens of thousands of cuts. He knew that sword better than any other and though he'd never actually fought with it, he believed that with that sword in his hand he could stand up to just about anyone. Or any*thing*. On impulse he packed his two cheaper but still sturdy training swords, putting all of them into an oversized tournament duffel. Then he locked up his shop and went to war.

(5)

Ferro drove; Vince sat, arms folded, head turned away to look out of the passenger window at the darkness rushing by. He'd been like that most of the way back to Philly, had barely said a word while they were gathering their weapons and equipment—a process that would be creating a lot of questions they would have to answer at some point—and hadn't said a single word since they'd headed back north.

"Vince . . . ?" Ferro finally asked as they headed north through Abington. They'd be in Pine Deep in forty minutes. Dawn was coming late today as a dense cloud cover remained locked down over the region. "Vince . . . you okay?"

LaMastra turned slowly to face his partner and gave him a long stare that was filled with a bottomless sadness.

"We're going to die, you know," he said softly. "All of us." He turned back to the window. "We're all going to die."

Ferro opened his mouth to say something reassuring, but ultimately held his tongue. He didn't like to lie to his partner.

(6)

About five minutes after Crow pulled away from his store the back door to his apartment opened and a hunched figure shambled slowly inside. It was streaked with blood and dirt and it moved with slow, shuffling steps from the kitchen into the living room, then into Crow's bedroom.

It stopped, head raised as if sniffing the air.

"Crow," it said in a hoarse, dry voice.

The three cats cringed back from it, hissing.

The figure turned slowly toward them and stood there, swaying like a scarecrow in a breeze, then it leaned back against the wall and slumped wearily to the floor. The cats kept their distance for a while, eyeing the intruder warily. Then one of them— Muddy Whiskers, the oldest—took a tentative step forward, paused, took another step, and another, always ready to run. Finally the ginger cat was right there, sniffing the mud-caked shoes and torn jeans.

The figure raised one hand, offering scabbed and filthy fingers for the cat to smell. Muddy Whiskers looked past the fingers at the face, at the bloodred eyes, but he didn't shy away. After another few seconds he came closer still and pushed his head against the proffered hand. He started to purr.

The figure bent forward and scooped the cat up, pulled him to his chest, buried its mouth and nose against the cat's head, and began to cry.

The other cats watched for a while, and then they, too, came closer and took the strange-yet-familiar scent. Muddy Whiskers let himself be held, and he didn't even struggle as Mike Sweeney began rocking back and forth as he wept.

Chapter 32

Crow peered into the oversized duffel bags the detectives laid out on a table in the lab Weinstock had ordered set aside for their use. "Gee, you think you brought enough guns?"

"If it has fangs we want it dead," Ferro said, "not just pissed off."

"Works for me."

There were two short-barreled Remington 870s with pistol grips and folding stocks of the kind favored by some of the more hard-core narcotics units; a Mossberg Bullpup with a twenty-inch barrel and an eight-shot clip; a venerable old Winchester Defender with a standard stock and a Parkerized finish; an Ithaca Deerslayer; and one monster of a ten-gauge shotgun that LaMastra fondled with familiarity. This was an Ithaca Mag-10 Roadblocker with an augmented clip that allowed him to carry seven shells instead of the usual three. It was a bull of a gun useful only in the hands of a bullish man.

Ferro had somehow procured a thousand rounds of 12-gauge and two hundred for the Roadblocker, and over the last few hours they had worked in teams to doctor them up by injecting pure garlic oil into the casings, sealing the needle holes by melting the plastic with a lab burner. Ferro, LaMastra, and Val handled that job, marking each shell with a felt-tip pen to indicate the ones that were enhanced. Crow worked on the five hundred 9mm pistol bullets Ferro had brought. The concave mouths of the dum-dums needed only a small drop to fill, and Crow sealed in the oil with a drop of hot wax, blew on the wax, and smoothed the tips to make them round and even. When they had doctored six hundred shells and three hundred bullets, Ferro called a halt to it. They all gathered around the autopsy table, staring in fascination at the weapons and the ammunition that they hoped would help them survive the coming war.

"Okay," Ferro said as if instructing a class, "the plain red shells are standard twelve-gauge double-ought buckshot. The ones marked with the black arrows are filled with deer slugs. If we have to concentrate on head shots, that'll do'er."

"What about those?" Crow asked, touching a shell marked with thick black bands.

"Shok-Lock rounds," Ferro said. "Inside is a kind of ceramic minishell that explodes on impact and discharges bits of metal."

LaMastra nodded. During the hours of work he'd shaken off some of his funk and had started talking again, though his eyes were still spooked. "Fire one at a lock and *poof!*—no lock. Fire one at a head, and all you have is a lingering cloud of pink mist."

Crow winced. "Thanks, that image is going to stay with me."

"The rest are for Vince's Roadblocker."

"Standard double-ought," said LaMastra with a grin, "but at ten-gauge it's a real crowd-pleaser."

They loaded all six of the shotguns. Crow selected the Bullpup, liking its weight; Ferro took a Remington. They stowed their shotguns in one of the duffel bags, along with Crow's Japanese sword and a collection of knives. LaMastra opened one of the bags of garlic bulbs and poured several dozen into a plastic bag and stowed this in the duffel.

Ferro finished the last of his cold coffee, "Does anyone know when sunset is today?"

"6:47," said Val. "I checked the paper."

"Then let's go," said Ferro.

Val told them to wait and quickly searched the cabinets until she found some small plastic specimen vials with pop-off lids. She filled a half dozen of them with garlic oil and gave two to each of them. "You never know," she said, and they nodded their thanks.

Ferro and LaMastra stepped out into the hallway, leaving

Crow and Val alone in the morgue. Crow wrapped her in his arms and kissed her.

"I know this will tarnish my Captain Avenger image," he said, "but I've never been this scared before."

"Me, too."

"We could leave, you know. Pack up my car . . . just go. You, me, and the baby."

"Sounds great. I hear Jamaica's great this time of year."

They smiled at each other, letting the lie make the moment bearable. They kissed very tenderly. Val leaned back and searched his face for a long time. "Crow, I'm not going to make any more speeches, okay? Just promise me that you'll come back. Give me your word and I'll be able to let you go. Otherwise—I think I'll just go crazy."

Very seriously he said, "Val, you know that poem I like, "The Highwayman" by Alfred Noyes? The one Loreena McKennitt did a song about? Remember what the hero says to his love? *'I'll come to thee by moonlight, though hell should bar the way.'* That's me, baby. Mr. Hero Guy. Nothing's going to stop me."

She pulled his face close to hers. "Swear to me, swear you'll come back."

"I swear," he whispered.

"Swear on our baby."

"I swear."

"Swear," she said again and again, and each time he swore, and each time he kissed her face, tasting tears. "I love you," she said.

"I love you, too." Then she pushed him back and turned away and walked across the room where she leaned with both hands on the edge of a counter. He understood and didn't say anything else. As he pulled the door closed behind him he heard the first of her deep, terrible sobs.

The cops saw his face and didn't comment.

Crow nodded and he and the cops headed out to assault Dark Hollow.

Chapter 33

The three ATVs stood in a row in the clearing at the top of Dark Hollow, the gray light of dawn brightened by the intense yellow paint jobs. "Nice," LaMastra said, nodding approval as he ran his hands over the controls; Ferro eyed the machines dubiously.

"They're gassed and ready to go," Crow said. He strapped the sprayer units to the back of each vehicle. Crow took his *katana* from his duffel, drew it from its sheath, fished a vial of garlic oil from his pocket, and smeared it all over the blade.

"Will that hurt the sword?" Ferro asked.

Crow shrugged. "At this point, who cares?"

Finished with the sword, Crow poured more of the oil into his palm and rubbed it all over his throat, wrists, and face. "Eau-de-stinko," he said, holding up the vial and wiggling it in Ferro's direction. "It's what everybody's wearing these days. Besides, I'm under orders from Val to come back alive."

"Good idea," Ferro said, taking it.

Crow went through the particulars of the ATV with Ferro; LaMastra needed no instruction, having owned motorcycles all through high school and college. They mounted, fired up the bikes, and tested them out by driving in and out of the parking lot for a few minutes; then they lined up behind Crow.

"Let's kick some undead ass!" Crow yelled and gunned his engine. He went over the edge of the pitch, feeding it gas, zigzagging to keep ahead of the pull of gravity. The others followed,

engines shattering the stillness of the morning. It was steep enough
to terrify Ferro, and the path was littered with stones and potholes, but the big low-pressure tires of the ATVs seemed indifferent to the terrain. One by one they swept down the hill,
speeding through the morning light toward the veil of shadows
that marked the boundary of Dark Hollow.

At the top of the hill, a lonely figure stood and watched them
go, his black funeral clothes flapping in the breeze.

"You go get them sonsabitches, Little Scarecrow!" he shouted,
screaming it with all his might, yelling in a desperate voice; but
only the crows in the nearby trees could hear him. The cry was
stretched out onto the breeze and blown into silent fragments.
"God keep you boys safe."

(2)

Val wandered around the hospital for an hour, too nervous to
just sit and watch Weinstock sleep. She went down to the cafeteria for a plate of eggs but ate less than half of them. Morning
sickness wasn't a severe problem for her, but it was there. Newton called on her cell. "Hey . . . how are you?" she asked.

"We spent the night throwing up," the reporter said with a
bitter laugh. "How about you?"

"Pretty much the same," Val said, though she noted Newton's
use of "we." "How's Jonatha? I imagine she's heading back to
Philly after what happened."

"Actually," Newton said, "she's not. She wants to stay and
help me document this. Which is reporter geek-speak for saying
that we both want to help, but not in any storming the castle
sort of way. We can do research, help with intel, as they say in the
military."

"Were you in the military?" Val asked hopefully.

"No . . . I watch 24 and The Unit. Heading over to the hospital now. Jonatha's getting dressed and we should be there in a few."

"I don't know what to say except . . . thanks. I know this
must be terribly hard for you both. It's not your fight—"

"We talked about that, Val, and we both pretty much agreed that it is our fight. It's everyone's fight."

"Thanks, Newt. I'm sorry I was so hard on you before."

"As it turns out, you had every right to be. See you soon."

She bought a paper and a big decaf in a go-cup and carried it back up to Weinstock's room and frowned when she saw that the door was ajar; she'd definitely closed it when she left and the nurse wasn't due for her rounds until seven. Val hurried over and opened the door quietly to see a small mud-splattered and disheveled figure standing over the sleeping doctor. Even though his back was to her, Val recognized him at once.

"Mike . . . ?" she said.

(3)

Crow crouched above the seat as the ATV slammed into unseen potholes and jerked over unavoidable rocks. Far behind him he could hear Ferro cursing and yelping as his body thumped painfully over and over again onto the saddle.

At the base of the long hill Crow braked to a stop to let the others catch up. LaMastra was right behind him the whole way, but it took Ferro an additional couple of minutes to pick his way laboriously down the hill toward them. He looked exhausted and miserable and his crotch and tailbone hurt like hell from the bumpy ride. Crow suggested that he try standing up off the seat next time and Ferro told him what he could do with his belated suggestions.

Crow pointed. "See that path there, where the trees form a kind of archway? That's where we're going. Be prepared, because when Newt and I were here we got a really bad feeling as soon as we entered it."

"Can't be as bad as the way I felt when we crossed over from sunlight to shadows on that hill," LaMastra said.

"He's right," Ferro agreed, "if I wasn't already a believer that would have done it. It was stepping out of who I am and into being a frightened five-year-old kid. Very . . . basic emotions, a primitive fear. Does that make sense?"

"Yeah, that says it." Crow nodded along the path. "Down there . . . it gets worse." He gunned his engine and took off.

LaMastra looked gloomily at Ferro. "Great pep talk."

They followed, and as each of them motored down the path an identical feeling of unease and claustrophobia clutched at their hearts. Ferro found himself reaching back to touch his slung shotgun over and over again; LaMastra kept murmuring prayers to the Virgin Mary that he learned in Sunday school. The path was so narrow that dry branches whipped at them and plucked at their sleeves with skeletal fingers, but this eventually emptied out into a wide clearing and Crow stopped again. The others drew alongside, flanking him as he examined the terrain ahead.

"Holy Jesus," gasped LaMastra, staring at the expanse of twisted and diseased trees and hairy vines that hung like loops of intestine from every branch. Leprous toadstools were littered across the mossy floor of the swamp, and the whole place smelled like rotten eggs and spoiled meat. The stench was overpowering. Gagging, Crow opened up his second vial of garlic extract and rubbed some on his upper lip. He passed the vial to Ferro and LaMastra, who copied this trick.

"What's wrong with this place?" LaMastra asked, unknowingly repeating the question that Newton had asked two weeks before. Crow shook his head.

"Everything," he said.

They rode on through the twisted woods for another half an hour and then suddenly the side of the old farmhouse loomed up before them, rising out of the shadows in tangles of diseased ivy. Crow felt his gut tighten at the sight of it. They all slowed as they emerged from the forest into the overgrown side yard and then stopped in a patch of sunlight in the front yard about eighty feet from the porch. They turned off their engines and the silence was immediate and enormous.

"Doesn't look like much," said LaMastra, examining the house through narrowed eyes.

Crow snorted, "It grows on you."

The pile of debris on the porch made the house look deceptively frail and shabby, but Crow knew that the place was a near fortress of sturdy stones and seasoned timbers.

Ferro nodded. "I expected something a lot more rustic, you know? Older, deader, more like a haunted house from a scary movie."

"You think this place doesn't look haunted?" Crow asked, surprised.

"It's not that . . . I expected it to be a dead old house. This place feels . . . *alive.*"

"Thanks," LaMastra muttered, "'cause I wasn't nearly scared enough before."

He and Crow got off their ATVs, but Ferro lingered. "It's a lot bigger than I expected, too. I'd guess fifteen, eighteen rooms." Somewhere behind them a dozen crows sent up a cawing chatter. Ferro dismounted and unslung his shotgun. "We're burning daylight, gentlemen. Let's be about our business."

They unstrapped one of the sprayer units and Ferro volunteered to carry it. "You two can provide cover."

LaMastra raised his big shotgun and jacked the first round into the breech. The sound was startlingly loud. "Let's get it done."

With a grim smile, Crow bent to the duffel bag and removed the two pinch bars he'd brought along for just this purpose. He handed one to Vince. "Before we go in there, I'm for letting the sun shine in."

"So am I," agreed Ferro, "or I would be if there was any sun." Above the clouds which had been gradually forming since late morning had coalesced into a gray-white ceiling. The small patch of daylight that shone down on their parked vehicles grew gradually fainter as the clouds draped the sun in gauzy layers.

"It doesn't have to be actual sunlight, though, right?" LaMastra asked. "I mean . . . it's still daytime, so these assholes are going to be sleeping. Right?"

Crow didn't meet his gaze. "Yeah, well, Jonatha was a bit hazy on that point."

"Terrific," LaMastra said.

Crow stalked toward the porch, shotgun in one hand and pinch bar in the other. As he climbed the steps he carefully examined the debris, staring at every dark spot to see if it scuttled or moved, but there were no signs of cockroaches. Ferro stood on the top step of the porch and shined his flashlight into crevices and under shingles, following the light with the nozzle of the sprayer. Nothing moved.

"No creepy crawlies," he said.

Crow braced his feet and drove the heavy claw of the pinch bar between plywood and brick wall and threw his weight against it; LaMastra went around to the left side of the house and attacked that panel. Soon the air was torn by the squeals of protesting nails and percussive grunts and curses as they pried the gleaming sixteen-penny nails out of the sheet of plywood; then suddenly there was a splintering crack and Crow's panel slid straight down the wail, nail heads skittering on the brick like fingernails on a blackboard. It came down at an angle, struck the porch floor on one corner, stood on end for a moment, and then toppled backward onto the debris as Crow danced out of the way.

Crow threw down the pinch bar. "Well, kiss my ass!"

"What's wrong?" LaMastra called, racing around the corner.

The window frame was splintered and devoid of glass, but they couldn't see into the house because the entire frame was securely blocked by neat rows of new red bricks. Crow reached up and touched the cement, and though it looked recent it was cold and hard. He shook his head. "This son of a bitch thought of everything."

"Yeah?" asked LaMastra. "I'll bet he didn't think of this." With that he took Ferro's shotgun, fed in a Shok-Lock round, aimed the weapon at the length of shiny steel-welded chain, and pulled the trigger. The chain leapt like a scalded snake, spitting sparks and metal splinters, then the weight of the lock on the inside of the door yanked the ends through the holes and they heard the chain slither into a heap behind the door.

Crow nodded his appreciation. "Wow. That gives a whole new slant to breaking and entering."

LaMastra handed the Remington back to Ferro and picked up his ten-gauge. "Shame I can't get them for Bessie here." He stood four-square in front of the door, shotgun leveled. "You guys ready?"

Crow jacked a fresh round into the breech and Ferro drew his Glock. They stood on either side of LaMastra, and Ferro said simply: "Kick it."

LaMastra slammed his heel against it and the door flew inward, swinging all the way around to smash against the inner walls, sending the chain skittering across the floor of the entrance foyer. LaMastra stepped forward and fired a shot into the doorway, pumped, fired again, jacked in another round, and crouched to fire again. "Who has light?"

Ferro moved to LaMastra's side and aimed a flashlight beam inside. LaMastra moved inside cautiously, with Crow closed behind. The living room was big, intensely dark, and totally empty, without furniture or carpet, nothing but darkness and dust. Ferro held the light above their heads and fanned the beam slowly back and forth; wherever the light went, two shotgun barrels and the sprayer followed. It was a big living room with a high ceiling and a hardwood floor. The flashlight showed the brickwork that denied entry through the windows. Some old wiring drooped through the torn plaster of the ceiling, and there was a piece of new plywood nailed to the ceiling, ostensibly to cover a hole. The repair job on the ceiling had been the first really bad bit of carpentry they'd seen because the tips of the dozens of nails used to affix it from the second floor had come poking through the wood and stood out in little tufts of wood splinters.

Crow exchanged a look with LaMastra, who nodded, and the two of them moved through the living room toward the doorway to the adjoining room, careful where they stepped in case the floor was rotten, listening intently for any sound. Their hearts hammered in their chests. Ferro lingered by the front door and directed his light in front of them as Crow and LaMastra inched toward the doorway to the next room. There were French doors connecting the two rooms, and all of the little panes of glass were painted flat black. Crow reached for the handle and turned it. The handle turned easily, but as he pulled there was a springy resistance.

"It's not locked, but feels like it's caught on something."

"Give it a good yank," said LaMastra. "If that doesn't work knock out a pane and reach through."

"Be careful," Ferro said from the doorway. "I don't like this."

"Wait," said Crow, "I think I have it." He gave the handle a sharp pull and it abruptly gave, sending him staggering back a step. LaMastra caught him and almost as an aftereffect they heard the snap of strong twine. The sound was followed by a brief rumble that shook the house and then a rasping sound from overhead. They looked up in horror to see the sheet of plywood that was nailed to the ceiling detach itself at one end and swing down with a high-pitched squeal of hinges and pulleys.

"Frank! Watch out!" LaMastra called, lunging toward Ferro, but the heavy panel slammed into Ferro even as the detective turned to run. LaMastra and Crow saw the gleam of the long nails as they caught the flashlight's glare. There was a thump and Ferro screamed as the nails struck him in the back, driving him back through the doorway, and then the panel slammed into place and all light was extinguished.

Chapter 34

"Here, drink this," Val said, handing Mike a cup of hot tea. It was vending-machine tea, but if it tasted bad there was no sign of it on Mike's face. He sipped it and then cradled the cardboard cup between his palms, body hunched over the rising steam, his face pale and unspeakably sad.

"Crow isn't here?" he asked.

"No, he . . . had something important he had to do this morning."

Mike nodded, not looking at her. "He went back to Dark Hollow, didn't he?"

Weinstock gave Val a sharp glance; she shook her head. "Mike?" she said softly, laying a hand on his knee. "What makes you think Crow's gone out to the Hollow?"

"He's gone out there to try and find Griswold."

When they didn't answer Mike raised his head and looked at them. Both of them had horrified, stunned expressions on their faces, but these worsened as they got their first clear look at Mike's eyes.

"God!" Val recoiled. "Mike . . . what's *happened* to you?"

He managed the slightest of smiles, but his voice quavered as he said, "Don't worry . . . I'm not one of them."

"You're not one of . . . what?" she asked, and without realizing she was doing it she moved her right hand down toward her purse, where she had a .32 pistol she'd taken from her father's gun collection.

Mike's eyes followed her, his smile flickering. The gold rims around his blue-red eyes seemed to flare for a second. "You going to shoot me?"

Her hands paused, fingertips just over the closed mouth of the bag. Narrowing her eyes, she said, "Do I need to shoot you, Mike?"

"I hope not," he said. "I've already been dead once today. Don't know how many times I can take it."

"God, Val, he's a vampire!" Weinstock hissed.

Mike turned to him. "No," he said softly, "I'm something . . . else."

Val paused a moment longer and then pulled her hand back. "What happened to you?"

He lowered his eyes. "I don't know. I told you, I'm not one of them . . . but I don't really know what I am."

"Mike, tell me what happened."

Tears pearled the corners of his eyes. "I . . . ," he began and a sob broke his word in half. Mike slid off the bed toward her and suddenly wrapped his arms around her; one sob became a flow of them and they built and built until he was sobbing uncontrollably, hanging on to Val as if he'd fall into the abyss if he let go. His thin body shook and bucked and after a moment of stunned hesitation Val gathered him in and held him as tightly as he clung to her.

He kept saying one word over and over again as he wept. "Mommy . . ."

(2)

Since he'd awakened in his grave a month ago the Bone Man had spent most of his time wandering the roads and fields of Pine Deep searching for some kind of purpose, for a reason that he was back. Some of the time his mind seemed to be opening up and filling with insights, with knowledge he could not have acquired while he was alive; but these moments of insight were always brief and they never let him look deeply enough into the mysteries. It was insanely frustrating.

He knew, for example, that Griswold was a psychic vampire and that Mike was a *dhampyr*, but he didn't know the limits of what each of those things was, which didn't exactly help him plan his next move.

He knew that the Red Wave was coming and that it was going to do great harm to the people of Pine Deep—but he didn't actually know what form it would take, or the actual moment it would start. He knew it was going to be on Halloween, and he *guessed* that it would be sometime after sunset, but that's where the whole process showed its rust: it was half knowledge and then guesswork.

He knew that he was here for a purpose, and that it was tied to Mike, certainly more so him than anyone; and along the way he'd learned that he could blind the eyes of that Bible-thumping tow truck driver any time he tried to put Mike in his sights. Yeah, mission accomplished there at least, but now he felt that there was a bigger, greater purpose.

He wondered if somehow Griswold was blocking him off from understanding his greater purpose. That wormy old bastard was strong enough—strong in ways that the Bone Man didn't always understand. He was *old* strong, an evil intelligence centuries in the making.

Twice now he'd told that poor boy Mike the truth, first about his parentage, and then as much of the story as he knew. He knew, knew for a sure-thing certainty you could take to the bank, that it was the right thing to do, that telling Mike was part of why he had come back; but now, looking back on it, he was filled with doubts. The boy hadn't taken the news well. Who would? The first time he'd crashed his bike and nearly died out in the fields. The second time the kid actually *had* died. That had scared the Bone Man worse than anything he'd known in life or death, and for a lot of long confused hours he'd sat by the boy's body as it cooled. He'd never felt so lost and alone, so Judas guilty as he did then. Surely this boy was not meant to die. How could that make any kind of sense? And there *had* to be sense somewhere in this madness or why else had he been brought back? Granted, the kid was probably going to die during the

Red Wave or maybe later when the strange genetics of the *dhampyr* wore the kid down and killed him as it did everyone cursed with that legacy, but the kid just up and had a coronary right there and then.

Sitting by the boy's body the Bone Man cursed God until even the crows in the trees looked aghast.

Then Mike had stopped being dead.

From wherever it had gone the kid's spirit came and re-claimed his body. Just like that.

Thinking about it as he walked through the woods toward Griswold's house, the Bone Man cast an angry eye at Heaven. "Moves in mysterious ways, my ass."

When Mike had opened his eyes, the Bone Man tried apolo-gizing, but the kid looked through him as if he wasn't there. Like he didn't see him anymore, which made no sense. If the dying could see him, and the dead could see him, then Mike should have been able to.

But the kid had gotten up and wandered off, heading back to town. The Bone Man yelled at him, had strummed his guitar—something that always seemed to work before—but the boy just didn't hear, as if whatever bond had existed before the kid died had burned away once he woke up.

Now, everything was in motion. The Bone Man could see what Vic and Ruger were doing and now he understood the time frame of the Red Wave. If there was ever a time when he needed to be heard, it was now . . . and wasn't that just the way? You need something, you get a kick in the nuts by God.

Now the boy was on his own and the Bone Man was almost to Griswold's house. L'il Scarecrow was walking in harm's way and he hoped there was something, however small, he could do to help. "This being a ghost shit just sucks."

(3)

The room was totally black and after that huge crashing impact of the trapdoor swinging down everything settled into an ugly silence. Crow felt the floor under him, but he couldn't see it.

"Frank?" he whispered.

Nothing. Then, "Crow . . . ?"

"Vince? Where are you? Where's Frank?"

There was a rustling sound and then bright white as La-Mastra turned on his flashlight. Shielding his eyes from the glare, Crow looked around. LaMastra was on his knees, the light in one hand while he reached down to pick up his fallen shotgun.

"Are you hurt?"

"No" LaMastra answered. "You?"

"I'm good. Where's Frank?"

LaMastra swept the light toward the door. "I think he's outside. Damn, look at that shit."

Crow got to his feet and examined the doorway, running his hand over the massive panel that now sealed the door shut. He fished out his pocket Maglite and played its beam over the ceiling. "Son of a bitch set a good trap. Look." He pointed with the light. "See there? He made it look like someone had done a bad patch job on the ceiling, with nails sticking down through from upstairs like some shithead carpenter did it using nails that were too big." He turned the light back onto the doorway. "It's a perfect fit. That whole panel was a trapdoor attached to the ceiling. Soon as we tripped the wire it swung down on hinges and slammed itself flush into the doorframe. No way for us to pry it out, no angle for leverage even if we had the pry bars." He pounded on it. "Solid as a bitch. And those nails . . . they were the teeth of the trap. Holy shit . . ."

LaMastra set down his flash and used the side of his fist to pound on the door. "Frank!" he yelled. "Frank—you out there?"

There was no sound at all from the other side.

"I think he got hit," Crow said. "When it fell, it looked like he got hit."

"Must have knocked him out, otherwise he'd answer."

Crow didn't think so. Not all of the nails in that trapdoor were intended to seal the door. There were a couple of dozen right in the middle. He saw the light shine on them a second before it hit Ferro. The trapdoor must weigh half a ton; nothing less would have made it move so fast or hit so hard. All that weight pushing those nails? Crow's heart sank.

"We have to get out of here, Vince."

"Give Frank a minute . . . he'll get us out."

"I don't think so."

LaMastra half turned and shot him a vicious look. "What's that supposed to mean?"

"Just what I said. Maybe Frank's okay, maybe he's not, but right now you and me are locked in this friggin' place. No way I'm going to stand around and wait. What if the roaches come back?"

The big detective glared at him, his features made harsh by fear and the glare of the flashlights. "Frank's okay," Vince said stubbornly.

"Whatever you say, Vince . . . but I'm going to look for another way out of here."

He turned away and surveyed the room. To his left a staircase led upward into total blackness, to his right were the French doors that had been part of the trap. The doors hung open, their tripwire snapped. Crow peered cautiously through into the next room. "Looks empty. Maybe we can get out through the kitchen door. It should be through there."

Grudgingly, LaMastra joined him, "What if the back door's bricked up?"

"Then we'll find the stairs, go up, see if maybe there's a way out. If we have to maybe we can blast a hole in the roof and climb the hell out."

"No other option?"

"We find the cellar stairs, go down there. See if there's a way out."

LaMastra looked at him like he was crazy. "Why on earth would we want to do that?"

"We don't. I'm for the direct route, right through the house and out. But we have to expect more booby traps."

"You think anyone's here?"

"No way to know, but if there is, they sure as hell know we're here. C'mon, let's move."

"I see anyone, man, I'm gonna kill them."

"Works for me." Crow used his shotgun barrel to push open the doors. They fanned back from the doorway just in case there was another wire, but nothing happened; after a moment they moved into the next room. A threadbare area rug lay on the floor, rumpled and smelling of rat droppings; an old-fashioned couch was pushed back against one wall. Two doorways led from this room: one was naked of any door and emptied into a dark hallway that jagged right out of sight; the other had a heavy door that was tightly shut. Crow moved to the closed door and examined it and the ceiling above. No visible traps.

"Go slow," LaMastra warned as Crow reached for the handle. The knob turned easily with no telltale resistance, and it swung open on creaky hinges; but there was nothing on the other side besides a neat wall of new-laid bricks.

"I guess we go the other way," Crow said, aware that there was the clear sense of being herded into a more complex trap. Their options were limited, so he moved through the open doorway. They shined their lights over every inch of it and saw no trip wires.

They moved down the hallway and this emptied out into another room filled with dust and shadows. A water-damaged breakfront sagged on three legs against one wall, and on the opposite wall a battered old oak table stood, supporting a stack of red bricks. Another huge pile of rotted carpet filled the center of the room. Before they moved farther Crow shined his light across the room and could see the white bulk of an old refrigerator beyond the far doorway.

"There's the kitchen," Crow said. "Let's get the hell out of here."

They moved slowly, hugging the walls in order to keep a clear line of fire across the whole room. At the kitchen door they peered in and saw the faintest line of pale daylight seeping in on one side of the boarded window.

"Finally," LaMastra said, "it's about time we caught a break."

He took a step forward and his leg passed through an almost invisible infrared beam that cut across the doorway an inch off the floor. Neither man saw it; neither of them expected anything that sophisticated. LaMastra's heel cut the line and at once there was an audible click and then a sound like a firecracker and suddenly a section of the kitchen floor lunged up at them, nailheads tearing through old linoleum. It was the reverse of the front-door trap and Crow, a half step behind LaMastra, saw the movement and grabbed the bigger man's shoulder and yanked back, screaming as he backpedaled them both away from the trap.

They staggered back onto the rumpled carpet—which immediately buckled under him. Crow fell backward and down, and with LaMastra's weight accelerating the rate of fall they plunged through the massive and perfectly disguised hole in the dining room floor and plummeted into blackness.

(4)

Vic looked down at his wristwatch. 1:18 P.M. Above him the sky was clouding up nicely, and he nodded approval. Right on time.

A car rumbled across the bridge and Vic waited, looking up at the tiny particles of dust that drifted down from the heavy timbers, then peered down at the wires he held in his fingers. He twisted the leads onto the terminals of the heavy-duty battery. Once the wires were in place he slid the whole assembly into the niche he'd carved out of the bank. Vic removed a diagram from his shirt pocket and consulted it, glancing up to check that the lines on the map matched the long strands of wires that trailed up the supports to the three bundles that were each nestled into their proper places.

He picked up the clock and set the time, then very carefully pulled the button that primed the clock to ring at just the right moment.

"Boom!" he said softly as he backed away from the timer.

As he trudged up the bank toward his truck he tugged a notebook out of the back pocket of his jeans, humming as he walked. There was still a lot to do, but he was ahead of schedule, and that made him happy. He wanted the Man to see that he was still the most reliable of his army, still his right hand. Yeah, he thought as he opened the truck door and climbed in, he'd get all of it done in time, and maybe a little more besides.

He was grinning as he spun the wheel and headed back toward town.

(5)

There was an unreal moment of mingled darkness and trapped flashlight illumination, a sensation of floating that did not feel at all like falling. Then they hit the cellar floor so hard it sent agony shrieking upward through Crow's whole body; the carpet padded their fall to a degree, but Crow landed badly, hitting first on the edge of his heels and then falling backward to slam the flat of his back on the concrete floor. Instantly the world exploded in white light and thunder as LaMastra accidentally jerked the trigger of his shotgun and blasted a hole in the carpet inches from Crow's cheek. Small flecks of gunpowder sizzled into his skin.

The rug collapsed on top of them, and Crow groaned as the weight of the heavy material drove the hard scabbard of his sword case into his spine. Beside him, LaMastra snarled in confusion as he thrashed at the carpet, and with every movement he elbowed or kicked Crow.

"Vince, stop it, for Christ's sake!" Crow bellowed and emphasized it with his own elbow. It caught the detective somewhere soft and there was a whoosh of air and a grunt of pain.

They both stopped thrashing and let the moment settle around them.

"Are you hurt?" Crow asked.

"Everything hurts," was LaMastra's muffled reply.

"Let's get this frigging carpet off us . . ."

But that fast the folds of the carpet were whipped away from Crow by unseen hands. While LaMastra still struggled to get free of the carpet, Crow scrambled around onto his hands and knees, his heart hammering in his chest, scrabbling for the fallen flashlight, but his desperate fingers sent it rolling away. The light pinwheeled around and then came to an abrupt stop as someone caught it with the toe of a polished shoe.

On all fours, Crow stared at the face of the man who stood over them. The blood turned to ice in his veins and the world seemed to spin sideways into unreality as he watched the man bend down and pick up the Maglite.

Jimmy Castle held the light in his bone-white fingers. He held the beam under his chin the way a prankish child might at a campfire.

"Boo!" he said, and his mouth stretched wide to show two rows of jagged white teeth.

Chapter 35

It took a long time for Val to soothe Mike. Clinging to her, he seemed to regress to an almost babylike state, his words reduced to an inarticulate wordless noise that was drenched with tears. She stroked his matted hair and kissed his dirty face and rocked him back and forth until his terrible sobs slowed to a whimper and then he felt silent. Jonatha and Newton came in and when they saw Mike they kept silent; Weinstock waved them over to the far side of the room. Jonatha sat in a chair and Newton leaned against the wall, both of them looking as confused and uncomfortable as Weinstock.

When Mike finally lifted his head, he sniffed, accepted the tissue Val gave him, then slowly looked around the room as if he'd never seen it. He wiped his nose and blotted his eyes. He offered no weak smile or embarrassed apologies for his tears. People in wartime don't need to do it, and their fellow refugees don't require it of them.

Because his eyes were now so red and puffy Jonatha and Newton didn't immediately notice their unnatural look.

Val helped Mike to his feet and led him to the bathroom. "Why don't you clean yourself up, honey? Take your time. You know Mr. Newton, he's a friend. He knows what's going on. Professor Corbiel is also a friend. She's from the University of Pennsylvania." She put her hand on his cheek. "She's a folklorist. She knows about vampires."

That made Mike's eyes flicker and he turned to look at her

and she saw his eyes. Jonatha gripped Newton's knee and her fingernails dug deep.

Mike went in and closed the bathroom door.

Val and the others huddled around Weinstock and she told them what Mike had said.

"What's with his eyes?" Newton asked.

"We don't know yet," Val admitted, "but something terrible must have happened."

They heard the toilet flush and the door opened. Mike came into the room and sat down on the edge of the bed. His face was composed, but the abiding hurt was there in the stiffness of his posture and the profound sadness of his face.

"Mike," Val said, sitting down next to him, "you know what's going on in town, don't you?"

He nodded. "Some of it," he said. "Maybe a lot of it, but not all of it."

"What do you know?" Newton asked.

Mike sighed. "This is going to take time."

Val wrapped her arm around his shoulders. "We have to know."

"Before I tell you what I know I guess I should tell you *how* I know." He took a breath, held it, let it out slowly. "You know that there are vampires in Pine Deep, don't you?"

Val just squeezed his shoulder.

"My mother is one of them."

"God . . ." Weinstock breathed.

He told them what happened at his house and didn't dare look at the horror on their faces. "She saved my life," he said, and sniffed back some tears.

"So . . . Vic Wingate's involved in this," Jonatha said. "If he knew about Mike's mom—"

Mike snorted. "Vic isn't just 'involved' . . . he's *his* right hand."

"Who, Mike?" Val asked.

He gave her a quizzical look. "Why . . . Ubel Griswold, of course. Don't you know?"

"How do you know that?"

"That's the other thing . . . the other way I know about what's going on. I know because the Bone Man told me."

"The Bone . . . ," Val put her hand to her mouth. "Mike . . . tell us everything."

He did. He started with the Massacre and how Griswold began hunting humans after his cattle were killed by the first blight. A blight, he said, that was different from the current one because it actually was just a freak of nature, a real plague. "This new one is something Griswold did," he told them. "The first plague just gave him the idea."

He told them about how the Bone Man, who knew a thing or two about the supernatural from his childhood in the deep South, was able to piece together what Griswold was doing, and what Griswold was. He told them how the Bone Man hunted Griswold that day, trying to catch and kill him before he turned into a monster as the moon rose. He told about the fight they had in Dark Hollow, and how the Bone Man killed him with his old blues guitar and buried him in the swamp a couple of miles from Griswold's old house.

Val said, "Crow went down there with two police officers, the detectives from Philadelphia who were here during the man-hunt."

"Can you call him, tell him to come back?"

"I tried, there's no cell phone reception. But they have guns and other stuff. Garlic to use against the vampires, and gasoline to burn the house down."

Mike looked uncertain. "I hope that works."

"Go on, kid," Newton said, "tell us the rest."

"After Griswold died he was just gone for a long time. There wasn't any trace of him, even in the swamp, except maybe like a, I don't know—a presence, if that makes sense. Then sixteen years ago he just woke up. Just like that. He was weak, confused, and he didn't even understand exactly that he was dead. He was really scared, too, and he called out for the one person he knew would always be there for him." He paused and his mouth twisted into an ugly shape. "Vic." He took another steadying breath. "Vic started coming out to the swamp every day, and he started doing research about the supernatural. Griswold told him everything about what he was, about being born to a race of werewolves in Serbia."

Jonatha glanced at Newton, who nodded.

"Griswold always believed, you see, that when he died he'd just come right back to life as a vampire right away, but that didn't happen because somehow when the Bone Man killed him it weakened him really badly. The Bone Man thinks it was some magic in his guitar. I don't know, that sounds kind of stupid." He wiped his nose again. "Anyway, Griswold was scared, thinking he was just going to be a spirit without a body, trapped there in the swamp, but Vic found something in one of his books, a kind of ritual that sometimes allows a ghost to kind of possess a human body. Not like in the movies, not green pea soup and all. This was more like hijacking a car. Neither of them knew if it would work, or how long it would last. They tried it over and over again, but nothing happened. Vic *killed* people and Griswold tried to inhabit their bodies. Vic even let Griswold try and take over his own body, but it didn't work, but then Vic came up with the idea of Griswold trying to use a blood connection to make the process work better. That's when they decided to try and have Griswold possess the body of his only living blood connection in town."

They all exchanged puzzled looks. "A blood relative?" Newton asked. "In Pine Deep?"

"Oh . . . Christ," Val said, making the connection. Mike looked at her and nodded. She said, "You're talking about . . . Terry!"

Mike kept nodding. "During the Massacre, when the mayor was just a kid, his sister was attacked and he tried to save her. She died and Mr. Wolfe was almost killed. He was *bitten* by the werewolf and was in a coma for weeks. He never turned into a werewolf himself—the Bone Man says that's because Mr. Wolfe's spirit is too full of light, or something like that, I don't really understand that part—but the blood connection was established, and because of that link, Griswold was able to hijack Mr. Wolfe's body and use it as his own. He . . . um . . . well, the way the Bone Man put it—Griswold went out for a night on the town. Drinking, partying, and, um, sex."

"Good God!" Weinstock stared at Mike. "I feel sorry for whatever poor gal wound up in the sack with him!"

"Do you know who it was?" Val asked.

Mike turned to face her and his eyes burned like flame. When he spoke his voice was bitter and tight. "Take a look at me, Val. All of you take a good look and figure it out for yourselves."

Her eyes became as big as saucers. "Oh. My. God! A long time ago, when Terry and I were dating, he told me that he got drunk and had an affair. We were . . . in love at the time, and it's what broke us up. He tried to tell me that he didn't remember any of it, that he just woke up in bed with a woman. It was someone I knew, someone I'd been friends with in school. He said that he had no memory at all of what happened, or how he got there. I thought that was a weak, bullshit excuse and I kicked him out." She reached out and gave Mike a fierce hug. "Oh, Mike . . . oh you poor kid! I never noticed . . . none of us did."

Mike gently pushed Val back. "Why would you? How could anyone know? I didn't know, even though I delivered the mayor's paper every day. The mayor doesn't know, either. Only my mom and Vic know that I'm Mr. Wolfe's son."

"But . . . but . . . ," Newton stammered, "wait a goddamn minute here. If Griswold was using Mayor Wolfe's body, doesn't that mean that, in part at least, you're . . . you're . . ."

"Yes. That means that I'm also Ubel Griswold's son." He gave a bitter laugh. "You all look like you just ate a bug. Imagine how I feel. But, let me tell you the rest of it before I . . . well, let me just get it out, okay?" Val handed him another tissue, and Mike launched right into the story of how Vic Wingate engineered the death of Big John Sweeney and married Lois shortly after, and then settled in to watch the boy, to study him. "At first Vic hoped that I was going to be like Griswold—another *monster*. Maybe he even thought I was going to be Griswold reborn. After a while, though, either he or Griswold figured out that I wasn't a chip off the old block. Vic was furious and he wanted to

kill me, but Griswold didn't. By now Griswold had figured out
what I was."

"A *dhampyr*," Jonatha said, and Mike nodded.

"Griswold always expected to become a vampire one day, always assumed he'd get killed eventually as a werewolf, so he
made sure he knew a lot about vampires. That's why he's so
good at being one. He *knows* what he is, and he began to suspect
what I was. He also knows the legend that if any evil hand kills
a *dhampyr*, then its energy is scattered throughout the region.
That means that everything in Pine Deep would have had the
same powers as a *dhampyr*." Newton opened his mouth, but
Mike cut him off. "Before you ask, no I don't have superpowers.
I'm not any stronger than I was, I can't fly or leap tall buildings.
The Bone Man said that the *dhampyr's* two main strengths are
his ability to sense the presence of evil—and, yeah, I got that
going overtime, but there's so much of it I don't know where to
look—and the other thing is that anything I pick up—a stick, a
stone, anything—becomes like a supercharged weapon against
evil. I don't need garlic or any of that. Supposedly."

"Why 'supposedly'?"

"Because my biological father carries a werewolf bloodline,
not a vampire bloodline. His blood and Griswold's spirit are in
me, and my mother was a weak woman who was a slut for Griswold and Vic. A *dhampyr* is supposed to be pure, untouched by
evil, unable to become evil . . . but look at my family tree, guys.
What are the odds that I'm going to be so pure that I'm going
to be a real threat to any of these things?"

"Are you guessing, or do you know?" Val asked.

He shook his head. "Even the Bone Man doesn't know. He
says that I'm different than he expected. That's kind of funny,
don't you think?"

No one laughed.

"If you're not supposed to be harmed by any evil," Newton
said, "why did he give you to Vic? Pardon me for saying this, but
Crow told me that Vic knocks you around a lot."

"Oh yeah, Vic loves to hit, but he never killed me. He wanted
to, more than you can imagine, and I think he was trying to

make life so bad for me that I'd kill myself. That would remove the threat without any danger to Griswold." Mike paused. "Don't think I haven't thought about it, too. A lot of times."

Val bent forward and kissed his forehead. "I'm glad you didn't, sweetie."

Jonatha said, "Mike, I don't know you, but from what I'm hearing it sounds like you've certainly taken a side in all this. You may have the worst heritage anyone's ever heard of, but you're here with us. You're not with Vic."

He didn't meet her eyes, but his cheeks colored. "I guess."

"The *dhampyr* aren't usually fighters," she said, changing tack. "They're more like witch-sniffers—beings that can sense evil and are dedicated to revealing it. Among the Gypsies the *dhampyr* usually goes from town to town and offers his services to detect and destroy vampires or other evil. Not in single combat or anything . . . it, um, involves some kind of ritual dance and the use of special charms, and so on."

"Oh brother," Weinstock said, rolling his eyes.

"Don't worry," Mike said, "I don't see myself breaking into a dance number any time soon."

"But there's a downside to being a *dhampyr*," Jonatha said gravely. "Did the Bone Man tell you that?"

Mike gazed at her for a long time before nodding. "Yeah, he told me that."

"Told you what?" Weinstock asked.

Jonatha cleared her throat. "Well, in folklore, the *dhampyr* is the antithesis of a vampire. Where a vampire is evil, the *dhampyr* is not; where a vampire preys on humans, the *dhampyr* preys on supernatural creatures; and, where the vampire is immortal . . . the *dhampyr* is not. In fact, the *dhampyr* generally only lives into his early twenties."

"What happens?" Val asked, leaning forward. "Is it a matter of a high mortality rate for someone so young fighting those kinds of odds? Because you're going to have a hell of a lot of backup here if it comes to a fight."

Jonatha shook her head. "No . . . it's worse than that. Beginning with late puberty the *dhampyr's* skeleton begins a process of degeneration. It . . . um . . ."

"What she's trying to say," Mike said, "is that my skeleton is going to turn to jelly by the time I'm in my mid-twenties. It'll stop supporting my organs, and eventually I'm just going to collapse into a big mooshy mass and die."

"Holy . . . God!" Newton said.

Val reached out and put her hand on Mike's arm and he shied away.

"I'm so sorry, kid," Jonatha said softly. "Maybe that part of the story's just bullshit. Maybe the different biology here . . . Mayor Wolfe and all . . . it might make things different."

"Yeah," Mike said brightly, "and maybe Santa will come and sprinkle elf-dust on me and make everything all better."

"Well don't forget you're in a hospital and this is the twenty-first century, not fifteenth-century Romania." Weinstock said, reaching out with his good arm and patting Mike's shoulder. "I'll bet there's a whole we can do, so let's not dig a hole quite yet."

Mike's eyes searched the doctor's face, then he nodded.

"Is there more?" Newton asked.

"Sure," Mike said softly, "I haven't even gotten to the part where I died, yet."

(2)

The crucified man hung there in the shadows and felt his life run out of him. He could barely feel his limbs; his hands and feet were distant countries from which he received little communication. Most of the time he was not conscious, lost in blackness but still aware of his own body, of the tether of pain that still held him to the world. Sometimes he could find his way into the light, but he had to blink away tears of blood just to catch a brief glimpse of the weak gray daylight. He coveted those momentary glimpses because he was sure they were the last ones he would ever have.

His head felt heavy. He wanted to lay it down, let his chin fall on his chest, let his neck rest from carrying that improbably heavy burden, but he couldn't. Something burned in the back of his head and he felt as if that burning pinpoint kept his head from falling forward. There were other burning spots as well, little fires in his hands, along his sides, down one leg, in the heel of his other, twisted leg. The skin around each point of fire was warm, too, but the warmth was wet and ran in long lines down his limbs.

When he was up in the light he could smell things that didn't make sense, a cacophony of odors. Distantly he thought that they should make sense, but it was so hard to think with that constant burning. He struggled to separate the smells. There were four of them, he thought. One smell was sweet and thick and reminded him of freshly sheared copper. Another smelled like his mother's kitchen and her spicy food, of Sunday dinners with Uncle Tony and the pot of gravy always simmering on the stove. He could remember that kitchen to the tiniest detail, though he could not, for the life of him, remember his own name, or how he came to be there. Or where he was. Or anything useful.

His thoughts drifted back to the smells. The third smell was an outhouse stink of urine and sweat, and he knew that those smells came from him. He wondered if he had made a mess of himself; he wondered if he should care. The last of the smells was an aroma from his teenage days long ago. How long ago? He wasn't sure. A long time? Yesterday? He could not be sure, but he knew that smell was the gasoline stink of cars and grease and filling stations. The four smells were all around him, covering him, clogging his nose, filling the air that drifted past his bloodied nose and mouth and eyes.

He tried to move, and from a thousand miles away he felt the fingers of one hand twitch. Was it his right hand? He wasn't sure. Just fingers, moving.

He coughed once. A short, sharp cough choked with bloody phlegm, and the brief convulsion of the cough ignited each of those burning points into white-hot searing suns that fried his nerve endings. He wanted to scream, to run away from the burning points of agony, but he could not throw his head back to utter the shriek that welled in him; instead his jaw dropped down and a stuttering, gagging growl bubbled out of the back of his throat.

Gradually, gradually, the intense flare of pain subsided, the fires banking back down to the burning points of heat. Then he coughed again, unexpectedly, sharply, a deeper cough that knotted his guts as if he'd just been punched. He doubled forward and the burning pain in the back of his head flared again, but the resistance was immediately gone. As his heavy head sagged forward, his shoulders followed, igniting more of the burning spots again, but with each flare more of his body became unstuck. He crumpled forward and he could see the ground reaching up toward him. He could see the puddle of gasoline and blood and urine that pooled around his shoes. He toppled forward, finally pulling free of the nails that had held him to the trapdoor.

Frank Ferro collapsed onto the porch of Griswold's house.

The punctured sprayer leaked high octane down his sides and onto the floor, and blood pumped sluggishly from twenty-six deep punctures in his body. The hole in the back of his head glistened red and there were tiny flecks of bone and brain tissue mingled in with the flowing blood.

One pierced hand flopped out, scrabbling feebly toward the light. He tried to find his feet, tried to recall how they worked, and after long minutes of trying managed to kick weakly backward against the door. He managed to shove himself six inches forward, six inches farther toward the yard. He tried again, and this time his fingers closed around a thick piece of debris from the fallen porch. He pulled with all his strength and slid another five inches forward. He coughed again and blood began streaming from his nose. The light flickered off and on and the point of burning pain in the back of his head became white hot again.

Ferro laid his face down on the floor and tried to remember how to pray. He knew he should be able to remember. But it was so hard to think.

★ ★ ★

When the thin black man in the dirty suit came walking out of the woods, Ferro looked up, hope flaring in his chest, but then the insight of the dying told him who this man was—this young man in cheap funeral clothes, with a nappy old-fashioned Afro and a blues guitar.

The man sat down on the porch rail, swinging the guitar around in front of him. He had a kindly face, though his eyes were like dusty marbles.

"You can see me, can't you?" the man said.

Ferro couldn't find his voice. He tried to nod, but even that was so hard.

"Yeah, you can see me. And I think you know who I am. Something tells me you do." He picked out a couple of notes on his guitar. "Listen, my brother, 'cause time is short. There's someone coming out here who you're not gonna want to meet, but he'll be here just the same. He's the peckerwood son of a bitch did this to you, and he's the one laid the traps for your friends." He bent closer. "I hope you can understand me, man, 'cause if you do, then you got one last chance to stick it to the Man."

(3)

The sight of Jimmy Castle standing there jerked Crow sideways into an unreal world where nothing made sense. If he had seen Ruger he could probably have dealt with it . . . but Castle was dead and *buried*. He and Weinstock had opened his coffin, had seen his putrefying corpse, had confirmed that Castle was dead. He *could not* be here.

Castle tossed the flashlight over his shoulder, where it struck the wall and clattered to the ground, the lens cracked but the bulb still lit.

Even though he was still bundled up in the carpet, LaMastra nonetheless made a gagging sound, which is when the spoiled-meat stink of Castle registered in Crow's stalled brain. It was as rancid as the leavings in the corner of a bear's den.

"Man, the look on your face is priceless," Castle said, laughing. "Almost as bad as when you and Saul Weinstock opened my casket. You both looked like you swallowed frogs."

"You . . . were dead!"

"I'm *still* dead, asshole. I'm a fucking vampire. You think sleeping in a coffin for a few days was gonna bother me? Nels and I—we thought it was a gas. Fooled *your* ass."

"But you were all . . ."

"All what? De-com-posed?" He made each syllable sound like a separate word. "Yeah, well, we can do all sorts of things and regenerating is part of the luxury package. Soon as I chomp down on you and your butt-buddy I'll be right as rain."

Castle shook his head and laughed. Other voices laughed, too. Behind them . . . near them, around them in the dark. Crow turned slowly to see other white faces emerge from the shadows. Crow saw Nels Cowan, and he had a flash of memories of their days together as policemen. The thickset man had always been funny, quick-witted, thoroughly in love with his wife and kids, and just crooked enough to accept free dinners at the Scarecrow Diner and a Christmas bottle of Jim Beam from the owner of Friendly Spirits. Now, dressed in the torn and filthy black suit he'd been buried in, he shambled through the shadows, drool hanging pendulously from his bloodless lips. This was the Nels Cowan of Weinstock's video, but worse—purpled by expanding gasses, visibly rotting.

LaMastra finally punched and wrestled his way out of the carpet and flopped around onto his hands and knees. He stared upward in furious indignation and instantly the look of fury on his face changed to one of stark terror. LaMastra screamed.

Without warning Jimmy Castle grabbed the front of LaMastra's Kevlar vest and jerked him off the floor and pulled him toward his grinning mouth, teeth gleaming like yellow knives. He held the big detective as easily as if he were a little child. LaMastra punched and squirmed, but Castle was far too strong. The vampire bent forward and ran a colorless tongue along the bloody seepage along the line of stitches on LaMastra's jaw; a moan of deep, almost sexual pleasure escaped Castle's throat. His eyes were totally black and as he pulled LaMastra even closer his jaws opened impossibly wide. Castle took one handful of the detective's hair and jerked his head to one side, exposing his throat.

Castle suddenly gagged and staggered, his grip going from rock hard to weak in the space of a second; LaMastra sagged down to his knees and Castle reeled back, pawing at his own mouth, spitting and hissing like a snake.

Crow stared in shock and confusion. Around him the other vampires sent up a howl of anger and confusion. Then Crow got it. The word sprang right into his head.

Garlic! All three of them had smeared it on their throats! The realization was like a shot of adrenaline to Crow and as he watched Castle retch in disgust and pain he felt sense and control flood back into him. He twisted sideways and dove for the shotgun. Encumbered by the sword strapped across his back, his tumble was awkward, but he rolled away and came up with the weapon in his hands.

Despite his pain, Castle sneered at him. "I'm going to rip your goddamn heart out!"

Crow raised his shotgun and pointed it at Castle's heart. Around him all the waxy white faces turned toward him, and all the hungry mouths laughed.

"Go ahead and shoot, asshole!" Castle jeered. "Take your best shot 'cause then I'm going to tear your eyes out and drink from the sockets."

"Blow me," Crow said, and fired.

The blast caught Jimmy Castle in the chest, plucked him off the ground, and threw him ten feet backward. He slammed into Nels Cowan and they both went down. Cowan was up again in an instant, laughing at the joke, reaching down to pull Castle up, sharing the prank Castle had just played on the stupid human with the gun. But Castle's hand was limp in his grasp and Cowan stared down, still not getting it. Castle lay in a ragdoll sprawl, arms and legs twisted, head thrown back in surprise, his chest a bloody pit of mush.

Crow jacked another round, the sound as distinct as any insult or challenge that's ever been. Cowan's snarl started as a whimper of fear, but instantly intensified into a predator's hunting shriek as he turned and lunged forward at Crow.

The first shot tore away Cowan's left shoulder and sent his arm spinning back into the shadows trailing a line of blood. For a moment Cowan froze there in a posture of attack, weight on his toes, one arm still reaching, but his face was blank with shock, his mouth agape. Crow's second round caught him in the throat and Cowan's body fell straight backward while his head struck the ceiling joist and then landed with a smashed-melon crunch on the ground.

The gunshot echoes boomed like thunder from every wall and then died into a breathless nothing, freezing them all in a monstrous tableau. But just for a second. Then the other vampires swarmed toward Crow from three sides of the cellar. Crow spun, jacking another round, but immediately there was a titanic bang as LaMastra—finally jarred from his shocked stupor—brought up the heavy Roadblocker and opened fire.

One of the vampires went down with a hole as large as a basketball punched wetly through his stomach; the recoil drove LaMastra back against Crow, and from then on there they stood, back to back, shotguns firing, impacts making them collide, the garlic-soaked pellets filling the room as the pale creatures, driven past fear by hunger and hate, rushed at them. Everywhere they looked there were white faces and clawed hands and black eyes and red mouths.

LaMastra fired his gun dry, but Crow kept shooting his, screaming all the while, jacking round after round into the breech, jerking the trigger, feeling the kick and hearing the concussion and jacking in the next round, and the next, until suddenly the gun clicked and nothing happened. Crow pumped it again. Click. Pump. Click. Pump. Click. Doing it, over and over again, screaming and dry-firing and pumping and staring into the blackness of shock and death.

And then Vince LaMastra tore the gun from his hands and belted Crow across the face. "Crow!" LaMastra shouted, "STOP IT!"

Instantly Crow sagged to his knees, panting like a dog, mouth working to form words but unable to make any come.

"Crow!" said LaMastra again, this time with less force. "It's over. Crow, man . . . it's over."

Slowly, very slowly, Crow came back from that black place to which his mind had fled, back to the shadows of the cellar and to the musty carpet on which he lay, and back to himself. He looked around . . . and everywhere there was death. White bodies lay sprawled in improbable heaps, mouths thrown wide, eyes open or closed, hands splayed, flesh torn but bloodless. Dead. All of them. Dead.

Jimmy Castle. Dead. Nels Cowan. Dead. By the boiler, that was Carl Jacobsen, who owned a small farm down by the reservoir. Carl, with five kids at home. Dead. Over by the stairs, wasn't that Mitzie Grant who had just graduated from nursing school? Dead. The others were strangers. Dead. All dead.

Upstairs Frank Ferro was probably dead, too; and down here in the center of it all—Malcolm Crow and Vince LaMastra. Alive. By some miracle, by a chance. Maybe by skill and luck, too. But alive amid all that death. They looked at each other, shaking their heads, unable to speak because how could human speech make any kind of sense of this? They should have been dead, but they had survived. They were alive.

Alive, but still trapped in Ubel Griswold's house.

Chapter 36

Vic's Ford pickup bounced along the back road, through the tall stands of oaks and pines, his wheels crushing October leaves into fragments. He had a sulfur-tipped kitchen match between his teeth and he was grinning. On the radio Gretchen Wilson was telling him that she needed to get laid. Sunset was hours away, but that didn't matter. Not to him, not to the Plan, and not to the *Man*.

Despite his earlier blues Vic felt pretty sporty and he couldn't prevent nasty little smiles from popping onto his lips every few minutes as he rolled through the forest toward the Man's house.

At one point in the trip he stopped on the crest of the last large hill before the road dropped down into the valley beyond which was Dark Hollow. Vic took a sheet of onionskin from his shirt pocket, unfolded and smoothed it out, and then used a drop of spit to stick it to the dashboard. He consulted the row of numbers and checked them against the screen display on the laptop that lay on the front seat next to him. Most of his stuff was on timer, but the timers were inactive until he sent a master signal, which he did now by typing in a password and hitting Enter. The computer whirred for a moment and then returned a message: Completed. A clock appeared in a pop-up window and began counting down.

Vic took his cell phone from his shirt pocket and made the last call he would ever make on that phone. Even though the cellular relay tower would be the last to go because some of

Ruger's team needed their phones to coordinate troop movements, Vic had no one else to call. Lois was with *them* now. Vic
didn't have any friends left among the living.

It rang three times and then Ruger answered.

"You ready, Sport?" Vic asked.

"Yeah, as soon as your wife's done blowing me." Vic heard
Lois burst out laughing in the background.

"Yeah, that joke never gets old, asshole," Vic said. "The clock's
ticking."

"Don't worry," Vic said, still chuckling, "we're ready."

Ruger clicked off the phone, his good mood suddenly soured.
His fist closed so tightly around the cell phone that his knuckles
popped and the case cracked. "Yeah, well, enjoy it while you
can, asshole," he muttered, "'cause this town ain't the only thing
that's going to die today."

He cranked down the window and threw the phone into the
weeds, then threw the truck back in gear and ground down the
road toward the Man's house.

(2)

Sarah Wolfe did not know her husband was awake though
he'd been conscious for almost ten minutes now.

It had taken most of that time for him to realize where he
was and what had happened. At first he had been frightened by
the strangeness of it all: the intrusion of plastic tubing into his
nostrils, the feeling of confinement around his limbs, the re-
straint of suspension straps, the pounding ache in his head, the
small, alien beeps of machines. Then it came to him. He was in a
hospital. He was hurt and he was in a hospital.

That realization began the process of looking inside to try
and understand why he was in a hospital. Was it a car accident?
A heart attack? Then . . . all at once the memories came to him
like a computer coming online. Images flashed onto a movie
screen in his head: the face he saw in the mirror, the face that
had changed each day, become more horrific, more alien each

day. The voice of his little sister, first on the phone, then beside him. In the elevator at the hospital. On the street, in the shadows of his office. In his own home. Mandy's little bloodstained face, so sad, so frightened, but also so hard and angry. Her words, her desperate pleas for him to kill himself. Then Sarah's face and Sarah's pleas that he see a doctor, a psychiatrist. Sarah again, staring at him with pity as he stood amid the broken fragments of mirror in their bathroom. Sarah recoiling in horror as he began to change from man to animal.

He felt the horror surge up in him as he remembered that awful moment when the thing in the mirror had taken control of his own flesh, his very soul. He remembered feeling with the thing's senses, thinking with its instincts, aching with its lusts, hungering with its passions. For those brief moments he had seen Sarah—his beloved Sarah—as prey. As *meat*.

There was the memory of how he had torn control back from the thing, back to himself, and the utter horror of knowing that this control was a weak and fragile thing; holding it was like holding an oiled snake. Then there was the memory of the bedroom window, of glass and cold morning air and the pavement leaping up at him. After that it was just darkness and darker dreams.

He lay there in the bed, feeling his body, trying to understand why he was still alive. Why hadn't the fall killed him? More important, why did he not feel like he had even taken that fall? His head hurt, sure, but nothing else did. He searched his nerve endings, trying to feel for muscles and shattered bones under the two forearm casts, but his limbs felt strong and whole. His skin itched in some places, and felt tight in others, but nothing hurt besides his head. How had he not been hurt? How had he not been killed, not have been at least crippled?

Terry slowly opened his eyes. The room was bright with fluorescent light, though the daylight from outside seemed weak. Sarah sat in an armchair reading a copy of the *Pine Deep Evening Standard and Times*. It was the early edition. Terry was amazed that he could read the print on the paper from what seemed to be at least twelve feet away. He stared at the blocks of black print and realized that he could read every single word as if the newspaper were only inches away. He could not see Sarah's face behind the paper, but he could smell her perfume. It seemed strong, far too strong, as if she'd bathed in it. Her sweat seemed strong, too. Terry frowned.

Outside in the hallway someone chewed noisily on the plastic cap of a pen. The sound was crashingly loud and it annoyed him, but worse were the grunts of someone defecating in a bathroom farther down the hall. It smelled, too.

Fear wrestled with wonder as he realized that he could hear everything, smell everything. Not just strong odors, but subtle ones, distinct and sorted in his nostrils, identified and labeled by some strange new part of his brain. As much as the strangeness of it terrified him, the *naturalness* of it felt so deliciously right.

He turned his head toward the wall and there was Mandy. Terry almost screamed, but he didn't. For some reason he did not want Sarah to know he was awake. Mandy stood there in her tattered green dress, with her wan face streaked with dark lacerations and bright blood.

"I know you tried," she said sadly. "I know you tried to do the right thing. But you waited too long."

Terry did not say a word.

"Now it's all too late." She looked over to the window beyond which purple-black clouds poised like fists above the skyline of the town. "It's going to be awful, Terry. So awful. I tried to help, but I messed it all up and now they're going to win. I'm sorry, Terry."

Terry did not trust himself to speak. He didn't know who "they" were, and he didn't much care. He was tired of ghosts and their cryptic messages, tired of madness and possession and curses. All he cared about was Sarah, and he knew that he would never be able to touch her again.

Mandy moved closer to him. "I love you, Terry. I never wanted to hurt you, you know that, don't you?" She searched his face for a long time, but he never let her see his feelings, and she slumped with an even greater sadness. "He's taken everything from us, Terry. And even though he's won, he won't let it end, won't let it be over for us." She touched his face and he flinched. "There are so many ghosts in this place, Terry. We're lonely, and we can't rest. Not while he lives, and he'll live forever."

Tears fell like rain from her blue eyes. "I thought God would save us. I thought that's why I was able to come back, because God wanted me to help you stop the curse. That was stupid." Her voice was crushingly bitter. "What does God care?"

Terry felt a tear form in the corner of his own eye.

Mandy seemed paler, less substantial as if she was fading away like morning mist. "I know that you don't want to do this, Terry, but you won't be able to help yourself. You're a monster now, Terry. *His* monster. He owns you, Terry, and he'll make you do terrible things. It's not your fault. No one is strong enough to stand up to him. I wanted to help, but I can't even do that anymore. There's not enough of me left." She bent forward and kissed him. "I love you, Terry," she said again and then faded completely from his sight.

Terry almost cried out as she vanished. The single tear rolled down across his cheek. Sarah rustled the newspaper as she opened to a new page. Outside the room the world ticked another second toward the Red Wave; inside his body Terry could feel the beast clawing to be unloosed.

(3)

"Come on, come *on*," she muttered into the phone, urging Crow to pick up. It rang once and then went right to voice mail. "Shit, still no signal!"

Over the last couple of hours Mike had told them the whole story as he knew it. The whole story, including the parts with Tow-Truck Eddie—which none of them could explain.

"Eddie's a religious nut," Weinstock observed, "but even Crow always said he was a stand-up guy. He's about the last person on earth I'd pick as someone likely to side with Ruger."

"He's not," Mike said. "Not exactly. The Bone Man told me

that for years now Griswold has been talking to him in his thoughts. Maybe it's a kind of telepathy, but Griswold has been pretending to be the voice of God, and he's basically brainwashed the guy into thinking I'm the Antichrist. He calls me the Beast."

"Beast of the Apocalypse, sure," agreed Jonatha. "That makes a kind of twisted sense. Think about it—if this tow-truck guy is really a devout believer, then he is, by that definition, neither corrupt nor evil. That means that if he were to kill Mike then it would have the opposite effect of, say, Vic or Ruger killing him."

Newton looked from her to Mike. "Which is what?"

She shrugged. "Mike would just be dead. None of the qualities he has as a *dhampyr* would be infused into the local landscape."

Weinstock grunted. "So . . . he's a sick, twisted, murderous bastard but a *good guy* sick, twisted and murderous bastard?"

"More or less, yes." She held up an emphatic finger. "That doesn't make him any less dangerous. If he's been this badly brainwashed, then he's on a par with a suicide bomber . . . a total fanatic."

Val made an ugly sound and they all looked at her. "I don't care if he's Saint Jude reborn—if he comes near Mike again I'll kill him."

No one doubted her.

"Try calling Crow again," Newton suggested after a moment. "And maybe those cops, too."

Crow's phone went right to voice mail again, so she tried La-Mastra's cell and got the same thing; but when she called Ferro's phone it rang six times before going to voice mail. A signal, but no response.

"This is bad," Mike said.

"You know that," Weinstock asked, "or are you guessing?"

"Some of both, I guess. The Bone Man told me that Griswold was going to do something today. Something called the Red Wave."

Newton turned away from the window where he'd been watching the storm clouds thicken and darken. Even though it was only three o'clock it was as gloomy as twilight outside. "Which is what exactly?"

"I'm not sure. He wasn't sure, either. All we know is that Vic and Ruger have been working hard to make as many vampires as possible so that the Red Wave will work, and that whatever it is will be bad. Really bad."

Val cut a look at Weinstock. "The Festival?"

"Has to be . . . damn it!"

"And it's supposed to happen tonight?" Jonatha asked.

"Yeah, but I don't know what it'll be or when it'll start." He put his head in his hands. "It's so frustrating to know some things in so much detail and not other things. I feel like I'm trying to put a puzzle together and I don't know if I have all the pieces or even if the pieces are part of the same puzzle."

"I have to go and warn Crow. If he's walking into a trap . . ." The hunting hawk look was back on her face even though her eyes were bright with terror. She looked at Newton, expecting him to say something, perhaps offer to guide her to Dark Hollow, but he blanched and even backed up a step.

"I . . . can't . . ." he said.

"Val," Weinstock said, "no, we could never get out there and find him. Not in time. We have to do something to stop the Festival. If Ruger and his goons show up tonight, it could be a slaughter. Everyone's going to be in costume . . . Ruger could walk right up to someone and no one would know who he was until it was too late."

Chapter 37

"**D**ear God!" gasped Crow as he climbed to his feet. Tears streaked his cheeks, but not just from the cordite. "Dear sweet Jesus God."

Beside him, LaMastra was furiously reloading his shotgun, flicking frequent nervous glances around at the shadows as he worked. The vampires were sprawled like dolls knocked off a shelf by an earthquake, their white faces strangely empty of malevolence. Kneeling, Crow peered in wonder at the face of Jimmy Castle.

"He doesn't have any fangs," he said softly. LaMastra looked up from his shotgun. "They must have gone away after he died. Anyone finds these bodies it'll just look like we murdered them all."

"I don't care," LaMastra said, and Crow turned and gave him a sharper look. The big man's eyes were twitching and jumping, and he had a nervous tic that made it look like he kept trying to smile.

Christ, thought Crow, *don't wig out on me now*. But then LaMastra's eyes hardened. "Hey . . . reload, damn it! Get your head out of your ass."

"Right, sorry . . ." He dug in his pockets for shells.

Slotting the last shell into his shotgun, LaMastra said, "We have to get out of this place." He picked up the fallen Maglite. His own flash had shattered when they fell through the floor, but Crow's sturdy little flash was still working. LaMastra held it above him as they began to explore the cellar.

Crow looked around at the walls, trying not to look at the bodies. "These old farmhouses usually have a yard entrance to the cellar. I saw one outside, but it was chained shut just like the front door."

"Good call," said LaMastra. "So let's find it, blow the lock, and get the hell out of here."

"Works for me."

The cellar was a thirty-by-eighty-foot oblong with a seven-foot-high unfinished ceiling and a badly poured concrete floor. Five doors were set into the walls, ostensibly leading to storerooms. A set of rickety wooden stairs bisected the basement, but they ignored them—upstairs held nothing but traps and frustration.

"The cellar door has to be behind one of these," Crow said.

"Shit."

The awareness of what could be behind any one of those doors was daunting and they were both sweating badly despite the deep cold of the room. The fact that there was no sound other than what they made and no movement other than their own was no comfort. The basement had a sneaky, crouching, waiting feel to it.

None of the cellar doors had locks, though they were all closed. Three of the doors were hinged to open out; the others opened in. Before they approached them they shone the light on the ceiling and all around the frames, looking for trip wires, but they could see nothing.

"Vince . . . I'll grab the handle and pull, you get ready to shoot anything that so much as twitches, okay?"

LaMastra wiped sweat from his face on a hunched shoulder and nodded. He set himself and aimed the shotgun at the center of the first door. Licking his lips, Crow reached out for the handle, took a breath, and then turned the knob and pulled the handle as he stepped back to yank the door open.

LaMastra almost fired just from sheer nerves, but Crow shined the light inside and they were looking at a filthy but empty toilet stall.

Neither sighed in relief; there were still four to go. They moved eight feet to their right and stopped before one of the two doors that opened inward.

"I'll kick it," LaMastra said and gave it such a massive stamp that the door crashed inward and off its hinges and fell flat, sending up clouds of dust. They sprang into the room and instantly LaMastra saw a figure lunging at him with the same speed and aggression. He fired without thinking and there was a boom and the sharp crash of shattering glass.

"Nice shooting, Tex," Crow said. "You just killed a mirror."

"Shit."

The room was cluttered with old chairs, wardrobes, tables, and boxes of bric-a-brac. "Nothing," Crow concluded. "Just Griswold's old junk."

They exited and crossed the cellar to the far end where the last three small rooms were.

"Your turn," LaMastra said, shifting to a flanking position, gun ready. Crow nodded and braced himself for the kick, but just as he raised his leg the door was whipped open and children poured out of the shadows, laughing insanely and reaching for them with black-taloned hands.

(2)

Vic saw the three ATVs and immediately jammed on his brakes, bringing the pickup to a screeching stop. Dust plumed up from his tires and panic leapt up in his chest.

The Man's in danger! The thought was like a hot wire in his brain.

He was out of the truck and running, low and fast, making maximum use of the tall grass, toward the house, his Luger in his hand, eyes cutting back and forth across the field for signs of movement. He couldn't see anyone, but just one glance at the house told him there was trouble. One of the plywood sheets was down, exposing the red brick he'd laid.

As he drew closer he could see that the front door was open.

"Shit!" he hissed, then changed his angle of approach so that he came at the house obliquely. It had to be Crow—they used ATVs at that stupid Hayride—but who was with him?

Crow being here could be very bad or very damn good, especially if he was actually inside. Vic had rigged the place pretty well last time he was here. He crabbed sideways from where he was squatting and tried to get a clearer look at the front of the house. The pile of debris from the fallen porch roof hid most of his view of the door.

He heard a sound and froze, listened. Heard it again. A kind of moan. Definitely human. By now he knew the sounds the Dead Heads made and the Fangers didn't moan. Vic rose to three-quarters of his height, just enough to see over the pile of debris. What he saw made him smile.

There was a man lying on the porch at the top of the steps. Even from where Vic stood he could see that the man was covered in blood. Vic felt a flush of pride at knowing that at least one of his little booby traps had worked. Still cautious, he moved closer, though he knew that if a man that badly injured had been left to lie there and bleed, then his companions were in no position to help.

Vic didn't understand what he was seeing at first, because the wounded man had a landscaper's insecticide sprayer on his back, but then he got a whiff of gasoline and he understood. His smile faded slightly. The presence of the gas confirmed the fact that these intruders understood something of the nature of the problem. Not good, he thought, but at least the problem appeared to be contained for the moment.

He stood over the bloody man and admired the effects of his little booby trap. The nails of the trapdoor had caught him good; one had even punched right through his skull. Vic nodded in satisfaction at that. It had taken a lot of hard work to rig that trap; nice to know it had worked as planned.

He climbed onto the porch and pushed on the front door, but the panel was as solid as a rock. Good. Crow and whoever else came with him were probably trapped inside.

He turned looked down again at the corpse. The man had obviously crawled out of the vestibule, trailing blood and piss and gasoline all the way, leaving a slimy trail like a slug. Blood was still mostly wet. Vic figured the guy hadn't been dead long.

Even with all the blood Vic recognized the dead man. Frank Ferro, the black cop from Philly who'd been hunting Ruger. Vic chuckled. Well, this wasn't the first spook he'd killed over the years. He saw a bulge in the man's rear pants pocket and was reaching for the wallet when the dead man moaned.

Startled, Vic jerked his hand back and brought up the pistol. The man reached out one feeble hand and fumbled at the edge of the top step, closed his fingers around it, and then tried to pull himself forward. Vic was impressed. Hole in the back of his head and the son of a bitch was still trying. He took a wooden kitchen match from his shirt pocket and put it between his teeth.

"Howdy, partner," Vic said. "Having a little trouble there?"

The bleeding man slowly turned his head. His eyes were half-closed and crusted with blood, but Vic could see one brown eye come slowly into focus and stare at him. The man struggled to speak, and managed it only marginally. "H . . . help . . ."

Vic laughed. "Yeah, I'll get right on that." He lowered his pistol. "Christ, you are one sorry-looking nigger. That hole in your head's gotta hurt."

"Help . . . me . . ."

"Nope, can't do that. Tell you what, why don't you tell me what the hell you're doing here. Or should I guess?" He bent close and sniffed. "Doing a little vampire hunting, are we?"

Ferro's eye gave a slow blink. "You . . . you're part . . . of it."

"Yeah, you could say that, but don't worry, I don't bite. Even if I did I wouldn't bite dark meat. Eww." He sat down on a broken porch beam. "No, I'm what those boys call the Foreman. If you know about the Fang Gang, then you probably know about the *Man*, about Ubel Griswold. Yeah, I can see it on your face that you know. Well, I'm his right hand, you see. He's always said so."

"Why?" Ferro croaked. His voice was almost nonexistent.

For a moment Vic's eyes shone with a different kind of light. "For reasons you would never understand, not if you lived a million freaking years." He glanced at the house. "Your friends are probably dead, you know. No one's coming to help you. I planned for everything."

"Kiss . . . my ass . . ." Ferro breathed.

"Suit yourself." He stood up and walked down off the porch and went over to examine the ATVs. "Wow, you guys brought a lot of nice toys. Too bad you're all shitheads."

As soon as Vic's back was turned Ferro used all of his strength to shift position, tucking one hand under his body and straining with the other to reach his fallen pistol that lay among the rubble.

Vic finished examining the bikes and climbed back up onto the porch, saw Ferro's reach, and plucked the pistol out of reach. "Nice try, Bojangles," he said with a grin and kicked Ferro in the ribs.

Ferro's body constricted into a ball; his cry of pain instantly turned into a string of wet coughs that misted the floorboards with red.

Vic chewed on his match, smiling with real pleasure as he watched Ferro die moment by moment; but that smile was immediately wiped off his face by the distinctive sound of a shotgun blast.

He leapt to his feet, pistol in a two-hand grip, head cocked to listen. The sound had come from inside. He was sure of it, but from *where* inside? After almost a full minute he heard another shotgun blast, and another. There was a barrage of blasts, and now he knew that they had to be coming from beneath the house. In the cellar. It worried him that there were so many shots. *They* should have been able to rip the intruders to shreds after the first shot, but the blasts went on. And there were pistol shots, too. Then silence. He waited it out and there were no more sounds from beneath the house.

It worried him that it had taken *them* so long to bring down two men, but he had no doubt that it was now a feeding frenzy in there. He relaxed slowly, lowering the pistol.

"Serves 'em right, the dumb shits." He turned back to Ferro, who was trying to use the side of a clenched fist to raise himself off the floor. "You guys should have stayed out of the Man's business, you know that? You think I put in thirty frigging years of hard work to have that jackass Crow and a dumb-shit nigger like you just muck things up? You can't be that stupid, even for a jig." He gave Ferro another vicious kick.

Ferro felt his ribs explode. Breathing became suddenly impossible as the fragments of shattered ribs tore gashes in his lungs. Ferro could feel himself beginning to drown as his lungs filled with blood.

But he felt his mouth twisting upward into a savage smile as he looked down at the object he held, the small bright blue thing he'd managed to claw out of his pants pocket while Vic was rooting through the duffel bags on the ATVs.

Vic kicked him once more, and the lights of the world began going out in Frank Ferro's mind. He could not feel the blows anymore. He was drowning in the blood that clogged his throat. He wanted to say something: a prayer, a curse, anything. He wanted to mock the man who was killing him, to tell him that he was not going to kill anyone ever again; but there was just not enough life left in him to do it. All he had left was the strength to roll back the striker-wheel with the pad of his thumb. The motion pressed the lighter's tiny valve and the spark ignited into a small blue flame.

Poised in midkick Vic looked down in overwhelming horror as Frank Ferro plunged the lighter down into the pool of garlic oil, blood, urine, and high-octane gasoline.

(3)

Crow fired the shotgun even as he stumbled backward, shouting a warning to LaMastra, but the sergeant was already in trouble as two slender forms leapt at him and bore him down. There were a dozen of the children. The oldest were twins who looked to be around twelve or thirteen, and the youngest, Crow saw to his absolute horror, was a baby who crawled as quickly as a scuttling beetle, its angelic face split to reveal only two needle-sharp fangs protruding from otherwise smooth gums. The sight of the children almost froze Crow and LaMastra into fatal immobility, but their fingers were already on their triggers and as the creatures swarmed at them they fired out of reflex. After that it was easier to shoot, their hands working in mechanical independence from their stunned minds.

Crow's first shot caught a little girl in the chest and she just flew apart into red rags. The sight of her just exploding like that nearly drove him mad. It was too horrible, too impossible a thing to be allowed. As the shotgun pellets tore her apart it was as if the blast ripped open the fabric of all reality and everything from here on would be nightmares and insanity.

Then another creature lunged at him—a Chinese boy of about ten, who dodged the falling body parts and leapt at Crow, hissing like a rat. Crow barely had time to work the pump and so fired the blast an inch away from the child's throat. The decapitated head spun away into shadows, but the body kept falling forward to strike Crow's chest; as it collapsed down in death the monster's talons slashed down the front of Crow's trousers, opening two deep gashes.

The smell of fresh blood drove the others insane and two of the smaller creatures dove in, straining to be first at the open wounds. Crow hammered down on the back of a seven-year-old little girl with the stock of the shotgun and kicked the other, a ten-year-old boy, forcefully in the face. Both fell away, driven back only by Crow's greater weight, but neither was injured. The girl had been driven to her elbows and knees by Crow's shotgun stock, and from that position she leapt like a cat at his leg. He screamed as her spiked nails sunk into the back of his thigh and then there was a searing burst of white-hot agony as she drove her tiny fangs into the bleeding wound. Crow hammered at her twice more with the stock as he lumbered back to dodge another attack by a reedy black boy in a Cub Scout uniform.

"GET OFF!" Crow screamed as he jammed the barrel of the shotgun down against the top of the little girl's head and pulled the trigger. Her head exploded, and the force of the blast drove a handful of the pellets down through her body, where they erupted from just below her shoulder blades. She flopped away and Crow turned to see the Cub Scout leap at him. The boy, though small and slightly built, caught him unawares and collided with Crow's head and shoulders. They went down in a churning heap.

Closer to the door of the utility room, LaMastra was still struggling with the twin vampires. They were good-looking kids with luminous green eyes and angelic faces, and LaMastra could not make himself accept that these lovely kids were monsters. Then they snarled at him, showing their fangs and their flicking tongues, and as they did this their eyes flared from green to an unholy red. They fanned out on either side of LaMastra; he fired and missed, fired and missed, and each time the twins mocked him with high-pitched laughter. They were incredibly fast, but then LaMastra faked toward one of them and pivoted to fire point-blank at the other. The vampire twisted out of the way so that only a third of the pellets tore through his hip and upper thigh, but it was enough to make the boy pirouette like a dancer in some macabre ballet.

The other twin watched, startled for a moment, and then dodged in at LaMastra and with one extended hand slashed him from shoulder bone to hip, tearing open the Kevlar vest and most of the shirt beneath. The injured twin screamed like a banshee as the garlic worked like poison to burn its way through his veins. His heart exploded in his chest, ripping out through his breastbone in a spray of blood and bone.

The sight of this jolted the other twin, who stopped and

stared at his brother and at the bloody ruin of his chest. LaMastra took that moment to step forward and ram him in the stomach with the wide barrel of the Roadblocker and then hoist him up into the air, using the shotgun like a tent-peg to pin the vampire hard against the cellar ceiling. The boy writhed and spat and then LaMastra pulled the trigger. The full blast of the ten-gauge weapon blew a fist-sized hole through the thin body and punched a hole in the ceiling so that blood and bits of vertebrae geysered into the room upstairs.

LaMastra reeled back from the falling corpse and the rain of blood.

"God!" he cried as the thought that he had just killed two children stabbed him through the heart.

A second later something hit him between the shoulder blades and he fell; the shotgun flew from his hands and went spinning off into the shadows. He landed hard on his knees, the concrete shooting pain up through his kneecaps; but even as he landed he reached over and back to grab a handful of hair in his fist, then with a growl of mad fury dashed a red-haired boy of eight or nine onto the floor in front of him. The impact flattened the back of the child's skull, but did not stop him from immediately whipping around onto all fours and baring his teeth. The boy lunged again, and LaMastra used the side of his left fist to parry the biting mouth away from his inner thigh as he drew his Sig Sauer with his right. He racked the slide and as the child flew at him again he fired twice. Two black holes appeared in the child's chest as the body flew backward, arms and legs swinging brokenly.

LaMastra dodged another small scuttling form and saw that it was a toddler, no more than two or three. Its mouth was smeared with day-old blood and it had red rat-eyes. The tiny hands clawed the air as it waddled toward him. Vince shot it once in the head and spun away, vomiting onto the wall. But as he turned he had a brief, fleeting image of something black floating toward his head and then there was an explosion of pain and stinging lights and he could feel his body falling. Small, sharp fingers clutched at him as he fell hard. Instantly he felt tiny teeth bite deep into the soft flesh at the crook of his arm, and another bite on his inner thigh. He was helpless, dazed by the fall, and they were feeding on him. He could hear the slurping sounds as tiny mouths drank his precious blood.

Crow rolled over and over with the Cub Scout on his back, the creature's arms and legs wrapped around him like steel bands. Crow's samurai sword impeded the roll and with each ungainly revolution it pressed painfully into his floating ribs; his shotgun was gone. The child couldn't have been more than nine years old and yet was immensely strong. The vampire tore at Crow's shirt collar, trying to get at his neck—then suddenly stopped, gagging as he encountered the smears of garlic oil on Crow's skin. Undeterred, the little creature started ripping at the softer flesh of Crow's armpit. Crow managed to fight his way back onto his knees and then threw his weight backward into the boiler. The metal cylinder made a huge hollow booming sound and Crow felt the pressure release just for a second; he took that second. He slid his hand up between his body and the child's forearm, wrapped fingers around the thin wrist, and then bent forward sharply and flipped the child off with great force, using the grip on the child's arm to snap him all the way forward like cracking a whip, and at the end of the movement he yanked back with a sudden jerk. He could feel and hear the bones and tendons of the child's arm tear and break, and the extended feet of the Cub Scout caught another vampire, a fat boy of twelve, right in the face. The fat vampire fell back and Crow released the Cub Scout's forearm.

The child's arm was unnaturally distended, but his face showed no trace of pain, only an intensified hatred. He scrambled back to his feet and ran at Crow, but Crow dodged to one side, diving toward his fallen shotgun. He did a complete roll and came lightly back onto the balls of his feet, shotgun in hand, jacking a round into the breech as he turned. His first blast caught the Cub Scout in the stomach, tearing him into two parts.

Crow heard a cry behind him and saw LaMastra on the

ground with two small creatures kneeling on him—*feeding on him!* With an inarticulate cry of disgust, Crow waded in, clubbing the small bodies aside with the shotgun. One, a pretty little girl with blond braids, hissed at him with a mouth filled with LaMastra's steaming blood. Crow shot her in the face.

Wheeling, Crow saw that the other vampire, a small olive-skinned boy with a yarmulke bobby-pinned to his hair, was already creeping back toward the dazed sergeant. Crow kicked the vampire in the ribs to knock him back against the wall and shot him in the chest.

Crow wanted to check LaMastra, to see how bad he was, but there was still the fat kid. Crow turned quickly and saw that the child was advancing on him, holding a shovel in two hands. Crow had no way of knowing that it was the same shovel that had been used to knock LaMastra to near-unconsciousness. The boy lunged forward, swinging the long-bladed weapon clumsily but with great force. Crow dodged back, sucking in his gut and evading the shovel's blade by less than an inch.

As he dodged, Crow caught sight of the kid's face in the glow of the flare and realized that he knew the kid, knew him well. It was Kurt Bernhardt, the son of Chief Gus Bernhardt. Crow had seen the kid just two days ago in the Crow's Nest when the boy had come in to buy a Hunchback of Notre Dame costume for Halloween. He opened his mouth to say something, to try to make the kid understand, but the kid swung the shovel again and knocked the shotgun out of his hands.

Crow backpedaled as he clawed his clawed his Beretta out of his shoulder rig. He had to lunge backward to dodge the next swing of the shovel—a slicing blow that would have torn his throat out—and he saw the murderous delight on Kurt Bernhardt's face as he advanced, swinging the shovel like the Grim Reaper's scythe.

"I'm sorry," Crow said and put three rounds into the kid's head.

Before the kid was even down Crow whirled around, then the world froze in horror as he saw a sight that would haunt his nightmares for the rest of his life. The big sergeant lay sprawled in the same position as before, with his arms and legs thrown wide and his limbs streaked with blood. A creature knelt on his chest and was tearing at the stitches on the detective's jaw. Blood welled and the little thing began sucking at it with desperate greed, then it must have heard Crow's moan of horror and it raised its head to stare at him with baleful, inhuman eyes. It was the infant who had come crawling out of the utility room with its bloodstained diaper drooping from its desiccated little body, and its two needlelike fangs sprouting from the otherwise toothless mouth. Blood was smeared on its lips and dripped thickly from the fangs as it stared at Crow. The infant could not have been more than a few months old. Just a baby, and they had done this to him. They had corrupted the innocent flesh of an infant and made it into a monster more horrible than anything Crow had ever imagined. The baby lowered its head again to the wound and began drinking.

A sound—a mingled cry of horror, disgust, and appalling sadness—burned its way out of Crow's chest as he heaved himself back to his feet. He kicked the creature away from LaMastra's chest and it fell roughly onto the ground, where it landed on its back, arms and legs wriggling. Crow staggered after it, holstering his pistol and then drawing his sword. As the little creature struggled to turn over, Crow braced his legs and raised his sword

"God forgive me," he said and sank to his knees. The sword fell, and his heart fell with it. He could hear it fall, feel it drop from the anchors in his chest. It toppled down into a lower, darker place, and there it would remain.

Crow heard LaMastra moan and he turned away to see that the detective had managed to get into a sitting position. He was covered in blood and breathing heavily. LaMastra looked around the cellar . . . at the bodies, adult and children, littered like trash. The violence that had been forced out of both men was humiliating and dehumanizing. LaMastra put his head in his palms and began to cry.

Crow stood in the center of the cellar, feeling the grief twist in him, but they were still trapped in the land of the dead, and neither of them knew what other dreadful things they would have to do in order to escape.

(4)

A moment later the cellar was rocked by a *BOOM!* as something outside exploded.

It jolted them both back into the moment, and Crow grabbed LaMastra and hauled him to his feet.

"What the hell was that?" LaMastra demanded.

Their eyes met.

"Frank!" LaMastra said, a smile leaping onto his face. "He's still alive and he's trying to get us out of here."

"Goddamn!" Crow said. "But let's not sit here and wait. There has to be a way out of here."

Shaky and sick to their stomachs, they nonetheless picked up their guns—careful not to look too closely at the bodies—and reloaded. They went over to the fourth door, braced it, opened it . . . and saw the short flight of stone steps leading up to the yard. Crow used his flash to find the lock and LaMastra blasted it apart. The cellar doors flew open and a waft of fresh air buffeted them.

They stumbled up out of the darkness and collapsed with weary gratitude on the withered brown grass behind the house. The wind was cool and damp and the stormy clouds above looked ready to open. They heard a sound and looked up to see hands of flame reach up from the roof of the house, and a great column of smoke twisted its way into the sky.

"Jesus Christ!" LaMastra yelled. "Frank's torched the place. Is he out of his *mind*?"

Crow scrambled to his feet, pulling LaMastra, and together they raced along the side of the burning house and then slid to a halt a dozen feet from the porch, stopped by a wall of intense heat. The entire front of the house was ablaze; sheets of flame raced up the wooden columns, eating the timbers and blackening the bricks. The big pile of rubble that had been the porch roof was a bonfire, and lying next to that mass was a single blackened form, wrapped in a cocoon of orange flame.

They stared in horror. The figure was completely burned, the skin charred to a withered skeleton. On its back was the ruptured and melted remains of a garden tank sprayer.

"Oh, no," said Crow. "No . . . please no . . . don't do this. . . ."

"FRANK!" Vince LaMastra screamed. "Frank. . . ." He sank slowly down to his knees and beat his big fists on the hard earth, calling his friend's name over and over again.

Crow stood by helpless and appalled.

There was a roar of a truck engine and Crow spun around to see a battered Ford pickup racing away from the burning house. Crow bolted and ran, cutting across the field in a direct line toward the small gap in the trees toward which the truck was heading. If he had had another three or four seconds he might have made it in time, but the pickup was gathering speed as the driver pushed it beyond all sense, driving with reckless abandon over the lumpy earth. Crow screamed at the driver to stop, but the truck rolled on, gaining the entrance to a road Crow had never known existed. The truck spun and jolted onto the road and in seconds it was gone, lost in a cloud of dust.

Crow fired three shots after the truck, hitting it once and obliterating the left taillight, but then the truck was out of range behind trees. LaMastra came pounding up behind him, shotgun at port arms, eyes fierce with the need to kill, to avenge his friend, but Crow shook his head.

"He's gone."

"Shit! Who was it?"

Crow had only gotten one good look at the driver's face, but it was taking him a few seconds to work out who it was. The man had been horribly burned and covered in soot, most of his head hair was gone, melted by the heat of the fire, and one eye was nearly closed, but Crow was almost positive that he knew the man.

"That was Vic Wingate," he said.

LaMastra ground his teeth. "He killed Frank!"

"I think so . . . and I'll bet he's the one who rigged the house, too. I think we know who Griswold's human helper is. Goddamn it. I should have seen this."

LaMastra wheeled on Crow, chest heaving as if he'd just run a mile. "We have to find him. We have to find him and then I want him. For what he did to Frank, for what he put us through in there . . . I *want* him. I want to find that bastard and cut his heart out."

"I'll hold him down for you."

They turned and sprinted back to the ATVs.

Chapter 38

In the minutes before the first explosions the crowds on Corn Hill and Main Street had reached maximum density. Thousands upon thousands of tourists thronged the streets, milling in numbers that made last night's Mischief Night celebration seem like a rehearsal. There was laughter and music, shouts and screams as kids in costumes chased each other through the swarm. No one cared that the sky was heavy with storm clouds—if it rained, it rained—and the early darkness really jazzed the Halloween mood.

The Halloween Parade was just starting, the balloons and bands waiting their turns on the staging area of the High School track. The big floats with their orange-and-black paper flowers and faux funereal drapings pulled onto Corn Hill one at a time while the first band played the theme from *Buffy the Vampire Slayer*. Baton twirlers dressed like scarecrows spun their flaming batons high into the air and pirouetted before catching them behind their backs. Acrobats costumed like Renaissance jesters cartwheeled and flipped along the sides of the Grand Marshal's limousine. Actors from classic TV horror shows waved to the crowd.

Above the town the flocks of shapeless night birds circled in slow patterns, watching everything, waiting for blood to perfume the air, drawn by the dead smells that mingled strangely with the vital scent of the people below.

Within the crowd itself certain figures moved slowly, often at odds with the flow, occasionally with it, sometimes just watching from the black mouths of alleys or through the opened windows of parked cars. Most wore costumes; all wore masks that hid their pale faces and fiery red eyes. Beneath their masks they licked their red lips and waited for the word, watching as the herd of prey thundered by unaware.

Ruger and Lois came out of the back of a store on Main Street and walked hand in hand toward Corn Hill. He wore nothing more outré than an expensive suit—black, single breasted, with a white shirt and red tie. Nothing ostentatious, just elegant—something Ruger never had been before. Lois was poured into a tight red silk dress that clung to her in ways that drove Ruger nuts. She'd put in some time on her hair and makeup and she was a stunner. Lois had added one little touch that Ruger loved—a small diamond tiara that was nestled into her dark curls. She looked every bit the red queen that she was.

Since he'd turned her, since he'd taught her to drink and to hunt, Lois had come alive in ways no one could have predicted. She was every bit Ruger's match for vicious intensity, and he loved her for it. Really loved her—something Ruger had never let himself feel. His red queen.

They strolled along without hurry, waiting for the word, and behind them came a phalanx of others. A quarter of Ruger's army was seeded throughout the crowd; more walked with him. The rest were positioned all around town—at the Hayride, on the campus, in the movie theaters, strolling the side streets that saw the heaviest traffic of trick-or-treaters. Those that walked behind Ruger and his queen were the elite, the sharpest of them, the most indulgently vicious. The fun-loving ones handpicked by Ruger. When spectators saw them all walking toward the parade, they laughed and fell into step, thinking it was part of some kind of entertainment.

That made Lois laugh, and anything that made Lois laugh made Ruger happy. He started waving to other partygoers to come and join them.

"The more the merrier," he said and gave Lois a kiss. She pulled him close, tilted up both their masks, and tore his lips open with

her fangs. The smell of blood was so intoxicating that he wanted
to take her right there and then. He bit her back as they walked,
and no one noticed, no one saw. Their wounds opened and
bled, and closed as they licked and sucked at each other as they
walked.

Somewhere away to the southeast there was an explosion, but
it was almost lost beneath the weight of the music and shouting.
A few people looked up at the sky, searching for lightning or
fireworks.

"Here it comes, baby," he said to Lois, who hissed with joy.

When the second explosion hit, nobody ignored it. The
whole brick front of the Pine Deep Fire Company seemed to
leap up into the air just as the Grand Marshal's limo was passing
it, and then everything inside the station exploded outward in a
massive fireball that seemed to lunge at the crowd. Costumes instantly ignited, windows on the other side of the street blew
apart, and glass daggers slashed through the crowd. The paper
flowers on the floats caught fire. All of this within the space of a
second.

Ruger raised his left hand, fingers splayed, and every one of
his people stopped amid the terror and panic to watch him.
Ruger looked at his watch and then snapped his fingers. As if
commanded by that snap the three bridges that connected Pine
Deep to the surrounding towns exploded. And Ruger's army *attacked*.

(2)

When the Bone Man left Frank Ferro at the farm, he flowed
like wind back to the hospital, resuming his perch on the roof,
flanked on either side by a line of crows. From there he saw the
first of the explosions, long before the fall of night, and he
understood now the subtlety of Griswold's plan. There was no
way to stop the Red Wave.

"No way in hell," he told the crows.

(3)

A few minutes before . . .

"Hey . . . kid?" Newton said, touching Mike lightly on the arm. "You said that you can sense evil? I mean, are we talking some kind of supernatural spider-sense here?"

Val shot him a look.

"No, I'm not being flip. If something's coming, if Griswold and all these vampires are about to attack the town, can Mike give us some kind of early warning alert? I mean . . . do we have time to try and sound an alert, or evacuate the town?"

"I don't know how it works," Mike said. "I don't know how to turn it on and off. I mean . . . I feel it all the time, it feels like ants crawling all over me and I know, in some weird way that I can't explain, that that means that there's evil around."

"So you *do* have a spider-sense."

"Newt," Val warned.

"I don't know how to . . ." Mike waved his hands around, "to filter it. It seems to be coming from everywhere. It started after I, y'know, came *back*. I wanted to ask the Bone Man what to do, but he was gone."

"Mike," Weinstock said, "you told us that you think you died out there, that you were *gone* for at least half a day. You do know that this is impossible, right? You'd be brain damaged in minutes. You'd have cell breakdown and—"

Mike shrugged. "I was dead. I was out of my body. When I came back to my body I was ice cold and I couldn't move. I actually think I was in whatchacallit? Rigor mortis."

"And, what? You just got better?"

"Yeah, I think that's what happened." When no one said anything, Mike added, "Okay, I know that sounds ridiculous because this is such a normal world where nothing weird ever happens. It's not like we have ghosts and vampires and were-wolves here in sunny Pine Deep."

"Kid's got a point," Newton said to Weinstock.

"Well, if that's the case, then what does that make you? A zombie? I mean . . . human beings don't just shrug off rigor mortis. I thought you were supposed to have a degenerative bone disorder as a *dhampyr.*"

"You sound like you're pissed off that I'm alive, Doc." Mike almost looked amused.

"Oh hell, it's not that. Believe me, kiddo, I'm happy as hell to see you walking and talking, but I just want to understand it."

"Get in line," Mike said. He gave his face a vigorous rub with both hands. "God!" he shouted, "how do you think I feel about this? Yesterday I found out my mother was a vampire! A *vampire!* Then I find out my father is not only a vampire but also a were-wolf and the worst mass murderer in history. He's personally killed thousands of people. Not by sending an army like Hitler— he turned into a monster and killed them himself. *Then* I find out that I'm not even exactly human and that if I make it through the next couple of days then I'm going to die in just a few years. But wait—it gets worse. Yesterday I freaking well *died.* I lay down and stopped breathing. Do you think I'd make some-thing like that up? Do you think it makes me feel special? I'm a freak. Look at my eyes, for God's sake! Do you think that's nor-mal? You're adults, you're all smart . . . why don't you try and understand that?" He kicked the guest chair halfway across the room, then stomped over to glare out the window, his face a match for the furious storm clouds.

As if in agreement thunder rumbled overhead so loud and sudden that it shook the hospital, rattling the windows.

"It doesn't matter anyway," he said in a softer voice. "It's al-ready too late."

Val took a step toward him. "What do you mean?"

Mike turned from the window and the fiery rings around his eyes were as bright as a welder's arc. "Mr. Newton . . . you asked me if I could sense what was going on so we could prepare. That kind of just got flushed down the toilet."

Another shockingly loud boom rattled the windows.

"That wasn't thunder," he said, and as if to emphasize his

words they could all see the plume of fire and smoke that rose from just north of town.

The third explosion knocked out the lights.

(4)

Vic's plan for the opening event of the Red Wave was meticulous. Ten seconds after the power plant blew, the TV and radio stations went next, then the phone company. Some of Ruger's sharper soldiers were detailed to toss Molotov cocktails into the backs of the news trucks, and among the first victims to be torn down were the reporters doing stand-ups along the parade route. Some fragments of footage got out, but everyone was in costume and nothing would make sense, no matter how many times the techs back at the regional offices ran the playback. The cell towers were next on the list.

By the time all that was happening, at least one tourist in fifteen was feeling the first effects of the massive doses of the psychedelic drugs in the candy. Confusion was a tool, and Vic was a master craftsman.

(5)

Magician Rod Leigh-Evans was having a bad night. The motor on his big electric table saw conked out during dress rehearsal and the whole trick had to be scrapped, which sucked because it was the centerpiece of his act. That meant that he had twelve minutes to fill with no major routines. He rushed home to get some of his older, less exciting tricks out of his garage. Stuff the crowd had probably seen a hundred times, but it was all he had left.

It didn't help that his assistant, the Incredible Wanda, had called him from an ER in Abington where she was having her foot stitched up following what she called "a bathroom misadventure." Wanda declined to explain what that meant.

Stuck for an assistant, Leigh-Evans badgered one of the Festival staff to take Wanda's place. The only staff member not assigned to something that couldn't be switched was Chris Maddish, a young man hired to translate for a group of Japanese tourists whose plane was delayed in Chicago. When Leigh-Evans explained that Chris would have to go on as the Incredible Wanda there was one hell of an argument. Two hundred dollars later Maddish was squeezed into Wanda's dress and wig. All things considered, Leigh-Evans thought, the kid looked better as a sexy woman than Wanda ever did; but the bribe money meant that the magician was now doing this gig for free.

When the show started, it was a rolling disaster. Some of the scarf tricks were so old the material was disintegrating during the performance, so he tried to sidestep into shtick as if being the world's worst magician was all part of the show. The audience looked uncertain because he had started well and you can't change a theme after you've set the expectations of the audience.

The rabbit he pulled out of the hat peed on his cummerbund—which at least got a laugh out of the audience, though he was pretty sure they weren't laughing *with* him. Then he segued into a trick that at least promised a nice visual—one of the appearing dove tricks. Doves were pretty and they didn't pee on you.

The trick here was to have the Incredible Wanda hold a wooden platform that was an inch thick and thirteen inches square, blow up a balloon, place it in the center of the platform, do some hand waving, and then pop the balloon to reveal the dove. All very clever, all pretty easy, but with popping the colorful balloon and the serenity of the cooing dove, it had very nice sounds and visuals.

The crowd, already restive, barely paid attention while Leigh-Evans ranted through his patter and did the hand gestures, but halfway during the trick Chris dropped the platform. The sound of it hitting the stage silenced the crowd, but also drew their complete attention. None of them had ever seen a magic act as overwhelmingly bad as this. The magician was horrified because of what was *inside* the platform.

He started again, his voice breaking on a couple of the lines in the patter and his hand gestures looking a bit less assured. When he popped the balloon and cried, "Voilà!" the crowd stared at the dove.

Instead of cooing and flapping its wings, the dove flopped dead onto the stage, rolled once, and then fell off the platform into the popcorn cup of a seven-year-old girl. Who screamed.

"Well," the magician thought as the crowd started screaming, "at least it can't get any worse."

All of this took place on a small stage in front of the town's electrical power substation, which then blew up.

(6)

Deep beneath the mud and muck of the swamp, Ubel Griswold felt the explosions vibrate through the bones of the earth. He opened his mouth and howled with delight as the Red Wave began.

Chapter 39

Crow and LaMastra made it back to the base of the pitch in less than an hour. If it had been a straight run it would have been fifteen minutes, but the terrain was cluttered with roots and rocks. Even so, they hit the pitch at full tilt and the two ATVs swept up the steep hill and leapt over the edge like dune buggies, landing hard and slewing around to kick dust pillars in the parking lot. They didn't even bother to switch off the bikes, and instead leapt off and ran for Crow's car, piled in, and went screaming out of the Passion Pit in a spray of gravel, jouncing and bouncing along the rutted length of Dark Hollow Road.

At the crossroads Crow spun the wheel to put them on A-32. There were plenty of cars on the road—some heading toward town, most racing away from it at dangerous speeds. Then a huge rolling *BOOM!* buffeted them from behind and LaMastra twisted around in his seat to see a massive fireball plume up behind the farthest hills.

"What the Christ was that?" Crow demanded, steering in and out of traffic with no regard for blaring horns. Many of the cars on the outbound side of the road were slowing or pulling off onto the verge. There were several rear-end collisions as drivers gaped at the fireball.

"Something big just blew the hell up. What's down that way?"

"Just the bridge."

LaMastra turned back around. "Maybe not."

Before Crow could reply his cell phone rang and he steered one-handed while he dug it out of his pocket.

"Crow! My God . . . tell me you're okay!"

"Val, honey, I'm okay. Are you okay? What the hell's happening? Everyone seems to be trying to get out of town?"

"I don't know. We keep hearing explosions. I lost count of how many."

"Where are you?"

"I'm at the hospital, in Saul's room. We're all here. I—"

"Val, listen to me," he interrupted. "Listen really carefully. Frank's dead."

"Oh my God! How?"

"Vic Wingate killed him. Vic's part of this, and—"

"I know about Vic. Mike told me."

"Mike?"

"Crow . . . he's here with us. He's changed, Crow, he's—"

There was another explosion, this time well ahead of them, and the cell signal just died.

"Val! VAL!" He yelled, but he was talking to dead air. He hit RECALL, but nothing. He looked at his phone. No bars. "My phone just died. Try yours," he said to LaMastra, who already had his out.

"Nothing. I was trying to call my friend Jerry Head to see if he could give us some backup . . . and then nothing. As soon as that last explosion hit."

Crow drove, swerving around a swelling rush of cars racing away from town. "The bridge . . . and now what? The cell phone tower? Val got cut off, but she said that there were a lot of explosions."

"Oh man."

"You'd better reload us, Vince. This is going to be bad."

"It's already bad."

"Then it's going to get worse."

(2)

Billy Christmas heard the screams and grinned. "The tourists are really loving this stuff." He sipped hot mint tea from his travel mug and parked a haunch on the empty flatbed that had just come back. The returning customers were being herded toward the concession stand, a second tractor was pulling a fresh group of victims out, but the third was deep in the attraction. Weird theremin music filled the air.

"Yeah, they're eating it up," agreed BK. "Guess no one needs it to actually be dark to get into the mood."

Thunder rumbled in the sky. "Dark enough," Billy said.

"Not supposed to rain, though. I checked the weather . . . it's clear everywhere else. Probably just a passing system. Lucky us."

There was more thunder, a shorter burst not preceded by a lightning flash. BK looked east over the miles of waving corn. He saw the glow on the horizon and almost dismissed it as lightning—but the glow was too orange and it didn't flicker, merely tinted the undersides of the clouds.

"Christ!" BK pointed, but Billy was already climbing up onto the flatbed's deck.

"Something just blew up real good. Damn! There's another!"

They watched a small fireball sear its way upward in the distance.

"That's near the town," BK said. He pulled his cell phone out and hit the speed dial, calling Jim Winterbottom, his point man for the parade. The phone rang and rang and then went to voice mail. When he tried again, his own phone went dead. "That's weird . . . suddenly I get no bars."

There were four more explosions, none of them close to the hayride.

"Yeah, me too. Try the walkie-talkie." Sarah Wolfe had arranged for the police department to loan the security force a set of walkie-talkies—older models that had been in storage but which would still work as a backup. The signals were bounced by relay towers and routed through the department's switchboard.

"No signal," BK said. "This is too weird for me, Billy. Let's—"

Two things happened right then. The lights in the whole attraction suddenly went out—and with the murk under the late
afternoon clouds, the whole place went very dark—and then
the screams began. Not just the screams of the kids out in the
field . . . but screams everywhere.

Billy turned. "What the f—?"

A figure rushed at them. White face, red eyes, fangs—and an
orange and black PINE DEEP HAUNTED HAYRIDE STAFF T-shirt.

"Mr. Kingsman!" yelled the vampire. "Something's wrong. All
the power's out."

"It's okay, Danny," BK said. "Get one of the ATVs out of the
barn and run the circuit. Everyone comes back here."

"What's going on?"

"Don't know yet, but let's round everyone up. Come on,
Danny, chop chop."

The kid nodded and dashed for the barn.

Billy said, "I'll take the haunted house. The emergency lights
should have kicked in, but I'll bring everyone out." There were
more explosions. He ran up the path.

Another white-faced figure in an orange T-shirt was coming
around the far end of the tractor. BK waved him over. "Chet,
good . . . listen, something's going down so we're pulling everyone in. Do me a favor and—"

Chet, grinning with his mouthful of fangs, just leapt at him
and clamped black-taloned fingers around BK's throat as he
drove him back against the flatbed.

(3)

Film actor Ken Foree was nearing the end of his lecture about
the allegory and social commentary in the George Romero *Living Dead* films when the drive-in's big screen changed from an
image of a younger Foree dressed like Philly SWAT shooting it
out with a bunch of zombies at a rural shopping mall to a flat
expanse of silver-gray emptiness.

"In *Dawn of the Dead* the consumerism of the American—" he said, and then his microphone cut out along with all of the lights throughout the drive-in's big lot. Annoyed, he turned toward the projection booth mounted above the bunkerlike concession stand, but it, too, was dark. Instantly fifty cars started honking their horns and people began to grumble loudly.

Foree held up his hands to try and quiet the crowd. "People, people!" he called, pitching his theater-trained baritone above the din. "Let's all calm down. Give the man a chance to fix the problem."

As they quieted down, he continued talking, telling some jokes about mishaps on the sets of the monster movies and TV shows he'd worked on. Folks began to get out of their cars and draw closer, and Foree encouraged them with come-here gestures. Not surprisingly, many of the attendees were dressed in bloodstained clothes and made up to look like the living dead. Foree took it in stride. *Star Trek conventions get Klingons, I get the walking dead,* he mused.

He saw that more people were coming around from the far side of the concession stand, and these new arrivals seemed to be more in the vampire motif: fangs, bloody mouths, dark eyes, though they had the classic zombie vacant expressions and slow, shuffling gait down perfectly. He waved them in, too.

(4)

They'd put Tom Savini in the main house of the theater department and there were two sets of attendees. The general admission crowd sat in the theater seats while the MFA film students were onstage. One by one Savini was transforming them from ordinary college kids into monsters or victims of monsters.

The makeup effects man was a legend in the business and had pioneered many of the wound effects that were now standard in horror and action films. He was describing how latex and other materials were used to create the effect of a zombie tearing a chunk out of someone's arm when the lights went out.

The theater went totally dark.

Savini sighed. The crowd immediately started getting restive, so he pitched his voice loud enough to carry and said, "Apparently the dean didn't pay the electric bill." It had the desired effect of getting the startled students to laugh with him rather than to panic. "Everyone sit tight. There should be emergency lights . . . ah, there we are."

The lights came on. The screaming began a moment later. The blood that sprayed the walls was not stage blood.

(5)

The tingling ant-crawly feeling on the back of Mike's neck intensified and just as the hospital emergency lights kicked on he turned away from Val and Weinstock and looked at the window for what seemed like an hour but was really a fragment of a second.

"Down!" he screamed as he spun and dove at Val, tackling her so that they collapsed between the bed and the bathroom wall; even before they landed Mike reached up and grabbed the front of Weinstock's hospital gown and pulled him right out of the bed. Jonatha staggered back from them as they fell and she bumped into Newton, who tripped backward, dragging her with him—a clumsy move that saved both their lives because in the next fragment of a second a new blast ripped through the town and the big tempered-glass window imploded, sending thousands of flying glass daggers scything through the room. The window side of Weinstock's bed was shredded, glass needles jabbed into the walls, and the shock wave swept the vase of flowers off the bedside table and smashed them against the wall. Then, as if drawing a deep breath after a scream, the hot air from the blast was sucked back out, leaving Weinstock's room a darkened and glittering debris field.

394 Jonathan Maberry

There was glass everywhere. They all crouched where they had fallen, more terrified of all the glass than of the blast.

Val was the first to move, and she pushed back against Mike, who still lay half on top of her, his weight on her lower back, pressing her stomach into the floor. "Mike," she said urgently, "the baby . . ."

He instantly arched up over her, balancing on fingers and toes while glass tinkled off his back; Val wormed carefully out from under him. Weinstock was tucked into a tight corner, his face contorted in agony as he clutched his wounded arm to his chest. Blood seeped through his bandages, evidence of ruptured stitches, and he curled his body up like he was stuffed into a box of pain.

"Is anyone hurt?" Val asked as she used the edge of the chair to pull herself to her knees.

Jonatha gasped as she sat up. "I think I'm cut."

Newton scuttled out from under her and fished a keychain flashlight out, playing the tiny beam over her. There were at least a dozen small cuts on her arms, but nothing serious. Newton crunched over glass to the bathroom and returned with a thick wad of toilet tissue and began blotting at the cuts.

Val swept off the seat and sat down, wincing at the pain in her lower back and stomach. Mike helped Weinstock up and stood him against the wall. Weinstock was barefoot.

"What the hell is happening?" the doctor demanded, but nobody had any answers. Instead they each stopped moving and listened to the sounds coming through the empty window. The screeching of car horns. Gunshots. And screams. Lots and lots of screams.

The door opened and a nurse rushed in, her face smeared with blood, clothes littered with glass fragments, eyes wild. She had one hand pressed to her throat. "Doctor! Oh my God . . . they . . . they . . ." Then she sank to her knees and fell forward, her hand slipping away to release an arterial spray.

Behind her in the half-lit corridors, it was sheer pandemonium as patients and nurses and doctors staggered through the shadows, most of them bleeding from the shattered windows.

Jonatha tore the wadded tissues out of Newton's hand, but as she bent to press it to the nurse's throat the artery pumped a last feeble splash and then stopped.

"What the hell is going on?" she screamed, turning toward Mike. "What's going on?"

Mike looked out the window. There was more light spilling into the room from the fires out there than from the emergency lights. "It's what I was trying to tell you," he said. "This is what Griswold and Vic have been planning all these years. The Red Wave."

"But what is it? What does he want? Just to kill us?"

Mike turned. "Don't you get it? This isn't about us. It's never been about us, not really. We're just in his way. You said it yourself—Griswold is a psychic vampire. Every time someone is killed by those *things* he created, every time someone dies in pain and terror, he feeds on it. Every death makes him stronger. He's been getting stronger and stronger all these years, and now with this . . ." He waved at the window. "With this, he'll be strong enough."

"Strong enough to do what?" demanded Val, rising.

Mike's fiery eyes burned in the darkness.

"Strong enough to rise from the grave. That's what this is all about. He's using all this raw power to remake himself. He wants to come back, not as a ghost or as a psychic vampire, but with a new body."

Weinstock stared at him, then looked out the window at the inferno that was Pine Deep. "What kind of body can he make by feeding on pain and death?"

Mike shook his head. "I don't know. There's never been anything like this. The Bone Man was sure of that, and I *know* it. Just like I'm the first of whatever I am . . . when Griswold rises he'll be the first of what he is. Something really powerful." He paused as if listening to voices in his head. "I think he wants to be a god."

The others just looked at him, not getting it.

"This isn't just about Pine Deep, either, any more than it's been about us. The Red Wave is going to break Griswold out of the grave, but it's also going to spread outward. The Bone Man told me that there are a lot of things that make Pine Deep what it is, and it's what drew Griswold here in the first place. This place is like a battery for storing spiritual energy. I don't really understand it, but it's something about its geography. The Bone Man called it geo-something."

"Geomancy?" Jonatha ventured.

"Yeah. Pine Deep's surrounded on all sides by running water. That keeps the spiritual energy here in town, concentrated, and over time that energy just builds on itself. Griswold's drawing on that just as he's drawing on a release of energy from everyone who gets killed. When he rises, though, he'll have enough power to cross the water boundaries and take all that energy with him because all of it will *be* him. The Red Wave is not another plague, it's more like a tsunami, and when he rises everywhere he goes that power is going to be unstoppable." Mike closed his eyes. "Griswold is going to destroy the world and we're too late to do anything about it."

"No . . ." Val said, touching her stomach.

Mike opened his eyes and laughed. "Welcome to the apocalypse."

Chapter 40

Missy, Crow's old Impala, rocketed down the black road at seventy miles an hour. Crow was hunched over the wheel, his face set in a grim mask, his eyes intent on the road. Beads of sweat were scattered across his brow. Beside him, LaMastra was as rigid as stone. Only his big fist moved, pounding down repeatedly on his thigh as he muttered, "Go! Go!"

All Crow heard was Val's name echoing in his head. He wanted to scream.

Several more explosions blew bright red holes in the night. Thunderous echoes buffeted the car as it crested another hill. Crow cried out and jammed on the brakes; the wheels screeched and the car slewed and fishtailed before finally coming to a stop at the top of the last hill before they reached the town proper. Crow and LaMastra felt their minds freezing with shock as they stared at the road and the town. Cars by the hundreds clogged the road, crowding both lanes, clawing along the shoulders as they fled from the town. Behind the mad exodus the town itself was ablaze. Fires whooshed upward from dozens of spots, and the undersides of the clouds writhed with red snakes of reflected fire. Buildings and trees burned vigorously; telephone poles flamed like torches all along Corn Hill.

"Who's doing all this?" LaMastra punched the dashboard. "This can't all be Vic Wingate. I mean—these are vampires we're dealing with! Vampires don't blow shit up. Do they?"

The flaming debris was raining down onto the rooftops of

the houses near the elementary school. Already some of the houses were burning. "They do now," Crow said in a drum-tight voice. "I guess they do whatever serves their purpose?"

"Purpose? *Purpose?* What purpose? I mean, why blow shit up if you just want to drink blood? I don't get it."

A line of cars three abreast were heading right for them, horns blaring, high beams flashing on and off. "Hold on," Crow said as he spun the wheel. "This is going to get tricky." Missy left the road and crunched along on the outside edge of the shoulder, at times clinging to the edge of the drainage ditch that ran parallel to the verge. He reached the line of cars and shot past; the drivers cursed at him and shot him the finger, but Crow spun the wheel back and shot back onto the road, accelerating into an open slot, racing into the burning town.

(2)

Ruger had kill zones set up at each of the big event areas that made up the Festival, using the handy tourist brochures so thoughtfully provided by the borough to locate the right spots. One of them was the Dead-End Drive-In, and that was already a slaughterhouse; another was the Hayride. He had teams hitting the college campus, the two movie theaters, the high school gymnasium, and the banquet hall of the Harvestman—everywhere tourists were gathering in large numbers with some possibility of containment. Vic's fireworks were keeping things hopping. The bridges were gone, which meant that no one was getting out of Pine Deep. If they fled into the farms and state forest, then that would be a happy hunting ground for later on. By the time anyone on the outside figured out what was happening—if that was even possible—and mobilized any kind of police or military response, it would be way too late. The Man would be up by then.

(3)

Brinke Stevens flashed a bright smile as she handed the signed 8x10 studio portrait of her in a seductive pose. The young man she'd signed it for was blushing so hard he couldn't speak.

"Don't forget your candy," she called, and the guy reached out a sweaty, trembling hand to take the bag of Pine Deep Authentic Candy Corn. Everyone who got a picture got some candy. The fan pressed the picture to his chest and sort of scuttled away, already tearing open the plastic bag.

Brinke cut a look at Debbie Rochon, who was signing her own stack of pictures, and they both cocked a knowing eyebrow.

"Gotta love the fanboys," Debbie said under her breath.

"Each and every one."

The seats were all filled with fans who already had their pictures and who were stuffing handfuls of candy corn into their mouths. They all looked strangely happy.

"Ladies?" They turned to see Dave Kramer, one of Crow's friends, who was the liaison between the Festival and the actresses. "We're going to run the first film in forty minutes. You need a break from this . . . ?"

Brinke shook her head. "Nah. These guys have been waiting all day."

"We're good," agreed Debbie. "We can do a pee break after the movie's on."

That's when the lights went out. The lines of fans groaned, milled, mumbled. A few of them tittered as if this was all a wonderful kind of fun.

"Someone get the tent flaps!" Kramer yelled, and when nobody moved he hustled over and did it himself, pulling back the pumpkin-colored canvas to let in the pale afternoon light. Thunder boomed over and over again and a wet breeze swept into the tent.

A Pine Deep cop was on post outside and he turned when the flap was opened.

"Everything okay in there?"

"Lights went out."

"Okay," said the cop and pushed past Kramer. He turned on his big flashlight and headed right to the signing table, playing the beam over the two actresses. "Hello, ladies . . . sorry for the inconvenience."

They shrugged. "Not a problem," Brinke said. "You know what's going on?"

"Don't sweat it . . . it's all under control." The cop kept his light right in their faces.

"Officer," said Debbie, "you mind with the light?"

The cop grinned, and they could see the white of his teeth even past the harsh glare of the flash. "You bitches are the scream queens . . . aren't you?"

A half-dozen bulky figures crowded the tent's opening; college football team sweatshirts and pasty faces. They shoved Kramer roughly out of the way. At the table, Officer Golub bent toward the actresses, his white grin stretching wider and wider.

"Let's hear you scream," he whispered and then snapped his teeth at them.

(4)

Jim O'Rear wasn't scheduled to give his demonstration of film stunt techniques until that evening. Knowing that Crow was shorthanded he volunteered to spend the afternoon walking the grounds at the Hayride to make sure all the attractions were in top shape. There were reporters from all the big papers as well as from the major horror magazines—the last thing Crow would need was a shot of tourists stuck at, say, the Cave of the Wolfman with no werewolf, no spooky lighting, no smoke effects.

He had just completed the circuit and was heading to the Haunted House to give BK the thumbs-up when he heard screams coming from the Scream Queen tent, which, despite its name, was not scheduled for anything loud until the marathon started, and according to his clipboard that was nearly forty minutes from now. He listened. O'Rear had heard a lot of screams—as an actor and stuntman on movies and on dozens of haunted attractions; he knew the difference between canned screams and real. This sounded way too real. Even for a theme park designed by Malcolm "I-have-no-limits" Crow.

He stared in the direction of the tent. The screams kept going, on and on.

"Shit," he said, and started running.

(5)

The creature hit BK like a missile and together they crashed backward onto the flatbed's deck. The thing lunged at him, trying to bite him.

"What the fu—?" BK started to say, but the hands around his throat were like steel bands, instantly cutting off his air. Black poppies started blooming at the edges of his vision.

Though he did not understand what was happening, or even recognize the nature of the person attacking him, BK had been in too many fights to go down this easy. He jammed his left fist under the attacker's jaw and shoved upward, pushing the teeth away from his throat, then hooked a sharp right-hand hooking palm heel into the creature's ear. BK was a very big, very strong man and the shot should have taken all the steam out of this guy, even if he was hopped up on crack. The openhanded blow should almost certainly have popped the eardrum, but the snarling thing on top of him shook it off with barely a moment's loosening of its grip.

BK's mind was going dark from oxygen starvation. So, his next hit was a killing blow, a two-knuckle rising punch into the attacker's Adam's apple. He heard the hyoid bone crunch; instantly the pressure slackened and the attacker reeled back, clutching his throat. BK came off the flatbed and was expecting to see the son of a bitch go down dead. Instead he shook himself like a wet dog and raised his head.

That's when BK got his first real look at him.

His attacker was a teenage boy, maybe seventeen, with a pimply face and shaggy hair. His eyes were dark, his mouth full of fangs . . . but suddenly BK realized, with a sick and terrible certainty, that this was not another Halloween costume.

The monster rushed him again.

(6)

Screenwriter Stephen Susco was yelling at the projectionist. The power had gone off barely ten minutes into screening of his film, *The Grudge 2*. The house lights were out and the emergency lights were next to useless. Now there was some kind of fight going on in the back rows of the theater.

The projectionist never appeared; neither did the ushers. Susco turned to fellow screenwriter-director James Gunn, who was scheduled to screen his flick *Slither* in a couple of hours and in a low voice said, "This is the sort of shit you'd expect in LA."

Gunn spread his hands. "Small Town, America. What can I tell you?"

"Hey, I grew up near here. Don't bust on Bucks County."

A sound made them look up to see a dark, round object come sailing out through the projectionist's window, arc over the crowd, and land with a wet thud on the stage. Both screenwriters looked at it, smiling at first because this was Halloween and they thought it was a joke. The object rolled toward them and came to a wobbly stop five feet away. The smiles drained away from both their faces as they recognized the face—and head—of the projectionist.

The back doors of the theater burst open with a crash and a dozen pale-faced strangers filled the doorway. Dixie McVey led the way. He pointed at the men on the stage. "Fetch!" he said. The killers rushed past him and the dying began.

(7)

The woman in the party dress staggered out of the firelit shadows with a ragged bundle in her blood-streaked arms. Her dress was torn, and tears had cut tracks through the soot stains on her face. It had probably been a pretty face once, but not now.

"My baby!" she screamed as she lurched toward the hospital entrance. Flaming fragments from the TV station next door fell all around her. "God! Please help my baby!"

Most of the crowd that had been thronged outside of the ER entrance had bolted and fled when the station blew up. Only three people were left—a nurse, an EMT, and a pizza delivery guy with a bloody rag pressed to his face. They stood in a loose knot watching the rain of flaming debris, but they turned as the woman staggered toward them.

"My baby!" The woman's voice was shrill with anguish, and the watchers could see that the baby she carried in her arms was horribly limp. She stopped walking and just stood there. "Help my baby!"

The pizza delivery guy took a tentative step toward her. "Lady! Come on! Get in here." A chunk of steaming pipe crashed down only yards behind the woman, but she was too out of it to even twitch.

The pizza delivery guy looked at the EMT and together they sprinted across the parking lot toward her. The nurse lingered by the door, but screamed for all of them to get inside. She tried not to look at the small, slack limbs that hung from the bundle of bloody rags the woman clutched to her chest.

The two men braced her and each took an arm to hurry her along. A flaming shoe slapped down in front of them. "Christ," growled the EMT.

"My baby's hurt!" wept the woman as they hustled her along. The nurse came out to meet them, making shushing noises to soothe her, reaching out for the baby. The woman screamed and huddled over the baby, shielding it from the nurse's touch.

"Get the door," ordered the nurse, and the pizza delivery guy ran forward to pull open the heavy door. The emergency power did not extend to the hydraulic doors.

The woman stopped outside, jerking back, her face suddenly frightened and suspicious. "No! You'll hurt my baby!"

"No, no," the nurse quickly assured her. "We're going to help you. We're going to help your . . . baby. Come on, sweetheart."

"That's right, Miss," said the EMT, trying to urge her on. Still the woman hesitated, clearly afraid of the yawning doorway.

"My baby?"

"There are doctors in here," said the nurse. "They'll take care of your baby. They'll fix you both up good as new." The lie burned like acid on her tongue.

The woman turned and looked at the nurse, her eyes almost blank except for haunted shadows. "Doctors?"

"Yes, Sweetheart. Very good doctors. The best. Now come on in so we can help you."

"Come inside," the pizza guy called, half watching her and half watching the seemingly endless fall of flaming debris.

Reluctantly, the woman began moving again, letting the driver and the nurse guide her inside. They crossed the threshold and left the danger of the falling debris behind. There were other people milling around in the ER entrance now, including a young resident from Pakistan who was already moving toward them with a look of deep concern on his face. The woman stopped just inside the entrance and slowly lowered her arms. The tattered blanket fell from her hands onto the floor, and a limp form flopped out into the light. The nurse and the driver stared. The pizza delivery guy and the resident stared. All of them wore identical frowns of surprise and confusion.

On the hospital floor lay an ordinary child's doll, with a plastic smiling face and soft rubber arms and legs. The driver was the first to lift his eyes from the doll to the bloodstained woman. She was no longer staring wide-eyed with shock. She was smiling. Her smile was wide and white and impossible.

Lois Wingate threw back her head and laughed as behind her the doors were yanked open by powerful hands. All of the vampires who had been hiding in the shadows behind parked cars in the lot now came howling into the hospital to share in the fun. They swarmed past Lois. Last of all came Karl Ruger, twirling Lois's tiara on a long white finger.

"Now that was just plain mean," he said with a grin.

Lois flew into his arms and their kisses tasted of blood.

(8)

Vic stumbled away from the open door of the pickup toward the weak lights that spilled through the glass doors of the Emergency Room entrance. Twice he tripped and fell. A thin whimpering cry bubbled from his lips as he tottered toward the doors, one hand pressing a greasy rag against the melted skin of his face and the other batting at invisible nothings that he believed flew around him. He was deep in shock and his shoulders twitched every few steps.

He pulled the door open, screaming in effort and pain, oblivious to the carnage around him. The vampires looked at him but did not dare approach. They knew who he was, and even if he was burned and out of his mind with pain, not one of them dared to attack him.

At times during the nightmare drive from Griswold's house to the hospital Vic thought that his skin was still on fire—it felt like it was still blazing—and he beat at his skin. But that only made the pain worse. He wept and mumbled and cried out for the Man to help him, but the darkness in his head was silent except for the roar of open flame.

Inside the hospital he reeled and lurched toward the ER. He didn't know if any doctors would still be alive or not. He didn't care. There would be morphine.

All the way to the hospital he kept calling the Man, using that old mind connection to try and reach him . . . but it was like shouting into a well. The Man didn't answer, didn't say a word.

The silence burned him far worse than the damage to his skin and he had to will himself not to sob. It wasn't right . . . it wasn't fair. None of this was fair.

The right side of his face looked normal, but the left was a horror show. If a waxwork dummy had been worked over with a blowtorch, the effect would have been about the same. Skin sagged in melted folds, drooping over one eye, hanging loosely from the bone on withered strings of damaged muscle. His left eye was not blind, but all he could see was a milky whiteness shot with threads of scarlet. Most of his black hair had burned away to reveal a worm-white scalp splotched here and there with lurid red marks. His clothes had burned, too, but they had kept his body from the worst of it. He had rolled around in the tall grass near the house to extinguish the burning jacket and jeans before the flames could do crippling damage to his body, but his face was ruined. His hands were puffed with leaking blisters from swatting at the flames.

Thirty feet inside the ER he tripped over a kid's rag doll and went down in a sprawl, cracking his chin against the marble floor. He bellowed for help, unable to work out the mechanics of how to get back to his feet. His bladder let go and Vic Wingate lay sprawled in his own piss, his face a Picasso mask, wheezing air in and out through a seared throat.

And Vic Wingate started to cry.

(9)

They all heard the screams change from shock to terror to pain. Val ran out into the hall with Mike behind her just as the door to the fire stairs opened and half a dozen white-faced vampires came dashing out, laughing and yelling like frat boys on rush night.

(10)

Terry could feel everything that was happening to him. He was acutely aware of the shift in body temperature as his system jumped into a whole new dimension of cellular activity. His respiration quickened and his pupils dilated as hormones were pumped furiously into his system. In his brain new glands formed and old ones faded away; his heart hammered with tremendous force, sending his blood coursing through his veins to carry strange new chemical mixtures to organs and bones. His entire nervous system was like a supercomputer running a massively complex program and redesigning itself as it functioned, expanding its memory, discarding useless files, accessing new and bizarre data.

Terry could feel his body shifting, altering as mass was reassigned. His bones became heavier to support muscle tissue that had thickened and grown more dense. His skin tingled as new hair follicles formed and began sending stiff red shoots through the flesh. His jaw ached horribly as the configuration of his teeth changed; his molars shifted forward to allow the growth of strong new carnassial teeth, and the incisors and canines became decidedly more pronounced. Externally his face looked no different. If Sarah had been looking at him instead of out in the hallway trying to get answers about the noise and confusion, she would not yet have seen anything beyond the last of the fading bruises that marked his face, but inside Terry, nothing was the same.

When the first explosions rocked the hospital, Terry's mind registered them but did not focus. His window faced east and only rattled as the shock waves hit, and Terry's reforming senses did not register any immediate threat. He remained submerged in his internal world of physical change, but Sarah had leapt to her feet and gone rushing into the hallway. She was out there for a long time, and when the changes in Terry's body began to affect his surface anatomy, he was distantly glad that she was not in the room. There was just enough of him left to care.

When the windows on the other side of the hospital blew inward, the changes were starting to accelerate. His window only shuddered in its frame and its dark surface reflected the chameleon changes taking place on the bed.

Outside, Sarah, the staff, and scores of patients choked the hallway. Every third person had a cell phone and people were shouting into them as if it would do some good. Rumors buzzed back and forth like agitated flies. There were screams and yells, and the sound of bodies colliding in the poorly lit halls.

A nurse started yelling for everyone to go back to their rooms, for visitors to help get their family members back to their beds, while down the hall a doctor was yelling for everyone to get out of their rooms and away from the windows. Suddenly terrified for Terry, Sarah began to fight her way through the darkness toward his room. The whole hospital shook as blast after blast rocked the town. People staggered into her, and twice she tripped and fell in the darkness. Just as she reached for the handle to his door there was a tremendous shattering crash from inside and she screamed and shoved her shoulder against the inrush of wind. She fought her way inside and then stopped, hand to her mouth to stifle a scream.

The window was an empty hole through which the night air blew with stinging coldness. Shredded curtains whipped and danced in the breeze. On the bed the blankets were torn to ribbons, and the IV stand lay on the floor in a puddle of solution.

Sarah stood in the doorway and screamed again.

The room was empty. Terry was gone.

(11)

The Bone Man stood on the roof of the hospital and watched the town burn. His guitar hung from his limp right hand and his left palm was pressed to his chest as if his heart could actually beat. It felt like it was breaking nonetheless.

Two floors below he could feel the thing that had been Mike Sweeney, could feel the energies surging and flowing in him like tidal waters. Above him the cloudy sky was dense with thousands of circling crows. Down there in the streets he saw the thing that had been Terry Wolfe racing through the flickering shadows. Out beyond the edge of town, down in the Hollow, he could feel that other *thing* twisting and writhing in the muddy darkness. This is what that poet must have meant, he mused, when he wrote about a beast slouching to town to be born.

Chapter 41

Val went out of the room to see what was going on. There was no sense or order to the melee in the halls. Some of the patients and staff were screaming; some crouched down against the base of the walls, arms wrapped around their heads like kids used to do during air raid drills in school. There were at least three people lying on the floor, either dead or unconscious, and no one seemed to notice or care.

Then the door to the fire stairs opened and a knot of figures dressed in Halloween costumes came creeping out. Immediately they split up and went in different directions, and as Val watched two of the figures leapt at a pair of elderly patients and tackled them to the floor. A nearby nurse screamed, and in the dim light cast by the emergency floods Val couldn't exactly see what was happening, but she knew.

The screams changed then, transforming from shouts and shrieks of confusion and fear into true screams of pain and terror. More figures came out of the stairwell, and one of them turned in her direction. He was only a silhouette, framed by the weak lights in the stairway, but an icy fear reached into Val's chest and closed its cold fingers around her heart. Her lips formed a word, a name, and even though she didn't speak it aloud it soured her mouth like bile.

Ruger.

She wasn't sure if he saw her, but just the possibility of it—and the reality of his presence here—made the unborn embryo in her womb scream in psychic terror. Val fled back into Weinstock's room.

"*He's here!*" she gasped.

(2)

"Crow! Watch!"

Crow already saw the body lying in the street and wrenched the wheel hard over so the wheels missed the prone figure's outstretched hand by inches. He skidded to a stop and threw it into Park. The rest of the street was choked with running people and burning debris. Every store along the street had lost its glass to the explosions, the windows yawning wide and black like gasping mouths. LaMastra reached for the door handle.

"What are you doing?" demanded Crow.

"I'm going to see if that person is . . ."

"No you're not!" Crow reached past him and hammered down the door lock with his fist. "That person is dead. So's that one over there. I can see more of them down the street—just look!"

LaMastra did look, seeing what he hadn't taken in before. There were bodies everywhere. A few moved feebly, but most were clearly dead. People ran by in panic, sometimes pausing to pound on the car's hood and try the door handles before fleeing into the night.

"Vince, I don't know what's happening, but I think it's suicide to get out of the car before we get to the hospital. We have to get to Val."

LaMastra stared out at the riot. He saw a white-faced creature leap from the top of a parked news van onto a running man. The two of them rolled over and over in the middle of the street, and then the vampire tore out the man's throat in a geyser of blood.

"*Jesus Christ!*" LaMastra cried.

Crow punched him in the arm, hard. "We can't save them. We have to go!"

Crow put the car in Drive and stepped on the gas, but as he did so LaMastra cranked down the window and laid the barrel of the big shotgun across the frame; as the car passed, the cop fired and splashed the vampire against the side of the van.

"Drive!"

Crow drove.

A naked man staggered out into the middle of the street, his body bleeding from a dozen sets of small punctures. Four children ran after him, their laughing mouths bright with fresh blood. LaMastra shot two of them, but the others fled.

Crow had to weave in and out of the oncoming traffic, blaring his horn, flashing his brights. Cars and people buffeted him and one of his headlights went blind; but with LaMastra maintaining a nearly constant barrage even the panicking people started dodging out of the way. LaMastra fired his gun dry and rolled up the window while he reloaded. He fished Crow's shotgun out of the duffel and as Crow threaded his way toward the hospital, LaMastra emptied both guns again and again.

"Christ!" he gasped, hastily reloading again. His shoulder ached from the kick of the two guns. "How many of these things are there?"

When they entered the parking lot they saw a pair of vampires holding the struggling body of a young woman in their arms. Her body was naked and crisscrossed with freely bleeding gashes. The vampires moved from victim to victim, first cutting their own skin to dribble their own blood into slack, dead mouths, and then dripping the woman's blood into the same mouths. At once Crow and LaMastra understood not only the reason for the impossible numbers of the living dead but the overwhelming horror of the invasion. The sheer scope of it was impossible to grasp.

"Get those two bastards!" Crow bellowed as he gunned his engine and raced across the lot. Hearing the roar of the engine, the vampires dropped the woman's corpse and turned snarling faces at the single headlight of the big Impala. LaMastra crammed his beefy head and shoulders out the window and his first shot took one of them off at the shoulders, but the other—seeing his comrade fall—fled into the darkness with incredible speed and agility. LaMastra fired and missed.

"Leave it!" Crow yelled as he pulled around to the ER entrance. The car rounded the corner and burst into the main section of the parking lot. There were more bodies, and more vampires laboring at their task of increasing Griswold's army. Crow stamped down on the accelerator and rammed the closest one, who almost—but not quite—managed to leap out of the way. The vampire thumped across the hood and landed behind the car, but he was up again in a moment and running after them, spitting with fury. LaMastra leaned out the window and blew his legs off.

Crow squealed to a stop a dozen yards from the hospital entrance and they gaped at the carnage. There were bodies everywhere, lying twisted and dead, littering the opening and strewn about in the lobby.

"Everyone's dead," he said, gagging on it.

But as they watched, the bodies began to rise.

"Oh, shit!"

The corpses stirred and rolled over, jerking back into a new and terrible wakefulness. There were at least twenty of them, and as they rose some of them wandered off into the hospital, but many of them turned toward the front door, staring past the single remaining headlight of Crow's car.

"This is not good," said LaMastra as he hurried to reload.

There was a thud and the whole car shook as something heavy landed on the roof. Crow could see white fingers hooked around the edge of the door. He drew his Beretta and put two slugs up through the roof. A white body fell past his window.

Crow made a low, feral noise, his lip curling. He said, "Hold on to your ass!"

LaMastra stared in horror as Crow began gunning the engine. "Oh . . . no, don't even think about it!"

"This ain't the blues anymore, partner, this is rock and roll!" Crow slammed the car into drive and kicked down on the accelerator. Missy shot forward, the hot engine ready for the challenge, and with a howling cry of rage, Crow plowed into—and through—the big double doors, tearing metal and glass and slamming into the crowd of newly risen vampires.

(3)

"Are you sure it was him?" Weinstock demanded. The shock of what Val had seen was worse than the agony in his arm. He was dressed in pajamas and the dress shoes he had worn down to the morgue. The others pushed the chairs and the bedside table in front of the door.

Val didn't answer; instead she yanked open the big clothes closet and started pulling out the duffel bags of weapons that Crow and Ferro had left behind. Sweat was pouring down her face despite the cold air blowing in through the window and her hands shook visibly as she passed the bags to Mike, who laid them on the bed.

"Jonatha, Newt . . . can either of you use a gun?" Val asked as she ripped the zippers down. She and Mike emptied the contents fast and sloppy.

"Not well," Jonatha said dubiously, "but I know how to pull a trigger."

Newt shook his head. "Somebody will have to show me."

"Learn fast." Val handed each of them a 9mm pistol and half a dozen magazines.

"I can shoot," Weinstock said. "One hand still works."

Val gave him a pistol. "Saul, get dressed fast. Newt, help him. You'll need pockets for ammo." She began stuffing her own pockets with shotgun shells and 9mm mags. Her eyes were fever bright as she looked at Mike.

"Let me have a gun," Mike said. "I used a shotgun once. I went skeet shooting with my friend Brandon."

"Take it."

"And . . . can I have one of Crow's swords?"

Despite her haste, Val hesitated and gave him a searching look.

"He's been teaching me how—"

"I know. That doesn't mean you're good enough."

"Doesn't mean I'm not, either."

They held that stare for a moment, then Val gave him just a flicker of a smile. She looked down at the weapons and grabbed more shells. "Take whatever you want. Crow took his good sword with him, and he told me that he was going to coat the blade with garlic oil."

Mike shook his head. "I don't have to worry about that."

Her gaze flicked up again. "What do you . . . oh."

The *dhampyr*'s eyes were like torches. "I just hope I have some superpowers after all."

Right then a heavy fist began pounding on the door.

Val stiffened and turned. The pounding was so hard it shook the heavy institutional door in its metal frame. A wave of sickness twisted in Val's stomach.

"Come owww-owwt!" someone called in a singsong. There were screams outside, but even through that they could hear the snickering laugh of whoever was beating on the door. "Come owwwwwww-owt!"

Val snatched a pistol off the bed and took a step toward the door.

"No, Val—don't!" Newton cried. He was holding Weinstock's pants and the doctor had a leg poised to step into them.

"Shut up," Val snarled, and it wasn't clear if she was talking to Newton or the monster outside. Then she racked the slide and put four rounds through the center of the door.

The next scream they heard was inhuman.

And Val Guthrie smiled.

(4)

Even though his guts were turning to gutter water, BK stood his ground as his attacker rushed him. Three times he'd nailed this psycho son of a bitch with crippling blows to the head and throat. Three times the attacker just shrugged them off. BK was not a spiritual guy, and he didn't much believe in the boogeyman, but he wasn't an idiot, either. Something was way off the sanity radar here and whether he wanted to believe it or not he had to accept the fact that this guy was not acting human. No, he corrected himself in the microsecond between the time the guy sprang and when he leapt, not *acting* human, this weird-ass motherfucker was *not* human.

Belief and acceptance are sometimes very different concepts.

The teenager jumped from too far away and yet still covered the distance between them—and the impossible reality of that nearly got BK killed—but BK was a fighter and he'd been in hundreds of scrapes from schoolyard scuffles to extreme martial arts bouts to back-alley knife fights. His conscious rational mind was not always allowed to be in the driver's seat; reflexes and gross motor skills are better for the battlefield.

As the attacker slammed into him, BK shifted slightly to one side, accepted the grab with one of his own, pivoted, and let the killer's mass and momentum do all the work. The pounce turned into a pirouette and then the killer was falling with BK's bulk on top of him. They hit the ground hard and fast, with BK's muscle and mass driving downward to smash the attacker's bones with the impact. BK didn't stop there, didn't even pause; as soon as his hands were free of the need to steer the attacker's body, he let go of the teenager's trunk, grabbed him by the chin and the hair, and then threw himself into a tight roll through the air. BK's bulk, plus the twisting grip, created a savage torque that more than just snapped the neck—it wrenched the killer's head around more than two hundred degrees.

The attacker went limp in an instant.

BK rolled all the way to his feet but froze in a crouch, staring at what he had just fought, and what he had just done.

"Oh my God . . ." He dropped to his knees, gagging at the taste of the bile in his throat. The moment was unreal; he could feel his pulse pounding like a muffled surf in his ears.

He heard screams off to his right and rose and he turned. A woman ran out of the cornfields, her blouse torn and bloody, and two men chased her. Both of them were as pale-faced as the teenager he'd just killed. The woman reached the Haunted House and got inside, slamming the door; immediately her pursuers began hammering their fists on the door. It buckled and splintered and they tore the flimsy wood away and went inside. There were more screams.

BK was running with no awareness of having wanted or intended to. He pelted across the lot, noting with strange detachment that many tourists were milling around, some of them singing and others dancing in the unstructured way mental patients will. They all looked stoned. He recorded that, but couldn't deal with it now.

He reached the Haunted House just as one of the pursuers came hurtling back out through the doorway with a short length of broken wood rammed up under his chin, his shirtfront glistening with blood. The man fell flat on his back and didn't move, so BK vaulted his body and dashed inside. Billy had gone in there.

Just inside he saw the young woman huddled in a corner by a bandstand that had instruments but no musicians—they weren't scheduled to play until eight that night and it was just turning six now. There were bodies on the floor. One was a younger teenager whose throat had clearly been torn out; the other was a red-haired woman dressed in a den mother's uniform. Her mouth was smeared with blood and there was a drumstick jammed into the socket of her right eye.

On the far side of the bandstand the second of the two pursuers was locked in a mutual stranglehold with Billy Christmas, and they rolled over and over, their feet kicking out to send guitars and hi-hats crashing to the floor. Billy's face was streaked with blood and his shoulder was slashed from the deltoid to the elbow.

BK rushed over and grabbed the attacker by the hair and hauled backward with all his weight, pulling him away from Billy, whose face had started to turn purple. BK kicked the man in the back of the calf, dropping him to his knees, then grabbed hair and chin and, standing wide-legged, he wrenched the man's head over and up. The vertebrae popped like a drumroll, and BK let the body flop to the ground.

Billy was already climbing painfully to his feet, eyes dancing with shock, and yet he was smiling the weirdest smile BK had ever seen.

"You okay?" BK asked.

"Dude," he gasped, the blood on his face mingling with sweat and tears, "I killed a v—vam—" He couldn't quite get the word to fit into his mouth.

"What the hell is going on here?"

Billy rubbed his hands across his face. "I tried to, you know, stake him through the heart." He shook his head. "Sternum's a bitch." He coughed, spit blood onto the floor, wiped his mouth with his uninjured arm. "Eye socket," he said, nodding emphatically, "works." He dropped to his knees and threw up.

"Note to self," BK said softly while he stood over his friend.

(5)

Crow and LaMastra stood amid the carnage in the entrance hall to the ER. Everywhere around them was death. There had been over a dozen vampires—newly risen—in the hospital entrance; now there were only corpses. The air was thick with a gunpowder stink and the two of them were nearly deaf from the gunfire.

Crow covered LaMastra while the big detective reloaded both of his guns, and then did his own as LaMastra's Roadblocker tracked up and down the hall. Crow bent into the car and fished out his *katana* and slung it across his back.

"Once we find your lady and the others," LaMastra said, "we'll need new wheels."

Crow nodded. His car was a smoking wreck. "I saw Sarah Wolfe's Hummer out in the lot. If we can find the keys—"

"I can hotwire anything with wheels," LaMastra said. "Benefits of an inner-city education."

"Good to know." Crow took out his last bottle of garlic oil and smeared half of it on his throat and wrists before handing it to LaMastra. As an afterthought he licked some off his wrist so the taste would be in his mouth. "You ready?"

"No. You?"

"No," Crow said. "Let's go. Elevator'll be out. Stairs are over there."

"What now?" LaMastra asked. "We seem to be alone for the moment."

The lobby led to a hall that ran the whole length of the building, and they followed it as fast as good sense would allow, Crow walking point, LaMastra back-walking to cover their asses. The hall broke to their left in three places, toward the ER triage rooms, to the main bank of elevators a hundred feet farther along, and then jagged off into the labs and X-ray department. They saw nothing moving at all. There were corpses everywhere, but they didn't know if they were truly dead, waiting to rise, or shamming it as part of some kind of trap. If anything had so much as moved they'd have blasted it to red slush.

"Well, we have two choices, as I see it," LaMastra said quietly as they came to the fire tower.

"They being?"

"Val and the others are either upstairs in Weinstock's room or down in the morgue. She's your fiancée, so you pick."

"Shit. What would your choice be?"

Crow took a few paces down the hall and looked briefly into the triage rooms. There was a dead nurse on the floor of the waiting room and a few corpses slumped into the chairs, but no one else. "My first guess would be the morgue. It has the strongest door and that's where we left all the ammunition and the rest of the garlic. Given a choice of where to make a stand, I'd hole up there."

LaMastra pursed his lips. "Given a choice. Look around . . . this all happened fast. You think Val had time to go down there?"

Crow felt his stomach lurch. "No."

"Then we go up." They moved to the first stairwell. LaMastra said, "Okay, the same game plan? If it's pale and we don't like the way it looks, shoot it?"

"What if we shoot a patient by mistake?"

LaMastra's face was wooden. "If we live through this we'll light a candle."

They fanned out and flanked the doorway to the fire stairs. To both of them it seemed as if their whole lives consisted of going through doors with fear and violence playing tug-of-war in their hearts.

The fire door had a heavy crash bar and Crow raised his leg and pressed his right foot on the steel bar. They did not have to worry about booby traps now, but an ambush was a real possibility. With a quick glance at LaMastra, Crow gave the door a powerful kick and it flew inward, and they rushed through, Crow aiming straight and then up, LaMastra aiming straight then low, but the stairwell was empty. The dim emergency lights flickered and the two men listened to the rasp of their own breathing magnified by the acoustics of the stairwell. They started climbing, moving as quietly as they could. There were bloody handprints smeared along the walls, very fresh, droplets worming their way down to the floor. Crow led the way, taking each step with great caution, eyes barely blinking despite the stinging sweat that trickled down from his forehead. He was moving on the razor edge of awareness, his senses tuned and focused, ready for anything. And yet, he was still surprised when Karl Ruger stepped out from around the corner.

They jerked to a halt and brought their guns up fast, barrels pointing at the killer, but Ruger just grinned at them and tickled his black talons along the slender, unmarked throat of the young child he held in front of him.

Behind Ruger, and below them on the steps, there came the whispering footsteps of vampires hurrying to close the trap.

The killer smiled. "Trick or treat," he said softly.

Chapter 42

Vic Wingate sat on a plastic chair with his back to a cool concrete wall, a wet towel against his face and morphine dancing in his eyes. On the floor in front of him was a dead nurse with her throat ripped away. She had given him the towel and told him to wait, and she'd smiled at him like he was a real person, not a circus sideshow freak. Not the Incredible Melting Man. She had been nice. Now she was dead. As dead as everyone else in the waiting room.

Vic sipped from the can of Coke she'd bought him from the vending machine. It felt soooo good on his burned throat.

Two vampires came past him, shooting him a brief and uncertain glance as they bent toward the dead nurse. One of them cut his own forearm and moved to hold it out over the nurse's slack lips.

Vic shook his head. "No. Leave her be."

The vampire who had cut himself looked up, surprised. "She's meat for the master."

"Leave her be!" Vic barked, lowering his towel.

The second vampire made a rude sound. "Ruger said—"

Vic's one good eye was like a blue laser. "*Ruger* said? Ruger? Who the hell is Ruger to say shit?" The morphine was dulling the pain and giving him some of himself back. "Do you know who I am?"

The vampires said nothing.

"I'm the Man's right hand, you pasty-faced shitbags. Ruger

doesn't tell you what to do—I do. And if you don't like it, then why don't you take it up with the Man?"

Terror blossomed in their faces.

Vic got up and walked over to the closest one and crowded him. Vic's burned face was a more frightening spectacle than their pale masks, and in Vic's eyes the vampires could imagine the face of the Man. They shrank back.

"This one stays dead," Vic told them. "You two had better make sure no one else screws with her or I'll bury you both down deep and tight and you'll never be able to feed, never be able to rise. You'll stay down there and rot—forever!"

The two vampires fled, leaving Vic in the ER waiting room with the dead nurse. There were other corpses there as well, but Vic didn't give a damn about them. He only wanted the nurse left alone. She had been kind to him. He found the towel and pressed it against his face as he sat.

(2)

Susco and Gunn watched the slaughter from the stage, the two of them rooted to the boards as the vampires tore into the audience. Each of them wanted to believe that this was some kind of publicity stunt, some elaborate prank being played on them by Crow. But when they saw the reporter from Channel 3 go down with half his face torn away any chance they had for self-deception, and any hope there was of this being a joke, died right there.

There was sound and movement to their right and they turned to see a big man come lumbering onstage, moving with the slow, mindless shuffle of a zombie from one of their own films. This one was real, though, and his face was smeared with bright blood, his eyes not completely vacant, but rather filled with a feral and primitive predatory lust.

Gunn grabbed Susco and hauled him back as the big man swiped at them with black-taloned hands. Susco nearly tripped, but turned the stumble into a crouching run and bolted for stage left, with Gunn—who was taller—catching up with long-legged hustle.

"This way!" Susco yelled, pointing toward the emergency exit, but just as they reached it, the door flew open and two more of the shambling Dead Heads crowded in, moaning with hunger and reaching for them

Susco ducked under their grab, but as he dodged out of the way the leading creature caught the shoulder of Gunn's jacket. Susco kicked at the thing's knee hard enough to buckle it. It fell and dragged Gunn down with it.

As Gunn fell he rolled onto his back and kicked up and caught the monster's face, driving it back.

Susco saw a toolbox sitting open on a pair of sawhorses and he snatched a handful of tools and began throwing them as fast as he could; he hit the monster who was grappling with Gunn with a hammer and the other one with a big pair of channel locks. The blows did no damage but made the creature holding Gunn stagger, and that gave his prey the chance to hastily shrug out of his jacket and make a break for it. Susco picked up the whole toolbox and threw it, catching the monster in the face, knocking him backward into the orchestra pit.

Gun caught up to Susco and shoved him toward the far exit. They slammed into the crash bar—and rebounded. The door, against all fire regulations and common sense, was locked.

(3)

Val kept her gun trained on the door while Newton, Mike, and Jonatha overturned the heavy medical bed and used it to re-inforce their barricade. There was still pounding on the door, but it was sporadic now, more a hit-and-run-away teasing. That or the creatures had learned caution.

Weinstock, dressed now but standing in shoes that were filled with blood from the cuts on his feet, stood next to her.

"Crow will come," he kept saying to her, "Crow will come."

"I know," Val said, wanting to believe it.

None of them were watching the window. The open, gaping, inviting window.

(4)

Terry ran through the streets faster than a galloping horse. At first he dodged from shadow to shadow, but as he changed he grew bolder. The crowds on the street were thinning as the tourists and residents of Pine Deep fled into houses or out into the country, or died. Many hundreds of them wandered around in a drug-induced haze or had become so intensely freaked that they ran screaming into the shadows—victims of Vic Wingate's psychedelic-laced candy. Terry could smell the drugs in them, could smell how it flavored and distorted their sweat. He ignored them as he ran.

Around him the people of the town—of *the* town, no longer *his* town—died in the thousands. Corpses littered the ground or slumped over wrecked cars or drifted through the night with red smiling mouths. Fires burned everywhere, raging in some places with inferno fury. The air was thick with the mingled smells of smoke and blood.

No one tried to stop him as he ran. A few people saw him and ran screaming into the darkness, the very sight of him tearing apart what little sanity they still possessed after the explosions and the mass killings. One or two just stared at him with eyes that were filled with nothing, reflecting the emptiness of minds blown dark by too much horror.

The pale-faced ones shrank away, yielding to him, letting him pass.

Through the city streets he ran on two feet, even though those feet were not structured for the job, but if he kept his weight far forward, then the very speed at which he moved kept him balanced, and every once in a while he would tap the ground with his hands to steady himself. As the burning stores and houses thinned out and he broke out into the clearer, cleaner country air, he finally dropped to all fours and ran along at an amazing speed, his powerful muscles rippling and bunching under his tough new hide. Moonlight shone down on him, sparkling on the silvery tips of each of the hairs in the fur along his shoulders and back. His claws left crescent-shaped divots in the blacktop as he raced along the dark road.

Far overhead a flock of night birds had begun to follow him. They began riding the lofty thermals, but he was moving too fast for that, and so they dropped lower and began flapping their ragged wings to keep pace.

Mile after mile unfolded beneath him as he ran, and the manor houses gave way to the long stretches of farmland. Vast avenues of blighted corn and wheat rustled in the breeze; knobbed rows of diseased pumpkins watched as what was no longer Terry Wolfe passed on its way to Dark Hollow.

(5)

There was no Pine Deep Police Department during the Red Wave. By the time the first explosions had rocked the town, the only living members of the department were Gus Bernhardt, Ginny—who ran the switchboard—and Jim Polk.

Now it was just Polk. Well, maybe Tow-Truck Eddie, too, but Polk didn't care much about him either way.

The volume of the screams was fading now as the tide turned from the hundreds with Ruger against the thousands in town for the Festival, to the thousands with Ruger hunting the hundreds who were trying to flee. The math was working out the way Vic had planned. All of the explosions had gone off. The bridges were gone, along with the power plant, the gas lines, the cable, phone lines, cell towers, all the police cars, and the TV and radio stations. All exactly according to plan, and it was getting a bit quieter in town—not that Sergeant Polk noticed. When it had all started he'd clamped earphones over his head and waited it out with the Grateful Dead screaming in his ears. He thought the irony would amuse him, but it just made his stomach feel worse.

He sat in Gus Bernhardt's oversize swivel chair, crossed ankles propped on the chief's desk, a nearly empty bottle of Wild Turkey cradled against his crotch. On the computer table that jutted out from the desk, Polk's pistol sat gleaming in the light from a pair of candles. The gun was fully loaded with hollow points and ready to hand. He'd already replaced the two rounds he'd used on Ginny. Her plump body lay sprawled under the desk, but some of her was splashed all over the front of the dispatcher's console. As for Gus, the vampires had taken him in the first minute. The fat bastard probably fed a dozen of them.

Polk looked up at the clock. 7:33 P.M. Just a little over three hours since it all started.

He took a long pull on the Wild Turkey and stared out the windows at the havoc. Some people still ran by screaming, some in Halloween costumes, some in funeral dress with horror-movie faces. In the distance, against the darkness, he could see the glow of fire molded around the soft edges of the twisting column of smoke rising from the phone company building. The front window of the chief's office had a long jagged crack that ran crookedly from upper left to lower right. Polk had watched in fascination as the original blasts had sent that crack skittering across the glass. He was amazed that it held, even when the power station blew. It still might go, he figured, since the wind was picking up outside. He knew that he should move, that he was dangerously close to the glass, but he just sat there and took another sip of bourbon.

Out of the corner of his eye he saw the doorknob jiggle, and he turned to watch Jennifer Whitelaw from the CVS down the block desperately trying to work the handle. There was a long line of blood trickling down from her scalp and it ran alongside of her nose. A few drops had splashed onto her blouse. She beat on the door and even kicked it. Polk watched as her face changed from hope to confusion to anger and then to a revelatory mask of accusation. Then she was gone. A white hand appeared out of the gloom and snatched her away. Two tiny droplets of blood had flown from her face as she was jerked back and they splattered against the glass. The splashes were head-high to the door and Polk thought they looked like red, condemning eyes.

He drank the bourbon.

By his crossed heels was the thick manila envelope Vic Wingate had dropped off that afternoon. Fifty thousand bloodstained dollars in tight bundles. Another big chunk of Ruger's drug money. Polk had counted the money and as he turned over each bill he saw at least one drop of old, dried blood. Fifty thousand dollars, and a half-pound bag of coke to sweeten the deal. And the note: FOR SERVICES RENDERED. Vic's little joke.

Vic had smirked as he handed it over, had given Polk a neat little bow and a sly wink, like he was giving a dollar to a kid, sending him off to the movies so he could screw his big sister. That kind of a sly wink.

The bottle was almost empty and so was Polk. He nursed the whiskey and listened to the Dead, watching the dying outside. Beside him the pistol ached to be held, it longed to be kissed. There should always be a last kiss, he reflected, after you've collected your blood money.

(6)

Tonight Pine Deep's Dead End Drive-In lived up to its name. Every single car was an island of death. Shattered windows, doors standing open, upholstery splashed with blood, the gravel around the cars littered with shreds of torn clothing, cracked eyeglasses, broken cell phones.

Pine Deep's nature made the slaughter so successful; the tourists believed what was happening was a joke, all part of the show. By the time the truth of it was impossible to deny, half of the them were dead; the rest fled and were hunted.

Perhaps because he was on a stage and had a different perspective on the events as they unfolded, or perhaps he'd been in too many movies that dealt with this exact sort of thing, Ken Foree alone managed to keep his head. He knew the difference between stunts and real violence. When he witnessed the slaughter he knew that this was no stunt. He didn't know what it was, but it was real.

As one of the mindless Dead Heads began crawling over the edge of the stage, Foree snatched up the heavy microphone stand and swung the weighted steel base with every ounce of strength he possessed. The disk-shaped base crushed the creature's skull. As it fell dead, he leapt down from the stage and charged the second creature.

When that one went down he started shouting for the patrons to run, and when those who could still move got into gear he led them in a mad dash to the projection booth. He was able to cram eighty people in the concrete pillbox. That's all that could make it before he had to slam the steel door in the face of five more of the shambling killers. The projection window had metal shutters, and Foree slammed them shut and threw the slide bolts.

The creatures beat on the door and screamed in rage and hunger. The people packed inside screamed, huddling down in the dark, pressing their hands to their ears.

The person nearest him clutched his sleeve. "Can they get in?" she begged.

"No," he said, "no, they can't get in." He hoped he wasn't lying.

(7)

Crow pointed his shotgun directly at Ruger's grinning face.

"Go ahead, hotshot—splatter me and you splatter Junior here." Ruger gave the kid a fierce shake.

Beside Crow, LaMastra braced himself against the wall and aimed down the stairs at the four vampires who clustered at the lower landing. Five others milled hungrily behind Ruger. The trap was a good one and they had walked right into it.

"Well, well," murmured Ruger, "this is a hoot. I'm so happy to see you I could shit daffodils."

The child, a thin boy of about nine, struggled against the

white hands that held him, but he might as well have been trying to work loose from iron shackles. The killer kept one arm wrapped around the kid's body, pinning his arms; with the other hand he traced little lines across the boy's slender throat. The kid winced and wriggled helplessly.

"Let him go," Crow said, twitching the barrel of the shotgun.

"Sure, I'll get right on that."

"Let him go and then you can have me."

Ruger shook his head. "I already *have* you, asshole. Both of you. And soon as I'm done kicking your ass I'm going to go upstairs and take that broke-nose bitch of yours. Oh, don't look surprised. You think I don't know she's here? I can smell that piece of farm-girl snatch a mile off."

"I'm going to kill you," Crow said softly.

"What . . . again?" Everyone laughed at that except the living. "Unless you haven't figured it out by now, dickweed, you *can't* kill me."

"Third time's the charm, Karl. Let the boy go, then you and me can dance a bit."

"Or," Ruger said, enjoying this, "we could just tear your arms off and beat you with them. Really, no joke. We've already done that tonight. Twice."

"Three times, boss," someone said, and they all cracked up again.

"Crow . . ." LaMastra said under his breath.

"Tell me something, Karl . . . what's with all the fireworks and shit? What's the point? This part of some bullshit evil master plan? You think tearing down a small town like this makes you—what, some kind of vampire king or some shit?"

Ruger pretended to be interested. "Actually we do have a master plan. And, funnily enough, it's actually pretty darned evil."

"Oh? Like what? You take over Pine Deep and then you turn it into a vampire tourist trap?"

"No, dumbass, we take over Pine Deep and then we take over the whole shitting world."

Now it was Crow's turn to laugh. "Yeah, right. And when the

National Guard start dropping napalm on your ass, what then? You going to hide behind a kid then, too, you cowardly piece of shit?"

Ruger's smile didn't falter. "Don't worry, boy, we have plans for that. The Man has plans for everything."

"Yeah, yeah, yeah, whatever. Put the kid down."

"Blow me." Ruger gave the kid's throat a quick squeeze; the kid winced again, his face screwed up; he bared his teeth as he fought against the killer's iron grip.

"Crow . . ." LaMastra said again.

"Don't be a pussy, Karl. You're supposed to be the über-tough guy . . . put the kid down."

"Sorry, can't do it."

Ruger pushed the kid forward and took a step down toward Crow. Below, the vampires moved up a couple of steps, smiling at how Ruger was playing this.

LaMastra flinched away from them so that he and Crow were tight back-to-back.

"Rock and a hard place," mocked the killer. "You can't kill the kid, and that popgun can't kill me."

"Don't be too sure," Crow said, putting some edge to his voice.

Ruger's smile flickered just the faintest bit. "Well, well, you think you have some kind of secret weapon to use against the big bad vampires. Oooo . . . scary. Look at me ready to piss myself I'm so scared." He jostled the kid as he took another step. "Let me guess . . . silver bullets?"

"I'm not that dumb, Karl."

"You're not that smart. So . . . what is it? Holy water? I wash my dick with holy water."

"Take a sniff, jackass."

The killer's smile flickered again, longer this time. The other vampires shifted uncomfortably, and still they all took another step down toward Crow.

"Yeah, well, you still can't shoot, smartass." Ruger lifted the kid off the floor to provide maximum coverage.

"Watch me," Crow said.

And he fired the shotgun.

Ruger was startled, but he was fast. So incredibly fast. He watched Crow's eyes, saw the tightening of his finger, and then he threw the boy at Crow as he dodged sideways. The blast caught the kid in the chest and flung his small body backward against the other vampires. Ruger ducked back behind one of the others, shoving two of them into the path of Crow's next shot. Then he was gone up the stairs.

"NO!" screamed LaMastra as he watched the child's body tumble down the stairs. The vampires stared, as stunned as the detective was, but Crow jacked a round and the sound of it broke the tableau. He fired and the closest vampire was hurled back against the other, his face torn away. Garlic-soaked pellets hit the creatures behind them and they screamed in fear and agony.

Crow spun around and fired past LaMastra down the stairs. "Vince! Snap the hell out of it! Kill the bastards!" He fired again and that broke the detective's trance. They both opened up as the vampires, caught between Ruger's orders and the reality that these men had weapons that could kill their kind, hesitated. That was enough for Crow. In the narrow confines of the stairwell the two shotguns cut them to ribbons.

Then it was over except for the echoes of thunder that rolled up and down the concrete tower. Crow sagged back and sat down hard on the blood-slick steps, not caring that he sat between the outstretched legs of a dead monster. LaMastra stood over him, chest heaving as he stared at the carnage. He shifted the shotgun to his left hand, grabbed Crow by the front of the shirt, jerked him to his feet, and slammed him against the wall with such force that Crow felt the world explode in a blinding fireworks display.

"*You bastard!*" he screamed. "You sick murderous bastard!" With each word he banged Crow against the blood-splattered wall.

"Vince . . . !"

"I should have let that son of a bitch kill you!"

"Vince!"

"You shot that kid!"

Crow had just about enough of it. As LaMastra hauled him forward and began to slam him back again, Crow crunched the stock of the shotgun hard against the side of LaMastra's ribs and at the same time pivoted his whole body sharply around. The speed of the pivot and the force of the blow spun LaMastra into the wall; then it was the sergeant who crashed into the wall, and Crow brought the barrel of his shotgun up under LaMastra's chin hard enough to lift the detective onto his toes.

"The kid was already dead, you stupid shit!"

LaMastra blinked. "W—what?"

"He was a vampire! He was part of Ruger's trap. Christ, do you think I'd actually kill a kid, for Christ's sake?" He stepped back, resisting the urge to butt-stroke LaMastra with the shotgun stock, but he knew that would only be transference for what he was feeling.

"How . . . how—?"

Crow pointed with the shotgun at the twisted, broken corpse. "Don't you pay attention? The kid had teeth like a rattlesnake."

LaMastra turned and looked down. The kid was in a broken sprawl, his mouth open. The fangs hadn't yet completely retracted into the gums.

"I . . . didn't. I was looking down the stairs, man—"

"Save it. We have bigger fish to fry." Crow said. "Just reload and let's go find Val."

Chapter 43

They crept up the outside of the building like roaches, scuttling up along the brickwork in the dark, silent, patient, fired by hunger and purpose. Five of them went up—the lightest of the pack, the ones with the strongest fingernails, the ones who could dig into the cement between the bricks. Four more waited below, smiling up through the firelit darkness.

When the climbers paused at one window, one of the watchers below cupped his hands around his mouth and softly called, "Next one up."

The five climbers looked up to the big window fifteen feet above them. There was a boom and a flash. A gunshot. Another, and another.

The climbers grinned and as one they reached up for the next brick, and the next.

(2)

LaMastra led the way up the stairs, whipping the shotgun barrel around every corner, whispering "Clear!" at each bend. The tower was littered with debris as if it belonged in a town where there had been strife and warfare for months rather than hours. Torn clothing, nameless junk, broken glass, and blood. In smears and splashes it was everywhere. The copper stink of it was making them sick; the higher they climbed the fresher and stronger the smell.

They were both sweating heavily and breathing like marathon runners. The gunshots still seemed to echo in their eardrums, and their shoulders were swollen and bruised from the recoiling guns, but need and fear and rage kept them going.

The fourth-floor door was ajar, blocked from closing by an empty shoe. LaMastra shifted over and crouched, aiming through the opening. He nodded to Crow, who carefully opened the door. They could see the nursing station forty feet down the hall. There were bodies on the floor, but nothing moved in their line of sight. Crow stepped out first with LaMastra covering him, and moved over to the station. A nurse was sprawled on the counter, her throat torn out. Farther back in the large cubicle was a man in surgical scrubs. He had a bullet hole in his forehead.

Crow leaned closer and whispered, "That's the nurse who helped stitch up Saul, and this guy here's Gaither Carby. Local farmer. His son Tyler's a friend of Mike's."

"Val?" whispered LaMastra.

"Don't know."

There were still sounds around the corner, down near Weinstock's room. A whimpering cry, a pleading voice, and laughter.

They looked at each other, nodded, and just as they started to make their play a voice bellowed out: "Freeze! Police!"

They spun around and Officer Eddie Oswald, his uniform torn, his limbs streaked with blood, stood wide-legged in the fire tower doorway holding his pistol in a two-hand grip.

(3)

Jim O'Rear rushed into the Scream Queen tent just in time to see Debbie Rochon run by, screaming. When he saw what was chasing her he almost screamed himself.

There were two of them after her, both of them big, both of them with bloody mouths. The inside of the tent was a madhouse. People fought together on the ground, their thrashing legs kicking over the folding chairs. One of Crow's pals, Dave

Kramer, was using an overturned table to block the attackers long enough for some of the patrons to crawl out from under the skirts of the tent. In the middle of all this, some of the tourists stood looking at colors in the air no one else could see; one was sitting cross-legged on the stage pushing candy corn into his drooling mouth as his eyes jumped and rolled; a few had completely freaked out and were yipping like dogs and batting away at invisible attackers. At least a dozen of the customers were slumped in death, their throats torn to red tatters, their eyes seeing nothing at all.

None of it made sense. It was insane.

There was a cop there, but he was not trying to stop the carnage. Instead he was bending Brinke over a table, pushing her chin up to expose the tender flesh of her throat.

"Leave her alone!" O'Rear snatched up a folding chair and crashed it down on Golub's back. The big cop fell to his knees, releasing the actress, who slid from the table, gasping.

Instantly the cop turned, hissing and showing his teeth to O'Rear.

"Holy shit!" O'Rear staggered back, horror and disbelief twisting his face.

Golub was laughing as he got to his feet. "This is going to be fun—"

O'Rear kicked him in the balls as hard as he could. It dropped Golub, supernatural or not, back down to his knees.

"You bastard!" Brinke snatched her pen off the signing table and rammed the point into Golub's neck.

The cop howled and swung a heavy backhanded blow at her that sent her flying over the table. O'Rear cursed and kicked Golub in the throat with the heavy toe of his Timberlands. It only slowed Golub for a few seconds, but it was long enough for O'Rear to reach down and grab the cop's sidearm. He racked the slide and put two in the side of his head.

Golub went down and stayed down.

O'Rear spun around, searching for Debbie. She had a folding chair in her hands and was trying to beat back the football players, but her blows did nothing more than slow them down. O'Rear settled into a shooter's stance and shot them both in the back. They barely noticed. He raised the pistol, corrected his aim, and put the next four rounds in their heads. They dropped like rocks.

"Headshots," O'Rear breathed. "Freaking headshots . . ."

He helped Brinke, who was more scared than hurt, to her feet, and they hurried over to Debbie. There were more of the football players in the tent, and Kramer was throwing chairs at them, hoping for a lucky shot. O'Rear fired as he ran and brought down three more, but it took the rest of the magazine to do it. Kramer grabbed Debbie and pulled her toward O'Rear.

"I'm out!" O'Rear threw the gun in the face of the next closest vampire and the four of them made a dash for the exit. A dozen others followed, but there was nothing more they could do for the people inside except stay alive long enough to get help.

(4)

The Pine Deep library looked like the old church it had once been. Narrow, with arched gables and a tall bell tower, it sat like an echo of the last century, parked between a New Age candle shop and a computer store.

When the killing began there were forty people in the main room, most of them kids who were listening to spooky stories read by local actor Keith Strunk. When the big explosion hit, Strunk was telling them how the clever creature F. F. Manny Thing escaped from a snorgle-beast. Then the lights went out and the windows blew inward.

Strunk did his best to keep the kids from panicking, but everyone was screaming, some in terror, some in pain. Two little girls, Helena and Rebekah, were seated in the corner with a black-and-white dog named Lady. Before anything happened Lady stood up and the hair along her spine rose as stiff and straight as a brush. She looked toward the front door and started growling very quietly. The girls dragged the dog into the corner to try and quiet her, and that saved their lives, because after the windows blew in, *they* came in, hungry and vicious.

The screams became much worse. Worse terror, deeper pain.

"Come on!" Rebekah yelled and grabbed Helena's hand and they bolted for a door set into the corner near them; Lady backed up with them, barking at the snarling things that moved through the room.

Helena pulled the door open and they ducked inside, pulling Lady with them. Rebekah slammed the door and shot the bolt and for a terrifying minute they stood there at the top of the cellar stairs, listening to sounds. Dreadful sounds. Wet and awful.

When they heard something bump against the door, something that sounded like an elbow or a knee but with a limp, sliding quality, they ran down into the darkness of the basement, trying not to scream, trying not to cry.

When the library had bought the old church property most of the inside of the building had been renovated, but not the basement. Used for storing books and old furniture, it was a warren of stacks of boxes and bags, but even in the dark the girls knew every inch of it. They'd played hide-and-seek here, had invented games of being archaeologists in ancient tombs—and in this they weren't far off the mark. Beneath the floor of the backmost closet, under a layer of concrete poured by accident during an earlier renovation when the church passed from Baptist to Methodist hands in the 1970s, the centuries-old crypts had been inadvertently hidden. Now that room contained disused file cabinets filled with paperwork no one could even identify. That's where the little girls went with their dog. They ran in there, stifling their sobs, trying not to think about what was happening upstairs to their friends.

Helena, the taller and stronger of the two, slammed the door and began pushing at the filing cabinets. She was seven and a half and her little body was tough, but not tough enough—not until Rebekah realized what she was doing and threw her weight into it. Between them it was just enough, and the first cabinet slid twenty inches and thudded against the door. They found another and pushed that, and another. It took them fifteen minutes, and all the time the sounds of mayhem continued from above, and Lady kept growling.

When there was nothing else they could push in front of the door, the two girls sank down with their backs to one cabinet, holding each other, and they both broke down into helpless, hopeless sobs.

Much later, when the newspapers were telling the story of what happened in Pine Deep on the night that became known worldwide as "Hellnight," there would be a number of articles written about two little girls and their dog who hid among the dead and as a result got to live.

(5)

"Val! I heard shots," Mike said. "Listen."

"Crow!"

They crowded as close to the door as the barricade would allow, Mike and Val pressing against Jonatha and Newton, with Weinstock behind them. Huddled together they could each feel the trembles rippling through each other.

"I think I heard two guns at the same time," Val said.

Mike closed his eyes, trying to focus on his hearing even though his ears rang from the shots Val had fired through the door. The crawly sensation was constant now and he knew that there were many of them out there. Then the sensation spiked up like someone jabbed a hot electric wire in the back of his neck; he stiffened.

"Mike," Weinstock said behind him, "what is it?"

"I feel—"

His eyes flew wide and he tried to spin around, but Weinstock was pressing forward too hard. A warning was rising to Mike's lips and then suddenly Weinstock was whipped backward away from him. White hands seemed to appear out of nowhere and they snatched Weinstock, tearing at his skin.

"NO!" Mike screamed, bringing up his shotgun, but there

was no clear shot; Jonatha and Newton seemed to turn in slow motion, but Val lunged forward, grabbing Weinstock's hand as he fought against the four vampires that had him. A fifth was climbing through the empty window frame—a boy the same age and size as Mike—his friend Brandon.

Val fired two shots and one of the vampires went down, but the others were moving backward so fast and Weinstock was flailing too much. Mike leapt forward and grabbed the doctor by the hand.

"Help me!" Weinstock and Mike screamed it at the same moment. A vampire clamped his hands around Weinstock's throat and Val fired again; the round clipped Weinstock's shoulder, but it also caught the vampire in the throat. Weinstock shrieked in pain and suddenly there was blood on his throat and chest.

They were at the window now. Jonatha and Newton beat at them with their fists, Val hammered with the butt of her pistol. She leaned over Weinstock as the whole crowd of them, human and inhuman, hung teetering on the windowsill. She jammed her pistol into a white face and fired, jammed it into a belly and fired. Mike dropped his gun in order to use both hands. Weinstock kept screaming and screaming.

Val shot at Brandon and he fell backward, either hit or falling from loss of balance. He plunged into the darkness.

And then it was over. Two vampires lay dead on the floor. Two others, dead for sure, had been blasted out the window. Mike held Weinstock's hand, and Jonatha and Newton had handfuls of the doctor's pajamas. They clung to him, pulling him back from the abyss.

"Saul!" Val said, casting around for something to use as a bandage for his bleeding throat. "He's hurt—Newt, Jonatha, help me get him to the bed. Mike, watch the window."

Mike snatched up his weapon and went back to the window, but the assault was over. Two bodies lay on the ground four stories below, but there was no sign of anyone else. He looked up and sideways, just to be sure, but nothing. His friend Brandon's body was not among the dead and Mike thought he could hear Brandon's laughter on the wind.

"Christ, he's bleeding bad," Newton said. Jonatha started tearing off pieces of sheet for Val, but as soon as she pressed them against Weinstock's throat they became soaked with blood.

"I think they got the artery," Val said. Her face was spattered with blood. "How do I stop it? Saul! How do I stop it?"

Panic was in Weinstock's eyes and he kept trying to speak, but every time he opened his mouth all that came out was blood.

"Saul . . . what do I do?" she begged. The wad of torn sheeting was soaked; blood ran down her wrist. "Oh, God, Saul . . . please . . . *help me,* please!"

The panic in his eyes was fading now, flowing out of him as the blood flowed. He tried to speak, tried to say something, and Val bent close, listening with all her strength for some clue, some magic trick of medicine that he could give her.

All he said was, "Rachel."

His eyes stared at Val and maybe in that last moment he was seeing the face of his wife, and maybe the faces of his children; he did not see Val's face, or the faces of the others who clustered around him, each face shocked as white as the faces of the monsters who had done this. Saul Weinstock stared through them and through the walls and through the night with a fixity of vision so intense and so pure that he might have looked on the face of God.

"No, no, no, no!" Val pleaded, fumbling under the bandages for some trace of a pulse, finding none, finding nothing. Weinstock's body seemed to relax back, the tension and fear of everything that was happening leaving him. Val bent over him, hugging him to her chest, crying so hard that it shook the whole bed.

Then she threw her head back and screamed.

Chapter 44

"**P**ut the guns down and put your hands above your heads."
Crow and LaMastra both had their shotguns aimed at
Tow-Truck Eddie. Everyone else in that part of the wing was
either dead or dying.

"Put them down!"

"Not going to happen, Eddie," Crow said.

"Stand down, Officer," growled LaMastra. "We're all on the
same team here."

Oswald's blue eyes cut back and forth between them. His face
was florid, his eyes bright. One sleeve of his shirt was torn and
there were long scratches carved into the sculpted muscles of his
arms. "Crow . . . I don't know who's who or what's what right
now. I just know that everyone in this town has gone crazy. People I know—people I go to *church* with—have been *killing* each
other!" He took a step forward—half threatening, half pleading.
"I saw the organist from my church, Cubby Sanders, a man I've
known since I was five years old, I saw him bite the throat out
of the reporter from Fox News. He killed him and . . ." He
made a sick sound and swallowed several times. "He killed him
and drank his blood." A tear broke from his left eye and rolled
slowly down toward his chin. "I don't understand."

Crow lowered his shotgun, then reached out and pushed
LaMastra's barrel down.

"Look, Eddie . . . I don't how to begin explaining this to
you, but there are monsters in Pine Deep. Vampires."

Eddie lowered his gun, too. "Vampires. God save our souls . . ."

"Who else is with you?" asked LaMastra. "Where's Chief Bernhardt? How many men can we count on?"

The big man shook his head. "They're all dead. Except . . . except those that are with *them*. I saw Shirley O'Keefe trying to kill a child, a little boy. I . . . shot her. In the chest."

"She didn't die, did she?" Crow asked, stepping closer.

"No. I had to shoot her again and again. The *evil* in her was so strong that she didn't want to die."

"How many of them are there?" asked LaMastra, looking up and down the hall. "Do you know that, Officer? How many of these things are we facing?"

Eddie straightened. "The gates of Hell have opened and the host of Satan walks the earth."

"Oh brother," LaMastra said softly.

"How many, Eddie," Crow insisted.

"Thousands," Eddie said dully. "There are thousands of them." Then his eyes brightened. "But I know who is behind this. If we can find him . . . and *kill* him, then Hell will recall its armies."

Crow looked at LaMastra, who shrugged. "Yeah, we know, too, and if you want to kill that evil son of a bitch, then we're all on the same team here."

"Amen to that," LaMastra agreed.

Down the hall, behind one of the doors, gunfire erupted.

Crow spun around. "Val!"

(2)

BK led the way and Billy Christmas brought up the rear; between them were over a hundred customers and staff. BK had a heavy tree branch in his hands, the jagged end thick with blood. Billy had a piece of rebar he'd uprooted from a fence line. Fewer than a dozen of their charges carried weapons. Peppered through the group were customers who had eaten some of the candy corn; these were the only ones in the group who didn't look scared. A few them even sang happy, trippy songs; some were crying and jabbering in invented languages.

"Incoming!" Billy yelled. "On your three."

BK spun to his right as a group of figures rushed at them from the shadows. He put himself between them and his group, club raised and ready. The lead figure in the other group had a chair leg. Everyone froze.

"BK . . . ?" asked the leader of the other group.

"Jim?"

Jim O'Rear stepped out of the dense shadows beneath a big oak. Behind him Brinke and Debbie fanned out; each of them had clubs. Kramer was at the end of the line, herding the group forward.

"What the hell is going on here?" Brinke asked as Billy trotted up.

"Christ if I know."

"I think it's something in the water," Debbie said. "Drugs or something."

"Maybe." BK looked over the newcomers and saw that some of their party were showing the same dazed detachment. He caught Billy's eye; Billy gave a small shake of his head. Drugs may account for some of it, but some of what they'd seen could not be explained away by drugs. No way.

BK pointed up the hill. "We're making for the barn. Two doors, plenty of tools. We can hole up there."

O'Rear nodded. "Outstanding."

The groups merged together, friends seeking out friends and giving hugs; strangers embracing the way victims of a shared catastrophe will. The night around them seemed to be expanding—there were fewer screams and they were farther away.

Debbie had her head cocked to listen. "I think it's . . . stopping."

"God, I hope so," BK said. "But let's get the hell out of the open. Jim, left flank, Kramer on my right. Billy, watch our backs. Come on—let's go!"

They started running, heading toward the barn, each of them praying that would be the end of it.

(3)

"Shhh," Foree said, holding a finger to his lips, "let me listen."

He pressed his ear to the steel door of the projection booth. The terrible screams that had torn the night for the last two hours had quieted. The woman who had first asked him if the monsters could get in still huddled close to him. Her name was Linda—a retired phys ed teacher who had come to hear Foree speak because she had gone to see the original *Dawn of the Dead* with her husband nearly thirty years ago; now she was trapped in the utter blackness of the booth with the star of the film, and everything was so surreal that she felt like she was in a dream. She touched his arm.

"You . . . you're not going to open the door, are you?" Her voice was filled with appalling fear.

He reached for her in the dark, found her shoulder, gave it a reassuring squeeze. "Don't worry, I'm not opening that door until I know damn sure that the cavalry has arrived. I want to hear bugles blowing."

She leaned her head against his arm, an act entirely devoid of flirtation. It was based entirely on the need to believe in the solidity of hope. Foree stroked her hair, calming her the way he would soothe a frightened child. The booth was so intensely dark that all that was left to the cowering survivors was patience and prayer.

(4)

"Anything in there?"

"Lotta corpses."

The vampire who had once been a real estate salesman opened the door to the lecture hall so his companion, who had once been the assistant football coach at Pinelands College, could look inside. The room was awash in blood. It streaked the walls, pooled on the floors, glistened on the faces and bodies of the dead people who lay scattered on the floor or slumped in chairs.

"Someone had fun," said the real estate man. "Looks like eighty, ninety kills. Shame we missed it."

The coach smiled. "The cleanup guys should be here soon, then we'll have eighty or ninety more playing for the home team."

"Works for me. C'mon, there's still time to hunt before the ritual. I'm still hungry."

Grinning like schoolkids, they closed the door and headed out to the campus grounds, where screams and shouts still filled the air.

It was at least five minutes before a voice said, "Everyone stay down."

One of the slaughtered bodies moved, first raising his head, which moved quite well despite the gaping ruin that was his throat, then getting to his feet. He surveyed the room. There were eighty-seven bodies, but only fifty of them were dead. The others just looked it.

He moved quietly to the door, listened, opened it and looked out, then closed and locked it. "Okay," he said crisply, "everyone up. We have to move fast."

Thirty-seven murder victims stood up. All of them looked terrified, but in each of their faces was a spark of hope. The trick had worked. When the attack started the killings had been horrendous. The attackers swarmed in and there had been no warning, no challenge, no hesitation . . . just slaughter. Panic swept the room and the attackers used that, herding the people back toward the corners, cutting off their lines of escape, killing and moving to the next person packed into the corner.

Then one man—the one who now stood by the door—turned all that around. He grabbed a hot soldering iron from his worktable and had leapt at one of the killers, swinging the burning needle over and down onto the back of the monster as he bent over a woman to drink from her throat. The creature screamed once and then went limp. When a second monster saw this and closed on him, the man ripped the soldering iron out of the dead creature's skull and went straight for the new-comer's eye socket.

Battles sometimes turn like that. A rout becomes a rally when one person takes a stand and shows how to kill the enemy that everyone else thought was impervious. Instead of a dozen ter-rorizing several dozen, the survivors became the attackers. One to one the creatures were too strong, but when five or six peo-ple tackled them, the physics of overwhelming mass and mo-mentum kicked in. It wasn't an easy win, and the fifty-nine that had started the counterattack had been stripped down to thirty-seven by the time the last killer went down. Thirty-seven plus the man with the soldering iron.

He tried to lead them outside, but the campus was a war zone. So, he herded his small army back inside and came up with a plan.

Tom Savini had made a career out of making people look dead, look like victims, look like monsters had been at them. He was here in Pine Deep to lecture on that very subject. He had everything to hand. There was enough real blood to reinforce the illusion, and though he had to cajole, browbeat, and, more than once, actually deck one of the survivors to keep them from losing their heads and to encourage cooperation, in the end they all followed his lead.

While Savini was painting wounds on a grad student, the young woman started to cry. "This is real . . . isn't it?"

He paused and searched her eyes, then smiled. "I've been to 'Nam and I've spent my life in the movies. Nothing's real."

She gripped his wrist. "Thank you," she said, her voice low and urgent.

Savini glanced at the door, then back to her. "Thank me when this is over."

"You got it."

(5)

Crow pounded his fist on the door. "Val . . . VAL!"

LaMastra and Tow-Truck Eddie had his back, both of them facing outward to check the hall. The light was bad and half of the emergency bulbs had been smashed. As Crow beat and kicked the door, LaMastra squinted and brought up his shotgun.

"Crow . . . we got company."

"Crow! Is that you?" Her voice was muffled, but it was Val.

"Baby, it's Vince and me. Open the door."

There was noise and the squeal of something being dragged and then the door flew open. Val was there, completely drenched in blood, her face pale, her eyes dark.

For just a moment—for one terrible slice of time—Crow thought that she had been taken, that she had been consumed by the terror; but then she flew into his arms, and the warmth of her, the heat of her tears, the firm and full-blooded reality of her told him the truth. He pulled her close and kissed her bloody face and lips.

"I told you I'd come back for you, baby."

"Oh, God, Crow . . . it's been so awful."

"We got company!" LaMastra said again and he broke their moment by firing into the shadows. Something screamed and fell back into the darkness.

Crow and Val brought up their guns and the others in the room tried to crowd into the doorway, which is when the big man standing to Crow's left turned around and looked into the room and locked eyes with Mike Sweeney.

"No!" Mike cried and staggered back a step.

"The Beast!" hissed Eddie. "Crow, there he is! There's the monster who has opened the gates of Hell!"

Crow looked the wrong way first and saw nothing in the hallway, and then he turned and saw Eddie pointing his gun into the room, right at Mike. He saw the look on Eddie's face and knew he was going to shoot, so he let go of Val and slammed Eddie's arm against the doorjamb. The gun fired and the bullet missed Mike's head by inches.

LaMastra grabbed Eddie by the collar and Crow shoved his chest and they hurled him out into the hallway. Eddie slipped on blood and went down hard, sliding five feet on his ass. LaMastra kicked the gun out of his hand and screwed the hot barrel of his Roadblocker into Eddie's temple.

"Don't fucking move," LaMastra warned.

"Mike, what's going on? Crow asked. "Val, somebody . . . what's this shit?"

Mike pressed past Jonatha and Newton. "Crow . . . he's the one that's been chasing me on the road. He's the one I told you about."

"Are you sure?"

"He's sure,"Val said. "He told us all about it. Eddie even came into the store once."

"He's the Beast of the Apocalypse!" Eddie looked pleadingly at LaMastra. "He's the one responsible for all of this. You have to let me—"

"Crow . . . ?" LaMastra asked.

"Keep him there. Val, Mike, tell me what's going on. Make it fast."

They told him a very abbreviated version of what Mike had learned from the Bone Man. They both spoke loud enough for Eddie to hear. While they spoke Crow became aware of Mike's eyes, and a chill rippled up his spine.

"Holy shit," he said. He glanced at LaMastra. "Vince?"

"You call the play, man. I'm not emotionally invested in this bozo. Just say the word."

Crow turned to Eddie and squatted down. "You heard what Val and Mike just said. You got fifteen seconds to give me a reason not to let Vince paint your brains all over the floor."

"I am the Sword of God." He said it as if it explained everything.

"And you think this kid is the Antichrist?"

"He *is*."

LaMastra nudged him with the shotgun. "One twitch of the finger, Crow, and we're done with this shit."

Val came over and knelt down. "Eddie, I want you to listen to me. Mike is not the Antichrist or any other kind of evil. He's an innocent boy who is as much a victim of all of this as we are. You've been lied to by Ubel Griswold, over and over again."

"No! Satan is the Father of Lies and—"

Val slapped him across the face. "Listen to me, Eddie Oswald; if Mike Sweeney is evil, then you're a dead man." She straightened and turned to Mike. "Mike . . . kill him."

Mike said, "What?"

"Go on, kill him. If you're the goddamned Antichrist, then kill this fool, so we can get the hell out of here."

Mike stood there, holding his shotgun loosely in his hands. "No, I—I mean, can't we just tie him up or something?"

"Some Antichrist," LaMastra muttered, mostly for Eddie's benefit.

Mike came over and gently pushed Crow and Val aside. He knelt down in front of Eddie.

"Careful, kid," said LaMastra, then to Eddie he said, "And you behave."

Mike laid his shotgun down. "Mr. Oswald . . . when you were in the store the other day you came looking for me, didn't you? You thought it was me, but then you came and met me and I could tell that you weren't sure. Well, I have to tell you that I don't give a rat's ass if you live or die. I really don't. You've been trying to kill me for a month now, and I didn't do anything to you to deserve it. Everything in my life is shit. Everything. My mom's a vampire and my dad . . . well, my dad is the kind of guy you *should* be going after. If you were really on some kind of holy mission to rid the world of evil, then you should be standing with us rather than against us." He leaned closer. "I could kill you. They'd let me. They'd do it for me if I asked."

"Damn skippy," agreed LaMastra.

"Our friends have been dying. My best friend, Brandon, tried to kill me just five minutes ago. I'm probably going to die sometime tonight; and if not tonight, then sometime soon. So, I don't have a lot to lose."

Eddie's eyes kept trying to meet the stare of Mike's goldrimmed red-blue eyes, and each time they fell away.

"Look at me," Mike said.

Eddie looked at the floor.

"I said *look* at me."

It took visible effort, but Eddie finally raised his eyes to meet—and hold—Mike's stare.

"I have every reason to kill you. No one will say 'boo.' I have every reason to kill you, but one."

Eddie licked his lips. "Wh—what's that?"

"Because I'm not who you think I am."

"You're not a little boy. You're not—"

"Human? No, I think I left that kind of thing behind. I'm born from monsters, Eddie, but I'm not a monster. Look me in the eyes."

Eddie looked for as long as he could.

Mike leaned over, stretched, and picked Eddie's pistol off the floor. He offered it butt first to the big man.

"Hey, kid, what the hell you doing?" LaMastra barked, but Mike shook his head.

"Put the gun down," he said to the detective. "Please, just put it down. I want Mr. Oswald to see that he's free to make up his own mind."

LaMastra looked at Crow, who hesitated and then nodded; LaMastra moved the barrel away and down, but he didn't like doing it.

"Mr. Oswald," Mike said, "I'm giving you a chance here to do the right thing. We're fighting against these monsters. We could use your help."

Tow-Truck Eddie stared at him, wide-eyed for what seemed like an eternity, and everyone could see the warring emotions as they passed like clouds across his face. His eyes were watery, his lips trembled.

"I . . . I'm sorry," he said weakly. Mike smiled at him. "I'm so sorry!"

And he whipped his pistol up toward Mike and fired.

It was Willard Fowler Newton who saved Mike's life. Why him and not the others was a question none of the survivors could ever adequately explain. It was as if an invisible hand shoved him hard from behind and he lurched into Mike and knocked him out of the way even as Oswald was pulling the trigger.

Then the world exploded as LaMastra, Crow, and Val all fired simultaneously, each from point-blank range, all of them shooting to kill. Oswald's body was plucked off the ground and torn to red rags.

Then everyone was crowded around Mike, who lay half inside Weinstock's room.

"Mike!" Crow saw blood on him and started pulling at Mike's shirt, looking for the wound. But there was nothing.

"I'm okay," he said, pushing himself up to a sitting position. "He missed."

"Thank God!" Val turned to Newton, who had fallen down and was sitting against the wall. "You saved his life!"

"Finally a hero," Newton said with a small smile, and then he pitched over on his side as blood poured from his chest.

"Christ," Crow said, "Newt's hit."

"No!" cried Jonatha, trying to push past, but Val pushed her back as she and Crow tore at Newton's clothes. They found the entry wound high on the right side. It was well away from the heart, but it was bleeding freely. Crow pressed his palm flat on the hole.

"Mike," Crow yelled, "see if you can get Saul out here. He can tell us what to do."

When Mike didn't move, Crow looked at him. "Come on, damn it—he took that bullet for you. Move your ass!"

Val touched Crow's cheek. "Crow . . . honey . . . Saul's dead."

Crow closed his eyes—first lightly and then he squeezed them shut, not wanting to look at the world anymore.

"I'm sorry," Mike said, and it wasn't clear if he was expressing sympathy for Crow's grief or apologizing for Newton's injury.

When Crow could talk past the stricture in his throat, he said, "Jonatha, get me something to use as a compress. Towels, anything. Val, keep the pressure on right here. See, just like that." He guided her hands, then looked up to accept a folded towel from Jonatha. "Vince, see if Eddie there is wearing a belt. I need it."

With Tow-Truck Eddie's belt and the towel, Crow made a tight compress over the bullet wound. Newton was in and out of consciousness. "Jonatha, keep your eye on him. If he wakes up, don't let him move that compress, and don't let him move. There's no exit wound, so that bullet's still there. If he moves it could shift around and do damage."

He stood and walked into Weinstock's room. Val followed him and held his hand while Crow looked at his friend's body, ugly and graceless in death.

"How?" he asked, and she told him.

Crow inhaled and exhaled very deeply, as if trying to abrade his lungs. He bent over Weinstock and kissed his friend on the forehead. "I'm so sorry, man." Then he turned and pulled Val close and they just stood there, not kissing, just holding on to keep from drowning.

From the doorway, Mike said, "Crow . . . something's happening."

Crow had to tighten his mouth to respond to that, biting back everything he wanted to say, to yell.

"What is it, Mike?" Val asked.

"It's that feeling I've been getting. What Mr. Newton calls my spider-sense? It's, um, *changing*." When Crow and Val were both looking at him, he said, "The vampires—I think they're going."

Crow frowned. "Going? Going where?"

"Going to *him*."

Chapter 45

Vic wandered through the shadows of the hospital corridors looking for a living doctor or nurse, and came up empty. Most of the corpses had been revived and were gone now; the rest were the ones too badly torn up by the Dead Heads to be worth bringing back. Armless, legless, headless junk.

He heard a quiet footfall behind him and whirled, bringing his gun up. High as he was on morphine, his gun hand was still steady as a rock. Three figures came out of the darkened office, their smiling mouths rouged with blood.

"Oh," Vic said, lowering the gun. "It's you clowns."

Dixie McVey gave him a toothy grin. "We've been looking for you."

"Yeah?" Vic gave them a narrow-eyed appraisal. McVey was the only one of the three he knew; the others looked like tourists who had been impressed into service. "Why would that be?"

"Ruger said that you was hurt, that you burned yourself playing with matches or something. His words, Vic. He said for us to make sure you was looked after."

"Nice to hear he's concerned about my health. Sends three Fangers to babysit me."

McVey shrugged. "Hey, man, I'm just following orders. Ruger says jump and I'm in the air."

"Is that a fact?"

"Hey, Vic, I'm on the clock here. Ruger tells me to find you and bring you out, then that's what I'm going to do. If I'm out of line here, then tell me."

"Bring me 'out'?" He looked at the other two vampires, both of whom were giving him *the stare*. He almost laughed in their pasty faces.

"To the Hollow, man. The Ritual's probably already started. I can feel the Man calling." A dreamy look floated around in his eyes. "I got a car outside."

"Okay," said Vic brightly. "Let's go for a nice ride in the country." He gestured with his burned hand. "Lead on, McVey."

"Cool, man." McVey turned and began leading the way and the other two vampires, neither of whom had uttered a single word, fell in behind Vic. They went about ten paces and then Vic stopped.

Vic said, "Oh, wait a minute." MacVey turned to face him. "You know what I forgot?"

"What's that, man?"

"Just this," Vic said and jammed the pistol against McVey's face and pulled the trigger. The garlic-filled dum-dum punched a neat round hole beside the officer's nose and then blew the whole back of his skull off. McVey's amazed face went blank with death as he toppled backward; Vic turned and stepped back, covering the other two.

"Do you think I'm fucking *stupid*?" he shouted. "Is that it? What did Karl arrange for me? A car accident? Or maybe I was gonna fall down a flight of steps and break my neck. I know it wasn't going to be a fang job because the Man would know about that. So what was it gonna be?"

The vampires shifted and looked scared. One of them looked ready to bolt, the other just stared at the barrel, trying to work out why the gun had been able to kill one of their kind when that was supposed to be impossible.

"Car accident," one said, and the other nodded.

Vic snorted. "So, what's the deal here? You boys working for Ruger now? Is that it? You guys don't give a shit that I'm the Foreman and that I'm tight with the Man?"

"We just did what we were told. Ruger told us that the Man was through with you."

"And you *believed* that?" Vic asked with more incredulity than he felt.

"What do we care?" asked the other vampire. "We don't know you—we just do what we're told."

Vic shifted the gun to point at that vampire's face. "Tell me, son, how much do you want to live? I mean even as a piece of shit like you are, how much do you want to go on living?"

The vampires exchanged a glance. "A lot."

"Good," said Vic, and he lowered the gun. "Then from now on you do what I say. You got that?"

After a long hesitation, they nodded.

"Then come on. I think there's still some time for fun and games around here." And he thought, *I want the Man to see how I'm still part of this. Ruger's not the only one who racked up a body count for the cause.*

(2)

Val and Mike brought Crow and LaMastra quickly up to speed on everything that had happened. Crow took the news better than LaMastra did, but they both remained on their feet even with the enormity of it all.

"Then we have no choice," Crow said hollowly.

Val met his stare and the fear he felt was reflected in her eyes. She absently touched her stomach.

"We have to do it," Crow said. "We have to try."

"Yes."

LaMastra just stood there shaking his head. Not in refusal of what Crow was proposing, but in denial of a world where such things were necessary.

Crow turned toward Newton and Jonatha. The reporter was lying with his head in her lap. Newton tried to speak, but Jonatha shushed him. Over his head she gave Crow a significant look. "I think he'll be okay—the bleeding's slowed down. He can breathe, but it's hard for him to talk and he's in a lot of pain. There's no way he can go with you."

Crow knelt next to Newton. "Hey, Newt, how's things?"

The reporter raised a shaky hand and gave it a seesaw shake.

"Hey, buddy, you know what we're going to do, but listen to me—you two are out of it. Val and Vince will go with Mike and me. You two stay here and hold the fort. Jonatha, if there's anyone alive on this floor, then round them up and move them all into any room you think you can defend. We'll leave you plenty of guns and ammo. Just hole up and wait for us to get back."

Jonatha looked doubtful. "What if you don't get back?"

"Then as soon as you think it's safe, go find some way to call the State Police, the National Guard, and anyone else you can think of. They're probably on their way already anyway. If we aren't back by then, send someone to look for us in Dark Hollow. After that, you guys get as far away from this place as you can. If we don't make it back, it's 'cause we failed. If that happens, then you don't want to be within a thousand miles of here. Okay?"

They both nodded, looking scared. Crow patted Newt's leg. "Don't forget, Champ, we still have a book to write. I'm expecting to go on *Oprah* and brag about it, so let's all make sure we're around come morning."

Crow rose and joined Val, who was squatting by the open duffel bag reloading her shotgun. Her face still looked pale and sickly.

He kissed her. "How are you doing, babe?"

Her eyes were dark with damage. "About the same as you."

"You mean you're boyishly handsome, full of youthful energy, and unbelievably charming and witty?"

"No, I said that I'm about the same as you."

"Bitch."

"So they tell me." She managed a small smile as she finished loading the gun; she picked up a game pouch filled with shells and strapped it on.

"It's going to be tough," he said lamely. "You could stay here with them . . ."

She adjusted the straps. "It's been tough all along." She picked up the shotgun again and jacked a round into the breech. "Crow," she said in a voice that was a strange blend of softness and hardness, "I'm never going to let you out of my sight again."

"Fine with me."

"Are you ready?" Mike asked, and Crow turned to look up at the boy. Mike had wiped the blood off his face, but his clothes still glistened with red. Crow had tied his spare sword over Mike's shoulder and the boy was practicing drawing it. Crow was encouraged by how fast the kid was.

"Let's go," LaMastra said. "Let's kill this evil son of a bitch and have done with it."

(3)

From the womb of darkness he called out and they came to him. Tens of thousands of them, seething and scuttling in the shadows, wriggling out of holes, crawling up from forgotten wells, clawing their way out of old cellars. They swarmed into the night and raced toward Dark Hollow. He waited for them, needing them, hungry for them, willing them to come.

Into the forbidden place they swarmed. The rats came first, chittering and squeaking as they scurried on quick feet; behind them came the roaches and beetles, covering the earth like a shiny black carpet, hissing along on their million legs, crawling over each other, driven by the irresistible power of his call. Here and there were a few larger animals: stray dogs with shaggy coats, scarred farm cats, raccoons and opossums and rabid squirrels. There were a few black goats that had been born wild and mean in the deeper reaches of the state forest. All of them surging forward to answer that compelling call.

Beneath the tons of muddy earth he waited, and as the first armies of vermin flooded into the swamp he sent fingers up through the soil, seeking the surface with limbs made from roots and vines and old bones and maggots. A single finger broke the surface of the swamp; muddy water dripped from its bleached whiteness. The finger rose, reaching up into the moonlight, extending itself until it became impossibly long, jointed in dozens of places like a grotesquely articulated insect leg. It was absolutely without pigment, a limb born in the womb of thirty years' darkness, and it curled over the bugs and rats and spiders, swaying in the damp breeze. Antenna-like, it sensed the mass of life around it and quivered with expectant agitation. The rats leapt up in frenzy, throwing their bloated bodies at it, driven to madness by the call of the presence of this flesh.

One rat, older and fatter than the others, waddled through the press toward the swaying finger, crying out with an imploring trill. The exploring finger became aware of it, and the tip of the finger turned slowly toward the rat. A long nail, sharp as a talon, tore though the fingertip, forming as it grew. The finger trembled with anticipatory delight and then snapped forward and downward, piercing the fat body with a single powerful thrust. Blood exploded from the wriggling body as the nail stabbed deep into the rat's belly and wormed its way toward the heart. The rat screeched in a death ecstasy that made its entire body shiver. It rose up as the finger lifted its weight and shook it, then the rat's empty corpse was hurled aside. Blood dripped from a tiny mouth that had formed on the finger's pad; the finger immediately plunged down into the press, impaling another rat, splashing the ground with blood. Another finger tore through the surface, spearing a raccoon as it rose out of the ground; another appeared, and another. Within seconds the entire clearing was a writhing mass of white stalks of maggot flesh and fossilized bone. Dozens of articulated fingers rose and fell, tearing and rending, piercing and slashing, crushing as the vermin of the forest flooded in and crowded forward to die. Living bodies of dogs and goats and cats were torn to bloody rags and the pieces dragged beneath the surface, down to where Griswold's new body was forming. Their torn meat was added to his, lending mass, sheathing his skeleton with new muscle, new flesh.

Still the creatures poured in, denuding the forest of all life except for the birds, who stayed in their trees and watched with black, emotionless eyes.

It did not take long, perhaps an hour, and then the frenzy of slaughter was done. The bone-white fingers missed nothing, overlooked nothing. Each dead form, each insect, each rat and goat was dragged down into the dirt. The ground swelled with all of the thousands of pounds of matter, the whole surface of the swamp trembled and bubbled like a hot cauldron over a fire, and in that cauldron a witch's stew was brewing.

One by one, the articulated fingers slithered back into the mud, whipping downward like tongues sucked into well-fed mouths. A terrible silence fell down and smothered the swamp.

Chapter 46

LaMastra hotwired Sarah Wolfe's H1 Alpha—there was no sign of the Hummer's owner, a fact that twisted the knife in Crow's heart by another full turn—and they headed out of the hospital lot. The skeletal remains of a burning building lay sprawled across Corn Hill, totally blocking it. "Cut through the school yard," Crow said. "We can use the side streets to cut over to A-32."

LaMastra spun the wheel and scraped sparks off his left quarter-panel as he squeezed through the narrow gap in the chain-link fence and cut through the empty school yard.

Mike gave the school a bleak stare but felt no real sense of loss. He had never been happy there, and he'd not expected to ever go back. In his heart, he did not expect to live through the night. He gripped the handle of the sword tightly and said nothing.

As LaMastra reached the far side, he glanced by force of habit into the rearview mirror. "Uh oh," he said softly. "We have company."

They all turned to see several cars following.

Val and Mike turned to watch. "Vampires? In those cars?" Val asked.

The detective grunted. "That'd be my guess."

"They're after me," Mike said.

LaMastra glanced at him in the mirror. "I thought they couldn't kill you."

"No, but they can run us off the road, kill you guys, and just tie me to a telephone pole or something."

"Vince," Crow said, "this would be a good time for reckless driving, wouldn't you say?"

"Way ahead of you, boss." LaMastra scraped through the gate and made a hard right, kicked down on the pedal, and shot down the street at sixty miles an hour. Crow yelled out the turns and Val and Mike watched the dark street behind them. The pursuing cars had vanished into shadows now that they were on streets unlit by fires, but they all knew they were there.

They reached A–32. To their right the road led fifty yards to a twisted tangle of smoking metal that had been the Crestville Bridge; to their left the hardtop cut through shadows toward the farmlands and the forest. LaMastra made a hard left.

As they left the town proper the moonlight bathed the road in a cold light. Far behind them the first of the cars emerged from shadow.

"There's five of them now," Val said,

"Persistent sonsabitches!" LaMastra groused. He pressed his foot down even harder and the H1 seemed to laugh with the freedom of speed and power. The big car shot up the hill, gathering speed despite the steep climb. The pursuit cars fell behind. "Crow, this is pretty much a straight run from here to Dark Hollow. I doubt I can lose 'em."

"Do what you can."

The H1 clawed its way to the top of the hill, crested it, and began the long plunge. "CHRIST!" LaMastra yelped and stood on the brakes and the Hummer smoked to a stop. A hundred yards ahead three cars were jammed across the narrow road, blocking it entirely. Hungry white faces leered at them through the windows, and a handful of vampires stood on the road. As the H1 rocked on its springs from the sudden stop, the creatures began running toward them.

LaMastra stared at the road. On either side of the obstruction was a narrow verge and then a sheer drop into a drainage ditch. "I'll take suggestions," he said hastily.

Crow racked the slide on his Beretta. "Ramming speed."

LaMastra threw him a tight smile. "Okay, kids, buckle up for safety."

The running vampires had almost reached the car when the H1 lunged forward. Crow leaned out his window with his pistol and emptied the clip into the pack. Three went down with holes in chests and stomachs, and two more were smashed into the shadows by the grille and weight of the H1, but these two got up and began chasing the car as it rolled toward the roadblock. Behind the H1, the five pursuit cars crested the hill and swooped down like predatory birds. The lead car did not even try to veer around one of the running vampires and the creature was smashed down and then crushed by each succeeding vehicle.

LaMastra bellowed like a bear as the muscular H1 smashed into the roadblock at the point where two smaller cars, a Fiat and a Saab, sat nose to nose. With all the weight and momentum behind it, the Hummer punched through, swatting the smaller cars aside. Crow leaned out the window with his shotgun and fired round after round of the metal-vaporizing Shok-Lok rounds into the lead pursuit car, hitting the grille and turning the engine instantly into junk. The car lost control and slewed sideways into one of the barricade cars, catching a vampire between the two machines and crushing him from crotch to knees. The other pursuit cars tried to jam on brakes, tried to swerve, but they were going too fast, and they hit, one after another in a collapsing accordion of torn metal and ruptured gas tanks.

Behind the H1 the world erupted into towering flame as a fiery fist of smoke and burning gasoline punched upward into the sky and shock waves chased down the hills.

"Goddamn!" yelled LaMastra in triumph. Crow was nodding as he reloaded the Remington. Val and Mike were twisted around backward, watching the tower of flame.

(2)

Jonatha led the way, the shotgun's unfamiliar weight heavy in her sweating hands. Behind her was a straggling line of patients, staff, and visitors she'd gathered from the top four floors. Many of the visitors were dazed and followed her with glazed eyes and vapid smiles. One tried to give her some candy corn, but Jonatha had long since lost her appetite. A staff nurse—whom Jonatha had found hiding in a utility closet—had tried to take charge of the exodus, but after a good look at Jonatha, who was covered in blood, over six feet tall, and carrying a shotgun, the nurse just shut up and helped round up the survivors.

For as busy a hospital as Pinelands Hospital, there were pitifully few ambulatory survivors, and of those fewer still would be any good in a fight. Even so, it didn't take a lot of strength to pull a trigger, so Jonatha handed out handguns to the weakest and the long guns to the strongest.

The elevators were out, but the nurse told her that there was a zigzag ramp in the back of the east wing, which had long sloping ramps for use during fires or other emergencies when the elevators were out. Jonatha led her charges that way, gathering other survivors along the way. Newton was on the front gurney, crowded in with an old lady who had just had her knee replaced; Dr. Weinstock's heavy pistol was clutched in his hands. At the end of the line was a farmer who had come to the hospital to visit a friend and who now carried Eddie Oswald's service Glock, the spare magazines stuffed in the pockets of his bib overalls.

Every floor of the hospital was a shambles, but there did not seem to be anything moving, alive or dead, except the people who joined her parade.

The nurse leaned close to Jonatha, "We can get to the old triage unit—it's where they do seminars on ER techniques. It's not used for patients except if we get overflow. It's on the next floor down and it will have been closed tonight."

"Sounds good," Jonatha said, "let's get everyone in there and barricade the door."

But the triage room was already occupied when they got there. A man sat on the edge of one of the tables, a can of Coke in his hands, a pistol lying next to him.

Jonatha gasped and brought the shotgun up to cover him. She

could see that he was not a vampire. One side of his face was burned and bubbled, the skin hanging in melted folds; one eye was as white as a boiled egg. He waggled the soda can at her.

"Hey," he said with a smile that made his disfigured face look positively hideous. "Come on in."

Jonatha waved the others back and entered the room very cautiously. Just because the man was not one of *them* did not immediately allay her fears. Even under the burned skin he looked mean and there was a twinkle to his one good eye that made Jonatha feel stripped naked. His gaze crawled up and down her body, lingering appreciatively on her chest, and then finally staring boldly into her eyes. "Yeah, you can definitely come in."

"Who are you?" she asked nervously, peering around the room to make sure there was no one else lurking in there.

He watched her examination and chuckled. "Ain't no one else, darlin'. Just me. Just the Incredible Melting Man." He giggled like he was stoned. "Come on in."

"I . . . have a bunch of people with me. We all need to come in."

"Sure, sure, bring 'em in." He waved the bottle. "I was wondering when you'd get down this way. I was in the hall a few times and heard you talking."

She narrowed her eyes. "You weren't in the hall. I didn't see you."

"No," he said with a sly smile, "but I saw you."

Jonatha frowned. "And you sure you're all alone?"

"Honest to God, sweetie," Vic Wingate said, "aside from you I'm the only living soul in this room."

(3)

They came to him, flooding in from the town, from the farms, from the lonely houses that now stood empty of life along the fringes of the black highway. Those that did not have cars came running, their tireless limbs carrying them across the miles, their powerful muscles helping them leap and dive and climb and drop. They came down the long hill, and they came over the tops of the mountain; they came through secret ways in the forest, drawn to the forbidden swamp deep in the heart of Dark Hollow, compelled by the force of Ubel Griswold's dark desire.

The farmers came first, their overalls and jeans and flannel shirts splashed with their own blood and the blood of neighbors and family. Sometimes they came in whole family groups, each white face eager to be in the presence of their new father. They lumbered into the clearing and fell prostrate before the bubbling swamp, overwhelmed with Griswold's nearness, lost in the aura of his power. Then came the teenagers from the Haunted Hayride. Scores of them with slashed throats and black eyes full of hunger. They laughed and smiled, delighting in their freedom, in their strength, intoxicated by the blood that thundered through their veins. The town folk—residents and tourists—came later, most of them in Halloween costumes, and they cavorted like jesters in the court of the king.

They gathered and danced and leapt and sang out in their joy, feeding off the energies released by the Ritual even as Griswold fed off each of them, off each of their kills. It was a sharing of energy, an orgy of parasites.

Two figures stood at the edge of the clearing, and between them slumped a third. The two watchers were as deeply moved as all the others, but they were not allowed to join in. It was their special task to wait, to watch, and to be ready with the sacrifice that sagged in a dead faint in their cold hands.

Ruger stroked the hand he held, delighting in its warmth, knowing that it was the quickly flowing blood that kept it warm even in this cold place. He was glutted, having killed and fed so many times tonight that he had lost count, satiating himself so fully that he had many times had to vomit up the mingled human wine in order to be able to keep on feeding; yet still he hungered for this unconscious woman's blood. Not that he desired her in the way he had desired his grinning consort, who stood holding this woman's other hand. No, he desired her because she was the chosen sacrifice, because she was taboo. She was reserved strictly for the Man, and that made Ruger hunger for her with a fierce passion. He knew that Lois felt it, too, and as he turned to her she hissed at him, smiling as her tongue lolled between her fangs. Her pale body was ripe and white, as hard as polished stone. They had used each other over and over again since last night, since the moment when Ruger had forced innocent blood into her mouth and released her into a world of dark delight and bloodred pleasure. That act had driven the soul out of her, had freed her. Now she was his and he was hers; their hungers were equal and incredibly intense.

Ruger had known from the very moment he'd first tasted her vampire blood that she would be like him, a killer who delighted in the joy of the kill, who craved the fear, the hurt, the desperation that could be provoked in the struggling victim. In that way they were more like Griswold than like the rest of the revelers gathered here. A darker power burned in their hearts, and they delighted in it.

Together they watched the writhing bodies. Some of them had stripped and were abusing each other in every possible way, and in some ways only possible for creatures of their kind, creatures with their strength and endurance. There were screams of pain and ecstasy, and Ruger felt himself getting hard as the children of the Man went insane with passion, became frantic with want, as they glutted themselves on blood and violence. All in *his* name. Ruger thought it was all a blast. As much as he wanted to defile this woman, he also wanted to discard her and throw himself into the press, to rend and tear and take. He wanted to watch Lois as she rutted and bit and tore and screamed. She was so vicious and cold and passionate that it made Ruger dizzy just to think about her at the moment of a kill.

Then a tremble seemed to ripple through the earth under his feet, something different, not caused by the twisting bodies. The first contraction of the swamp's dark womb as it readied its unholy child for birth. He flashed Lois a razor-sharp smile.

"It's happening, baby! Can you feel it?"

Lois ran a tongue over the serrated line of her fangs and ran her fingers over her blood-gorged loins. Beneath their feet, the earth groaned in pain.

(4)

They encountered no other roadblocks as they swept along the road, though they passed dozens of wrecked cars. Beside the road a few farmhouses burned like lonely torches, but most of the houses stood dark and empty, surrounded by fields of blighted corn and shadows.

The road unraveled under the car and the miles fled away behind them. Mike closed his eyes and leaned back against the cushions. His hands were still clamped around the intricate hilt of the *katana*, and his lips moved as if in prayer. He realized he was doing that and stopped, and try as he might he could not recall what words his lips had formed or what prayer he had said, if it was a prayer at all.

Mike felt totally alienated from the others, as if he were from another world or part of a different species; then, darkly, he realized that indeed he was. Ever since he had opened himself up to what he was and who he was, ever since he had let the *dhampyr* within him emerge, his whole world had changed. He looked at the others and wondered how it was that they could not hear the screams that constantly shrilled in his ears, how they could not sense the huge, pervasive atmosphere of total malevolence that was clamped down over the entire town.

Crow reached back and took Val's hand and their eyes met. She mouthed the words *"I'm scared."* He nodded and gave her hand a reassuring squeeze, and his own lips formed the words *"I love you."* It wasn't much to offer each other, but it was the only talisman they had to share.

As LaMastra drove, he tried not to think about what was going to happen. The sight of Frank Ferro charred and blackened in death was burned into the front of his brain, regulating his rage, keeping the gas turned up. It kept the fear banked.

He flicked a glance now and then at the others, seeing them in the rearview mirror, watching as they prepared for what was ahead. Twice he saw something weird and almost spoke up. It was there and gone, just a shimmer in the air of the backseat between Mike and Val. There and gone when he blinked.

"We're here," LaMastra said quietly, and Crow turned as the H1 approached the turnoff to Dark Hollow Road. "God help us all."

There was no reception for them, no guard unit of vampires. Griswold was incredibly confident, or arrogant.

LaMastra made the turn. Everyone checked their weapons for the twentieth time and slapped pockets to feel the reassuring bulges of extra ammunition. Val took a jar of garlic oil from her pocket, smeared some on, and handed it around. When Crow was finished, he handed it back to Val, who reached forward and dabbed some on LaMastra's throat and face as he fought the car along the rutted road.

Then, suddenly they were in the clearing. LaMastra eased the car to a stop and switched off the engine.

Crow turned in his seat and faced the others, though inside the shadowy car he could barely see them; even so they all felt each other's presence. "No pep talk, no rousing speech," he said. "We go in fast and dirty, and we kill as many of them as we can. Val, if I die, you can't go to pieces, just as I can't if you're killed. That's the way to lose a war. If any of us dies, then the others have to stay focused."

"They killed my family," Val said tightly. "I want them all dead."

"Vince?"

The cop grunted. "Frank may have been a stuffy old fart, but he was a good man. And he was my friend. I think I deserve some kind of payback." He paused and grunted again; maybe it was a laugh. "Besides, we LaMastras are hard sonsabitches to kill."

"Yeah, so I noticed." Crow turned to where Mike's silhouette crouched on the edge of the back seat. "Mike?"

"You know what I think," he said and jerked open the door.

LaMastra glanced at his retreating back. "Buffy the Vampire Slayer there's got attitude."

"Lay off him, Vince," said Crow.

"Hey, it's not criticism. I just don't want to have to waste time protecting him, you dig?"

Val jacked a round into her shotgun. "This is war. Everyone pulls their own weight."

They got out. The ATVs were out of gas, but Crow picked up the gasoline sprayer unit and slipped it on as they all looked down the hill. He took coils of rope from the duffels strapped to the ATVs, tied them to the bumper of the Hummer, and tossed the ends over the edge. Overhead the storm clouds had thinned and there was a hint of moonlight, just enough to paint pale silver on the descending line of shrubs. They lingered at the top for only a moment, and then without a further word they started down the hill, using the ropes as guidelines but moving fast, hurrying toward the swamp.

Chapter 47

"Party time!" Vic said.

Jonatha heard the faint squeak of a hinge and turned to see the two tall cabinets beside the door open. Two men stepped out, both of them grinning at Vic's little joke.

"Jonatha! Look out!" she heard Newton shout through the open doorway, but his call ended in a choking cough.

Jonatha screamed and brought her shotgun up as one of the monsters lunged at her. There was a huge explosion and the recoiling stock hit her hard in the stomach. The vampire fell on her and bore her to the floor; she landed hard and shoved at him, and was surprised when the creature just rolled off and lay still. Then she saw the ragged red hole in its chest, and understood.

She scrambled to a sitting position and swung the gun around, but the trigger clicked empty. She'd forgotten to jack in a new round, and the other vampire simply snatched the weapon from her hands.

"Stupid bitch," Vic said.

"She killed Marty!" complained the remaining vampire. "What the hell she have in that gun?"

"Probably garlic," Vic drawled, and laughed as the vampire suddenly thrust the gun away, not wanting to be anywhere near it. "Go outside and play," Vic suggested. "I'll take care of LaKisha here."

The vampire looked from her to its dead companion, and

then with a hiss it leapt past Jonatha and plowed into the crowd of stunned onlookers. The creature grabbed the nurse and clamped its jaws around her throat; blood sprayed the wall. The patients screamed and panicked, colliding with gurneys and wheelchairs and each other. The vampire laughed wildly, tossed the nurse's body against the wall, and laughed like a happy kid as he chased an old lady down the hall.

Jonatha screeched in horror and fury and made a try for the shotgun, but Vic Wingate backhanded her with shocking force and speed. She pirouetted dizzily and crashed into a row of cabinets, but before she could fall Vic caught her under the armpit, spun her around, and jammed his pistol into her stomach.

"Whoa there, girlie-girl," he wheezed. "I've been having a really bad day. I've been just hoping and praying for something to come along to cheer me up. Shows you I'm still in the groove." He held the pistol in his burned hand and with his other he caressed the curve of her cheek.

In the hall, the vampire was bent over, feeding off the old lady, ignoring the other patients. When he felt the old woman's heart give out, he plucked her off the floor and threw her at two other patients, who went down in a bone-breaking tumble. He rose and kicked a wheelchair over and stomped down on the head of the old man who toppled out of it. The old man's head exploded and the vampire smiled. He was at the height of his powers after the long night of killing and feeding. He could kill all of these people if he wanted. He glanced over his shoulder and saw Vic playing with his new toy, and he smiled.

The vampire turned back to the crowd and grabbed the struts on the nearest gurney, on which lay a small man with a pain-gray face. The vampire froze in place, his hands still on the struts. The little man on the gurney was pointing a pistol at him. It was a huge Ruger Blackhawk and its mouth stared blackly at the vampire from less than six feet away. There was no way for the vampire to know if the gun was loaded with ordinary bullets or more garlic, and he paused in uncertainty. Terror and pain were painted all over the patient's features and his eyes were glassy with fever.

The vampire smiled.

The man smiled.

The vampire lunged at him and the man shot him through the eye.

The blast threw the vampire backward, all life extinguished in a single moment as the garlic-filled dum-dum punched through his brain; the recoil pitched the patient back onto the bed with a chest-jarring thump. Newton dropped the pistol and clutched his shattered chest with both hands as new pain detonated within him.

Vic Wingate made Jonatha back up step by step until they were both at the door. He could see the hallway beyond and he saw the last of his bodyguards go down with his head half blown away. Vic kicked the door shut in the faces of the terrified patients. Keeping the gun in place, he released Jonatha with the other and reached out to turn the lock.

Jonatha knew she was going to die. She knew she was going to die badly, because she had a good idea who this man was—a man with a burned face who worked with the vampires. It had to be the kid's stepfather. It had to be Vic Wingate. The thought terrified her so severely that she felt horror trying to pull her down into darkness. What was it the kid had said? Vic is Griswold's right hand. It was Vic who rigged all the explosions. It was Vic who took care of Griswold all these years, who protected him. Vic had been behind most of what happened all along.

Vic saw the defeat in her eyes and licked his blistered lips. His good eye crawled up and down her. "My, my," he said, "You are something. Just what the doctor ordered, 'cause it's been a real bitch of a day."

He backed her up to the examination table; her hip hit it hard and he moved so close to her that she breathed his exhaled breath. Vic put his free hand on her chest, cupping her breasts and hefting their weight. "My oh my oh my, but you are something else. You're half unreal, you know that, girlie-girl? You're like a gift from Heaven, you are. You just came down from Heaven to be with ol' Vic. You're what a sick man needs to feel good. Shame you're a nigger, but what the hell, it's all pink inside." Open sores oozed clear mucus on his face as he leered at her.

"Please don't hurt me," she begged as tears welled from her eyes. Her heart hammered to get out of her chest. "Please."

"Well, well, it is nice to hear you say please." He licked his lips again and his hand never stopped touching her. He sought out her nipples and pinched them and laughed as she yelped and flinched. Jonatha wanted to throw up. She wanted to run, but she felt as if all the power had been sucked out of her muscles by his invading touch. "Say it again. C'mon, girlie-girl, say it again."

"P . . . please . . ."

"Again."

"Please!"

"Again."

"Please, for God's sake! Please!"

"Well, since you ask so nice . . ." and he grabbed the collar of her sweatshirt and gave it a vicious and powerful jerk. Cloth ripped and his fingernails scraped painfully across her sternum. The gun barrel pressed harder as he ripped and tore at the cloth, shredded it, exposing her upper breasts and the white bra, and all the time he muttered a kind of chant that sent cold chills racing up and down her spine. "Here it comes. Oh boy, here it comes. Here it comes now . . ."

She saw the specter of death looming above Vic's shoulder, she saw it grinning through his melted face and burning in his eyes. She saw the future in those fiery eyes. She saw rape and pain and humiliation, and at the end of it all, she saw her agonizing and pointless death. In all her nightmares of vampires and werewolves, in all her research into demons and beasts, in all of her studies into the nature of evil, she had never conjured an image more terrifying than this madman with the scorched face. She could understand monsters that killed because it was their supernatural nature, she could understand beasts that were trapped within the dictates of an ancient curse, or driven by primal instincts that were completely beyond control, but this was an ordinary man. A human being capable of making his own choices, capable of understanding right from wrong and good from evil. This was a chosen, deliberate evil, and Jonatha suddenly understood that this was the worst kind of evil. In this man she saw all the evil of the human kind seething with life and power, glaring at her with lust and hunger, ready to rip her life away.

"Here it comes, girlie-girl. Oh boy, here it comes . . ." His strong fingers hooked inside the edge of one bra cup and began to pull. Jonatha screamed.

And then she hit him.

Before she was even aware that she was going to do it, one hand smashed the pistol aside and the other slammed into Vic's burned face with her rigid palm and hooked fingernails. It exploded the blisters and drove spikes of red-hot pain into his head—and he screamed even louder than Jonatha had. His finger jerked on the trigger and the gun fired, but the bullet tore into a cabinet.

"Get away from me!" Jonatha shoved him with both hands and Vic stumbled and stumbled back, but instead of taking the chance to run, she chased him and hit him again and again, pounding on the gory ruin of his face, screeching so shrilly that it hurt Vic's ears almost as much as the blows that kept raining down. Vic's blood splashed abstract patterns across her torn shirt, across her screaming face; it sparkled like rubies in her short hair; and he swung wildly with the pistol and caught Jonatha on the arm, spinning her halfway around.

Vic was in such immediate pain that he didn't even try to shoot her—he just wanted to get away; so with blood in his eyes and his head in a bag of thorns he tore free and staggered toward the door and clumsied it open just as he heard a sound that chilled his boiling blood. Jonatha had retrieved her shotgun and jacked a round into the breech.

"Bastard!" She fired a shot that chopped a hole the size of a dinner plate out of the jamb a yard from his head, but Vic was ducking and weaving, and then he plowed into the crowd of patients, bashing and kicking at them, tossing them behind him to block pursuit and give her no chance at a shot.

In the hall, Newton lay on the gurney, nearly as blind with pain as Vic. He was frozen in the act of digging into his pants pocket for a tissue to wipe sweat from his eyes. He didn't know who this guy was—but like Jonatha he could make a reasonable guess. His pistol tangled in his sheets where he'd dropped it after shooting the vampire and after the shock of that act had buried a knife of pain in his chest. The gun wasn't visible to this killer, but reaching for it would draw his fire.

Jonatha stood in the doorway, her shotgun aimed and ready, the barrel moving back and forth like a viper searching for exposed flesh to bite.

Vic grabbed a young girl, a bald chemo patient, and wrapped a thick arm around her throat, laying his pistol arm on her shoulder to steady it as he backed away from Jonatha. He squeezed off two shots; the girl screamed and the bullets hit the metal door frame and zinged off through the hallway. Jonatha ducked back inside and everyone else dropped to the ground.

Newton took the only chance he could. If he could distract Vic, draw his attention—even if meant drawing his fire—then it would give Jonatha at least a chance.

So he took out the one solid object in his pocket and flicked it at the back of Vic's head. It was small, just an old dime—scraped and faded, with a hole through it so that someone could wear it around their ankle on a piece of twine—and it pinged off Vic's skull doing no harm at all, but Vic spun that way, swinging the gun away from the girl and aiming it at Newton. There were two simultaneous blasts—one from Vic's pistol, and his bullet punched a hole right into the wall an inch from Newton's head, and the other was the deeper boom of Jonatha'a shotgun. The blast took Vic in the wrist and blew off half his arm.

A few of the birdshot peppered the arm of the chemo patient, and she cried out and fell, but Vic seemed painted into the moment, his body immobile, his face white with shock, his eyes bugging out at the ruin of his arm, which ended in a red tangle just below the elbow.

He opened his mouth to scream, to whimper, to say something . . . but nothing came out. Vic didn't even seem to be registering the pain. He was frozen into a moment of total, horrified disbelief.

That gave Newton all the time he needed to pick up Weinstock's heavy gun, steady his arm on the rail of the gurney, and aim.

"You're Vic Wingate," he said.

Vic's eyes flicked to him. Tears burst from his eyes and rolled down his cheek. "I . . . I . . . please!"

"This is for Mike," Newton said, and shot him four times in the face.

(2)

The Bone Man felt it happen. He felt Vic die. It sent an electric thrill through him that lifted some of the deadness from his heart. It was similar to what he had felt when Polk ate his gun, and when the vampires killed Gus Bernhardt. He'd even felt some of it—less of it—when Eddie Oswald died.

Now, every single one of the men who had murdered him thirty years ago was dead. Since he'd come back he'd prayed for something like that, for the twisted release that came from rough justice. It made him feel more free, less tied to the blood and nerves of this goddamned town.

As he drifted down the hill behind Mike Sweeney, Val, Crow, and Vince LaMastra, the Bone Man felt even less substantial than he had since he'd risen.

I could leave now, he thought, *I could go and rest*. Without knowing how, or where that insight came from, he knew it was correct. His own murder was avenged, even if indirectly. He had saved Mike from Tow-Truck Eddie—several times in fact, whether by standing between the boy and the killer, or by whispering in the boy's head at the right moment, or by drawing on all of his nearly exhausted reserves of energy in order to push Newton into the path of Oswald's bullet. He'd done that; and as far as he could figure, that's why he'd been brought back. Not to get justice, but to give justice some kind of fighting chance.

He'd tried to help Henry Guthrie's family, but he certainly failed at that. On the other hand he'd stood between Crow and the roaches that day and maybe that had saved his life.

Yeah, he mused, *I could step out of this ball game and sleep.*

With Vic dead, the Bone Man knew that all he had to do was want it bad enough and he'd be gone. Leave the living to fight the dead, even though that fight was probably lost anyway.

I could go . . . but what if I stayed?

The climbers were nearly down to the floor of the Hollow. The endgame was about to start, win or lose. It wasn't his fight anymore. He'd already saved the town once, and died for it. Been *damned* for it.

This ain't my fight no more.

Overhead, invisible against the sky, the crows were circling, circling.

The Bone Man looked at Mike, who was trying hard not to scream, trying hard not to run from this—because who on earth would want to go forward and embrace that kind of heritage? And yet he kept going.

He looked at LaMastra, who had already lost a friend and who would probably be haunted by this every day of his life. It wasn't even his town, and yet he kept going.

He looked at Val, who had the most to lose of any of them because of that little babe that was just starting to grow in her belly. She *should* leave, she most of all should just turn around and find some way out of this town. She'd already lost too much, and yet she kept going.

Then he looked at Crow, who had been tortured by this since Griswold had killed his brother and then tried to kill him. Crow had been in and out of the bottle, had wrestled with enough personal demons. Maybe he had the biggest stake in this because he always believed that the evil had never gone away. Even so, he could have left; he should have packed Val and maybe Mike into a car and driven out of town after they discovered who and what Boyd was. He knew that he was on a suicide mission, that there was no foreseeable way that the four of them could stand against all those monsters, let alone against Griswold and what he was about to become. He should leave, and yet he kept going.

They reached the bottom of the pitch and stood facing down the long corridor of twisted trees. The sounds of shrieks and laughter from the Hollow filled the air, even from this distance. The Bone Man, invisible, stood behind them and watched them brace themselves, check their weapons, exchange handshakes or hugs, and then head down the road toward death.

The Bone Man was done here, he had no reason to even stand and watch, let alone follow. He was nearly powerless, and he was free. And yet he kept going.

Chapter 48

They stopped at a point a hundred yards back from the cleared space around the swamp, squatting down behind a clump of wild rosebushes. Beyond was a sight out of Hell itself.

Hundreds of vampires writhed together in a perverse orgy of unbound passion and violent ecstasy, throwing themselves at each other, sometimes biting, sometimes kissing. They dragged each other to the ground and fed on the stolen blood in each other's veins; they did unspeakable things to each other and enticed others to do the same or worse to them. It was a celebration of their strength, of their powers to do and take harm, of their supernatural endurance, of their vampire nature. If any human had been a part of that press or caught in those acts of fervent cruelty, he would have died within the first few moments,

LaMastra clutched at Crow's sleeve. "There's too many of them!"

"I know." He nudged Mike. "Do you see Griswold? Has he risen yet?"

"No," the boy answered in a tight whisper. "We still have a few minutes. I didn't even think we'd be in time. It'll happen soon, though. I can feel it."

LaMastra made a noise. "What is it, a disturbance in the Force?"

"Vince," Val said.

"Sorry."

Crow closed his eyes and tried to picture the landscape as he

remembered it during the day. "I have an idea," he said and outlined it quickly. Val gasped, but she kept her comments in check.

"As plans go," LaMastra sighed, "that really sucks."

Mike said, "It's the best we got."

"Right." Crow looked at Val. "I . . . don't know what to . . ."

Her eyes glittered like polished onyx. "Say 'I love you, Val
Guthrie,' and then get your ass in gear, Mr. Crow."

He grinned. "I love you, Val Guthrie."

"I love you, too."

She turned away from him and focused her attention down
on the writhing mass of undead bodies. Crow lingered for a
moment longer, staring at her profile, then he rose, nodded to
LaMastra and Mike. "Give me five minutes."

"I don't know if we have that much time."

"Then give me what you can."

Mike rose and walked the first few yards with him. "Crow,"
he said quietly, "if I don't get a chance later . . . I just wanted to
say thanks."

"For what?"

"For being there for me when no one else was. I mean before
all this happened. You were always cool, you always treated me
like a person, like I was worth something."

"You are."

"You were the only one who acted like I was. I'll never forget it, man." Awkwardly, he extended his hand. Smiling, Crow
took it, but then pulled the boy close and gave him a hug.

Before he let him go, Crow whispered, "Iron Mike Sweeney,
the Enemy of Evil."

Then Crow turned away and melted into the shadows.

(2)

On the floor of the Hollow, Ruger and Lois were swaying together as they watched the bodies, moving as if to the pulsing of
tribal drums, but the only music was made by the cries and
screams and moans of the vampires. The level of agitation in the

crowd was at a fever pitch and still it climbed higher with every moment, carving out new levels of passionate intensity. Ruger could hardly bear to just watch; his craving was so acute it was physically painful. Suddenly one scream rose higher than all the others. It was a shrill, piercing cry that stabbed upward from the press with such naked power that the revelers were shocked to an abrupt silence, and the scream exploded outward from the center of the press. Shock waves of force rolled outward, buffeting the bodies roughly backward.

Ruger crouched in a shocked silence, Sarah's limp wrist momentarily forgotten in his grip. He looked at Lois, whose face was wild with animal excitement.

In the center of the crowd a space appeared occupied by only one of the vampires. Ruger frowned at the vampire, trying to understand what he was seeing. The creature in the center of the clearing was standing straight, his body stretched, his legs wide, feet arched so that only the tips of his shoes touched the muddy ground. What Ruger couldn't understand was how the man was standing at all: the contact his toes made with the ground was only tenuous, and his body shook and trembled, but did not fall. The vampire's head was thrown back in such a demonstration of total ecstasy that the corner of his mouth had begun to tear; his scream was constant and droplets of blood shot upward from his rupturing lungs, seeding the air above the Hollow with a fine red mist.

The revelers lay or stood or crouched or sat in postures of awe, their ears deafened by the shriek, their eyes filled with the glory of the event. They knew that this was some signal, the trumpet blast of something wonderful to come. The screaming went on and on, tearing apart the throat of the screamer, ripping loose the vocal cords, shattering the larynx. Blood ran in lines from the wide staring eyes of the revenant; blood dripped from both nostrils and from both ears; blood spurted from around each black fingernail and it flowed from his penis and anus and soaked his trousers, it filled his shoes and overflowed to drip onto the ground. The skin of his face seemed to ripple and roll and then blood burst from every pore, showering the supplicants, who surged forward to taste it as it fell. The screaming went higher and higher and then faded as the throat filled with blood. A fountain of gore erupted from the upturned mouth and shot upward with great force. The body continued to shake and tremble with ever greater agitation as the force within it built to critical mass—and then it exploded. The vampire's body literally flew apart as if a stick of dynamite had detonated in its chest. Limbs and parts of limbs, bits of shredded flesh, indefinable chunks of viscera smashed like a grisly hail onto the vampires, and they gasped in shock and then screamed in exultant joy.

Ruger was the first to see what now occupied the center of the clearing; he was standing too far back to be blinded by the shower of blood and meat. He saw a tall white stalk like the trunk of a slender sapling rising out of the ground. It was splashed with blood and bile and other foul fluids from the center of the vampiric body it had impaled, and it swayed above the crowd. Gradually the revelers became aware of it. They turned to stare up at it, every pair of eyes becoming fixed and unblinking; each mouth gaped wide in unspoken cries of wonder.

The white stalk was slightly thicker than a human arm and jointed in a dozen places so that it could bend and twist in any direction, though at the moment it stood as tall and straight as pale bamboo. At the top of the stalk was a large bud which slowly blossomed to reveal five long petals. Each petal was a man-jointed finger tipped with a hard claw as shiny black as a beetle's carapace. The fingers flexed wide to reveal a palm in the center of which gaped a hungry red mouth lined with dozens of needle-sharp teeth. One of the revenants took a tentative step toward the stalk and immediately the huge hand whipped around and closed with crushing force on the vampire's face. Blood erupted between the multijointed fingers, but the vampire did not try to pull away. Instead he pushed forward to increase the contact with the hand and the hungry palm, helping the hand crush him and bleed him. The trapped vampire tore at his own flesh, opening dozens of cuts that bled freely, and the others around him flocked forward, feeding off him even as the hand drained him dry.

A second hand punched upward through the mud and closed around the throat of another vampire, lifting her wriggling into the air. The stalk of the arm twisted around her like an anaconda, crushing her bones and splattering everyone around her with her blood. She screamed and screamed until there was nothing left of her but pulverized bone in a shapeless envelope of desiccated skin. A third hand came up, and a fourth, and the slaughter began in earnest.

Ruger felt the pull, felt the need to throw himself into the press, felt the command deep in his mind that compelled him to die so that Griswold could live, but he stayed rooted to the ground at the edge of the clearing. Whether the power that held him there was some higher command by Griswold or his own powerful need to survive, he could not tell. Lois stood with him, and Ruger could see the look of naked hunger in her glazed eyes, saw drool hanging in streamers from her lips. Her grip on Sarah Wolfe was so tight that Ruger could hear the woman's forearm bones grind together and then snap.

Up on the hill, Val, Mike and LaMastra watched the spectacle with minds frozen by horror. Even Mike, who had peered into the darkest parts of his *dhampyr's* mind, had not seen this. In his astral wanderings during his brief detachment from life he had never foreseen such an alien horror. Yet he knew that this was part of the Ritual, part of the blood sacrifice that would open the doorway between death and life and allow Griswold to return.

"My . . . God!" LaMastra was clutching his shotgun to his chest as if it afforded some sacred protection. "What are those things?"

"They're . . . that's all part of him." Mike wanted to close his eyes, to look away, but he could not.

"What are you talking about? There must be twenty of those things! What is he? An octopus?"

Mike shook his head. "There are images in my head. I can . . . almost see him. He's still changing. He's changing all the time. I don't know what he is, but he's coming now. He's about to re-turn."

"I just hope he keeps doing what he's doing. He's butchering the whole lot of them."

"No," Mike said. "He won't kill them all. He still needs an army. He just needs to get strong enough, and he's almost there. I can feel it. But there's one more thing he needs. Innocent blood. That means that down there is a human who—oh no!" His scanning eyes had fixed on the three figures standing by the edge of the clearing. Val looked to where Mike pointed with a trembling hand. "I thought she tried to save me," he murmured wretchedly. "I thought she was different than the others."

"What is it?" LaMastra asked. "What do you see?"

Mike pointed. "The one on the right, that's Karl Ruger."

"Shit! You're right."

"The woman he's holding, that's Mrs. Wolfe—the mayor's wife."

Val had to clamp her hands over her mouth to keep from cry-ing out. She pressed forward and stared, and even with the crazy movements and bad light she could make out the familiar lines of her friend's face. "No . . . God, no!"

Mike's voice was dead. "And the other woman, the one help-ing Ruger hold her . . . that's my mom."

LaMastra snapped his head around and gaped at Mike. "Oh, Jesus, kid, I'm so sorry . . ."

Mike shook his head and then raised his eyes to look at both of them. "I'm only fourteen," he said softly, and that said it all.

Val wrapped her arm around him and LaMastra put his hand awkwardly on the boy's shoulder and in the midst of the horror they shared his grief. Mike closed his eyes and tried not to be completely crushed by everything; then he winced as LaMastra's hand tightened painfully. He looked up and saw what had jolted the detective. In the clearing things had suddenly changed. The murderous white arms were no longer slaughtering the vam-pires, and things had become still.

More than two-thirds of the vampires had been butchered

and their crushed and lifeless bodies littered the swamp; but there were still scores more of the creatures scattered around, their faces suffused with joy even though their bodies were drenched in the blood of their own kind. One by one the towering artic- ulated arms slipped back into the swamp until only the one that had first emerged remained. As they watched the arm seemed to swell, first at its base and then expanding upward as it struggled toward a greater uniform thickness, taking on more mass as if matter was being pumped into it from below. The stalk slowly took on color, too, displaying a mottled appearance like the skin of a slug. It stood hovering above the ground, the long fingers opening and closing spasmodically. With each outward flex the mouth in the center of the palm gaped with a snakelike tongue that flicked in and out.

Ruger and Lois were no longer standing idle at the edge of the clearing; they were moving slowly forward, dragging Sarah down to the edge of the swamp and dumping her unceremoni- ously in front of the stalk. Sarah had been unconscious before, but the nearness of such power must have roused her, because as the stalk drew close she shifted painfully on the ground and then slowly sat up. She was still dazed and seemed not to register the movement all around her. From where they were crouched, Val could see the exact moment when Sarah became aware, and it broke her heart.

Sarah must have heard something behind her and she turned slowly, blinking with confusion, then froze slack-jawed at the throng of wax-white figures clustered around her, their faces more terrifying than any Halloween mask. Sarah scrambled away from the vampires as they advanced on her, but they did not attack her, did not even touch her; they just wanted to be closer to the thing that was waiting for her. Sarah kept backing, sliding on mud, half-sinking in the muck as she fought to es- cape, and then her shoulder thumped against an obstruction and she glanced briefly back, saw that it was a sapling, and turned quickly back to face the advancing throng. Then Sarah froze and a quizzical expression came over her face and she turned again and looked more closely at the tree trunk, letting her eyes travel up its length. She saw the bloom at its crest, saw the long white petals, and frowned as the petals stretched wide and then clutched into a tight fist; and she watched in awful fascination as the petals opened again, turning toward her, revealing the whole hand. The red mouth in the mottled palm hissed at her.

Sarah's scream shattered the stillness as the hand reached for her.

"NO!" Mike leapt to his feet and before either Val or La-Mastra could grab him he was gone, running wildly down the hill, screaming and shouting. Below, all of the creatures in the Hollow jerked around and stared at the small figure racing through the shadows toward them. A few of them even laughed when they saw his size. As he burst into the clearing he opened up with the shotgun and two of the vampires went spinning away into death. Seeing their companions fall, a few of the others jumped forward to make the kill, but the white arm lunged at them and smashed them into the mud and then swept around to knock the others around like tenpins.

Lois gripped Ruger's sleeve. "That's Mike!" she hissed, her face showing confusion and some fear. No compassion, not even a flicker of it, touched her face.

"The *dhampyr*?" Ruger smiled, intrigued.

"We have to do something. If he's killed, then the Man could be destroyed! The others, they'll tear him to pieces."

She took a step forward to try and intervene, but Ruger snagged a handful of her hair and jerked her back. She whirled on him, spitting with rage. Ruger gave her a bland smile. "Think for a minute, you silly bitch."

Lois slapped his hand away from her hair. "What are you talk-ing about? We have to do something now."

"Do we?" He grabbed her and pulled her close, whispering into her ear. "Let's just watch and see what happens, 'cause ei-ther way we can come out of this higher up on the food chain."

Her red-black eyes searched his for a moment, and then Lois's full, red mouth blossomed into a smile as dark and as wicked as Ruger's.

★   ★   ★

Mike fired his shotgun empty and the ground was littered with the dead. A huge figure rushed at him and Mike realized with horror that it was Chief Bernhardt, his grossly fat body moving with inhuman speed, his mouth rimmed with fangs. Mike swung the empty shotgun like a club, but the chief caught it and jerked it fiercely out of Mike's hands. The chief grinned, tossed the shotgun away, and then reached for Mike as the vampire next to him was smashed aside by the reaching white hand. With a snarl Mike reached over his shoulder—just as he had seen himself do in dreams a hundred times—and whipped the *katana* from its scabbard; there was a contrail of silver in the night air and Bernhardt staggered back, his beefy hands pawing at the red gash that was sliced inches deep into his mammoth belly. Mike stepped to one side and brought the sword down at a new angle and the chief's bald head went tumbling to the ground.

Another vampire rushed him and Mike turned sharply on the balls of his feet and stepped to one side as he slashed laterally across the vampire's middle. The creature folded in half and crumpled to the mud. Mike turned again, raising his sword to a high guard position as the many-jointed white arm snaked by. Mike slashed at it, but it moved too fast and all he accomplished was a long shallow surface cut. The white arm slithered back into the mud so fast that it seemed to simply vanish, only to reappear yards away, where it knocked down a vampire who was rushing at Mike's blind side.

Mike turned again and instantly two figures slammed into him, bearing him down to the ground and knocking the sword out of his grip.

LaMastra and Val were nearly at the clearing when they saw Mike fall; LaMastra opened up with the Roadblocker to cut a path through the crowd.

"Mike!" Val yelled as she blasted her way into the crowd at LaMastra's right. The shotgun jumped in her hands and with each blast her sore shoulder and injured eye socket throbbed. One vampire seemed to rise up out of nowhere and grabbed the shotgun, yanking the barrel hard enough to pull Val forward off balance, but the pull jerked her finger that much harder against the trigger and the blast killed the attacker and another vampire behind him.

It was LaMastra who noticed first that they had a slight—ever so slight—advantage. They did not need to shoot to kill. Their bullets and shells were laced with garlic and it was like firing poison into their opponents. Any wound was fatal, even if a single pellet lodged in the undead flesh; so he stopped trying to aim and just kept firing. The problem was, there were more vampires then they had ammunition, and there seemed to be no chance at all of reloading.

Two vampires rushed at Val, and she was shocked to see that they were both young teenage girls wearing the bloodstained remnants of Halloween costumes: one was Elvira with fake cleavage showing through her skintight black dress, and the other was Dorothy from Oz. Val hesitated, but only for a moment, and then she bit down on her horror and fired. Elvira's artificial bosom blossomed with blood and she did a neat pirouette, falling across Dorothy's feet, but Dorothy hopped over her and turned her evasion into a diving attack. Val managed to sidestep, and as she twisted she brought the folded metal stock of the shotgun around in a bone-smashing blow to the girl's jaw. The shock of the impact sent darts of pain through the bones in Val's forearms and she almost dropped the gun. Dorothy shook off the blow and the bones in her face were re-forming even as she rose and rushed again at Val. Val fired from point-blank range and Dorothy's face vanished.

Something hit Val hard between the shoulder blades and she staggered and went down, turning as she fell. Marge, the red-haired waitress from the town diner, stood over her, still in her waitress whites but splashed with blood and mud. Marge reached for Val, knocking aside the barrel of the shotgun so that the blast went up into the night sky, and reached for Val with clutching fingers.

LaMastra stepped forward and knocked the waitress away with a vicious kick to the ribs and then shot her as she turned on him. Immediately three pairs of hands seized him from behind and LaMastra was yanked backward into a screaming, hissing tangle of monsters.

Then the whole swamp seemed to explode with light and heat. Instantly flames shot up all around the clearing, casting the battling figures into sharply etched white-and-black caricatures. The vampires scattered away from the blaze, fleeing toward the safety of the hillside, and then screamed as the flames chased them up the slopes. Everywhere they went, every direction they turned in, new fires appeared. A dozen of them were caught in the first wave and became shrieking torches that ran madly around the clearing, igniting trees and bushes and other vampires.

By the edge of the clearing, safe under a stand of diseased pines, Ruger and Lois watched the battle. They were the only ones who saw and understood what was happening. They saw the figure that ran along the perimeter of the clearing with a burning cloth-wrapped stick in one hand and the nozzle of some kind of sprayer in the other. The tank of the sprayer jiggled and sloshed on the man's back, and the smell of gasoline was thick in the air. As the man ran he sprayed everything with gasoline and touched the torch as he passed. Fires sprang up behind him. Some of the fires raced quickly up the hill, evidence that he had left a trail behind him.

Even from the other side of the clearing, Ruger could see the man's face clearly. "Crow," he murmured. "That sneaky son of a bitch." His voice held a trace of admiration and there was even a smile on his colorless lips.

Lois shrank back from the advancing wall of flames. Fire and smoke rose into the night and leapt from tree to tree. The steady night breeze and the dryness of the autumn plants and bushes stoked the fires into an inferno in just seconds. The white articulated arm whipped back and forth, shying away from the fire, and finally slithered back down into the mud of the swamp, safe from the flames. Sarah Wolfe lay over the spot where the arm had vanished, and her body shook and trembled with the palsy of shock.

Ruger ground his jagged teeth together and his smile of appreciation metamorphosed into a more predatory grin.

Lois clutched Ruger's arm. "Come on, baby, let's get out of here."

"Oh, *hell* no!" snapped Ruger. "I want him so bad I can already taste it."

Lois gave the fire a fearful look and then stared over to where Griswold's arm had vanished into the mire. "To hell with this," she said, and instantly turned and ran toward the only gap left in the towering ring of fire.

"Bitch!" Ruger called after her, but he wasn't crushed by it. They were predators and predators did what they had to do to survive. Afterward he'd find her, and if he did horrible things to her to make her pay for running out, he knew it would only make her hotter for him.

Mike dodged a lunge by a vampire that had once been his gym teacher, Mr. Klinger. He spun away from a second grab and whirled in a slashing turn like a helicopter's blades, and the top of Klinger's head leapt a foot into the air. Others came at him and he cut and cut and cut. It was not pretty swordplay. It wasn't something from the samurai movies Crow watched; it wasn't dynamic like those *Blade* movies, or acrobatic like Buffy. It was raw and savage hack and slash, subpar for any martial arts class, but it had all the power of his fury and the speed that comes from need; and it was a weapon in the hands of a *dhampyr*, and that counted for a lot. Like the garlic in the guns, a weapon in the hands of a creature such as Mike delivered fatal cuts every time. It would have been very useful for him to know that, to understand that he did not need to be as precise with his cuts, but there was no way he could have known. Even the Bone Man didn't know that, not that he could tell him if he did.

Mike cut and killed as if he had been born to it; his face was a mask of strife, his soul was lost in the total acceptance that this was what he was put on earth to do. And if he died doing it . . . then so what? There would be no one left alive to mourn his death. To some degree he'd always known that, but to die this way would at least mean something.

Then, in one of those moments that seemed designed by a God who is as perverse as he is vicious, Mike turned around, sword raised—and his mother stood not eight feet away. She was more beautiful than he'd ever seen her, pale and intense, smiling without any of the cowed or drunken shame that he'd always seen in her eyes. For a crazy moment, seeing her so alive, so in command of herself, lifted Mike's heart, but that gladness was fractured at the core and as soon as his mother smiled her wicked smile, he felt his hopes shatter in his chest.

"Mom . . ." he said, holding the sword in one hand and starting to reach for her with his other.

For a moment—and maybe it was Mike's breaking heart that played a trick on him, or maybe there was a single thread of humanity still sewn through the twisted fabric of what Lois Wingate had become—the ugliness of his mother's smile wavered and the hungry light in her eyes dimmed. She started to say something . . . then stopped herself, her smile fading, and without attempting any attack she backed away from him and fled into the flickering black-and-yellow shadows.

He needed to stand there and deal with the grief; he needed to repaint his understanding of the world so that it matched this reality—but there were more vampires to fight, more killing to do, and so he turned away from the hole in his life where she had been and kept cutting.

Val struggled to her feet and aimed her shotgun at the nearest vampire, who dodged and then rushed her as she pumped in the next round. She aimed at the last moment and pulled the trigger. The hollow click was lost beneath the tumult, but Val felt the weight of it chunk down on her heart. The vampire bowled her over and they went down together. She tried to jam her forearm under its jaw, but it was far too strong, and inch by inch the snapping fangs came closer to her throat. The stink of the garlic slowed the monster, but its desire was murder, not feeding, so he began clawing at her throat with his nails. Abruptly he stopped and blood splashed Val's face. Spitting the foulness of it out of her mouth, she shoved at the body and it fell away. The grinning head fell to one side and the body to the other.

Val looked up in stunned surprise and saw Mike standing over her, his sword blade trembling from the tension in his hands. He kicked her shotgun toward her and stood over her as she hastily reloaded. A vampire staggered drunkenly toward Mike, the look of fear and confusion on the creature's pale face tightening into abject terror as he saw the long blood-smeared blade move in a silvery flash. Mike kicked aside the sagging corpse, his face hard and his eyes as cold and sharp as the razor edge of the sword.

Val rose behind him and looked around for Crow. She saw him chasing a trio of vampires with jets of gasoline. Then a shadowy figure slipped up behind Crow, and Val screamed, "RUGER!"

She began running, but a dozen vampires swarmed at her and Mike and suddenly all she could think about was fighting and killing.

Crow heard Val's cry just as he felt someone behind him. He whirled around to bring the sprayer up, but Ruger was already too close. He caught Crow's hand, ripped the plastic pistol grip out of his grasp, then backhanded Crow so hard and fast that it was just a blur. Crow spun down to the ground, the torch flying away, and his shotgun slipped from his shoulder.

"Come on, Kwai Chang," Ruger taunted, "let's try for round three here."

Crow shrugged out of the tank straps. He made a play for his holstered pistol, but Ruger kicked it out of his hand and then short-kicked him under the chin so hard it turned the firelight around him to sparkling party lights. Hard hands caught Crow under the armpits and he felt himself pulled roughly to his feet. Through pinholes in his dancing vision he saw Ruger's leering face, heard his whispering voice.

"I can't even begin to tell you how much I'm gonna enjoy this." Ruger licked his lips and grinned.

"Fuck you," Crow said and kneed him in the crotch, then

thumbed him in the throat. That wiped the leer off the killer's face and Crow iced that cake by hitting him in the face with a hard two-handed shove that sent him stumbling backward. Crow made a dive for his shotgun, which was lying in the dirt, but Ruger beat him to it; he shouldered Crow out of the way, snatching up the weapon, took the shotgun in both hands, and with a grunt of effort bent the barrel to a crooked forty-degree angle. He tossed the ruined weapon to Crow. "Go ahead, ass-hole, shoot me."

This time Crow wasted no time on banter. He dropped the useless gun as he pivoted and kicked Ruger in the knee as hard as he could, the crack of bones audible even through the surrounding noise. Ruger cursed and dropped to his good knee. That gave Crow time to reach for his sword and he whipped it out in a fast draw that beat anything he'd ever managed, but Ruger grabbed the shotgun up and parried the blade. The man's speed was unbelievable, faster by far than when they had first fought in Val's front yard—and he was plenty fast then—and even faster than Ruger had been when they'd battled it out at the hospital. Both times Crow had tried to kill Ruger; both times he thought he'd succeeded. Now he was up against a Ruger who was pure monster and at the top of his powers. Crow watched in horror as Ruger rose to his feet, no trace of pain on his face; Crow could hear the bones snapping back into place in the killer's leg.

"Yeah, kickbox a vampire—that's clever," Ruger said and swung the shotgun like a cudgel, and though Crow was able to bring the sword up in time to parry it, Ruger was only using the attack as a ruse to step in close. He clamped one icy hand around Crow's sword wrist and with the other he punched him in the stomach hard enough to knock all the air out of the world. Crow managed to turn enough to deflect most of the force, but what connected was still like a bullet in the gut. Crow felt something tear inside. There wasn't enough air to scream and Crow sank down to his knees.

Ruger bent down and leered at him. "Ooo—where's all the fancy kung-fu moves now, dickhead?"

Ruger raised his fist to punch again and hesitated as the ground beneath them suddenly trembled with the rumbling thunder of an earthquake. Crow stared stupidly down, trying to decide whether it was really happening or if he was going into some kind of convulsion. The tremor passed and Ruger's smile returned as he reached down and once more jerked Crow to his feet, slapped him twice across the mouth, and then pulled him close.

"You know what I'm going to do, asshole? I'm going to break your arms and legs and while you're lying there in the mud I'm going to strip that broke-nose bitch of yours and take her in every hole she's got. Right in front of you. I'm going to split her open and make you watch it. Maybe I'll let all my boys here pull a train on her, ass-hump her until she's begging me to kill her and screaming at you for being a cowardly, ineffectual little small-town piece of shit. Then, when we've used her all up—I'm going to *turn her*. Ohhh, yeah, baby. I'm going to turn that prissy bitch into one of my sluts. Then I think I'll let you two have a nice reunion."

Crow's mouth was filled with blood and he gagged on it. All Crow could do was hock up the blood in his mouth and spit it at Ruger. The garlic was all but gone, but there was just enough to make Ruger wince and cough.

"Yo! Asshole!"

Ruger looked toward the sound and right into the swing of the stock of LaMastra's shotgun. It caught him across the mouth and the vampire's face seemed to disintegrate as he whirled down to the ground. Crow sagged, too, but LaMastra caught him with one hand and kept him up.

"Come on, man, we got to fall back and regroup." LaMastra's face was crisscrossed with scratches and cuts, his clothes were torn, and he looked nearly spent. "Gotta find some space to reload. I'm dry."

Crow felt the ground firming under him and he started to say something, but then something punched him in the stomach again. It was impossible with LaMastra standing face-to-face with him just inches away, but Crow looked down and when he saw what it was the whole world twisted sideways into madness. It was a fist. A fist covered with blood that steamed like soup, a fist wrapped in coils of purple intestine and red strings of muscle fiber, a fist that seemed to have sprouted like magic from LaMastra's stomach. Crow looked slowly up from that fist to LaMastra's face. The detective seemed confused; he frowned, gave Crow a weary half-smile, and then coughed up a dark pint of blood onto Crow's chest. The detective's big body sagged down and Crow saw Ruger standing close behind him, smiling. Always smiling.

With a grunt, Ruger yanked his fist out of LaMastra's body and let the big man slump all the way to the ground. Ruger raised his fist to his mouth and licked off some of the blood.

"VINCE!" Crow screamed as he tried to hold on to LaMastra, tried to keep the life in the young man by sheer force of will, by sheer need, but the lights in LaMastra's eyes flickered like candles. He stared into Crow's eyes, and his mouth formed a single word.

"No—" Then more dark blood bubbled onto LaMastra's lips and poured out of his mouth and the flood of it extinguished the fragile light in his eyes. Crow held his friend in his arms and looked up in despair to where Ruger stood above them.

"And now it's your turn," Ruger whispered and took a single step forward.

Instantly a thunderbolt flashed across the flame-torn darkness and struck Ruger in the side, barreling him over, and he went down in a fighting, hissing ball with something monstrously huge and immensely powerful. The impact knocked Crow back a few steps and he stared in shock as the two bodies came to rest against a heap of sword-slashed and fire-burned corpses.

Ruger was pinned under something that was bigger and far stronger—something whose body was packed with knotted cords of muscle and whose hide rippled with a pelt of coarse red hair. Four vampires—survivors of Ruger's elite guard—rushed in and tackled the thing and it went down as Ruger scrambled out from underneath. He rose to his feet, visibly shaken and slashed to the bone in a dozen places, but even as Crow watched the wounds began to close, the skin knit.

One of the other vampires was less fortunate, or perhaps less powerful, and he flopped onto his back with a head that was connected by a few grisly strands of meat. A second vampire catapulted back with a smashed skull. The creature just shook off the other two as it rose into a fighting crouch, facing Ruger. Instantly they began stalking one another, circling, snarling. The thing that had attacked Ruger was gigantic as it rose onto its hind legs, and even with its hunched back and misshapen legs it towered above Ruger. It had large piercing yellow eyes with catlike slits, and tall fur-covered ears that rose straight to tufted points high above the sloping skull. It had a long lupine muzzle that was wrinkled back to reveal spit-flecked teeth as sharp as spikes. The thing stood there, its chest heaving with predatory lust, its daggerlike claws rending the air. Crow stared at it and his mind nearly toppled into a shocked faint.

It was a werewolf.

For an insane moment he thought he was seeing Ubel Griswold reborn, and an atavistic terror threatened to tear the guts out of him. He reeled backward from it, but the creature's whole attention was focused on Ruger.

A dozen more of Ruger's guards circled the monster, but the creature didn't wait for them to attack—it lunged at them and Crow flinched back as blood and torn chunks of meat showered him.

Val and Mike stood with their backs to a wall of flame. She fired her guns dry time and again, and while she reloaded Mike fought with the sword. Twice they felt the ground under them rumble, but there was no sign of Griswold. Even the articulated limbs had receded into the mud. Some of the vampires screamed at one another to kill the woman, but not the boy, and that gave Val and Mike a bit of an edge. When Mike rushed the attackers, they scuttled back, learning from the death of their fellows about the danger of being near this boy.

"I'm nearly out," Val whispered to Mike as she slapped her last magazine into her pistol. Mike nodded, too exhausted to speak. The sword, which had been so light in his hands before, now felt as heavy as a sledgehammer. He looked around for Crow and LaMastra, but they were somewhere on the other side of the clearing, behind pillars of flame, if they were even still alive.

"I'm sorry, Val," Mike said, and he fumbled one hand toward her. For just a moment their hands met and held, and Val gave a fierce squeeze.

"Hold on, honey," she said, and then there was more killing to do as a fresh wave of vampires rushed them.

The werewolf slashed at his face and Ruger dodged back a little too late. He dabbed at the furrows torn on his chin. He sneered at the werewolf. "Well, well, if it isn't the Man's lapdog."

The beast growled low in its throat.

"I thought you were supposed to be on our side. Guess the Man was wrong about that." Ruger ran his fingers along the gash that was already nearly healed. He sniffed his fingers, smelled blood, and licked off the taste. "Mmm. Yummy." Ruger glanced across the clearing to where Sarah lay sprawled, then he cocked his head at the beast. "Ah. I know why you're so pissed. The Man really was wrong about you. You don't want to share at all. You want her all for yourself. Bad doggie. No rawhide chew toys for you tonight." He looked at Sarah again. "It's a shame she's already dead." The beast's head snapped around toward Sarah and it sniffed the air as if trying to smell the exhalations of her breath.

Instantly Ruger attacked, slamming into the monster with all of his inhuman strength and speed. The creature was larger and stronger, but Ruger was faster and far more cunning. He drove the werewolf back and down and then scrambled on top, straddling the beast's barrel chest and pinning its arms with his knees. Ruger's fists began their favorite game—smashing, pulping, destroying—and his speed was blinding. Blood danced up from torn flesh; the crack of bones sounded like gunshots. The werewolf howled in agony and surprise.

Snarling with fury, the beast twisted its hands on its powerful forearms and forced them up behind Ruger, then dragged those claws sharply downward from shoulder blades to waistline. Ruger howled in agony and threw himself away, trailing blood. The werewolf gave him no chance and dove at him, landing claws-first into the vampire's chest and knocking him down. But as Ruger fell he snatched the pistol from his belt, the one he had taken from Crow; he dug the barrel into the monster's gut and fired two shots.

The werewolf was lifted off him and pitched over onto its back, gasping in terrible pain. They were not fatal wounds, but the werewolf was momentarily helpless. Its metabolism could repair almost any amount of damage, but not with the miraculous speed of the vampire.

Ruger got back to his feet and stood over the beast. His body was a mass of long slashes, but they were healing quickly and the pain was inconsequential to him. His clothes glistened with blood that looked black in the firelight. He stared down at the beast, watching it struggle against its own pain and damage, and he grinned in triumph.

"So much for *Lassie Come Home*," he said. "So much for the big dramatic entrance. Stupid shit." He kicked the werewolf, and the creature made a feeble swipe at him, but Ruger easily evaded the claws.

He aimed the pistol at the werewolf's skull. "Let's see how much this hurts."

There was a flash of silver and then the pistol and the hand that held it went flying off into the night. They landed in a burning patch of dry grass and the dead flesh instantly caught fire. Ruger stared at the stump of his right wrist, at the blood that jetted from it, seemingly unable to comprehend what had just happened. He turned slowly, his mouth working in soundless shock.

Crow stood on wide, trembling legs, his sword in his hands. Firelight glimmered on the garlic-coated edge of the weapon. Crow's face was a mass of blood and dirt, his lips trembled with shock, but his eyes were infernos hotter than the fires that raged around him. "You're a piece of shit, Ruger," Crow wheezed. "You were a piece of shit when you were alive, and you're a piece of shit now."

Ruger's face changed from shock to fury in the space of a heartbeat. Howling in uncontainable frenzy, he leapt forward and before Crow could raise the sword for another blow, Ruger used his bleeding stump to batter the weapon aside. There was a sharp metallic *crack!* and ten inches of the sword went spinning into the smoking shadows, the reflective edges striking sparks in the air. Crow staggered back as Ruger swung again and he could feel the cold force of the blow slice the air an inch from his chin.

"You took my hand!" Ruger cried in wonder. *"You took my fucking hand!"*

Crow swung the broken sword at him, and this time Ruger jumped back, evading the cut easily. He laughed as Crow slashed again and again, the jagged stump of the *katana* cutting nothing but smoke and air. Crow lumbered forward doggedly, slashing, cutting, hacking, but each time Ruger lunged backward, and each time the blade missed.

Then something happened that Crow was never able to adequately explain. Ruger took another step backward as Crow lunged in once more, but this time Ruger's evasion jerked up short as if he'd hit an invisible wall, so when Crow's blade came slashing it caught Ruger across the middle. A deep red line, like an impossibly wide mouth, yawned in Ruger's chest and more blood splashed into the air. Ruger looked down at his right leg, and Crow found himself looking, too.

Ruger had backed up to where Vince LaMastra's corpse lay sprawled in a lake of blood. Ruger's retreating foot had brushed against the sergeant's dead, slack hand—*and that hand had closed around the ankle.* The fingers were clamped as tight as a steel shackle.

It was impossible, of course. LaMastra was dead, and there was no power left in his limbs; he was dead, and his dead brain could not have sent the signal to clutch or to hold. Ruger's face was knotted in confusion, and as he gradually raised his eyes to meet Crow's, there was fear in those dark eyes as well.

"I killed you twice, you miserable prick," Crow said in a hoarse voice that sounded like Ruger's own graveyard whisper. *"This time, stay dead!"* The broken sword rose and fell with all of the dwindling strength in Crow's battered body. It caught Ruger on the side of the neck and chopped downward into the chest and sliced Karl Ruger's black heart in half.

Ruger stared at him in disbelief for a long time.

Then he fell. The fierce predatory light in Ruger's eyes that had burned so brightly for so long, a light that had shone on so much death and destruction, went dark forever.

Crow stood there, unable to grasp the reality of what he had just done. After all of this, Ruger was actually, finally gone. It hit him as hard as Ruger's punch and for a moment the enormity of it made him dizzy. The invincible, unbeatable Karl Ruger was gone. Really gone this time, but would anyone ever really know? He looked around, expecting to see death rushing at him, but for the moment he stood alone over Ruger's corpse.

Then he looked down at LaMastra's hand and for the briefest moment there was a shimmer in the air that seemed to rise from the dead man's back, and then LaMastra's fingers relaxed open and were still.

Forty feet away the werewolf was struggling to get to a kneeling position, blood streaming from its wounds; near him, Sarah lay on the ground and shook with palsy. Her face was gashed and bleeding badly and blood dripped onto the mud at her knees. The werewolf began crawling slowly toward her, making low plaintive sounds in its throat. It left a pattern of gore behind it like the trail of a slug.

Crow's mind could not handle the thought of the werewolf. There was something about it that he did not want to understand even though he *did* understand, so he turned away. He picked up the Roadblocker and patted LaMastra down for the last of his ammunition, then Crow hastily reloaded and went to find Val and Mike.

There were far fewer vampires now. The smoke from the fires was so thick it was hard to see. Crow skirted brush fires and he killed anything that got in his way, though each time he fired the big gun it made his gut hurt. Something was definitely wrong in there. He could taste blood in his throat. Then he heard three pistol shots and angled in that direction, blundering through the smoke.

And there was Val, with Mike beside her.

Around them were mountains of the dead. The last remaining vampires yielded and fled as Crow came screaming into the clearing. Crow staggered toward Val and she cried out his name and ran to him, wrapping her arms around him, weeping and saying his name over and over again as they both collapsed down to their knees.

Mike Sweeney stood above them, searching the smoke for movement, his body crisscrossed with cuts, his face a red and nearly unrecognizable mask. Then he also slumped to his knees, looked blankly at Val and Crow, and fell forward onto the bloody hands that still held the sword. His face was bright with fever and his eyes stared at nothing.

"Ruger's dead," Crow whispered as he showered Val's matted hair with dozens of quick, light kisses. "But he killed Vince."

"Oh, God . . ." Val huddled against him. "Is it over?" she asked.

He kissed her lips. "I think so," he murmured.

Beneath them the ground exploded.

Chapter 49

The whole swamp seemed to lift into the air, propelled by titanic pressure from below. Crow felt himself rising into the night, hurtling through shadows and flame and confusion; he felt Val being pulled away from him, heard her scream. Mike was screaming, too. He pitched end over end and landed in a thick holly bush. The bush softened the impact, but Crow could feel something twist in his lower back. Dirt and wormy mud continued to geyser up, shooting high into the smoky sky before raining down heavily all around him. The corpses of the vampires were thrown around like dolls.

A great roar filled the air. Dirt and mud fell all over Crow; he sputtered and spit it out as he shouted for Val and tried to scramble around to find her. The act of turning sent daggers of pain through his back and stomach; pain darted and sparked along the backs of his legs. Fiery light swarmed like fireflies around his head, but there was a narrow corridor of clear vision and he strained to see what it was that had caused the fearful eruption. The muddy earth in the center of the swamp had been churned and torn away. Huge masses of it were clumped around, displaced and discarded, piled up to create a crater rim like the earthworks of a volcano. A few of the surviving vampires, seared and battered, crawled like grubs away from the hole.

There was another deep rumbling sound, and as he watched something impossibly massive began rising from the mouth of the crater. It rose slowly, unfolding from the mud, assuming a shape like a man's and yet unlike anything that had ever lived. Legs like Greek columns lifted its bulk, and the colossal torso straightened by slow degrees to raise the gigantic head; vast arms stretched wide and as the monstrosity reached its full height it stood over fifteen feet tall. Its skin was mottled and slimy, covered with a pale and leprous flesh that oozed and glistened with open sores and pustules; its legs were like those of a great towering goat and seemed to be composed of twist upon twist of braided tree root and warped bone, all of it wrapped in layers of raw muscle fiber that shone wetly with blood and mucus. The torso itself was man-shaped, but its wet flesh was a horrifying patchwork of rat and dog skin, splotchy with patches of bloody fur. The shoulders were covered with writhing hair composed entirely of living maggots that were fused into the skin. The neck was as thick as a bull's and was topped with a face more horrible than any medieval gargoyle: there were two burning red eyes that fumed and smoked and glared out over a boar's snout on either side of which rose thick tusks. Thinner fangs, like those of a rattlesnake, curled downward on the insides of the tusks and hot venom dripped onto the heaving chest and sizzled on the squirming flesh. The beast's brow was heavy and sloped, giving the skull a simian cast, but the ears were large and came to sharp points. Writhing atop the head was a gorgon's nest of twisting snakes.

Crow stared up into the face of pure evil, and he could feel the hope run out of him like water from a punctured barrel. His mind twisted and struggled, trying to accept what he was seeing, and he knew terror on every level of his consciousness, from the coldest facets of his logical mind to the primal instincts buried deep within every cell. This was the face of nightmare defined, this was the dark at the top of the stairs, this was the monster in every child's closet. This was the darkness of the human soul released and given immeasurable power; this was the human potential taken to the ultimate degree of corruption. This was the fear of death and all the monsters out of legend. This was the devil himself.

Here was the architect of all their grief, all of their loss. Here was the cruel intellect whose awful desires had conceived the campaign of hurt against the town and its people. This was Ubel Griswold reborn, the god of the dark new world to come.

(2)

Griswold looked slowly around at the devastation he wrought. He stood in a fiery temple whose smoky pillars seemed to lift the entire heavens. Beneath his skin the vermin of the earth writhed in constant agony so that his skin appeared to shimmer. When he looked out upon what his hand had made, he was well pleased.

Crow lay nearest, groaning, hands clamped to his stomach; Val was fifty feet away, slumped against LaMastra's corpse. Ruger's dead body lay over the rim of the crater and near it the were-wolf crouched, still weak and bleeding, its yellow eyes filled with fear and hate. Mike was the farthest away, his sword hilt inches from his hand; his eyes were wide and staring and all hope was struck from his face.

Ubel Griswold threw back his head and laughed. It was a sound too deep, too loud, too jarring to be real. Crow jammed his fists against his ears and cried out as blood burst from his nostrils.

Griswold took a single step forward and the whole clearing shook; another step and the sound was like the fall of an artillery shell. Crow felt his body lift and thump down with each cloven footfall, and his mind rebelled against such a creature. The world was never meant to endure the weight of such a thing as this, and Crow knew that if it was here, if had been allowed to manifest itself, then everything was lost, that all sense and order were gone from the world.

Griswold eyed them all with amused contempt. "What a collection of useless shit," he said in a voice that boomed like thunder.

Crow remembered that voice, that thick accent, from a million years ago.

"Did you really have the conceit to think you could stop me? That you could stop my Red Wave?" He stamped down a yard from Crow's head and the shock wave threw Crow five feet into the air. "I was leading armies before this sewer of a country was even born! I was with the Aryan hordes that burned Rome! I've walked a thousand battlefields, ten thousand!" He spat, and the spittle was alive with beetles and maggots. "You all deserve death just because you're too stupid to be allowed to live." Griswold said all this in a voice filled with contempt, but his face was bright with pleasure. He was enjoying this on a profoundly sexual level; this was better than anything he'd felt in thirty years. To smell blood on the air, to taste the richness of pain on his tongue—it was wonderful.

He bent toward Crow and pointed one taloned finger, and as Crow watched in helpless horror the finger extended, became one of the multijointed limbs that had sprouted earlier from the mud. The claw stretched toward Crow and touched him, but the touch was light, a caress. "Yesss. I know you. I know your blood. Your brother squealed like a little girl when I gutted him."

He sneered with malicious delight as he turned toward Val. "I know you, too. I had your uncle. Very tasty. He screamed for mercy, did you know that? He begged and screamed and pissed in his pants, and I took him anyway. Weak, cowardly piece of garbage. But his blood was oh so sweet. And when Boyd killed your brother . . . I *tasted* that, too. It was delicious."

He turned again, this time to the werewolf, who tried to stand erect, but failed and slipped back down to all fours. The werewolf snarled at him and Griswold shook his head slowly. "You disappoint me," he said. "You were supposed to be at my side, and yet you turn on me. I even brought your woman here to be my sacrifice—a sacrifice I would have shared with you—and yet you kill my servants. That will cost you."

Finally Griswold turned to Mike. "And you. My son. My betrayer. *Dhampyr* indeed! I may not be able to kill you, but I can hurt you. I can make your world a screaming hell until you take your own life. I will delight in finding ways to torment you, *dhampyr*. Perhaps I'll lock you and your *other* father in the same cellar and see what happens. He isn't evil, it seems, and that means he can kill you and it won't harm me at all. Very droll, don't you think? Yesss, I will lock you away together and wait until he gets hungry enough. That will be sweet."

Crow saw Mike stare across the clearing to where the werewolf crouched, saw the sight of the creature register on Mike's face, and Mike scrambled into a defensive crouch.

"I used his body once. I wore it like a suit of skin and in it I used your mother. Oh . . . she was sweet, my little *dhampyr*! Would you like to know the things she did? Would you like to know the things she liked? Would it shock you? Would it make you scream the way I made her scream?"

Mike snatched up his sword and rushed at Griswold. The sword flashed and Griswold reached down from his towering height and simply smashed the boy into the mud. The sword fell from his hands and he lay gasping in the muck, his eyes wide and staring from the enormity of the pain.

Griswold sighed. "God! I've wanted to do that since you were born, you worthless waste of blood."

"Leave him alone!" yelled Crow as he lurched to his feet, took one decisive step toward Mike, and immediately fell flat on his face. He coughed and blood flecked his lips.

Griswold's laugh shook the world. In the air above tens of thousands of crows screamed as the echo assaulted the sky. Around him the forest was ablaze.

Then Griswold bent down and from behind the ridge of the crater he lifted the limp, sagging body of Sarah Wolfe. Crow looked up and tried to call her name, but his voice was only a faint croak. Sarah stirred in Griswold's grasp, but did not wake. Blood trickled from both of her ears; her eyes were half-open and sightless with shock.

"Ah, my sweet," Griswold murmured, stroking her with a long talon. He sniffed at her, smelling her blood, and his eyelids fluttered as if he had just inhaled the most potent of opiates. "You are a gift for a god. Just a little sip, just a taste, and then I can leave this place. Just a tiny drop of your blood and I will leave here forever and this world will be *mine*." He sniffed her again and then caught sight of Crow worming his way brokenly through the mud. "Did my son tell you what is going to happen? Oh, I know he looked into that *schwartze* musician's mind— do you think he could have done that without me letting him? It amused me to have him look and to feel his pain at what he saw. Do you know what he saw? Shall I tell you? He saw the end of your world. He saw the coming of a new Dark Age. I will darken your skies and your lives forever. I will build my armies and spread out across the face of this world, and every nation will fall because they will not know how to fight what I am. Do you think the cross will stop me? I piss on your cross! Do you think garlic and rosewood will stop me? Weeds and garbage! I'm above such nonsense. There is *nothing* in your world that can stop me, and my army will be vast and powerful. How can your armies hope to stop mine with guns and tanks? I can raise all of the dead across the whole of the world. Every cemetery is a fresh battalion for me, and as I kill my enemies they will become my newest recruits. Nothing can stop me. Not now, not ever again."

He closed his flaming eyes for a moment and drew in a deep lungful of air through the dripping nostrils of his porcine snout. "Can you smell the fire and blood? That is the perfume of Armageddon." He opened his eyes and raised Sarah once more to his mouth. A fat, mottled tongue lolled out and licked her throat. Even unconscious she gagged and shifted instinctively away. Griswold looked down at the werewolf, his voice filled with mockery. "To think I was going to share her with you. I was going to let her death be the bond between us. I would have made you a general in my army, equal to Wingate and Ruger. Together we would have washed all the nations of the world in blood. But you are too stupid, too small of mind to understand or appreciate those gifts. Well, see your woman die! See how her blood will set me free, set me on the road to conquest!" His mouth yawned wide and the serpent's fangs dripped with venom and Sarah's eyes snapped open and she shrieked with such a deep and overwhelming terror that it filled the whole world and lifted up into the smoky air.

The werewolf's shriek was almost human as it leapt at Griswold.

If Terry's mind was still in that hulk of a body, then at that moment, hearing those words, it snapped. Hate can sometimes transcend everything, even injury and fear of the grave. Love is a powerful force that can move mountains.

As Griswold bent to consume Sarah, Terry Wolfe threw himself at Griswold, slashing and tearing and biting in an insane frenzy of murderous need; his talons opened great rents in the diseased hide and instead of blood it was a torrent of ants and spiders and roaches and slugs that poured from the wounds.

But love and hate were not enough and in the perverse scheme of things on which the universe was built this was not Terry's fight to win; as powerful as he was, he was no match for the thing that Ubel Griswold had become.

Griswold bellowed in pain and struck out at the werewolf, knocking it dozens of feet through the air; his monstrous hand opened reflexively and Sarah dropped to the torn mud by the massive goat legs, and she lay there as still and silent as the dead. Griswold bent toward her and then recoiled when new pain flared in his chest as Val knelt by the edge of the crater with Crow's Beretta held in both hands firing spaced shots, punching dark holes in Griswold's flesh, trying to hit a heart that didn't exist. There was no blood for the garlic to pollute, no nervous system for the oil to disrupt—but Griswold's flesh was alive and he could feel pain, even if he could not be killed. He swiped angrily at Val and she scrambled backward, but not fast enough. Just the edge of Griswold's massive hand struck her forearm, but it was enough. There was a loud *crack!* and the pistol dropped into the mud. Val screamed as she fell, clutching her broken arm to her stomach.

"Val!" Crow yelled. "Look out!"

Val looked up as Griswold took another thunderous step forward and reached for her, but she was already slithering away through the mud, pushing herself backward with her heels. The huge cloven hoof came down right where she had been and the whole floor of the Hollow shook. Val stumbled to her feet and ran.

The werewolf lunged again, and as it attacked, Crow could see that half of its face was smeared with fresh blood and one ear was hanging by a few red threads; but the claws and fangs were undamaged and it flew at Griswold with supernatural ferocity, catching the towering monster in the back. Griswold hissed in pain and staggered with the impact; he reached around with both hands, trying to dislodge the werewolf, but the creature had buried its fangs into the putrid flesh of Griswold's waistline and was shaking its head back and forth, worrying the flesh into tatters. Griswold tilted backward as if overbalanced by the werewolf's weight, and for a moment Crow's heart leapt in his chest. It looked like the werewolf was winning, was ripping the giant down, was killing him. Griswold tipped backward and only as he fell did Crow realize that Griswold was making himself fall. His gargantuan body crashed backward onto the ground with the werewolf under him. Tons of weight crashed down onto the werewolf's chest and drove Terry's body inches into the mud. Crow could hear the snap of bones and a canine yelp of pain.

Griswold rolled over and got to his knees. The werewolf was nearly buried in the mud, pushed deeply into the swampy earth in a tangle of fur and blood. Sharp edges of white bone stood like cactus needles all along the creature's body, and the chest labored to breathe with tattered lungs. Griswold reared above him and curled his right hand into a powerful bucket-size fist, then with a growl of triumphant hate he punched downward, driving the fist into the werewolf's chest. The whole rib cage exploded in a spray of blood. A pitiful howl of defeat and agony burst from the creature's mouth, propelled by a bright red jet of gore. Griswold grinned and punched down again and again and again. Blood splashed the entire clearing and bits of bone flew up and bounced off Griswold's chest.

Crow was sickened by what he saw, but was helpless and compelled to watch.

Griswold paused for a moment to admire his work. The werewolf was clearly dead, its body destroyed beyond any hope of its superhuman ability to cure. Its spine was shattered in a dozen places, its skull was smashed in, the heart and brain pierced.

Griswold peered at the beast and a look of pleasure dawned on his features, then he and Crow watched as a sudden and awful change came over the werewolf. In the space of just a few seconds the thick red fur was sucked back into the body, the musculature shifted, and the shattered bones reoriented themselves even; it was as if Crow was watching some splatter-house film speeded up to superfast motion. In just seconds the werewolf completely vanished and the man emerged.

Crow looked down at the dead man and his heart tore itself to pieces. "Oh my God . . . *Terry!*"

Griswold laughed as he raised his fist for a final blow. He put all of his incalculable strength into it and slammed down so hard that blood flew everywhere and the ground shook with earthquake force and the body of Terry Wolfe was driven totally into the ground, out of sight, buried forever in the wormy earth.

"Be damned," Griswold snarled, "as I was damned." He punched again, driving the corpse farther down. "Be buried, as I was buried." And a final earth-shaking blow. "Be forgotten, as I was forgotten."

Crow looked up at the giant and then down at his own empty hands. His shotgun and pistol were gone, his sword was broken. All he had left was the dagger in the sheath on his belt. A good strong weapon, the blade coated with garlic. He drew it and looked at it. It was a pitiful toy matched against the monster that Griswold had become.

"God help me," he prayed as he rose to a trembling crouch.

A gunshot startled him and he saw that Val had found the pistol and was holding it in her left hand, her right curled protectively around her stomach. She stood well back from Griswold and was again firing well-aimed shots, hitting every time. Griswold roared in renewed anger and hauled his great bulk to his full height and took a step toward her, but she ran. He lumbered after her, taking a single step for each half-dozen of hers. She ran toward the fires and dodged around them, and Crow scrambled after, calling her name. He realized what she was doing: she was trying to get to the gasoline sprayer, but Griswold was already closing in, bending to grab her.

Crow broke into a run, feeling pain shoot down his legs with each step, feeling something slide hot and wet in his stomach. He was closer to Griswold than he was to Val, and he caught up first. He raised the dagger. *"Leave her alone!"* he bellowed and drove the blade into the back of Griswold's right knee. The point of the dagger stabbed deep, severing corded muscle and tendon, and the goat leg buckled and Griswold went down onto the knee; the motion tore the blade out of Crow's grip and caused the dagger's point to drive deeper into the joint. Griswold swung around and grabbed at Crow. Crow tried to run, but Griswold was too fast and Crow cried out as the huge hand clamped like a vise around his waist. He was snatched off the ground. He beat at the fist, but he might as well have been beating on a chunk of granite.

"CROW!" he heard Val cry and he looked down to see her fumbling to reload the pistol, making a clumsy job of it with one good arm.

"I'll tear your soul out of you for that!" promised Griswold and he squeezed harder still. Crow gritted his teeth and tried to beat at the hand, but the pressure only increased. Blood drowned Crow's vision and roared in his ears; he heard a sound and realized that it was his own voice, screaming a high, shrill note of agony as the fist squeezed tighter and tighter until the bones in Crow's hips began to crack. Crow could feel his legs dying, he could feel the nerves rending as the bones shifted and splintered.

"Oh . . . *God!*"

Griswold leaned close and laughed. "I spit on your God!"

Crow heard a feral growl and turned to see Mike Sweeney slowly rising to his feet, lips curled back from his teeth, his face a mask of unfiltered hate. He clawed through the mud until he found his sword hilt and tore it free.

Griswold turned toward him, a mocking laugh on his lips, and then Mike was at him. The sword slashed in under Griswold's reaching hand and cut the kneeling giant across the inside of his undamaged leg; immediately that leg buckled and Griswold began to cant sideways. His hand opened and Crow felt himself falling, felt his body land, but he felt it only as a jolt to his upper body; his lower body was dead. He thumped down and saw Mike dodge in again, saw the sword flash out again and another long line open in Griswold's stomach, near where the werewolf had cut him, though those earlier cuts had long since healed. The same torrent of squirming insects poured out, and Mike danced around them, cutting and cutting. All the time Mike kept screaming "NO! NO!" over and over again at the top of his voice. He was mad, insane, driven to a point of rage beyond anything he had ever imagined, beyond anything Crow had ever witnessed.

Griswold struck at him and again Mike went down, but the boy's rage was so great that he clawed his way back to his feet and attacked again. Each time his sword licked out another gash appeared on Griswold's body. Lice and maggots and worms spilled out into the glow of the brush fires and burning corpses. Mike came in again and slipped on a twisting pile of centipedes and started to go down; Griswold howled in triumph and reached for him, moving faster than anything his size should be able to. His hand closed around Mike's waist the way it had ensnared Crow, but at that moment Val opened up with her reloaded pistol. The first two shots hit Griswold in the face and he reared back in pain, pawing at the damage. Mike seized the opportunity to slash downward with the sword over and over again, half severing the thick wrist. The tendons parted and the hand sagged open, spilling Mike to the ground. Instantly the boy was up again, his fury unabated, his killing frenzy stoked even hotter. The sword slashed and slashed and great stinking chunks of Griswold flew into the night, landing with wet thuds on the torn ground, or falling into the fires, where they popped and sizzled.

"Val!" Crow yelled, "The sprayer . . . the *sprayer!*"

He didn't know if she heard him or had just run out of bullets, but there were no more shots. Mike was still fighting, still holding the moment. Crow looked wildly around for a weapon and saw something on the ground near him; he set his teeth against the pain and used his hands to pull himself toward it. He grabbed it, kissed it, and rolled onto his back, bracing the butt of the Roadblocker against the ground.

Griswold's roars were ear-shattering; they tore chunks out of the night. And each one sounded stronger. Mike's arm was tiring, his strength failing, and Griswold was regaining his strength despite the wounds the *dhampyr* inflicted. Whatever supernatural force the boy possessed was not doing the job; he just wasn't causing enough damage.

Crow pulled the trigger of the big Mag-10 and the recoil buried the stock four inches into the mud. The bear-shot caught Griswold under the chin and snapped his head back like a boxer's when he stepped into an uppercut. Half of Griswold's porcine snout was gone, the raw meat seething with insects.

The air in front of Crow shimmered—just like it had after LaMastra died—and for a moment, just for a fraction of a second, Crow thought he saw a man standing there. Gray skin that had once been chocolate brown, intelligent eyes that were now dusty, a smile that Crow still remembered after all these years. The Bone Man looked at him and his mouth formed the words, "Little Scarecrow."

The Bone Man turned and leapt at Griswold, flying high into the air as if he had no weight. Then he was gone, but Griswold staggered as if struck and Crow knew that the Bone Man had dealt his blow. But there was far more to the Bone Man's attack than that. Suddenly the air was filled with a new sound and Crow looked up as the air was rent by the screams of ten thousand birds and the dry, hysterical rustle of countless wings. The night sky above the clearing coalesced into a funnel of black that spiraled down and down and down as all the night birds of Pine Deep came at the Bone Man's call.

Griswold turned his ruined face upward—a face that even now was starting to reconstruct itself—and Crow saw fear on those features. Real fear. Crow jacked a round into the breech and fired again just as the wave of crows hit Griswold like a fist. The combined impact drove Griswold to the ground with a thunder that shook the valley. Hundreds, thousands of the birds died in that first moment, their skeletons shattered as they hit, but the birds kept coming in wave after wave.

Crow jacked another round and fired, knowing that the blast would kill some of the birds, too, but it had to be done. He fired, pumped, fired.

Mike stood his ground on the far side, slashing at his father's flesh, releasing the vermin, watching as the crows attacked them.

There was a hissing sound and Val was there, the spray tank on the ground where she'd dragged it, the pistol grip in her left hand, the gasoline splashing Griswold's torso and throat and chest.

Crow fired his last shot and dropped the gun. He dug into his pocket for his lighter and started crawling again, needing to be near for this. Mike was sobbing as he hacked at Griswold; Val was screaming. The noise of the birds was maddening, and throughout it all Griswold's voice shook the heavens and his fists smashed down and slaughtered the birds.

Crow yelled and he tasted blood in his mouth as he flicked the lighter on and slammed it down onto the gas-soaked mud.

"Go back to hell!"

The night opened its great dark mouth and roared with a tongue of flame. A sheet of fire shot into the air and Crow rolled away, beating at the flames on his arm and hair. Val dropped the sprayer and rushed to him, and they clung together in the furnace heat. Griswold roared in terror and pain as the fire attacked him like a living thing, like a white-hot predator. Together they crawled over to where Sarah lay, and when Crow pressed his fingers to her throat, there was a slow but steady rhythm.

The heat slammed into Mike like a fist, but he stood his ground. Even when his eyebrows singed to ash and his hair began to melt Mike held fast and his sword cut and cut through the flames. Mike knew—if he knew nothing else in life for sure—that this was his moment. This truly was what he was born to do. Griswold had not yet fed on Sarah Wolfe's blood; he had not yet tasted the innocent blood that would send his power soaring off the scale. He could still be hurt, as the flames were hurting him; and he could still be killed, as Mike so dearly wanted to do. If the sword in the hands of a *dhampyr* was a holy weapon, then so was the fire so long as he touched it, shared the essence of what he was with it. And with the birds. He felt the wings brush him and he knew that it was deliberate, that something—or perhaps some*one*—was orchestrating the moment. The air shimmered around him and Mike thought he heard the sweet sound of blues music like a calming eye of this dreadful storm. The music put iron back into his muscles and deep in Mike's soul the eye of the *dhampyr* finally and completely *awoke*. Power raced through him like lava, burning through his veins, igniting in his muscles, and as he renewed his attack the inferno around Griswold flared brighter, and the birds plunged and died.

Ubel Griswold screamed even louder, a shriek that rose up to the heavens.

The fire burned Mike's sword black as it cut, and then the metal began to glow as if it had been buried deep in a forge. He rent and tore at his father as the crows in the air ignited and fell onto Griswold, their own mass adding fuel to the blaze. Thunder cracked above and lightning forked through the sky as if nature itself, finally appalled at the perversity of what had come to life in Dark Hollow, now cried out in protest.

Griswold climbed back to his feet, a flaming god wreathed in fire; he opened his mouth to cry his rage and the flames flooded inside. He thrashed and beat at the birds and the fire, but the fire burned with a greater will even than his. As Val and Crow watched, Griswold's mighty legs buckled and he dropped to his knees. For a long time he knelt there, burning, his arms still flailing, but with each moment there was less power in his fight, less belief in his own survival. Val and Crow lay there in the mud and the blood and watched the oldest evil, perhaps the oldest sentient thing on earth, burning to death as above them the remaining night birds circled and circled endlessly.

All around Griswold, around the swamp and through the woods to where his house still stood, the trees were on fire. Despite the thunder and lightning, the clouds overhead had parted and a swollen orange moon rode the heavens above the pyres of Halloween.

Mike's clothes were catching fire, but he stepped closer still so that he could bring his sword high over his head and with a final grunt of effort he chopped down, cleaving between the horns and cutting all the way into Ubel Griswold's brain. There was a burst of black light that flashed outward and struck Mike like a shock wave so that he staggered back, his eyes rolling up in his head; his sword fell from his twitching fingers as he stumbled backward and finally fell.

It seemed to take forever, but Griswold finally toppled forward onto his face and as he did so the force of will that held his shape together failed. The flesh blackened and burned away and the millions of insects that made up his body popped and hissed and steamed as they were charred to ashes. What the fire did not consume the surviving birds did.

After thirty years of planning, after centuries of hunting as man and wolf, after the meticulous ambition of the Red Wave, Ubel Griswold was dead and all his dark dreams with him.

Crow heard a sound and saw that Mike was crawling painfully toward them, and when he was near Val and Crow pulled him close and slapped out the embers on his clothes. He curled up like a child against them, weeping uncontrollably, clinging to them with absolute need, and they in turn held him, and each other.

"Now it's over . . . ," Crow whispered, kissing Val's face, her hair.

She pressed his hand to her chest over her heart.

Above them the thunder boomed again and the clouds closed once more, and then the rain fell as if Heaven itself wept.

EPILOGUE

Midnight in Hell

The SERT Tactical Team came in from the east in a pair of Bell Jet Rangers. They made a full circuit of the town, using nightscopes when they could and standard binoculars where there was too much fire. There were over a hundred buildings burning, cars overturned, corpses everywhere. Lieutenant Simons, the team leader, had spent two tours in Iraq; this looked worse. Before his advance team was even on the ground he called it in as a possible terrorist attack by forces unknown. That rang bells all the way to the governor's residence in Harrisburg, and he was on the phone to Homeland within two minutes.

The governor declared a state of emergency before the first SERT chopper set down in the high school playground, and by the time Lieutenant Simons had deployed his Tac-Teams, Homeland had issued an elevated Terror Alert.

Each Tac-Team had four men, all of them in woodland camouflage battle dress and tactical body armor; each team leader and his coverman carried the HK MP-5 9mm SMG, the point man had a Glock .40 caliber pistol and a ballistic shield, and the fourth man backed their play with a short-barreled Remington 870 12-gauge shotgun. They were fighting fit and elite, each one of them pumped with adrenaline and ready to take down any armed resistance.

But apart from the fires and the towers of smoke, the streets of Pine Deep were as silent and still as the grave. For the first twenty minutes all they found was death.

The next wave of choppers swept in from Trenton and Philly, their blades scything through the towering columns of smoke that rose from the town, and they skirted the bigger wall of smoke that was an almost featureless gray screen across the forested hills beyond the town. The state forest raged out of control and the fingers of flame seemed eager to reach up and touch the helicopters.

The news choppers got there first, having been scrambled when the live feeds went down. They beat the first of the police units by ten minutes and so were able to tape nearly all of the rescue operation. Even the police were already on their way when Joe Bob Briggs called them from a gas station telephone in Black Marsh. He'd met up with screenwriters Susco and Gunn and the three of them had rowed a fishing boat past the smoking ruins of the bridge and called from the first phone they found.

Residents of Crestville and Black Marsh had reported the blasts to 911 and local news; planes in flight had radioed in descriptions of the widespread fires. Boats of every description pushed off from Crestville and Black Marsh, and an armada of them cruised up the Delaware, disgorging press, cops, EMTs, and lots of rubberneckers.

Police from the neighboring towns and the regular Staties were ordered to hang back well outside the perimeter of the town proper. Orders had come from the governor; the National Guard was being mobilized and Homeland would take over as soon they had a team on the ground.

The SERT teams moved out into the streets, hugging the shadows, sticking close and low to the buildings, each team cross-spotting for the other. As tough and hardened as these men were, what they saw began to wear on them very quickly. Buildings lay in ruins. Bodies littered the streets. Then there was movement off to the left and Simons held up his closed fist and the team froze, weapons shifting to cover the pale-faced figure that moved out of the smoke. It was a woman holding a dead child in her arms. Even from across the street Lieutenant Simons could tell that the baby was dead—nothing that twisted and broken could, please God, still be alive. The woman was white with shock, her eyes hollow, and she walked with a mindless shuffling gait.

Simons detached two men to get her and bring her over and down behind cover. She allowed herself to be nearly carried out of the street; she made no sound, registered no trace of recognition.

And that's how it started. First her, then a pair of little girls and their dog climbed out through a cellar window of the library. A small family came out of an alley, the father holding a golf club like a weapon until the SERT team members made him put it down. The father looked at the club and then began to cry.

"We have multiple survivors," Simons called in. "No hostiles visible. We need backup and med teams on the ground right now."

From then on choppers landed one after another in parking lots and in fields. The sounds of their rotors brought more and more people out of hiding, and they staggered out of their houses, their faces slack with shock and black with soot, their mouths trembling, eyes rimmed with red, minds too numb to even speak. Dozens of people were clearly drugged, but how and by what was not yet known. Some of the tourists and residents rushed up to the rescue teams, heedless of the guns and the warnings, and clung to the police as they wept. By the time the first team reached the hospital parking lot, some of the officers were weeping, too; the rest had faces like stone masks but with eyes that burned as hot as open furnace doors. If there had been any terrorists in Pine Deep, there would have been a second bloodbath.

It took Simons almost forty minutes to find someone who was lucid enough to tell the story of what happened, but the story turned out to be impossible, just a psychotic delusion. Monsters, vampires, and zombies. The witness was a big man, a blues singer who identified himself as Mem Shannon, who was in town for a Festival gig, and though the man didn't appear to be as dazed or stoned as some of the survivors, his story was ridiculous. By the time Shannon described how he beat a vampire's head in with his electric guitar, Simons had already tuned him out and was looking for a more credible witness. But everyone who could talk told the same story, or some version of it.

Two SERT Tac-Teams entered the hospital as if they were entering a combat hot zone, which was not far from the truth, although by dawn there was no heat left. Inside the hospital everything was cold: the building, the bodies, the blood splashed high on the walls. The team made their way in through the ER entrance, past a wrecked car that had been driven right into the building. They saw spent shotgun shells and 9mm casings; they saw bullet-riddled bodies. They followed the trail of bloody footprints that led away from each successive battle site, down the hall, into a stairwell choked with the dead, up the stairs and unerringly to where they found a room filled with patients and injured staff members.

Until that point Jonatha had been in control of her emotions, but when she saw the first SERT officer appear in the doorway to the examination room, she lost it. She laid her head down on Newton's lap and wept like a child. Newton, his eyes dreamy with the morphine one of the surviving nurses had given him, feebly stroked her hair.

The SERT team swept the hospital and found fifty-six living people and three times that many dead; many more were unaccountably missing. Some of the survivors had barricaded themselves in storage rooms or utility closets in remote corners of the hospital; ten were in the chapel, clutched together behind the altar; and the rest were the survivors of Jonatha's group. The stories they told were frantic, chaotic, and often contradictory except for those people who had been with Jonatha. Everyone in her group talked about terrorists.

Jonatha had conjured the story and coached them all in the specifics, clearly explaining what the consequences would be for their lives and credibility if they even breathed the word *vampire*. After everything that had happened, the people were more than willing to buy her fiction and by the fifth or sixth retelling, most of them actually believed it. It was easier to believe.

Newton was evacuated along with a handful of others who were seriously wounded. A Medivac chopper flew him to Doylestown Hospital and he was in surgery fifteen minutes after touchdown. The doctors had to sew up and reinflate his left lung, reset four ribs, more or less rebuild his sternum, and treat him for countless abrasions, contusions, and a dangerous dose of shock. When they asked him what had happened, he muttered dazedly about vampires taking over the world, and the staff all smiled to each other about that.

Jonatha stayed in town and tried to explain how important it was to send a team immediately out to Dark Hollow. She was ignored at first, but then she found the right spur and dug it deeply into their collective flanks. She told them that Dark Hollow was the base camp of the terrorists, and that the leader of the group might still be there. She told them that a local policeman had gone out there with a detective from Philadelphia, and that a second Philly cop had been murdered out there the day before. They had uncovered the terrorist plot, but by the time they knew what they were up against, the lines of communication had been cut.

It was a good story, something to react to, something to get behind. The SERT teams saddled up, eager for the chance to actually find some of the sick bastards who had committed the atrocities, to rescue some fellow officers, and maybe even to get a little payback.

Seventy minutes after the first choppers had landed in town, three helicopters lifted off—the two SERT Bell Rangers and a heavier medevac bird—and flew southeast at top speed. Fire planes were already ordered from every field in three counties, but the Tac-Teams had to go in while the forest was still ablaze. The closer they got to the fires the more the rescue team began to lose hope of finding anyone alive. They found a big field by a dilapidated old house and set down there. The front porch was charred and as they moved past they saw the remains of a corpse on the porch, and Lieutenant Simons knew that, from Jonatha's description, they had just seen the body of Detective Sergeant Frank Ferro.

The Tac-Teams were trained to move fast and they passed down the forest trail at great speed but with almost no sound. Night-vision glasses painted the landscape a lurid green, but as they neared the burning swamp area they switched back to standard eyesight—the fires provided more than enough light.

As they enter the clearing, Simons stopped, his troops fanning out to either side of him.

"Oh my God," he whispered. His shock was reflected on the faces of each officer and medic. This was like nothing any of them had ever seen.

The fires in the clearing had died down from lack of fuel, the bushes having burned down to the mud and sizzled out. Wisps of smoke drifted up from charred corpses and mingled with the predawn mist to create a surreal landscape. There were thousands of corpses. Thousands.

And in the middle of it all, there were four living people.

Val was the only one conscious. She sat in a huddle, clutching a broken and bloated arm close to her body. Crow had passed out and his hands were icy and slick with sweat. Sarah Wolfe looked like she was sleeping, but as soon as the medics touched her she began to scream—her eyes were still closed, but she screamed and screamed for nearly three minutes. Mike was in worse shape. His body was crisscrossed with many deep cuts, each of which was caked with blood and dirt; some of the cuts were already red and hot with infection. His eyes were strangely discolored—blue, flecked with red, ringed with gold—and the pupils were fixed and dilated, his breathing shallow and rapid. One of the boy's hands was badly broken, and there was evidence of bleeding from his ears.

The medics worked like heroes and two-man teams hustled everyone out on stretchers, running through the woods as fast as safety would allow toward the waiting choppers.

"Will he be all right?" Val begged one of the medics.

"I'm sure he will," the medic lied.

They found the body of Philadelphia police detective Vince LaMastra lying in a bloody pool, his dead hand clutched tightly around the ankle of another corpse. Simons stared down at the big detective's body and tried to understand how such a huge hole could have been torn through the man's muscular stomach. The wound did not look like any kind of gunshot wound, but it was too rough for a knife. Val was standing beside him and she surprised Simons by kneeling and bending forward to kiss LaMastra on the forehead. She did it gently, as if she were saying good night to a sleeping child. The act touched Simons and his eyes burned with tears.

The man whose ankle was caught in LaMastra's grip had obviously been killed by some kind of weapon, and Simons was startled to find a broken Japanese sword hilt near the body. His surprise doubled and then tripled when he took a closer look at the face of the dead man. As impossible as it seemed, he looked exactly like Karl Ruger, the man who had been the focus of the manhunt the month before, but whose body was stolen from the Pine Deep morgue. Simons had to force himself to shelve his wonderment so he could continue with the search.

When it was clear that there were no additional survivors to discover or identify, Simons ordered a stretcher for Val.

"I'm pregnant," she said as they secured her to the board. They promised to be careful.

While they worked, Simons squatted down next to her, pulling off his Kevlar helmet. "What in God's name happened here?" asked the corporal in an awed whisper.

Val looked at him for a moment. She opened her mouth to speak, but then shook her head.

"I don't know," she said.

(2)

It took two days to put out all the fires, though water was pumped onto the buildings for much longer. Nearly a week passed before all of the survivors were found and counted. Some of them had been hiding in root cellars under their farmhouses; others in any shelter they could find. A dozen farmers and their families had crowded into a big shed that was piled with huge sacks of garlic bulbs. The entire congregation of a synagogue had boarded themselves up in the sanctuary. Over a hundred people, mostly teenagers, had been herded into the barn at the Haunted Hayride by a couple of actresses and a stuntman. A Bucks County blues band, Kindred Spirit, and their entire audience hid in the pool house at the country club and for some reason no one was even injured. A group of moviegoers had barricaded themselves in a drive-in projection room, and on the college campus a bunch of students from the theater department had survived by covering themselves in fake wounds and hiding among the dead. Those were the kinds of stories that emerged as the days went on.

But not all of these stories ended well. Four stock boys, three checkers, and half a dozen customers had tried hiding in the walk-in refrigerator of a ShopSmart, and though they survived the night, they were trapped in the cold darkness and found two days too late. Several people had apparently fled into the woods but were killed by smoke inhalation. Three teenage girls were found locked in an old 1950s bomb shelter that was sealed by a combination lock they apparently couldn't open, and they never turned on the air filtration system.

There were other stories of survival and disaster, and with each day the tallies of both living and dead rose. When the official counts were finally checked and rechecked a dozen times, the survivors numbered 6,532. The death toll stood at a staggering 11,641, making it one of the worst disasters in U.S. history. Nearly two-thirds of all the people in town for the festival had died—a mix of residents, tourists, entertainers, and reporters.

Somewhere, no one ever discovered where, there were eighty-four people missing, among them Lois Wingate, the mother of the boy rescued in the forest. No trace of them was ever found by the authorities; no remains were ever discovered.

Over time the hundreds of forensics investigators from dozens of local, state, federal, and military agencies put together a clear picture of what happened. Blood tests showed that a large number of the survivors had ingested dangerously high doses of LSD, haloperidol, PCP, and other hallucinogens. Bags of tainted candy corn and other treats were found in the pockets of many of these people. They found even larger quantities of these drugs in the town's water supply, in beer kegs, even in locally bottled well water. Autopsies revealed that a number of the victims died from massive overdoses of these drugs, particularly among the children; another group had lapsed into comas. It didn't help matters much that haloperidol was known for disrupting memories, so some survivors had no recall of anything happening.

They found weapons caches, and background checks allowed the authorities to tie the weapons to over a dozen militant groups ranging from the Aryan Brotherhood to Al Qaeda. They found anti-Semitic literature that espoused a violent call to arms to stop the "Jewish takeover of America." They even found Internet downloads of schematics for making a low-yield dirty bomb—this in the garage of a Syrian doctor who was killed at the hospital. In short they found absolute proof of a hotbed of terrorism right there in Small Town, America. Homeland jumped on this and released it to the press in an attempt to counter the wild stories of vampires and monsters. It was a far more reasonable explanation for the witness reports, and for the most part it worked.

Vic Wingate would have been pleased. Setting up that smokescreen had taken years to plan and implement.

Depending on who was looking at the evidence, and how much of the evidence he was looking at, it either made perfect sense or no sense at all. That, too, would have been fine with Vic. He had left good leads to follow and some that were obvious red herrings. He wanted misdirection and that's exactly what he got. Except in transcripts of eyewitness reports—which were always privately discredited by physicians and psychologists—the word "vampire" never made it into any official report. If it did, it was on an eyes-only level, and at that level no one was particularly chatty.

Even so, Homeland's press blackout did little good, so eventually the story got out. Reporters descended on Pine Deep like an invading army, and once entrenched they could not be budged for weeks. *Nightline* began nightly reports from Pine Deep that went on for forty-six days. Every detail of information released by the authorities was minutely picked over and endlessly debated by experts in fields ranging from pharmacology to international politics. Every person in town was interviewed over and over again. Every avenue of investigation was explored with unflagging enthusiasm.

No army of terrorists was ever discovered, though some of the less credible terrorist organizations tried to take credit for the catastrophe. That at least gave the current administration someone to shoot at.

When the press found out that the body of Ruger, the infamous Cape May Killer, was discovered at the scene of the Dark Hollow slaughter, that hyped things up again. Just what his involvement had been was never determined, and the coroner's report was sealed by order of Homeland Security.

The official story, given to a prime-time audience by the president, was that a small domestic terrorist cell had been formed by Vic Wingate, Karl Ruger, and Kenneth Boyd. Drug money financed the cell and it received support of various kinds from other terrorist organizations around the world. Wingate and Ruger had known ties to white supremacist organizations, so overall this was seen as "terrorism from within," a sound-bite-friendly phrase that got great coverage. The president saw this as a clear sign that America "must increase its vigilance within our own borders" and "never back down even in the face of great personal harm" and "that every citizen must join" with him "in responding appropriately." It was not the worst lie of that administration, but it was close. When another U.S. carrier battle group was dispatched to the Middle East as part of the appropriate response, even the president's usual critics applauded the action. At the time.

The government breathed a sigh of relief that the Official Story had been successfully swallowed because of the collective gullibility of the people. But the investigators in the government were still deeply afraid because they knew they were lying; they really had no idea what had happened in Pine Deep and they were terrified that it would happen again.

Only a handful of people knew the full and complete story, and one of them wrote it down and waited for just the right moment to spring it on the world.

(3)

One year later, on the anniversary of the Pine Deep Massacre, Willard Fowler Newton published his first book. It was called *Hellnight: The Truth behind the Destruction of Pine Deep*; and it told the true story of what had happened in the town from an insider's point of view. He wisely changed many of the names. Crow and Val were downplayed in the story and their later actions ascribed to townsfolk who had died—a literary license that created new heroes for the public. Mike Sweeney was not mentioned at all, and his role in the story was given to Brandon Strauss, who would forever be remembered as the *dhampyr* in the Pine Deep catastrophe, and who was one of the eighty-four people still unaccounted for.

The book was not a sensationalized piece of writing, not like the dozen or so terrorist-themed books punched out by tabloid writers for the hungry paperback crowd. If anything, *Hellnight* was understated, the prose a little dry. The book didn't just chronicle the events of that one night, but instead presented a backstory that jumped decades and even centuries into the past. Newton's book did not focus on white supremacists, psychedelic hallucinations, or mass hysteria.

Newton told a monster story.

The immediate result was a media outcry and a universal panning of the book by every critic in the country. Within a day of the first reviews Newton was fired from the *Black Marsh Sentinel*.

Newton took the backlash stoically. He no longer cared what

his editor thought, and he didn't give a damn what the critics wrote or said. In the first two weeks *Hellnight* sold out its modest first printing. The small publishing house that had bought the book—the forty-third Newton had approached—hammered out a second printing, this time putting one hundred thousand copies on the shelves, and in a little over ten days those shelves had been swept clean. By Christmas of that year, *Hellnight* was into its fifth printing and it showed no signs of slowing down. It leapt to the top of the nonfiction best-seller list and nothing seemed to be able to shift it until well into the spring. During this time some of the townspeople began coming out in support of the book—a few at first, and then more and more as the book's fame and topic rekindled a whole new interest in the town. Suddenly everyone was talking about vampires. The Sci-Fi Channel was the first to do a special on the town and its haunted history, and soon every basic cable station with a van and a steadycam was producing their own. Reporters who had previously mocked *Hellnight* were rushing their own books to print.

The government very vocally denied that any of the events in Newton's book happened and saying so publicly was tantamount to issuing a mandate for conspiracy theorists to shout "cover-up!" This was further fueled when fragments of video footage from the first few moments of the massacre began appearing on the Internet; officials again denied their authenticity, but the story persisted.

There were some odd cultural side effects of this new notoriety. The word *dhampyr* came into popular usage and even, in one of those pop-culture quirks, became *the* word to describe an up-and-coming executive who was likely to replace a well-seated CEO. A band called Missing 84 had a modest hit with a song called "Haunt Me" that was later covered by the blond gal from *American Idol* and it hit the number three spot on Billboard.

Did the public actually believe the story? Did they truly believe in vampires? Psychologists and sociologists went head to head over that for months. The consensus was that people believed what they wanted to believe, and vampires, it seemed, were what they wanted to believe. It was like the UFO craze of the eighties and nineties. Still, the sales of garlic rose steadily all through that year and well into the next, and in some rural areas, never quite dropped back to normal.

Newton and his fiancée, Dr. Jonatha Corbiel, a noted folklorist from the University of Pennsylvania, were regulars on *Oprah* and *The Tonight Show* with Jay Leno; Jon Stewart and Stephen Colbert got a lot of mileage out of the story. Newton's scarred and grimly smiling face appeared on every magazine cover from *Fortean Times* to *Newsweek*. Fifteen movie companies courted him for the movie rights to the book. Newton hired a particularly predatory agent who negotiated an excruciating contract that left Newton with extraordinary artistic control over the project, and gave him a check that was so astounding that Newton had it copied and framed for his office. When the book finally went into paperback release, thickened by a new chapter on the reconstruction of the town, it started out as a bestseller and just simply stayed there. His second book, *Ghost Road Blues*, was a biography of the now legendary Bone Man. The film rights to that became the subject of a bidding war eventually won by Don Cheadle, who planned to direct and star in the picture.

When the *Hellnight* movie came out the following Halloween, two years after the massacre, it opened nationwide on 3,144 screens and had the twelfth biggest opening weekend in movie history. Newton was delighted that they got Jason Alexander to play him in the film. Jonatha found it absurd that Beyoncé was signed to play her, the actress being nearly a foot shorter. The hunky young soap opera actor who played Brandon—local newspaper delivery boy and eventual slayer of the monster—parlayed his movie role into a three-picture deal that ultimately made him a big screen star. In later years he would generously tell E! that it was his role in *Hellnight—The Movie* that gave him his first good role. It would have amused Ferro and LaMastra, Newton mused, that their parts were played respectively by Denzel Washington and Owen Wilson who, though they did fine jobs in their roles, were as unlike the two cops as

Beyoncé was unlike Jonatha. It made a hell of a movie, though, with a great blues soundtrack by Mem Shannon and Eddie Clearwater—both of who had been in town that terrible night.

As the books and the film became famous, newspapers tried every wheedling trick in their repertoire to try and discover the true identities of craft store owner "Jessie Hawkins," and local farmer "Mary Perkins." None of them ever succeeded. The town hall had burned down, more than half the townsfolk were dead, and none of the residents interviewed after the release of the book seemed to have a clue as to who these people really were, or had been. It was often speculated that they were just ciphers, characters blended from several sources to give the book a point of focus. After a long time, the newspapers gave up and went in search of fresher news.

Malcolm Crow and Val Guthrie were happy with the fiction and wanted no part of the celebrity.

BK and Billy Christmas didn't spend much time with Crow after that night. They buried a lot of their friends after the massacre and after the funerals they drifted. And on one drunken evening when BK and Billy were together down in Philly, staring into their beers, Billy said, "I'm good if we never talk about that shit again."

BK nodded. "Works for me." Nor did they, though it privately haunted each of them because it made the world fit wrong.

The surviving celebrities stopped returning Crow's calls when he kept trying to apologize. Val figured that Crow had upped everyone's therapy bills by several hundred percent. Acting in horror films is one thing, living one is a bit different; eventually Crow let it go.

In took four years for the whole *Hellnight* hullabaloo to settle down. By then, rebuilding of the town was well under way. Since the governor had declared the town a disaster area, a decision supported by the White House and FEMA, the surviving residents were able to obtain federal funds with which to rebuild and restart their lives. Willie Nelson and John Mellencamp did a Farm Aid concert there one year and that helped a lot as well. After an event that that seemed certain to destroy the town for good, Pine Deep began coming back. The notoriety of the book and movie helped enormously. Sarah Wolfe was elected mayor a year after her husband's death and ran unopposed; and working with a team of investors and corporate donors, she rebuilt the town's economy and partnered with Rachel Weinstock to acquire funding for the Saul Weinstock Memorial Wing of the Pinelands Hospital. Sarah did not, however, reopen the Haunted Hayride. It remains abandoned to this day.

Pine Deep, even in its half-rebuilt state, became the place to visit. Souvenirs such as bricks from the dynamited buildings became hot novelty items; authentic Pine Deep garlic oil was a top seller. The bottom line was that the town itself was coming back bit by bit, brick by brick, life by life.

By then Newton was comfortably wealthy and living in a restored New Orleans antebellum mansion with his wife and their baby girl, whose name was Valerie. The house was set back into the lush countryside in St. Martinville, not too many miles from where Jonatha had grown up. The estate had a wall and a security gate and there was always a guard on patrol. Always.

On a spring morning five years after the burning of Pine Deep, a Lexus with Pennsylvania plates passed through the gates and drove the winding quarter-mile to the house. Newton and Jonatha saw the car coming and were there with smiles and hugs as the passengers got out. Then all had a lazy picnic under the pecan trees.

There were seven of them. Newton and Jonatha sat in cane chairs the servants had brought down for them, and little Valerie tottered around behind twins with black hair and blue eyes. The twins, a boy and a girl, were four-and-a-half years old, and their names were Henry and Faith. Their mother sprawled in a lounge chair and she was hugely pregnant. She wore a floral-pattern sundress and her long legs were tanned and pretty. Her husband sat on the deck of the redwood picnic table and kept his eye on the kids, who were throwing pieces of sandwich bread at the ducks. Butterflies flitted placidly among the bougainvillea and ground orchids, and the pecan trees cast them all in cool shade.

Malcolm Crow bit into a piece of *boudin* and washed it down with lemonade that had cherries and mint leaves in it. He looked older than five years should have made him, but his mouth was still prone to smiling, and he called the extra creases in his face laugh lines. He wore an ancient Phillies cap and a sweatshirt with an R. Crumb picture of Blind Lemon Jefferson on the front.

Without glancing away from the running children, Newton said: "How is he?" Newton never needed to specify who *he* was.

"About the same," Crow said after a few moments.

"Has he decided about college yet?"

"Nope." A yellow jacket landed on Crow's arm; he blew on it to chase it away.

"Did you tell him that Jonatha and I would pay his way? Anywhere he wanted to go?"

"Uh-huh." Crow munched a cookie. "He's just not sure he wants to go."

"I don't think he will go," said Val. "He just isn't interested."

Jonatha shook her head. "College would be good for him. He's smart enough."

"That has nothing to do with it."

"But it would give him a chance to meet other people, to get away from that place."

Val took a sip of her lemonade. "I don't think he wants to get away."

"That's insane, though!" said Jonatha. "After all he's been through, why would he want to stay?"

Val and Crow exchanged a brief glance, but said nothing.

"Hey," said Newton, changing the conversational tack, "have you guys given any more thought to moving down here?"

"Uh-huh," said Val.

"And . . . ?"

"Gets awful hot here during the summers," Crow said. "Makes it hard for Shamu here to get around." He winked at his wife, who mouthed the words *"You will pay for that."*

"Which means what?" asked Jonatha "You're not going to come live with us? Why not stay at least until the baby's born? We do actually have air conditioning, you know."

Val reached over and took Jonatha's hand. "Thanks, sweetie, but the time's not right. *He* won't leave, and we won't leave without him."

As Newton turned to say something, Crow held up his hand, "Now, now, don't go off on a lecture tour on us, dude. You guys have been terrific to us, and more than generous. With the insurance money from the store and the cash you guys send us—which you don't have to do, but which I will keep taking anyway, you filthy rich bourgeois snobs—we have the new house just about finished."

"The farm's coming along, too. I made an offer on a couple of hundred acres of what used to be the Carby place. If it goes through next year we'll become the second largest garlic farmer in the state."

"You guys are nuts," Newton observed. He wore shorts and boat shoes and there was an old dime on a string around his ankle. "I wouldn't live there for all the—"

Val shook her head. "Our life is in Pine Deep."

"Still?" Jonatha asked, cocking her head to one side. "After everything?"

Val reached over and took Crow's hand. "Yes," she said. "Especially after everything. It's different for you two, it always was. Pine Deep wasn't your home. It *was* our home, and it still is. We fought for it, and we won't walk away now."

"Or hobble away," added Crow, tapping the cane that lay beside him. After that hellish night he'd spent eighteen months in a wheelchair, another year on crutches, but was now able to get around with only a cane to help him up stairs and slopes. The doctors said he would always have a bit of a limp. A souvenir, one of them had said, and after the look Crow gave him he hadn't repeated the joke.

"Has there been any sign of . . ." Newton gestured vaguely.

"No," Crow said quietly. "I think the fire, the birds . . . and Mike . . . whatever Mike brought to that fight seemed to turn the tide. I've, um . . . even been down there a few times. Now that I know a back way I can drive in. Beats climbing that friggin' hill."

Newton paled. "You went *back?*"

"I had to see. Once I was up and around I had to *feel* the place, you know? I brought in the heavy equipment and we tore his house down." He laughed. "I even sowed the ground with salt. The swamp, too. But I don't think it was necessary. The place felt—I dunno . . . diminished."

"Still doesn't feel right, though," Val said. "I've been there, too. Once, to lay flowers in memory of Terry, Vince, and Frank. I won't go back again. But to answer your earlier question . . . yes, we'll stay there. We earned that right."

Crow reached over and took her hand, then gently kissed the hard ridge of her knuckles.

Jonatha lapsed into silence, but Newton said, "And you'll keep Mike with you?"

"For as long as he wants to stay," Crow said.

"Is there any sign of skeletal degeneration? Anything like that?"

Crow and Val shared a look. She said, "He doesn't like to go for his tests. So far he looks strong . . . really strong, but I know that sometimes he's in pain."

"What kind of pain?" Jonatha asked.

"He doesn't talk about it," Crow said. "Whatever it is, he just eats it, just deals."

Val looked at the sunlight through the leaves. "After the adoption went through we talked about moving away—we thought he'd want to—but he wants to stay even more than we do. He has a good job with Pinelands Reconstruction. He likes building; he likes making things whole again. He's helping to rebuild the town. It'll take years, you know, but you'd be amazed how many people want to move in and raise families there. It's weird, but the place has really come alive. Property is selling for ridiculous amounts of money."

"It'll be a different town, though," said Crow. "New faces, new families."

"But it's always going to be the 'Most Haunted Town in America,' " reflected Newton.

A shadow passed over Crow's face and he looked away at the

geese and ducks and the bright sunlight glinting off the gently rippling water. It was only after he heard his children laughing as they chased a butterfly that the shadow gradually passed and for a moment he thought he heard the faintest echo of sweet, sad blues drifting on the breeze.

"Yeah," he said very softly. "It'll always be that."

(4)

It was just breaking dawn when he emerged from the forest near the farmhouse. He trudged along, his feet heavy with exhaustion, his face haggard. There was a small cut above his left eye that still bled sluggishly and the shoulder of his black pullover was torn.

He crossed the fields where Val would soon be planting corn, turned onto the winding road, and plodded slowly toward the house. He was tired, but he wasn't in a hurry. There was no more need for haste, the sun was already up, the night's work was done.

On the back porch he stamped clumps of dried mud from his boots and slowly climbed the steps that led to his own back entrance to the house. Val and Crow understood his need for privacy, for a private entrance. At the door he stopped and leaned forward to sniff the strand of garlic bulbs. They were stale, the aroma faint. He tossed them over the railing into the yard. He'd replace them this afternoon. There was always enough garlic around; Val saw to that.

Inside he unbuckled his army-surplus web belt and tossed it and the holstered Beretta onto the bed. He shrugged out of the shoulder sling that held his sword, a three-year-old Paul Chen original. The blade would have to be cleaned, but that could wait, too. Right now he was just too tired. He stripped off all his clothes, stuffed them into a hamper, and then stretched his aching muscles, ignoring the popping sounds from his joints. Mike was a big man, tall and muscular. The growth spurt that had started when he was sixteen had rocketed him up to six-three, and he suspected he might make it to six-four. Long hours with weights and punching bags, with Nordic-Trak and bicycles, had sculpted his physique into lean hardness. The last five years' worth of boxing, wrestling, and jujutsu had given him quickness and balance and an economy of movement that made some people wonder if he was a dancer.

He padded into the bathroom and removed his contact lenses. They were tinted to make his eyes look blue—an ordinary blue. Without the lenses he avoided looking into the mirror whenever possible. He drank four glasses of tap water, turned on the shower, adjusted the temperature mix, and came back into his bedroom. He put an old Robert Johnson CD on the changer and turned the volume all the way up.

He opened a small cupboard. On the inside of one door was a chalkboard, the slate cluttered with numbers that had been chalked in and wiped out. The number 84, long since erased, could be seen faintly, just a ghost of a mark. The clearest number, the latest number, was 41. Mike used the side of his balled-up fist to wipe out that number, and with a piece of chalk he wrote 39. He set the chalk down, rubbed his weary and unsmiling face, and went back into the bathroom to scrub away the dirt and the blood and the memories of the night before.

AFTERWORD (2008)

If you're reading this, then you've stuck with me for three long novels and I thank you. The Pine Deep Trilogy—*Ghost Road Blues, Dead Man's Song,* and *Bad Moon Rising*—were a hell of a lot of fun to write. If you're reading this without having first read this novel, I suggest you read no further until you've finish the book. There are some spoilers here and no author wants to ruin the fun in their own book.

At book signings and appearances I'm frequently asked how and why I chose to write this kind of story. The backstory for the books—the legend of the *Vlkodlak* of Serbia, the Gypsy legend of the *dhampyr,* and the different species of vampires—was something that I've been researching since I was a kid. You see, I had a very spooky grandmother. She was born in the "old country," which for her was Alsace Lorraine, on the border of France and Germany, but she was of Scottish ancestry. Maude Blanche Flavel, descendant of the MacDougall and Gunn clans of Scotland, grew up in the late 1800s during the last great era of folklore and superstition. When she was forty she had my mother, and my mother was about forty when she had me. So by the time I was old enough to ask questions, Nanny (as we called her) was close to ninety years old.

I spent a lot of time with her, absolutely swept up in the folkloric tales of Western Europe. By the time I was twelve I was a little walking encyclopedia of ghosts, werewolves, vampires, and other things that go bump in the night. My grandmother *believed* in all these things. For me, the jury's still out, but I keep an open mind.

In 2002 I had a chance to make a career break from writing books on martial arts and took a shot at doing something on the supernatural. My first book on the subject, *The Vampire Slayers' Field Guide to the Undead,* was published by a small press and has since gone out of print. It made only a modest splash at the time—just enough to get me booked into libraries and museums as "the vampire guy." It was also published under the pen name of Shane MacDougall, partly as a nod to my Nanny's forebears, and partly because my editor at the time thought my martial arts readers would think I'd suddenly gone round the bend if I started writing about monsters.

While I was doing the research for that book I thought how interesting it would be if real people encountered the versions of supernatural creatures as they appeared in folklore, rather than the versions seen in popular fiction and film. There are so many bizarre and even shocking aspects of folklore that have never (or at best, seldom) been utilized in fiction that I had to give it a shot.

Ghost Road Blues, however, was my first novel. I had no personal blueprint for constructing a book and when I sat down to plot and write the story it quickly became apparent that for the tale to include the folkloric elements as well as the degree of character development I felt compelled to include, it was going to be either a very big book—a monster of a book, in fact—or it was going to be several books. Turns out that three is just the right number. *Ghost Road Blues* did very well when it came out, both in terms of sales and notoriety. It was very well received by readers and enthusiastically reviewed.

Exploring the folkloric within the framework of fiction allows for the author to create a mythology for the story that won't necessarily take the reader in expected directions. The ghosts in my story don't act the way readers expect, as can be seen in the case of the Bone Man, who rises from the grave, but doesn't know how to *be* a ghost, and Mandy whose haunting of her brother misfires in a big way. The characteristics of the werewolf as explored in the book are drawn from a number of different legends, notably the *Benandanti* in Terry's story and (perhaps) in Mike's. And certainly the vampire mythology of the story represents something of a worldview of vampirism, particularly in that there are a number of different species of vampires, ranging from psychic monsters like Griswold, to the more traditional revenants (Ruger, McVey, and others of the "Fang Gang.") and the mindless zombielike eating machines—the Dead Heads—like Boyd. In this last case it's worth taking a look at the legend of the *craqueuhhe*, a flesh-eating species from France.

Much of this folkloric backstory is covered in my 2006 nonfiction book *Vampire Universe: The Dark World of Supernatural Beings That Haunt Us, Hunt Us, and Hunger for Us* (Citadel Press). A handful of readers (those who'd read that nonfic book) were cleverly able to put together several pieces of the Pine Deep puzzle, and gold stars to them. A second book, *The Cryptopedia: A Dictionary of the Weird, Strange & Downright Bizarre* (Citadel, 2007) contains additional folkloric and occult clues. I have at least two more folklore books coming out from Citadel that will allow readers to further explore the complex and fascinating world of supernatural predators: *They Bite!: The Darkly Delicious World of Supernatural Predators* (Citadel, 2009) and *Vampire Hunters and Other Enemies of Evil* (September 2010). The *benandanti* are covered there in some depth.

The folks who have come with me to the end of the series — first readers, editors, and others—have asked me if this is the end for Crow, Val, Mike, and the town of Pine Deep. Will Mike succumb to the slow death talked about in the *dhampyr* legends, or will his rather complex family history change that? Is the Bone Man gone for good now? What happened to Mike's mom? And are the nights in Pine Deep really safe now?

Well, folks, I guess time will tell. Maybe I'll come back to Pine Deep someday. I suspect there are a lot of stories that wait to be told. After all . . . it is the most haunted town in America and who knows what might still be out there amid the rustling corn and the rows of pumpkins? If I do return to America's Haunted Holidayland, I hope you'll come along for the ride.

—JM

ACKNOWLEDGMENTS

Thanks to my wonderful agent, Sara Crowe of Harvey Klinger, Inc.; my terrific editor at Kensington, Michaela Hamilton; and to the great Doug Mendini.

Thanks to Chief Pat Priore of the Tullytown Police Department; Peter Lukacs, MD; Dale Blum, RPh; Lisa and Eric Gressen, MD; and Larry Kaplan, DDS, for extensive technical information. Any errors that remain in the book are purely the author's doing.

Thanks to my crew of first readers: Arthur Mensch, Randy Kirsch, Charlie Miller, and Greg Schauer, and to my devious and highly weird webmasters, David F. Kramer and Geoff Strauss.

Thanks to Gus Maris of Red Lion Diner and Erin and Danny Da Costa of Graeme Pizza for letting Crow and Val visit for a spell, and thanks to my friends in the HWA (Horror Writers Association) and the Garden State Horror Writers for dropping by Pine Deep's Halloween Festival.

Thanks to the many wonderful bookstore managers and community-relations managers who made the tours for my previous books such a joy!

Thanks to Stephen Susco, Brinke Stevens, Joe Bob Briggs, Ken Foree, Tom Savini, Tim O'Rear, James Gunn, and Debbie Rochon for dropping by to make an appearance.

Thanks to Sam West-Mensch, Chris Maddish, Elizabeth Little, Mischa Wheat, Jim Winterbottom, David Pantano, Rick Robinson, Brandon Strauss, Helena Penfold, Rebekah Comley, Keith Strunk (and F. F. Manny Thing), Mark DeSousa, and all of the wonderful friends of Pine Deep.

My author homepage is www.jonathanmaberry.com, which has links to the website for this series and for my nonfiction books.

Connect with U(s)

Visit us online at
KensingtonBooks.com
to read more from your favorite authors, see books
by series, view reading group guides, and more.

Join us on social media

for sneak peeks, chances to win books and prize packs,
and to share your thoughts with other readers.

facebook.com/kensingtonpublishing
twitter.com/kensingtonbooks

Tell us what you think!

To share your thoughts, submit a review,
or sign up for our eNewsletters, please visit:
KensingtonBooks.com/TellUs.